MURDER MOST
MOST
Romantic
MEDIEVAL
DIVINE

Other Titles in Random House Value's
Murder Most Series

Murder Most Postal
Murder Most Delectable
Murder Most Feline
Murder Most Confederate
Murder Most Celtic
Murder Most Merry

MURDER MOST *Romantic*

EDITED BY MARTIN H. GREENBERG
& DENISE LITTLE

MURDER MOST MEDIEVAL

EDITED BY MARTIN H. GREENBERG
& JOHN HELFERS

MURDER MOST DIVINE

EDITED BY RALPH MCINERNY
& MARTIN H. GREENBERG

GRAMERCY BOOKS
NEW YORK

This 2005 edition published by Gramercy Books,
an imprint of Random House Value Publishing, a division of
Random House, Inc., New York, by arrangement with
Cumberland House Publishing, Nashville, TN.

Pages 271, 573, and 931-932 constitute an extension of this copyright page.

Gramercy is a registered trademark and the colophon
is a trademark of Random House, Inc.

Random House
New York • Toronto • London • Sydney • Auckland
www.randomhouse.com

Printed in the United States of America

Catalog records for these titles are available from the Library of Congress.

ISBN 0-307-29020-4

CONTENTS

MURDER MOST ROMANTIC
1

MURDER MOST MEDIEVAL
273

MURDER MOST DIVINE
575

MURDER MOST MOST *Romantic*

Passionate Tales of Life and Death

Contents

Introduction ♦♦♦ 5
   Denise Little

Homicidal Honeymoon ♦♦♦ 9
   Laura Resnick

The Scottish Ploy ♦♦♦ 29
   P. N. Elrod

www.gonnahavekelly.com ♦♦♦ 47
   Diane A. S. Stuckart

The Perfect Man ♦♦♦ 71
   Kristine Kathryn Rusch

Celtic Cross ♦♦♦ 107
   Yvonne Jocks

Hostage to Love ♦♦♦ 123
   Mary Watson

Dizzy and the Biker ♦♦♦ 145
   Susan Sizemore

Night Hawks ♦♦♦ 169
   Jody Lynn Nye

Keeper of the Well ♦♦♦ 181
   Deb Stover

Dearly Beloved ♦♦♦ 201
   D. R. Meredith

The Show Must Go On ♦♦♦ 217
   Neesa Hart

Twelve Days ♦♦♦ 235
   Laura Hayden

Authors' Biographies ♦♦♦ 255

Copyright & Permissions ♦♦♦ 271

Introduction

Denise Little

Murder and romance are an unlikely combination...or are they? If given a choice in the matter, most of us would prefer them to remain entirely separate. Yet, there's no denying that an edge of danger can heighten tension and intensify feelings, particularly romantic feelings. Love, after all, is often at its most intense when it is threatened. And when that threat is mortal, well...it gives a whole new meaning to the phrase *a love to die for....*

That's exactly what this collection of stories is about—romance experienced in the teeth of mortal danger, when every decision is life-or-death and the smallest mistake could kill you. Many award-winning writers have joined together in this volume to bring you the best in romantic suspense. From Laura Resnick's heart-stopping story of a honeymoon gone very wrong, to Diane Stuckart's look at the scary side of cyber, to D. R. Meredith's tale of love and death in small-town Texas, and beyond, every story adds a new twist to *Murder Most Romantic*. It's a collection guaranteed to make your heart beat faster...in more ways than one. So sit back, put your feet up, and take a ride along the knife-edge where love and murder meet.

Enjoy!

MURDER MOST
MOST
Romantic

Homicidal Honeymoon

Laura Resnick

As soon as she woke up next to the corpse, she knew it was going to be a bad day.

Her first words were, "Blagh! Argh! Murrrrgh!"

She followed this with a more articulate arsenal of curses: "Jesus H. Christ! Holy shit! What the hell! Ohmigod, ohmigod, ohmigod!"

She only realized she had leaped out of the sagging double bed and staggered backward across the room when she stepped on something that made her yelp in surprise. Cold and hard, it slid out from under her foot, causing her to fly up in the air, flail briefly, and then land heavily on the hard tile floor. She lay there winded and dazed, her head throbbing, her heart pounding.

"Ohmigod," she murmured weakly when she could speak again. "Ohmigod, ohmigod, ohmigod..."

Stop panicking! Think this through.

She was utterly bewildered. Rational thoughts were hard to seize, never mind formulate and examine.

Maybe he's not really dead. Maybe he just looks dead.

After all, all that blood would make *anyone* look dead.

"Ohmigod, ohmigod, ohmigod..."

She opened her eyes and stared at the ceiling. High overhead, a tropical fan whirled lazily. She rolled her head sideways, looking for the object she had slipped on. The big white tiles she was lying on were old and worn, but relatively clean.

Where the hell am I?

She saw the object she'd stepped on. It lay a few feet away, its smooth, cold surface gleaming a dull metallic gray.

A gun.

He'd been shot. The dead man in the bed had been shot.

All right. Get up and look. Then call the cops. And...

"Oh, my God!"

And get dressed!

She was naked. And alone in a strange room with a corpse and a gun.

I was naked in bed with a dead man.

Jesus, Mary, and Joseph, I beg you, don't let my mother ever find out about this.

The thought came as a reflexive response to the scene...but once she examined it, she realized she couldn't form an image of her mother. Some unconscious instinct suggested this was probably a blessing, but it nonetheless worried her. Particularly when she realized, a moment later, she couldn't even remember her mother's name. Or...her own name.

"Oh, my God."

She sat bolt upright, stark naked in the humid warmth of the shabby room as the realization hit her with full force.

My name? What's my name?

Nothing came to her.

What's my goddamn name? Who am I?

She stood up, looked around, and shivered despite the heat.

Where was she? What was she doing here? Who was the guy—oh, Jesus, the dead naked guy—in the bed?

The room possessed few amenities. No TV, no phone, no refrigerator with overpriced beverages and fattening snacks. Just the sagging double bed (complete with bloody male corpse), a nightstand, a smashed lamp lying on the floor next to the dead man's crumpled clothes, an armoire that had seen better days, a sink, a mirror, and a few towels.

She walked over to the mirror and looked into it. She was brown-haired, brown-eyed, slim, perhaps thirty. Not a knockout, but attractive enough that, were there not a corpse in her bed, she wouldn't even consider flinging herself off the balcony in hopeless despair now.

Balcony...

She looked around for her clothes. Not seeing them—*good grief, did I come here naked?*—she reached for the sheet on the bed and gave it a tug. The sight of its red-stained folds slithering down the dead man's body brought her to her senses.

"Not a good idea."

She turned in the direction of the sink again. The sudden movement made her head ache painfully. The room swam in and out of focus. That wasn't just from waking up in a panic or falling on the floor, she realized suddenly. She reached up to gingerly examine her scalp and discovered a big lump beneath her hair.

She developed a theory.

Someone hit me over the head and killed him....

But who? And why? And what should she do now?

Trying to ignore her aching head, she wrapped a threadbare towel around herself, turned, and went out onto the balcony. Her room, she discovered, was on the second floor of a grubby pale building in a rundown semi-urban street.

She looked around, starting to feel like she might throw up. There were a few street signs, mostly garish and hand-painted. She couldn't read them.

Am I illiterate?

Two young men were walking down the opposite side of the street, partially hidden in the shadows. The sun was low in the sky, and she didn't know if it was dawn or sunset.

"Excuse me," she called. "Hello? Excuse me. Could I ask you a few questions? Hello! Excuse me!"

They finally paused, looked up, and saw her. After a moment of immobile surprise, they both grinned broadly and started across the street toward her building. It suddenly occurred to her that a woman wearing only a towel who summoned two strange men to her bedroom balcony could conceivably create entirely the wrong impression.

She took immediate steps to correct any misapprehension on their part. "I've just got one or two questions about—"

"*No hablo inglés.*"

"Huh?"

The young man who had spoken repeated himself and, it seemed, added an apology. The other simply shook his head and kept grinning at her.

"Um...is that Spanish?" she ventured.

"*Sí, señorita. Español.*"

"Now that's just lovely," she muttered. She was pretty sure she didn't speak Spanish, whoever she was. Was everyone here Hispanic, or just these two guys? Unfortunately, there didn't seem to be anyone else on the street whom she could ask.

The young man who had spoken now said something else. She didn't understand the words, but the suggestive tone was unmistakable. The silently grinning one looked like he was trying to find a way to climb up to her balcony.

"No!" she said, backing up a step. "No, thanks. I mean, sorry. I mean...Everything's fine up here, thanks." She gestured vaguely behind her. "I've just got a...There's a man who...No!" she uttered when she realized they seemed to regard her gesturing at the bedroom as an invitation. "No!" she repeated forcefully, holding her hands out as if to ward them off. Fortunately, *no* was a word they seemed to understand. Looking disgruntled and perplexed, they started muttering comments that she was certain weren't complimentary. However, the moment her gaze was caught by a glimmering reflection on her outstretched left hand, she stopped listening.

A wedding ring?

Good grief, a wedding ring? She was *married*? She had forgotten an entire husband?

"Oh, no!" She forgot about her two young swains as she raced back into the room and, forbidding herself to be sick, examined the dead man's left hand. Yes, there it was: a wedding ring. One that matched her own.

"Oh, my God..."

We're married?

Her head was pounding. Her stomach churned. Panic raced through her veins.

Or we were married? I guess I'm a widow now.

She forced herself to study the dead man.

Evidently she wasn't shallow, since she certainly hadn't chosen this man for his dashing good looks. He had been ten or fifteen years older than her, a little jowly, with a small mouth and a bland face. His thin, mousy hair was long enough in front that she guessed he usually tried to comb it over that big bald patch now so carelessly exposed. He clearly didn't work out or get much sun, and it looked like he enjoyed fatty foods.

He was also wearing a diamond-studded pinkie ring on his right hand—a particularly cheesy-looking one, even by the standards of pinkie rings.

"Good God," she muttered. This was her husband?

She wondered if she had loved him very much. It seemed that if she had, surely there ought to be at least some quiver of recognition in her heart when she gazed at him, but she felt nothing. Well, nothing except panic, revulsion, fear, and bewilderment—which was really quite enough, for now, anyhow.

She wondered what she should do now. One thing she was certain she shouldn't do was pick up the gun. Her memory might be gone, but she was nonetheless pretty sure she had seen any number of movies wherein the heroine, suffering from shock and a lack of common sense, picked up the murder weapon in confusion, only to be immediately pounced upon by some cop who jumped to the inaccurate (but, frankly, understandable) conclusion that she was the murderer.

She went to the sink and splashed cold water over her face. Her head throbbed. Her stomach contracted threateningly.

Try to remember. There must be at least one thing you can remember.

She closed her eyes and concentrated on breathing in a slow, soothing rhythm.

Relax, relax... Think...

The image of a man penetrated her thoughts. He was tall, dark, and handsome.

Don't fantasize—think!

His image grew stronger, though. Clearer. Coming fully into focus. He had dark piercing eyes, lush brown hair, a sexy smile, broad shoulders....

Was I cheating on my husband?

She was an adulteress married to a balding, jowly man who wore a pinkie ring. An adulteress without any clothing, it seemed.

Perhaps losing her memory had been an unconscious choice, an escape from reality, rather than a result of this bump on her head.

"Ohhhhh..." Trying not to weep in frustration and despair, she buried her face in her hands and wondered who had murdered her husband. Wondered who the handsome man in her memory was.

She suddenly gasped as she realized that the most likely person for her to remember, at this particular moment, was...her husband's murderer!

"Oh, no!"

She needed to get the cops. Whoever she was, wherever she was, she needed to report her husband's death. She also needed to seek police protection until the murderer was caught. What if she had seen the killer? What if the killer knew she had seen him?

She didn't even think, just reacted. She gave in to her panic and ran for the door. She had to get out of this room! She had to find a phone, a police station, a safe place! Preferably a place at some distance from the corpse of her forgotten husband—at least until she could compose herself. She reached for the doorknob, and then—

And then leaped backward in startled fear when it rattled slightly. She stared stupidly at it, watching it turn slowly. The door latch gave a soft click. Her heart pounded with blind terror. She stood frozen on the spot, incapable of motion, as the door swung open.

The tall, dark, handsome man whom she remembered now stood in the doorway, his familiar eyes blazing with some powerful emotion.

The killer!

Her mouth worked silently in mindless, breathless terror.

He stepped into the room and swiftly closed the door behind him. "You're here," he said with almost violent intensity.

He reached for her. Unable to scream, she finally gave in and fainted.

Someone was dousing her with bitterly cold water. It was inhumane! It was *outrageous.*

She sat up shivering, sputtering, and waving her arms around.

"Come on," he said. "Get it together. We have to talk."

She opened her eyes, saw him, and—feeling much better now—screamed her head off.

"Stop that," he snapped. "You want to bring everyone in the whole hotel crashing through that door?"

"Yes!"

He put his hand over her mouth. In that same instant, she realized she was stark naked again. Her towel lay beneath her in a lumpy heap. Renewed terror gave her strength to act. She bit him. Really hard. He gasped and snatched his hand away, giving her a wounded look. She screamed again, more forcefully this time.

"What's the *matter* with you?" he demanded.

"Arrrrgh!" She snatched the towel up, jumped to her feet, covered herself, and staggered away from him.

Still cradling his hand, he stared at her as if she had gone mad. "What is it?" he demanded.

"Stay away from me!" she ordered.

His increasingly bewildered gaze raked her from head to toe.

"Don't look at me!" she shrieked.

"O...kay...," he said slowly. "Want to tell me why not?"

"Because I'm not dressed, you idiot!" she raged, momentarily forgetting that modesty should really be the least of her concerns at this particular moment.

He frowned. "Huh?"

"Clothes! Clothes!" she cried. "I don't have any clothes on!"

"Yes, I noticed that." He sounded testy again. "And, believe me, I was planning to ask about that."

"Turn around!" she shrieked, beside herself now. Bad enough that he should murder her, but ogling her, too, was really beyond the limit.

"Will you stop?" he snapped, going over to the bed to examine the corpse. "It's not as if I've never seen you naked before."

That stopped her. "It's not?"

"Christ," he muttered, studying the body, "what happened here?"

"You...you've seen me naked before?"

"Did *you* kill him?"

"Are you sure?"

He glanced back up at her. "Sure about what?"

"That you've seen me naked before?"

He squinted at her. "What are you talking about?"

"I don't..." She spread her hands helplessly for a moment, then scrabbled at the towel as it started to slip. "I don't know who you are."

"*What?*"

"I don't know who he is." She shook her head, then winced as it throbbed again. "I don't know who *I* am."

"What are you talking about?" he repeated.

"And I don't remember what happened here."

His jaw dropped. "You're kidding."

"Oh, good grief, do you think I would kid about a thing like that?" she snapped.

"At least you're starting to sound more like yourself." He eyed her uncertainly. "So all this screaming and this, um, modesty....It's because you..." He tried out the phrase with obvious difficulty: "You don't recognize me?"

"No. I thought you might be...you know."

"No, I don't know."

"The killer."

"Jesus." He looked down at the corpse again. "We're in even more trouble than I thought."

She ventured, "Who exactly *are* you?"

Something about the corpse made him suddenly exclaim, "Hey!" He seized the dead man's left hand and stared at it with an expression of outrage. "I'm the guy who normally wears this ring."

She staggered toward the bed and stared at it, too. "It, um, matches mine." She held up her own left hand, careful not to touch the corpse.

"I know," he snapped.

"What?"

Still staring at the dead man, he murmured, "We got married six days ago."

"Huh?"

He looked up at her, then suddenly dropped the dead man's hand and said, "You and me, I mean."

"You're my husband?"

"You don't really think you'd have married a guy who wears a pinkie ring, do you?"

She sat down on the edge of the bed. "Oh, this is a big relief."

"I think I'm flattered," he said dryly.

"Really, you have no idea." She sighed and felt some of her panic dissolving. "I'm not married to him. I'm not a widow. And I'm not an adulteress."

"Well, it's only been six days." When she gave him an irritated look, he said, "Kidding, kidding."

"And I haven't killed my husband." She paused and added, "Of course, it's only been six days."

He ignored that. "You're sure you didn't kill him?"

"I'm not sure of anything," she admitted.

There was a sudden pounding on the door accompanied by what sounded like a trio of confused Spanish voices. She looked at him in mingled fear and confusion.

"I *asked* you not to scream like that," he muttered. "Get rid of them."

"I'm not dressed," she argued.

"They're more likely to go away if *you* tell them to than if *I* tell them to," he pointed out. "You're the one who screamed for help."

She experienced another moment of doubt as she looked at him. He was tall and well-built, and she wouldn't have a chance against him, she suspected, if he was lying to her.

He caught her dubious expression and said, with the exasperation only a spouse could muster, "Will you *stop*?"

She nodded. "I'll get rid of them."

She went to the door, opened it slightly, and found two men and a very fat woman in the hallway. The two men looked concerned. The woman looked annoyed. It took some effort, but she bridged the language barrier with enough tenacity to assure them there wasn't a problem, after all. She might have been more convincing, she thought, if she were wearing more than a towel.

After closing the door, she turned to find him searching the room.

"What are you looking for?"

"Where are your clothes?" he demanded.

"I don't know." She studied him and said slowly, "If you're my husband, then you should remember what I was wearing when I disappeared."

"You were wearing..." His dark eyes went wide and he said, "Oh."

"What?" she pounced.

"You were naked the last time I saw you."

"What?"

"In our room," he added. "We were, uh, consummating the marriage. Yet again."

"Oh."

"Then we had some wine....And that's all I remember until I woke up alone." He plucked the dead man's shirt and trousers off the floor. "You're going to have to wear his things."

"Yuck! No!"

"Don't worry, he wasn't wearing them when he was shot." He glanced at the naked corpse and added, "Obviously." He sniffed the clothing briefly and made a face. "But I'm afraid they reek of aftershave."

"Figures," she muttered. She took the clothes from him, started to lower the towel, then paused and made a gesture asking him to turn his back.

He looked insulted. "But I look at you naked all the time! You *like* me to look at you naked."

"Even so—"

"You like me to do a lot more than look."

"Nonetheless—"

"Just before you disappeared, you tore off all my clothes and we—"

"I don't want to hear this right now!" She took a steadying breath and said more calmly, "Right now, I don't really know who you are, and I'd appreciate it if you'd turn your back. Surely I wouldn't have married a man who would refuse me that much?"

He sighed. "Fine. Whatever." He turned his back and, while she got dressed, spoke over his shoulder. "Tell me what you *do* remember."

"Nothing. Well, no," she amended, "I remember you."

"But you just said—"

"I mean, I remembered your face."

"Yeah?" He sounded pleased.

"Yeah, but nothing else. I woke up a few minutes ago. Here. No memory. No clothes. With a dead man."

He was silent for a long moment before asking, "Woke up where?"

"Here," she repeated, pulling the dead man's trousers up over her hips. "Gosh, he was chubby. Give me your belt."

"Here, *where*?" he demanded, unbuckling his belt.

"In bed. With him," she admitted reluctantly.

He went still for a moment. His voice was strained as he said, "His name was O'Mallory."

"Oh."

"You didn't like him."

"What a surprise. Did you?"

"No."

He finished taking off his belt and held it out to her, still keeping his face averted. Instinct told her that he probably was indeed her husband, because she didn't need to see his face to know exactly what expression was on it right now.

While she put on his belt, he lowered his head and studied the floor with intense concentration. Still standing behind him, she realized she recognized that posture, too.

After a moment, he said, "Did he, uh...Do you remember if...I mean, if he...Oh, Jesus."

She looked at the dead man. "If anything happened, then I sincerely, truly, profoundly hope that I never ever remember it as long as I live."

"Do you...feel okay?" he asked.

"Somebody hit me on the head," she complained.

"Hit you?" He turned his handsome face and looked at her, his brown eyes soft and concerned.

Now this is more like it.

She had evidently married well, after all.

"I think that's why I can't remember anything," she opined.

"Let me see," he murmured.

She stood still while he came to her and examined the bump on her head, a dark frown on his face. His fingers were gentle, and his touch stirred a memory.

"You like sailing," she murmured.

His frown lifted. "Yeah."

"And you cook."

"That's right," he encouraged.

"I like to watch your hands...." She took one of his hands between hers and tried to remember more. "And you're so good at unbuttoning things that the first time...." A wave of heat washed through her. "Oh."

"Hmmm?"

"I think I remember the first time," she whispered.

"That's good," he murmured. "I worked hard, after all. I'd hate to think—"

"We're...on our honeymoon," she ventured.

He nodded. "We flew here the day after we got married."

"Wait." It was coming back to her. "The honeymoon suite at the Hilton?"

He nodded again. "The night we got married." He grinned and added, "Some complaints about the noise."

"We knocked over furniture," she said suddenly.

"Ahhhhh, you're remembering."

"And then we came here...wherever this is."

"Costa Rica. Because you like wildlife. Especially—"

"Birds," she interrupted, pleased she was recalling more details now.

"Birds," he repeated with a notable lack of enthusiasm. "I really wanted to go to the Virgin Islands, but *nooo*. You said if there was one place you'd alw—"

"Do you have to bring that up now?" she snapped. Her eyes flew wide as she realized, "Wow, I really am married to you, aren't I?"

"Is that a problem?"

"No, no, I'm sure I'll get used to it—"

"Thanks."

"But how did I wind up here? And who the hell is O'Mallory? And how did you find us?"

"O'Mallory is a creep who turned up at the hotel—"

"Please tell me this isn't our hotel."

"No, no," he assured her. "We're staying at a nice place on the coast."

"That's a relief."

"Yesterday morning, I came to. It was late, I felt really hung over—"

"You were drunk?"

He shook his head. "The bottle of wine in our suite must have been drugged. I woke up face-down on the floor, naked and alone. You were gone." He glanced at the bed and added between his teeth, "So was my wedding ring."

"But why?"

"O'Mallory called and said if I ever wanted to see you alive again, I had to get one million in U.S. dollars, in cash, and have it ready."

"Ready for what?"

"His next call."

Her eyes widened. "You've got a million dollars on you?"

"No." He shook his head. "I couldn't get my hands on that much money in one day, especially not in Costa Rica."

"But if we were at home—"

"If we were at home and I had a week or two, then I could do it."

"Wow, I really married well, didn't I?"

"Mind you," he added, "then we'd have to live in a tent and clip lots of coupons for a while."

"But I'm worth it?" she prodded.

"Usually," he agreed with a smile. "Anyhow, when O'Mallory called again last night, he told me to meet him in the lobby of this hotel. After I got here, I waited downstairs for thirty minutes. When he didn't show up, I thought he might have you hidden in one of the rooms, and so I started searching for you."

"That's it?"

He shrugged. "He sounded really scared during that second call. He didn't even seem to care that I didn't have the money yet, just wanted me to come anyhow."

"You didn't call the cops?"

"He said you would die for sure if I did." He shook his head. "All

I could think of was getting to you. So I got a car and drove all night to get here."

She looked out the window. The sky was brighter. "So it's morning."

"You didn't know that?"

"I don't know anything," she reminded him.

"Not even how he wound up dead?"

"No. Or whose gun that is."

His gaze followed hers to the weapon lying on the floor. "Or what he was scared of, I guess?"

"Well, I think we can safely deduce he was scared of winding up like this."

He nodded. "Good point."

"What do we do now?" she wondered.

"Go to the cops." He went back to the bed and grabbed O'Mallory's left hand.

"What are you doing?" she demanded.

"I want my wedding ring back."

"Oh, yuck! No! Eeeuuuw! Leave it."

"But it's my wedding ring!"

"You can afford another," she said with forced patience.

"But this is the one you put on my hand when we got married. This one has sentimental value. It's—"

"It's on a dead man's hand!" she snapped. "Leave it there!"

"But—"

"If you put it back on now," she informed him through gritted teeth, "you will never again touch me with your left hand."

He dropped the corpse's hand. "I see amnesia hasn't affected your stubborn streak at all."

"Why did he even take your wedding ring, for goodness' sake?"

"To pass himself off as your husband, of course."

She shuddered. "But why?"

"He had to haul your naked unconscious body from our suite to his car, and later from his car into this hotel." He shrugged. "With matching rings, all he had to say was that you were his wife and you'd had too much to drink."

"If I were his wife," she said with feeling, "I would indeed drink too much."

He glanced down at the big tangle of blood-soaked bedsheets and said, "I suppose he stole one of these from our room and wrapped you up in it."

"So there's no doubt that he saw me—even touched me—naked." She felt faint again. "Oh, God."

Someone pounded at the door again. There was more shouting in Spanish. Deep male voices this time, and what sounded like a stern warning.

Her husband sighed. "Get rid of them."

She nodded and turned to do so. Before she reached the door, however, it suddenly flew open with a loud crack of splintering wood and snapping metal. Four uniformed policemen stampeded into the room, all of them armed and clearly ready to shoot.

She raised her hands. They stared at her. She stared back. When she could finally make a sound, it came out as, "G...ga...gahhh..."

A short, stout, smirking man walked in slowly behind the four cops. He seemed to be their superior officer.

She gasped. "Oh, my God! Wait minute!" She stared. "Yes! I remember you! You ambushed us! O'Mallory was afraid of you! *You're* the one who hit me on the head, you jerk!" Her eyes flew wide as she realized, "You killed him!"

"Ah, Mrs. Smith," he said. "A pleasure to see you again."

She glanced at the bed. "Smith? He checked us in under the name Smith? Of all the unoriginal, clichéd, hack—"

"Uh, honey," her husband interjected, "that's *our* name."

She squinted at him. His hands were raised, too. "I'm really Mrs. Smith?" she asked.

He nodded.

She shrugged. "Oh, well. At least it's easy to spell."

The stout man cleared his throat. When he had their full attention, he introduced himself. "I am Captain Lopez."

"I'm not at all happy to see you," she replied.

Her husband said to the other cops, "Listen to me. My wife has been kidnapped and—"

"Your wife, *señor*," Lopez interrupted, "is a murderess."

She gasped. Her husband argued. The cops, in response to a command from Lopez, handcuffed both of them, then went around the room gathering evidence. When they collected the gun, her husband swore.

"Her fingerprints are on it," he guessed, "aren't they?"

"A very astute prediction," Lopez replied.

"I didn't shoot him!" she snapped at her loving spouse.

"I know," her husband said, his gaze still fixed on Lopez, "but he means to prove otherwise."

"He can hardly prove otherwise," she argued, "since I never touched the gun...." She choked and whirled to stare at Lopez. "You planted my prints on it while I was unconscious!"

"I'm afraid it was necessary."

"No wonder O'Mallory said I would die for sure if...if what's-his-name here went to the cops!"

"Scott," her husband supplied. "It's Scott."

"The cops are in on it!" she continued.

"No, no," Lopez said. "Just me."

She looked at the four cops busily tearing apart the room in search of damning evidence against her. "What about them?"

"They don't speak a word of English," Lopez advised her. "They just follow orders."

"So O'Mallory prowled the resorts in search of wealthy victims," Scott guessed, "and you gave him police protection in exchange for a cut of the take."

"Sadly," Lopez said, "he was inept at his duties, so there hasn't been much 'take' so far. I've been obliged to find a replacement."

"O'Mallory found out," Scott surmised. "He realized you'd try to get rid of him."

"Of course!" she said, understanding now. "You couldn't just fire him and count on him to go away quietly."

"So you're framing his final kidnap victim for his murder," Scott concluded.

"Especially since," Lopez said with a noticeable quiver of outrage, "his final victim is not the surgically enhanced young trophy wife of Alan Scott Smith, the fifty-six-year-old heir to a mining fortune worth four hundred million dollars. Noooo!" Warming to his theme, Lopez went on, "Instead, that incompetent moron O'Mallory zeroes in on Scott Alan Smith, a newlywed from Seattle with a wife who—may I be excused for saying?—has the temper of an angry cobra and a head as hard as granite!"

"You may be excused," Scott said.

"Hey!" she said.

"Love isn't blind," Scott told her, "it's just incredibly tolerant."

"If we could return to the subject of my upcoming murder trial," she prodded.

"I'm open to bribery," Lopez said with the air of a man trying to demonstrate goodwill and a desire to cooperate, "but I fear that you can't meet my price."

"Which is?" she prodded.

"One million, U.S., cash."

Scott sighed. "Well, as you've remarked, I'm not the mining fortune heir with the trophy wife, so I'd need time to get that much money together."

"We're not giving a penny to this slimy worm!" she snapped.

Scott glared at her. "There goes my whole 'give me time' ploy."

"It wouldn't have worked anyhow," Lopez assured him.

"You can't convict me of a murder I didn't commit!" she insisted.

"Of course I can," Lopez said. "I am an expert at manufacturing evidence."

"Oh." She thought she was going to throw up.

"Yes, I'm afraid things do look really bad for you," Lopez said with a touch of sympathy. "And on your honeymoon, too. Such a shame, but it can't be helped."

"Look, why don't you arrest *me* for his murder?" Scott suggested desperately. "Say I found them here together, and in a jealous rage I—"

"Sorry," Lopez said. "Your gallantry is admirable, but the gun is covered with her fingerprints, not yours.... However, we'll be happy to arrest you, too."

"On what charge?"

"I'm sure I'll think of something."

"You won't get away with this!"

"What that warning lacks in originality it makes up for in sincerity," Lopez replied. "However, sincerity is unlikely to prevent your conviction or—"

There was a sudden shout behind her, so loud it made her jump.

More men came pouring through the door, and there was a great deal of yelling, confusion, and shuffling around. When a gun went off, Scott knocked her to the floor and landed on top of her. She gasped for air and struggled to see what was going on. She saw scuffling feet coming toward her. She tried to roll away, but Scott's weight pinned her down. One of the feet kicked her in the head.

"Ow!"

"What? What's wrong?" Scott demanded.

"Someone kicked me! Get off of me!"

"Stay down!" he ordered.

"What's going on?"

When Scott finally let her up, Lopez was face-down on the floor with his hands cuffed behind him. The four cops who had come here with him were spread-eagled against a wall and submitting to a search, all the while protesting (it seemed) their innocence. And a dozen heavily armed men in combat fatigues were in charge of the scene.

"What's going on?" she said again as someone helped her and her husband to their feet.

"O'Mallory must have betrayed Lopez," Scott said.

She looked around. "You mean...he realized you might not get here in time to save him—"

"To save you," he corrected.

"—and so he blew the whistle on Lopez!"

"Does anyone here speak English?" Scott asked.

"*No, señor.*" An earnest-faced uniformed man apologized for this, then spoke at great length in Spanish.

They tried to understand, but their efforts at communication were frustrating.

"Oh, mother of God!" Lopez exclaimed from his undignified position on the floor. "He's saying you have to accompany him to the station and give your statements to an interpreter! Really, if you people can't even learn a few words of Spanish, why not honeymoon in a place like the Virgin Islands?"

"You see?" Scott said to her.

"Oh, will you drop it?" she replied.

"Didn't I tell you—"

"Saying 'I told you so,'" she warned him, "would be a bad way to start off our marriage."

He seemed ready to argue for a moment, but then all the fight went out of him. He leaned down and kissed her. "I'm just glad you're safe now," he whispered.

She tried to put her arms around him, then winced when the hand-cuffs bit into her wrists. "Hey, Lopez, we need the key to these cuffs."

Lopez grumbled, then gave some instructions to one of his captors. A few moments later, someone removed the handcuffs, and she sank into her husband's arms—an embrace that now felt wonderfully familiar.

"You stink of O'Mallory's after-shave," he murmured.

"Nothing happened," she muttered in relief.

"You remember now?"

"It's coming back to me."

He tightened his arms around her for a moment, then said, "I don't think we should tell your mother about any of this."

She froze for a moment, and then groaned, "My mother."

"What's wrong?"

"Oh...I had just mercifully forgotten her for a little while there."

She felt him shake with laughter, and then he kissed her hair. He ran a hand down her back and over her bottom, snuggling her hips against his. A bunch of other memories started returning, and she felt her skin flush.

"Come on," she whispered. "Let's go give our statements and get this over with. We have a honeymoon to get back to."

"Okay, Harry."

She flinched and pulled away. "Harry?"

He nodded. When she continued to stare blankly, he said, "Harriet. Harriet Bryniarski Smith. You didn't know?"

"Harriet Bryniarski." She put a shaky hand to her brow. "No wonder I forgot."

"Honey..."

"What else have I forgotten?" she demanded.

"I don't know."

"You're not a bigamist?"

"No!"

"Or a serial killer? Or the leader of some kind of perverted cult? Or—"

"No! Will you *stop*?"

"Just give me the bad news now. I can take it."

He sighed. "There is no bad news."

She studied him hard. "We'll see."

"The bad news," Lopez insisted, as his captors hauled him off the floor and out of the room, "is that he is not the heir to a mining fortune worth four hundred million dollars!"

"On the other hand," Scott pointed out to Harriet, "*that* Smith is a notorious bisexual philanderer. Whereas I'm straight and entirely monogamous."

"Well, it's only been six days," she pointed out.

He kissed her hand, a courtly gesture that she now remembered was typical of him. "In sixty years," he promised, "I'll still be able to say it to you."

She smiled. "I think today has sort of spoiled Costa Rica for me. So if you still really want to go to the Virgin Islands..."

"That's a good idea." He looked around and grinned. "But I swear to you, I don't normally go this far to win our fights."

The Scottish Ploy

P. N. Elrod

Cassie Sullivan slammed her clipboard onto the props table, causing the sword collection that lay there to jump. One fell to the floor with a solid clank. The abrupt noise startled everyone, giving her the undivided attention of the whole cast and crew. "If just one more thing goes wrong, I'm calling in an exorcist!"

Nell Russell left off wiring together tree branches that were to be part of Burnam Wood. "What's happened now?"

"Trevor Hopkins backed out."

"What?" Similar expressions of dismay flowed from the others who stopped work on the set to come closer, faces tense.

"Hopkins got a starring role in a straight-to-video horror movie and grabbed it."

Nell's mouth twisted. "He chose that over the lead in *Macbeth*? Why?"

"Money. They can pay him more. The option's in his contract."

Everyone nodded, understanding perfectly. The Sullivan Theater Company, for all its members' sincere enthusiasm, was small change to an actor like Trevor Hopkins. Apparently his commitment to keeping theater alive wasn't deep enough to survive the lure of Hollywood dollars. Cassie herself could side with Hopkins to a degree, but there was such a thing as fair warning.

Opening night was only a week away.

"What'll we do for a new Macbeth?" asked Willis Wright, the stage manager.

"Hopkins' agency is sending over Quentin Douglas as a replacement."

"Who?"

Cassie shrugged. "He's done some commercials."

A general groan. Nell joined in. "What kind of commercials?"

"Who knows? Foot powder, shaving cream, talking sandwiches— I don't care so long as he can project the lines. They said he played Macbeth in college—"

Another groan.

"—so he knows the part. If Isabel likes him, he's in."

"Great. Did he save his old costume?"

Cassie glowered. "Don't get me started. At this point I may do a nude production."

"That would sell more tickets. Think of all the sword jokes."

"Argh!" Cassie looked around for something else to slam or throw, but nothing non-breakable presented itself. The company watched her, somewhat wall-eyed. Her tempers were infrequent and short-lived, but infamous for their intensity. Everyone knew to get out of the line of fire for the brief duration, but this time no one seemed to know which way to jump.

She put her hands palm-out in a peace gesture. "It's okay, boys and girls. I just hate surprises. Chalk this up to the production poltergeist and get back to work. Let's keep it to one life-and-death crisis every ten minutes instead of every five. Okay?"

A rumble of agreement. They resumed their tasks. Nell hung close, though. "When's the foot-powder wonder boy due?"

"Sometime today. I just got the call from—"

"Miss Sullivan?" Baritone voice. Rich. Chocolate-smooth delivery. Built-in projection. No need for a body microphone.

Cassie turned to take in the owner of the voice. *Oh, my gawd.* Hair like jet, soap opera hero's face, body of personal trainer, thin line of beard edging his jaw—perfectly in keeping with a Shakespearean character—straight white teeth in a friendly, open smile.

"I'm Quentin Douglas—the Gilbert Agency sent me?" Hand outstretched. Expecting her to respond.

"Yes, they certainly did," she murmured, still goggling. She put her own hand out and connected with his firm grip.

The vision spoke again. "I hope I can work out for you."

His "hope" momentarily sparked a variety of emotions in Cassie, which she quickly snuffed out. *You're off actors, Cassie-girl, you are immune no matter how gorgeous they are. Anyone that good-looking is going to be attached or gay.* "I'm sure you will, Mr. Douglas." She was still holding his hand. Belatedly, she released it.

"Please, call me Quentin."

Before she could call him Quentin, she felt an urgent tugging on her shirttail; Nell obviously wanted to be included in the first-names fan club.

"Quentin, this is Nell Russell, she's playing Lady MacDuff, Hecate, and Young Siward."

"I'm very versatile," Nell purred, oozing forward to shake his hand, too. She had no misgivings about fraternizing with actors, usually bestowing one broken—or at least slightly bruised heart—per production.

Quentin tendered another easy smile, his royal blue eyes twinkling.

"Glad to meet you. Is there much doubling up for roles in this one?"

"A few," Cassie answered, since Nell seemed to have forgotten her next line, basking as she was in his presence. "None of the principals, of course. Go through there to my office, the red door. I'll be right along."

Quentin Douglas departed, walking smooth as a panther on ball bearings. Nell made a low moan of appreciation deep in her throat, ogling at the snug fit of his jeans on his perfect backside—not to mention the muscular set of those sculpted shoulders....The view wasn't lost on Cassie, but she made herself look elsewhere, gritting her teeth.

"Oh, I didn't think they made them like that anymore," Nell sighed.

"Down, girl, I don't want you breaking him before we even start."

"But he's the one."

"What? Your own true love? You've said that on every—"

"No, I mean I know who he is! He's the sports drink shower guy."

Cassie blanked. "O—kay."

"You know, that commercial where the guy takes the shower and they pour sports drink all over his sweaty body. Relief from the heat in slooooow-mooootion."

"I'm surprised you even noticed his face." Not much of a TV watcher, Cassie had no recollection of the ad. She quelled a sudden feeling of deprivation.

"I've seen him in *As the Planet Revolves*, too. He can act."

"On TV. I've gotta find out if he's any good for stage work."

"Cassie, he looks like he'd be good for all kinds of things!"

"We'll see." Cassie hurried to her office before she caught Nell's terminal case of carbonated hormones. Yes, Quentin Douglas was a prime physical specimen; yes, he could probably act, but having once fallen far too hard for that type, Cassie had sworn them off forever. Of course, that was difficult to remember when face-to-face with Quentin across her cluttered desk. He had an energy that beat against her like a sunbeam. She refused to be burned by it, but quietly rejoiced; that sort of dynamism was highly valuable. He just might be able to make a whole theater feel it.

"Here's my résumé," he said, handing over a sheet of paper stapled to a head shot.

She compared the photo to the reality. Usually publicity pictures were an idealized improvement of the subject. Not with this guy, though. Would his looks detract from the production? On the other hand, it couldn't hurt to have a drop-dead handsome, extremely virile Macbeth leaping around the stage waving his sword. "Know how to play with your weapon?" she asked. "I mean—do you know stage combat?"

"It's a passion of mine." He flashed those perfect teeth. "I don't get much call for it in commercials."

"This job doesn't pay as well as TV work."

"It's experience. I'm always looking to hone my skills." He kept up with the eye contact.

Is he flirting with me? she wondered, conscious she was only in her second-best work shirt, her third-best jeans, with her blazing mane of red hair piled every which way from its hasty morning pinning. But Quentin had live theater in his background; he'd know how grungy things could get. No matter. *I'm immune to his type now. Stick to business.* She found a copy of *Macbeth* and handed it over. "Let's have a reading, then."

"Sure. What would you like to hear?" Quentin was remarkably self-possessed. Most of the actors she'd dealt with had panic attacks at the prospect of a cold reading. Not this wavy-haired cool cucumber.

"How about Act Three, Scene Four? Macbeth's talking with the First Murderer at the banquet." There, a highly charged scene to work with; would he know the right level to hit?

Quentin found the spot in the book right away, indication that he knew the play well. She fed him the lines of the First Murderer. After a glance at the pages, he delivered flawlessly and in such a manner as to make the arcane language easily understandable to a modern audience. He also got the emotions across without snacking on the scenery.

Cassie tried not to look too enthusiastic. "Okay. I'm happy, but the decision rests with the show's angel, Miss Isabel Graham. I'm directing, but she's the producer and star and has final say." She expected some sort of response from the name. Millions of people knew of her. Even Cassie had seen an episode or three of Isabel's hit comedy series, *I Love Isabel.*

"Shouldn't be a problem," said Quentin, not batting an eye. "I've worked with Bel before."

"Really?" Cassie did not miss the affectionate diminutive of Isabel's name. Only a very select few had the privilege of calling her that.

"She and I were in college together," he explained. "In fact, we were in *Macbeth* one semester. The same roles."

"How...convenient." Cassie spotted the confirmation of this on the résumé.

"Bel's career took off faster than mine. I did a stint in the navy to pay for college, which delayed things for a couple of years. I'm catching up."

"That's great." *I think*. "So Isabel already knows you're here?"

"She's the one who recommended me to the casting agency. But I wanted to get the part on my own, not just because she told you to put me in."

"That's very considerate of you. What if I'd turned you down?"

"Then I'd go back to New York and nag my agent for other jobs. No point being in a show if the director doesn't think I'm right for the part."

Her respect for him went up a few notches. "Just as well it all worked out, then. Let's introduce you to the others. Rehearsal starts in an hour. We'll go over the blocking for Act One."

"All right. How's the curse going for this production?"

At this out-of-nowhere shot, Cassie paused in mid-boost from her desk, and sat down again. Rather abruptly. "Curse? Who told you?" she blurted before thinking.

"This is the bad-luck play," he said, his eyes twinkling again. "So what troubles have you had?"

"I don't believe in the curse," she answered dismissively.

"The Weird Sisters' spells are supposed to be real, and it's always been bad luck to quote from the Scottish play while backstage."

"Only because in the old days it meant the current production was about to close. Companies could quickly throw *Macbeth* together to fill up the schedule gap. If an actor heard anyone rehearsing lines from it backstage, it meant his show's run was doomed."

"I've not heard that one." He fixed her with a rather intense look. "But you've not really answered my question, Miss Sullivan."

"Cassie," she said automatically, and let it hang there between them for a very long moment. Or did time just telescope when he looked at her like that? *Oh, but he does have riveting eyes*. She broke out of their spell and came up with a reluctant response. "We've had a few glitches that we blame on the production poltergeist, but there's been no more now than for any other show."

"Forgive me, but that's not what I've heard."

She could fix people with a formidable look herself and did so now with Quentin, her green eyes stiletto-sharp. "And just what have you heard?"

Unlike others she'd ever used it on, he didn't seem to recognize the danger signal and leaned forward, quite unintimidated. "When I found out I was going to be sent to replace Trevor Hopkins, I phoned Bel to thank her for the boost. She gave me an earful. I know about the missing costumes, props breaking, sets falling down, electrical shorts, flooded bathrooms—the works."

"We found the costumes in the trash and put that down to cleaning staff error, the rest is just accident and coincidence. It's an old building. It would be odd if things didn't go wrong with…things."

"What about the rash Bel got from her makeup?"

"Allergic reaction to a new brand. We changed it."

"And Trevor Hopkins finding that dead rat in his codpiece?"

"It crawled in there to die. We made him a new one and set out traps."

"And the needle that turned up in Bel's corset? She got a bad scratch from that."

Good grief, he knew everything. Cassie fought down her anger. "The costume crew was careless. They apologized. The rest is coincidence. What are you getting at with all this, Mr. Douglas? Do you think someone is after Isabel?"

"I think Isabel thinks someone is out to kill the production."

"That's ridiculous. I've been with the people here for years, there's no way—"

"Bel worked herself into a good upset once she started talking. She's willing to lay the blame on the play's traditional curse, but she's also willing to consider non-supernatural alternatives. You may know and trust everyone here, but she's an outsider."

"Mr. Douglas, I can tell you right now that all the people in this company are two hundred percent behind this production. We're working to make it a success because we need her money. Isabel's agent approached me with her offer to foot the bill for the whole thing so long as she gets to play Lady Macbeth, and I gratefully accepted. The publicity this playhouse will get from her name will give us the financial help we've always needed. There is no way anyone here is going to jeopardize that."

"But maybe talk about a curse might embarrass her in some way? The tabloids love this kind of thing."

Ouch. He knew how to hit low. "Miss Graham wants to prove to the world she can play high drama as well as middle-America comedy, and a little bad publicity is not going to stop her. She's a total professional and knows that the show must go on."

Quentin, his gaze still steady, nodded slowly, as though he'd found something he'd been looking for and liked it. "You seem to be aware of just how important this is to her."

"If she blows it the critics will be merciless. She's put a lot of trust in me, an unknown backwater director—"

"Whose parents were the darlings of Broadway once upon a time."

It was no secret, but she was surprised he knew that. "Yes, they were, and they taught me everything they knew when they invested in this theater. I want to do proud by their memory, and I will give Isabel my best effort."

"Then we're all in accord." He suddenly relaxed and smiled.

She couldn't help but smile back. "Yes, I suppose we are, but—"

Someone banged urgently on her red door. "Cassie! Emergency!" It was Willis Wright, stage-managing in overdrive from the sound of him.

Heart thumping, she shot from her chair, on full alert. In any given production there were a hundred emergencies, but his tone of voice made this one serious. She tore the door open and nearly collided with him. "What is it?"

"We've found a body up on the gridwalk."

"*What?*" She pushed past, tearing toward the stage. There she saw the whole company staring upward to the dark heights of the grid, the steel construction that held the lights and backdrops. She stared herself, trying to pierce the shadows. "Flashlight!"

Willis slapped one into her hand. Its beam was pale from use and didn't reach far, but she saw a man-sized shape dangling ominously over stage center.

"Oh, my God. Is that for real? Someone get up there and find out."

Willis himself saw to it, scrambling up the metal ladder affixed to the backstage wall. He reached the grid and gingerly stepped onto it. The hanging figure swung heavily. Several of the people around her gasped.

"Everyone back out of the way!" she snapped.

Still staring up, they reluctantly moved clear.

And only just in time. Willis yelled, "Look out!"

The thing high above suddenly plummeted. The body smacked into the stage with a resounding thud, inspiring screams. Cassie jumped in reaction, but held her place. She became aware of someone looming close behind her. Quentin. Generating a lot of heat. He stared over her shoulder at the body.

It was only a dummy—for which Cassie heaved a great sigh of relief—but its appearance sent a chill right up her spine. Female, with a hangman's noose around the neck, it was dressed in her own private working uniform of jeans, cowboy boots, and her best blue work shirt, which had gone missing yesterday. Topping all was a red wig, the color matching her own wild mane. Most disturbing was a huge prop butcher knife, smeared with dark red paint, sticking out of the thing's chest.

She felt Quentin's warm hand on her shoulder, gripping tight. "Good God...that's supposed to be you."

She recoiled at the suggestion. "I hope not."

"That's sick!" Nell all but shrieked. "Absolutely sick! Which one of you did this?"

No one stepped forward; no one looked the least bit guilty or smug, but then, most of them were actors.

No. I'm not going to go there, Cassie thought. *These are my friends, they're family!* An unfamiliar hollowness invaded her guts. Fear. Real fear. That fake knife had been buried right to the hilt in her effigy's chest. She steeled herself, went over, and pulled it out. All eyes were on her as she held it up like a trophy.

She fully milked the moment, making a slow turn to take them all in, keeping her voice rock-steady. "All right. Listen up. I am not amused. Somebody could have been killed if this thing had fallen at the wrong time. There's no harm done, but no more tricks. I'm talking zero tolerance, folks. I find anyone, absolutely anyone, screwing around like this, and I will personally bury them. Is that clear?"

Nods of comprehension all around. She tried to read their faces for any clue as to who might be the guilty party, but it was impossible, so she concentrated on not trembling from the adrenaline rush. Rule One for any good dramatic scene: never let them see you sweat.

"Cassie? What's going on here?"

She turned to face Isabel Graham, the show's patron, producer, and leading lady. Though known as a brilliant comedic star by means of her hit TV series, at the moment Isabel truly resembled Lady Macbeth. Her blue eyes were wide with shock, her mouth set in a grim downward turn. She looked at the bloody knife, then at the dummy.

"Just a sick joke, Isabel," Cassie wearily explained, wishing she could lose the knife.

"Another one?" This came from Isabel's manager, James Keating, also her most recent fiancé. Like Nell, Isabel fell in love a lot, but had been careful not to follow through to marriage just yet. According to the tabloids, though, Keating just might be the one to break the rule. He was movie-star handsome, had a shark's attitude when it came to business, and was totally devoted to Isabel. He stared at the dummy sprawled all over center stage.

"Cassie, this isn't a joke."

"That's supposed to be you?" asked Isabel, horrified.

"It's a rotten likeness. I have a much better figure."

Isabel puffed out a short, mirthless laugh. "Not funny."

"Absolutely not," agreed James. "This is a deliberate and cold-blooded—"

"Quentin!" Isabel squealed, suddenly noticing her new co-star standing behind Cassie. Cassie dodged clear just as Isabel launched herself at him. He obligingly grabbed her up in a full body hug and spun her slender form around.

Short attention span, thought Cassie. Isabel had loads of talent, but when she wasn't performing she was as easily distracted as a kitten was by a new piece of string.

"You've grown!" crowed Isabel when Quentin set her down.

"Nope, you just got shorter."

"Did not! You get those big muscles in the navy?"

"They're rented, but if they work out, I might buy them."

James Keating watched the exchange between the two old friends with thin-lipped tolerance. Cassie knew how he felt. Her last—completely last—actor-boyfriend had thrown her over for someone else. He'd been just as public about it, too. Was James worried about a rival?

Willis came up then, or rather down, having just quit the metal ladder. He also inspected the "body," especially the noose rope. His focus served to draw Isabel back to the immediate problem.

"What is it, Will?" Cassie asked.

He shook his head. "This was set like a booby trap. I found fishing line leading from the dummy's noose to the ladder and down the rungs on the inside. The noose was just barely snagged on a hook up there with a fancy knot; one good pull on the line and it's off and dropping. I accidentally tripped the gag when I got to the top. Whoever set it wanted to pull it down from a distance. It would have worked, but the setup was clumsy. If there'd been a good draft it might have come tumbling down beforetime and killed someone."

She felt cold. All over.

"Cassie, you should call the cops on this. James is right, this isn't a joke anymore. Maybe the rest of the stuff you can fob off on the poltergeist, but somebody put work into this thing—and it had to be somebody with free access to the building. This came from the basement props and costume storage."

"Not the clothes," she said.

"Those are your own clothes, aren't they?" asked Isabel.

"Don't hold it against me. I'll buy something nice for opening night."

"Stop with the joking already," said Nell. "This a deliberate act of terrorism!"

"I agree," said Quentin. "You need to report it."

"And have the tabloids eat us for lunch? I don't think so." She'd already had to deal with several overly friendly reporters looking for the inside scoop on a perfectly ordinary—well, almost ordinary—production of *Macbeth*. They'd been interested in any sort of dirt on Isabel, of course.

Isabel shook her head. "Never mind the so-called press. I can take a little heat so long as they spell my name right. This could be a life-threatening situation. You have to call the police!"

Cassie raised her hands in a placating gesture. Unfortunately, the prop knife was still in one clenched fist, causing everyone to back away a step. "Okay! I'll phone them, but I am not terrorized, I'm mad as hell. Everyone here should get mad, too."

Nell visibly thought that one over. "What? Like an acting exercise?"

"No! I mean if you put all the poltergeist stuff together, most of it doesn't mean squat, but this is different. I think that someone wants to kill this show, for reason or reasons unknown."

"Over my dead body," said Isabel, her eyes flashing blue fire. "I'll call in a security firm and lock this place up like Fort Knox before I let that happen."

"Right," said Cassie. "That's what I'm looking for—I want you and everyone else mad and on red alert. If we all play watchdog, look out for each other, anticipate problems before they happen, then they can't happen. Am I brilliant, or what?"

"Or what," Nell deadpanned. "You want us up here twenty-four/seven to revoke Murphy's Law? Lemme tell you, girl, when it comes to theater, Murphy was an optimist."

For the rest of the rehearsals Cassie concentrated on directing, which almost made her forget about the poltergeist. For whole minutes at a time.

It helped to have really good actors to work with, though. Quentin Douglas's romantic, hot-blooded—if slightly psychotic—Macbeth quite overwhelmed the brooding, anger-driven version Trevor Hopkins had attempted. Even without the drawing power of Isabel Graham's star name, this production was shaping into something special. Cassie was thrilled. She wanted the audience to see the characters, not the actors playing them.

Complications still arose. Mostly in the form of Quentin finding all kinds of ways to stick close to her when he wasn't busy killing people on stage. She pretended not to notice his attentions and focused on rehearsal business, which drove Nell up the wall.

"He likes you, Cassie! Are you nuts? Total studs like him are thin on the ground."

"He's an actor. Actors are off my menu."

"Unbend a little, girl. At least have coffee with him sometime so he doesn't think you hate him."

"I don't hate him! I'm being professional. Go for him yourself."

"I tried—but all he did was get me to talk about you. The least you can do is date him so I can have a vicarious thrill when you tell me all about it."

"I've no time. The play opens soon, and in four weeks it closes; he'll be history. End of problem."

"You wish."

Despite everyone looking out for each other, Murphy's Law continued with a vengeance. Opening-night jitters became the norm days too early, with more missing or damaged costumes, broken props, and damaged scenery flats. Frustration rose, tempers shortened, and arguments were frequent. Isabel's presence helped; she could stop a fight with her star-powered smile alone. At her own expense she had all the locks changed and hired off-duty policemen to keep an eye on things. To no avail, with so many crew and actors milling hurriedly about trying to bring the production together it was impossible for the security types to watch everything. The incidents continued.

After the effigy business, Cassie started sleeping over in the theater. She'd often done so when work had gone too late to drive home. With spare clothing, a comfy couch in her office, and showers in the dressing rooms, it was no hardship.

She didn't tell anyone, having gotten over her fit of denial to face the ugly fact that someone in the group was out to kill the show. Cassie absolutely hated the idea, but she found herself looking at familiar faces with new eyes. She began to come up with motives for each and had to bite her tongue to keep from blurting out an accusatory question that could destroy a lifetime of friendship.

So she kept quiet about her after-hours guardian duty, hoping that if she did discover the culprit they could settle things privately.

As for the possibility that an anti-Shakespearean ghost had taken up residence in the theater...well, Cassie had yet to meet a poltergeist who was any match for a furious redhead armed with a baseball bat.

The first two nights were uneventful, giving her much time to think back on all the various pranks—especially the deadliest. The guilty party behind the effigy had to have access, time, and privacy to set it up. The knot made her think of sailors, but ex-navy man Quentin Douglas, so newly come to the show, had no motive. Besides, most of the company knew how to do special knots; it was part of their normal stagecraft training.

That clue shoved to the side, she thought seriously about motivation. Why would anyone want to kill the production? Not one of her people would benefit if it died—quite the contrary.

What about Isabel? She believed in this show, but was that just cover? Her plan to prove herself to be a powerful dramatic actress as well as a comedy star was backfiring in the tabloids. Derisive articles were surfacing without any of the writers having seen her work. Unfair, but bad news sold. If Isabel stopped the production in the face of the mishaps, then maybe the critical feeding frenzy would never happen. Of course, she lost the chance to disprove all that derision with a solid performance, as well.

Perhaps James Keating? He'd more than once voiced the thought that they should quit and close down the show before anyone got hurt, but he always deferred to Isabel's wishes. Could he be tired of playing second banana?

By the third night at watch, Cassie was exhausted. At eleven she locked out the last of the crew and made a round of the dark and silent theater. While others might find its cavernous quiet and deep shadows ominous, she was in her home element, each creak as familiar as her own breath. When no boogeyman obligingly leaped out so she could whack him with her bat and solve her problems, she retired to the dressing room area to get a much-wanted shower.

Having seen enough Hitchcock movies to be sensible about the vulnerability of bathing females, she not only locked the dressing room door, but propped a chair under the knob. Any would-be Norman Bates would have a tough time of sneaking up on her, especially if the toolbox she'd balanced on the chair fell off.

Just as she finished her final rinse and cut the water, a terrific crash nearly made her leap out of her freshly scrubbed skin. Dripping, she struggled frantically into a terry robe and grabbed up her bat. Her heart hammered so loud she could barely hear anything else as she approached the dressing room door, which was being forced open inch-by-inch by a powerful hand.

Swallowing her fear and outrage, she nipped quick as a cat behind the door and raised her weapon high.

The chair abruptly tumbled over, and a black figure cautiously edged inside. She gulped again. He was awfully big for a poltergeist.

No matter. He was a trespasser and she was within her rights. She brought the bat down hard on the back of his head, giving a banshee yell for good measure.

He whirled just in time to whip his arm up, deflecting the blow to the side. He yanked the bat from her grasp and drove bodily toward her. She buried her fist into his belly, using plenty of knuckle. The man doubled over. Cassie ducked, rolled, and grabbed up the bat again, coming to her feet with it ready in hand as he recovered enough to turn on her.

"*You?!*" she screamed, caught between disbelief and rage.

"*Grrg!*" said Quentin Douglas, holding his gut.

"What the hell are you doing here?"

He waved one hand, palm out, backing away from her threat. "Uh-afh-ooo?"

"I'm watching the place," she answered, understanding the question even if articulation was lacking. "Why are you here? You're the poltergeist? I don't understand!"

He violently shook his head, then found a chair and dropped into it. He didn't look like a poltergeist. *But then he's an actor,* she reminded herself.

"I'm here to watch out for trouble," he wheezed out a few moments later. "With the stuff that's going on…it seemed the right thing to do. I was worried about you."

Wow. Her last guy would never have done *that* for her. "I can take care of myself."

"I noticed," he said, rubbing his gut.

"How long have you been here?"

"Since the first night I arrived."

"What? You've been creeping around every night without me knowing?!"

"I happen to be very good at it. That's why Isabel recommended me when Hopkins gave notice. She knew about my navy training. She thought it might be an asset to theater security."

Cassie relaxed. Marginally. She still held her bat ready. "Are you all right?"

"Just bruised pride. If my service buddies ever found out I was decked by a half-pint like you—"

She growled and tightened her grip on the bat.

"Take it easy! That was a compliment. You've got a great punch. If red hair is mentioned they won't hassle me."

Mollified, she eased off. "Why'd you come in here? Trying to cop a peek?" She tightened the tie on her robe, suddenly aware of drafts.

"That would be great, but I saw someone lurking in the hall outside. I chased him, then lost him. When I returned I found the lock jimmied, so I thought I'd better check to make sure you weren't hanging from a coat rack with a knife in you."

"Oh. Well. Thanks. Shouldn't we go looking for the lurker, then?"

"We—sure, when you've dressed for the part, but don't go to any trouble on my account. In the meantime, I'll start looking around."

Growling, she retreated to the shower area and threw on clothes, then went to find Quentin.

Apparently recovered from the blow to his gut, he reported that all was quiet. "He's probably gone by now. I didn't get a good look at him. It was too dark. It might even have been a woman."

"Let's turn on all the lights and see what we find." She headed for the master switches backstage.

"Wait a second...do you smell gas?"

She sniffed. He was right.

"Basement," she said decisively, pivoting and running for the stairs. "We have butane tanks there to fuel stage-fire effects, but they're locked up in a cage. I don't see how—"

Quentin followed her, using the flashlight he carried to light the way down the stairs for them both. "Who has the keys to the cage?"

"There is no key, just a trick padlock, it's a joke around here—" She stopped cold. On the bottom step was a single candle burning in a holder. She scrambled the rest of the way down the stairs and slapped the flame out. The gas smell was worse here; she felt a headache coming on from it.

Quentin surged past her. Some of the cage wire had been cut through. He thrust his hand into the hole and shut off the valves on the hissing tanks.

"Out!" he ordered, and she did not argue with him.

An hour before the final rehearsal Cassie called a meeting. She was mad as hell, but not showing it. In fact, she looked quite pleasant and rested. That was enough to alert her people that something was up.

"We're going to have the best show we've ever put on," she said as an opening.

Nell, who knew her very well, showed alarm.

"We can also relax, our troubles are over. The poltergeist blew it. I know who's been trying to kill this production."

"Who?" demanded James Keating, holding tight to Isabel's hand.

Cassie grinned. "Someone who didn't know all the ins and outs of this old place. One of the jokes here is the fact that there is a huge dummy padlock on the butane cage." She quickly explained about what she and Quentin had discovered the night before. "This place was supposed to blow up, or at least be so damaged as to make the show impossible. The culprit, not knowing that a trick catch on the padlock would open it, didn't have time to cut through the hasp, and smashing it would have been too noisy, so he cut the cage wires instead—and that was his giveaway."

"How so?" asked Isabel.

"A woman or a small man could have got a hand through the cage wires without too much trouble, and wouldn't have needed to cut the wires to turn the tank valves on. Anyone inside the Sullivan company would have known to just pop the trick padlock. Only an outsider, a man unable to get his big hand through, would have thought it necessary to cut the wire to get to the tanks. So why the hell were you trying to kill this production—Mr. Keating?"

Keating, no actor, went a sickly gray. "That—that's slander!" he finally stammered out. "My lawyers will strip you to the bone!"

Isabel shot to her feet. "You bastard!"

"B-but, sweetie-pie—it was getting too expensive, even as a tax write-off. And the critics were eating you alive even before opening night. Besides, you're a *star*, not an *actress*...."

Cassie calmly fitted her baseball bat into Isabel's hand. "Here, honey, have a party."

The Graham-Keating engagement, along with James Keating's right arm, which he'd raised to ward off the blow, was officially broken. Despite his threat of legal reprisal for slander, assault, and battery, no one in the company would admit a thing, so the police investigation into his broken arm stalled, while the show went on. Isabel Graham, drawing from that afternoon's inspiration, gave a riveting performance as one of the most vicious, bloody-minded Lady Macbeths the critics had ever had the pleasure to cower from; they also enthused about newcomer Quentin Douglas, sparking talk of a Broadway revival of the play.

"Four weeks and he's history," chided Nell to Cassie at opening night's celebration party. "Yeah, sure. You change your mind about dating actors yet?"

"Maybe," Cassie admitted, returning Quentin's look from across the stage. He started toward her, eyes twinkling again. "He didn't seem to mind too much when I clobbered him, so there's some hope...."

"Then you go, girl!" Nell pushed her forward. "And give him one for me!"

www.gonnahavekelly.com

Diane A. S. Stuckart

He had been there for the past half-hour, perched atop an empty bicycle rack in front of the West End art gallery where Kelly Winslow worked part-time. *Waiting for someone*, she tried to tell herself, noting his scrutiny of the pedestrian traffic in this, one of Dallas's most popular historic districts. Indeed, he looked little different from the typical West End hanger-on with his black T-shirt, black jeans, and fashionably cropped black hair. Just some thirty-ish Goth-wannabe...maybe a neophyte hit man who hadn't yet learned the art of blending with a crowd.

Then he turned his black sunglasses in her direction, and Kelly shivered.

"Get a grip, girl," she muttered, deliberately focusing her attention on the inventory list she was compiling. Chances were, the man couldn't even see past the reflection of sun against glass to make out who might be standing behind the gallery window.

No reason to assume he was staring at her, in particular. No reason to suspect he was the same person who, unbeknownst to her until a few days before, had been following her for weeks now. No

reason to fear that he was the Internet stalker who had a website dedicated completely to her, a frightening little corner of cyberspace he
called www.gonnahavekelly.com!

Come visit my website, Kelly. I think you'll find it very interesting, the
message appearing in her e-mail box a few days earlier had read. She
had almost deleted it, certain it was one of those invitations to a porn
site halfheartedly disguised as an e-mail from a friend. But some
impulse had made her click on the link, anyhow.

Its unsettling domain name notwithstanding, the website appeared
to be nothing more sinister than an unauthorized tribute dedicated, as
it claimed, "to the beauty and power of Kelly Winslow's extraordinary
paintings." Three page links each suggested that she click. Feeling
rather smug, Kelly had.

The first link, entitled See Who Kelly Is, consisted of the same
photo she used in her gallery publicity. A box of statistics followed: age,
28; eyes and hair, brown; height, 5´5˝; and so on. At the bottom of the
page was a list of various galleries that had shown her work, information that, while hardly secret, must have taken some effort to compile.

Next was See What Kelly Has Painted, featuring perhaps a dozen
photos of the various oils she'd displayed over the past year. Under
each, the unknown webmaster had added comments of his own...all
complimentary, some surprisingly insightful. She had clicked from
there onto the final if oddly titled page See What Else Kelly Does, and
her initial satisfaction had swiftly deteriorated into dismay.

The images that had followed would, under other circumstances,
be dismissed as innocent, even boring: shopping at the health food
store; drinking coffee at a table outside Starbucks; dancing with friends
at a Greenville Avenue bar. Nothing special about them, at all...save for
the fact they had been taken without her knowledge or consent!

"Kelly, darling, be a lamb and ring up Mrs. Criswell," an affected
voice abruptly broke in on her thoughts.

The speaker was a tall, thin man with shoulder-length blond
hair...Billy Criswell, the gallery's flamboyant owner and, in a manner
of speaking, Kelly's employer. He displayed her works in his gallery
in return for her few unpaid hours a week helping him run the place.
It was a setup that benefited them both.

So what would he say if she told him about the website? she

wondered as she wrapped the aforementioned Mrs. Criswell's new watercolor. Probably, not much. *Free publicity, darling,* he'd likely declare, dismissing her fears as casually as the police had.

There's not much we can do, ma'am, the polite voice that had identified itself as Detective Ted Ralston, of the Computer Crimes Division, had told her. *Unfortunately, it's not illegal to post pictures of someone without their consent. I can record your complaint but, unless this person ever actually threatens you, I suggest you don't worry.*

That, basically, had been the good detective's advice in one neat package. It had been easy enough for him to say...and a hell of a lot harder for her to do. In the past week, she'd been certain at least half a dozen times that some man or another was following her, only to realize after a few nerve-wracking minutes that she simply had let her imagination run wild. So, maybe the detective had been right. Chances were that he'd be too shy ever to approach her, anyhow. Fantasizing about her in cyberspace was likely as far as this wacko would ever go.

But he *had* wanted her to know about this fantasy, she reminded herself.

Which brought her back to the man in black. Was he her stalker, or just another victim of her paranoia? *If he's not there when you look out the window again, then that means he's not the one.* The mental bargain with herself made, she began counting to ten—very slowly— then dared another glance back out at the street.

The man was gone.

She breathed a thankful sigh that was loud enough to draw the attention of Billy, who had just hustled another, non-buying customer to the door. "Really, darling," he drawled, shaking back his bleached mane, "if you're that bored, why don't you go home early. Heaven knows they're not rushing in to buy *your* work."

His snide reference was to her pair of as-yet-unsold abstracts that had been on display for the past week. *Love Is a Pain,* she had wryly named the second of the two, with its tortuous angles in shades of charcoal and red that captured the essence of a bleeding heart...hers, to be exact. The other, painted well before the romantic breakup that had spawned its bleaker companion, was a study in brilliant primaries and more optimistically titled, *Love Is Bliss.*

"If you won't mind closing up alone, then I will go. If I hurry, I can catch the early bus."

A few minutes later, she was out on the sidewalk. Though freshly released from her air-conditioned haven, she still felt sweat begin trickling from her temples before she'd gone a block. For once, however, the oppressive heat might be considered a friend. *No stalker in his right mind would be following someone around on a day like this*, she told herself in satisfaction. Not with the June sun as hot as a ripe jalapeño, and no breeze in evidence to help cool the fire.

If she had a choice, she wouldn't be walking, either. She'd be tooling around town in her car like any other good Dallasite, with the windows rolled up tight and the a/c cranked down to polar. Unfortunately, said vehicle required $600 worth of repairs to be drivable, according to the local shop. Kelly grimaced. Since she didn't have the spare cash this month, she had reconciled herself to getting around on foot and on public transportation, for the time being.

She paused at a sliver of shade provided by the awning of a trendy clothing store window, and sighed. She damn well couldn't afford this place's three- and four-figure price tags, either; still, it didn't cost anything to look. But barely had she begun to lust after a bright red leather halter-top—on sale at $295—when a movement in the window reflection caught her eye. Her could-be stalker was behind her now, standing perhaps twenty feet away!

Kelly took off toward the next corner at a pace somewhere between race-walking and jogging. All she had to do was reach the bus stop unscathed, and she'd be home in half an hour. Just one more block, she reassured herself and stepped into the crosswalk.

Barely had she registered the blat of a car horn before a strong hand clamped around her upper arm and jerked her back onto the curb. A heartbeat later, a beat-up yellow mustang made a swift right turn in front of her, tires squealing and exhaust belching. When the smoke cleared, she found herself staring in dismay at the fresh tread marks now laid over the very spot where she'd been standing on the crosswalk.

Wincing a little at the pressure of his fingers, she slowly turned to face her rescuer. Had he not pulled her back, those tire marks would have been decorating her body, instead. But now he had her where he probably wanted her...firmly in his grip. They were close enough so that she could see the faint beading of sweat on his brow from the heat, could breathe in the faintest hint of the expensive-smelling after-shave he wore. And he was even more attractive than she'd realized, Kelly thought in dismay.

At least, I'm not being stalked by some butt-ugly loser wearing a pocket protector.

Just as quickly as the irrelevant thought flitted through her mind, she mentally tromped it down. *Damn it, Kelly, focus.* To her advantage, half a dozen cars now were stopped at the light alongside them, their occupants all potential witnesses to any altercation. The man could hardly carry her off without being noticed, so she didn't have to panic...at least, not yet. But she damned sure wasn't going to stand there playing helpless victim, either.

"All right, asshole," she declared in a voice that squeaked only slightly. "You've got exactly two seconds to let go of me, or else I'm going to start screaming."

"No need to scream, Ms. Winslow. I was just keeping you from being roadkill...nothing more sinister than that." A faint smile tugged at his lips. "It's okay, I'm one of the good guys."

Releasing her, he slipped a finger beneath the gold neck chain he was wearing and pulled it up to reveal a badge that glinted in the sunlight. Then he reached into his jeans pocket and extracted a business card stamped with the Dallas Police Department logo. "Detective Ted Ralston, Computer Crimes Division," he said and handed it to her. "We talked on the phone last week."

"I—I remember."

She glanced from the card to him, and then back to the card again. *This* was the cop she'd talked to? Maybe she should call the police on a more regular basis. Perhaps his voice was a bit different—deeper, sexier—from what she remembered but, then, their conversation had lasted maybe all of two minutes. But if he was a cop, then what in the hell was he doing...

"...Following me," she finished aloud. "Damn it, you were following me, weren't you?"

"My apologies if I alarmed you, ma'am."

He pulled off his sunglasses to reveal a pair of the sexiest blue eyes she had ever seen on a man. They were rimmed with thick black lashes that would make any model in a mascara ad weep with envy, while a fine spray of squint lines radiated from each corner, as if those eyes were habitually crinkled from grinning. Unfortunately, his expression now as he stared down at her was anything but amused.

"Actually, I wasn't so much following you, as hoping to spot your cyber admirer," he went on, that blue gaze making a quick sweep of the street around them before locking on her again. "You see, I did another check on that website you reported to us. Turns out there have been a few significant...well, changes...since the last time I looked at it."

"Changes? What kind of changes?"

He hesitated, and then nodded in the direction of the Starbucks across the street. "Why don't you let me buy you a cup of coffee, and I'll tell you about it."

❦　❦　❦

"He's been inside my house!"

The few sips of iced latte that Kelly had managed to swallow threatened to come back up in a fear-laced spray of milk and coffee. With an effort, she managed to hold back that unseemly tide, even though Detective Ralston would have been the only witness. At his urging, they had eschewed the air-conditioned comfort of the coffee-house for the hot if relatively private sidewalk patio, with its row of empty, umbrella-shaded tables. Even so, she leaned across the table and dropped her voice to a whisper.

"He's been inside my house," she softly repeated. "How do you know that?"

"He added a few new pictures to the website this morning. Pictures of your studio, your kitchen, your living room...your bedroom."

Her bedroom. Dear God, surely he hadn't come prowling in the night, snapping pictures of her while she was sleeping! She briefly shut her eyes as she steeled herself to ask the next question. "What about...I mean, did he—"

Ralston shook his head. "He didn't take any pictures of you, if that's what you're asking. They're just shots of empty rooms. I don't suppose you've noticed any signs of a forced entry in the past few days?"

"No, nothing...but then, it's not like the place is a fortress," she faintly answered, picturing the tiny, tree-draped bungalow off Greenville Avenue that she called home.

The single-story house was just large enough for one person to spread about comfortably, with its combined living/dining room, two bedrooms—one of which she had converted into her studio—a bath, and a kitchen. Furnished with garage sale oddities and vintage store leftovers, the place dated from the thirties. Its door locks were original hardware; flimsy things that she'd always meant to replace with deadbolts, but never had gotten around to doing so. And the wood-sash windows with their little thumb locks weren't much better, considering that a couple of them didn't even close completely to start with. Breaking in would be an easy feat for anyone with a couple of spare minutes and a nail file.

"...think we've discovered his identity," Ralston was saying, and Kelly snapped her attention back to the detective. "He covered his tracks pretty well, but I was able to trace the website back to a guy by the name of Jason Todman. He's twenty-nine, single, makes pretty good bucks. By all accounts, he's smart, successful, not bad-looking—"

"So why in the hell does he need to stalk me? Can't he get a date?"

The detective had slipped his sunglasses back on, so that the cool black barrier was between them again. "It's not a matter of not being able to get a date," he replied, and a matching coldness crept into his tone. "I don't think even he could completely explain his reasons, except that it's a power trip. Controlling women that way makes him feel, well, sexy."

"I see. So how do you know all that, Detective Ralston? Did my friend Jason send you an e-mail or something?"

"Nope, just guessing. Must be those psych classes I took at the academy, kicking in after all this time."

Another grin tugged at his lips, dispelling the momentary chill between them...if, indeed, it had even existed. Kelly allowed herself a wan smile in return, even as she persisted, "But I don't understand. If you know who the guy is, why don't you just go arrest him? After all, he broke into my house. Surely that's still against the law, even if his webpage isn't."

"But unless we have a witness, or some physical evidence he was there—fingerprints, hair samples—we can't charge him with anything. For all we know, he took those pictures while he was in the house on legitimate business. Or maybe he got them from you."

Right. Like she was in the business of handing out photos of her living quarters to every guy who rang her doorbell. She didn't say that aloud, however, but merely swirled a straw in her latte—already thawed into a lukewarm brown concoction—as she strove for a reasonable reply.

"All right, Detective, let me make sure I understand what's happening here," she finally said. "Some crazy computer nerd has the hots for me; he takes pictures inside my house when I'm not there and posts them on a website; the police know who he is...and they can't arrest him for a damn thing. Does that about cover it?"

"That about covers it."

She shoved aside her half-full drink and stood. "Fine. Thanks for the coffee. Now, if you'll excuse me, I think I'll go home and wait to be murdered in my sleep."

To her dismay, those last few words verged dangerously on a wail. Blinking back tears of frustration, she started at a swift walk toward her bus stop. Just wait until the next time the issue of police pay raises came up on a city bond issue, she silently fumed. She'd check off a big fat "no" faster than Detective Ralston could blink those sexy blue eyes of his!

"Wait, Ms. Winslow..."

She heard the soft scrap of athletic shoes against pavement, and then Ralston was beside her again. "Just because we can't arrest the man, doesn't mean there's nothing we can do. At the very least, I can check out your place, make sure your friend isn't hiding in the closet."

She halted in mid-step and shot him an outraged look. "Excuse me?"

"Sorry, bad joke," he quickly amended. "What I really mean is that I can look things over for you, see if I can figure out how he got in, and fix it so he can't do it again. Besides, I'm parked down the block from your place, so I have to ride back with you, anyhow."

Yeah, or you could wait and take the next bus.

Still, the detective had a point. The thought of returning home alone, knowing that some stranger had been prowling within its walls, was more than unsettling. It made sense to let a professional make the rounds with her; maybe recommend a few security tips. And if her cyber stalker did happen to be lying in wait with his camera, it wouldn't hurt for him to see a man around the place...particularly a hunk like Detective Ralston.

The heat that abruptly warmed her cheeks wasn't entirely from the afternoon sun. *Don't get ahead of yourself, Kelly.* Probably, cops had rules about getting involved with crime victims. Of course, since they weren't going to arrest this Jason Todman unless he killed her, or did something equally vile, then maybe she didn't yet count as a victim.

She ventured a sidelong glance in Ralston's direction. He flashed her another smile, and she wondered if maybe he was thinking the same thing. Or maybe he was just feeling guilty about his earlier flip comment, and wanted to make amends. For now, either was fine by her, so long as it meant she didn't have to walk into her house alone.

She nodded. "All right, you win. Might as well get my taxpayer's money's worth."

"Might as well," he agreed, and his smile broadened into a grin that, to her consternation, did quite interesting things to her insides. "If nothing else, I'll pull a few strings and get you the city discount on new locks."

Detective Ralston...or Ted, as she had called him for these past two weeks...had been as good as his word. The day after their first meeting, he had returned to her place with two shiny new deadbolts, which he proceeded to install on both front and back doors. He'd also fixed the sticking windows, so that she could close them all the way. And since he'd done all this work on his off-hours, Kelly had offered to reciprocate by picking up the tab for Tex-Mex at one of Greenville Avenue's hot spots that night.

Not a date, she had hurried to clarify, when he had begun to mumble something about departmental policy. *Just a little thank-you for your help.* But a shared pitcher of margaritas, combined with the sight of him in snug jeans and an equally tight black T-shirt, had proved a devastating combination. Halfway through a platter of fajitas, she'd gathered the courage to point out that, technically, she wasn't yet a crime victim...so maybe it was okay if they counted this as a date, after all? And matters had proceeded quite satisfactorily from that point on.

He had left her place early the next morning, but not before retrieving the business card he'd given her at their first meeting.

"Don't bother trying to get hold of me at the precinct," he told her, scratching through the printed phone number with a felt-tip pen, and scrawling in another number above it. "You call there, you get someone who transfers you to someone else, who transfers you to another someone else, who'll probably end up having to take a message for me. Anytime you need me—day or night—call my cell phone."

But she'd had little need to dial that number, for he usually called her first...sometimes, while she filled in at the gallery; other times, just before she settled in for the night. Unfortunately, he'd been able to break away from work for a full evening only twice more in that time, but both those occasions had ended quite satisfactorily in her bed. In the meantime, though, and to her very great relief, her cyber stalker finally seemed to have tired of his game.

Two days after her first date with Ted, she had checked the Kelly website again, only to find a lone THIS SITE UNDER CONSTRUCTION banner. When she'd gleefully told Ted what she had learned, he merely flashed her that sexy grin and mentioned something about having sent an official, unofficial "cease and desist" e-mail to the site. Thus, by the end of the second week, her cyber stalker had become all but a distant memory.

That was, until she came home from the gallery that afternoon to find her latest painting askew on its easel.

It was the oil she'd begun work on just a few days earlier, rounding out her series of abstracts with love as their theme. Rather than using the brilliant shades of *Bliss*, or the stark, contrasting tones of *Pain*, she had opted for a more thoughtful feel with this as-yet-unnamed work, indulging in muted primaries and softer lines. While the painting was but half-finished, she had been so pleased with the results that, yesterday, she had done something she rarely did...allowed someone other than herself to view a work in progress.

"Don't take this wrong, but I'm beginning to see your friend Jason's fascination with you," Ted had told her as he studied the canvas from all angles. "You have a wonderful gift, this ability to turn your own emotion into something we all can recognize." Then he'd unleashed his sexy grin on her, adding, "Actually, it's a bit scary, just how well you can do it...but, then, I'm the kind of guy who likes being scared."

Half an hour later—and after an impromptu session on the floor of her studio that was anything but frightening—Ted had returned to work, and she had covered up the wet canvas until she could return to it the next morning. Unfortunately, she'd ended up putting in an entire day at the gallery, so that it had been late afternoon before she went back again into her studio and made the unsettling discovery.

Perhaps Ted had taken a final look at the canvas before leaving yesterday, she tried to tell herself as she stared now at the painting, its protective cloth hanging slightly askew, like a curtain that had been twitched aside. But she remembered walking him to the door immediately after their impromptu lovemaking. Certainly, he couldn't have stopped by while she was at the gallery, since he had warned her yesterday that he was going to be working a double-shift today.

Cautiously, she lifted the cloth, half-fearing to find the canvas beneath damaged. The painting, however, was just as she had left it. No one had been prowling about her studio in her absence; no one had been splashing about with her oils. She shook her head at her paranoia, straightened the picture...and only then noticed a smudge of robin's-egg blue along one edge.

It was a small defect, as if someone's thumb might have slipped as he held the canvas, and smeared the still-wet oil. The damage was easily repairable, something she could have caused herself. Reflexively, she glanced at both hands but saw no telltale blue paint. Somebody else, then. But, who?

The stalker, that's who.

Impulsively, she grabbed for the phone and began dialing Ted's cell number. Maybe she was being paranoid, but she'd feel a lot better if he were the one to tell her so. When the call finally rang through, however, instead of Ted's familiar voice, or even his crisp message—*You've got me. Leave a message*—coming on the line, a prerecorded voice explained that all circuits were busy, and asked that she please try her call again later.

Kelly slammed down the receiver. Of all times for the system to be overloaded, why did it have to be now? She could call the local precinct, but would they have any better luck than she in getting through to him? Swiftly, she reached into her desk drawer for Ted's business card. She could still make out the original number, despite the heavy black line he'd drawn through it. She'd try him there, and she would leave as many messages as it took for them to find him.

A moment later, an efficient female voice answered, "Dallas Police" and, at her request, promptly transferred her. She heard a click; then her call rang through but a single time before a voice answered, "Computer Crimes Division, Detective Ralston speaking."

"Ted, it's me, Kelly. I think he's been in the house again," she began in a rush, only to hesitate as she registered what she had just heard. The voice on the other end of the line was oddly familiar...but it wasn't his.

"Kelly?" the voice questioned with an air of professional reserve. Then, abruptly, the polite tone took on an urgent edge. "Is this Kelly Winslow?"

"Y—Yes...but who—"

"I've been calling you for the past three days, Ms. Winslow," the voice went on. "Didn't you get any of my messages?"

She glanced over at the answering machine beside her phone, frowning. No flashing red light signaled any unplayed messages. Come to think of it, there hadn't been a single message on her machine for almost a week now. And surely she'd misheard the name this person had given when he'd answered the phone. "I—I'm sorry, who is this again?"

"This is Detective Ralston," the voice replied. "I'm the one you talked to a couple of weeks ago about your cyber stalker, remember?"

Kelly sank back in her chair and tried to corral her rapidly racing thoughts. Large as the Dallas Police Department was, surely there weren't two detectives by that same name in the same precinct. So who in the hell was the man on the other end of the phone? Deciding it was best to play along with him, at least for the time, she hesitantly replied, "Y-Yes, I remember. So, why were you trying to get in touch with me?"

"I've tracked the Kelly website back to its owner, and I think we need to talk about this guy." He paused, and then went on, "Look,

Ms. Winslow, maybe I shouldn't be dumping all this on you over the phone. My shift's about up, anyhow, so why don't I just drive over there and tell you the rest? Besides, I've got a picture of him that I think you should check out, just in case."

"Sure...good idea...that'll be fine," she heard herself agree. "You have the address?"

"In your file. With traffic, I should be there in, say, thirty minutes."

It wasn't until she heard the buzzing of the dial tone over the sound of blood pounding in her ears that Kelly realized he had hung up some moments earlier. With shaking hands, she slowly returned her own receiver to its cradle. What had just happened here...and who in the hell had she been talking to?

The phone rang again, the unexpected sound practically sending her leaping from her chair. She snatched up the receiver and put it to her ear, then ventured, "Hello?"

"Kelly?"

It was Ted. Or, she abruptly wondered, was it merely the man she thought was Ted? She pressed the heel of her palm to her forehead and tried to think. Was it a good sign that a wave of relief had swept through her at the sound of his voice...or was it merely an indication that she'd been thoroughly taken in by a suave stranger who was pretending to be someone he was not?

"I'm between shifts," he was saying, in the meantime, "and since I'm just a few blocks from your place, I thought I'd stop by, if that's okay with you."

She choked back a laugh that was perilously close to a sob. Hadn't they just had this conversation, she and one of the two men who called himself Ted Ralston? "Sure, why not?"

"Kelly, is everything all right?" he replied, and she heard the frown in his voice. "You sound kind of strange."

"Well, that must be because strange things are going on. By any chance, did you accidentally erase my phone messages for the past couple of days?"

"Erase your phone messages?" he echoed. "No, not unless I did it in my sleep."

"And I don't suppose you remember smudging my painting when you looked at it yesterday, do you?"

"No, I never touched it. And what the hell kind of questions are these, anyway?"

Kelly took a deep breath, aware that she must sound like a stereotypical hysterical female. "Sorry, Ted. It's just that I found a thumbprint on my painting that I'm sure wasn't there yesterday. And if I didn't put it there, and you didn't, then someone was in my studio today."

"That's it? A thumbprint?" he asked, the tension in his voice easing. "I'll take an official look at it but unless you've been handing out door keys, I'd almost guarantee you it's yours. But why didn't you call me, instead of worrying yourself into a frenzy?"

"I tried, but all the cellular lines were all busy. I had to call you at the precinct, instead."

"You did?" Something momentarily sharpened his tone—surprise...anger?—before he went on in the same unconcerned tone. "Let me guess. They transferred you from department to department, and then cut you off before you could leave a message, right?"

"Not exactly. I got transferred to the Computer Crimes Division right away. Someone answered the phone who said he was you, and told me that he's been trying to get hold of me for days. He's on his way over here right now to talk about the cyber stalker."

"I see."

"You see?" she echoed in disbelief. "Well, that's great, because I don't. What am I supposed to do now? He says *he's* Ted Ralston...you say *you're* Ted Ralston. So who am I supposed to believe, him or you?"

Me, she waited for—prayed for—him to say. Rather than answering her, however, he said in a very deliberate voice, "Kelly, I want you to think back very carefully to that phone call. When the dispatcher transferred you over, did you hear anything on the lines...any tones, any clicks...before you were connected with this guy?"

"It did click once," she recalled in a puzzled tone, "but what does that mean?"

"It means our cyber stalker friend is a hell of a lot more clever than I gave him credit for being. Damn it, Kelly, he must have tapped into your phone line, maybe through your modem. That's why, when you dialed the precinct, he could intercept the call and pretend to be me."

She hesitated, wanting desperately to believe he spoke the truth. After all, if computer hackers could shut down multimillion-dollar corporations with simple e-mail viruses, surely they could play equal havoc with phone lines.

"I know it all sounds crazy," he went on, "but you've got to trust me on this one. The guy you just talked to is your stalker, not me...and he damn sure has crossed over the line if he's ready to meet with you in person."

Crossed over the line. She'd read the papers enough to know what happened when a stalker did just that. Usually, the headlines blared words like *shot* and *dead*. But even as she shut her eyes against those disturbing images, she heard his voice take on a more urgent note as he went on, "Listen, Kelly. This is very important. When you talked to this guy, did you give him any reason to imagine that you already knew me?"

She opened her eyes again and shook her head; then, remembering that he couldn't see her through the phone lines, she replied, "I don't think so. I was too shocked to do anything but listen to him talk, and then tell him it was okay when he asked to come over. I—I didn't know what else to say."

"Don't worry, you handled it just right." She relaxed a little as she heard a note of warmth replace the earlier sternness in his voice, only to gasp in disbelief as he added, "That means he won't suspect a thing when you let him inside the house."

"You really want me to let him inside the house?" she repeated a few minutes later, after Ted—wearing very uncop-like jeans and a torn white T-shirt—had slipped in through the back door and joined her in her tiny living room.

He nodded and twitched back the front window curtain just enough to give them a glimpse of the street beyond. A few battered sedans were parked along the curb, but Ted's sleek black BMW was nowhere to be seen, as he'd taken care to leave it on the next street over.

"We already went over this on the phone," he answered, his attention fixed on the encroaching dusk. "Sure, I could arrest him the minute he knocks on the door, but hosting a website—or even pretending to be me on the phone—isn't enough to justify charging him with a crime. The judge would kick him free, and you'd be right back at his mercy. The only way I can make anything stick is if we can prove some sort of threat against you."

"And what if he *does* threaten me, and you try to arrest him, and he resists?" she wanted to know, still not convinced this idea was anything but insane.

He glanced over and flashed her his sexy grin. "I'm pretty sure I can handle him...but just in case I can't, I've got backup waiting." Then he returned his attention to the window, and his grin abruptly faded. "All right, it's showtime," he murmured, indicating the dark green pickup that was pulling into her driveway.

He let the curtain drop, and turned to her. "Remember, I'll be in the hallway, just out of sight, but where I can hear everything. Now, chances are he's going to throw you a few curves, show you some reports or pictures that make him look like he's the genuine article. But don't let him rattle you with smoke and mirrors...just keep him talking until he says something to incriminate himself, okay?"

Keep him talking. She silently repeated those words as she opened her front door, letting out a blast of air conditioning into the muggy dusk. The man who stood on her porch was maybe a year or two older than she, of medium height and build, and with features that were pleasant if rather ordinary: straight nose, sandy hair, mild brown eyes behind wire-rim glasses. His clothes were equally run of the mill, blue slacks and a white shirt, topped by a tan jacket that was slightly too heavy for the day's remaining heat.

The single, irreverent corner of her mind that wasn't currently frightened shitless by the entire situation chortled. He might be believable as the guy delivering UPS packages, or as the person who sold printers and peripherals in the local computer superstore, but as a cop...never. The question for the moment was, however, was he also her cyber stalker?

"Ms. Winslow?" he politely inquired. At her nod, he flipped open a leather wallet to reveal a badge remarkably similar to Ted's, then reached into his jacket and pulled out a business card. It was identical to the one on her desk, save that it lacked the handwritten phone number.

"I'm Detective Ralston. May I come in for a moment?"

Nodding again, she opened the door wider. He stepped into her living room, his gaze taking in each detail as he casually paced it, a thick manila folder clutched in one hand. He paused at the darkened hallway, and for a heart-stopping moment she feared he would keep going. To her relief, however, he turned and asked, "You're here alone, ma'am?"

"Yes...I live here by myself." She gestured toward the balding horsehair sofa, which was well away from the hall, and suggested rather breathlessly, "Maybe you'd like to sit down now?"

He took the seat she'd indicated and set his folder on the old steamer trunk she used as a coffee table. Kelly perched on a straight-backed chair a cautious distance from him; then, conscious of the man in the hallway listening to every word, she went on in as casual tone as she could muster, "I believe you said you had some information?"

The man who called himself Detective Ralston nodded. "The first time we spoke, I told you there wasn't much I could do about the situation," he began. "I checked out the website, anyway, and got the name of the domain owner...one Jason Todman. When I ran a check on him, nothing came up, but since he's only been in Dallas a few months, I decided to dig deeper."

He flipped open his folder and pulled out what appeared to be an official-looking form, its numerous blanks filled in with blue-inked writing. "His last known addresses were Chicago and L.A., and it turns out that both departments had pretty thick files on the guy. You see, you're not the first woman he's stalked."

"So you mean he's put up websites like the Kelly one before?"

"Not exactly. The common denominator is that our friend Jason has a thing for women in the arts...dancers, musicians, painters. He finds a woman who catches his fancy, and picks a role to play with her, something that would fulfill an immediate need for the victim.

"Usually, he chooses an actual person to impersonate," the man continued, "someone whose name people might have heard before, but who doesn't have an immediately recognizable face, someone he can re-create with a handful of stolen business cards and an answering service. Then he arranges to meet his victim, and he usually ends up dating the woman for a while...under his assumed identity, of course. It's a real cozy arrangement, until she decides to call it quits."

"Th—Then what happens?"

He pulled out a photograph from the file and slid it toward her. *Smoke and mirrors*, Kelly reminded herself, steeling herself to see a gruesome crime scene photo. To her relief, however, the picture was instead a black-and-white publicity still. Its subject was a dramatic-looking woman about her own age, her bleached hair chopped and spiked in last year's style.

"Her name was Millie Donovan," he said, and she shivered a little at his use of the past tense. "She was the lead singer with one of the local club bands in Chicago. She died in a house fire a month after she broke up with Todman, though he was using the name Kurt McAfee at the time. The arson guys ruled it an accident, said a lit cigarette caught the bed on fire. Odd thing was, her friends all insisted she didn't smoke."

He pulled another picture from the file and flipped it toward her. This woman was a brunette wearing a leotard and long, gauzy skirt, posed gracefully on pointe. "Tammy Jacobs, partner in a struggling dance company based in Los Angeles. Two days after she broke up with a guy named Ben Tresome—who turned out to be Todman— paramedics pulled her out of a one-car wreck. The skid marks and some paint damage indicated that her car was run off the road, though she wasn't able to tell us much about what happened." He glanced up at Kelly's unspoken question and added, "Oh, she sur-vived the accident...but she doesn't dance anymore."

"My God," she breathed, letting the photographs drop back to the table as she strove for calm. If this man truly was Detective Ted Ralston, and he simply was trying to convince her she was in danger, he was doing a damn good job of it. And if he actually was Jason Todman trying to scare the hell out of her, just for sick thrills, he was succeeding with that, as well.

"But I don't understand. If this Jason Todman has done what you say he has, why isn't he already in jail?"

"The local cops picked him up, but he had alibis in both cases, and there was absolutely no physical evidence to tie him to either crime scene. Even the fact that he'd used a false name to get close to those women wasn't sufficient cause to hold him." Ralston quirked a wry brow. "Like it or not, it's not a crime to use a fake name just to get laid."

Kelly would have blushed at that last, save that she was struggling against the sudden sick feeling that had enveloped her. "You said he assumed roles with these women," she managed in a voice that shook only slightly. "What exactly did you mean by that?"

"With the Donovan woman, he claimed to be the owner of a record label looking to sign new talent. Turns out that Kurt McAfee really is a record executive, but he happened to be out of the country during the time that Todman was using his name. He told Tammy Jacobs that he'd just sold out his dot-com company to a big conglomerate and was looking for places to invest his profits. With a couple of others, he played a surgeon, and the son of a well-known televangelist. He makes a point of choosing positions of power...of trust."

Positions of power...of trust. She briefly shut her eyes, then softly asked, "Like, maybe pretending to be a cop?"

"That's possible. Listen, I know the website is upsetting, but I don't think you're in any immediate danger. Those other women had been involved with Todman awhile, and it wasn't until they dumped him that all hell broke loose. So, as long as you don't start seeing the guy—"

He broke off abruptly, frowning, and then casually pulled another photograph from his file. "I guess that, between your painting and your work at the art gallery, you meet all sorts of interesting people," he resumed in a conversational tone as he slid the sheet toward her. "Are you currently seeing anyone...involved in any relationships?"

While he was speaking, she'd had time for a clear look at the page before her. Unlike the others, this one was a police booking photo, complete with dual views and the requisite identifying numbers across the bottom. The suspect had worn what appeared to be jail issue, and looked as if he hadn't slept in a couple of days; still, he had stared into the camera with the hint of a grin, as if confident this was the closest he'd come to paying for his crime.

Kelly slowly looked up from the photo of the man she'd been sleeping with these past couple of weeks, to the man before her. Steeling herself, she gave Ralston the barest of nods, even as she said, "I have been going out with someone, but it's nothing you'd really call serious."

"You're hurting my feelings, Kelly," a cool voice spoke up from the direction of the hallway. "And here I thought we had something real...something special."

Jason Todman—or was he Ted Ralston?—was leaning against the doorjamb, the blue steel finish of the revolver he held glinting dully in the room's low light. Kelly gasped and scrambled from her chair. The man beside her rose more slowly, still clutching the incriminating folder as he eased away from the sofa.

"I can't believe you're listening to this loser," he addressed Kelly in the same chill tone. "Everything he's shown you, he could have pulled off a website, or created himself. Real cops carry guns...and I'm the one with the gun. And you saw the badge, and the business cards with my name on them. They all looked pretty damn real to me."

"You can buy replica badges a dime a dozen on the Internet," Detective Ralston—or was he Jason Todman?—countered calmly. "Guns are just as easy to get. As for the business cards, whenever I give a seminar at the local community center, mine are always there for the taking."

"Yeah, but you're forgetting one thing. Who looks more like a guy who has problems getting women...me or him?" the other man demanded, and jerked a thumb at his rival.

Kelly didn't reply, her attention held by a hint of color...a tiny smear of robin's-egg blue paint on his extended hand. He followed her gaze, and then allowed himself a wry smile.

"Stuff's a bitch to get off without turpentine," he casually observed, shaking his head in mock dismay as he let his hand drop again. "I didn't even notice I'd gotten any on me until after I left. By then, you were already on your way home from the gallery, so I couldn't come back."

"Convinced now, Ms. Winslow?" the detective softly asked. At her frightened nod, he returned his attention to Todman. "All right, Jason, it's over with. Now, why don't you hand the gun to me, and we can talk about what to do next."

"I've got a better idea. Why don't we quit talking?" Todman countered and pulled the revolver's trigger twice in swift succession, catching him squarely in the chest with both shots.

By the time the sound of gunshots and Kelly's answering scream had faded, Ralston lay slumped against the far wall. A folder's worth of scattered pages had settled over him in a bureaucratic drift, mercifully obscuring any blood or gaping flesh. She probably should check to see if he was still alive, she faintly told herself, but surely there wasn't a need.

"Well, that's settled," Todman observed with a final look at Ralston, and then turned to her, pistol raised. "Unfortunately, it also means that things are over between us, too, Kelly."

"This isn't necessary," she protested in a voice that sounded weak to her own ears, even as she tried to summon a smile. "You know I don't want to see you go to jail...not after what we've had together. Maybe we could—"

"Cut the bullshit, Kelly," he interrupted in a conversational tone that was far more frightening than any overt threat. "I've just killed a cop, and I'm not about to leave you around to testify against me. Now, why don't we go into your studio and get this over with."

He gestured with the pistol in the direction of the hallway, and she took a deep breath. She had little hope of a police rescue; gunfire was common enough in this part of town not to draw undue interest from the neighbors. If she tried to flee, he would shoot her down long before she made it to the door; once in the studio, however, she'd be effectively trapped. Still, the latter choice left her with a few more precious moments in which to come up with a plan.

"I'm thinking murder-suicide," Todman went on in the same casual tone as she walked on shaky legs into the studio. "That seems to be a pretty popular cause of death with couples in this town. Oh, yes, people will think you're a couple," he confirmed as she shot him a confused look. "You see, I borrowed one of his credit cards and set up the cell phone account in his name. When they check, they'll find plenty of activity between that number and yours. And, of course, there'll be a few personal possessions of his scattered about your house."

So saying, he reached over to the wall switch and flipped on the light, illuminating the half-finished oil that sat upon the easel. "You know, I really do like that painting," he mused, gripping her by the arm as he walked her over to it. "Such beauty, such power. Too bad you didn't get to finish it. But those are the breaks."

His gaze lingered on the abstract a moment longer before he let her go and took a step back. His tone was businesslike once more as he said, "Since your friend Detective Ralston was shot from a distance, we're going to have to make you the suicide instead of the murder victim. Powder burns, angle of bullet entry, and all that. But we have to make it look right."

"Please," she whispered, "don't do this. Leave, and I'll never mention your name to the police. I swear it!"

"I've read that women commit suicide differently from men," he went on, as if she'd never spoken. "They never put the gun to their temple, or in their mouth...guess they don't like the idea of blasting their pretty faces all over the place. So, how do you think they do it?

"They go for the heart," he answered his own question, and she gasped as she felt the sudden, painful pressure of the muzzle directly over that wildly beating organ. "It's quick, it's clean, and they can still have an open casket at the funeral. So tell me, Kelly, does that work for you? Because I'm equally comfortable with the head, if you were planning on being cremated—"

"Lower your weapon, and step away from her!"

The words lashed whiplike through the room, momentarily jerking Kelly from her terror. Todman stiffened, and she heard his swift intake of breath before he slowly turned to look over his shoulder. Cautiously, she raised her own gaze to look in the direction of the voice.

Detective Ralston—minus his jacket and glasses—stood in the doorway of her studio, looking remarkably alive and unbloodied for a man who had just taken two bullets in the chest. Except that Kelly barely recognized him as the mild-mannered guy she had dismissed as harmless only minutes before. Maybe it was just the automatic pistol he gripped with businesslike efficiency in both hands. Or maybe it was simply the way his ordinary features had hardened into the cold, implacable expression of a man prepared to finish an unpleasant job.

"You were right, Jason," he said in the same chilled tone. "Real cops carry guns. They also wear body armor when they know they're going up against scumbags like you." And, indeed, Kelly could see where the bullets had torn two holes through the fabric of his shirt. As she stared at him in something akin to awe, she heard him repeat,

"Now lower your weapon and step back."

Before Kelly realized what was happening, Todman had slipped behind her so that he now faced Ralston. "I'll kill her," he threatened, his pistol pressed into the back of her ribs as he used her for a shield. "You put down *your* gun, and let the two of us walk out of here, and maybe I'll let her go once we're out of the county."

"Not a chance. It ends here, now."

Ralston moved one step closer, then two. Abruptly, Kelly felt her captor's free hand grip her shoulder, pulling her closer to him as he raised his revolver and leveled it at the detective.

"You'll have to shoot her to get at me," he shouted. "You don't want to be responsible for the bitch dying, do you? Now, put down the gun and get the hell out of my way before I—"

He broke off abruptly as Kelly reflexively slammed an elbow into his gut, and then dived for the floor. She had barely landed in an ungainly heap when she heard the crack of gunfire for the second time that day. She lay where she was, waiting for the sound of a second bullet, the one that would rip through her body. Instead, all she heard was the thunk of something small but heavy landing on the wooden floor beside her.

Cautiously, she lifted her head just enough to see that the object was a familiar blue steel revolver. Next to it was a rapidly widening puddle of crimson. Biting back a gasp, she raised her head still higher to see Jason Todman swaying as he clutched his gut, blood dripping from between his fingers and splashing at his feet. He moaned once, and then sagged to his knees.

As she scrambled a safe distance from him, his dull gaze met hers. He managed a brief, sickly shadow of his familiar grin. "I had you, Kelly. I had you," he whispered and collapsed against the easel, tumbling the painting on top of him.

In the silence that followed, Ralston reached down and picked up the fallen revolver. Wincing slightly as he clutched at his bruised ribs, he straightened again and stuck the gun in the waistband of his trousers, then walked over to where she still huddled on the floor.

"Are you all right, Ms. Winslow?" he asked as she tentatively took his proffered hand and scrambled to her feet.

She nodded. "I—I'm fine," she managed in a halting voice, adding as she looked over at the body in the middle of her studio floor, "but I guess he's not, is he?"

Even as Ralston shook his head, Kelly heard a faint wail of sirens and raised her brow in surprise. Apparently, there was a limit, after all, to the amount of gunplay that her neighbors would tolerate before calling the cops. "Backup will be here in a minute," Ralston told her unnecessarily as he reached for her fallen oil painting, and then settled it back on the easel.

Careful not to look down at the dead man again, Kelly moved closer to the painting, gasping a little at what she saw. A large smear of drying blood now bisected the canvas, almost obliterating the abstract heart that, moments before, had glowed so brightly. At her sound of dismay Ralston—who had shrugged off his torn shirt and now was unbuckling his bulletproof vest—glanced over at her. "Sorry about the painting. It looks like it was something special. What did you call it?"

"*Love Takes a Chance*," she softly replied, belatedly dubbing it with the title that had come to her just this very afternoon, as she worked at the gallery. "It was the last of three, but I guess I'll never finish it now."

"Are you sure? I rather like the title, myself."

Kelly glanced back over at him. By now, he had shed the vest and the T-shirt beneath it, and was gingerly examining the pair of purplish bruises on his chest. *Not a bad body, especially for a computer geek*, her inner voice irreverently decreed. *I wonder if he likes Mexican food.*

As if feeling her gaze on him, he looked up and flashed her a faint grin. While not as devastatingly sexy as Jason Todman's had been, Ralston's grin hinted at definite possibilities. Feeling far more cheerful than she should have, considering that she'd almost been murdered a few moments before, and a dead man was lying practically at her feet, Kelly smiled back.

"Actually, I was considering expanding the series to four paintings," she said over the blare of sirens that was now right outside her window. "So tell me, Ted, what do you think of this for a new title...*Love Tries Again?*"

The Perfect Man

Kristine Kathryn Rusch

Paige Racette stared at herself in the full-length mirror, hands on hips. Golden cap of blond hair expertly curled, narrow chin, high cheekbones, china blue eyes, and a little too much of a figure— thanks to the fact she spent most of her day on her butt and sometimes (usually!) forgetting to exercise. The black cocktail dress with its swirling party skirt hid most of the excess, and the glittering beads around the collar brought attention to her face, always and forever her best asset.

Even with the extra pounds, she was not blind-date material. Never had been. Until she quit her day job at the television station, she'd had to turn men away. Ironic that once she became a best-selling romance writer, she couldn't get a date to save her life. Part of the problem was that after she quit, she moved to San Francisco where she'd always wanted to live. She bought a Queen Anne in an old, exclusive neighborhood, set up her office in the bay windows of the second floor, and decided she was in heaven.

Little did she realize that working at home would isolate her, and being in a new city would isolate her more. It had taken her a year to make friends—mostly women, whom she met at the gym not too far from her home.

She saw interesting men, but didn't speak to them. She was still a small-town girl at heart, one who was afraid of the kind of men who lurked in the big city, who believed that the only way to meet the right man was by getting to know him through mutual interests—or mutual friends.

In fact, she wouldn't have agreed to this blind date if a friend hadn't convinced her. Sally Myer was her racquetball partner and general confidante who seemed to know everyone in this city. She'd finally tired of Paige's complaining and set her up.

Paige slid on her high heels. Who'd ever thought she'd get this desperate? And then she sighed. She wasn't desperate. She was lonely.

And surely, there was no shame in that.

Sally had picked the time and location, and had told Paige to dress up. Sally wasn't going to introduce them. She felt that would be tacky and make the first meeting uncomfortable. She asked Paige for a photograph to give to the blind date—one Josiah Wells—and then told Paige that he would find her.

The location was an upscale restaurant near the Opera House. It was The Place to Go at the moment—famous chef, famous food, and one of those bars that looked like it had come out of a movie set—large and open where Anyone Who Was Someone could see and be seen.

Paige arrived five minutes early, habitually prompt even when she didn't want to be. She adjusted the white Pashmina shawl she'd wrapped around her bare shoulders and scanned the bar before she went in.

It was all black and chrome, with black tinted mirrors and huge black vases filled with calla lilies separating the booths. The bar itself was black marble and behind it, bottles of liquor pressed against an untinted mirror, making the place look even bigger than it was.

She had only been here once before, with her Hollywood agent and a movie producer who was interested in her second novel. He didn't buy it—the rights went to another studio for high six figures—but he had bought her some of her most memorable meals in the City by the Bay.

She sat at the bar and ordered a Chardonnay that she didn't plan on touching—she wanted to keep her wits about her this night. Even with Sally's recommendation, Paige didn't trust a man she had never met before. She'd heard too many bad stories.

Of course, all the ones she'd written were about people who saw each other across a crowded room and knew at once that they were soul mates. She had never experienced love at first sight (and sometimes she joked to her editor that it was lust at first sight) but she was still hopeful enough to believe in it.

She took the cool glass of Chardonnay that the bartender handed her and swiveled slightly in her chair so that she would be in profile, not looking anxious, but visible enough to be recognizable. And as she did, she saw a man enter the bar.

He was tall and broad-shouldered, wearing a perfectly tailored black suit that shimmered like silk. He wore a white scarf around his neck—which on him looked like the perfect fashion accent—and a red rose in his lapel. His dark hair was expertly styled away from his chiseled features, and she felt her breath catch.

Lust at first sight. It was all she could do to keep from grinning at herself.

He appeared to be looking for someone. Finally, his gaze settled on her, and he smiled.

Something about that smile didn't quite fit his face. It was too personal. And then she shook the feeling away. She didn't want to be on a blind date—that was all. She had been fantasizing, the way she did when she was thinking of her books, and she was simply caught off-guard. No man was as perfect as her heroes. No man could be, not and still be human.

Although this man looked perfect. His rugged features were exactly like ones she had described in her novels.

He crossed the room, the smile remaining, hand extended. "Paige Racette? I'm Josiah Wells."

His voice was high and a bit nasal. She took his hand, and found the palm warm and moist.

"Nice to meet you," she said, removing her hand as quickly as possible.

He wore tinted blue contacts, and the swirling lenses made his eyes seem shiny, a little too intense. In fact, everything about him was a little too intense. He leaned too close, and he seemed too eager. Perhaps he was just as nervous as she was.

"I have reservations here if you don't mind," he said.

"No, that's fine."

He extended his arm—the perfect gentleman—and she put her arm through his, trying to remember the last time a man had done that for her. Her father maybe, when they went to the father-daughter dinner at her church back when she was in high school. And not one man since.

Although all the men in her books did it. When she wrote about it, the gesture seemed to have an old-fashioned elegance. In real life, it made her feel awkward.

He led her through the bar, placing one hand possessively over hers. This exact scene had happened in her first novel, *Beneath a Lover's Moon*. Fabian Garret and Skye Michaels had met, exchanged a few words, and were suddenly walking together like lovers. And Skye had thrilled to Fabian's touch.

Paige wished Josiah Wells's fingers weren't so clammy.

He led them to the maitre d', gave his name, and let the maitre d' lead them to a table near the back. See and Be Seen. Apparently they weren't important enough.

"I asked for a little privacy," he said, as if reading her thoughts. "I hope you don't mind."

She didn't. She had never liked the display aspect of this restaurant anyway.

The table was in a secluded corner. Two candles burned on silver candlesticks and the table was strewn with miniature carnations. A magnum of champagne cooled in a silver bucket, and she didn't have to look at the label to know that it was Dom Perignon.

The hair on the back of her neck rose. This was just like another scene in *Beneath a Lover's Moon*.

Josiah smiled down at her and she made herself smile at him. Maybe he thought her books were a blueprint to romancing her. She would have said so not five minutes before.

He pulled out her chair, and she sat, letting her shawl drape around her. As Josiah sat across from her, the maitre d' handed her the leather-bound menu and she was startled to realize it had no prices on it. A lady's menu. She hadn't seen one of those in years. The last time she had eaten here had been lunch, not dinner, and she had remembered the prices on the menu from that meal. They had nearly made her choke on her water.

A waiter poured the champagne and left discretely, just like the maitre d' had. Josiah was watching her, his gaze intense.

She knew she had to say something. She was going to say how nice this was but she couldn't get the lie through her lips. Instead she said as warmly as she could, "You've read my books."

If anything, his gaze brightened. "I adore your books."

She made herself smile. She had been hoping he would say no, that Sally had been helping him all along. Instead, the look in his eyes made her want to push her chair even farther from the table. She had seen that look a hundred times at book signings: the too-eager fan who would easily monopolize all of her time at the expense of everyone else in line; the person who believed that his connection with the author—someone he hadn't met—was so personal that she felt the connection, too.

"I didn't realize that Sally told you I wrote."

"She didn't have to. When I found out that she knew you, I asked her for an introduction."

An introduction at a party would have done nicely, where Paige could smile at him, listen for a polite moment, and then ease away. But Sally hadn't known Paige that long, and didn't understand the difficulties a writer sometimes faced. Writers rarely got recognized in person—it wasn't their faces that were famous after all but their names—but when it happened, it could become as unpleasant as it was for athletes or movie stars.

"She didn't tell me you were familiar with my work," Paige said, ducking her head behind the menu.

"I asked her not to. I wanted this to be a surprise." He was leaning forward, his manicured hand outstretched.

She looked at his fingers, curled against the linen tablecloth, carefully avoiding the miniature carnations, and wondered if his skin was still clammy.

"Since you know what I do," she continued in that too-polite voice she couldn't seem to shake, "why don't you tell me about yourself?"

"Oh," he said, "there isn't much to tell."

And then he proceeded to describe his work with a software company. She only half listened, staring at the menu, wondering if there was an easy—and polite—way to leave this meal, knowing there was not. She would make the best of it, and call Sally the next morning, warning her not to do this ever again.

"Your books," he was saying, "made me realize that women look at men the way that men look at women. I started to exercise and dress appropriately and I..."

She looked over the menu at him, noting the suit again. It must have been silk, and he wore it the way her heroes wore theirs. Right down to the scarf, and the rose in the lapel. The red rose, a symbol of true love from her third novel, *Without Your Love*.

That shiver ran through her again.

This time he noticed. "Are you all right?"

"Fine," she lied. "I'm just fine."

Somehow she made it through the meal, feeling her skin crawl as he used phrases from her books, imitated the gestures of her heroes, and presumed an intimacy with her that he didn't have. She tried to keep the conversation light and impersonal, but it was a battle that she really didn't win.

Just before the dessert course, she excused herself and went to the ladies' room. After she came out, she asked the maitre d' to call her a cab, and then to signal her when it arrived. He smiled knowingly. Apparently he had seen dates end like this all too often.

She took her leave from Josiah just after they finished their coffees, thanking him profusely for a memorable evening. And then she escaped into the night, thankful that she had been careful when making plans. He didn't have her phone number and address. As she slipped into the cracked backseat of the cab, she promised herself that on the next blind date—if there was another blind date—she would make it drinks only. Not dinner. Never again.

The next day, she and Sally met for lattes at an overpriced touristy café on the Wharf. It was their usual spot—a place where they could watch crowds and not be overheard when they decided to gossip.

"How did you meet him?" Paige asked as she adjusted her wrought-iron café chair.

"Fundraisers, mostly," Sally said. She was a petite redhead with freckles that she didn't try to hide. From a distance, they made her look as if she were still in her twenties. "He was pretty active in local politics for a while."

"Was?"

She shrugged. "I guess he got too busy. I ran into him in Tower Records a few weeks ago, and we got to talking. That's what made me think of you."

"What did?"

Sally smiled. "He was holding one of your books, and I thought, he's wealthy. You're wealthy. He was complaining about how isolating his work was and so were you."

"Isolating? He works for a software company."

"Worked," Sally said. "He's a consultant now, and only when he needs to be. I think he just manages his investments, mostly."

Paige frowned. Had she heard him wrong then? She wasn't paying much attention, not after she had seen the carnations and champagne.

Sally was watching her closely. "I take it things didn't go well."

"He's just not my type."

"Rich? Good-looking? Good God, girl, what is your type?"

Paige smiled. "He's a fan."

"So? Wouldn't that be more appealing?"

Maybe it should have been. Maybe she had overreacted. She had psyched herself out a number of times about the strange men in the big city. Maybe her overactive imagination—the one that created all the stories that had made her wealthy—had finally betrayed her.

"No," Paige said. "Actually, it's less appealing. I sort of feel like he has photos of me naked and has studied them up close."

"I didn't think books were that personal. I mean, you write

romance. That's fantasy, right? Make-believe?"

Paige's smile was thin. It was make-believe. But make-believe on any level had a bit of truth to it, even when little children were creating scenarios with Barbie dolls.

"I just don't think we're compatible," Paige said. "Sorry."

Sally shrugged again. "No skin off my nose. You're the one who doesn't get out much. Have you ever thought of going to those singles dinners? They're supposed to be a pretty good place to meet people...."

Paige let the advice slip off her, knowing that she probably wouldn't discuss her love life—or lack of it—with Sally again. Paige had been right in the first place: she simply didn't have the right attitude to be a good blind date. There was probably nothing wrong with Josiah Wells. He had certainly gone to a lot of trouble to make sure she had a good time, and she had snuck off as soon as she could.

And if she couldn't be satisfied with a good-looking wealthy man who was trying to please her then she wouldn't be satisfied with any other blind date, either. She had to go back to what she knew worked. She had to go about her life normally, and hope that someday, an interesting guy would cross her path.

"...even go to AA to find dates. I mean, that's a little crass, don't you think?"

Paige looked at Sally, and realized she hadn't heard most of Sally's monologue. "You know what? Let's forget about men. It's a brand-new century and I have a great life. Why do we both seem to think that a man will somehow improve that?"

Sally studied her for a moment. "You know what I think? I think you've spent so much time making up the perfect man that no flesh-and-blood guy will measure up."

And then she changed the subject, just as Paige had asked.

As Paige drove home, she found herself wondering if Sally was right. After all, Paige hadn't dated anyone since she quit her job. And that was when she really spent most of her time immersed in imaginary romance. Her conscious brain knew that the men she made up were too perfect to be real. But did her subconscious? Was that what was preventing her from talking to men she'd seen at the opera or the theater? Was all this big-city fear she'd been thinking about simply a way of preventing herself from remembering that men were as human—and as imperfect—as she was?

She almost had herself convinced as she parked her new VW Bug on the hill in front of her house. She set the emergency brake and then got out, grabbing her purse as she did.

She had a lot of work to do, and she had wasted most of the day obsessing about her unsatisfying blind date. It was time to return to work—a romantic suspense novel set on a cruise ship. She had done a mountain of research for the book—including two cruises—one to Hawaii in the winter, and another to Alaska in the summer. The Alaska trip was the one she had decided to use, and she had spent part of the spring in Juneau.

By the time she had reached the front porch, she was already thinking of the next scene she had to write. It was a description of Juneau, a city that was perfect for her purposes because there were only two ways out of it: by air or by sea. The roads ended just outside of town. The mountains hemmed everything in, trapping people, good and bad, hero and villain, within their steep walls.

She was so lost in her imagination that she nearly tripped over the basket sitting on her porch.

She bent down to look at it. Wrapped in colored cellophane, it was nearly as large as she was, and was filled with flowers, chocolates, wine, and two crystal wine goblets. In the very center was a photo in a heart-shaped gold frame. She peered at it through the wrapping and then recoiled.

It was a picture of her and Josiah at dinner the night before, looking, from the outside, like a very happy couple.

Obviously he had hired someone to take the picture. Someone who had watched them the entire evening, and waited for the right moment to snap the shot. That was unsettling. And so was the fact that Josiah had found her house. She was unlisted in the phonebook, and on public records, she used her first name—Giacinta—with no middle initial. And although her last name was unusual, there were at least five other Racettes listed. Had Josiah sent a basket to every one of them, hoping that he'd find the right one and she'd call him?

Or had he had her followed?

The thought made her look over her shoulder. Maybe there was someone on the street now, watching her, wondering how she would react to this gift.

She didn't want to bring it inside, but she felt like she had no choice. She suddenly felt quite exposed on the porch.

She picked up the basket by its beribboned handle and unlocked her door. Then she stepped inside, closed the door as her security firm had instructed her, and punched in her code. Her hands were shaking.

On impulse, she reset the perimeter alarm. She hadn't done that since she moved in, had thought it a silly precaution.

It didn't seem that silly anymore.

She set the basket on the deacon's bench she had near the front door. Then she fumbled through the ribbon to find the card she knew had to be there.

Her name was on the envelope in calligraphic script, but the message inside was typed on the delivery service's card.

> Two hearts, perfectly meshed.
> Two lives, perfectly twined.
> Is it luck that we have found each other?
> Or does Fate divine a way for perfect matches to meet?

Those were her words. The stilted words of Quinn Ralston, the hero of her sixth novel, a man who finally learned to free the poetry locked in his soul.

"God," she whispered, so creeped out that her hands felt dirty just from touching the card. She picked up the basket and carried it to the back of the house, setting it in the entryway where she kept her bundled newspapers.

She supposed most women would keep the chocolates, flowers, and wine even if they didn't like the man who sent them. But she wasn't most women. And the photograph bothered her more than she could say.

She locked the interior door, then went to the kitchen and scrubbed her hands until they were raw.

Somehow she managed to escape to the Juneau of her imagination, working furiously in her upstairs office, getting nearly fifteen pages done before dinner. Uncharacteristically, she closed the drapes, hiding the city view she had paid so much for. She didn't want anyone looking in.

She was making herself a taco salad with Bite-sized Tostitos and bagged shredded lettuce when the phone rang, startling her. She went to answer it, and then some instinct convinced her not to. Instead, she went to her answering machine and turned up the sound.

"Paige? If you're there, please pick up. It's Josiah." He paused and she held her breath. She hadn't given him this number. And Sally had said that morning that she hadn't given Paige's unlisted number to anyone. "Well, um, you're probably working and can't hear this."

A shiver ran through her. He knew she was home, then? Or was he guessing?

"I just wanted to find out if you got my present. I have tickets to tomorrow night's presentation of *La Bohème*. I know how much you love opera and this one in particular. They're box seats. Hard to get. And perfect, just like you. Call me back." He rattled off his phone number and then hung up.

She stared at the machine, with its blinking red light. She hadn't discussed the opera with him. She hadn't discussed the opera with Sally, either, after she found out that Sally hated "all that screech-ing." Sally wouldn't know *La Bohème* from Don Giovanni, and she certainly wouldn't remember either well enough to mention to someone else.

Well, maybe Paige's problem was that she had been polite to him the night before. Maybe she should have left. She'd had this problem in the past—mostly in college. She'd always tried to be polite to men who were interested in her, even if she wasn't interested in return. But sometimes, politeness merely encouraged them. Sometimes she had to be harsh just to send them away.

Harsh or polite, she really didn't want to talk to Josiah ever again. She would ignore the call, and hope that he would forget her. Most men understood a lack of response. They knew it for the brushoff it was.

If he managed to run into her, she would just apologize and give him the You're-Very-Nice-I'm-Sure-You'll-Meet-Someone-Special-Someday speech. That one worked every time.

Somehow, having a plan calmed her. She finished cooking the beef for her taco salad and took it to the butcher-block table in the center of the kitchen. There she opened the latest copy of *Publisher's Weekly* and read while she ate.

During the next week, she got fifteen bouquets of flowers, each one an arrangement described in her books. Her plan wasn't working. She hadn't run into Josiah, but she didn't answer his phone calls. He didn't seem to understand the brush-off. He would call two or three times a day to leave messages on her machine, and once an hour, he would call and hang up. Sometimes she found herself standing over the Caller ID box, fists clenched.

All of this made work impossible. When the phone rang, she listened for his voice. When it wasn't him, she scrambled to pick up, her concentration broken.

In addition to the bouquets, he had taken to sending her cards and writing her long e-mails, sometimes mimicking the language of the men in her novels.

Finally, she called Sally and explained what was going on.

"I'm sorry," Sally said. "I had no idea he was like this."

Paige sighed heavily. She was beginning to feel trapped in the house. "You started this. What do you recommend?"

"I don't know," Sally said. "I'd offer to call him, but I don't think he'll listen to me. This sounds sick."

"Yeah," Paige said. "That's what I'm thinking."

"Maybe you should go to the police."

Paige felt cold. The police. If she went to them, it would be an acknowledgment that this had become serious.

"Maybe," she said, but she hoped she wouldn't have to.

Looking back on it, she realized she might have continued enduring if it weren't for the incident at the grocery store. She had been leaving the house, always wondering if someone was watching her, and then deciding that she was being just a bit too paranoid. But the fact that Josiah showed up in the grocery store a few moments after she arrived, pushing no grocery cart and dressed exactly like Maximilian D. Lake from *Love at 37,000 Feet* was no coincidence.

He wore a new brown leather bomber jacket, aviation sunglasses, khakis, and a white scarf. When he saw her in the produce aisle, he whipped the sunglasses off with an affected air.

"Paige, darling! I've been worried about you." His eyes were even more intense than she remembered, and this time they were green, just like Maximilian Lake's.

"Josiah," she said, amazed at how calm she sounded. Her heart was pounding and her stomach was churning. He had her trapped—her cart was between the tomato and asparagus aisles. Behind her, the water jets, set to mist the produce every five minutes, kicked on.

"You have no idea how concerned I've been," he said, taking a step closer. She backed toward the onions. "When a person lives alone, works alone, and doesn't answer her phone, well, anything could be wrong."

Was that a threat? She couldn't tell. She made herself smile at him. "There's no need to worry about me. There are people checking on me all the time."

"Really?" He raised a single eyebrow, something she'd often described in her novels, but never actually seen in person. He probably knew that no one came to her house without an invitation. He seemed to know everything else.

She gripped the handle on her shopping cart firmly. "I'm glad I ran into you. I've been wanting to tell you something."

His face lit up, a look that would have been attractive if it weren't so needy. "You have?"

She nodded. Now was the time, her best and only chance. She pushed the cart forward just a little, so that he had to move aside. He seemed to think she was doing it to get closer to him. She was doing it so that she'd be able to get away.

"I really appreciate all the trouble you went to for dinner," she said. "It was one of the most memorable—"

"Our entire life could be like that," he said quickly. "An adventure every day, just like your books."

She had to concentrate to keep that smile on her face. "Writers write about adventure, Josiah, because we really don't want to go out and experience it ourselves."

He laughed. It sounded forced. "I'm sure Papa Hemingway is spinning in his grave. You are such a kidder, Paige."

"I'm not kidding," she said. "You're a very nice man, Josiah, but—"

"A nice man?" He took a step toward her, his face suddenly red. "A nice man? The only men who get described that way in your books are the losers, the ones the heroine wants to let down easy."

She let the words hang between them for a moment. And then she said, "I'm sorry."

He stared at her as if she had hit him. She pushed the cart past him, resisting the impulse to run. She was rounding the corner into the meat aisle when she heard him say, "You bitch!"

Her hands started trembling then, and she couldn't read her list. But she had to. He wouldn't run her out of here. Then he'd realize just how scared she was.

He was coming up behind her. "You can't do this, Paige. You know how good we are together. You know."

She turned around, leaned against her cart and prayed silently for strength. "Josiah, we had one date, and it wasn't very good. Now please, leave me alone."

A store employee was watching from the corner of the aisle. The butcher had looked up through the window in the back.

Josiah grabbed her wrist so hard that she could feel his fingers digging into her skin. "I'll make you remember. I'll make you—"

"Are you all right, miss?" The store employee had stepped to her side.

"No," she said. "He's hurting me."

"This is none of your business," Josiah said. "She's my girlfriend."

"I don't know him," Paige said.

The employee had taken Josiah's arm. Other employees were coming from various parts of the store. He must have given them a signal. Some of the customers were gathering, too.

"Sir, we're going to have to ask you to leave," the employee said.

"You have no right."

"We have every right, sir," the employee said. "Now let the lady go."

Josiah stared at him for a moment, then at the other customers. Store security had joined them.

"Paige," Josiah said, "tell them how much you love me. Tell them that we were meant to be together."

"I don't know you," she said, and this time her words seemed to get through. He let go of her arm and allowed the employee to pull him away.

She collapsed against her cart in relief, and the store manager, a middle-aged man with a nice face, asked her if she needed to sit down. She nodded. He led her to the back of the store, past the cans that were being recycled and the gray refrigeration units to a tiny office filled with red signs about customer service.

"I'm sorry," she said. "I'm so sorry."

"Why?" The manager pulled over a metal folding chair and helped her into it. Then he sat behind the desk. "It seemed like he was harassing you. Who is he?"

"I don't really know." She was still shaking. "A friend set us up on a blind date, and he hasn't left me alone since."

"Some friend," the manager said. His phone beeped, and he answered it. He spoke for a moment, his words soft. She didn't listen. She was staring at her wrist. Josiah's fingers had left marks.

Then the manager hung up. "He's gone. Our man took his license number and he's been forbidden to come into the store again. That's all we can do."

"Thank you," she said.

The manager frowned. He was looking at her bruised wrist as well. "You know guys like him don't back down."

"I'm beginning to realize that," she said.

*   *   *

﹏ ﹏ ﹏

And that was how she found herself parking her grocery-stuffed car in front of the local precinct. It was a gray cinderblock building built in the late 1960s with reinforced windows and a steel door. Somehow it did not inspire confidence.

She went inside anyway. The front hallway was narrow, and obviously redesigned. A steel door stood to her right and to her left was a window made of bulletproof glass. Behind it sat a man in a police uniform.

She stepped up to the window. He finished typing something into a computer before speaking to her. "What?"

"I'd like to file a complaint."

"I'll buzz you in. Take the second door to your right. Someone there'll help you."

"Thanks," she said, but her voice was lost in the electronic buzz that filled the narrow hallway. She opened the door and found herself in the original corridor, filled with blond wood and doors with windows. Very sixties, very unsafe. She shook her head slightly, opened the second door, and stepped inside.

She entered a large room filled with desks. It smelled of burned coffee and mold. Most of the desks were empty, although on most of them the desk lamps were on, revealing piles of papers and files. Black phones as old as the building sat on each desk, and she was startled to see that typewriters outnumbered computers.

There were only a handful of people in the room, most of them bent over their files, looking frustrated. A man with salt-and-pepper hair was carrying a cup of coffee back to his desk. He didn't look like any sort of police detective she'd imagined. He was squarely built and seemed rather ordinary.

When he saw her, he said, "Help you?"

"I want to file a complaint."

"Come with me." His deep voice was cracked and hoarse, as if he had been shouting all day.

He led her to a small desk in the center of the room. Most of the desks were pushed together facing each other, but this one stood alone. And it had a computer with a SFPD logo screen saver.

"I'm Detective Conover. How can I help you, Miss…?"

"Paige Racette." Her voice sounded small in the large room.

He kicked a scarred wooden chair toward her. "What's your complaint?"

She sat down slowly, her heart pounding. "I'm being harassed."

"Harassed?"

"Stalked."

He looked at her straight on then, and she thought she saw a world-weariness in his brown eyes. His entire face was rumpled, like a coat that had been balled up and left in the bottom of a closet. It wasn't a handsome face by any definition, but it had a comfortable quality, a trustworthy quality that was built into the lines.

"Tell me about it," he said.

So she did. She started with the blind date, talked about how strange Josiah was, and how he wouldn't leave her alone.

"And he was taking things out of my novels like I would appreciate it. It really upset me."

"Novels?" It was the first time Conover had interrupted her.

She nodded. "I write romances."

"And are you published?"

The question startled her. Usually when she mentioned her name people recognized it. They always recognized it after she said she wrote romances.

"Yes," she said.

"So you were hoisted on your own petard, weren't you?"

"Excuse me?"

"You write about your sexual fantasies for a living, and then complain when someone is trying to take you up on it." He said that so deadpan, so seriously, that for a moment, she couldn't breathe.

"It's not like that," she said.

"Oh? It's advertising, lady."

She was shaking again. She had known this was a bad idea. Why would she expect sympathy from the police? "So since Donald Westlake writes about thieves, he shouldn't complain if he gets robbed? Or Stephen King shouldn't be upset if someone breaks his ankle with a sledgehammer?"

"Touchy," the detective said, but she noticed a twinkle in his eye that hadn't been there before.

She actually counted to ten, silently, before responding. She hadn't done that since she was a little girl. Then she said, as calmly as she could, "You baited me on purpose."

He grinned—and it smoothed out the care lines in his face, enhancing the twinkle in his eye and, for a moment, making him breathlessly attractive.

"There are a lot of celebrities in this town, Ms. Racette. It's hard for the lesser ones to get noticed. Sometimes they'll stage some sort of crime for publicity's sake. And really, what would be better than a romance writer being romanced by a fan who was using the structure of her books to do it?"

She wasn't sure what she objected to the most, being called a minor celebrity, being branded as a publicity hound, or finding this outrageous man attractive, even for a moment.

"I don't like attention," she said slowly. "If I liked attention, I would have chosen a different career. I hate book signings and television interviews, and I certainly don't want a word of this mess breathed to the press."

"So far so good," he said. She couldn't tell if he believed her, still. But she was amusing him. And that really pissed her off.

She held up her wrist. "He did this."

The smile left Conover's face. He took her hand gently in his own and extended it, examining the bruises as if they were clues. "When?"

"About an hour ago. At San Francisco Produce." She flushed saying the name of the grocery store. It was upscale and trendy, precisely the place a "celebrity" would shop.

But Conover didn't seem to notice. "You didn't tell me about the attack."

"I was getting to it when you interrupted me," she said. "I've been getting calls from him—a dozen or more a day. Flowers, presents, letters and e-mails. I'm unlisted and I never gave him my phone number or my address. I have a private e-mail address, not the one my publisher hands out, and that's the one he's using. And then he followed me to the grocery store and got angry when the store security asked him to leave."

Conover eased her hand onto his desk, then leaned back in his chair. His touch had been gentle, and she missed it.

"You had a *date* with him—"

"A blind date. We met at the restaurant, and a friend handled the details. And no, she didn't give him the information, either."

"—so," Conover said, as if she hadn't spoken, "I assume you know his name."

"Josiah Wells."

Conover wrote it down. Then he sighed. It looked like he was gathering himself. "You have a stalker, Ms. Racette."

"I know."

"And while stalking is illegal under California law, the law is damned inadequate. I'll get the video camera tape from the store, and if it backs you up, I'll arrest Wells. You'll be willing to press charges?"

"Yes," she said.

"That's a start." Conover's world-weary eyes met hers. "But I have to be honest. Usually these guys get out on bail. You'll need a lawyer to get an injunction against him, and your guy will probably ignore it. Even if he gets sent up for a few years, he'll come back and haunt you. They always do."

Her shaking started again. "So what can I do?"

"Your job isn't tied to the community. You can move."

Move? She felt cold. "I have a house." A life. This was her dream city. "I don't want to move."

"No one does, but it's usually the only thing that works."

"I don't want to run away," she said. "If I do that, then he'll be controlling my life. I'd be giving in. I'd be a victim."

Conover stared at her for a long moment. "Tell you what. I'll build the strongest case I can. That might give you a few years. By then, you might be willing to go somewhere new."

She nodded, stood. "I'll bring everything in tomorrow."

"I'd like to pick it up, if you don't mind. See where he left it, whether he's got a hidey-hole near the house. How about I come to you in a couple of hours?"

"Okay," she said.

"You got a peephole?"

"Yeah."

"Use it. I'll knock."

She nodded. Then felt her shoulders relax slightly, more than they had for two weeks. Finally, she had an ally. It meant more to her than she had realized it would. "Thanks."

"Don't thank me yet," he said. "Let's wait until this is all over."

All over. She tried to concentrate on the words and not the tone. Because Detective Conover really didn't sound all that optimistic.

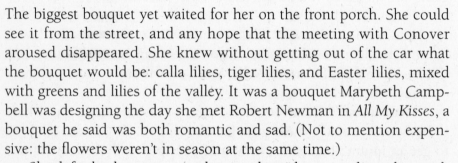

The biggest bouquet yet waited for her on the front porch. She could see it from the street, and any hope that the meeting with Conover aroused disappeared. She knew without getting out of the car what the bouquet would be: calla lilies, tiger lilies, and Easter lilies, mixed with greens and lilies of the valley. It was a bouquet Marybeth Campbell was designing the day she met Robert Newman in *All My Kisses*, a bouquet he said was both romantic and sad. (Not to mention expensive: the flowers weren't in season at the same time.)

She left the bouquet on the porch without reading the card. Conover would be there soon and he could take the whole mess away. She certainly didn't want to look at it.

After all this, she wasn't sure she ever wanted to see flowers again.

When she got inside, she found twenty-three messages on her machine, all from Josiah, all apologies, although they got angrier and angrier as she didn't answer. He must have thought she had come straight home. What a surprise he would have when he realized that she had gone to the police.

She rubbed her wrist, noting the soreness and cursing him under her breath. In addition to the bruises, her wrist was slightly swollen and she wondered if he hadn't managed to sprain it. Just her luck. He *would* damage her arm, which she needed to write. She got an ice pack out of the freezer and applied it, sitting at the kitchen table and staring at nothing.

Move. Give up, give in, all because she was feeling lonely and wanted to go on a date. All because she wanted a little flattery, a nice evening, to meet someone safe who could be—if nothing else—a friend.

How big a mistake had that been?

Big enough, she was beginning to realize, to cost her everything she held dear.

That night, after dinner, she baked herself a chocolate cake and covered it with marshmallow frosting. It was her grandmother's recipe—comfort food that Paige normally never allowed herself. This time, though, she would eat the whole thing and not worry about calories or how bad it looked. Who would know?

She made some coffee and was sitting down to a large piece, when someone knocked on her door.

She got up and walked to the door, feeling oddly vulnerable. If it was Josiah, he would only be a piece of wood away from her. That was too close. It was all too close now.

She peered through the peephole, just as she had promised Conover she would, and she let out a small sigh of relief. He was shifting from foot to foot, looking down at the bouquet she had forgotten she had left there.

She deactivated the security system, then unlocked the three deadbolts and the chain lock she had installed since this nightmare began. Conover shoved the bouquet forward with his foot.

"Looks like your friend left another calling card."

"He's not my friend," she said softly, peering over Conover's shoulder. "And he left more than that."

Conover's glance was worried. What did he imagine?

"Phone calls," she said. "Almost two dozen. I haven't checked my e-mail."

"This guy's farther along than I thought." Conover pushed the bouquet all the way inside with his foot, then closed the door, and locked it. As he did, she reset the perimeter alarm.

Conover slipped on a pair of gloves and picked up the bouquet.

"You could have done that outside," she said.

"Didn't want to give him the satisfaction," Conover said. "He has to know we don't respect what he's doing. Where can I look at this?"

"Kitchen," she said, pointing the way.

He started toward it, then stopped, sniffing. "What smells so good?"

"Chocolate cake. You want some?"

"I thought you wrote."

"Doesn't stop me from baking on occasion."

He glanced at her, his dark eyes quizzical. "This hardly seems the time to be baking."

She shrugged. "I could drink instead."

To her surprise, he laughed. "Yes, I guess you could."

He carried the bouquet into the kitchen and set it on a chair. Then he dug through the flowers to find the card.

It was a different picture of their date. The photograph looked professional, almost artistic, done in black and white, using the light from the candles to illuminate her face. At first glance, she seemed entranced with Josiah. But when she looked closely, she could see the discomfort on her face.

"You didn't like him much," Conover said.

"He was creepy from the start, but in subtle hard-to-explain ways."

"Why didn't you leave?"

"I was raised to be polite. I had no idea he was crazy."

Conover grunted at that. He opened the card. The handwriting inside was the same as all the others.

My future and your future are the same. You are my heart and soul. Without you, I am nothing.

Josiah

She closed her eyes, felt that fluttery fear rise in her again. "There'll be a ring somewhere in that bouquet."

"How do you know?" Conover asked.

She opened her eyes. "Go look at the last page of *All My Kisses.* Robert sends a forgive-me bouquet and in it, he puts a diamond engagement ring."

"This bouquet?"

"No. Josiah already used that one. I guess he thought this one would be more spectacular."

Conover dug and then whistled. There, among the stems, was a black velvet ring box. He opened it. A large diamond glittered against a circle of sapphires in a white gold setting.

"Jesus," he said. "I could retire on this thing."

"I always thought that was a gaudy ring," Paige said, her voice shaking. "But it fit the characters."

"Not to your taste?"

"No." She sighed and sank back into her chair. "Just because I write about it doesn't mean I want it to happen to me."

"I think you made that clear in the precinct today." He put the ring box back where he found it, returned the card to its envelope and set the flowers on the floor. "Mind if I have some of that cake?"

"Oh, I'm sorry." She got up and cut him a piece of cake, then poured some coffee.

When she turned around, he was grinning.

"What did I do?" she asked.

"You weren't kidding about polite," he said. "I didn't come here for a tea party, and you could have said no."

She froze in place. "Was this another of your tests? To see if I was really that polite?"

"I wish I were that smart." He took the plate from her hand. "I was getting knocked out by the smell. My mother used to make this cake. It always was my favorite."

"With marshmallow frosting?"

"And that spritz of melted chocolate on top, just like you have here." He set the plate down and took the coffee from her hand. "Although in those days, I would have preferred a large glass of milk."

"I have some—"

"Sit." If anything, his grin had gotten bigger. "Forgive me for being so blunt, but what the hell did you need with a blind date?"

There was admiration in his eyes—real admiration, not the sick kind she'd seen from Josiah. She used her fork to cut a bite of cake. "I was lonely. I don't get out much, and I thought, what could it hurt?"

He shook his head. That weary look had returned to his face. She liked its rumpled quality, the way that he seemed to be able to take the weight of the world onto himself and still stand up. "What a way to get disillusioned."

"Because I'm a romance writer?"

"Because you're a person."

They ate the cake in silence after that, then he gripped his coffee mug and leaned back in the chair.

"Thanks," he said. "I'd forgotten that little taste of childhood."

"There's more."

"Maybe later." There was no smile on his face anymore, no enjoyment. "I have to tell you a few things."

She pushed her own plate away.

"I looked up Josiah Wells. He's got a sheet."

She grabbed her own coffee cup. It was warm and comforting. "Let me guess. The political conferences he stopped going to."

Conover frowned at her. "What conferences?"

"Here in San Francisco. He was active in local politics. That's how my friend Sally met him."

"And he stopped?"

"Rather suddenly. I thought, after all this started, that maybe—"

"I'll check into it," Conover said with a determination she hadn't heard from him before. "His sheet's from San Diego."

"I thought he was from here."

Conover shook his head. "He's not a dot-com millionaire. He made his money on a software system back in the early nineties, before everyone was into this business. Sold his interest for thirty million dollars and some stock, which has since risen in value. About ten times what it was."

Her mouth had gone dry. Josiah Wells had lied to both her and Sally. "Somehow I suspect this is important."

"Yeah." Conover took a sip of coffee. "He stalked a woman in San Diego."

"Oh, God." The news gave her a little too much relief. She had been feeling alone. But she didn't want anyone else to be experiencing the same thing she was.

"He killed her."

"What?" Paige froze.

"When she resisted him, he shot her and killed her." Conover's soft gaze was on her now, measuring. All her relief had vanished. She was suddenly more terrified than she had ever been.

"You know it was him?"

"I read the file. They faxed it to me this afternoon. All of it. They had him one hundred percent. DNA matches, semen matches—"

She winced, knowing what that meant.

"—the fibers from his home on her clothing, and a list of stalking complaints and injunctions that went on for pages."

The cake sat like a lump in her stomach. "Then why isn't he in prison?"

"Money," Conover said. "His attorneys so out-classed the DA's office that by the end of the trial, they could have convinced the jury that the judge had done it."

"Oh, my God," Paige said.

"The same things that happened to you happened to her," Conover said. "Only with her those things took about two years. With you it's taking two weeks."

"Because he feels like he knows me from my books?"

Conover shook his head. "She was a TV business reporter who had done an interview with him. He would have felt like he knew her, too."

"What then?" Somehow having the answer to all of that would make her feel better—or maybe she was just lying to herself.

"These guys are like alcoholics. If you take a guy through AA, and keep him sober for a year, then give him a drink, he won't rebuild his drinking career from scratch. He'll start at precisely the point he left off."

She had to swallow hard to keep the cake down. "You think she wasn't the only one."

"Yeah. I suspect if we look hard enough, we'll find a trail of women, each representing a point in the escalation of his sickness."

"You can arrest him, right?"

"Yes." Conover spoke softly. "But only on what he's done. Not on what he might do. And I don't think we'll be any more successful at holding him than the San Diego DA."

Paige ran her hand over the butcher-block table. "I have to leave, don't I?"

"Yeah." Conover's voice got even softer. He put a hand on hers. She looked at him. It wasn't world-weariness in his eyes. It was sadness.

Sadness from all the things he'd seen, all the things he couldn't change.

"I'm from a small town," she said. "I don't want to bring him there."

"Is there anywhere else you can go? Somewhere he wouldn't think of?"

"New York," she said. "I have friends I can stay with for a few weeks."

"This'll take longer than a few weeks. You might not be able to come back."

"I know. But that'll give me time to find a place to live." Her voice broke on that last. This had been her dream city, her dream home. How quickly that vanished.

"I'm sorry," he said.

"Yeah," she said quietly. "Me, too."

He decided to stay without her asking him. He said he wanted to sift through the evidence, listen to the phone messages, and read the e-mail. She printed off all of it while she bought plane tickets online. Then she e-mailed her agent and told her that she was coming to the City.

Already she was talking like the New Yorker she was going to be.

Her flight left at 8:00 A.M. She spent half the night packing and unpacking, uncertain about what she would need, what she should leave behind. The only thing she was certain about was that she would need her laptop, and she spent an hour loading her files onto it. She was writing down the names of some moving and packing services when Conover stopped her.

"We leave everything as is," he said. "We don't want him to get too suspicious too soon."

"Why don't you arrest him now?" she asked. "Don't you have enough?"

Something flashed across his face, so quickly she almost didn't catch it.

"What?" she asked. "What is it?"

He closed his eyes. If anything, that made his face look even more rumpled. "I issued a warrant for his arrest before I came here. We haven't found him yet."

"Oh, God." Paige slipped into her favorite chair. One of many things she would have to leave behind, one of many things she might never see again because of Josiah Wells.

"We have people watching his house, watching yours, and a few other places he's known to hang out," Conover said. "We'll get him soon enough."

She nodded, trying to look reassured, even though she wasn't.

About 3:00 A.M., Conover looked at her suitcases sitting in the middle of the dining room floor. "I'll have to ship those to you. No sense tipping him off if he's watching this place."

"I thought you said—"

"I did. But we need to be careful. One duffel. The rest can wait."

"My laptop," she said. "I need that, too."

He sighed. "All right. The laptop and the biggest purse you have. Nothing more."

A few hours earlier, she might have argued with him. But a few hours earlier, she hadn't yet gone numb.

"I need some sleep," she said.

"I'll wake you," he said, "when it's time to go."

He drove her to the airport in his car. It was an old bathtub Porsche—with the early seventies bucket seats that were nearly impossible to get into.

"She's not pretty anymore," he said as he tucked Paige's laptop behind the seat, "but she can move."

They left at five, not so much as to miss traffic, but hoping that Wells wouldn't be paying attention at that hour. Conover also kept checking his rearview mirror, and a few times he executed some odd maneuvers.

"We being followed?" she asked finally.

"I don't think so," he said. "But I'm being cautious."

His words hung between them. She watched the scenery go by, houses after houses after houses filled with people who went about their ordinary lives, not worrying about stalkers or death or losing everything.

"This isn't normal for you, is it?" she asked after a moment.

"Being cautious?" he said. "Of course it is."

"No." Paige spoke softly. "Taking care of someone like this."

He seemed even more intent on the road than he had been. "All cases are different."

"Really?"

He turned to her, opened his mouth, and then closed it again, sighing. "Josiah Wells is a predator."

"I know," she said.

"We have to do what we can to catch him." His tone was odd. She frowned. Was that an apology for something she didn't understand? Or an explanation for his attentiveness?

Maybe it was both.

He turned onto the road leading to San Francisco International Airport. The traffic seemed even thicker here, through all the construction and the dust. It seemed like they were constantly remodeling the place. Somehow he made it through the confusing signs to Short Term Parking. He found a space, parked, and then grabbed her laptop from the back.

"You're coming in?" she asked.

"I want to see you get on that plane." He seemed oddly determined.

"Don't you trust me?"

"Of course I do," he said and got out of the car.

San Francisco International Airport was an old airport, built right on the bay. The airport had been trying to modernize for years. The new parts were grafted on like artificial limbs.

Paige took a deep breath, grabbed her stuffed oversized purse, and let Conover lead her inside. She supposed they looked like any couple as they went through the automatic doors, stopping to examine the signs above them pointing to the proper airline. Conover was watching the other passengers. Paige was checking out the lines.

She had bought herself a first-class ticket—spending more money than she had spent for her very first car. But she was leaving every-thing behind. The last thing she wanted was to be crammed into coach next to a howling baby and an underpaid, stressed business-man.

She hurried to the first-class line, relieved that it was short. Conover stayed beside her, frowning as he watched the people flow past. He seemed both disappointed and alert. He was expecting something. But what?

Paige stepped up to the ticket counter, gave her name, showed her identification, answered the silly security questions, and got her e-ticket with the gate number written on the front.

"You've got an hour and a half," Conover said as she left the ticket counter. "Let's get breakfast."

His hand rested possessively on her elbow, and he pulled her close as he spoke. She glanced at him, but he still wasn't watching her.

"I have to make a stop first," she said.

He nodded.

They walked past the arrival and departure monitors, past the newspaper vending machines and toward the nearest restrooms. This part of the San Francisco airport still had a seventies security design. Instead of a bank of x-ray machines and metal detectors blocking entry into the main part of the terminal, there was nothing. The secu-rity measures were in front of each gate: you couldn't enter without going past a security checkpoint. So different from New York, where you couldn't even walk into some areas without a ticket. Conover would have no trouble remaining beside her until it was time for her to take off.

She went into the ladies' room, leaving Conover near the depar-ture monitors outside. The line was long—several flights had just arrived—but Paige didn't mind. This was the first time she'd had a moment to herself since Conover had arrived the night before.

It seemed like weeks ago.

She was going to be sorry to say goodbye to him at the gate. In that short period of time, she had come to rely on him more than she wanted to admit. He made her feel safe for the first time since she had met Josiah Wells.

As she exited the ladies' room, a hand grabbed her arm and pulled her sideways. She felt something poke against her back.

"Think you could leave me?"

Wells. She shook her arm, trying to get away, but he clamped harder.

"Scream," he said, "and I will hurt you."

"You can't hurt me," she said. "You can't have weapons in an airport."

"You can bring a gun into an airport," he said softly, right in her ear. "You just can't take it through security."

She felt cold then. He was as crazy as Conover said. And as dangerous.

"Josiah." She spoke loudly, hoping that Conover could hear her. She didn't see him anywhere. "I'm going to New York on business. When I come back, we can start planning the wedding."

Wells was silent for a moment. He didn't move at all. She couldn't see his face, but she could feel his body go rigid. "You're playing with me."

"No," she said, letting her voice work for her, hoping it sounded convincing. She kept scanning the crowd, but Conover was gone. "I got your ring last night. I decided I needed to settle a few things in New York before I told you I'd say yes."

Wells put his chin on her shoulder. His breath blew against her hair. "You're not wearing the ring."

"It didn't fit," she said. "But I have it with me. I was going to have it sized in New York."

"Let me see it," he said.

"You'll have to let me dig into my purse."

She wasn't sure he'd believe her. Then, after a moment, he let her go. She brought up her purse, pretended to rummage through it, and took a step toward the ladies' room door, praying her plan would work.

He was frowning. He looked like any other businessman in the airport, his suit neat and well tailored, his trenchcoat long and expensive, marred only by the way he held his hand in the pocket.

She waited just a split second, until there were a lot of people around from another arriving plane, and then she screamed, "He's got a gun!" and ran toward the ladies' room.

Only she didn't make it. She was tackled from behind, and went sprawling across the faded carpet. A gunshot echoed around her, and people started screaming, running. The body on top of hers prevented her from moving, and for a moment, she thought whoever had hit her had been shot.

Then she felt arms around her, dragging her toward the departure monitors.

"You little fool," Conover said in her ear. "I had this under control."

He pushed her against the base of the monitor, then turned around. Half the people around Wells had remained, and two of them had him in their grasp, while another was handcuffing him. Plainclothes airport police officers. More airport police were hurrying to the spot from the front door.

Passengers were still screaming and running out of the airport. Airline personnel were crouched behind their desks. Paige looked to see whether anyone was shot, but she didn't see anyone lying injured anywhere.

Her breathing was shallow, and she suddenly realized how terrified she had been. "What do you mean, under control? This doesn't look under control to me."

Security had Wells against the wall and were searching him for more weapons. One of the uniformed airport police had pulled Wells's head back and was yelling at him. Some of the passengers, realizing the threat was over, were drifting back toward the action.

Conover kept one hand on her, holding her in place. With the other, he pulled out his cell phone. He hit the speed-dial and put the small phone against his ear.

"Wait a minute!" Paige said.

He turned away slightly, as if he didn't want to speak to her. Then he said into the phone, "Frank, do me a favor. Call the news media— everyone you can think of. Tell them something just happened at the airport....No. I'm not going through official channels. That's why I called you. Keep my name out of it and get them here."

He hung up and glanced at Paige. She had never felt so many emotions in her life. Anger, adrenaline, confusion. Then she saw security lead Wells away.

Conover took her arm and helped her up. "What's going on?" she asked again.

"Outside," he said, and pushed her through the crowd. After a moment, she remembered to check for her laptop. He had it, and somehow she had retained her purse. They reached the front sidewalk only to find it a confusion of milling people—some still terrified from the shots, others just arriving and trying to drop off their luggage. Cabs honked and nearly missed each other. Buses were backing up as the crowd spilled into the street.

"Oh, this is so much better," she said.

He moved her down the sidewalk toward another terminal. The crowd thinned here.

"What the hell was that?" she asked. "Where were you? How did he get past you?"

"He didn't get past me," Conover said softly.

She felt the blood leave her face. "You set me up? I was bait?"

"It wasn't supposed to happen like this."

"Oh, really? He was supposed to drag me onto the nearest flight? Or shoot me?"

"I didn't know he had a gun," Conover said. "He was ballsier than I expected. And he wouldn't have taken you from San Francisco."

"You know this how? Because you're psychic?"

"No, he wanted to control you. He couldn't control you on a plane. I had security waiting outside. A few plainclothes cops have been around us since we arrived. He was supposed to grab you, but you weren't supposed to try to get away."

"Nice if you would have told me that."

He shook his head slightly. "Most people wouldn't have fought him. Most people would have cooperated."

"Most people would have appreciated an explanation!" Her voice rose and a few stray passengers looked in her direction. She made herself take a deep breath before she went on. "You knew he was going to be here. You knew it and didn't tell me."

"I guessed," he said.

"What did you do, tip him off?"

"No," Conover said softly. "You did."

"I did? I didn't talk to him."

"You booked your e-ticket online." His face was close to hers, his voice as soft as possible in all the noise. "He'd hacked into your system weeks ago. That's how he found your address and your phone number. Your public e-mail comes into the same computer as all your other e-mail. He's been following your every move ever since."

"Software genius," she muttered, shaking her head. She should have seen that.

Conover nodded. Across the way, reporters started converging on the building, cameras hefted on shoulders, running toward the doors. Conover shielded her, but she knew they would want to talk to her.

"Why didn't you warn me?" she asked again.

"I thought you'd be too obvious then, and he wouldn't try for you. I didn't expect you to be so cool under pressure. Telling him about the ring, pretending you were interested, that was smart."

One of the reporters was working the crowd. People were turning toward the camera.

"Where were you?" she asked. "I looked for you."

"I was behind you all the time."

"So if he took me outside…?"

"I would have followed."

"I don't understand. Why didn't you tell me not to get the ticket online?"

"The ticket was a gift," Conover said. "I didn't realize you were going to do it that way. You told me when you finished. His file from the previous case mentioned how he had used the Internet to spy on his first victim. He was obviously doing that with you."

"But the airport, how did they know?"

"I called ahead, said that I was coming in, expecting a difficult passenger. I faxed his photo from your place while you were asleep. I asked them to wait until I got him outside, unless he did something threatening."

She frowned. More reporters were approaching. These looked like print media. No cameras, but lots of determination. "You could have waited and caught him at home."

"I could have," Conover said. "But this is better."

She turned to him, remembering the feel of the gun against her back, the screaming passengers, the explosive sound when the gun went off. "Someone could have been killed."

"I didn't expect a gun," Conover said. "And I didn't think he'd be rash enough to use it in an airport."

"But he did," she said.

"And it's going to help us." Conover watched another set of reporters run into the building. "First, his assault on you in an airport makes it a federal case. The gun adds to the case, and all the witnesses make it even better. Then there is the fact that airports are filled with security cameras. There's bound to be tape on this."

She frowned, trying to take herself out of this, trying to listen like a writer instead of a potential victim.

"And then," Conover said, "he attacked you. You're nationally known. It'll be big news. Our DA might have lost a stalking case against Wells, but the feds aren't going to let a guy who went nuts in an airport walk, no matter how much money he has."

"You set him up," she said. "If this had failed—"

"At the very least, I would have been fired," Conover said. "But it wouldn't have failed. I wouldn't have let anything happen to you. I didn't let anything happen to you."

"But you took such a risk." She raised her head toward his. "Why?"

He put a finger under her chin, and for a moment, she thought he was going to kiss her.

"Because you didn't want to leave San Francisco," he said softly.

"I get to stay home?" she asked.

He smiled, and let his finger drop. "Yeah."

He stared at her uncertainly, as if he were afraid she was going to yell at him again. But she felt a relief so powerful that it completely overwhelmed her.

She threw her arms around him. For a moment, he didn't move. Then, slowly, his arms wrapped around her and pulled her close.

"I don't even know your first name," she whispered.

"Pete," he said, burying his face in her hair.

"Pete." She tested it. "It suits you."

"I'd ask if I could call you," he said, "but I'm not real good on dates."

That pulled a reluctant laugh from her. "Obviously I'm not, either. But I make a mean chocolate cake."

"That's right," he said. "Let's go finish it."

"Don't we have to talk to the press?"

"For a moment." He pulled back just enough to smile at her. "And then I get to take you home."

"Where I get to stay." She couldn't convey how much this meant to her. "Thank you."

He nodded. "My pleasure."

She leaned her head against his shoulder, feeling his strength, feeling the comfort. It didn't matter how he looked or whether he knew *La Bohème* from Don Giovanni. All that mattered was how he made her feel.

Safe. Appreciated. And maybe even loved.

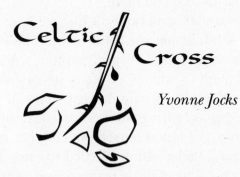

Celtic Cross

Yvonne Jocks

"**S**omeone's going to die," whispered Didi, staring at the tarot card.

Her new employer, Annie Tregaron, glanced down from where she stood by the cash register. "The death card doesn't always mean death," she prompted gently. *Too gently*, Didi thought, considering the garish picture of a skeleton that she'd just drawn from the store's sample deck.

"I asked the cards what I should know about taking this job, and then I drew *this*!"

"It usually means beginnings and endings." Annie plucked the card neatly from Didi's hand, tucked it back into the deck, and shuffled all seventy-eight with practiced hands. With her gauzy skirts and all those rings and bracelets and all that brown hair, Annie Tregaron looked like some kind of high priestess. She sounded so sure, and yet…

Someone's going to die, thought Didi again. And she had the sick feeling it might be her.

Was taking this job a mistake?

Annie handed back the cards with quiet confidence. That confidence had drawn Didi back to her store, Avalon, again and again, even before the clerking job became available. Didi liked other things about the store, too—the incense and candles, the Celtic and Native

American music, the crystals and jewelry. It felt like maybe magic really worked, in here, like a place where the harshness of the world could never intrude....

Didi O'Sullivan longed to believe such a place existed. But...the card!

"Try again," advised Annie, since Didi had already learned her tasks for the day and now was just killing time. "A whole spread, not a one-card pull. It'll tell you more."

Didi didn't understand tarot all that well yet, despite the books she'd bought—books her husband had pitched a fit about. As she laid cards out on the glass-topped counter, she murmured a chant beneath her breath to remember the basic spread: "Cover me, cross me; over me, under me; behind me, before me."

But instead of admiring the knot-work design that backed the face-down cards, she found herself noticing her gold wedding band. *Had* she made a mistake? Annie seemed so safe, so capable of taking up anybody's problems in those many-ringed hands!

Inhaling scented air, Didi turned the first card, called the significator, which represented the center of the matter. The breath whimpered out of her. She stared down at the same picture of a horseback skeleton.

Death.

Someone...

"Well," said Annie steadily. "That *is* what you were asking about, right? Let's see what the cross card tells us." While Didi sat on the stool behind the counter, near to paralyzed, Annie turned the next card. It lay across the first, indicating obstacles. "Ah..."

It was a face card, the Knight of Swords.

Even without books, Didi knew what—or who—that card represented. Apparently, so did Annie.

"Your husband?"

Didi's gaze again dropped to the wedding ring, with a mixture of misery and hope.

Conn...

"I've never loved anyone like I love my wife, Mr. Delaney," said the man sitting across the desk from Sawyer, earlier that day. "Maybe nobody has. I'd die if anything happened to us."

Die? That seemed extreme, but Sawyer was no expert on true love. All he said was, "And you're hiring me to...?"

Connor O'Sullivan shifted restlessly. He had shaggy black hair, a long and shadowed jaw, stubborn blue eyes. He wore jeans and a WWF T-shirt. "This isn't real comfortable for me, you know. Coming to another guy for help."

Sawyer could've guessed that from the shirt. "So don't think of me as a guy, Mr. O'Sullivan," he advised, leaning farther back in his chair. He opted against propping his booted feet up on his desk. *Too gumshoe.* "Just think of me as a private investigator."

O'Sullivan scowled at him a long moment more.

"Is it your wife you want investigated?"

"*Yes.* I mean—" O'Sullivan closed his eyes, shook his head. Either he really was upset, or he was an excellent actor. "It's not that I think she's cheating on me or anything. Didi would never in a million years do something like that."

Sawyer had heard *that* before. It was usually a lie.

"*Never!* She knows it would kill me."

Again with the dying. "So..."

O'Sullivan opened his fists, spread his fingers. "My wife's gotten sucked into some kind of cult."

Suddenly, this wasn't just another is-my-wife-cheating case after all. "A cult," Sawyer repeated, propping his elbows on his wood-veneer desk.

"People are always taking advantage of Didi. That's why she needs *me*. About a month ago, she starts bringing home weird books and crystals and shit, you know? From this hocus-pocus bookstore she's found down on 7th Street. Next thing I know, she's following her horoscope and talking about the freaking moonphase and just going *spacey* on me."

Sawyer considered that. "New Age spacey is one thing, Mr. O'Sullivan. But a cult has to have a leader. A figurehead. Like David Koresh, or that Jim Jones bastard. Remove the figurehead, you end the cult."

"Yes!" agreed O'Sullivan. "There's this woman at the bookstore, Annie something-or-other. She gives classes in fortunetelling and shit, and women get together there after hours in some kind of *coven*, and...and they've got my Didi."

"Kidnapping is a job for the police." Only as he heard himself all but turning down money did Sawyer admit the truth. As much as this case intrigued him, he had a bad feeling about it. A *real* bad feeling. No crystal ball required.

And yet...

"I mean, they have her brainwashed or something," insisted O'Sullivan. "But the way they're turning her against me, she might as well be kidnapped. She even got a job at the place—can you believe it? Like I haven't been providing for her just fine! Like she has any business hanging around those lesbo crazies doing their voodoo shit."

Lesbo crazies? How sad—yet Sawyer was intrigued. "What exactly is it you want *me* to do, Mr. O'Sullivan?"

"You probably wouldn't go for killing them all, huh?" asked his client, with a sudden, awkward laugh.

Sawyer just stared, unamused. *You couldn't afford me.*

"Never mind," said O'Sullivan quickly. Dropping his gaze, he scraped his open hands down his blue-jeaned thighs. "Bad joke. What I need is information on this Tregaron woman and what kind of a woo-woo cult she's running. I need to show Didi what a batch of loonies she's getting into, before it's too late. I don't...I don't think she'll listen anymore, if it comes from me. They've got her that turned around. But cold, hard proof..."

"From a professional like myself," clarified Sawyer, not smiling.

"Yeah," said O'Sullivan. "Look, I'm desperate. If this doesn't work, I don't know what else I can do. Get me something to make my wife see sense, okay? Before I wake up one morning and find her dead and mutilated, some kind of satanic sacrifice. We...this isn't the kind of love that you just let go of, you know? This is the kind of love a man's got to fight for—or die trying."

There it was again, the bad feeling. But...Sawyer *did* need the business.

"I'll give it a day and see what I can find out," he said. By quoting his price, he mentally accepted responsibility for whatever came of it.

He just hoped whatever-came-of-it didn't end up being his fault. Again.

"Calm down," repeated Annie. "You won't hear anything the cards are advising if you overreact."

"Over*react*?" squeaked Didi.

Annie had found herself drawn to the redhead's vulnerability early on, drawn to the potential of it. She would be interested to see what Didi could become—with the right influences, of course.

But the woman wasn't particularly well grounded.

"Remember what I said about the Death card." If she spoke steadily, she could help slow a listener's brainwave cycles toward the alpha end of the spectrum. It was like a mild form of hypnosis. "You said you were asking about the job, so that makes sense. You're leaving remnants of the old Didi behind. That's not such a bad thing, is it?"

Didi shook her head, but reluctantly. She still looked pale.

"Standing in your way, though—the cross card—is a man, possibly dark-haired. He makes up for his insecurities by pretending to know everything, no matter whom he hurts in the process. You think that's your husband?"

Annie thought she saw a nod hidden in Didi's shrug. She'd figured as much, ever since the day Didi brought a moon pendant back to the store, claiming that her husband wouldn't let her wear it. Wouldn't *let* her! It bristled Annie's every female instinct.

"Your hope for the situation, its highest good, is…" Annie's bracelets jingled as she turned the card that made the top of the cross shape. "Justice. Well…maybe it has to do with you paying your own way, like you said you wanted to."

That didn't feel quite right, but Didi nodded again, so Annie continued.

"And the foundation of the situation is…" *Huh. Eight of Swords.* She never had liked the drawing of a woman, bound and blindfolded, blades on all sides. "Isolation," she murmured. "Confusion. Self-doubt…"

How could *that* have led to Didi's life change, registering for classes at Avalon, getting involved with the woman's circle, *taking this job*?

That *was* what this spread was about, wasn't it? Didi taking this job? *Something didn't feel quite right, at that…*

Annie turned over the card that symbolized the immediate past— the Devil, humanity's tendency to chain itself with negativity or obsession.

But whose? Didi's, or her husband's? Or someone else's?

Faster now, Annie turned the next card to reveal the immediate future—and stared.

It showed a tower, lightning blasting the roof off, innocents tumbling from its windows toward their death. A portent of devastation, the Tower was arguably the worst card in the entire deck.

Oh, crap, she thought, taking in the main body of the tarot spread. *Maybe someone IS going to die.*

Great. Absolutely peachy.

"What is it?" asked Didi. "What's wrong?"

"I...I'm not sure," Annie admitted. She'd already made Didi more susceptible to suggestion by easing her brainwaves down toward alpha state. She could too easily plant prophecies for the girl to self-fulfill. "The future is fluid, after all."

"It's bad news," guessed Didi.

"It—" Annie took a deep breath. "It shows that there could be some kind of blowup in your near future, because of these cards." She indicated the Devil, the Eight of Swords. "They indicate self-denial, unwillingness to take responsibility, a tendency to dwell in negativity." Annie considered her new part-time clerk. "What the heck's been going on in your life lately, anyway?"

Didi drew herself up straight. "That's my own business."

Now she grows a spine.

To complicate matters, the bells over the doorway chimed and an auburn-haired man walked in.

He didn't look like Annie's type—or Avalon's. She sold to black-lipsticked Goths, RenFaire types, hold-over hippies. She also helped housewives, dentists, college professors, computer programmers.

And yet, despite the jeans and scuffed bomber jacket, this man *still* didn't look like her usual customer.

"We'll talk in a minute," she instructed Didi. "In the meantime, go choose a nice black crystal—jet, or obsidian—for extra protection. On the house. And *don't worry.*"

Nodding, Didi headed for the back of the shop.

Annie turned to the not-a-customer, a tallish man with sideburns and gray eyes and an air of purpose about him that she didn't fully trust. "May I help you?"

"I hope so," he said. He looked her up and down—but like a regular guy would. *That* part didn't set off any warnings. Then he offered his hand. "Sawyer Delaney. Can I ask you a few questions?"

What Connor O'Sullivan couldn't stand was the not knowing. He tried to just go on to his job like nothing had happened, like he could just sit behind the office building's security desk with his video feeds and his badge and his headset and not care. He tried to distract himself by laying out his umpteenth game of solitaire, using a worn pack of casino cards. But how was a man supposed to stay calm when crazies were threatening his *wife*?

It wasn't like he could take off his worry the same way he changed out of his T-shirt and into the stupid white monkey-shirt management forced him to wear. Uniform or not, he could barely think past his upset.

Didi...

From the moment he saw her, he'd known they were meant to be together. Within weeks of their first date they were living together; within months, they'd married. Something like that didn't happen any old day, right? But he and Didi, they were special.

What kind of unfeeling bitch would turn a man's wife, his soul mate, against him like this?

Connor split his attention between the playing cards and the video feeds, a voyeurism he normally enjoyed. Did the people he watched know what he was going through? Were any of them involved with that Tregaron woman's cult?

He wrenched his attention away from the vid-screens and, since he couldn't concentrate anyway, scooped the playing cards off the counter and into the trash.

The ace of spades fluttered to the floor, a stray. He wondered what the Tregaron woman would make of that?

Anyone who put a stop to her kind of craziness was a real man, in his book.

* * *

Most of the con-artists Sawyer had run into didn't stay anywhere long enough to get caught—or prosecuted, anyhow. They tended to decorate in such a way that they could pull up and move on.

In contrast, a computer check from his office told Sawyer that the store called Avalon had been in business at the same location for over three years. It had its own website, announcing new merchandise and listing classes and retreats for the next six months. The store itself had stained glass worked into its display windows and murals on the upper walls.

The proprietor clearly had no intention of moving anytime soon. Either she was legit, or…

Or she had her own, less legal reasons for confidence.

Two women occupied the store. One, a pale young redhead, fit Didi O'Sullivan's description. The other had long, wild brown hair, and a wide mouth, and clear green eyes so direct that he could think of no other word than "wise."

So this was the Jim Jones of the New Age set?

He'd have thought she'd be taller.

"Sawyer Delaney," he said in a neutral voice. "Can I ask you a few questions?"

"Annie Tregaron," she said back. "You can *ask*."

No promises about answers, though…

"I'm a private investigator, Ms. Tregaron, looking into some concerns about the, um, *occult* stores in town."

She kept her expression remarkably neutral, but her eyes cooled. *Something to hide, Dark Lady?*

"'Metaphysical,'" she said. "The word *occult* means 'hidden,' and as you can see, we aren't hiding anything."

"Well, that should make my job easy." Fun though the hard-boiled private-eye routine was on TV, he generally caught more information with honey than with vinegar. "Do you have a few minutes? We could talk here, or go across the street for a cup of coffee—my treat."

She glanced over her shoulder toward the redhead, who was sorting through a bin of colored rocks. "I have a new clerk today."

At least that meant she'd talk to him. Then again, after her "occult means hidden," speech, she'd look damned suspicious otherwise.

More damned suspicious.

"Here's fine," he said.

"Do you have an ID?" she asked.

He dug it out for her.

As he was showing her his credentials, he noticed the tarot cards laid across the glass counter. "Have I interrupted something?"

"Nothing to worry about."

But the skeleton card drew his interest. "Death, huh?"

"The Death card," said Ms. Tregaron, "doesn't always mean death. It usually means endings and beginnings."

Sounded like a line to him.

"But sometimes it means death, right?"

She met and held his gaze for what felt like a very long moment. She was a helluva lot prettier than Jim Jones.

Sawyer looked away first. Because he didn't want to alienate her, he told himself.

"Sometimes," she admitted.

"So," he asked, his voice coming out deeper than usual. "Who's going to die?"

"So," she countered. "What is it that has *'people'* so concerned?"

"You don't know?"

"Folks usually complain that we're Satanists, sacrificing babies and having orgies in the back room."

"I hadn't heard the orgies part," he admitted—and she smiled. Annie Tregaron had a hell of a smile. *Oh, hell,* Sawyer thought. He was in trouble.

"You needn't sound so intrigued, Mr. Delaney," she chided, her own voice deepening.

He was in deep, deep trouble.

Annie answered the private investigator's questions with her usual speech—the we're-not-witches, we're-not-Satanists, we-don't-target-minors speech. She never knew if a person would actually buy it, of course, but she found herself hoping the investigator would. He could be trouble, otherwise.

And, okay, he *was* attractive in a lanky sort of way.

"Could I see the back room where you hold your classes?" he asked, and she led him back through the curtains, only briefly glancing toward Didi O'Sullivan.

Annie was proud of her "classroom" in back. A storage area opened off of it, but she knew Mr. Delaney's peek would show him nothing more damning than a lot of boxes and empty shelving. The main room had dark blue linoleum, a large table and a dozen chairs, and a refrigerator, which Mr. Delaney checked.

"No dead bodies," she said, and he spun around, as if surprised by her voice. "But there's a Dumpster out back, if you want to be sure."

"I'll keep that in mind," he said, looking down at her. She could feel his nearness against her, like an expectation.

"Will there be anything else?"

"*Would* you like to get a cup of coffee?" he asked. "Maybe after you've closed up for the day?"

"I don't drink caffeine."

"Herbal tea, then."

"Wouldn't that be a conflict of interest? What about whoever hired you to dig up proof about our brainwashing, child-sacrificing, demonic orgies?"

He narrowed his eyes, cocked his head suspiciously. "I hadn't mentioned brainwashing."

"Goodbye, Mr. Delaney," she said. She headed for the front door, confident that he would follow her. He did.

"Can I call you if I have more questions?" he asked.

"You can *call*," she demurred.

He stopped in the doorway, folded his arms, looked her up and down like a man who knew what he was doing.

Annie waited for it.

"Are you a good witch," he asked, "or a bad witch?"

"I told you, I'm not a witch."

He glanced toward the tarot spread on the counter.

"Witches," she said, "have too many rules about ethics."

Then she smiled her best, most evil smile, and turned away from him. She didn't need him distracting her any further.

She had Didi to take care of.

The more frightened Didi felt, the more dangerous her magic bookstore seemed. She tried not to be scared, but…a private investigator? He'd asked Annie some scary questions.

Had she made a mistake, taking this job?

It didn't help when Annie glanced at her with those all-knowing eyes and predicted, "You're having second thoughts?"

"I…"

"How long have you been married?"

Then Didi understood. "Second thoughts about *Connor*?"

"You said your husband wasn't happy with you taking this job," said Annie. "He made you return that amulet."

Both of which were true, but…

"Well, we'd agreed that he'd work, and I'd stay home and take care of the house." Or the one-bedroom apartment, as the case may be. "Conn's family thinks it's an insult to the husband if his wife works. That's not *his* fault."

Annie looked unconvinced.

"And he *didn't* tell me to return the moon amulet." True, he'd yelled at her about it. Worse, he'd thrown her new crystal ball across the living room, right through the window. It had shattered on the concrete outside, so of course she couldn't return *that*. He'd gone off to the bar to cool off. Afterward he'd apologized for losing his temper, held her tight, told her she was the most important thing in the world to him.

Didi loved it when Conn told her things like that.

Since she had to somehow pay the apartment complex for a new window, she'd decided on her own to get the money back on the moon pendant. Did Annie resent the return? Was that it?

"I suppose," said Annie slowly, "that I misunderstood."

But she sounded suspicious, and that made Didi mad.

"Conn and I have our problems, but he loves me," she insisted. "He loves me more than anything in the world. He says so."

Annie, she remembered, had never married. Didi had admired her quiet confidence...but maybe it was a ruse.

She didn't want to be like Annie, if it meant alienating Connor. She didn't want to be empowered, if it meant being alone.

"I should probably go," Didi said. She wasn't sure she would come back, either. But she would rather tell Annie that over the telephone. "It's after four."

"What about the tarot reading? Don't you want to finish it?"

"No." For all she knew, Annie had arranged the cards to lay out that way on purpose. "It's probably nothing. Like you said, endings and beginnings."

Didi retrieved her purse from behind the counter.

"See you tomorrow," said Annie.

And Didi, hurrying out the front door with a jingle of bells, called back, "Bye."

When she remembered the onyx in her pocket, she decided to worry about it later.

She wasn't likely going back.

The cards said scary things in that place.

"You cheat!"

One of the suits crossing the marble foyer glanced nervously toward Connor O'Sullivan. Well, the hell with him. *He* wasn't the one on the phone with a no-good PI.

"I checked Tregaron out thoroughly," said the cheat. "Court records. Credit report. Better Business Bureau. She's clean."

"You didn't look hard enough," protested Conn. "Didn't ask enough questions."

"I've worked all day on this! I spent a half-hour at the store myself, and Ms. Tregaron was..."

Delaney hesitated, which made Connor immediately suspicious. "What already?"

"Impressive. And I, uh, found no bodies in the Dumpster."

Connor felt suddenly cold. "She got you, too."

"What?"

"You son of a bitch!"

Another passing businessman cleared his throat.

"Mind your own damn business," Connor snarled at him.

"Look," said Delaney into the phone, "I know this isn't what you were looking for—"

"And don't expect to get paid for it, either!" Connor slammed down the phone, dug for his car keys with a shaking hand. He needed a beer. It wasn't quite time for him to go off shift, but he didn't give a rat's ass about the time.

If you wanted something done right, you did it yourself.

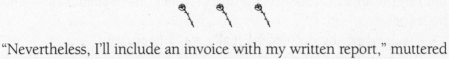

"Nevertheless, I'll include an invoice with my written report," muttered Sawyer to dead air as he hung up the phone. "You paranoid *jerk.*"

But he had a bad feeling about this.

Maybe he was just bummed about Annie Tregaron. It was dicey, pursuing a woman when he'd seen everything from her credit report to her spotless driving record.

Too spotless, maybe?

But, no, that wasn't the same kind of bad feeling.

On a hunch, he leaned over his computer and ran another check. But this time, he typed in a different name entirely.

Within minutes of seeing the results, Sawyer was on the phone to Avalon. When he just got the answering machine, he headed out the door.

At a run.

Annie used Didi's job application to find her clerk's apartment complex—one of the rundown types from the sixties building boom, with smaller windows and communal balconies. Once she'd spotted the apartment, she parked her car, but she didn't get out right away. Instead, she used her cell phone to try Didi's number one last time.

Not even an answering machine.

After turning over the last four cards of Didi's Celtic-Cross spread, Annie knew she had to find her new clerk. As Mr. Sawyer Delaney had so simply pointed out, sometimes the Death card really *did* mean death.

And sometimes you did what you had to do.

Annie got out of her car, locked it, and headed toward the apartments. She heard a car screech to a stop in the parking lot behind her; heard a door slam shut. "Annie!"

Speak of the devil—Sawyer Delaney!

"What are you doing here?" But she couldn't help glancing over her shoulder, toward Didi's apartment, as she asked.

"I followed a hunch." Delaney took her by an arm, tried to guide her off the cement walkway, tried to stop her. She pulled away—and he let her.

That's when she decided he really was a good guy.

Bad guys didn't let go.

"Look, I've got to check on Didi. Her car's here, but she's not answering the phone."

"Let me do it," insisted Delaney.

"She doesn't even *know* you."

"Yeah, well, her husband knows *you*. By reputation, anyway. And he's not real happy with you today."

Then Annie understood who had hired Sawyer Delaney. She understood her certainty that something was wrong with Didi's marriage.

She hesitated, glanced toward the stairs.

"Look, he's got a record," insisted Delaney. "Bar fights. Threats. Battery."

Annie nodded. "Fine. You check. But get her out of there."

He searched her eyes, then nodded, turned. He took the stairs two at a time, like someone who could get the job done.

But he couldn't reach the landing before the gunshot.

The gun just went off—and now there was a body on the floor. They'd been fighting about the job again. Didi said she would quit, but Connor lost his temper worse than ever, and…

Yes, that was it. They'd been fighting about the job.

Somehow they ended up in the kitchen, with its sink full of dirty dishes and its overflowing trash can. He'd started yelling. She'd yelled back—Annie Tregaron's influence, maybe?

He'd screamed his frustration and grabbed a knife.

Even that didn't seem real, even as he slashed at her, even as she cowered behind bloody arms, because after all he loved her. He loved her more than anything—kept trying to tell her that. They would be together forever. But there was the knife, and there was the pain, and his gun hung off the chair where he always put the holster after work....

With a loud, crisp *bang!* the body crumpled, too neat, too sudden. Then someone was at the front door, banging on it and yelling something about calling 911. The bloody, shaking hands couldn't hold the gun steady.

It was now starting to feel horribly real after all.

But...he'd loved her!

The gun clattered onto the table—so much heavier than you'd think, guns—and the banging at the door got louder until shaking feet found their way across the living room, until blood-slick hands fumbled the lock, until the door swung open.

Then Didi O'Sullivan looked into the panicked eyes of the man who'd been in Annie's shop this afternoon, and she didn't know why he was there at her apartment. But she guessed she knew what had happened, after all.

"I killed him," she whispered. "He's on the floor. The cards said someone was going to die, and it was Connor."

Then she began to weep.

"She said he loved her," whispered Annie Tregaron, staring down into her cup of herbal tea.

Sawyer glanced around the all-night diner. "This is not what I meant about taking you out for coffee."

But she'd been so shaken in the aftermath of the shooting—after the ambulance had taken Didi to the hospital, after the police cars, after the reports—that he'd had to do *something*. Attraction aside, he owed her that. As angry as he'd been, Connor O'Sullivan could have gone after Annie almost as easily as he'd gone after his wife.

His wife was just the safer target.

"He said he loved her, too," Sawyer offered. "For what it's worth."

"So why'd he try to kill her?"

"Why did she stay with him?" He shrugged. "Love's not all hearts and flowers, you know? Women are more likely to be killed by a husband or boyfriend than a stranger. When people's emotions and self-image get involved…"

She was staring at him, but she didn't look empowered or wise. She looked scared.

Sawyer said, "That's probably the worst possible lead-in to asking a woman out that I could ever come up with, huh?"

She said, "Yes."

He nodded, and looked down into his mug of coffee. *Oh well.*

Then she said, "But *any* date would have to top this, right?"

He nodded, looked up, grinned.

Annie's face twisted into a kind of wince. She wasn't ready to smile quite yet. She'd held Didi until the paramedics showed up, putting pressure on the towels they'd wrapped around her lacerated arms, wiping tear-streaked spatters of blood off the girl's face. Only when Didi's parents had arrived at the hospital, had Annie agreed to leave her.

Finding someone like that really *was* a kind of magic. Sawyer had no intention of letting her slip away, after all that.

Unless, of course, she told him to.

"So…," he prompted. "What do the tea leaves say, anyway?"

"I don't read tea leaves." But she inhaled deeply, then straightened her shoulders, sat up a bit. "Give me your hand."

Sawyer did.

Annie Tregaron studied his palm, stroked a single finger across the lines of it. He enjoyed her touch, firm and purposeful but not clinging.

She nodded and looked up, still holding his hand. "Yes. I'll go out with you."

So he had to ask. "Just what did you see?"

"Nothing," she admitted, with the barest of smiles. "I don't read palms, either. Just cards."

Their fingers interlaced.

It was a beginning. A good one. ✒

Hostage to Love

Mary Watson

"Promise we won't stay long."

Brand-new Assistant Prosecuting Attorney Jo Haynes heard the hint of desperation in her voice, but there was nothing she could do about it. Anticipation of the ordeal ahead made her restless and fidgety. She jabbed a button on her armrest to lower the power window and sucked humid eighty-degree air into her lungs.

Sharon Hancock, Jo's part-time secretary and full-time friend, used the driver's control panel to close the window. "Want me to park at the curb and leave the engine running?"

Jo reminded herself that Sharon was barely twenty-five, and that most of the time her flippancy was one of her more appealing traits. Still, if she hadn't been driving, the crack probably would have earned her a punch on the arm.

"No one appreciates your impudent wit more than I," she said dryly. "But I don't think *you* appreciate how much I hate these places. They give me the creeps."

"Then you shouldn't have agreed to come with me," Sharon replied. "We have to stay for a decent amount of time. The whole purpose of visiting a funeral home is to pay your respects."

"Well, yes, sure," Jo muttered. "I know *that*. But—"

"It would sort of defeat the purpose to dash in, blurt 'So sorry for your loss,' then race for the nearest exit."

Jo grimaced, conceding the point. "I would never blurt out 'So sorry for your loss.' Ugh. Sounds like a chintzy generic sympathy card."

"Well…yeah. But what should you say? What would be appropriately sympathetic, compassionate, but not schmucky?"

"You're asking the wrong person. Not knowing what to say is one of the reasons I avoid funeral homes. That, and besides—"

"They give you the creeps."

"Big time. Think about it—you stand around with a bunch of other people who don't want to be there, all of you uncomfortable as hell, trying to think of nice things to say about a dead person most of you barely knew and maybe didn't even like that much…."

"Like how good she looks."

"As if! How can dead look *good*?"

Sharon grinned. "But that's what a lot of people comment about. The makeup, the hair, how natural the corpse looks, what an attractive dress she's wearing…that kind of thing."

"Creepy," Jo declared, feeling vindicated. "At least we won't have to listen to that sort of asinine drivel."

"Probably not. I doubt Flo's casket will be open. You never know, though. Last year, when Ralph Forstner fell headfirst into that corn auger? His mother insisted on an open casket, said his friends should have one last chance to see him before they put him in the ground."

"Oh, Lord," Jo murmured, wiping suddenly damp palms on her skirt. "Surely they won't—" Her right hand levitated in an involuntary gesture of dismay. "—*show* her."

She thought Sharon's mouth tried to twitch into another grin before she got it under control. "I wouldn't think so. If it was *my* family, I know they'd want a closed casket. But cosmetologists can work miracles nowadays, so maybe."

Jo closed her eyes and offered up a heartfelt prayer that she wouldn't have to think of something appropriate to say while gazing down at Flo Johanssen's dead, painted face. The biggest reason funeral homes gave her the creeps was because they were always occupied by dead people. Who were usually wearing too much rouge. By the time Sharon found an empty space in the Bates Mortuary parking lot, Jo's stomach felt like a giant clenched fist.

"Looks like half the town is here," Sharon said as they headed up the sidewalk toward the entrance. She sounded a little too enthusiastic in Jo's opinion, as if they were about to enter the Elks Lodge on singles night.

Sharon was right, though. The joint wasn't exactly jumping, but a sizable crowd spilled out of the "parlor" that held Flo's mortal remains and into the large foyer. While waiting in line to sign in as a visitor, Jo spotted the mayor, the bank president, the owners of several local businesses, three ministers, approximately half the high school faculty, and about a jillion teenagers. The number of teachers and students wasn't surprising. The recently departed Flo and her husband, Bob, both taught at the high school. Most of the kids looked as miserably uncomfortable as Jo felt. Of course it was possible that their misery was actually caused by grief.

"Quite a turnout, huh?"

Recognizing the deep, sonorous baritone, Jo turned to face Sheriff Angus McCormick. Damn. Of all the people she'd have wished *not* to run into....

"Hello, Sheriff. Yes, evidently Flo had a lot of friends."

One side of his full mouth lifted in a mocking half smile. "C'mon, Madam Prosecutor. We both know most of these people are here just to get a look at her, see if the rumors are true."

Jo ducked her head and studied the glossy gray marble floor, caught between the impulse to agree with him and a more politically correct conditioned response. Of course he was right, but damn! The man was either the most scrupulously honest person she'd ever met, or the most tactless, insensitive clod. Unfortunately, she didn't know him well enough to make the call. This was only the third time they'd met, and he'd managed, with no apparent effort, to completely discombobulate her the first two times. He was on a roll, three for three, batting a thousand.

Deciding that any response would be better than stupefied silence, she murmured, "That's a pretty harsh judgment."

"I wasn't passing judgment."

Jo tilted her head to give him a skeptical look.

"Curiosity isn't a crime, or even a sin, so far as I know." He lowered his voice and leaned a few inches closer. "And considering some of the rumors...." He trailed off with a shake of his head that could have signified either disgust or amused disbelief.

"I know," Jo muttered. Although at the moment she wasn't really focused on the rumors about the circumstances surrounding Flo Johanssen's death. She was wondering whether the sheriff was wearing musk cologne, or if that was just his own natural essence. Whichever, the effect was potent, which only intensified her uneasiness. Belatedly realizing that all the people between her and the visitors' book had moved on, she seized the excuse to step away from him. McCormick and the pheromone cloud surrounding him followed her.

"Is the, uh...the casket, is it open?" Jo stammered as she scribbled her name.

"I don't know. I came in right behind you and Sharon. Funeral homes make you uncomfortable?"

"Gee, how'd you guess?" she said dryly. "Was it the sweat on my forehead? The desperate glint in my eyes?"

His grin was startling, wide and spontaneous, until he remembered where they were and replaced it with an appropriately solemn expression.

"No, it was the way you almost choked on the word *casket*," he said as he added his signature beneath hers. "Speaking of which..."

Casually planting a hand on the small of her back, he steered her toward one of four wide doorways leading off the foyer. A discreet sign on an easel beside the door identified this particular parlor as the temporary resting place of Floradora Johanssen.

"Floradora?" he murmured in surprise.

"She was named for a rose," Jo explained.

"No wonder she preferred Flo. What kind of person would name a baby Floradora?"

"An avid rosarian."

She knew what he was doing. The small talk served as a distraction while that hand on her back gently but firmly urged her forward, through the thinning crowd and across the room. She was pleasantly surprised that he made the effort. Maybe he wasn't such a hard case after all.

"You've done this a lot, haven't you?"

"Looked at dead people? Too many times."

She didn't doubt it; he'd served two tours in Vietnam and spent twenty years with the DEA before "retiring" to his hometown in southern Indiana and ending up as the county sheriff.

"I meant escorted people to places they'd really rather not go."

"That, too," he acknowledged. "So, what have you heard?"

Jo stopped so abruptly that his left shoulder collided with her back. "About Flo?" she said under her breath, at the same time thinking, *Surely not, he couldn't be asking what rumors she'd heard.*

"Yeah. I heard she had a delayed reaction to something the plastic surgeon gave her, and her face swelled so much the stitches ripped loose."

"Good God," Jo muttered.

She was appalled. What was he thinking, for heaven's sake—gossiping about Flo's death right there in the room where her casket was on display? Only a couple dozen feet from her grieving family! She pivoted to poke a discreet elbow into his solar plexus and gave him an exasperated look.

"Shush! Someone will hear you."

The admonition was a bit late. Mitch Pierce, who owned the town's hardware store, sidled up on McCormick's right to confide in what he probably thought was a whisper, "But that wasn't what killed her. I heard it was the liposuction she had last month. The thingama-jig they used to suck out the fat was contaminated, gave her a blood infection."

"No, no, that's wrong!"

This from Mitch's wife, Elaine, who suddenly materialized to join the discussion. "I just heard from Erma Hudgins that it wasn't the infection that killed her." Elaine paused a beat for dramatic effect, then declared, "It was a heart attack."

"That's what I heard, too," chimed in Pete Rautenberg, who had been headed for the door when Elaine's news flash snagged his attention.

Jo glanced around anxiously. Lord, how far were their voices carrying?

"Who'd you hear it from?" Mitch demanded. Evidently he didn't
consider Erma Hudgins a reliable source.

"Trish Eberhardt, who got it straight from Heidi West. Heidi
works for Doc Dennison, and he's Lloyd Bates's vet."

"Well, then," Elaine said with a "see, I told you so" nod at her
doubting husband. Lloyd Bates was the county coroner, so naturally
information that had originated with an employee of the veterinarian
who gave Lloyd's dogs their rabies shots had to be considered
irrefutable.

Pete suddenly grinned and reached out to tap Jo's upper arm with
his fist. "Hey, Jo, great to see you." Evidently he'd just noticed her
standing there.

Startled out of her dumbfounded spectator status, Jo stared at
him blankly for a second.

"Hi, Pete. Good to see you, too."

The pressure of the sheriff's hand, which had never budged from
her lower back, increased for a moment. A gesture of support? A
heads-up caution? (Pete did reek of gin, but he hadn't tapped her that
hard.) A signal for her to move?

"Sheriff, I'd think if anybody would know the cause of Flo's death,
it'd be you," Elaine remarked coyly.

McCormick smiled and shook his head. "Sorry, Elaine. The death
occurred in Vanderburgh County. All I know is what her obituary
said—that she died 'from complications following surgery.'"

This time there was no question about the message his hand was
conveying; it pushed so hard that Jo had to take a hasty step or land
face-down on the carpet.

"Excuse us," McCormick said as he moved forward with her.
"They'll be closing soon and we haven't paid our respects."

When they were several feet from Pete and the Pierces, he murmured, "God, I love this town." Jo looked over her shoulder at him
and saw laughter dancing in his eyes. "Never a dull moment," he
elaborated. "And the people are so…"

"Eccentric?" she suggested. "Nosy? Downright rude?"

"Honest. Plainspoken and often nosy, yeah, I won't argue that. But most of them are honest to the bone. I didn't realize how much I'd missed that—the knowledge that what people say to me is almost always going to be the unvarnished truth, as opposed to what they think I want to hear."

"Even the criminals and miscreants?" Jo asked.

"Especially them. My interview technique is very persuasive."

That was an understatement if she'd ever heard one. Even out of uniform, in khakis and sans tie, he radiated authority and physical strength. And of course there was that voice, which had a power all its own. A couple of weeks ago she'd seen him use it to quietly "persuade" an insolent, tattooed, two-hundred-pound jerk to make an abject apology to his wife for the verbal abuse he'd been dishing out, and then make an appointment to arrange for anger management counseling.

Just as Jo was reflecting on the restraint and diplomacy he'd demonstrated on that occasion, McCormick shoved her between two enormous floral arrangements. She opened her mouth to complain, then closed it when she realized he'd saved her from being trampled by the high school football team, who'd apparently decided to leave en masse and in a hurry.

"Sorry about that," McCormick said. "You okay?"

"Everything but my dignity seems to be intact," she replied from the depths of a miniature rain forest. All she could see of him was the hand that appeared between leaves the size of dinner plates. "Is it safe to come out?"

"Yeah, the stampede's over. So many people left that I can see Floradora's casket. You'll be relieved to know it's closed."

Jo was so gratified by the news that she grabbed his hand and started gingerly making her way out of the jungle…only to be roughly pushed back.

"Hey! What the—"

"Quiet! Stay there," the sheriff ordered. His voice was barely audible, but commanding enough to make her clamp her lips together midsentence.

A second later she heard a shriek—a startled, frightened cry that raised the hair on her arms. Then someone else shouted something unintelligible. Jo squeezed McCormick's hand, though she couldn't have said whether it was a reflex action or a wordless plea for explanation.

But apparently the sheriff was preoccupied with the disturbance, whatever it was. His only response was to yank his hand from her grip. Although Jo couldn't hear anything over the incomprehensible babble of alarmed voices, she thought he was moving away. Determined to find out what was going on, she parted the foliage in front of her face and peered out.

She was just in time to see Zane Wilkes point a gun at the ceiling and fire a round into one of the air-conditioning vents.

Jo ducked back behind the greenery, her heart pounding so hard that for a while the whooshing thud of her own pulse was the only sound she was aware of. She sagged against the wall at her back and breathed deeply through her mouth. Holy shit. Why in God's name had the president of the high school chess club brought a *gun* to the funeral home?

When her initial shock started to recede, two things became clear. First, a smart, levelheaded kid like Zane Wilkes wouldn't do something like this unless he'd completely flipped out. Second, and even more alarming, in addition to the handgun he'd fired into the ceiling, Jo was sure she'd seen another weapon—a hunting rifle, she thought—slung over his shoulder, alongside a large backpack. Which meant that whatever he was doing, it probably hadn't been a spur-of-the-moment decision.

She had no idea what *she* could or should do, but she was the assistant prosecutor, an officer of the court. She couldn't just stand there hiding behind a bunch of plants, despite McCormick's instruction to do exactly that. And where the hell was he, anyway? He was the county sheriff; he should be dealing with this situation. Jo scrunched into a half squat to peek through a gap in the foliage, hoping to see that he'd taken charge and "persuaded" Zane to hand over his weapons. Her view was severely restricted, but McCormick's khakis were nowhere in sight. The only person talking now was Zane. He pointed the handgun at David Nesbitt, who, if she wasn't mistaken, was the Johanssens' family physician.

"Over here, next to Mr. Johanssen. You, too, Reverend. Take a seat next to the doctor, but don't get too comfortable."

Not much chance of that, Jo thought. All three men looked terrified. Zane, on the other hand, seemed focused and in control. She had no idea whether that was a good sign or a bad one. McCormick would probably know. Where *was* he?

Zane was facing the opposite side of the room, gesturing with the gun for a fourth person Jo couldn't see to come forward. She might be able to slip out if she moved now. She backed up slowly, one hand behind her to locate the wall. Fortunately a lot of individuals and local businesses had sent potted plants and floral arrangements. Some sat on the floor, others on tables or pedestals of varying heights, so that they provided fairly dense cover almost all the way to the door. Almost, but not quite. She'd have to cross about six feet of open space, and hope that no one saw her and called attention to her.

She impulsively crouched to remove her shoes and set them behind a large vase filled with irises and oriental lilies. A tingly itch in her nose caused a moment of panic. Oh no, what a time for her pollen allergy to kick in. She hunched over and pressed a finger under her nose, exhaling through both nostrils to check the incipient sneeze. When she lifted her head, she was startled to find herself looking at a narrow door. It was covered with the same wallpaper that had been used on the walls, so well camouflaged that she might not have noticed it from five feet away even if it hadn't been hidden by the flowers. Holding her breath, she grasped the dainty porcelain doorknob, turned it, and gently pushed...just enough to create an opening she could fit through. Despite her fears, the hinges didn't screech and give her away. Still, she waited to exhale until she was on the other side of the wall and the door was closed behind her. She sank to her knees and rested her forehead against the smooth, cool wood framing this side of the door.

"Please, Lord, don't let this be the embalming room," she whispered.

A large hand covered her mouth an instant before a godlike voice murmured in her ear, "It's just an office."

Jo knew she would have died, right there on the spot, if the spot had been anywhere else—the county courthouse, a church, the Dairy Queen, a public restroom—but no way was she going to check out in a funeral home.

She pulled McCormick's hand from her mouth. "Give me a heart attack, why don't you!"

He grasped her upper arms and lifted her to her feet. "Sorry. Scaring you out of your wits wasn't my intention. I just didn't want you to scream."

"Well, I probably would have," Jo admitted as she hitched the strap of her shoulder bag back into place and turned to face him. "I guess we know what caused the stampede. How'd you get here?"

"I slipped out with a couple of other people during the initial confusion, right after the kid marched in waving his nine."

"His what?"

"He's got a nine-millimeter semiautomatic, plus God knows what else in the backpack." Taking her arm again, he pulled her toward a door on the far side of the office. "C'mon, we can't stay here.

"He was watching a group of people at the front of the room, near the casket," he continued as they hurried across the office and a small interior hallway. "Either he didn't notice us leaving, or he did notice but didn't care. I'm inclined to think it was the latter."

"His name is Zane Wilkes," Jo said as he ushered her into another, larger office across the hall from the one they'd just left. Kevin Bates, Lloyd's son and partner in the mortuary, was there, standing at one of three desks while he spoke to someone on the telephone. Also present were Erma Hudgins and Flo Johanssen's teenage nephew, Billy Merckle. All three were obviously distraught, but Billy looked like he might start weeping at any second.

"I know who he is," the sheriff said in reply. "Billy here identified Zane for me and was about to enlighten me about why he's using the ductwork for target practice, when I heard you open the door."

Jo stared at him in amazement. He'd *heard* the door open? A second later the rest of what he'd said sank in. She whirled on Billy.

"You knew Zane was going to do this?"

He flinched as if she'd struck him. "No! I thought it was just talk, you know, that he was blowing off steam."

His voice was thin and high-pitched, bordering on hysteria. Jo cast a worried look at the door to the hall, which McCormick had left standing open.

"Shouldn't we—"

"No, it's okay." He put a hand on Billy's bony shoulder and guided him to a chair, then moved another chair and took a seat facing the boy, so close that their knees were almost touching. "Would you please get Billy a glass of water."

He spoke to Jo, but Billy had a hundred percent of his attention. He was working to calm the boy's fear, his movements slow and non-threatening, his voice soft, patient. Jo placed her shoulder bag on one of the desks and looked around for a water cooler, a fountain, a restroom...

"I've got it." Erma bustled forward carrying a pitcher of water in one hand and a glass in the other.

Jo perched on the desk to the sheriff's left and restrained the urge to start bombarding Billy with questions. He wasn't in the witness box, though he might well end up there. McCormick gave the boy a brief respite, a few seconds to collect himself, while he took the phone from Kevin.

"Okay, Ed, I'm back," he said tersely. "Nothing, Ed, don't do anything, just stay on the line....No, dammit, don't notify anybody until I tell you to. Send one car—that's one car, Ed—to block the entrance to the property. No lights, no siren. Nobody gets closer than that. And Ed? I mean nobody....I don't care what the hell you tell people. Tell 'em we're having an orgy, or the place is under emergency quarantine. But understand this—if I look out the window and see any state police cruisers or television vans, it's your ass. Got it?"

Evidently Chief Deputy Ed Steinmetz replied in the affirmative, because McCormick handed the phone back to Kevin and once again focused his attention on Billy. The kid looked stunned. Not stunned as in intimidated or scared, but awestruck. Jo empathized. She was remembering why she had been less than thrilled to encounter Sheriff McCormick a half-hour or so ago...and reflecting that she was damn glad he was there now.

"Okay, Billy," he said as if the conversation with his chief deputy hadn't taken place. "What's Zane doing here? What provoked this?"

Billy drew a shuddering breath. "He's mad. Really pissed."

"Yeah, I sensed that," McCormick drawled. "Who's he mad at, and why?"

Billy hung his head. "Everybody who hurt Aunt Flo, or didn't do anything to help her. By rights, that should include me, I guess."

McCormick shot Jo a questioning look. She shook her head in response.

"Hurt her how, Billy?" she asked.

He shrugged. "Lots of ways. Uncle Bob was always criticizing, telling her she was getting fat and starting to show her age...said she was a lousy cook and she spent too much money on stupid things. Then Mr. Yellig gave her two bad evaluations in a row, so it was like he was on her case, too."

"Teacher performance evaluations, you mean?" Jo asked. Virgil Yellig was the high school principal.

Billy nodded glumly. "She was afraid she'd lose her job. Uncle Bob is...what do you call it?"

"Tenured," McCormick said.

"Yeah, right. He's been a teacher forever, but Aunt Flo just got her certificate a couple years ago and she was still on probation. She knew if she lost her job, Bob would blow his stack. 'Cause he was already gripin' about all the money she spent on clothes and makeup and stuff, I mean."

"Which she thought she needed because he'd convinced her she was a fat, ugly hag," Erma chimed in, sounding outraged.

The sheriff ignored the outburst, signaling his impatience and a sense of urgency with a quick glance at his watch. "Tragic as all this may be, Billy, it doesn't explain why Zane Wilkes is holding several people at gunpoint right now. Don't tell me he always reacts this way to emotional abuse."

"No," Billy mumbled. He lowered his gaze to stare at the water glass, which he was clutching with both hands. "Zane and Aunt Flo..." He squirmed in discomfort, his neck and face turning bright red. "They were...uh..."

"Lovers," Jo finished for him when it seemed he might choke trying to get the word out.

Billy's muffled "Yeah" was drowned out by Erma's strangled gasp and Kevin's shocked, "Lovers!"

The sheriff silenced them both with a freezing look. "I need you to think, Billy," he murmured, laying a hand on the boy's arm. "Besides Bob Johanssen and Virgil Yellig, who else does Zane blame for Flo's death?"

Billy shook his head in abject misery. "Lots of people. He didn't tell me who all of 'em are, just said a lot of people were to blame."

Jo abandoned her perch on the desk to stand beside McCormick. "Doctor Nesbitt? Reverend Tyler?" she asked. When Billy nodded, she explained, "Zane singled them out, made them sit with Bob Johanssen."

"Who else?" McCormick pressed.

But the boy had reached his breaking point. "I don't *know*!" he wailed. "Oh, Jesus, is he gonna kill them? He won't really kill all those people, will he?"

McCormick squeezed the boy's arm, at the same time pressing him back into the chair. "No." His voice was quiet but rock solid, his gaze locked with Billy's. "That's not going to happen. I'm going to go talk to him, and we'll straighten out this mess so everybody can go home."

His reassurance had begun to visibly calm the boy, but that last sentence made Billy bolt upright, eyes wide with panic.

"He won't talk to you! He won't *listen* to you! If you go in there, it'll just make him more pissed!"

The brusque shake of McCormick's head told Jo that he'd automatically dismissed the boy's opinion. Billy obviously thought so, too. He turned to her in desperation.

"You gotta believe me, Miss Haynes. A couple months ago Zane talked to one of the city cops. Don't ask me which one, 'cause I won't tell. Zane told him how Bob was treating Aunt Flo and said somebody should have a talk with him, tell him to either treat her right or leave."

Jo was fairly sure the city officer Zane had spoken to was George Kelly, Bob Johanssen's best friend since high school.

"The cop told Zane to mind his own business," Billy said bitterly. "Said it wasn't his job to make husbands and wives get along with each other, and if Aunt Flo wasn't happy, *she* could leave, or maybe talk to a marriage counselor."

"So Zane feels let down or betrayed by the policeman he went to for help," Jo murmured. Then, addressing the sheriff, "Billy's probably right. You may not be the best person to approach him."

"I bet he'd talk to *you*, though," Billy said before McCormick could reply.

The sheriff vaulted out of his chair and barked, "Absolutely not!"

at virtually the same instant Jo stammered, "Who...me?"

"He knows you," Billy pointed out. "He likes you, too. He says you're the smartest woman he's ever met."

Jo gaped at the boy. "Zane said that?"

"Don't even think about it," McCormick growled. "Get the idea right out of your head."

"He does know me," she argued, and wondered if she'd lost her mind. "I'm one of the chess club sponsors."

"Good for you," McCormick shot back. "Zane Wilkes didn't come here to take part in a chess tournament."

"Uh, excuse me, Sheriff," Kevin interrupted in his most soothing undertaker's voice. "Ed wants me to tell you that the patrol car is here, blocking the drive."

"Thanks," McCormick snapped without breaking eye contact with Jo.

"I could appeal to him with reason and logic," Jo suggested. "Zane is extremely intelligent. He has a real talent for strategic analysis."

"Which means he's probably anticipated that we'll send somebody in—"

"But he won't have anticipated that it'll be me."

"And it won't be. You aren't qualified—"

"I beg your pardon!" She interrupted him for the second time, indignation prevailing over courtesy. "For your information, I've questioned and cross-examined hardened criminals."

McCormick's left eyebrow rose a sardonic centimeter. "How many of them were pointing a loaded gun at you at the time?"

Jo couldn't immediately produce a retort to that, but Erma chose that moment to weigh in with her opinion.

"I agree with the two of them—Jo should go in there and try to talk some sense into him," she said confidently.

If looks could kill, the one McCormick shot her would have put Erma in intensive care. She didn't flinch.

"For heaven's sake, Sheriff, disconnect your stupid male ego for a minute and think. This boy is full of anger at the *men* he holds responsible for Flo's death. Now, who's he more likely to be willing to listen to—a male authority figure, or a woman he already trusts and respects?"

Jo managed not to smile, but she couldn't resist the impulse to remark, "I believe that would qualify as some of the plainspoken honesty you value so highly."

For a second she thought McCormick was going to let her have it, really rip into her. But then his mouth twisted in an ironic smile and she felt her tensed muscles relax.

"Tell Ed we're going in," he said to Kevin. "If we're not back in thirty minutes, he should call Captain Richmond at the state police post."

"Good luck," Erma called softly as they left.

They took the long way around, approaching the parlor via the front foyer so Zane wouldn't think someone was trying to sneak in and take him by surprise.

"Scared?" McCormick asked as they approached the end of the hallway.

"Oh, yeah," Jo murmured.

"Good. You should be. The nine-millimeter holds eleven rounds—enough for the two of us and nine other people."

"If this is your idea of a pep talk, I have to tell you, it sucks," she replied. "Anyway, he fired one round into the ceiling, so now he has ten, not eleven. Of course that's not taking the rifle into account. Please don't tell me how many bullets a rifle holds, I'd really rather not know."

McCormick grabbed her arm and yanked her to a halt halfway across the foyer. "He has a rifle?"

Panic flared in her chest. "Christ, I thought you knew that." She thought she might faint. "You didn't know about the rifle?"

He inhaled a long, deep breath, then released it in a rush. His lips compressed to form a taut seam. Jo could almost *feel* him suppressing the urge to shake her. "Damn it, I should've trusted my own judgment. You're going back to wait with the others."

He'd pulled her a couple of yards before she collected her wits and started resisting. Unfortunately, the feet of her pantyhose provided no friction whatsoever on the polished marble floor.

"No, stop!" she hissed. "I'm all right, really. I just got a little—"

"Hysterical." His harsh whisper made it an indictment, but at least he stopped dragging her across the foyer.

"Anxious," she corrected stubbornly. "Oh, all right, petrified, but only for a second. I'm okay now. Anyway, you *said* it was good that I'm scared!"

She saw a faint glint of surprise, and just maybe admiration, in his eyes. She quickly pressed on, not giving him a chance to argue.

"I can do this. I can. Back to the rifle—I could be mistaken; it might be a shotgun. I saw a long black barrel, hanging on his backpack. Come to think of it, it looked too fat to be a rifle barrel."

McCormick shook his head decisively and started walking again, but back in the direction they'd originally been headed, pulling her with him. As relief washed through Jo, she reflected giddily that his left hand had spent so much time pushing or pulling or grabbing or yanking her around tonight that it might as well be surgically grafted to her body.

"I saw it, too. But whatever it is, it isn't a gun," he whispered as they reached the parlor entrance.

They stopped simultaneously, frozen in surprise and confusion as they took in the scene before them. McCormick was right. The long black tube they'd both seen wasn't a gun. It was one leg of a tripod.

A video camera, which Zane had presumably carried in the backpack, sat on top of the tripod, beside Flo's casket. Sharon had been drafted to serve as vidcam operator. She sat on a chair behind the tripod, evidently using the camera to document individual statements. As Jo and McCormick watched, Zane instructed Reverend Tyler to take the seat Dr. Nesbitt occupied directly in front of the camera. The doctor got up without a word and moved to the last folding chair in the row, distancing himself from both the reverend and Bob Johanssen. He didn't appear to be in fear for his life, but rather completely demoralized.

Jo turned to the sheriff with a perplexed frown—were they witnessing what she thought they were witnessing? He nodded pensively, then inclined his head to indicate that they should enter the parlor. Despite a careful scrutiny of his eyes and his facial expression, she couldn't detect the slightest hint of uncertainty. Personally, Jo thought it might be better to wait until Zane finished taping what appeared to be a series of forced confessions, let him finish what he'd started. He probably wouldn't appreciate being interrupted. But on second thought, what if his plan was to force the men to confess and then kill them?

She might have stood there the rest of the night, seesawing between equally ruinous possibilities, if McCormick hadn't planted his hand in the middle of her back and given her an impatient push.

She drew a steadying breath and stepped forward as if she knew precisely what she was going to say and what the result would be.

"Zane?"

Her voice emerged so soft and embarrassingly timid that she wondered if he'd heard her. He looked up, blinked in surprise, then saw McCormick and scowled.

"Hi, Miss Haynes. You can come in, but he has to wait outside."

As Zane spoke he raised his right arm, which had been hanging relaxed at his side, and pointed the gun at McCormick. Jo was close enough to see that his hand trembled slightly. She wished she knew whether it was because he was on the brink of a total emotional meltdown, or because pointing a gun at the county sheriff scared the bejesus out of him.

"No, Zane, you need him here," she said with a lot more confidence than she felt. "If you're doing what I think you're doing, who better to serve as an official witness?" She continued into the parlor as she made the point, managing to put herself between the gun and McCormick. She could imagine how Mr. Macho Lawman was reacting to that, but he'd get over it. In her considered opinion, Zane was much more likely to shoot the sheriff than her.

Zane blinked again then raised his free hand to rub at his eyes. Jo was now close enough to see that they were red-rimmed and bloodshot, his complexion wan. She also observed that his clothes were wrinkled and his usually neat hair stood in spikes. Poor kid probably hadn't slept since he heard about Flo's death.

"Let him stay." She was careful to make it a request, not a demand.

The boy's head bobbed in agreement. "Sit back there, Sheriff," he directed. A sloppy waggle of the gun indicated a spot in the center of at least four dozen precisely arranged folding chairs. Smart, Jo thought; McCormick would have to clamber over several rows to get to him. She glanced back to check that the sheriff was complying. He was, though he didn't look happy about it.

"You come stand up front, between Sharon and me," Zane instructed. "I wish I'd known you were here. You could've got these bastards to confess a lot faster."

"So that is what you're doing." A quick glance at Sharon eased her anxiety somewhat. Sharon looked nervous, but not terrified. Of course, Jo couldn't imagine what it would take to terrify Sharon Hancock.

"All of these assholes are at least partly to blame for Flo's death," Zane told her, his voice hoarse with emotion. "All three of 'em either mistreated her or betrayed her."

Jo impulsively reached out to lay a hand on the boy's right shoulder. Realizing how close she was to the gun he was waving around as if it were a baton, she glanced at the sheriff. He glared back at her and gave an emphatic shake of his head, which she interpreted to mean: No, for God's sake, you idiot, don't try to take it away from him!

Jo administered a sympathetic pat to Zane's shoulder and withdrew her hand. "Billy gave us a little background information." She saw Bob Johanssen lean forward and start to blurt out something, then look at the gun. His Adam's apple worked as he reconsidered and sank back against the chair.

"Billy didn't know what I was going to do," Zane said. "I didn't tell anybody ahead of time, so nobody but me should take the blame for this."

"Nobody else will." McCormick's deep, imposing voice caused everyone but Sharon to give a nervous little start. "And Billy didn't rat you out. He's your friend and he's worried. He doesn't want anyone else to get hurt, that's all."

Jo caught that "else" and she was sure Zane had, too. McCormick was letting him know that they understood the reasons for his anger, but without endorsing his actions.

"We know why you're so pissed at Bob," he added after a slight pause. "But what about the others? What did the doctor and Reverend Tyler do?"

Zane eagerly seized the opportunity to catalog their sins, as the sheriff had no doubt anticipated. "He"—swinging the gun toward the doctor—"referred her to the butchers who gave her sepsis and caused a fatal heart attack!"

"But Doctor Nesbitt didn't perform any of the procedures, Zane," Jo murmured reasonably.

"He knew she was emotionally unstable!" he shot back. "He should have tried to talk her out of having cosmetic surgery, or at least recommended counseling beforehand. That's what doctors are supposed to do."

"He probably knew that cosmetic surgeons often require potential patients to talk to a therapist," McCormick told him, but Zane wasn't appeased.

"Those guys didn't know her...he did! He knew Bob had destroyed her self-esteem and turned her into an emotional basket case. Doctors are supposed to help people, not just take their insurance money and then pass them off to some other mercenary quack."

His agitation was beginning to alarm Jo. "All right, you've made your case against Doctor Nesbitt," she said briskly. "And you may have legitimate grounds for a malpractice investigation. What about Reverend Tyler? Why is he here?"

The minister, a tall, dignified man in his early sixties, spoke up before Zane could answer. "I failed Flo, too. Several weeks ago she came to me after a friend—" He paused to bestow a sad smile on Zane. "—urged her to seek counseling. Her marriage was deeply troubled. She wanted me to tell her it would be all right to end it."

"But you didn't," Zane accused. "You told her to stay and 'work things out,' be more 'tolerant and forgiving' of her husband's faults."

"Yes," Reverend Tyler admitted. "At the time I truly believed it was the best counsel I could give."

"At the time," Zane repeated bitterly.

"That's right, son." He lifted both hands, palms up. "Would I repeat the same counsel today, considering what's happened since she came to me? Probably not. But I believe strongly in the sanctity of marriage, so neither would I encourage her to file for divorce."

Zane's pale face flushed crimson and the hand holding the gun twitched in angry reaction. McCormick stood up and casually side-stepped to the end of the row of chairs.

"Easy, Zane," he said softly. "Hindsight is always twenty-twenty. We've all done things we regret or wish we could undo."

"Amen to that," Sharon murmured from her place behind the camera.

"But people should have to pay for their mistakes!" Zane cried.

"We do," Jo assured him. "Believe me, we all do pay, every day. Just because you don't *see* someone being punished doesn't mean he isn't suffering a terrible punishment."

"She's right," McCormick said. He'd taken advantage of the boy's distraction to move in front of Reverend Tyler. Zane backed up a step, raising the gun to the level of the sheriff's chest. Jo stopped breathing for a moment, but McCormick completely ignored the weapon.

"Take a look at Doctor Nesbitt," he said. "He's going to have to live with this particular error in judgment the rest of his life. Same for the reverend. He may have strong religious objections to divorce, but something tells me he won't be quite so inclined to dispense trite, simplistic advice from now on."

Zane's lower lip quivered and tears brimmed in his eyes. Jo was sure he was about to hand the gun over, or maybe drop it and collapse from sheer exhaustion. Instead, he suddenly spun toward Bob Johanssen, his arm flying up, elbow extended stiffly to aim the gun at Bob's head.

"What about that son of a bitch!" he demanded, his voice shaking with rage and grief. "Look at him, the arrogant bastard! He isn't *suffering*, he doesn't even feel guilty for the way he treated her! What's his punishment going to be?"

Everything happened so fast that only later could Jo reconstruct the sequence. Zane took an awkward step forward, lurching toward Bob. There was a startled yelp—presumably from Sharon—and the soft thud of the camera and tripod hitting the floor as Jo impulsively grabbed Zane's left wrist, the only part of him within reach. Reverend Tyler jumped up, frantically attempting to get out of harm's way, stumbled over his chair, and somehow ended up sprawled in the row of chairs behind him.

Fortunately McCormick moved faster and with much better dexterity than anyone, including Zane. His left hand closed over the gun and forced Zane's arm down, so that the barrel pointed harmlessly at the floor. Other than that, he did nothing to restrain the boy.

"No," he said gently. "No, Zane. His punishment will be having to live in this town." He didn't have to add, because everyone present was thinking it: "Where everybody he meets, every single day, will know what a bastard he was to his wife."

Zane made a strangled sound and fell to his knees, wrenching sobs tearing at his chest. Driven purely by instinct, Jo dropped to her knees beside him and wrapped her arms around him as McCormick removed the gun from his hand. Without a word, Sharon righted the tripod, removed the videocassette from the camera, and handed it to the sheriff.

"I...I wouldn't have shot him," Zane managed to say after a while. "I just...I just wanted to scare him, make the bastard *feel* something!"

"I know," McCormick murmured. Holding the gun high so that everyone could see, he explained. "He had the safety set to on."

The next hour passed in a blur for Jo, who felt so emotionally and physically drained that she could barely hold herself upright. McCormick had quickly and efficiently taken care of everything— phoning Zane's parents and arranging for them to be at the county jail when their son arrived, calling a couple of clerks to the funeral home to take the preliminary statements, fielding calls from three area television stations and two newspapers. The man was too damn capable by far, she reflected as she sat on the curb and contemplated the gritty asphalt in front of her. Surely he had a *few* faults or weaknesses.

"You still here?" the object of her thoughts said when he exited the funeral home a few minutes later.

"Believe me, it isn't by choice. I finished dictating my statement and went to collect my shoes. By the time I got outside Sharon had taken off without me. I'm giving her time to get home, then I'm gonna call and lay a humongous guilt trip on her."

"She probably thought you'd caught a ride with someone else."

"Probably." Jo pushed off the curb and his left hand—surprise!— slipped under her arm to pull her the rest of the way up. Suddenly she wasn't quite so exhausted. "But it's too good a chance to pass up," she told him. "Opportunities to make Sharon feel guilty are extremely rare."

He smiled and inclined his head toward his brown and tan county car, parked near the back of the lot. "So save it until you need a big favor. I'll give you a lift. I'll even throw in a hot-fudge sundae from DQ."

"Oh, God, you mean it?" Jo said with shameless eagerness. "I desperately need a sugar fix."

"Me, too," he said as his hand found its spot on her back and they started toward his car. "It's been a hell of a night."

"That it has," Jo agreed. "We deserve to indulge ourselves with some comfort food."

"Absolutely." They reached the car. He unlocked and opened the passenger door, waited till she was inside, then leaned down to add in a conspiratorial whisper, "Besides, don't tell anybody, but funeral homes give me the willies."

Jo smiled and leaned back against the seat. Now that was a weakness, and a man she could relate to.

Dizzy and the Biker

Susan Sizemore

"Report says the woman said her dog's a cat. That ain't right."

Detective Sergeant Mike Moran looked up over the computer screen. He was happy for the diversion. It was a hot summer afternoon, and the air conditioning wasn't working very well. A lot of work had piled up while he was on vacation. "What you working on, Charlie?" he asked the detective who had spoken.

Charles Boromeo came over with a suspicious eagerness and tossed a folder to him. "You're the animal guy. You tell me. Got a murder in a park. Dead end, so far. Witness got hit on the head. Says she doesn't remember anything. Storm washed away any physical evidence an hour after the crime. There's a kidnapped puppy—dog-napped puppy—involved."

"O—kaay." Moran leaned back in his chair and opened the jacket on the folder. A few seconds later he grinned up at Boromeo. "A murder at Franciscan Place. This is great."

Captain Cutler broke through a crowd of uniforms by the water cooler to join them as Moran spoke. "Great?" she asked. "Some poor old guy got whacked for his fancy dog and the only witness was assaulted."

"Well, yeah," Moran agreed. "That's terrible. We have to find the murderer, and the puppy." He ran his index finger up and down the report. "The guy, Alec Penhurst, was in his seventies, with no relatives. This happened a week ago." He couldn't help but sound gleeful. "His place is going to be up for sale—and I'm top of the waiting list!"

"Would that make you a suspect, Sergeant Moran?" Cutler was not happy with his attitude.

Moran was not fazed by her annoyance. "Got witnesses to my whereabouts on—" He checked the date. "June fourth. I've been trying to get into Franciscan Place since Dizzy was a pup. You know how you get a condo at Franciscan Place? Most people inherit them. The whole complex started out as a commune in the seventies. A group of urban animal lovers bought up some abandoned buildings in the warehouse district long before the area was trendy. They renovated the condo building on part of it. Turned the other forty acres into parkland." He gave a cynical laugh. "The last time a one-bedroom place was empty—the old lady died of natural causes—I was all set to move in, when, bam, out of nowhere, a great-niece from down in the bayou decides she wants to come and live in the big city. Association had to give the place to her rather than to me. I'm on a list for two years, then this backcountry Cajun cook moves into my home on a whim. Dizzy was heartbroken. But at least we still get to use the Franciscan Place exercise park. If your application is approved and you pay an annual fee anybody can use the park three times a week."

"That's where the murder took place," Cutler said. "Residents think somebody jumped the fence, grabbed the pooch—"

"A porcelain dog," Boromeo said. He scratched his head. "That makes as much sense as the woman claiming her dog's a cat."

Moran consulted the report again. "A Porcelaine. It's a fancy French breed. Very few in the States. Stupid motive for murder, but it is a rare breed. Are we sure that's the motive for the murder?" Moran wondered. He tapped the report. "No physical evidence."

"Hey," Boromeo asked, "if this was a dog park, how come the dogs didn't notice this old guy being attacked? How come this woman's cat dog didn't come to her defense?"

Moran consulted the witness statement, and quoted, "'You obviously don't know anything about dogs, Officer. They form an instant pack for playing when they're out here. Most of the animals were down by the front pond. And Harley—well, if you want some pigs rounded up from the swamp he's your dog. I don't expect him to be something he isn't—but if he thinks he's getting steak anytime soon after letting me get hit on the head he's sadly mistaken.'" Moran smiled. She understood dogs. He checked the name on the report. Yep, Sugar LaRoux. She was definitely the woman who'd stolen his condo out from under Dizzy's nose.

"Listen," he said to Cutler. "Why don't I take over the investigation? I've got an idea how to handle it...."

"Be good, Dizzy."

Moran slipped off her leash. She took off down the path, heading straight for the churned-up mud of the pond. Another dog was already splashing around in the reed bed near the stand of young willow trees. It was the middle of the afternoon, and it looked like Moran and the other dog's owner were the only people in this part of the Franciscan animal park. That was fine with Moran. He held back for a moment, studying the woman's profile while she watched her big dog wading in the water.

Frankly, she looked like a Sugar LaRoux. She had lush bosoms peeking above the scooped neck of a mint green T-shirt. She wore tan shorts that emphasized a heart-shaped bottom, and legs that went on for about three weeks. She had dark auburn hair, long and curling, and full lips that were so kissable they looked dipped in honey. He'd always had a soft spot for redheads. Moran would have recognized her as a "Sugar" from miles away.

Of course, the row of stitches and bruises that showed when she turned fully toward him was a strong clue as well. Somebody had hit her very, very hard, and the sight sent an unfamiliar jolt of anger through him. Moran had grown cynical in his job, but not so cynical that he couldn't still feel outrage and anger for a victim. He didn't usually get a sudden urge of protectiveness, though, or an electric jolt of desire when his gaze met that of a witness—who might be a suspect and was certainly...gorgeous.

"Will you get a look at that, Harley?" Sugar asked over the throbbing racket of frog mating ritual. "That is one pretty animal." She was referring to the sleek and happy Irish setter trotting toward them down the path, tongue flapping and a wide, doggie grin on its muzzle. Its dark red coat gleamed like silk in the sunlight. Harley's nose came up out of the mud at the appearance of a new dog. He gave a bark and took off like a shot.

"You be good," Sugar called after her big boy.

Then she looked past the dogs and saw the human following the Setter. She almost whistled. *That* was indeed one gorgeous creature, of the human male variety. Tall, dark, and handsome was the term, right? Well, he filled the bill on all three counts. Nice legs, too, she thought, sweeping her gaze up from his feet to long, strong thighs, narrow waist, broad chest and shoulders and back to the newcomer's face.

He was staring at her, so she didn't feel quite as rude as she might have for staring back. Of course he was staring. She touched her fingers to the bruises on her face, and the ugly aching marks on her left leg. She wasn't exactly an object of desire right now, but her current appearance certainly drew the eye. People usually looked quickly away, though. Not this guy.

The low, throbbing pain had been a part of her existence for several days now, so much so that she'd almost forgotten what it was like without it. What really worried her was that she'd forgotten several other things as well, which left her shaky inside despite her outward show of confidence. For example, this man she'd never seen before might be the one who'd hit her. She didn't *know*. That made her wary, and angry—with herself, and whoever the bastard was who'd smashed her skull and left her worried it would happen again. She was an open, voluble sort of person. Fear did not suit her lifestyle, but she couldn't help but be aware of being nervous at the man's interest in her, even though the slight fear was overlaid by an instant physical attraction.

So she fought down the visceral interest the man evoked, told herself that primal mating urges were on hold at present, and said to him, "Nice dog." If there was one thing that was a safe and neutral subject around here, it was pets—companion animals, babies, darlings—whatever you wanted to call them, love for animals was the one passion everyone indulged in at Franciscan Place. A hit man wouldn't have a pet as flighty as an Irish setter, would he?

She made herself look back at the dogs, and the man on the path did the same. Just as—

"Harley!"

"Dizzy!"

They leaped forward at the same time.

"Get off her!" Moran grabbed the male dog's heavy collar.

"Don't touch him!"

The dog growled. Dizzy snapped. The woman's shoulder banged solidly into Moran's, and the next thing Mike Moran knew he was lying on his back with the lush redhead's body on top of him. Under other circumstances this would have been a most pleasant sensation. Hot breath warmed his cheeks. His gaze went quickly from side to side and saw that the dogs were standing on either side of them. The animals were tense, but at least they weren't fighting, or—

"What kind of dog have you got, lady?" Moran demanded. He put his hands on her trim waist. The intent was to push her off, but his fingers and palms came into contact with warm bare skin, and lingered. "Having sex with a stranger is—"

"That was a dominance game." The woman shifted so that their gazes met. He was very aware of the soft weight of her breasts pressing against his chest. Her eyes were green, flecked with gold. One was swollen nearly shut.

"I know all about dominance games," Moran answered.

"I just bet you do."

His body tightened at the sultry sound of her voice, his body tried to disconnect all higher brain function. He saw that she'd shocked herself. The look on her bruised face told him that she didn't say such provocative things and didn't know where *that* had come from. The round O of surprise that shaped her mouth made kissing her mandatory. He would have, too.

Then Dizzy barked in his ear.

"Jealous bitch," he muttered. He and the woman helped each other up and brushed off the cedar chips and blades of grass that clung to their clothing. He noticed that where she wasn't bruised, she was blushing. That he found it charming bothered him. *Business*, he told himself. *She's an assault victim, murder witness, possible suspect. She's—*

"Cassandra LaRoux," she said.

He grinned. "But everybody calls you Sugar."

"How'd you know that?" She put her hands on her wonderfully curvaceous hips.

Mike tried hard not to look at those hips. "You're a famous celebrity chef."

She shrugged. "I'm a good cook."

Which was something else to find attractive about her. "Hey!" He pushed her dog's huge head away from his crotch. "What the hell kind of dog is that?" he asked Sugar LaRoux, but his attention was drawn away before she could answer as Dizzy took off, with Sugar's dog bounding after her.

"They like each other," Sugar said.

"He likes her all right," Moran said darkly.

"Now there's a protective daddy talking. Better to have them playing than mating, don't you think?"

"Maybe."

"Hey, Harley doesn't take to just any dog. Not usually without whupping 'em in a fight first. He's a rough, tough, stock dog raised in the bayous. Harley don't take nothin' from nobody. But I think we have love at first sniff here. Looks like he and—"

"Dizzy."

"Good name for an Irish setter. Harley's a Catahoula leopard dog. A cat."

"He looks like a biker." He shook his head. "Looks like my little girl's got a crush on a bad boy."

"That happens a lot."

Moran grinned at her as she gave a squeak of surprise and her hand flew to her mouth. "Maybe it's the concussion," he suggested.

Sugar damned her strangely loose tongue and ignored his mention of her injuries. She tried hard to focus on the dogs and not on how sexy his legs looked in his sporty athletic shorts. Harley and Dizzy were currently stalking a pair of ducks who floated serenely in the center of the pond. "There's instant attraction there," Sugar said as the dogs wheeled and chased each other back and forth along the shallow edge of the pond, tongues lolling and fur getting splattered with mud. She tried to keep her attention on the dogs, but was hampered by the same instant attraction Harley was showing toward the silky red-furred beauty who matched him for speed and energy.

"I'm Mike Moran," he finally introduced himself.

She gave him a direct look with her one good eye. "You're not a hit man by any chance, are you?"

He didn't show a bit of surprise. "I'm moving into Mr. Penhurst's place. Sorry to hear about Mr. Penhurst," he added. He whistled at his dog.

After a few moments, Dizzy split away from her new playmate and came running back up the path. Instead of stopping by her owner, she flew past where he and Sugar stood and trotted up the path that led to the rear of the exercise park. Harley followed the Irish setter.

"Walk with me," Mike Moran suggested.

"Look's like Harley's already made up my mind about where we're going today."

"Don't want to go back there where it happened, do you?" Moran questioned. He brushed fingertips lightly across her bruised cheek. "Don't blame you."

Which explained why he wasn't surprised at her silly hit man question. "Read it in the papers, saw it on television, or had a chat with Mrs. Beckett?"

"I haven't met Mrs. Beckett yet."

Which was not an answer. His fingers lingered on her cheek. She did not jump away from his touch. That was the crazy thing—she'd been jumping and ducking being touched by everybody but Harley since it happened. She didn't want to slap Mike Moran's hand away. She wanted to tell him to do it again. She said, "Welcome to the neighborhood. Don't let the murder and assault rate put you off our little community," she added as they climbed the wooded hill away from the pond.

He nodded and came with her. "I won't. Harley on the other hand..."

"Is a sweetheart. Okay, he's a bruiser, but he's mine and I love him. How much do you know about Penhurst?" He shrugged. Since he was moving into Penhurst's place, she figured he had a right to know facts. "He and I were talking while his puppy sniffed at a rabbit hole. I heard a noise behind us—thought it was a dog. I woke up in the hospital. At first I didn't remember being with Penhurst. At first all I recalled was coming out here with Harley, then waking up in the hospital."

She strode up the hill with flagging determination. The dogs ran on ahead, through bushes and intermittent stands of young trees. Mike Moran walked beside her with his hands thrust in his pockets. Swallows darted close overhead. Yellow butterflies fluttered nearer to the ground. The sun was as bright as a lemon in the clear blue sky.

"It's very hard to remember that we're in the heart of a city," Moran said, echoing Sugar's thoughts.

"This fenced forty acres is the most precious real estate in the city. I wouldn't have picked up and moved here without knowing Harley'd have someplace he could run free. With the park, I jumped at the chance to move here and open a branch of *Le Bon Temps*." In a few seconds they would crest the hill and be within sight of where it happened. She did not want to go into the back of the park.

"Come here every day, don't you?" Moran asked.

"No."

"But you try to. I know the feeling."

She stopped a step away from the top of the hill and their gazes met. He had chocolate brown eyes, and thick, dark lashes. Those eyes were very, very shrewd. She didn't see pity in them, or the sort of sick curiosity she was getting used to. The sympathy in his look was tinged with just the right degree of irony. "So, what happened to you?" she asked him.

"Got shot in the line of duty once," he answered. "Made myself go back to where it happened. More than once before I worked through it."

"You're a police officer?"

There was no hint of coldness or suspicion in her question. Moran appreciated Sugar's simple curiosity. What he didn't appreciate was the way Dizzy and Sugar's raw-boned hound started to rough-house. "Hey!" he shouted as Harley butted his Irish setter in the side. Dizzy went down on her back, feathered legs flailing. "Cut it out!" He turned a glare on Sugar, who laughed at his concern. "That dog of yours is a menace, LaRoux."

"They're just playing."

Dizzy's shining red coat was covered in dust and dried grass when Harley backed off and let her jump to her feet. She and Harley trotted away. "I raised her to be a lady," he complained to Harley's owner.

Sugar smirked, standing in the center of the path with one hand on her hip. "Harley loves the ladies."

"Him and me both," Moran said. She threw back her head and laughed a deep, sexy, infectious laugh.

The sight and sound of her sent a hot flash of desire through him that wiped out every bit of professional detachment he'd brought into this not-at-all-chance meeting. He looked at Sugar, and looking at her was a real treat even with the bandages and bruises, and his highly honed suspicious nature was overridden by lust, protectiveness, and genuine liking. Now, there was a deadly combination if there ever was one. Put those three components together and the chemical reaction could result in something serious indeed. He started to reach for her, to draw her into his arms and kiss her silly, but he stepped back instead. Not going to happen today, he told himself sternly. Fortunately, Dizzy ran up and bumped her head against his leg, which distracted him further from following his libido. He told himself the look of disappointment that briefly flashed across Sugar's face was his imagination. He looked at his dog and rubbed Dizzy's soft head. The two of them did just fine on their own up to this point.

"I never thought I was a dog person until Dizzy came along," he heard himself telling this stranger.

"I don't want to go over that hill today," Sugar said. Stepping around Moran, she called, "Yo, Harley. Let's go, boy!"

Harley came running toward her a few moments later, then spun around at the whirring of wings as a dove shot up out of the grass. He barked and took off toward the back side of the park again. Dizzy went with him.

"Cover me," Moran said, heading over the top of the hill. "I'm going in." He didn't look back, but heard Sugar follow.

Sugar stopped on the crest of the hill and watched Mike Moran explore the open expanse at the rear of the park. The examination he made was careful and professional. He even went over to the spot by the back fence where it was thought the assailant had climbed over and back out again with Penhurst's stolen puppy.

"He knows more than we do about this case," Sugar said to Harley, who'd come up for a bit of attention. She noticed her dog glance after the human male whose lovely Irish setter was now loping beside him, and smiled. "Jealous, huh?"

Moran was certainly a handsome devil, and she felt a definite buzz of attraction for him. She'd have liked him better if he'd said, "I'm a cop and I know about the Penhurst murder" immediately. This omission, plus his less than enthusiastic reaction to Harley playing with his precious Dizzy made her wonder if Mike Moran was someone she wanted to spend time with. She gave his backside one more appreciative look before she put the leash back on Harley and headed for the parkside entrance of Franciscan Place.

"It was something I said, wasn't it?" Moran asked Dizzy as they followed after Sugar and Harley. He knew damn well it was. He'd been friendly instead of professional and Ms. LaRoux caught on. Besides, he didn't like her dog. Well, he'd been nursing resentment because he and Dizzy could have moved in here months ago if celebrity chef Sugar LaRoux hadn't decided to exercise her auntie's option on her condo. Meeting her, he liked her instantly. Maybe he ought to keep some professional distance, but she was a neighbor, and all his protective instincts were kicking in. She was scared, and not just because she'd been traumatized by the attack. He could see it in her eyes, and hear it in some of the things she'd said. People didn't normally ask if strangers were hit men, even people who'd recently been struck on the head. And where had the marks on her leg come from? There was nothing in the hospital report or photos that showed anything but the head injury.

"You know, I didn't like you at first," he said, catching up to her at the door.

Sugar gave him a puzzled look over her shoulder. "At first? Ten minutes ago?"

"No," he said, and explained all about how he'd first heard about her. He didn't mean to do that, but talking to her came far too easily.

"Maybe I should have stayed in Louisiana," she answered, and swiped her keycard through the reader by the door.

When she opened the door, both dogs butted ahead, dragging their humans with them. Moran bumped shoulders and thighs with Sugar on the way through the doorway. He blessed Dizzy and the biker dog for this inadvertent contact, though he did manage a half-hearted, "Bad dog," just to let Dizzy know he expected civilized behavior even if she was running with a bad boy at the moment.

"I should have let you have the condo," Sugar told him as he followed her toward the hall that led to the front of the building and the elevators near the street entrance. "The place has been nothing but trouble."

There was a back stairs at the park entrance, and Sugar looked like the sort of active person who'd normally use them. He didn't think she was trying to dodge his company, but he did notice the glance she gave the stairway. She was nervous about using them. Why?

"Trouble how?" he asked as they reached the front of the building.

"Trouble like them," she said quietly, and tilted her pretty, pointed chin toward a trio of people already standing by the elevators. She looked like she was considering heading back for the staircase, but one of the trio noticed Sugar and waved. Sugar returned the gesture halfheartedly.

The group consisted of two women in their sixties and a man in his late forties. The man was thin and bald, nondescript in every way. He held a plastic bag in one hand. The old ladies reminded Moran of a couple of the fairy godmothers in the Disney version of *Sleeping Beauty*, only dressed in pastel sweatsuits instead of pastel fairy robes and pointed hats. One was thin and tall, the other short and plump. Neither woman looked happy with the thin man.

"Mr. Carlson, really, shopping outside the co-op is frowned upon," the plump one said as Moran, Sugar, and the dogs reached the elevators.

"There's nothing in the bylaws against it, Pansy," the thin woman said to the plump one. The thin woman held a fluffy white Maltese about the size of a longhaired rat in her arms.

"It's traditional, Esther," Pansy answered. Pansy had a definite cat person look to her. "Supporting all aspects of Franciscan Place is implicit in the charter."

"Implicit, yes," Esther replied. "But not required."

Moran looked from the women to the man. There was a stubborn set to Carlson's thin mouth, and deep anger in his pale eyes. Moran noticed that the white plastic bag the man held was imprinted with the logo of a big chain pet supply store. Moran knew there was a pet supply store here on the first floor of the Franciscan Place building. There were also a pet grooming shop, a pet sitting service, a dog training school, an animal psychologist's office, and a vet clinic on site. All these services were open to the public as well as to the residents, but residents manned the counters in the co-op enterprises and received a deep discount for bringing their business to the co-op stores. Looked like poor Mr. Carlson was busted by the tradition police. Moran noticed that while Pansy defended Carlson's rights, she didn't look happy about doing so.

He saw that Sugar looked pained as she pushed the button and waited for the elevator. Her big hound pressed against her leg and bared his teeth at the group, but didn't growl or show any other form of aggression. The Maltese yipped at the sight of Harley, but its owner didn't pay the cat hound any mind. Moran had the feeling that Sugar hoped they wouldn't be noticed and dragged into this conversation by the older folks. No such luck.

"Why, even Ms. LaRoux, here, with her busy schedule and her injuries, puts in time working at the co-op and on the hospitality committee," Pansy said.

"Not to mention taking over the board seat she inherited from her aunt," Esther added.

Sugar gave the women a wan smile. "Thanks."

Carlson glared at Sugar and said, "Once I'm on the board things will change."

"If you're elected to the board," Esther said.

"You won't win any votes if people know you're buying ferret food from an outside source," Pansy said. "It's not the Franciscan way."

Carlson continued to ignore the older women. He shifted his glare from Sugar to Moran, and his angry expression softened, just a little. "Another outsider. Penhurst's replacement, I suppose. Good to have new blood. What's your stand on the proposal?"

Before Moran could ask what Carlson was talking about Dizzy took it into her pea-brained head to notice the Maltese. He could almost hear her think, *a fluffy mouse!* as she gave a joyful bark—and leaped.

Of course she forgot she was on a leash. Dizzy never remembered when she was attached. She jumped forward—sixty pounds of brainless enthusiasm, and Moran, unprepared, went with her.

"Dizzy!"

Esther and Pansy got out of the way, but Moran slammed into Carlson. The plastic bag flew from the man's hand, busted, and cans of pet food went rolling down the hall.

"Dogs!" Carlson snarled, dropping to his knees to gather up the spilled cans. "I hate dogs."

"Sorry." Mike gathered Dizzy in with the leash and held her close. He would have helped Carlson, but the elevator doors opened, and Sugar pushed him and Dizzy inside. She and Harley followed quickly. Pansy and Esther resumed nagging Carlson as the elevator doors closed.

Sugar pressed the button for the eighth floor, then leaned her head against the back wall as the elevator began a very slow ascent. "Whew. Sit, Harley," she added, tugging on the heavy leather leash. "I mean it."

Moran was surprised when the big dog obeyed. "You, too, Diz." Dizzy sat for a moment, then scuttled over to Harley and started licking his ears. Harley accepted this grooming as his due. Moran concentrated on Sugar. "We both live on eight. That's nice." Penhurst had been her next-door neighbor, he recalled. Was there any relevance to that? "What's with Carlson and the old birds?" he asked. "And what proposal? I'm a cop," he added when she looked at him. "I like to ask questions. It's more of a compulsion."

She gave an understanding nod. "Sort of like my using hot sauce." She touched her swollen cheek. "Time for some pain pills. The old girls are a couple of founding members of the Franciscan commune. Carlson's the first outsider to buy into the place. You must be the fifth or sixth to get a condo that didn't go to an heir. The original residents are getting used to the idea of new residents, but there's still resentment against Carlson."

"For being the first?"

"For being a pain in the ass. Doesn't like dogs or cats or bunnies or snakes or birds or llamas."

"Llamas?"

"There are a pair of llamas living on the second floor. They're housebroken, I'm told."

"Okay. If he doesn't like animals, why does he want to live here?"

"He does like animals. He keeps ferrets. There's a city ordinance against keeping ferrets, Officer Moran. This is the only place in town he can have them."

"Detective Sergeant Moran. Is there? Then why—"

"He can keep them here because Franciscan Place has all sorts of special dispensations from city ordinances. Ferrets are really quite sweet, and clean. People have the mistaken belief that they're wild animals, but they've actually been domesticated for thousands of years."

He was impressed, and grinned to show her. She reacted by blushing a little, and that was impressive, too. He liked her skin all flushed and pink and— "How come you know so much about ferrets?"

"Because I volunteer in the pet supply store. You have to take classes in the history, care, and feeding of all sorts of critters to work in the co-op."

"Good for you," he said. The elevator creaked ominously as it passed the fourth floor. It was an old office building, he reminded himself. Renovated and added onto, but still old. "Tell me about the elections. Am I supposed to run for something?"

"Run from if you're smart. You moved in at a bad time, Moran."

Yeah, he thought, right after someone got murdered. "Afraid the dognapper's going to show up again?" Sugar touched her face, and then her bruised thigh. He wanted to ask her how she'd hurt her leg, but he left it for now. "What's with the election? What proposal was Carlson talking about?"

Sugar's head hurt. She wished Moran would stop asking questions. Then again, she didn't really want to stop talking to him. She liked his deep voice, and his humor, and his lively intelligence. The more time she spent with him, the more she liked him despite her initial skepticism. And she didn't like being alone. Soon they'd reach the eighth floor and go their separate ways. Then she'd be alone with her fears and suspicions, and the sense of helpless dread she hated.

She was probably just being paranoid. And bored.

She wished the doctors would let her go back to work. But kitchens were dangerous places. She was still getting dizzy spells and her vision went fuzzy sometimes. Not good conditions around hot stoves and sharp knives. So, she had at least another week of enforced vacation with only Harley—who was no great watchdog—to keep her company. Moran, she thought, might make a very good watchdog. Except that she was a strong, independent woman of the twenty-first century, and not some weak southern belle in need of a big, strong man's protection. And what a pity that was, she thought, giving Moran another once-over with her one good eye. He was not unaware of her scrutiny. Harley nudged her leg with his head, and got her mind back to the present.

"Where was I?" she asked him. "And where are we?"

"Sixth floor. Election. Controversy."

"Mr. Penhurst's death left a space open on the board. That's too bad, because there's an upcoming vote on whether to sell five acres at the back of the park for city development. Penhurst was against the sale. Carlson is running for the open board spot and no one so far is running against him. The election is next week. He's very much in favor of the sale. Those acres are worth millions. Every member of the owners association would receive a share of the proceeds, plus a great deal of the money would be used for needed repairs on the property. On the other hand, it would mean losing five acres of irreplaceable parkland. Some of the original residents argue that giving up a foot of ground goes against the spirit in which Franciscan Place was founded. They've vowed to tie themselves to trees in protest if the sale is approved. Everyone else is divided on the issue. I'm agin' it," she added. "Most of the dog owners are."

"Me, too." He rubbed Dizzy's head, then rubbed his square, masculine jaw thoughtfully.

He looked like he was about to ask another question, and she wanted to know what he was thinking. In fact, a stab of sudden suspicion went through her. But before Sugar could voice anything, an even sharper stab of pain knifed through her head, and then all she wanted was to get to her bathroom to throw up, and then take a painkiller and go to bed. Fortunately, the elevator drew to a halt and the door opened before the pain completely paralyzed her.

"Later," she managed to say to Moran, and she and Harley squeezed past him and Dizzy and hurried down the hall to her door.

"I brought you a pie."

Moran had made up his mind to pay a call on Sugar when the doorbell rang. She hadn't looked good when she got off the elevator. Maybe he should have gone with her to her condo. Instead he'd taken the chance to be alone. He'd given Dizzy a bath, then paced for hours. While he thought, Dizzy noisily groomed herself then curled up on the couch to sleep. When he opened the door Harley came in and promptly jumped up beside Dizzy. Dizzy didn't mind, and Moran was too intent on the human visitor to yell at the Catahoula.

Sugar was pale, but beautiful. He looked at the pie she held out to him. The crust was flaky and golden, and the scent of warm blueberries filled his nostrils. "I love you," he said to Sugar LaRoux. Then he added, "What kind of food do ferrets eat?"

He pulled her inside before she could answer and shut the door behind her. "Cat food," she said as he took the pie from her. She followed him into the kitchen. "Why?"

"Why'd you bring me a pie? And thank you. How'd you know I love pie?"

"You look like a pie kind of guy."

"Oh, I am."

The kitchen, like the rest of the condo, was pretty bare. Penhurst's furniture had all been donated to Goodwill, his papers and personal effects were in a police warehouse. Most of Moran's stuff was still at his old place. He had only the couch, his bed, his clothes, Dizzy's stuff, the microwave and a few dishes moved into his new home. He'd arrived to solve a murder first and settle down to enjoy living at Franciscan Place later. He hadn't counted on homemade pie. This was a real housewarming present. A treasure. He was glad he'd remembered to bring plates and silverware. He wouldn't have minded eating the pie with his bare hands straight out of the dish, but that didn't seem neighborly, somehow. He supposed he'd better offer the lady who'd made it a piece.

"You want some? How are you feeling? And how'd you bruise your leg?"

"Yes, please. Much better. Why do you want to know what ferrets eat?"

Moran busied himself with knives, forks, and plates. When he handed Sugar a slice of warm blueberry pie, he said, "You tell me first."

"Why should I tell you anything?"

"Why'd you make me a pie?"

"I like to cook. And I'm on the hospitality committee."

"Plus, you don't want to be alone." After a moment of strained silence, he added, "And you like me."

"Harley likes Dizzy," she answered. She looked at the dogs on the couch. "They make a cute couple."

"So do we."

His mouth said it before his mind could censor the words. He didn't know where those words came from, but he couldn't bring himself to apologize or back off. "At least, I think we do." She was blushing again. He took a step closer to her, and watched while she concentrated on eating her pie rather than look at him. He liked making her blush, seeing her pale skin take on heat. To get his mind off the thought of seeing more of her skin warmed by his words and his touch, he wolfed down his blueberry pie. The taste only made him wonder about how sweet her mouth would taste with her lips all covered in blueberries. To bludgeon down this thought, he went back into cop mode.

"Why don't you want to be alone? And what do ferrets eat?"

Sugar didn't know which question to answer first, or even if she should answer either of them. Maybe she shouldn't be here. Maybe she should have just dropped off the welcome present and gone back home. She glanced toward the door, but didn't seriously consider leaving. Maybe she'd only met Mike Moran a few hours ago, but there was an undeniable chemistry between them. Maybe the blueberry pie was only the beginning of showing how welcome he was at Franciscan Place. And maybe this was all moving too fast, and she was just reacting to him this way because she was lonely.

The ferret question seemed safer to address. "Cat food," she told him. "The expensive canned kind. There are a couple of kinds of ferret chow, but they're expensive, and vets say they aren't any better than good cat food. Why?"

"Carlson had dog food in his bag."

"Oh." Somehow that seemed ominous. She shrugged. "Maybe there's a dog food that ferrets like. Carlson's an expert on them."

He put down his plate and came forward to put his hands on her shoulders. Lovely, warm, big hands. "You're not exactly the suspicious type, are you?"

"I didn't used to be," she admitted. ""I'm really not a naive and trusting soul," she went on. "I've lived in New Orleans, not Mayberry."

"But you still get mad at yourself for being suspicious of people."

There was no arguing with this. It was like she and Moran had known each other forever. "And you get mad at yourself when you aren't suspicious of people."

"I really did think of you as a murder suspect before I met you," he admitted.

"And you met me on purpose." He nodded. She'd been annoyed about this at first, but her attraction to the man quickly overrode her outrage. "Are you the officer in charge of the investigation, or is moving in here a coincidence?"

"Yes. And yes." He shook his head. "I'm a good investigator, but I keep going off on personal tangents with you. Don't tell my boss, okay?"

She glanced back at the couch. "Would that be Dizzy?"

"She doesn't care right now." The dogs were tangled up in a pile, perfectly content to be with each other. One of them was snoring. "That biker of yours is making me jealous, Sugar."

"And here I thought I was Harley's only love."

"Guess we'll have to settle for each other." He'd done it again! And she was smiling at him with her lovely, kissable mouth. Moran carefully took his hands away from Sugar's shoulders and stepped away. He even put them behind his back to keep from touching her again. "I think it's time for the 'just the facts, ma'am' speech. I've got a murderer to catch."

Sugar had a teasing glint in her one good eye, and he sadly watched it fade. "You don't think Mr. Penhurst was killed by a stranger stealing his dog, do you?"

"You don't either," he answered her. "Why not, Sugar? Why don't you want to be alone?"

She put her hands up in front of her. "I've gotten a little paranoid since I got hit on the head. But—"

"What happened to your leg?"

"I fell down the back stairs. This old building needs some work, and we can't keep caretakers. Our last one left two weeks ago, and since Penhurst was in charge of the hiring committee he hasn't been replaced. The wiring's ancient. Sometimes there're power outages." She shrugged.

"You didn't fall, you were pushed."

"Harley probably knocked me off balance…except I was pretty sure he was a couple of flights ahead of me."

"Why didn't you tell the police?"

"Because I wasn't sure."

"If you weren't sure you wouldn't have even joked about my being a hit man."

"I can't remember what happened when I was attacked. How can I trust my judgment without any concrete proof?" She turned toward the couch. "Could it be that the dognapper is trying to steal Harley? Catahoula leopard dogs aren't too well known outside of Louisiana."

Moran laughed. "Hell, no, I don't think anyone's trying to steal your dog. They'd pay you to take that bruiser back." He ignored her outraged glare. "I think plain old greed's the motive. Why didn't you mention the fight over selling off part of the park to the investigating officers?"

She looked puzzled. "That's Franciscan Place business. You signed the non-disclosure agreement when you moved in, didn't you?"

Yeah, he had. The media was always trying to do cutesy stories on the weirdo hippie animal lovers that lived in the building, and the hippie weirdos were sick of it. Rule was nobody talked about Franciscan Place to outsiders. He considered pointing out to Sugar that non-disclosure agreements didn't count in a murder investigation, but it didn't matter now. Besides, every animal-loving hippie weirdo at Franciscan Place genuinely believed Penhurst had been killed for his dog. Every animal-loving hippie weirdo but one, but he was still an animal lover.

"That dog food is going to put Carlson away. He couldn't get rid of a dog as rare as a Porcelaine without even an animal shelter noticing, and it hasn't occurred to him to kill an animal."

Sugar looked stricken, but not really surprised. "You think Carlson killed Mr. Penhurst? Because of the proposed land sale?" She sighed. "I really didn't want to believe it was one of us."

"He bludgeoned a man to death because he was blocking the land sale Carlson wants. He tried to kill you twice. Don't feel sorry for him."

"And he stole a puppy," She added in outrage. "I don't feel sorry for him. Can I feel sorry for his ferrets?"

"I suppose somebody has to."

"What are you going to do? Search his apartment? Arrest him?"

"A couple of cans of dog food aren't probable cause for arresting the guy. I can start an investigation. Or..." He scratched his jaw. "Yeah."

"Was that a light bulb I saw go off over your head?"

"Uh-huh. Hey, Dizzy, wake up!" He looked at Sugar. "You and Harley want to show me around the building?"

❧   ❧   ❧

"Isn't he cute? The poor little thing."

Moran listened carefully at the door. "Shhh. I hear someone coming."

"Aren't you sweet?" Sugar whispered behind him. "Poor lonely thing. Been locked up in here all alone when you're just a baby. That's a good Dizzy. You lick his ears like a good mommy."

Despite the approaching footsteps in the hall, Moran took a moment to glance over his shoulder. There were no lights on in the caretaker's empty apartment, but Sugar and a pile of dogs were gathered in a patch of moonlight under a bare window. The place didn't smell so great, but Moran was used to dog mess. There were bowls of water and food on the floor and a stack of empty cans in a corner.

The Porcelaine puppy was in Sugar's lap, with Harley and Dizzy jostling to give the pup attention.

"Shh," he said again.

When Sugar glanced up he motioned to her to get out of the light. She scooted back, the dogs going with her. The steps halted outside the door. Then Harley's head came up, his attention on the door. A low growl started in his throat, but Sugar grabbed the big dog's muzzle to keep him quiet. Dizzy obeyed Moran's hand motion to sit and be quiet. Mostly she was good at obeying…for about fifteen seconds. Then whatever passed for thought in her pretty head would drift off and she'd be ready to play again. Fifteen seconds would do for now.

He stepped to one side and waited as a key turned in the door. A key. More physical evidence. They'd gotten into the basement apartment with the help of a credit card jimmied in the door. Sugar gave him permission to enter as a member of the board. The member of the board who had had a key to the caretaker's apartment was Penhurst. No keys had been found on Penhurst or in his condo. Moran's conclusions about where the puppy was hidden had proved correct. That the puppy was being taken care of by the murderer made sense—if you thought like a typical hippie weirdo resident of Franciscan Place. Which Moran did.

Now he waited to see if the person he expected would come through the door.

Sugar was glad to be in the shadows. She wasn't afraid, exactly. Not with Mike Moran standing there being large and competent. It was just that the idea of facing her attacker was—daunting—even if she'd been talking to him by the elevator only a few hours ago. She watched the door slowly open and hoped it wasn't Carlson. She didn't like the man, but it sickened her that someone she knew had tried to kill her. She held her breath, and a man stepped into the room.

She couldn't stop Harley's growl this time, or his lunge.

Carlson screamed.

Harley pulled so hard his collar came off in Sugar's hands. She shouted. The puppy trotted forward. Her dog drew up his heavy muscles and jumped. Dizzy began barking. Carlson screamed again.

Moran slammed the door and put himself between it and Carlson. Carlson ran into Moran. Harley leaped on Carlson's back. They all went down in a heap. Dizzy kept barking and the puppy yelped in distress. Sugar snatched up the puppy, then circled around the swearing, barking tangle of bodies to switch on the overhead light.

By the time the lights came on Moran was on his feet. Carlson was on his back. Harley straddled him, growling in his face.

"Get him off me! Get him off me!"

Moran looked at her. "I thought you said he wasn't protective?"

"Maybe he's trying to protect the puppy."

"Or Impress Dizzy."

"Get him *off*!"

Moran looked at Sugar's bruises, and enjoyed watching Carlson squirm in terror for a few more seconds. Then Sugar frowned at him in that civilized way women have of indicating they disapprove of such manly pursuits as torture and war, and he reminded her, "He's your dog."

"Right. Harley!"

Moran thought Harley backed off more out of boredom than obedience training. Harley turned to Dizzy, whose tongue lolled out in a way that indicated complete hero worship of Harley. "Sucker," Moran muttered. Carlson stared up at him, his face covered in drool. "You're under arrest for the murder of Alec Penhurst." Then he hauled the shaking Carlson to his feet and read him his rights.

When Moran was done Mirandizing his suspect, Sugar stepped forward, the white puppy still in her arms. "Why'd you try to kill me?" she asked.

Carlson would have been smart to wait for a lawyer before he did any talking, but he answered her. "To free up another liberal spot on the board." He sounded like murder was the most reasonable thing in the world. "You stand in the way of progress."

Moran added, "Besides, you thought she might get her memory back. That's why you tried the second time."

Carlson nodded. "That, too."

Carlson was hanging himself. Moran loved it, less work to make the case for him. He took out his cell phone and called in the collar.

A few minutes later a pair of uniformed officers arrived at the front of the building where he'd brought Carlson. He let the uniforms take Carlson away. He'd follow them to the homicide division soon. He went back inside the building.

Sugar and the dogs waited for him in his condo. The first thing he did was the one thing he'd been wanting to do since he first laid eyes on her. He took Sugar LaRoux in his arms and kissed her. It was as wonderful as he'd thought it would be, and went on for a long while.

"My head's spinning," she said when their lips parted. "And I don't think it's from the concussion."

"I have to go," he said. "That was a down payment for later."

She didn't object. "What's going to happen to the puppy?" she asked. "Penhurst didn't have any family."

Harley and Dizzy were on the rug. The Porcelaine was chewing on Harley's ear. Moran shook his head, and put his arm around Sugar's waist. "I think they've already adopted him."

She rested her head on his shoulder. "Looks like it."

"And I guess that means we'll have to stay together. For the sake of the children."

Night Hawks

Jody Lynn Nye

Footsteps came closer and closer to where Melina Lange hid, terrified, in the recess of the rough brick wall. Somewhere behind her was an assassin who had just killed her boyfriend. If she didn't keep moving, she knew she would be next.

She heard voices coming from the downslope side of Jasmine Garden Park. She left her hiding place and blundered up the hill in the dark. Twigs like fingers reached out of the bushes and pulled out strands of her long, curly hair. They scratched her hands, which were unprotected by her short trench coat. She ignored the pain and kept running.

Allen was dead! Melina's hazel eyes were blurred by tears as she stumbled on the white gravel path. She wished she could have been in love with him—truly, she did. She was ready for a plain, ordinary romance. That didn't mean she wasn't sorry someone had shot him, but at least it hadn't been her. She'd been instantly attracted to him. And what woman wouldn't have been, he was so handsome—muscular and tan with romantic, dark blue eyes and gorgeous sunstreaked hair. But what had really drawn her to him wasn't his looks, it was something else…something she couldn't quite define. He was intriguing, just a little offbeat, just a little dangerous. Though he wasn't more than a couple of inches taller than her five-foot-seven, he walked with a confident swagger, and he always seemed to have plenty of money. When she asked him about his business operations, he was so mysterious. He diverted her questions, or simply ignored them. She'd worried that he was dealing in something exotic and illegal. Now she was sure of it.

She had been titillated when Allen told her to meet him there in the Jasmine Gardens after dark. Twenty acres of fragrant, walled garden looking out over the white-tipped waves of the Pacific Ocean, it was a popular spot for couples seeking a little love fulfillment by moonlight. The Gardens offered plenty of intimate, private areas surrounded by low, mossy stone walls, where they could be alone. But when she arrived, eager and ready, wearing a sexy little dress she knew he'd like under the short raincoat, he'd spoiled the whole thing by telling her he had come there to meet someone—someone important, he'd said.

"And I'm not important?" she had asked, angry and disappointed.

So they'd quarreled, there in the most romantic spot in the city, while the waves tossed and crashed at the foot of the cliff far below the brick walls and night birds called in the trees. Everyone had heard Melina and Allen yelling at one another. Couples passing them to go deeper into the garden gave them pointed looks. If they weren't there to enjoy themselves, couldn't they at least take their noise somewhere else?

In the midst of the argument, Melina had caught sight of a figure, little more than a shadow, coming toward them. She ignored the stranger and continued arguing with Allen until a blue glint caught her eye as the silhouette's hand emerged from the inside of his raincoat.

After that, things had happened so quickly. Allen saw the gun at the same moment she had. With a single movement he'd shoved her into the bushes and dived in the opposite direction. The man—for it was a man—had a narrow, hatchet face and short-clipped hair. As Allen hit the ground and rolled, the gunman stuck his weapon out at arm's length. The gun's muzzle flashed. It made so little sound that Melina knew instinctively he'd used a silencer. Allen quit rolling and sprawled on the ground in a sad, boneless mass. The man moved up to his victim, kicked him to be sure of his kill, and turned and walked away. Melina had cowered for a moment until the assassin was out of sight, then flung herself at her boyfriend, turning him face upward. Allen's eyes stared sightlessly into the night. She could feel no pulse in his neck. Terrified, she groped for her cell phone. Her fingers fumbled on the keys several times before she managed to dial Emergency Response. She'd given her name, Allen's name, and all the details she could think of, her voice rising toward hysteria until the kindly operator on the other end of the line stopped her and calmed her down. He promised to send someone immediately. He asked her to wait where she was, and instructed her not to touch anything. It was too late for that, of course.

Melina switched off the cell phone, and sat down on the grass beside Allen's body, alone with the sounds of the night. Before, they'd been familiar and friendly. Now they were strange and frightening.

She heard footsteps approaching. Suddenly, it occurred to her that perhaps she hadn't waited until the assassin was out of earshot before calling for help. Perhaps he was coming back to eliminate the only witness?

Maybe it was just another lover looking for his beloved in the park. An enormous shadow passed by her suddenly, cutting off the light of a distant street lamp. Melina stayed still as long as her nerves could stand it, then fled into the trees.

The footsteps quickened as the mysterious figure behind her gave chase. Melina's heart pounded wildly with fear.

She'd missed the winding path, but felt it was smarter not to take it anyhow. The forest floor was uneven and slippery. Low, leafy plants whipped her legs, and she felt her stockings tear. The ever-present creak of tree frogs ceased as she disturbed them in her headlong dash through the park. She ran with her arms up, elbows out, to keep branches from striking her in the face. The footsteps following her got louder, feet crunching on fallen twigs as her pursuer plunged into the woods behind her.

She couldn't run forever. What could she use to defend herself? Searching her pocket with her free hand for her keys, she threaded them in between her fingers, points out. But she prayed it wouldn't come to that—mere keys against a gunman.

She ran toward the high stone wall that surrounded the garden. If she followed it, she might be able to get out of the park without being seen. A root caught the sandal strap over her toes. Her shoes weren't intended for sprinting, let alone running for her life. Melina grabbed for the tree to steady herself. Behind her, the following footsteps drew closer. She crouched down and wrenched her sandal free, then she sprang up, ready to run, when an arm wrapped around her from behind.

Her heart leaped in her throat, choking her. Melina almost passed out with terror, but some reflex, ingrained during a long-ago women's self-defense course, caused her to jab backward with her elbow. She caught the assailant in the belly. He, for it was a man, let out an *oof!*, but didn't let go. Frantic, Melina struggled to gouge her keys into his face. Her captor fought back, holding her pinioned with one arm. He pulled her farther into the brush, his other hand clapped over her mouth.

"Shh!" he hissed in her ear. "Don't make a sound."

This man had shot Allen in cold blood. He wouldn't hesitate to do the same to her. Melina had no intention of being dragged off and shot or strangled or knifed. She wriggled her jaw open, and bit the nearest finger of the enclosing hand.

"Crap!" the man growled, letting the hand fall. "No, don't yell," he began as Melina took a deep breath.

"Help!" Melina screamed at the top of her voice. "Help me!"

Her attacker sagged and released her. "I wish you hadn't done that," he said.

"Why shouldn't I have, you bastard?" Melina demanded, turning to face her tormentor.

Ping! A bullet struck the wall over their heads, showering them with stone shards. The stranger seized her hand and started running. She stumbled after him. For it wasn't the same man who'd killed Allen. This man was wearing jeans and a short, zip-up jacket.

"There're two of you?" Melina asked, fighting to free her hand. "Who are you? Why did you kill Allen? No, never mind. Don't tell me. Then you'll have to kill me. And I just want to go home. Please, let me go."

The strange man pulled her around a brick pillar and yanked her down to crouch beside him.

"I'm not going to hurt you. I'm just an innocent bystander here," he whispered. "A witness. My name's Mike Dillon. I'm a nature photographer. I've been working in the conservancy area up near the peak for three weeks. I've been trying to catch nighthawks in action for *Avian* magazine. I was on my way up there when I saw that guy shoot your boyfriend. I ran off to see if I could find a park warden. Old Boscombe is usually driving around at this hour. The park guys all know me, and they're armed and trained to deal with stuff like this. But I couldn't find any of them. I thought I'd better come back and help you."

Melina got a good look at him for the first time. He was thin, just the opposite of Allen, with longish black hair and light eyes. She couldn't tell their color in the meager moonlight that filtered through the bushes, but she found their expression sincere.

He had very pale skin, as though he often stayed up all night and never saw the sun.

"You're not an...assassin?" Melina's voice shook, and she hated herself for being so weak.

"I'm glad you're finally figuring that out," Mike said, a small, ironic quirk lifting the side of his mouth. "No. I'm one of the good guys."

"Oh." Melina swallowed, having to rearrange her thinking. "I'm Melina Lange."

She could see the glint of his white teeth when he smiled. "Pleased to meet you, Melina." He quit talking to listen to the night. The sound of the tree frogs diminished, then stopped again. "I think our bad guy is getting too close. We'd better move. Stay low, and use whatever cover you can find."

Melina had just taken a small step when an ominous *thunk* came from the tree beside them. Leaves flew in all directions. Melina let out a little peep of surprise and threw herself to the ground. Mike flattened himself over her. Another bullet whinged off the wall about twenty feet away from them.

"I think your friend's firing at random." Mike rose to a crouch and grabbed her arm. "Come on. This way!"

"He's not my friend!" Melina whispered furiously, as she ran after him.

"Well, he's sure not mine." He held up a thorny branch and gestured her underneath it into the heavily wooded landscape, then crept along beside her.

Melina bit her tongue as they finally stopped at the edge of a clearing. It was her fault that both of them were now in such danger. If only she had listened to this man and not screamed, giving away their location to the assassin. But what was she to think when he grabbed her? Was she supposed to believe he meant her no harm? For some reason, seeing her boyfriend killed before her very eyes had made her jumpy. Mike raised his head, getting his bearings.

"We're in the gazing pool garden," he whispered. "There's at least two or three ways in. We're not trapped, even if he's in here with us."

"If we can just keep hidden and out of the killer's way, we'll be all right," Melina said. "I called the police. We only have to stay away from him until they get here."

Another bullet ricocheted noisily off the wall, much too close for Melina's comfort.

"Damn," Mike said. "Or we can lay low until this guy runs out of bullets." He shoved her down into a patch of grass deeply shadowed by the surrounding bushes and flopped down beside her. He scattered handfuls of dead leaves over them both and motioned for silence. All too soon the sound of footsteps passed within a few feet of them. Melinda listened, her heart pounding so hard she was sure the killer would hear it. Soon, the sound of steps faded into the distance. Mike shifted.

"I think we're okay. He doesn't know where we are," Mike whispered. "What in hell was your boyfriend into, anyhow?"

Melina was too ashamed to tell him that she didn't really know. She put out a finger and touched his lips, signaling him to be quiet. His lips felt soft. She let her hand drop.

"I'm sorry," he said. "I didn't mean to snap. Are you all right? It's got to have been traumatic to see someone…"

…Die. He hadn't wanted to say the word, but it hung in the air between them. Melina shivered all over. Taking control of herself, she made a face.

"I'll be fine," she assured him. "You know, right now I'm so angry with him. Angry. Resentful. I'm sorry Allen…died, but I'm also totally

ticked off that he put me in this situation. He brought me here knowing something was wrong. He as much as told me that before the
gunman shot him." She looked up at Mike. His pale eyes picked up
the faint light and seemed to glow. "I'm sorry about all this. It's too
bad that you got involved, too, but I'm glad you were there. But
there's something I don't understand. If you were looking for hawks,
how'd you happen to see what happened to Allen? We were nowhere
near the wild parts of the park."

The light eyes dropped and were covered by long eyelashes. "I
was watching you," he said sheepishly. "I saw you, and I was just
wishing I had a someone as beautiful as you in my life when that guy
walked right up and pulled the gun out. I didn't hear anything, but I
saw a red flash, then…you know." Mike paused and looked at her. "I
suppose this is a bad time to ask you if you'd like to have coffee some
time?"

In spite of herself, Melina started laughing. The sound of it rang
out in the silent park. She knew her life depended on it, but with the
adrenaline rush from shock, fear, and relief she couldn't stop. She
covered her mouth with both hands. Mike wrapped himself around
her to muffle the sound. Suddenly, unexpectedly, inevitably, they
found themselves face-to-face, and all Melina could think about was
passionately kissing those soft, soft lips.

She pulled away from Mike with a little gasp and started crawling
away, into the undergrowth, moving as fast as she could so the
gunman wouldn't find them where the laughter had been. Mike followed her into a copse of thick, scratchy arborvitae bushes. He
reached for her, but she pulled away, welcoming the sharp prickles
against her back as a kind of penance for nearly making love to a
stranger when the man she'd been seeing was lying dead no more
than a hundred yards from her and a killer was stalking them.

"I'm so sorry," she said, hoping her face was in shadow so he
couldn't see how red she knew it was. "I didn't mean to laugh." It was
her turn to hang her head. "You know, I came here tonight hoping for
a nice romantic encounter. I just thought it would be with…someone
else."

Mike's light eyes glinted at her from the darkness. "So, under
better circumstances, would I do instead?"

She studied him, liking the way the spare planes of his face threw shadows under his brows and cheekbones. "Yes," she said in a very low voice. "You'll do nicely."

"Do you know who was shooting at your friend?" She could tell he didn't want to say 'boyfriend.' Maybe he was picturing himself in that role. To tell the truth, and she was ashamed of herself for it, given the events of the last hour, she was beginning to picture him in that role, too.

"I never saw that man before," Melina said.

"Neither have I. He's not a regular in the park. But I got a good look at him."

Melina made a face. "Well, *if* we live to describe him to the police, that will be useful."

"My camera bag's at the bottom of the hill. I threw it there when I went after you. I could try to go get it, and take his picture. You know, we ought to do that anyway, in case he leaves before the cops come."

Melina looked at him in astonishment. She wouldn't have been more surprised if he'd said he was going to sprout wings and fly them to the police station.

"Are you out of your mind? That's too dangerous," she said.

"All right," Mike said, his eyes dancing. "I'll draw his fire, you go get the camera."

"This is not an adventure story, Mr. Nature Photographer!" Melina hissed. "This is reality! We could get killed!"

"Fine," he said. "We'll die together, then. We'll both go."

This initiated a short, whispered argument. It ended only when Mike convinced her that staying there was even more likely to get them killed than moving back to the scene of the original crime, where his camera was. After all, he pointed out, the last place the killer would want to be found was right next to the body of his victim. And the killer knew the police were coming.

"I just wish they'd get here faster!" Melina muttered.

They tiptoed out onto the path. It was better that way, Mike had asserted, against Melina's protestations that they should stay under cover. The killer had searched this path, after all. They'd heard him. And they'd make a lot less noise walking on the compacted gravel than crawling around in the bushes. Here in the dark, noise was their enemy, silence their friend.

The camera bag lay exactly where he thought it would be. Mike took out a silver-cased camera, checked its film indicator, and handed it to her. He shouldered the bag, but carried in his hands a giant-sized flash attachment and a coil of wire with a palm-sized box at the end.

"Remote control," he told her as they trotted deeper into the park. His low voice soothed Melina's jangling nerves. "I don't need the flash when I'm using super-high-speed film. I like doing night photography. It's kind of a specialty with me. In the wild the hawks hunt at dusk and dawn, but what with streetlights everywhere in this park, as far as the hawks are concerned it's always dusk, so I have all night to get my pictures. The females are terrific hunters. You ought to see them. We'll stake this guy out, just like I would my birds. Then, we'll nab him."

We shouldn't be doing this, Melina thought, as the entrance disappeared farther behind them. We shouldn't be hunting the hunter. We should be getting out of this park, going somewhere safe, finding the police. But she could never resist that touch of danger. She was also glad to have something to do to help her keep from thinking about the cold reality of Allen's murder, and all those gunshots that had nearly ended her own life. She'd discovered she really didn't like getting shot at—and she wanted to make sure the assassin didn't get away. Until he was caught, she'd never have a moment's peace of mind. She owed it to Allen to find his killer. Surely she owed Allen that much.

At the edge of one of the smallest and darkest walled sections of garden, Mike set Melina in the shelter of a stand of thick bushes with the camera while he headed off into the darkness with the flash unit.

"How can you see where you're going?" she breathed.

"Practice," he said. "I've developed good night vision after stalking hawks."

Melina squinted into the shadows, feeling as though she missed him already. What an odd sensation…but understandable, perhaps. They'd shared something few people did: a life-and-death test of who they were. He'd cared about her during the crisis. He was friendly, funny, self-deprecating, and, as a bonus, good-looking. When this was over, *if* they both lived through it, she did want to go out with him. Maybe she'd join him photographing his hawks. That sounded interesting. She'd always liked birds and had a sympathy for raptors. They, too, had that taste for danger. Speaking of which...

Her heart started pounding again. Mike had been out of sight for a long time. The forest had gone quiet. That probably wasn't good. She stepped out slowly to see where he had gone and if he was all right.

Something crunched right beside the fence. Startled, Melina looked up. Silhouetted in the moonlight, the narrow-faced assassin was looking down at her. He'd come around the bend in the path at just the right time to catch her exposed in the pathway. His feral grin gave away his ill intentions as he drew the gun from inside his coat. Melina was hypnotized by the sight, unable to run away or even move. The barrel lowered toward her until she was looking at the black opening at its end. It looked big as a cannon. She was going to die.

"Hey, killer!" Mike yelled from across the path. The assassin spun around to face the new target.

The night blossomed into blinding light. Melina threw her hands up to protect her eyes. The assassin hesitated only a second, then fired shot after shot at the blazing target. She heard a crash in the dark.

"No!" she screamed, galvanized into action. Not twice in one night! Allen, and now Mike, murdered before she had even gotten to know him. She jumped the assassin, pummeling the back of his head and kicking the backs of his knees with every bit of strength she possessed. The man dropped to the ground, the gun flying out of his hand. Melina jumped on his back, kept pounding him even after he collapsed into unconsciousness until gentle but firm hands pulled her off.

They belonged to Mike. He was alive! A sob of relief burst out of her. She threw her arms around him and held him tightly. Then lights appeared everywhere around them. A couple of uniformed police officers moved in on the shooter, pinioning his hands behind his back with handcuffs.

"You hit him pretty hard, ma'am," the older officer said as they got out the smelling salts. A couple of moments later one of the policemen helped the dazed man to sit up while the other examined the man's wallet with a flashlight. Blood dripped into the gunman's eyes from a cut on his forehead. The cop turned his torch on Melina. "What'd you use on him?"

Melina looked down at her hand, struck dumb with shock. "Use?" She'd forgotten she'd been holding anything. A twisted metal box was clutched in her fingers. Twinkling glass shards peppered her sleeves and front of her coat.

Mike stepped in. "She nailed him with a Nikon F1 camera, Officer. Metal body. He might have a concussion."

The officer was amused. "A pretty expensive weapon, but effective. Couldn't happen to a nicer guy. I know this perp—he's got a blotter sheet you wouldn't believe. Stay here while I put him in the car. I'll need to get detailed statements from both of you in a minute."

Mike returned to Melina, who was staring, mortified, at the wreck in her hands. "I ruined your camera!" she exclaimed. "I'm so sorry. I'll get you a new one, I promise. But I thought he'd shot you."

Mike held up the little box. "Remote control. He got my flash unit. It was in a tree about six feet away from me. Don't worry about it. The equipment can be replaced. And it was worth it," he said with a grin, as he brought his soft mouth close to her ear. "You know, I've been waiting for weeks to catch a female nighthawk in action."

Keeper of the Well

Deb Stover

*R*ural Kansas—*present day.*

Hana Gillespie stared at the key cradled in her open palm as if seeking its permission to enter the rundown old farmhouse. *Face it, Hana—it's really yours.* She looked past the missing shingles and broken windows to sweep the landscape beyond the house, and released a contented sigh. This place was worth every penny it would cost to restore. It was her future.

She looked at the house again and pulled the newspaper article she'd printed from the microfiche at the library. When the woman at the hardware store heard which farm Hana had bought, she'd told her a bizarre tale of murder and ghosts. And, according to this article, at least the murder part was true.

A little girl named Annie had drowned in the well over fifty years ago, murdered by a farmhand. A few days after the man's execution, the girl's mother took her own life. Brokenhearted and alone, the grandmother had simply walked away from the farm.

This farm.

Despite the past tragedies, Hana was determined to make it a happy home for a child, once the adoption agency approved her application. Stuffing the article into her pocket, she faced her front door again.

Each time she entered, she realized what a disaster the place was. The downstairs was clean now, but still decrepit. Today she would explore upstairs.

Glancing across the parlor, she did a double take. In the doorway to the kitchen stood a child. She estimated the girl's age at around five. Bare feet and legs stuck out beneath a faded brown dress that reached just below her knees. Her blond hair hung straggly and unkempt.

Hana's gaze traveled back up to the child's smiling face. Something besides the endearing grin drew Hana's scrutiny. Need. The little girl needed something.

Or someone?

Why would anyone permit a child to roam around the countryside alone? Hana took a tentative step toward her, noting the physical characteristics of Down syndrome in the child's face. The little urchin grinned, crooked a finger in invitation, then simply disappeared.

Vanished.

Hana's blood turned cold and her heart slammed into her chest. She blinked, willing the child to reappear.

No such luck.

Was she imagining things? Was her desire to adopt a child threatening her sanity? Or had the hardware store clerk's tale planted the seeds of this hallucination?

Hana closed her eyes again for as long as she dared, then reopened them and walked into the kitchen. The child couldn't have been real. The way she'd dissolved into nothingness was impossible. But if she was real, Hana would have been aware of her turning to run away, not simply vanishing.

Like a ghost.

Educated, intelligent people like Hana simply didn't believe such nonsense. *It was only my imagination.*

Humming "Lions and Tigers and Bears" as a defense mechanism, Hana peeked around the corner at the back porch, where pails and other discarded items were stored. No little girls—only more evidence of the hard work Hana had ahead of her.

Squaring her shoulders, she walked purposefully outside to her car and opened the trunk. It was time for her to get her act together. Past time.

Ghost or no, Hana Gillespie was moving in.

She removed a box of cleaning supplies and placed it on the ground beside the car and retrieved her flashlight. Determined, she went back inside to open every unbroken window, then started up the stairs.

The old staircase groaned and creaked as she ascended to the second floor. This was an adventure—like Indiana Jones entering the "Temple of Doom." But no snakes, please.

At the top, she looked down a long hall at several closed doors. "There, that wasn't so bad," she said quietly, the sound of her own voice comforting. "What's behind door number one?"

A *real* bathroom. She whooped in delight upon discovering the antique plumbing fixtures. Though covered in fifty-plus years of filth, they were in fair condition. Now all she needed were new pipes, a water heater...and water.

Don't think about the well....

Hana stared for a few moments at the door across the hall. Taking a deep breath, she turned it. No bats. No mice. No snakes. "Whew." She walked around the room, touching the dusty dresser, running her hand along the rusted iron bed frame.

Only one of the three narrow windows had been boarded over. The other two opened rather easily once she released the rusted locks. The temperature lowered a few degrees almost immediately.

She dropped to her knees beside a trunk at the foot of the bed, running her hand along its intricate carving. Relief mingled with foreboding as she discovered it unlocked.

She closed her eyes. "God, please don't let there be anything that moves in here." Wary, she lifted the lid. "Aha." Papers, a Bible, and photo albums. A breeze came through one of the windows, several degrees cooler. Hana peered outside. Thunderheads loomed like harbingers of disaster to the southwest.

Sighing, she reminded herself to hurry through the trunk's contents, then she'd take some of it downstairs to examine more closely. Curiosity grabbed her by the throat and she removed a photograph album, catching a few loose photos as they fell.

Did these faces belong to the names from the newspaper article? The first was of a little girl standing between two women. Hana squinted as she studied the child's hauntingly familiar face.

"Annie," a small voice supplied from Hana's side.

Forcing herself to remain calm, Hana held her breath and looked at the little girl. Okay, so the ghost was real. She could handle this. Dead or alive, Annie was a child and Hana was a teacher. *No sweat. Yeah, right.*

Hana pointed at the photograph. "Annie?" she repeated, holding her breath.

The child nodded and pointed to the picture of herself. "Me."

"I see." Hana's eyes stung as she considered the little girl's tragic death. "Annie." She moved her finger to the young woman in the photograph. "Who's this?"

Annie giggled as if Hana's question was ridiculous. "Mama."

Hana pointed at the older woman's image. "Grandma?" she asked.

Annie nodded, then reached for the second photograph. "Kayub," she said, looking up at Hana to smile again. "Kayub fun."

Hana stared in silence at Caleb Dawes—the man who'd killed Annie? The skin around Hana's mouth tingled and the acid in her stomach hit a record high.

The photo showed the man smiling and leaning against the hood of an old truck. With his good looks, it was easy to see how Annie's mother, Mildred, might've fallen in love with him. Hana blinked and shook her head. Fictionalizing the missing pieces of this mystery wasn't smart.

Still, it made sense in a sick sort of way.

Caleb's eyes were light, probably blue. It was impossible to tell from the black-and-white print. His full lips were turned up in a grin that belied the morbid tale. This man looked...nice.

Swallowing her fear, she watched Annie take the photo and hold it close to her face. She displayed no fear, no anger toward the man. Surely Annie knew the identity of the person who'd pushed her into the well.

Maybe she just fell. Maybe...

"Kayub," Annie repeated.

"Did—do you like Caleb?" Hana asked.

The child looked up and nodded.

Hana had the overwhelming urge to hold Annie, to rock her, to protect her from a tragedy that had occurred over half a century ago. She closed her eyes.

I'm going crazy—having fantasies about mothering a ghost.

Her biological clock had taken control. Of course, it was beginning to seem more like a sundial at her age. Even so, Hana didn't have to resort to mothering a ghost.

Even an adorable ghost? Enough. When she opened her eyes again, Annie was gone. A protective urge evolved and grew within Hana, more powerful than any she'd ever known.

She had to find Annie. No, she had to save her...

Lightning streaked across the sky and thunder rattled the windows. Every sound sliced right through her, including the small voice crying out for help.

Annie.

Hana ran blindly down the stairs. It didn't matter that Annie Campbell was a ghost—that she was already dead. In Hana's heart, she was a little girl who needed her.

Nothing more, nothing less.

She rushed headlong into the storm. The wind whipped her face and stole her breath—rain penetrated her clothing. Hana leaned over the opening, ducking her head beneath the crumbling cover. She stared into the darkness. "Annie!" Her voice echoed back to her.

"*Annie!*" Tears burned her eyes and fell to join the water pooling at the bottom.

"Mama?"

Squinting, Hana prayed for any sign of the child. It wasn't her imagination. Annie was in the well. Leaning farther, Hana grasped the frayed rope with one hand and called out again. The stones suddenly crumbled beneath her and the rope snapped. A scream tore from her throat as she fell into the well.

She was either going to save Annie from something that had already happened...or become a ghost herself.

Hana struck the cold water and found Annie simultaneously. She grabbed the surprisingly solid child in one arm and held a much-appreciated rope with the other. She remembered the rope snapping and shook her head. Without it, she and Annie would both have—

Don't think. Saving Annie was all that mattered.

She looked up. How far had she fallen? "Help," she shouted toward the top of the well, though her nearest neighbor was a mile away. She had to *try.* "Help!"

Shivering, Annie wrapped her arms around Hana's neck. *Do ghosts feel cold?* It didn't matter—Annie needed her. Hana held her even tighter, fearing the child might disappear again before she could get her out of the well.

"Annie?" A face peered down from the top, and the masculine voice brought with it a surge of hope. "You down there, girl?"

He's calling for Annie?

Hana hugged Annie. "It's all right, honey," she whispered, then turned her attention upward again. "We can't get out."

Their rescuer moved away from the opening, returning within a few seconds. "I'm sendin' down another rope."

The rope landed in the water and she forced herself to concentrate on tying it around Annie's waist. It was no easy task considering how tightly the child clung to her. Hana struggled with the wet rope as her teeth began to chatter along with Annie's.

"We're ready anytime."

A shudder swept through Hana. Was she reliving Annie's death? Was the man at the top of the well another ghost?

Sure. Patrick Swayze to the rescue.

She slammed a mental door on such thoughts. Far more urgent matters demanded her attention now. Like her life...and Annie's.

She gave Annie a reassuring hug. "Did you hear? That man's going to pull us out."

"Kayub," Annie whispered.

Hana must have misunderstood. She kissed the top of the girl's wet head, banishing the crazy notion. She tied a loop in the second rope, large enough for both her feet and soggy tennies. She stood in it and wrapped one arm around both ropes, and the other around Annie.

"Ready," she called, praying their mysterious savior didn't turn out to be more terrifying than a watery grave. Within moments, the ropes grew taut and slowly lifted them up the narrow shaft. Hana held her breath. When they were above the water, she allowed herself a sigh.

Annie wept pitifully until someone reached into the well and pulled her to safety. A second later, those same, very human, arms hauled Hana onto solid ground.

She landed on her rear with an undignified plop, her gaze darting around in search of Annie. Had she vanished again after everything Hana had done to save her?

"Where'd you come from?" The man hovered over her, his legs spread apart as he stared down at her in obvious disbelief.

Hana lifted her gaze from his heavy work boots, traveled upward beyond a pair of overalls and a blue shirt to a familiar face. For a few moments, shock snatched her ability to speak.

"You're Caleb Dawes," she whispered in disbelief.

The man's expression changed to astonishment. "How do you know me?"

Hana struggled to her feet. This couldn't be happening—was it a nightmare? Caleb Dawes was dead. Of course...so was Annie.

"Where's Annie?" Hana demanded. Annie had drowned in 1949. Hadn't she? *God, I'm so confused.* What was happening? "Where's Annie?"

An older woman came out the back door of the farmhouse with Annie wrapped in a blanket. "She's gonna be fine, thanks to you," the woman announced, smiling at Hana.

If other people could see Annie, that meant Hana wasn't crazy. Didn't it? A wave of dizziness enveloped her. Swaying, she reached for the nearest means of support—Caleb's muscular forearm. His other arm circled her waist, preventing her fall.

"Miss Daisy, I think this lady better lie down a spell." He swept Hana into his arms and followed the woman into the house.

Daisy?

Of course. She remembered the name from the article. Daisy Campbell—Annie's grandmother.

Hana was dizzy, but not unconscious, so she couldn't blame this on a dream. She'd never fainted in her life. This was pure nonsense. Insanity.

And this was *her* house.

Wasn't it? Looking around the clean, well-maintained kitchen, Hana had her doubts. Where were the bird droppings? The dust? This couldn't be real. Her throat was dry; her eyes stung.

"P-p-put me down," she said, but the big man simply shook his head. He certainly didn't look or feel like a ghost—or a killer.

"Not 'til Miss Daisy tells me where to put you."

"I reckon we'd best put her in the guest room." The older woman—who also couldn't be real—led them up the stairs. "I swan. How'd that child fall in the well? Caleb, you fix that cover today. I ain't got eyes in the back of my head, and it's a sure thing Mildred ain't gonna watch her."

"Yes'm."

Mildred—Annie's mother?

Had Annie fallen in the well—or been pushed? And what had happened to Hana's old, decrepit farmhouse?

She stifled a gasp when she found herself carried to the first of the bedrooms she'd investigated. It was lovely and bright with a nine-patch quilt on the bed. Lace curtains fluttered in the breeze at the open windows.

Windows that had been broken and boarded over when she'd last seen them....

"Now, you shoo, Caleb," Miss Daisy demanded. "Tell Mildred to try'n get some warm broth into Annie while I tend our guest."

"I'll see to it myself," Caleb said with a frown, taking the child in his strong arms.

Hana blinked at the big man. Could he be trusted with Annie? She took a deep breath to quell her rising panic as Daisy turned to face her.

"What's your name, child?" she asked, assisting Hana in removing her wet clothing.

"Hana." She bit her lower lip when the woman turned to remove a soft cotton nightgown from the trunk Hana'd looked inside of earlier. The empty trunk.

"Hana what?"

The woman politely turned her back while Hana slipped out of her wet undergarments and into the gown. The dry flannel felt wonderful against her clammy skin. "Gillespie."

Daisy patted Hana's shoulder, then turned back the quilt. "How can I thank you for savin' little Annie? You rest and I'll get you something warm if you ain't asleep before I get back."

Hana obeyed the woman's gentle pressure at her back and climbed into the bed.

Daisy pursed her lips and shook her head. "Some folks just don't understand. Just 'cuz Annie ain't perfect don't mean she ain't a blessin' like every other livin' soul."

Living soul?

Hana blinked back her stinging tears, relieved to hear that little Annie was—had been—loved and wanted. *Wait a minute. This is impossible, remember?*

She looked up at the middle-aged woman. It was time to face facts. This woman was Daisy Campbell. *But how?* "What...is the date, please?" Hana asked, holding her breath as she waited.

Daisy moved around the room, looking perplexed when she picked up Hana's soggy Reeboks.

"The date...*please?*"

The woman smiled indulgently. "July 19, 1949. You get some rest now."

Hana slowly opened her eyes. Gazing around the dark room, she wondered where she was—then remembered with a start.

"Oh, my God." She sat upright and clutched the nightgown at her throat. This wasn't a dream. Even in the dark, she realized she was still in the small bedroom at the farmhouse. How could this be?

After crawling from the comfortable bed, Hana rushed over to peer out the window. Moonlight bathed the lawn in silver. She swallowed convulsively at the tranquil scene—so familiar, yet so strange.

Two vintage automobiles occupied the circle drive. A tire swing hung like a dark sentinel from a huge tree she remembered as nothing more than a stump. She rested her forehead against the cool glass.

A figure—a woman—darted across the lawn and climbed into a car parked on the dark road. There was something clandestine about the entire scene. Was it Mildred? But Mildred was dead.

"Am I dead? Are they dead?" She raked her fingers through her hair and shook her head. "Is this all a dream?"

She crossed the room and turned the knob on the wall near the door. The lights illuminated the floral wallpaper she'd last seen hanging in shreds. The soft pinks and blues were bright and pretty, no evidence of time's passage.

Time.

Hana slumped to the floor and covered her face. Tears didn't come, though they'd be welcome relief at this point. She rocked back and forth for several minutes.

"It can't be true," she muttered.

A cool breeze wafted through the window, extricating her from her daze. With a shudder, she drew a deep breath and stood. She had to get out of here. "I need some air."

And a shrink.

Quietly, she tiptoed into the hall and down the stairs to the front door, which opened on well-oiled hinges. The night was perfect—cooler than any since she'd left Kansas City. Taking a deep breath, Hana stepped off the porch and into the damp grass.

Okay. This isn't a dream and I'm not dead. What's left?

Insanity?

She chuckled out loud and continued her stroll toward the old barn she'd planned to have torn down. But here it stood, whole and perfect, silhouetted against the night sky. Mocking her. More proof.

Taking a deep, calming breath, Hana resumed her pace around the edge of the barn toward the fields. Despite the darkness, she needed to feel the wide open spaces surrounding her.

After stepping in something warm and squashy, she realized how foolish it was to traipse across a barnyard with bare feet—in the dark, no less.

"Oh, yuck." Hana backed up, wiping the manure off on the damp grass, then ran smack into something warm and solid.

And laughing.

She turned so quickly she nearly lost her balance, but he reached out to steady her. His grip on her upper arms was warm and strong. She wasn't frightened, even though she knew the impossible identity of the man who had his arms around her in the middle of the night.

In 1949.

She looked up at his face, a face that didn't resemble a murderer's in the least. Moonlight reflected off his blond curls, and his smile was plainly visible. Other than that, his features were a vague blur of light and dark. "Caleb," she whispered.

His smile faded, but his hands didn't move. "Who are you?" he asked softly, his voice melodic and unthreatening. "How do you know my name?"

Hana swallowed, staring at his face. A murderer? *This* man? Impossible. He'd saved Annie...and her.

He tilted his head to the side. "Miss Daisy said your name's Hana."

She nodded, wondering why his touch should feel so...powerful. Men hadn't been a big part of her life. She'd dedicated herself to her career, rarely finding time to even date. Was she so inexperienced that a simple thing like this could spark her libido?

Get a grip, Hana.

She recalled having seen Mildred—or rather a woman she'd assumed was her—leaving the house earlier to climb into an automobile for a midnight rendezvous. Obviously not with this man. Additional testimony of Caleb's innocence? If he wasn't involved with Mildred, then he had no motive to harm Annie. For some reason Hana was relieved that the evidence pointed away from this gentle, handsome man.

Suddenly, she realized something even more important. Annie was *alive*. And that miracle was because of this man's strong arms and her own recklessness. Relief flooded her. She smiled so suddenly it took even her by surprise.

"Annie's alive," she said in awe. "Thank you, thank you, thank you." Overcome with joy and relief, she threw her arms around Caleb's neck and kissed him.

He slid his arms around her and tugged her against him while his mouth returned her impromptu kiss with a raw, primitive hunger that seized her breath.

Hana's shock was quickly followed by a swift surge of yearning.

Her legs became rubber bands, and her belly tightened into a coil of blatant need.

She *should* be offended. He was bold. Impudent.

Marvelous.

Hana suddenly became aware of her state of undress, and the way her body molded against his. Intimately. *What am I doing?* Resurrecting her sanity, she pulled herself free and stared down at his tanned hand resting against the stark white nightgown at her waist.

Her face flooded with heat as she continued to stare at his hand. "Stop," she whispered, as much to herself as to him.

He stepped away, his magical hands falling to his sides. They stood staring at one another while the sound of their ragged breathing filled the night.

What had come over her? Hana Gillespie had never done anything so impetuous. She was vulnerable right now. Today's events tumbled over again in her mind. Her nerves were raw. She felt...exposed.

"I think you'd better go wash your foot," he whispered raggedly. "Before I forget my manners again."

"My foot?" Hana looked down, wondering why she should be concerned about her foot when the rest of her body ached for something she must deny it. Then she remembered and raced to the house as fast as she dared, since the moon had set and left her in a dark, lonely world.

A strange world...and an even stranger time.

She paused in the front yard to let her breathing slow as her pulse pounded. She wiped her foot in the damp grass again. The sound of a vehicle stopping out by the road made her dart behind the porch railing.

She heard a masculine chuckle from the vicinity of the road, but no telltale headlights shone in the darkness. Mildred's lover was being very cautious.

Hana remained hidden near the trellis, hoping she wouldn't be seen. The woman she assumed was Mildred stopped to remove her shoes, then quietly entered the house. The car drove away a minute later.

A well-orchestrated rendezvous.

Hana released a ragged breath and turned toward the house. Unless she wanted to explain her own nocturnal behavior, Hana needed to make certain Mildred was upstairs in her room before she went in herself.

But a lone figure caught and commanded her attention as she turned. An imposing figure, he stood in the field between the house and barn, staring toward the road. The fading moonlight distinguished the man's light hair.

Caleb Dawes.

Hana groaned and opened her eyes. Sunlight flooded the bedroom, shimmering through the snowy lace curtains to land in geometric patterns across the polished wood floor.

At least it was morning this time. But it was still 1949.

I'm not crazy. I'm not dreaming. This is real.

Completing her affirmations, Hana rubbed her head and swung her legs over the edge of the bed, struggling into a sitting position. Standing, she stretched and yawned.

The door opened just a crack, then Hana noticed the small hand gripping its edge just before a blond pigtail swung into the opening. After another moment, Annie's face followed, her blue eyes wide and curious.

"Hello, Annie," Hana said warmly, overjoyed to see the little girl alive.

The child came the rest of the way into the room. She wore a blue calico dress with black leather shoes. Her face was clean and shining pink, the blond braids neatly secured with ribbons.

Annie's fingers were in her mouth as she smiled at Hana. "Who you?" she mumbled.

"Don't you remember?" Hana frowned, then realized that the Annie who'd known her had been a ghost. A chill swept through her as she considered how very close the darling little girl had come to never seeing this new day. "I'm Hana."

"Hana," she repeated. "Annie." She pointed at herself, then swung left and right as she continued to stare at Hana with that impish grin.

She's alive, and she's going to stay that way. Hana couldn't begin to explain her fierce need to protect Annie. It was a simple fact—and, she decided, the reason she was here.

She needed facts to help her protect Annie. For one thing, who had Mildred been sneaking out to meet last night?

Jeez. I've fallen into an Agatha Christie novel.

Would the person who pushed Annie try again?

Shocked by her own bizarre thoughts, Hana reached out to touch Annie's shoulder, needing reassurance that the child was, in fact, alive. She mustn't permit her fears to transmit to Annie.

"So, Annie, do you know where your grandma hid my clothes?" Hana asked.

Annie walked over to the trunk and pointed. Hana followed and lifted the lid. Yesterday, in Hana's time, this trunk had held only photo albums and an old Bible. Now there were several old dresses, a pair of overalls, another nightgown, and a few undergarments that more closely resembled items one might expect to find in a torture chamber.

Voices raised in obvious disagreement reached Hana's ears. Two women—Mildred and Daisy, no doubt—were involved in a heated argument. She chewed her lower lip and cocked her head to listen.

Their words weren't discernible, and after a few moments the front door slammed. Remembering Annie, Hana glanced down at the little girl. Her blue eyes were wide and her lower lip trembled.

Hana knelt beside the child and tentatively pulled her into her arms. Annie hesitated for only a moment, then clung to Hana's neck and wept on her shoulder. "Don't cry, punkin'. It's all right."

Hana straightened and carried Annie to the edge of the bed. She sat there for several minutes, waiting for the child's tears to cease. It felt so right to hold this little girl. Fulfillment and contentment threatened to destroy all her efforts at logic. Annie's hair had a clean, little girl scent to it. Her small body was warm and filled a deep void in Hana's heart—a need she planned to fill by adopting.

"Well, I'd better get dressed," Hana said.

A short time later, Annie and Hana went downstairs to the kitchen. Daisy looked up from a letter clutched in her hands. Her eyes were red and puffy when she glanced up at Hana, and she stuffed the letter into her apron pocket.

Hana's gaze swept the tidy room, quite modern by 1949 standards. A Frigidaire hummed away in the corner, and the wood floor gleamed. A monstrous stove took up most of the far wall, and a huge sink sat beneath a square window. Arthur Godfrey's voice boomed to housewives across America from a radio.

The back door opened and Caleb came into the kitchen smiling. "How's my Annie this mornin'?"

The child flew into his arms and he whirled her in a circle. Hana watched them, knowing beyond any doubt that this man would never harm Annie. Yet, in the first history, he'd been executed for her murder.

Hana's journey through time had saved more than one life. She bit her lower lip and released a slow breath. None of this made sense....

Daisy hurried around the kitchen, and a few moments later, a huge breakfast filled the table. "Sit and eat before it gets cold."

Remembering the way she'd responded to Caleb's kiss, Hana avoided his gaze as she sat opposite him with Annie at her side. Daisy filled the coffee cups and poured a glass of milk for Annie, then took a seat.

"Hana, would you be willin' to stay on and help with Annie?"

As if she had anywhere else to go. Hana smiled and said, "I'd like that."

"Good," Daisy said. "Stay as long as you're willing. I'm gonna need the help."

The woman had a distant expression in her eyes. Why had she been crying earlier? Hana didn't want her to be unhappy. Daisy Campbell was a good woman who loved Annie.

As did Hana.

She glanced across the table at Caleb, whose gaze rested on her with warmth and something more that stole her breath. He turned his gaze to Annie and winked. "You gonna help me feed that ornery mule after breakfast?" he asked the girl.

Annie giggled and nodded. She held up some fingers and counted to three.

"Yep, he gets three scoops," Caleb said. "Good, Annie."

Hana's heart warmed as she watched the exchange between the man and Annie. How could anyone have ever believed him guilty of killing a child he so obviously adored?

They're both alive now. Hana sipped her coffee, vowing to keep them that way.

Hana bolted upright in bed, drenched in sweat. She scrambled from the bed and paced the room, raking her fingers through her hair. Then she heard it. Annie's voice crying out in her head, just like—

"Oh, God." Hana ran from her room and down the stairs to the back door. "Annie!" she shouted, racing toward the well, reminding herself that Caleb had sealed the well at Daisy's insistence.

Logic be damned—she heard Annie scream again just as the clouds parted and moonlight beamed on that wretched well like a spotlight.

The uncovered well.

"Annie!" Hana grabbed the rope and peered into the well. "Hold onto the rope, Annie."

"Mama!"

Hana had to save her. She shouted toward the house again for help. How had Annie—

Thwap. Something heavy slammed into Hana's shoulder and she fell down the narrow shaft. "Annie!"

The water felt like a million needles against her skin, and her wet nightgown dragged her under. She found Annie's arm and pulled them both to the surface, scrambling for the rope. Shivering, she held the choking but breathing child and clung to the rope.

Hana gulped in a breath to shout, then realized someone was standing over the well. Laughing.

The killer.

Would Annie *and* Hana drown this time? *No.* Tears swelled in Hana's eyes, but she blinked them back. The moonlight vanished as the killer slid the cover in place. Hana screamed and Annie cried.

They were being sealed alive in the well.

God help us.

Caleb heard the screams and raced from his bed and across the field toward the house. *Annie.* His little girl.

A car sped away as he neared the house, the lights vanishing down the dusty road. "Annie!"

He ran to the back door, but a muffled sound stayed him. His blood turned cold as he faced the well. The clouds shifted and the moon illuminated the cover he'd placed over it just yesterday. Nothing seemed amiss. Maybe he'd imagined the sound.

Still, something drew him to the well, and as he approached, he realized the cover wasn't latched, and it sat off-center. The muffled cry came again. Within seconds, he had the cover off and peered into the deep, black pit. "Annie?"

"Help us."

"Hana?" He didn't wait for her answer, but ran to fetch another rope. He shouted into the house for Miss Daisy, who joined him to help pull Hana and Annie to safety again.

Shivering and sobbing, they were both on dry ground again with his arms wrapped around them before he stopped to think. "What happened?" he asked, allowing Miss Daisy to take Annie and wrap her in a warm blanket.

"Talk inside," Miss Daisy said, carrying Annie into the house without waiting for an answer.

"Thank you," Hana said as he led her into the kitchen.

Miss Daisy had hot cocoa in front of Annie before she joined them at the table. "Now tell us what happened," she said to Hana.

"Something woke me." She looked at Annie, who had stopped shivering and crying now and seemed content with slurping her cocoa. "A nightmare."

"You saved Annie again," Caleb said. "I don't know how you knew, but—"

"I know how," Miss Daisy said, pulling two folded pieces of paper from her pocket. "This here's a letter from Mildred. She's gone and ain't comin' back." The woman's voice trembled. "She told me this morning that her lover wanted her to send Annie away. That he wouldn't marry her otherwise. That's when she told me she had to go away, because she wanted to marry him, but she was afraid he'd hurt..." Miss Daisy turned her gaze on Annie.

"Good Lord." Caleb glanced at Annie, who wasn't listening, thank goodness.

"Someone pushed me," Hana said. "Do you...think it was her lover?"

Miss Daisy nodded and bit her lower lip. "Yes."

"I saw a car just before I heard you scream," Caleb said, clenching his fist. "I'm gonna call the sheriff."

Miss Daisy agreed, but said it could wait until morning. Mildred and her lover were gone now, and Annie was safe. Then she looked at Caleb and gave him a sad smile.

"Mildred told me somethin' else," she said.

Caleb studied the older woman's face, realizing she knew the truth. He reached for her hand and squeezed it. "I wanted to tell you, Miss Daisy, but Mildred made me believe she'd send Annie away if I did."

"No child could ask for a better daddy, Caleb," Miss Daisy said, a tear trickling down her wrinkled cheek. "Maybe I lost a daughter today, but I think I got me a son instead. You'll stay?"

He looked at his daughter, who grinned through a cocoa mustache. "There's no place I'd rather be."

He felt and met Hana's gaze. Tears sparkled in her lashes and her dark hair had dried in tiny curls around her face. Right now she and Annie were the most beautiful people he'd ever seen. His heart felt tight in his chest and his throat clogged.

"That's settled then." Miss Daisy turned her attention to Hana. "And you're a guardian angel."

"Guardian angel?" Hana gave a nervous laugh and rubbed Annie's back.

Miss Daisy produced another piece of paper and handed it to Hana, who took it with trembling fingers. "Where did you get this?" Hana asked, her eyes wide.

"What is it?"

"Nothin' for you to worry about, Caleb," Miss Daisy said steadily. "It's between us womenfolk."

"You knew?" Hana asked, passing the piece of paper back to Miss Daisy.

"Like I said, you're Annie's guardian angel, child."

"What are you going to do with that?" Hana asked, a slight tremor in her voice.

Caleb didn't know what was happening, but he knew it was important. He reached across the table and took Hana's hand in his, giving it a firm squeeze. There was something powerful about his feelings for this woman. All he knew for certain was that he couldn't let her leave.

Miss Daisy rose and faced them all. "You both gonna stay here with Annie?" she asked in a no-nonsense tone.

Caleb nodded, knowing he could finally claim his daughter as his own. "Even President Truman couldn't drag me away from here now."

Miss Daisy smiled and said, "Praise be." Then she turned to Hana again, the folded piece of paper held in both her hands. "Hana...?"

Hana looked at Caleb with something burning in her eyes that made his heart do a little flip-flop in his chest, then she glanced down at Annie. When she looked up at Miss Daisy again, she drew a deep breath and said, "I'm here for a reason."

"That you are, child." Miss Daisy was still smiling when she tossed the folded paper into the stove where the glowing embers devoured it.

"Stowy," Annie said, yawning.

Hana gathered Caleb's little girl into her arms and looked up at him, "Tonight," she promised, "and forever."

Dearly Beloved

D. R. Meredith

Highwater, Texas, population 455, dozed in the shade of its own history. The town began as a division headquarters for the XIT Ranch in the Texas panhandle, considered the largest ranch anywhere ever, but according to the late Jake Palmer, when the XIT started selling off land at the turn of the last century, Highwater couldn't make it as an independent city. Everyone agreed that Jake exaggerated, because at no time in its history did Highwater qualify as a city. Village was more like it. Oh, it still had a post office, a small room on the west side of Highwater Grocery, where Butch Jones, the proprietor, was also the postmaster. There was always some argument down at Buddy's Café during the ten o'clock coffee hour that the postmaster ought to be somebody besides Butch. In a town the size of Highwater, you wanted to spread out the employment as much as possible. Butch already owned Highwater Grocery. It wasn't fair that he earn a salary as postmaster besides. There were whispers that Butch had turned Democrat just so he could get the appointment, but nobody wanted to insult Butch by asking him.

The ranchers and farmers and what businessmen as Highwater had that met every day at Buddy's listened closely to everything political Butch had to say to see if they could catch him supporting the administration in Washington. Highwater had voted Republican ever since Roosevelt declared a bank holiday, and First State Bank of Highwater closed its doors never to reopen them. The idea that one of their own would bolt Lincoln's party purely for the money was nearly more than Highwater could stomach, or at least those who met at Buddy's, which was everybody who mattered, meaning everybody who owned a business or land or had managed to stay out of bankruptcy court. They all knew that another bad drought like the 1950s, or one bad winter like the one back in 1886–87, and they were done for. So there was a smidgen of envy mixed in with principle whenever Highwater thought about Butch Jones being on the federal payroll as well as being proprietor of Highwater's only grocery store. Whatever the weather or the commodity markets did, Butch could always fall back on his government paycheck while the rest of the folks in Highwater and Bonham County would be hung out to dry. It stuck in Highwater's craw that it was so.

Butch Jones, his shadowy political affiliations, and his government check was the first topic of conversation whenever Butch missed the ten o'clock coffee hour—which was around the first of every month. Everybody figured he drove to Amarillo to get his check cashed instead of going to the bank in Troutman at the other end of the county like everyone else did when they had financial business. It was just one more way of thumbing his nose at Highwater, according to Buddy, who owned Buddy's Café where the coffee klatch met, and was therefore listened to with respect. By doing his banking in Amarillo, Butch put himself out of the reach of the local grapevine. One way or another, the ten o'clock coffee hour usually found out what a man had in his checking account and sometimes his saving account, too, if he did his banking in Troutman or one of the other towns near Highwater. "Information by osmosis," is what Sheriff Jim Hayworth called it, since every teller and every bank officer denied disclosing any information about any bank customer whomsoever, yet details seemed to float like the gossamer down from a cottonwood tree to be snatched out of the air by the men sitting at the round table by the front window in Buddy's Café at the south end of Main Street.

One woman sat at the round table—and she by special invitation of Buddy. But Elizabeth Walker had no illusions about why she was the only woman in Highwater history to be accorded the privilege of joining the coffee hour. She was there because she was the first elected official of the female persuasion. She was the Justice of the Peace for the Highwater end of Bonham County, and that made her a woman to be reckoned with. When investigating a death, she and not the sheriff or the commissioners' court or anybody else was in charge of the body and the evidence. Not until she determined the cause of death—natural causes, accident, suicide, homicide—was the case turned over to the sheriff. The fact was, Elizabeth had too much power to be excluded from the coffee circle. No one, including Buddy, was ever quite sure what Elizabeth might do if left to her own devices, so better to invite her into the circle than leave her out. That way they could keep an eye on her. Besides, now that she was an elected official, she had to be taught how the system worked, being that she was a woman and had no experience with public office and local government. They conveniently forgot the civic organizations that Elizabeth had been president of at one time or another, and that had, under her leadership, wrested town improvements out of the commissioners' court, frequently against the will of individual commissioners. Those were ladies' clubs and not on a par with elected officials.

"I don't see Butch Jones here this morning," said D. B. DeBord, a county commissioner forty-five of his eighty years.

"Reckon he's gone into Amarillo to cash his postmaster's check," said Buddy in a loud voice. D. B. had gotten hard of hearing the past year, so everybody had to speak up or get chewed out by D. B. for mumbling.

"I knowed Butch's granddaddy as well as I know my own name," said D. B. "I don't know what he'd think about the way Butch is carrying on."

"Somebody has to be the postmaster, D. B.," said Elizabeth, sipping her coffee and occasionally meeting the eyes of the sheriff. Lord have mercy, but there was no telling what her own granddaddy would have said about her own carryings on.

D. B.'s bristly white eyebrows drew together like they did every time somebody disagreed with him. "Don't have to be him. Plenty of people in Highwater could use a cushion like a government check. Ed and Jewel Carruthers sure could."

Everybody sipped their coffee and thought about the Carrutherses. Ed and Jewell had bought a quarter section—one hundred and sixty acres—after WWI. Everybody shook their heads at such foolishness. There was no way to make a living on a quarter of a section out in the western panhandle, not when the average ranch ran close to a hundred sections, and a farm, what few there were in Bonham County, averaged five sections. With little rain and hardly any surface water, a man had to dig wells and put up windmills just to water his cattle. But Ed Carruthers fooled everybody. He dug a well, put in Bonham County's first irrigation system, and raised vegetables that he sold to independent grocers. Nobody figured Ed and Jewell were making a killing, but they were sure making a living on that little quarter section.

"Ed and Jewel are close to eighty, D. B., if not already there," said Elizabeth, feeling just put out enough to start a fight. "And they live fifteen miles out in the country. Do you want to drive fifteen miles to pick up your mail? And they're too old to sit all day in that little room Butch has fixed up in the grocery store."

"I beg your pardon, missy, but I'm eighty myself and I ain't ready to put up the plow—and neither is Ed Carruthers," said D. B., his eyebrows now a solid bristly line above his eyes. "I seen him just the other day driving toward his place with a pickup full of lumber, so I guess he's fixing to build something, and if he's fixing to build something, then he's still got starch in his britches."

"That was last month, D. B.," said Buddy. "You seen him driving through town last month with lumber in his pickup. Yesterday you saw him drive through with something wrapped up and tied down in the bed of his pickup. Haven't figured out yet what it was, but it was awful damn heavy. His pickup was riding low to the ground."

D. B. flushed red. His memory had been slipping the last year or so, never about anything important, but he did tend to get his times mixed up—like the Saturday he went to the First Baptist Church thinking it was Sunday. "That's what I meant when I said the other day. That can mean last month same as it can mean yesterday."

"What do you suppose he's building?" asked Elizabeth.

"Well, how would I know?" asked D. B. in a testy voice. "Why don't you go out there and ask him if you're so curious?"

Elizabeth pushed back her chair and stood up. "I think I will. Ed and Jewel haven't been in church for a while, and since they have no family, somebody ought to check on them. Ed doesn't have any business climbing ladders or hammering, nailing, and sawing. And he doesn't have any business being postmaster either. His eyes are so bad, he really shouldn't be driving, much less trying to make out strange handwriting on an envelope. He and Jewel are really self-sufficient with their own water well and generator for electricity, and they have Social Security and Medicare. They don't need another government check."

"Any time you think Social Security pays for more than beans and flour, you're mistaken, Miss Elizabeth," said D. B. "Just ask any of us oldsters."

"I know about living close, D. B.," said Elizabeth. "Don't think I don't."

Embarrassed, D. B. looked down at the red-and-black-checked oilcloth on the round table. "My apologies, Elizabeth. I didn't mean to bring up hurtful subjects."

Elizabeth drew a deep breath to ease the sick feeling in her stomach. Her husband had died without insurance, without money, and without a will. Elizabeth was forced to sell most of her cattle and lease out half her ranch, and still wasn't through paying the inheritance taxes. That's why she had run for justice of the peace. Just like Butch Jones and the Carruthers, she needed a check just to get by.

She patted D. B.'s arm. "Don't worry about it. Everybody knows my situation. I shouldn't be so sensitive about it."

"In Highwater we all know one another's situations," said Buddy, "but we try not to talk about them. That's what good neighbors do. They help but they don't talk about it, and a whole lot they overlook because that's best." That was Buddy's way of apologizing for D. B. DeBord, and reassuring Elizabeth that nobody would allude to her finances again.

Elizabeth knew that she would find a vase of D. B.'s prize roses in front of her office door at the courthouse come tomorrow. That's what

men of his generation did when they hurt a lady's feelings. Not that
her feelings were hurt, exactly. She always felt sick to her stomach
whenever she thought of her finances. But today she was feeling contrary, and couldn't figure out why. Something was out of place in her
world and she didn't know what it was.

"Believe I'll go with you, Elizabeth," said Jim Hayworth, grabbing
his Stetson off the coat rack and following her out the door.

Jim Hayworth had been sheriff of Bonham County twenty-five of
his fifty years, and was nearly as whipcord lean and firm of flesh as
the day he got home from Vietnam if you ignored a little slackness
about the jaw—and Elizabeth Walker did. Lord knows, at forty-three
she had lines around the eyes and her chin wasn't as firm as it once
was and the forces of gravity were liable to attack her bosom any day,
so who was she to demand that a man have abs like steel? Of course,
chances were any man with a washboard belly didn't get it by working in Highwater, and Elizabeth had as much use for a glutton as she
did for a man who spent the majority of his time perfecting his manly
figure instead of using his brain and muscles to accomplish something that needed done.

Jim Hayworth was neither a glutton nor a fitness freak. He was a
man who worked hard at his job as sheriff and as a rancher in his off-
hours. Either one of those jobs kept you strong, but didn't necessarily
sculpt your body. Elizabeth didn't care. She would take Jim Hayworth
as he was, gray in his hair and gray on his chest when he whipped his
shirt off those days he came for supper and stayed for breakfast—
which was a couple times a week, or less frequently depending on
circumstances. She supposed everybody in Highwater knew exactly
when Jim stayed and when he didn't, despite the fact that Elizabeth
lived ten miles outside of Highwater, five of it dirt road meandering
across the prairie until it circled in front of her ranch house. But
nobody said anything, and as long as nobody said anything, then
she didn't plan on changing her ways. She was two years a widow,
and Jim had lost his wife some years before that, so it wasn't like he
was hanging his pants on another man's bedpost. He was her husband's best friend, and now he was hers, and they were best friends
who sometimes carried on a little. It wasn't anyone's business but hers
and Jim's, but Elizabeth didn't underestimate Highwater's interest in

the goings-on of their elected officials. Elizabeth figured it wouldn't be long before somebody mentioned that she and Jim were keeping too close company. Highwater was a town in which the word *seemly* was still in vogue.

She and Jim walked shoulder to shoulder toward the courthouse at the north end of Main Street where their pickups were parked. "I'll follow you to the Carruthers, and then maybe follow you home," said Jim in his slow, deep voice that always sent chills up her spine and set fire to her belly even though she figured she was old enough to be immune to those sorts of feelings. "I can throw a couple of steaks on your grill and help you set the table."

"How much setting does the table need for two people?" she asked with a sidelong look at him. "I figure I can handle it."

He leaned over and whispered in her ear. "Then how about I help you do a little house cleaning, maybe change the bed."

She felt the fire burning hotter in her belly. "I put on fresh sheets this morning."

He grinned at her, like Sam Elliott grinning at Katherine Ross in *Conagher*, and Elizabeth thought she might burn up from instantaneous combustion. "I meant I'd help you do a little housework tomorrow morning."

She wondered if he had any idea how lethal his grin and his voice were. She would hate to think that he did. It would take away from what they shared, and put her in the position of being seduced. She didn't much like that idea.

"What do you really think of me, Jim?"

He lost his grin and looked somber. "You make me hotter than any man my age ought to be, but that ain't the reason I like coming home with you." He grimaced. "That's a lie. I like you setting me on fire, but I like the way you warm me up when how we feel won't send us running to the bedroom. I feel comfortable with you, Elizabeth. You warm me down to the bone until I think I won't ever be cold and lonely again. And when I go home alone, I catch myself talking to you like you were there with me, telling you about my day and how I plan to spend the evening."

He fell silent and walked along with her past the vacant block where the Highwater Hotel stood before it burned down in 1928, and burned most of the town's aspirations with it. "That's as close as I can come to what I feel, Elizabeth. I ain't no Shakespeare. The words don't roll out of my mouth like diamond solitaires to make any talk between us sparkle."

There, in front of Highwater Grocery and Phil's Hardware and Variety Store, she raised up on her toes and kissed the sheriff on the mouth, and she took her time about it, too. If people were going to talk about her, then she would give them something to talk about besides her finances. "You might want to wipe your mouth unless you like strawberry cream lipstick," she said after breaking off the kiss.

Jim licked his lips, then pulled a handkerchief out of his pocket and wiped his mouth. "Always wondered why you tasted so much like strawberries." He tucked his handkerchief back in his pocket and opened the pickup door for her. "You know you gave the gossips enough to talk about for the next year. What do you say to that, Elizabeth?"

She slid into her pickup and rolled down the window so she could talk to him. "To quote my younger son, some folks in Highwater need to get a life, maybe take up watercolor or needlepoint. You'll follow me to the Carruthers place?"

Jim rubbed his jaw and looked off in the distance past the courthouse. "I been thinking about that, Elizabeth. Why don't you let me go out to see about Ed and Jewel. I think Ed would take a visit from me better than from you. Remember, Ed's kind of standoffish around any woman except Jewel. He thinks she hung the moon and the stars." He met her eyes, his a guileless blue. "Why don't you go get that table set while I see about the Carruthers?"

The fire abruptly went out in her belly. His eyes were too guileless, and she suspected he was trying to keep her from going to the Carruthers. Maybe if he had just asked her, she would have let him do it, but not now. "I don't like somebody trying to soften me up to get their own way, Jim. You can follow me to the Carruthers place, then follow me home for dinner, but don't count on anything else. I can change my own bed when it needs it, thank you very much, and it won't need changing for at least a week."

"Walt always said you could dig in your heels worse than a Missouri mule when it suited you," began Jim.

"Nice of you to tell me that my late husband was talking about me behind my back."

Jim looked exasperated. "God Almighty, Elizabeth, Walt told you that to your face. I heard him say it on several occasions. What's gotten into you today? You're snipping at everybody."

Elizabeth couldn't answer him because she didn't know what was wrong except that her intuition was telling her something was, but she could no more tell Jim why she thought so than she could fly. Feminine intuition was like that: reliable but inexplicable. "Why don't you want me going to the Carruthers place?"

"I never said I didn't want you going. I just said I'd run by if you were worried, but the fact is, Elizabeth, I was just out at Ed's place a couple of days ago. Ed's fine, but Jewel is laid up. MS is what the doctors told Ed. She spends a lot of time sleeping, according to Ed, and he said he could take care of her without any help, but I called the home health nurse anyway. She's going to check in twice a week to make sure Ed's managing."

"Why didn't you just tell me that to start with, Jim, instead of leading me down the garden path with talk about how hot I make you?"

"That was the truth, Elizabeth, and it doesn't have anything to do with the Carruthers. Maybe I was pushing a little hard about staying the night, but Lord Almighty, I don't need much of an excuse to do that."

"I'm going to go see the Carruthers for myself, Jim. You can come if you want to," Elizabeth said, rolling up her window and turning the ignition. She deliberately didn't look at Jim because she didn't want to see any expression on his face that might disillusion her further.

He followed her to the Carruthers'—she saw his pickup in the rearview mirror—but she resolutely kept her eyes on the narrow two-lane highway running arrow-straight through the prairie to the New Mexico border, glancing every now and then at the wildflowers along the road. The yuccas with their dagger-sharp leaves and beautiful long stalks of cream-colored flowers were in bloom. Black-eyed Susans and Indian blankets covered the earth in red, orange, and yellow tapestries. Indian paintbrushes with their brightly colored tips were scattered among them, looking like they had been dipped in red paint. By the time she turned off the highway and onto the Carruthers place, she felt better; in fact, she felt ashamed of herself for being so contrary with Jim, but too stubborn to turn back.

Elizabeth parked in front of the Carruthers' small, one-story frame farmhouse, and slid out of the truck. She knew for a fact that the house had three bedrooms, two for the children Ed and Jewel had wanted but never had. When Jewel reached menopause, and she and Ed knew for a fact there would be no late pregnancy as they had hoped, Jewel turned one bedroom into an office for Ed. The other she kept as a guest room, although to Elizabeth's knowledge, no guest had ever stayed under the Carruthers' roof. Elizabeth wondered how Jewel could have stood walking by those two empty bedrooms through all her childbearing years, always hoping for a miracle, always wondering who was at fault: her or Ed. More likely they believed children were a gift from God, and not a result of properly functioning reproductive organs, because Elizabeth had never caught a hint of a sour spot in the Carruthers' marriage. In fact, they acted so much like newlyweds that Elizabeth always expected to hear the echoes of "Dearly Beloved" whenever she was around them.

Jim parked his truck next to hers and joined her at the Carruthers' front door. Elizabeth knocked and called out, "Mr. Carruthers, it's Elizabeth Walker and Sheriff Hayworth."

The door opened and Ed Carruthers stepped outside on the porch. At past eighty he was a tall, stately looking man with silver-white hair and dark blue eyes, and must have been handsome in his younger days. "Elizabeth, Sheriff, what brings you out this way?"

His eyes were red-rimmed as though he had been crying, logical if his beloved wife had multiple sclerosis, thought Elizabeth. Soon her care would be beyond him even with the help of the home health nurse.

"Elizabeth got a bee in her bonnet because you and Jewel haven't made it to church lately," said Jim. "Nothing would do but for her to come out and check on you folks."

Elizabeth felt foolish, and because she felt foolish she wouldn't give in gracefully. That was part of her makeup and it used to drive Walt crazy, but she couldn't help it. Her stubbornness had solved some crimes in Crawford County that had been overlooked in the past. Not that she thought there was a crime here, she assured herself, but she just wanted to make sure everything was *right*.

"How is Jewel?" Elizabeth asked.

Ed Carruthers turned to Jim with a terrified look. "What does she mean?"

Jim laid his hand on Ed's shoulder. "I told her about Jewel having multiple sclerosis, and that she was spending a lot of time sleeping. I'm sorry but I had to tell her, Ed, or she might have led a platoon of the First Baptist Ladies' Missionary Society out here. Either that or she would have accused you of murder. You know she's done that on occasion, accused other people of murder, that is."

"I'm not accusing Ed of murder," said Elizabeth through gritted teeth. She wished Jim hadn't jumped in with an explanation as to why they had come. She would have liked to hear what Ed had to say without Jim's prompting.

"Of course, you're not," said Jim, seeming not to see her glaring at him.

"May I see Jewel?" asked Elizabeth. "I feel badly that she was so sick and I didn't know a thing about it. I didn't even notice obvious symptoms in her motor skills or speech."

"She is sleeping," said Ed. "Sometimes it's hard to wake her up and she is disturbed when I do."

"Disturbed how?"

"She doesn't make much sense, Elizabeth," said Jim. "Leave her alone, and leave Ed alone, too."

"I don't want you to bother a sick woman on my account," said Elizabeth. "I'm sorry I bothered you. Give Jewel my best when she wakes up." She turned and walked down the porch steps before turning. "By the way, Ed, what are you building?"

"Beg pardon?" asked Ed, his face blank.

"Everybody at Buddy's was talking about you driving through town with a load of lumber in the bed of your pickup. I just wondered what you were building, and if it wouldn't be best to have someone help you."

"I'm building shelves in the storm cellar," said Ed.

Elizabeth nodded and climbed in her pickup and drove off. She noticed Jim staying and talking to Ed Carruthers and wondered if they were getting their stories straight, because as sure as God made little green apples, Ed's story was full of knotholes. For one thing, MS generally hit women between the ages of twenty and forty, and by eighty they would either be dead or totally bedridden. Jim's wife, Carolyn, had died of multiple sclerosis, so Elizabeth supposed that's where that part of the story came from.

Elizabeth parked in front of her house, a two-story ranch with a wraparound porch and hitching rails still in place. She hurried into the house and consulted the phone book, then dialed a number while keeping her eye on the long dirt road that led up her house. She would see Jim coming long before he arrived by the cloud of dust his pickup stirred up.

She turned her attention to the phone when someone picked up on the other end. "Yes, hello, this is Justice of the Peace Elizabeth Walker. I was just checking to see if the home health nurse could possibly visit Ed and Jewel Carruthers more often than twice a week. They are such an elderly couple and the wife has MS. What did you say? You have no record of home health visiting the Carruthers at all? Sheriff Jim Hayworth was supposed to call, but something must have delayed him. Do I want to order the nurse to visit? No, I think I had better talk it over with the sheriff first."

Elizabeth hung up and began to pace the long living room with its old-fashioned furniture. Jim lied about the home health nurse, and Ed Carruthers lied about the shelves in his storm cellar, too. She and the other ladies of the Missionary Society had been in Ed and Jewel's storm cellar when they were helping Jewel last fall. The cellar already had shelves on all four walls. So that was two lies the men had told, and she would bet her bottom dollar that they had lied about the MS, too. There was no point in asking liars to repeat their lies. She would have to get to the bottom of this case another way, and the first thing she had to do was find Jewel Carruthers and talk to her—if she was still alive, and Elizabeth bet she was because Jim Hayworth would never cover up a murder. But knowing that, why was she so dead set on knowing what was going on? Because her best friend lied to her and she wanted to know why, or she would never trust him again or let him in her bed, either. And she didn't think she could stand dismissing him from her life.

After a tense meal, Jim dialed his answering machine at the courthouse to see if all was well in Bonham County. Elizabeth could have
told him it wasn't, but she didn't intend to tell him anything until she
ferreted out the truth. Then she would confront him, him and Ed
Carruthers both.

Jim hung up the phone and picked up his hat. "I gotta run, Elizabeth. One of the messages was from the XIT Bar. Eddie Gomez and
John Turley are liquored up and talking big. I figure I can get there
before the fighting gets started good and throw a loop around the two
of them and lock 'em up until they sober up. Then I guess I'll go
home. I don't figure there's any need in coming back here."

"You know when to take a hint," said Elizabeth, handing him his hat.

As soon as she could no longer see his taillights, she got into her
pickup and drove to the Carruthers place, parking halfway down the
long dirt road leading to the house. Grabbing a flashlight, she
climbed out of the pickup and began walking toward the house,
thankful that she hadn't noticed any dogs that afternoon. No lights
shone in the house, and Ed's old Ford pickup was parked close to the
barn. Elizabeth hesitated and wondered if she was being foolish.
Maybe Jewel did have MS and Ed really was building shelves in the
storm cellar. And maybe Jim just told her about the home health
nurse to keep her calm. But why would he do that? And why did Ed
need more shelves in the storm cellar when Jewel was unable to do
any home canning? For that matter, why would Ed lie about the
lumber to begin with?

Elizabeth stood irresolute in the shadow of a cottonwood tree in
the front yard. She needed to talk to Jewel—if Jewel was around to be
talked to. And *how* was she to find out? She couldn't very well go
around looking in windows like some sort of Peeping Tom. Or was it
Tomasina? On the other hand, she could peek into the barn and outbuildings and the infamous storm cellar to see if she saw the lumber.
Mind made up, she did exactly that. There was nothing in the barn
but a pickup covered by a piece of canvas. The outbuildings were
similarly innocent of anything suspicious. At last, she lifted one of the

double doors of the storm cellar and carefully walked down the steps. She shone her flashlight on an object sitting on two sawhorses in the middle of the cellar.

"Oh, God!" she cried, and turned to run up the stairs when two bright lights shone in her eyes. She turned her head and covered her eyes with her arm. "Ed Carruthers, is that you?"

"Yes, Elizabeth, I reckon it is."

"Who's that with you?"

"It's me, Elizabeth," said Jim Hayworth. "I'm surprised you didn't guess."

"I was hoping that it was Jewel!" retorted Elizabeth. "I was hoping that she wasn't in that pine casket on the sawhorses."

"She ain't in there," said Ed. "That pine box is mine."

"What! You built your own casket?"

"Jewel and I were from the Appalachian Mountains, and it was the custom there for the family to build a casket for the loved one who passed away. That's what I did for Jewel, but I built my own because I don't have no family left to do it for me. Me and Jewel never had anybody but each other. When she died, I built her a casket, the finest one I could. I stained it mahogany and lined it with pillows covered in velvet. But I wanted a tombstone for her—for both of us—so everybody would know we were buried together and nobody would dig us up someday and separate us."

"My God, you can't do that, Ed. You can't just bury somebody in a pine box anymore. By law the body has to be embalmed and the casket has to be set inside a vault. Tell him, Jim."

Jim walked down the steps and put his arms around Elizabeth, pulling her tight against him despite her pushing and shoving. "Hush, Elizabeth. Don't you believe in love stories? Don't you believe in two people planning their final resting place together?"

"This is not a love story!" shouted Elizabeth. "This is a violation of the law."

"Elizabeth, do you remember what Buddy said this morning? That we all know each other's situations, but sometimes we overlook things because that's best. I've been sheriff of Highwater and Bonham County for twenty-five years, and in that time I've learned to over-look some things. Ed's burying his wife by himself may not be the

American way of death, but it's the right thing for him and Jewel. And when he goes, I'm to see to it that he's buried next to Jewel in that very pine box you see. And I'll do it. I'm not arresting Ed for burying his wife. He had his reasons, some of which he's already explained. There's one more reason: Social Security. Jewel and Ed were too feeble to farm anymore, and they never made enough to save very much. In other words, they needed two Social Security checks to live."

"Ed's been cashing Jewel's checks even though she's dead," said Elizabeth. "That's welfare fraud."

"I prefer to think of it as Jewel's money," said Jim. "We're not talking about a couple of no-goods taking money they didn't earn from the government. We're talking about an elderly couple who've worked hard all their lives and made barely enough to survive."

"Jewel and me talked about it, and we agreed on what the survivor would do," said Ed.

"Take my hand, Elizabeth, and walk with me up the knoll in back of the house to that grove of cottonwood trees," said Jim. "I protected you from the truth as long as I could, but when I called for my phone messages this afternoon, there was one from home health asking about the Carruthers. I knew you had called, and I could pretty well guess you wouldn't let this lie, so I drove over here and hid my pickup in Ed's barn and pulled a tarp over it. Then Ed and I waited for you."

Jim released her and held out his hand. Elizabeth stared at him for a while, then finally placed her much smaller hand in his. Again, she couldn't fathom why, but her intuition told her it was right. She felt Ed take her other hand, and they climbed up the cellar steps and walked up the knoll.

Ed shone his flashlight on a pink granite tombstone. One side had Jewel's name and the date of her birth and death on it. The other side was blank except for Ed's name and his birth date. At the top of the stone were the words *Dearly Beloved*.

Jim stepped behind Elizabeth and put his arms around her. "Dearly Beloved, we are gathered here today to join this man and this woman in holy matrimony." He clasped her tighter and rested his chin on the top of her head. His voice seemed to echo inside her head. "Change holy matrimony to eternity, and I figure the words fit, don't you?"

Elizabeth swiped at the tears flowing down her checks. "How many laws do you figure we've broken?"

"This is Highwater, and the law works a little different here." ♪

The Show Must Go On

Neesa Hart

Scene 1:

For an opening day, things were going fairly well.

As usual, I'd arrived at the church auditorium three hours before the cast and crew were scheduled to arrive. I had checked and double-checked the props table. I'd posted a new sign-in sheet on the call board. I'd inspected the deck for possible tripping hazards and the occasional loose staple that could imbed itself into the sandalless foot of a shepherd or wise man. And I'd ensured that the ushers had everything they needed to seat the two thousand or so patrons who would soon arrive for the twelfth annual Majesty of Christmas Pageant and Holiday Spectacular at Cornova Baptist Church.

No last-minute crises—which seem to be the hallmark of opening days. The children's choir director knew where her angel costumes were, and, more important, wasn't bugging me about them. We'd managed to scavenge a relatively realistic-looking myrrh bottle. Our original prop got smashed at the previous evening's dress rehearsal when a member of Gaspar's entourage took exception to a comment from the Balthazar camp. One thing led to another, and the next thing we knew, we were minus one perfume bottle. Fortunately, the pastor's wife works part-time at a department store, and, at three this morning, I learned that fingernail polish remover will dissolve the ink on a display bottle of Calvin Klein's Obsession. Better yet, popcorn oil, it turns out, looks just like myrrh—not that any of us know what myrrh looks like, but the yellowish-orange tinge of the popcorn oil looks a thousand times more convincing than regular olive oil.

With that problem behind us, I felt fairly confident that we were in good shape for the opening. All the principal cast members had arrived early or on time for makeup and costuming, and I had just given the forty-five-minute call.

And then we found the body in the baptistery.

Forty-two minutes to curtain and there she was, floating face-down in the baptismal waters.

My assistant stage manager, Colleen Dufree, found her. The call light on my headset starting furiously blinking. I knew we had trouble when Colleen asked me to switch to a private channel. Usually, the entire technical staff remains on one channel. I have the control box and can ask someone to switch to a second channel if I think it's necessary. A little wary, I told Colleen to take channel five. I then switched my headset.

"Oh my stars," she was blubbering. "You aren't going to believe this."

"Calm down, Colleen. Where are you?"

"In the baptistery closet. I wanted to inspect the fog machine again to make sure the water was heating."

"Is there a problem with it?"

"NO!" She was starting to sound panicked. It is never a good sign when the assistant stage manager panics less than an hour before curtain. She's supposed to be well past the panic stage by then, and far into the automatic response mode. I heard Colleen draw a shaky breath. "The problem is," she choked out, "that Lisa Eggerston is floating face-down in the baptistery. Geez, Kel, I think she's dead."

Through some miracle of self-control, honed to a razor-sharp edge by years of doing this job, I managed not to visibly react. I did, however, immediately switch off my headset just in time to avoid swearing in Colleen's ear.

Well, great. We've got less than an hour to go and our director, in a final fit of melodramatics, decides to prove she really is in charge. If I didn't know better, I'd swear Lisa had done this just to get even with me. I switched my set back on. "I'll be right there, Colleen. Don't panic."

I wended my way through the milling actors, careful to keep my expression neutral. I answered questions, provided the occasional safety pin or strip of gaffer's tape. I assured Joseph that I'd repaired the loose board on the stable floor that morning, and then I ducked into the narrow hallway that led to the baptistery. I found Colleen, staring numbly at Lisa's body. "What happened?" I asked.

"I don't know," she wailed. "It's like I told you, I came back here to check the fogger—and there she was. The baptistery's not supposed to be full." She was wringing her hands, I noted. I was fairly certain I'd never actually seen anyone wring their hands.

"Are you sure she's dead?"

Colleen looked at me, wide-eyed. "I checked. Oh, Lord, Kel, this is horrible."

"Horrible," I concurred, and looked closely at Lisa's body. Now, I will confess to you that I was not overwhelmed with grief at this moment. And, as long as I'm being honest, I'll even confess that I was more than a little relieved.

Lisa Eggerston was the kind of director every production manager hates to work with—temperamental, demanding, and more than a little flaky. If I hadn't agreed to take on this show as a favor to the producer, a longtime friend of mine, I'd have quit weeks ago. Actually, I'd have quit the first time I met Lisa Eggerston. Like most church drama programs, this one had its institutions—and she was one of them.

"Control freak" didn't begin to summarize this woman's problems. Over the course of the past few months, she'd systematically angered or offended the costume designer, the set designer, the lighting designer, the props coordinator, most of the cast and crew, and generally everyone else she came into contact with. One night, a design meeting nearly ended in a fistfight when Lisa insisted on making the set designer justify his color choice for the stable interior. Last week, I'd spent several hours calming down the props coordinator after Lisa had delivered another six pages of props. Abstraction is lost on the woman.

Generally, the entire last two weeks of rehearsals had proved to be a miserable experience, and I had lived in dread of opening night, knowing full well that if I wanted Lisa to shut up and let me do my job, I'd have to put her in a straitjacket.

So maybe it was that pre-show numbness that sets in, where everything sort of runs on autopilot. More than likely, it was the sure knowledge that we'd get through the next two hours without listening to Lisa screech—the sound of her blistering lecture to the cast after last night's dress rehearsal still rang in my ears. Whatever the cause, I felt nothing but calm relief as I looked at her body.

She was still wearing the clothes she'd had on last night at dress rehearsal—a severe-looking black jumpsuit with silver trim that had made her resemble Cruella De Vil while she'd delivered her blistering lecture on commitment and duty before dismissing the cast three hours late.

Though she was face-down, there was no mistaking her identity. Her platinum hair, straight from a drugstore bottle, fanned around her head like an exotic lily pad.

"What in the world are we going to do?" Colleen insisted.

"Did you call 911?" I asked.

"Not yet."

I nodded and pulled my cell phone from my pocket. While Colleen and I watched Lisa float on the eerily calm pool, I made the call. I hung up and slid the phone back in my jacket. "They'll be here in ten minutes."

"I guess she must have slipped and fallen in last night after rehearsal. I can't imagine who could have filled the pool, or what she was doing back here."

"Isn't this thing computer operated?" I asked.

"I don't know. I guess so. We normally have baptisms on the first and third Sundays of the month. That would be tomorrow, but because of the set, we're not doing them. I guess someone might have forgotten to reset the programming. If that happened, the waters would have started filling during the night."

I touched the water. Cold. "Would she have had any reason at all to come back here?"

"Not that I know of, but you know Lisa." Colleen started to tear up. "Maybe she wanted to check the fogger herself. Oh, I don't know."

"Colleen," I said, my voice deliberately harsh. "You're not going to help anyone if you fall apart right now."

"I know." She visibly struggled for a minute. "I know, but..."

"Get a grip, Colleen," I ordered. "You need to stay in control here."

"It's just that I've never—" She drew a shaky breath. "Kelsey, what if—what if this wasn't an accident?"

"Of course it was an accident," I insisted.

"But what if it wasn't. What if someone killed her?"

"Why would someone do that?" At Colleen's disbelieving look, I coughed. "Well, er, you know what I mean. Sure, plenty of people are mad at the woman, but geez, Colleen, nobody would off her."

She shuddered. "I know. I know. I'm letting my imagination run wild."

"*In control*," I said again.

Colleen closed her eyes. Her black T-shirt made her face look especially pale, but when she looked at me again, her blue eyes were clear and dry. "Do you think we should, you know, pull her out?"

I thought it over. "No. Let's let the rescue squad do it."

"What should we do, then?"

I checked my watch. "I'm going to give the thirty-minute call. I want you to meet the ambulance at the rear entrance. Bring the paramedics in through the stage left door. No one will see them that way."

Colleen's eyes widened. "You aren't going to tell the cast?"

"Not right now," I affirmed.

"But, Kel, I don't think—"

I exhaled a calming breath. "Look, Colleen. There are two thousand people filling up that auditorium. We've got five hundred cast members ready to present a show they've been rehearsing for six months. They don't need Lisa Eggerston right now, and she certainly doesn't need them." I glanced at the body. "If we tell them, it will just cause chaos."

"But don't you think—"

"I think," I said calmly, "that we owe it to all those people to pull it together. Lisa would have wanted that. You know it."

"I know." She looked at Lisa's body. "I just can't believe this."

"I know." I laid a hand on her sleeve. "I can't believe it either. But you and I have a job to do. Go meet the ambulance, and I'll give the call."

"Okay." She grabbed my hand. "Kel—"

"I know," I said again. I gave her fingers a quick squeeze. "It'll be all right, Colleen. We'll get through this."

"I hope so."

"We will," I assured her. "Don't worry."

Colleen hurried down the hall toward the stage left door. I lingered a second longer, looking at the still form of our director. *I should feel something right now*, I thought. *I'm sure I should*. But to be perfectly honest, all I could do was tuck my clipboard under my arm, give the points of my black vest a firm, straightening tug, and think to myself, *The show must go on*.

SCENE 2:

Actually, considering the state of my concentration, not to mention poor Colleen's, I felt pretty good about the way things were going. We were three scenes into the show, and so far, no major bobbles—well, as long as you don't count Colleen's untimely discovery a half-hour before curtain.

I was trying especially hard to make out Colleen's facial expressions during the scene shifts. The near black-out conditions made it particularly difficult, but I strained anyway. I figured the look on Colleen's face was as close to a report as I was going to get on what had happened when the paramedics arrived. I knew Colleen well enough to know she'd followed my instructions to the letter. It's one of the things I love most about my job: I get to rule.

As a production and stage manager, I spend up to six months training the technical and design crews of a show to do exactly as I say. By three days before the show, they've even stopped asking me questions. I control the headset, and everyone on the other end does exactly what I tell them to.

So I knew that if the ambulance had arrived on time, then Lisa Eggerston's body was safely out the door and on the way to the hospital. Plenty of time to deal with the rest of the consequences later. However, though I'd spent significant time and energy training my people to simply follow my orders, I also knew that the paramedics, and heaven forbid, the police, weren't as likely to simply ignore the matter until after the last curtain call. I mean, a dead body *is* a dead body, and law enforcement and medical personnel have a way of taking that kind of thing very seriously.

Still, with three scenes behind us, I was beginning to relax. There was something comforting in the routine action of calling my cues and watching the drama unfold on stage. I kept one eye on the stage-left action, while I surreptitiously watched Colleen's crew make the difficult shift upstage left. They had to maneuver in the stable, complete with real hay bales, and the castors on the bottom of the flats tended to hang up on the loose hay. They seemed to have the large wagon almost in place, though, when I felt the hand on my shoulder.

This, I knew, was not good news. One of the most important jobs I do during a show is call the cues for the sound, lighting, special effects, and stage crews. *No one* tries to talk to me during a show unless it's an absolute dire emergency. Lisa and I had had several pointed, public arguments over this issue. She really wanted to be in charge of the show—even after we moved past rehearsals and onto stage. But that was my job, and, as I said, I get to rule. It's better for everyone when we all understand that.

So I knew this hand on my shoulder was nothing but trouble. I gathered my calm, made the last set of calls on the page of my prompt script, then slowly turned my head.

I half expected to find one of my shepherds whining about something like a lost prop, or, worse, a lost sheep. In twenty years of church productions, one thing I've learned: shepherds can never find their sheep. You have to put a prop person in charge of that.

What I found, though, left me feeling a little anxious, and greatly annoyed. A pair of intent blue eyes, set nicely apart in a sculpted face, studied mine in the split second before their owner flashed me his badge. Jack Maxwell, it read, homicide detective. He leaned forward. "I need to talk to you."

I glared at him, then called the next few cues on reflex. I switched my headset control to mute. "I, uh, can't right now." I indicated the audience with a nod of my head. "I'm a little busy."

"I don't think this can wait."

"It'll have to."

Detective Maxwell shook his head. "Can't."

"I'm in the middle of a show."

"I'm in the middle of an investigation."

"And it's not going to kill you to wait another hour. She's already dead, Detective."

He tilted his head to one side. The action caused a lock of dark hair to tumble across his forehead. He leaned closer to me. "I'm not a very patient man."

"Too bad," I muttered. My headset crackled, and I heard the sound technician ask me why I'd missed a cue. I flipped off the mute. "Right with you, Charley." Mute again. From the corner of my eye, I could see Mary and Joseph making their way through the streets of Bethlehem looking for a hotel room. Mary, just as she'd done every night in rehearsal, was spending more time playing with her head-piece than looking even remotely distressed that she was about to deliver the pregnancy pillow she wore under her costume. Great. Lisa had warned her a million times that if she didn't keep one hand on that pillow, it would drop like a basketball. Right now, it was hanging down near Mary's thighs. I groaned.

Jack Maxwell—with a name like that, I thought, no wonder he'd become a detective—didn't budge. Blast him. "Ms. Price," he insisted. "I really am going to have to insist."

"I've got a scene shift coming up."

"And there's a dead body in your baptistery."

"Still?" I asked.

An older woman seated near the imposing Mr. Maxwell leaned forward and rapped his shoulder with a set of bony knuckles. "Shhhhh."

He had the good grace to wince. "Sorry."

I looked at the stage again. Mary and Joseph had finally made it to the stable. There was a long song coming up. The choir director, I noted, had moved into place without my prompt. The song would take at least three minutes, and I didn't have any cues to call. I pulled off my headset. "I told my assistant stage manager to call the para-medics. What's the body still doing in the baptistery?"

He gave me a serious look. It would have been more serious if it hadn't made the dimple in his left cheek deepen. And if I hadn't been so annoyed with him, I might have thought he was cute. "I don't want to move it until I'm sure it won't disturb the evidence."

That had my eyebrows rising. "What evidence? She slipped and fell in the baptistery when she went to check the fogger. I'm guessing she hit her head and knocked herself unconscious. The computer must have turned the water on, and when the baptistery filled, she drowned. Case closed."

"You sound really sure about that."

He leaned back in his seat and draped one long arm across the back of two more. Obviously, he wasn't taking my hint that now was not the time for this conversation. I picked up my headset.

"Of course I'm sure," I told him. The song was ending, and I could see the shepherds moving into place. I did a mental count and noted there were two sheep missing. I flagged the page of my script and made a note to talk to Colleen. She had to find someone to handle those sheep before tomorrow night's show.

"Well, I'm not," Detective Maxwell insisted.

I shrugged and pulled my headset on. "Whatever." Flipping the switch to talk, I cued the lighting technician to illuminate the stable. A heavenly kind of glow shone through the wood slats and lit the manger from above. Nice effect. I really liked it.

"Ms. Price," Jack's face was so close to my ear, his breath tickled the back of my neck. "Do you have any idea what we're dealing with here?"

I ignored him and cued the sound operator to turn on Mary's mic for her solo. She sings remarkably well for someone who just gave birth in a pile of straw. Jack tapped on my shoulder. "Did you hear me?"

I nodded, but kept my eyes trained on the stage. The next set of cues was particularly tight, and I didn't want to miss one. I was making the third cue call when Jack seemed to lose his patience. "Ms. Price," he insisted again.

I held up a hand to try to hold him off. He ignored me. "For God's sake. Your director is dead."

My headset crackled to life. *Well, great,* I thought as I watched a lone sheep wander down the center aisle. I turned around to glare at Jack Maxwell. "In case you're interested, you just announced that to my entire crew."

* * *

SCENE 3:

Through sheer force of will, I managed to hold Jack, as I now thought of him, at bay until intermission. When he said he wasn't patient, he wasn't kidding. He fidgeted like a six-year-old. To make matters worse, my technical crew was falling apart. Not only were they missing cues, but I sensed the heightened tension through the limited conversation on the headsets. We almost reached a critical point when the rail crew flew one of the angels in too soon. One second earlier, and she would have collided with the flat we were flying out at the time. The increasingly anxious looks I was receiving from the actors told me all I needed to know. News of Lisa's death was spreading backstage with the alacrity of a three-alarm fire.

We persevered, though, and somehow got through two more songs, and the curtain came down on Act I. Feeling simultaneously drained and on edge, I picked up my script and exited the control booth. I walked toward the side door of the auditorium with Jack right on my heels. We stepped outside into a relatively gray December afternoon, but after the semi-darkness of the theater, the light seemed blinding. I had to squint. "All right, Detective, I have fifteen minutes of intermission. What do you want from me?"

He whipped out a notepad. That struck me as a little funny and kind of cute. I think that, right at that moment, I was losing my mind. My show was falling apart, my director was dead as a doornail, and all I could think of was that Jack Maxwell looked like a younger, hunkier version of Joe Friday. I kept waiting for him to mutter, "Just the facts, ma'am." If Jack noted my amusement, he ignored it, and certainly didn't share it. "Who found the body?"

"My stage manager, Colleen."

"What was she doing back in that area at the time?"

"Checking the fog machine to make sure it was heating. It's part of her job."

Jack jotted that down. "What were you doing?"

"Giving orders to the technical crew. That's part of my job."

He gave me a quick look to make sure I was taking him seriously.

In the outdoor light, his eyes were an even deeper blue than I'd first thought. "Giving orders?" he prompted.

"Yes." I braced one shoulder against the stone wall of the church. "I was going over the checklist with my audio technician when Colleen asked to speak to me on a private channel of the headset. We switched over, and she told me to come backstage."

He scribbled a few more notes. "Then what?"

"Then, I met her at the baptistery door, she showed me the body, and we agreed to call 911."

"Does anyone else know about this?"

"They do now that you told the entire technical crew over the headset." The door opened and Charley Constantine, my audio technician stuck his head out. "Uh, Kelsey, I hate to bother you, but I think you're needed backstage."

"I'm in the middle of an interview with Detective Maxwell, Charley."

"I know, but, um, everyone knows about Lisa. They're pretty upset. I think you'd better talk to them."

I glanced at Jack. He hesitated, then nodded. I motioned for Charley to lead the way. I followed him with Jack so close on my heels he might have been my shadow.

What I found backstage confirmed my worst fears. I had several cast members in tears, though to be perfectly honest, I'm not sure why. As far as I could tell, no one could stand the woman when she was alive. That's a particularly weird thing about death. People forget how annoying dead people were before they, well, died. As far as I knew, no one had even pretended to like Lisa Eggerston while she roamed the earth spreading theatrical terror.

But now, everyone was standing around in the backstage area doing a pretty good job of portraying hysteria, grief, horror, and shock. No one in the world exhibits these particular emotions quite as well as theatrical people. All the black they wear seems to add to the effect.

"All right," I said. "I need your attention."

"My God," one of the kings groaned. "This is just dreadful."

I ignored that. "You all know about Lisa," I said carefully. "I had wanted to keep the truth from you until after tonight's show. I'll take full responsibility for that."

The innkeeper's wife turned to Mary and threw herself against her shoulder. "Oh, I can't believe this." Mary wrapped a comforting arm around her.

I pulled Jack forward. "This is Detective Jack Maxwell. He's going to ask a few questions."

To my left, the angel Gabriel tried to move forward, but his wings caught on the wagon containing Herod's balcony. So he used what we referred to as his 'announcement voice' to get my attention. "Kelsey?"

I looked at him, almost expecting him to say, "Fear not." "What, Bill?"

"What kinds of questions?"

Jack cleared his throat. "Routine stuff. Just a few things we need to know about who saw her last, what time they saw her, that kind of thing."

Bill frowned. "My God." He looked at Jack. "You think this wasn't an accident, don't you?"

I had to stifle a groan. Just great. I'd suspected as much myself when I realized the water in the baptistery was cold. When the pool fills automatically, it also heats automatically. Since the water was cold, that suggested that someone had filled it deliberately. Under the best of circumstances, it had been a simple oversight by the custodial staff, but I was pretty sure that whoever had filled that pool had done it to drown Lisa Eggerston.

I glanced at Jack. His expression told me that he'd guessed the same thing. Well, good for him. Now his brilliant lack of timing had yielded a theater full of nearly hysterical actors—actors who are more than a little crazy under the best of circumstances. I decided not to help him out of the mess he'd created. I crossed my arms and shot him a knowing look. "*Do* you think it was an accident, Detective?"

He was tugging at the collar of his denim shirt, which he stopped doing long enough to glare at me. "Well, it might be a little too early —"

"You think she was murdered," Joseph insisted. "You think that one of us murdered Lisa Eggerston."

"I didn't say that," Jack said. "It wasn't necessarily someone in this room."

"But it could be?" That came from one of the extras.

Jack nodded. "It could be anyone."

"But you don't know," Balthazar asserted as he took a dramatic step forward, "do you?"

"I don't have any suspects at this time," Jack answered.

Gaspar pulled his crown from his head and began twirling it on his index finger. "Which means that the killer could still be loose in this theater."

A collective gasp filled the humid air.

"There's no need to panic." Jack surveyed the room, then his gaze landed on me. "I can't even say, conclusively, that Ms. Eggerston was murdered. It might have been a simple accident, and that's what I'm here to find out."

As if on cue, Mary clutched her throat and lurched forward. "But my stars. If she *was* murdered, and you don't know who did it, that means that any one of us could be next!"

I believe I mentioned the predisposition of theatrical people to histrionics?

SCENE 4:

I took my seat in the control booth again, having done the best I could to settle the nerves of my cast and crew. Thirty seconds before the curtain rose on Act II, I glared at Jack, who was still following me like a stray dog. "I hope you're proud of yourself. You've created total chaos back there."

He just shrugged, which, irrationally, riled my temper even more. Shrugging, indeed. The man obviously didn't have a clue what kind of havoc he was wreaking in my well-ordered world. I pulled my headset on and did my best to concentrate on my script, though it was hard with Jack leaning over my shoulder.

We were halfway through the third act when the kings' procession started. I had warned Jack to stay completely out of my way until after this portion of the program. It was by far my most challenging set of cues. With three kings, each with a multi-person entourage, live camels, one elephant, a pair of flying angels, and a two-year-old playing the young Jesus, the potential for disaster was enormous. We had multiple lighting and sound cues to navigate, moving scenery, and an elephant who'd proved to have a little stage fright. By the time the kings had moved into place, I was gripping my pencil so hard my fingers hurt. But, miracle of miracles, we got through the piece. The next song started and the mass of kings began to file off stage.

Belatedly, I noticed that Jack had left the control room.

The rest of the show passed without incident. I authorized two curtain calls, figuring my cast needed the extra encouragement after the night they'd had.

"Colleen?" I paged her on the headset.

"Yeah, Kel?"

I double-checked the control lights on my console to ensure that no one else had an active headset. The other members of my crew had all signed off. "You did a great job tonight. I know it was hard on you."

"Everyone's really upset, Kelsey. I can't believe something like this happened here."

"I know."

"Does Detective Maxwell know what he's going to do yet?"

"I haven't seen him since the kings' procession."

"He's been back here asking questions," Colleen told me.

"I see."

"Do you want to see the cast and crew again for any reason? You know, maybe talk to them about things some more?"

I thought it over. "I don't think so. Why don't you let them go home. They're all pretty stressed out."

"You aren't staying late are you?" she asked me. "I mean, not here? Not with this?"

"I don't think there's a murderer loose in the church, Colleen."

"I know, but it's creepy."

"A little."

"Listen, most of the cast and crew are headed over to Dom's Pizza Kitchen. It's going to be subdued, but I think they need to be together."

"That's probably a good idea."

"Why don't you come with us?"

I drew a deep breath and let my eyes drift shut. "I don't think so, Colleen. What I need is a good night's sleep."

"Are you sure?"

"I'm sure."

"Okay. Uh, Kel?"

"Yeah?"

"Things went well, all things considered."

"Yes, they did."

"I'll see you tomorrow?"

"Yep." I switched off my headset and leaned my head back in the chair. I'm normally energized after a show, but tonight, I felt nothing but bone-deep exhaustion.

I watched from the control booth as people filed out. Colleen was the last to leave. She waved at me just before she flipped off the lights. The glow from my console was the only light in my tiny little space.

Two hands landed on my shoulders. I wasn't startled this time. I'd been expecting him. "Hello, Jack."

"Hi, Kel."

"Learn anything backstage?"

"Some."

"Got any suspects?"

"A cast full." He started rubbing my shoulders. I let him do it because it felt too delicious not to.

"No one liked the woman."

I could see his reflection in the glass window of the room. He met my gaze with a knowing look.

"You warned me two weeks ago that this was going to happen. I should have listened to you."

A smile played across my lips. "I appreciate the fact that you didn't tell the cast I'd suspected this."

"Or that I knew you."

"Or that. If they'd known I'd talked to the police about my suspicions, it would have made things worse. They'd have felt like I was keeping some kind of conspiracy from them."

"Weren't you?"

"Don't frown, Jack," I said, and spun around in my chair to face him. "Part of my job is to keep things running smoothly. Can you imagine what would have happened if people had known what I was thinking?"

Jack dropped into the other chair. He took both my hands in one of his. "Do you think this was deliberate or not?"

"The water in the baptistery was cold."

"I know that. Someone filled it."

"She could have slipped and fallen in without the person who filled it knowing she was in there."

"Why would someone have turned the water on?"

"I don't know." I shrugged. "A prank, maybe. Habit. You don't have any proof it was deliberate."

"No." He shook his head. "I don't. And I'm not sure I can get any."

"Then what are you going to do?" I prompted him.

"Close the show," he responded. "At least until I have time to look around."

I jerked my hands away from him. "Close the show? Close the show? Are you crazy. You can't do that."

"This is a potential murder we're talking about here, Kelsey. I can't just let business go on as usual."

"I know that." I started to pace in the tight confines of the room. "But that doesn't mean you have to close the show."

"I don't see what other choice I have."

"All these people—they've worked so hard. It doesn't seem fair."

"They'll understand."

"You sound awfully sure of that," I accused him.

He shrugged again. It made his shoulders look impossibly broad when he did that. I forced the thought aside and ran my fingers through my hair. "Look, Jack," I prompted. "I'm not sure I can explain to you what a catastrophically bad decision this is."

"Why?"

"Why?" I stopped pacing. "Don't you think we say 'the show must go on' in show business for a reason? It's because a show isn't about one person, or a group of persons; it's the most collaborative of all art forms. It's about team work and sacrifice. It's about pulling together and sticking together, no matter what. It's the only place on earth where every member of the team, from the star to the stagehand, has an equally important role. And if you close the show, you'll take that away from them. This is months in the making, Jack. Months of these people's lives."

He studied me in the green glow of the LED lights. "I'm sorry, Kelsey. I know how much you care about this—and about them."

"But you're going to do it anyway."

"I have a murderer to catch."

"And there's no way I can talk you out of it?"

He leaned back in his chair and crossed his arms over his chest. "I'm afraid not. The only way I can let you raise the curtain tomorrow night is if I know I've got the killer behind bars."

ENCORE:

He looked so smug when he said that. But I also knew he was serious. Jack had believed he'd played his trump card at that moment, that I would finally give in and let him have his way.

But one thing he didn't count on: good production managers don't quit. And I like to think of myself as one of the best. It's my job to make sure the show runs smoothly. It's my job to solve problems and keep the ship moving steadily forward. It's my job to ensure that the cast, the crew, and the designers are cared for. I do it because I love it, and because I'm great at it. I do it because each time the curtain rises on a new production, I get to watch magic happen.

I knew there was no way that Jack was going to back down. If he didn't have the case solved by curtain time the next night, he'd shut down my show. I also knew that there was no way I'd let that happen. My people were very well trained. Colleen knew that show and its cues every bit as well as I did. So I did what any good production manager would at that moment.

I saved the show.

Which is how I ended up here at the Drysdale Women's Correctional Facility. Despite Jack's protests, and despite my lawyers howls of disbelief, I confessed to the murder of Lisa Eggerston. The judge was easy to convince. I repeated several stories of Lisa's antics in the final days of her life. I talked about her fits of temper, her demands, her unbelievable ego. I showed several examples of the memos she'd sent me, and the judge had no problem believing that I'd been driven to take action.

I explained that Lisa and I had fought backstage after dress rehearsal. One thing led to another. She shoved me. I shoved her. She fell in the then-empty baptistery and whacked her head. I didn't know, I said truthfully, how the pool had filled with water, but explained the computerized system that controlled it.

I was very convincing. The judge gave me involuntary man-slaughter with extenuating circumstances and sentenced me to two years at Drysdale.

I missed the closing of that show, but I've seen the video. Things went well. Colleen did a super job in my absence. And, I must con-fess, things haven't been nearly as bad here as I thought. Jack comes to see me fairly regularly. He's still trying to convince me to tell him what really happened that night in the church. I just shrug and ask him how he knows I'm not telling the truth. We usually fight after that. But then he comes to see me again so we can make up.

As of this morning, I've been here exactly thirteen months of my requisite twenty-four. It's been a long time since I sat down and really thought through those final few hours. I suppose it's only natural, though, that the memories would come to me now. After all, I've just given the forty-five-minute call to my cast and crew.

In less than an hour, the curtain—which is made out of several bedsheets stapled together—will rise on the first ever Drysdale Women's Correctional Facility production. The cast and crew consist entirely of my fellow inmates. I expect things to go well. My produc-tions usually do. From the makeshift control booth, I spot Jack. I'm glad he made it. I have a feeling he's going to appreciate my efforts more than most. We're debuting an original play this evening. Written and directed by my cellmate. It's a witty little murder mystery about a production manager who's finally driven to kill her director.

Next season, we're hoping to stage *The Pirates of Penzance*.

Twelve Days

Laura Hayden

I stared at Stik, trying to see features lost behind the hood of his dark sweatshirt. He had a "one with the shadows" thing going on. I'd stumbled into him twice already because I hadn't seen him. To his credit, Stik didn't curse either time, even when I'd stepped on his foot.

We slipped through the dense foliage, avoiding various detection devices. Our clothing had been impregnated with a chemical that the sci-tech adviser said made us invisible to vid and shielded our heat signatures.

God, I love science.

But technology couldn't protect us from all detection. We still had to avoid guards who patrolled with their own nifty high-tech gear.

Did I mention they had guns?

It wasn't until we'd landed that Stik told me he didn't trust technology so he'd chosen a challenging route into the compound. "Challenging" meant relying less on technology and more on crawling through impenetrable thickets and climbing sheer walls.

Evidently, he'd mistaken me for Spiderwoman.

My problem was—I hated physical activity. My life revolved like my office chair with everything in a 360° arm's-reach circle. But my office and equipment would be useless in twelve days if we didn't stop Doug Post.

Software ka-trillionaire Douglas Post had the world by the virtual gonads and wasn't threatening to squeeze; he'd gone straight to threatening all-out castration. Government brains had accurately anticipated his possible reaction to losing the lawsuit, realizing that—should Post's anger mutate into revenge—he could bring society to its technological knees. The hand that rocks the cradle isn't nearly as influential as the hand that holds the world by its *soft*ware.

When the gavel sounded on December 13, the founder/owner/president/CEO of MultiData was found guilty of creating a monopoly, stealing technology, creating an unfair and unethical marketplace—everything short of RICOH charges. Post dodged the press gauntlet and disappeared into his compound, a.k.a. the "Fortress of Silicon." A few hours later, he issued a warning: if the ruling wasn't reversed, Christmas Day would mark the functional end of every computer on the planet. Thanks to automatic upgrades, he could control every piece of MultiData software by remote. Short of a few antiques, every computer in the free and not-so-free world had at least one Multidata program embedded somewhere in its silicon bowels and one command from him could cause those computers to stop functioning and erase all their data.

A decade ago, we'd lived through the Y2k scare unscathed, but this time there'd be no fixes, no patches, no alternative software solutions. All we could do was surrender to Douglas Post and MultiData and make his Christmas very merry, indeed.

Or then again, we could break in, disable his computers and kill him....

Long story short, they chose me for the "disable his computers" part. Doug Post himself would be terminated by Stik, a man who looked as if he could kill without remorse, concern, or even breaking a sweat.

I shivered. The last thing I wanted to see was an execution—of Post or even a guard. Suddenly, I realized I'd seen no guards, none of the six hundred employees wandering around. Either Stik had picked the perfect route, or the world's richest boss had sent his employees home for a traditional family Christmas.

Yeah. Right.

Stik led us to the main building and it took over two minutes for the reconfigured Omni-Keycard to break the twelve-digit cipher lock. With advanced security like that, maybe Post didn't need guards. The lock clicked, the door opened, and Stik entered.

I counted to ten and followed, immediately tripping over something…someone. Sprawling to my knees, my hand landed in something warm and sticky on the floor. I looked down and stared at the victim, face-to-face. A dead guard. My throat closed until I glanced at my wet hand. Instead of the red stain of innocent blood, a bright yellow-green fluid coated my palm.

I bravely cleaned my hand on the android's sleeve before I scrambled to my feet. "CyberGuard, 2501 model," I said, wishing my voice didn't shake. "I didn't think they were on the market."

"They're not. These are beta-test units." Stik motioned for me to follow.

He negotiated the maze of corridors with ease, avoiding or disarming the security measures. So far, we'd seen only one inhuman guard. Had Post's megalomania grown so large that he'd replaced his human staff with programmable replicas?

I bumped into Stik when he stopped at a door that looked no different from the other doors we'd passed.

"He's in there. You ready?"

I gulped, nodded, then reached into my pack for my Silencer and set it up.

MultiData's most popular product was voice recognition software. Before we might reach him, Post could issue the command that would start a destroy-every-computer cascade effect. But my invention absorbed all sounds, stopping him from issuing any verbal commands such as "Make my coffee black," "Turn on the lights," or "Kill the intruders."

The unit registered a single voice beyond the door. "One," I mouthed. Stik nodded, readied his weapons, then stepped inside.

I waited, counting silently: one MultiData, two MultiData, three…

The Silencer absorbed any sounds of a fight—gunshots, screams of pain, pleas for mercy. At "ten," I entered, praying that Stik had overpowered whatever awaited him.

Sure enough, Stik stood unscathed, staring down at something hidden behind a large desk. I moved closer and saw an overturned chair and a pair of legs ending in Post's signature red Nikes.

I pointed to the shoes. "Post?" I mouthed.

Stik pulled back his own hood, revealing a remarkably average-looking face—certainly not that of a hardened killer. He scanned his victim, registering no emotion, no guilt, and no sense of satisfaction. He placed his large knife in the center of the desk. Instead of blood, a sticky yellow-green substance dripped from the blade.

I stared at the screen as my virus program infiltrated the central computer system. Rather than destroy the code, it rewrote it so I could access all levels and circumvent any passwords, inline booby traps or cyber-bombs. I tried not to worry about the body at my feet; it was just a bloodless replica, right?

"Where's the real Post?"

"Here. Somewhere," Stik said quietly. "Pull up a building schematic."

I poked around the computer and found a 3-D wireframe blueprint which I projected into the middle of the room.

Stik circled the hologram, analyzing the structure, then stalked over to a bookcase on the far wall. He wore a fleeting look of irritation; perhaps he was human after all and not a Robo-Stik sent in to do the Dirty Deed.

"Maybe he's in another building," I offered. "Or maybe he's hiding in one of the connecting tunnels between buildings. Or maybe..."

Stik held up his hand, stopping me. "Or maybe..." He pivoted and used that same hand to pull the bookcase from the wall. It teetered for a moment, then fell, scattering books and papers across the floor and landed on the mess with a substantial thud.

"—he's in here."

Behind the bookcase, we could see the outline of a door.

"I thought he was some Boy Genius. A secret room behind the bookcase?" I tried to laugh. "How clichéd."

"Smart men know to hide in plain sight." Stik pointed at the Silencer. "Set it up."

I hooked up the unit and it registered no audio sounds other than a cyclical click, probably something mechanical in nature. Thermostat? Watch? Time bomb? I shot Stik an "okay."

He pulled out his knife and a small hand laser, then disappeared into the room.

I fought the instinct to close my eyes as I counted. After "ten," I entered the dimly lit room. This time, I stumbled over no bodies, real or synthetic. The room's only occupant was a half-naked body on a med-lab monitor bed.

So where was Stik?

The temptation to retreat was almost overpowering, but our mission's importance superseded my instinct for self-preservation. I searched the shadows for Stik, spotting a single combat boot beneath the bed. I wanted to run—not to abandon him, but to retreat and reassess the situation.

Yeah, right.

I turned and tripped over a cable. Recovering, I scrambled toward freedom, but that same cable snaked around my ankle, tightened, and tugged me backward. I grabbed the door frame as a second cable wrapped around my other leg. The cables pulled hard enough to break my grip and drag me toward the bowels of the machinery.

If this animated jungle of wires and tubes killed Stik, I had no chance in hell of surviving. I couldn't even get satisfaction from screaming thanks to the Silencer.

Inspiration hit. Using the last of my strength, I batted the Silencer from the door, snagged its antenna wire and reeled it in like a fish. I slammed the off switch and suddenly could hear myself bellow in terror and blubber without shame. Between sobs, I screamed, "Computer! Sierra Mike Charlie override."

If my virus had invaded the system's protected core, it had embedded my control signature. If not, I was dead.

The cables grew limp.

"Sierra Mike Charlie override has been activated. Awaiting command." The computer spoke in its creator's voice.

I hyperventilated in relief as I untangled myself from the wires. I scanned the room. Where was Stik? Had the computer killed him, absorbing him into its components?

"Release the other intruder," I rasped.

An empty-looking wall shimmered with movement then spat out Stik's body. Like a cat, he landed on all-fours.

"Thanks," he muttered, sounding as if he seldom had need to thank anyone about anything. He stalked toward the med-lab bed and pulled out a second knife.

"Wait," I commanded.

He paused in mid-step. "Why?"

"Because you owe me a chance to sort this out before you kill him. What if this isn't Post?"

Stik gave me a curt nod. "One chance."

I stumbled toward the bed, trying to digest the medical telemetry. Wires and tubes covered his body, monitoring respiration, heart rate, brain activity—all bodily functions. A mirrored shield blocked his eyes and ears, allowing him to hear and see only what the computer supplied.

"Computer, what is the function of this facility?"

"To preserve the PostPrime."

So it *was* the real Douglas Post.

"Is he dead?"

"No."

"Explain."

"He is functioning within all parameters but one."

"Which one?" I ran through a mental list of physical complications—heart attack, other organ failure, cancer, disease...

"He is unhappy."

Hooboy...didn't see that one coming.

Stik stepped toward the bed.

"Please...not yet." I turned back to the terminal. "Computer, is PostPrime unhappy because he lost the court case?"

"PostPrime is unaware of outside concerns."

Prickles rose on the back of my neck. "Does he know about the court case?"

"No."

"Did PostPrime enter VR to be shielded from outside concerns?"

"No, we felt it was in his best interest. He was unhappy."

So the computer had shanghaied its own creator, maybe issuing the global threats itself without his input, much less permission. Simply put, he didn't deserve to die. Surely, Stik understood that....

"Computer, is PostPrime...happy in the world you have created for him?"

"PostPrime is not as unhappy as before."

I glanced at the monitor, and my heart rate hit warp speed. Post's computer had isolated and invalidated my virus. I couldn't break in. If I told Stik, Post was dead: innocent or not. "Computer, I want to talk to your creator."

"PostPrime is not communicating with the outside world."

I studied the body; he was an ordinary-looking man. Handsome in a sort of studious way. Okay, handsome in a "I'm-richer-than-any-body-on-Earth" sort of way. And he wasn't the hideous, destruction-unleashing Grinch we'd thought he was.

A shiver danced across my shoulders. "Let me enter his VR and talk to him."

Stik shook his head. "You don't know what you're doing."

"Yes I do," I lied. "It'll take time for my virus to give us control." A bigger lie. "I can go in, talk to Post, explain what's going on."

He glared at me as if x-raying my comments for the lie within. Finally, Stik sighed. "Do it."

It's not every day you fool a trained assassin.

"Highest priority status," I ordered. "I want to enter PostPrime's world."

In less than a minute, the computer generated everything I needed for VR.

Stik eyed the preparations with obvious distaste. "How long will this take?" In assassin-speak, it meant *"When can I go ahead and kill him?"*

"Give me eleven days"—I consulted my watch—"eighteen hours and forty-six minutes. If I don't succeed, make sure I'm cleared from VR before you kill him. If I'm there with him when he dies..."

Stik stared back with passionless eyes. "I know."

What I hate most about VR is getting motion sick during initialization, but MultiData's latest generation of VR had no ill side effects. I "landed" in a great hall packed with enough gold and treasure to finance a small monarchy. A decadent jewel-encrusted throne sat at the end of the room.

If Doug Post had conjured this for himself, I was in big trouble.

I heard a noise and hid as a band of women poured into the room, giggling and bouncing around like hyperactive cheerleaders. Their clothing or lack thereof reminded me of Victoria's Secret on parade.

If this was the way Post expected to see his women...

Post shouldered through the throng and plopped down on his throne. To his credit, he didn't ogle or touch them. In fact, he ignored them.

I focused my attention and "thought" myself into an appropriate costume—something with the right flavor but less exposure. Think Barbara Eden in *I Dream of Jeanie*.

I adopted an insipid smile and merged with the vapid audience of admirers. I thought he wouldn't notice me, but I was wrong.

"Oh God. A new one." He gave me a critical once-over. "Don't tell me. You're Jeanie, looking for a new master." He sighed and then grabbed my wrist. "Let's get this over with."

"Not so fast, buster." I pulled out of his grasp.

He looked as if he'd never met opposition before. "Excuse me?" Releasing me, he crossed his arms and frowned. "If this is a new programming variation, I don't like it."

I should've been more careful, but his attitude pissed me off. "What? The Lord and Master never hears the word, *no*?" I scanned the opulent room. "You must get your rocks off playing King of the World." *Yeah, while the rest of the world was sinking like the* Titanic.

A large gong interrupted his response. His harem swarmed in, separating us.

"Gift time!" they chanted, dragging him back to the throne.

One by one, they knelt at his feet in total adoration. A pile of presents grew: rare coins, electronic gadgets, keys to exotic cars—all sorts of expensive gifts, none that apparently pleased him.

After the procession, he glared at me. "What about you? Don't you have a"—he shuddered—"gift?"

I scowled. "It's not Christmas. At least, not yet."

He stiffened. "You know what *day* it is?"

"Gift day!" one nubile lass chortled, stroking his leg. "Let—"

"Quiet." He turned to me. "What day is it?"

"December 13th. Maybe the 14th. It's close to midnight."

He stared into the distance. "I've lost track of time."

I could have mentioned the lawsuit, but somehow I knew it wasn't the right time. *Time...?* I had an idea.

It took some concentration, but finally, a small box appeared in my hand. "Here." I gave it to him. "If this is Gift Day, this is for you."

I thought he was going to dismiss it like the others, but he didn't. He opened it and his dubious look changed to awe.

"A watch? For me?" He examined it carefully. "It works."

I shrugged. "It's no Rolex, but it'll keep time." I pointed at the dial. "And it has one of those calendar thingies so you'll always know what day it is."

He looked up, almost smiling. "Uh...thanks. I appreciate this."

I ducked my head. "You're welcome."

The harem suddenly swarmed the throne, pushing me away. They all sported new presents, coincidentally all watches. The computer learned fast.

"Look, darling. I've brought you a watch."

"No, look at mine. It has diamonds."

"Mine has emeralds..."

I backed away. So much for originality.

As the gaggle overwhelmed him, he looked up and mouthed, "Thank you."

At least he had manners....

VR is funny. Until you get settled, it's more like a dream where a warped logic allows abrupt changes in places, times, and people without question.

So it became tomorrow—December 14. I wandered around lost in a world that looked more like the Playboy Mansion than Alice's Wonderland. Finally I stumbled into the room where King Doug squirmed on his throne.

I tried not to laugh. "You look like my cousin after my uncle caught him smoking in the basement. Talk about a major whupping."

Post looked distracted by his discomfort. "My parents didn't believe in spanking."

Why was I not surprised?

"It's this damn throne," he continued. "I wish it had a cushion or something."

A blond carrying a red velvet pillow trimmed with gold tassels pushed me out of the way. "For you, darling."

And the harem descended, bringing cushions of every size and fabric and jockeying for the top position on the throne. The result? A four-foot-high stack of pillows that left Doug no place to sit.

"C'mere." I grabbed his hand and pulled him toward the door I'd created. His bevy squealed in protest, but he seemed relieved to escape.

When the screen door opened, the hinges made a reassuring creak. The scent of honeysuckle rode the warm fresh air along with the song of a meadowlark.

I led him across the worn plank floor, past terra-cotta pots brimming with red geraniums, and toward what I considered a better throne for His Royal rear end.

"Your choice." I showed him the swing that hung by chains at the end of the porch and beside it, a wooden rocking chair. Each sported one cushion covered in blue-checked gingham.

Doug selected the porch swing, leaving me the rocking chair. It didn't take long for us to start a complementary rhythm.

After a while, he spoke. "This reminds me of something. I'm not sure what, but I like it." Doug hooked his thumb in his waistband and leaned back with a contented sigh.

Ignorance was bliss. I'd always envied kids whose grandparents lived in bucolic countryside settings; mine lived in a midtown high-rise. Lacking suitable personal memories, I'd stolen this setting directly from *The Andy Griffith Show*.

And as long as Opie Post didn't figure this out...

Having witnessed their master's joy in the simplicity of a porch swing, the harem created their own swinging seats for him on the third day.

Unfortunately, something had been lost in the translation; they hung a wide assortment of chairs from the ceiling—stools, folding chairs, couches, office chairs....Every time a chair moved, it caused a domino effect, turning the throne room into a swinging hazard zone.

I had no problem coercing Doug into an escape. We headed for the door that led to a rose garden built from my memories of a park where I played as a child.

We strolled down a path between rows of bushes, and he paused to admire the colors. "I forgot flowers could be this pretty."

"You know what they say—take time to stop and smell the roses."

He knelt, selected a blossom and inhaled. "Nice." Suddenly he recoiled from the bush, staring at a drop of blood on his fingertip. "It's a thorn." Perplexed, he examined the bush. "They all have thorns. Why? You could've created roses without them."

"Then they wouldn't have been roses." I inspected his wounded finger. "They would've been...just pretend."

"Pretend," he repeated in a faraway voice, staring at his punctured finger.

"Here, let me." I conjured a Band-Aid and applied it to his forefinger. "There." I placed a maternal kiss on the boo-boo. "All better."

I forgot I had a mission.

I forgot he was a megalomaniacal madman.

I forgot this whole world was indeed pretend.

He turned and, for one moment, I thought he was going to kiss me. *So much for being maternal.*

He blushed and smiled. "Thanks."

I know what you're thinking. *Excuse me, Shelley. You're playing nice with a nutcase. Are you crazy?* In my defense, remember that in prolonged VR, it's easy to lose your train of thought, even when the universe's welfare hangs in the balance. But think about it—if my mission was to make PostPrime happy, I was on target.

The next day, the throne room overflowed with huge bouquets of roses, each stem filled with thorns. Not thorns. Spikes, large enough to puncture a tire. Talk about overstating a concept!

"Uh...excuse me?" Doug waved at me from his throne. "Could you give me a hand? I'm stuck."

The spiked roses ringed his seat like a barbed-wire corral. Had he tried to push his way out, the thorn-spikes would have shredded his hands. I imagined a pair of chain metal gloves and some leather boots and they appeared at his feet.

"Perfect." He tugged on the boots and the gloves, and now armed, made an easy path through the roses. When he reached me, he gave me a hug. "Thanks. These were exactly what I needed."

Okay, I'll admit it; I liked the hug. God help me, I liked the man. I grinned like an idiot. "Glad I could help."

He released me, stepped back, and gave me an expectant smile. "Wanna go for another walk?"

"To the garden?"

"Nope." He grinned. "A different type of park..."

As in Fenway Park. Baseball. Hot dogs. All-American entertainment.

Okay, I'll admit I'm no baseball fan, but I had something to cheer about; this was the first time I'd seen Doug actively manipulate VR, creating something for himself.

After the last batter struck out in this perfect shut-out game, the park faded away. We strolled back, hand-in-hand, stopping just short of the throne room.

"Did you enjoy the game?" he asked.

"I liked the hot dogs, the peanuts, the beer, the seventh-inning stretch, and especially the company." I thought I was being highly diplomatic, but he seemed crestfallen.

"But it was a perfect game. I made sure of it."

He swings...he misses. "The fun of baseball—of any sport—is not knowing the game's outcome before it starts. That wasn't a game; it was a predictable rout."

He looked as if he'd never contemplated such a notion. "Unpredictability..."

"Exactly. Constant predictability is boring. Surprises can be good."

Something dark crossed his face. He wandered toward the throne room without me, muttering, "Not always."

So if Doug Post hated surprises, how could I explain the big surprise waiting for him in the real world? Even worse, I'd lost track of the days and could count only by what presents I'd given him—the watch, the porch swing, the rose garden, and the gloves and boots. Four days. Maybe five if we counted the baseball game if that was a different day. Who knew?

It was time to play hardball, time to make Doug come to me. Sure enough, Mohammed came to the mountain. Doug appeared, holding out one red rose.

"For you. With my apologies."

I accepted the rose, noticing the small thorns along the stem. "Apologies for what?"

"For acting like an ass. I didn't even ask if you liked baseball. I'm sorry."

I sniffed the rose. "That's okay."

His look of contrition changed into a shy smile. "Willing to take another chance?"

"Sure. You lead."

We ended up sitting at the edge of the Grand Canyon, watching a brilliant sunset with the canyon changing its array of colors with each passing minute.

"I came here when I was ten," he explained. "I don't think I appreciated it, but I remembered it well enough to reproduce it."

Yahoo! Not only was he manipulating VR, but acknowledging his control. Definitely an improvement.

I tried to control my enthusiasm. "Nice sunset. Reminds me of one I saw on a business trip to Hawaii."

He cocked his head. "You've never told me what you do for a living."

Was it time to take an obvious opening? Maybe. "In the real world, I work with computers."

Shock flooded his features. "The real world..."

"You know...out there. Beyond VR. I work in system security and integrity."

Doug's eyes narrowed and he stood up. "You're a hacker." He stepped back as if putting distance between us would isolate him from danger. "You've broken into our system and are trying to steal data."

I remained seated. "I don't want to steal from you—just stop you."

His face hardened. "From what?"

I'd hoped this would be easier. "From destroying the world. You...or someone representing you, has threatened to release a viral code that will incapacitate every computer in the world loaded with any of MultiData software."

His voice remained harsh. "Why would I do something like that?"

"You lost the lawsu—"

Before I could finish, he closed his eyes.

"Computer, stop program."

When he opened his eyes again, he looked shocked to see me still there.

"Computer, I said *stop program*." He glowered at me.

I drew a deep breath. "I'm not part of the program. I'm real."

He raised his hand to shoo me away. "Then leave. I don't want real people here."

Defiant, I moved closer. "Why? Because we disappoint you? We bother you? We hamper your style? We make you unhappy?"

He almost responded, but instead, stormed off. I could've followed him, but didn't. I'd blown a big hole in his world. I could afford to be patient for a couple more days.

On day seven, I found him on his throne as usual. However, his harem were now his security guards, keeping me at bay. Rather than outmaneuver them, I allowed them to isolate me in a distant corner. After a while, Doug approached me, despite the harem's protests.

"I was unhappy," he said in a solemn voice. "Out there."

"I know."

"In here, I feel better."

"I know that, too."

He sat down beside me, and we remained silent until he spoke again. "I haven't been too happy here, either, but..."

I finished his unspoken thoughts. "But it's better than the real world."

"Sure. Look around." He made a sweeping gesture with his hand. "I have everything I could possibly want."

I gave his throne room a once-over, ignoring the harem girls' hostile glares. I noticed the empty chains hanging from the ceiling and the wilted rose petals scattered on the floor.

"Then maybe you ought to want *more* for yourself."

Doug peppered me with questions for the next three days. On the first day, he demanded to know everything about me: my life, my family and my job. Glossing over my job, I spent more time talking about childhood dreams, embarrassing stories about my evil cousin Patrice and anything that highlighted the ups and downs of my real world.

On the second day, he grilled me on current events, including bare details about the lawsuit.

The third day, he talked about himself. I learned he'd been labeled a genius at four and enrolled in college before turning eight, missing an entire childhood along the way. He waxed poetic about his first love, a fellow prodigy with whom he'd shared four magnificent weeks together before her parents stopped the affair. Listening to him, I realize he'd turned out to be much more stable than I'd anticipated. No chemical dependencies or obvious deviancy. No really extravagant lifestyle befitting his fortune.

I had to admit, I liked him. A lot.

But liking him wouldn't save his life. If Doug didn't willingly emerge from VR, Stik would kill him. Pure and simple.

I had to tell him. Time was running out.

Tomorrow...

When tomorrow came, everything changed. When I walked into the throne room, the harem girls were gone. Doug sat behind an old-fashioned desk, his throne replaced by an executive office chair.

He looked up from a stack of papers. "Morning."

"Is it? I've lost all sense of time." A chair magically appeared by the desk and I sat down.

He glanced at his watch. "It's December 23rd. 9:26 A.M." He shot me a brilliant smile. "You know, you couldn't have given me a better present."

Panic rose in my throat. December 23rd? I had less than forty-eight hours to come up with a solution...unless the solution had found me.

"I'm leaving," he stated in a calm voice.

My panic turned into elation. "VR?"

He nodded. "It's time to go back." He pushed the papers away. "I've been hiding from my problems, but they haven't gone away. You've made me realize I have a duty to fix things."

I couldn't believe what I was hearing. "Me? How?"

Doug Post smiled a smile I'd never seen before. "You showed me what it's like to be real, reminded me what I've been missing." A wistful look filled his eyes. "I'd forgotten how much I love life." He touched my hand. "Thank you, Shelley."

I swallowed my disbelief. "You're...you're welcome."

He pushed back from his desk and stood. "It's going to take me longer than you to extract myself since I've been here a while. You go first and tell your superiors I'm going to repair the damage done in my name."

It's exactly what I wanted to hear; not only had he'd recognized his errors and was going to rectify them, but it was all due to little ol' me. What an ego boost.

Something was wrong.

Maybe it was his resolute look, his businesslike demeanor...

This was too damn easy.

There was only one thing I could do. I threw my arms around him and kissed him.

Nothing happened.

All we'd done was talk...about life, liberty, the pursuit of...knowledge. I'd never even thought about kissing him. At least not too often. I had no basis of comparison.

But even if I couldn't predict Doug's reaction, I knew what mine should be. Something. But I felt nothing. Then I realized I'd never told him my first name, yet he'd just used it.

The only way he'd know it was if I'd just kissed a computer.

Maybe not the computer itself, but a simulated Douglas Post, formed for the purpose of stalling me.

What day was it? Maybe I'd lost twelve days and I was living inside the only functional computer on earth. Or maybe the computer figured Douglas Post was on the cusp of returning to the real world and had to distract me.

I had two choices: confront the computer or let it believe it'd fooled me.

"That's wonderful," I chortled, praying I sounded believable. "Let me get my things." I bolted from the room.

Okay, it was a lousy excuse, but I was desperate. I needed to find the real Douglas Post and I found him...

In the hallway.

Around the corner.

In the next room.

There were Doug Posts, everywhere, all dressed the same, sporting watches on their arms and bandages on their forefingers.

I needed the real Doug Post—now. I started kissing them.

The computer was smart enough to vary their responses to the kiss from tentative to ferocious. But none of them elicited the right response in me.

Until...

When I kissed the real Doug, he blushed, smiled, then kissed me back. A shiver crept across my shoulders. When we broke apart, we gasped for breath.

"Oh boy," we said simultaneously.

We grabbed hands and plowed our way through the Fake Dougs, running toward the door that led to Mayberry. Once outside, we vaulted the porch railing and sped toward the garden. We hid behind a row of rose bushes while a herd of Dougs thundered by.

I turned to whisper something and got a rather intoxicating kiss instead.

"Is this real?" he asked. "What I feel for you?"

"It's got to be."

"But what passes for reality here isn't necessarily real out there." He touched my cheek. "You willing to see if we can make it in the real world?"

"Definitely."

He stood. "Computer, command protocol Delta Delta Papa. Voice recognition verification."

The computer hesitated before answering. *"Voice recognition proto-col has been established."*

"Commence extraction of Delta Delta Papa and..." He turned to me.

"Sierra Mike Charlie," I supplied.

"Insufficient memory for simultaneous extractions."

"Reallocate memory."

"Insufficient memory for simultaneous extractions."

He sighed. "We'll have to do it in shifts." He bowed, slightly. "Ladies first."

"No way. What if the computer releases me, but keeps you? You go first. And tell the guy waiting for you that I'm sorry I stepped on his foot. You fix things there, then you get me out." I kissed him. "In that exact order. Got it?"

He stood. "Computer, commence extraction of Delta Delta Papa."

It wasn't a fancy procedure; he simply faded away. No sparks, no transporter effects like on Star Trek. Even though Mayberry had come from my thoughts, it faded, too. But I was too elated with my relative success to worry about that. After all, I'd saved the world and found love. Not bad for a hard eleven days' work. Or was that twelve?

Or unlucky thirteen?

My heart rate increased. Why? Because of desire? Anticipation? Fear? Whatever emotion spurred my heart also made it hard to breathe. I sat down, hoping to catch my breath.

It didn't work.

"Oxygen readout," I gasped.

Instead of a disembodied voice, a harem girl appeared beside me. "The oxygen levels are at minimum"—she gave me a malevolent smile—"and falling. With PostPrime gone, there is no need to continue life support."

"But...I'm in here."

"Insufficient memory. Fatal error. Would you like to reboot?"

Fatal error indeed. "No."

"Commence diagnostic programming and data compression."

The room began shrinking. The damn computer was going to take revenge one way or the other—suffocating me or squeezing me to death. I wanted to scream, but didn't have enough breath.

I started praying—that I hadn't lost track of time, that the world hadn't been rendered computerless, that Stik hadn't killed Doug the moment he awoke, that Doug could control his own computer and that I'd get out of VR alive.

As I grew weaker and dizzier, I prayed for Doug's survival more than anything else. All I knew was that if Doug hadn't survived, then it didn't matter if I escaped VR.

Didn't matter at all.

The world went black, then turned a brilliant white again.

Doug stood before me.

I drew in lungfuls of blessed air. "Is this heaven?"

He laughed. "Only if you want. You're still in VR."

I didn't have the energy to kiss him. "Are you real?"

"No. But I'm no computer pawn, either. It's a new feature of VR—being able to insert yourself into a running VR program without complete immersion."

"Cool. Wish I'd thought of that. I'd make a million."

"You ready to leave VR?"

"Definitely." I tried to sit up. "But I'm not working well."

"That's because the computer tried to kill you. You're still healing."

"Did we succeed?"

Doug gave me a brilliant smile that seared me to my soul's center. "Yes. Thanks to you." He pointed over his shoulder. "Ready to go?"

I nodded.

He twined his fingers through mine. "Commence extraction, Sierra Mike Charlie."

When I awoke again, I was on the med-lab bed, free of the telemetry equipment. Doug and Stik stood over me. Stik betrayed no emotion, but Doug smiled broadly.

"Welcome back." His kiss was long and deep. He reached behind him and pulled out a single red rose.

With thorns.

"A Christmas present for me?"

His grin flickered briefly. "You were in there longer than you think."

"How long?"

"Be my valentine?"

Authors' Biographies

P. N. "Pat" Elrod is best known for the critically acclaimed Vampire Files, featuring her wisecracking undead private eye, Jack Fleming, in his ongoing battle against the gangster underworld of 1930s Chicago. Beginning with *Bloodlist*, Jack's first head-spinning case is to solve his own murder! *A Chill in the Blood*, her seventh in the series, won the Lord Ruthven Award for best vampire novel of 1999 and her ninth, *Lady Crymsyn*, will be released in the fall of 2000.

She also authored four historical novels with the Jonathan Barrett, Gentleman Vampire series, set during the American Revolution and the best-selling *I, Strahd, Memoirs of a Vampire*, and *I, Strahd, the War with Azalin*, mixing vampirism and magic. All have won rave reviews from *Locus* to *Publisher's Weekly*.

One of her favorite projects has been collaborating with actor Nigel Bennett (LaCroix of TV's *Forever Knight*), on a series of books about the James Bondian vampire, Richard Dun, once known as Lancelot. *Keeper of the King* garnered wildly enthusiastic applause from both fans and critics. "Our premise," said Elrod, "is 'What if Lancelot had been a vampire?' No wonder he was Arthur's greatest knight!' Then we asked, 'What if he has to go after the Holy Grail—again? And this time he'd better find it!'"

Their second novel, *His Father's Son*, will soon be released. "Nigel has spoiled me for collaborations," reports Elrod with a big grin. "He's not only extremely talented, coming up with the best ideas, but has an enviable professional attitude, not to mention a great sense of humor. I am thrilled that our readers enjoy the books as much as we have." Elrod has also co-edited *Time of the Vampires* and the soon-to-be-released *Dracula's London* with Martin H. Greenberg, the latter featuring a short story by Bennett and Elrod.

Elrod has always been a fan of the romance genre and works a strong element of it into all of her novels. "I love a gutsy hero meeting a feisty heroine who not only keeps up with him, but passes him by so he has to work to win her heart. This is a favorite theme for me, especially when the characters take over and start writing their own lines, then I just sit back and relish the ride!

"I was delighted at the chance to contribute to this anthology. The idea of 'The Scottish Ploy' had been banging around in my head for some time and this gave me a means to combine my favorite elements, screwball comedy against a theatrical background. I was a drama major at university and have never lost the kick of working on productions. It has been a great help to my writing as it taught me how to visualize scenes and hear dialogue. I think every writer should take drama courses to enrich their work."

After this, her first foray into the world of romantic suspense, Elrod is planning out additional books in the genre—as soon as she finds the time! At present, she is working on two new Jack Fleming supernatural/mystery novels, two fantasies, and teaming with Nigel Bennett on their third Richard Dun adventure. "But not to worry," she tells her readers, "I'll fit in a romance or three, they're just too much fun!"

Neesa Hart writes contemporary romance under her own name and historical romance as Mandalyn Kaye. Her latest release, *You Made Me Love You*, is a contemporary single-title romance from Avon Books.

Neesa lives in Washington, D.C., where she writes full-time.

Sometimes, she lives other places around the country where she manages and produces theatrical presentations for churches large and small. "The Show Must Go On," she swears, is not based on a true story, though some of her former cast and crew do make cameo appearances. Neesa would like to dedicate this story to Ruth and Rose—who make her theatrical endeavors ever so much brighter.

Neesa's work has been honored with multiple awards by readers and her peers. She's a three-time HOLT Medal winner, a Romantic Times Reviewer's Choice winner, and a Gold Congressional Medal winner.

Neesa's books include:

The Promise, historical romance by Mandalyn Kaye. Pinnacle Books, 1995.

Beyond All Measure, historical romance by Mandalyn Kaye. Pinnacle Books, 1996.

A Matter of Honor, historical romance by Mandalyn Kaye. Pinnacle Books, 1996.

Restless, contemporary romance by Neesa Hart. Pinnacle Books, 1996.

Almost to the Altar, contemporary romance by Neesa Hart. Silhouette Special Edition, 1997.

Scandal's Captive, historical romance by Mandalyn Kaye. Zebra Books, 1997.

Seven Reasons Why, contemporary romance by Neesa Hart. Silhouette Special Edition, 1997.

"The Midnight Sky," a historical novella by Mandalyn Kaye in the *Scottish Magic* anthology. Kensington Books, 1997.

Priceless, historical romance by Mandalyn Kaye. Fawcett Books, 1998.

Halfway to Paradise, contemporary paranormal romance by Neesa Hart. Avon Books, 1999.

A Kiss to Dream On, contemporary romance by Neesa Hart, Avon Books, 1999.

Who Gets to Marry Max?, contemporary romance by Neesa Hart, Harlequin American, 2000.

You Made Me Love You, contemporary romance by Neesa Hart. Avon Books, 2000.

❧ ❧ ❧

Laura Hayden never lacks for a change of pace or venue in her life. The wife of an active-duty air force officer, she has, more than once, started a project while living in one state, sold it while on the road, and finished it while unpacking boxes and setting up a new household halfway across the country. Such versatility in her home life is also reflected in her writing career.

Laura claims 1993 as her banner year. She'd been writing for three years and had completed three manuscripts, two of which were under consideration by publishers. In March 1993, she sold her first project, "The Star of Kashmir," a lighthearted, action-adventure-romance novella written specifically for audio.

In May, she learned she had been selected as a finalist in the Romance Writers of America's prestigious Golden Heart contest for her time-travel manuscript *A Margin in Time*. The air force decided this was a perfect time to uproot her family from Colorado to Kansas for a one-year assignment.

Somewhere on I-70, she learned she'd sold her first novel, a romantic suspense to Harlequin Intrigue. A month later, she won the Golden Heart. Two months after that, her audio book came out to great reviews. A month later, her Golden Heart final-round judge bought *A Margin in Time* on a two-book contract for Pinnacle. Two months later, her first book was released and she sold a second Harlequin Intrigue novel.

After a year in Kansas, she moved to northern Virginia and wrote another romantic suspense for Intrigue and a lighthearted paranormal romance for Pinnacle. The next move was a one-year assignment to North Dakota where she wrote her fourth romantic suspense for Intrigue. When she sold her first short story "Nine Tenths" (featured in the *Dangerous Magic* anthology from Daw), she wrote it while using packing boxes as a desk since her family was moving to Montana. Laura finished the story on the road, somewhere in South Dakota. (She thinks it was at Mount Rushmore.)

It was in Montana that Laura got the idea for "Twelve Days." She reports: "I came up with this story while at the post office. I mailed packages several times a week and struck up a friendship with Doug, the guy behind the counter. We'd discovered some common interests, one of which was computers.

"When the first stories came out about Microsoft's legal troubles, Doug made an innocent observation: 'Boy, I bet Bill Gates isn't happy today!' I nodded, shot the breeze, mailed my package and trudged back through the January snow to my car. By the time I started the engine, I had the basic story—what if the world's biggest computer mogul got pissed and decided to take his toys and go back home? This was January 2000 and the gloom-and-doom warnings about the Y2K death of technology were still fresh in my mind.

"So here's to Doug at the C. M. Russell Post Office in Great Falls, Montana. Thanks!"

After two years in Montana, Laura is moving again, this time packing up three book projects with her household goods. Her next book, *Stolen Hearts*, a time-travel romance, will be available fall of 2001. It's part of the Hope Chest series from Zebra Ballad, a five-book continuity series being written by members of her critique group, the Wyrd Sisters.

She's also embarking on a new writing adventure—working as a ghostwriter on a big mystery series for a major publishing house. And as much as she'd love to tell you all about the project, her lips are sealed!

Laura credits her close ties to the Wyrd Sisters and the wonders of e-mail for keeping her focused on her career, despite all her moves. She enjoys hearing from her fans and welcomes them to e-mail her at: suspense@suspense.net

As she stands by her latest stack of cardboard boxes, she reminds her readers of the wise words of her screen hero Buckaroo Banzai: No matter where you go, there you are.

Yvonne Jocks believes in many magicks, particularly the magic of stories. She has written since she was five years old, and received payment of a transistor radio for her first short story, published by a local paper, at the age of twelve.

Soon after that, she decided writing wasn't lucrative enough to pursue professionally (transistor radios aside). Luckily, this decision did not last like the fun of writing did.

Under the name Evelyn Vaughn (E. Vaughn), Yvonne sold her first romantic suspense novel, *Waiting for the Wolf Moon*, to Silhouette Shadows in 1992. She promptly bought a larger television set. Three more books (*Burning Times*, *Beneath the Surface*, and *Forest of the Night*) completed her "Circle Series," which featured witches and monsters, before the Shadows line closed. The last won Favorite Science Fiction Romance in *Affaire De Coeur* magazine's 1997 reader's poll.

Yvonne's most recent writing project is a series of historical romance novels called "The Rancher's Daughters"—*Behaving Herself* and *Forgetting Herself*—for Leisure Books. She also enjoys writing short stories and novellas in the science fiction/fantasy and mystery genres, and her work has appeared in several books, including *A Dangerous Magic* from DAW books, which combined fantasy and romance.

A resident of Texas for twenty-two years (after living in places as diverse as Window Rock, Arizona, and Pearl River, Louisiana), Yvonne still loves the magic of stories, movies, books, and dreams. Her enjoyment of literature led her to earn a master's degree at the University of Texas in Arlington (her thesis traced the history of the romance novel). An unapologetic TV addict, she lives happily with her cats and her imaginary friends and teaches junior college English to support her writing habit…or vice versa. (All sentence fragments in her story are for effect. Really.)

"Celtic Cross" allowed Yvonne to delve into many of her own interests—she enjoys metaphysical stores such as Avalon and, like any good literature professor, owns a Shakespearean tarot deck. The difference between healthy and unhealthy love and romance has long fascinated her, as well as the emotions that lead to mutual empowerment within healthy relationships.

But mostly, it's the story. And the magic therein…

Feel free to write Yvonne at P.O. Box 6, Euless, TX 76039 or e-mail her at Yvaughn@aol.com.

D. R. Meredith, Doris to family and friends, has a split personality: one persona is that of an ordinary woman with husband, two children, two beagles, and a house in the suburbs; her other persona is a paid killer. After finishing such daily domestic chores as taking out the garbage, Meredith sits down at her computer and commits murder.

Famous for the unique ways in which her victims are "done in," she has created three highly acclaimed mystery series, all set in the Texas panhandle. One series features attorney John Lloyd Branson, another a Texas county sheriff named Charles Matthews, while the third and latest series features an unemployed paleopathologist and female sleuth named Megan Clark. Her first two sherriff mysteries won the "Oppie" for Best Mystery of 1984 and Best Mystery of 1985. Both *The Sheriff and the Branding Iron Murders* and *The Sheriff and the Folsom Man Murders* were selections of the Detective Book Club. Of the John Lloyd Branson series, both *Murder by Impulse* and *Murder by Deception* were finalists for Anthony Awards in 1988 and 1989. "Murder by Reference" was selected to be included in "Murder in the Museum III: A Bibliography," compiled by a panel of museum curators as a study in how the museum is perceived by the public.

A graduate of the University of Oklahoma, Meredith had been a teacher, a librarian, and a bookseller before the publication of her first book in 1984. She was regional director of the Mystery Writers of America, and is the National Liaison Chair for the American Crime Writers League.

She is the book editor for *Roundup Magazine* published by the Western Writers of America, a book reviewer for the *Amarillo Globe News*, has been a contributing editor for *Kirkus Reviews*, and is the current Western Fiction editor for *What Do I Read Next?*, a reference book for libraries and bookstores, published by the Gale Group. She has been a judge for the Spur Awards five times, an Edgar judge twice, and most recently a judge for the Western Heritage Award. She is one of three mystery writers featured in *Texas Monthly*. Meredith is a member of Mystery Writers of America, Western Writers of America, American Crime Writers League, and Sisters in Crime.

When not writing or being a literary critic, she teaches writing seminars at conferences and universities, most recently at the University of

Nebraska, or gives programs at libraries and book clubs. *Texas Almanac* names Doris one of the state's best mystery writers, an honor she considers makes her a valuable resource along with natural gas and beef. Both of Meredith's personalities live in Amarillo, Texas.

Jody Lynn Nye has always loved mysteries, from the first Agatha Christie she read to the most recent Tony Hillerman, and confesses that Dorothy L. Sayers's *Gaudy Night* is on her "if I were marooned on a desert island" list of books.

Jody was born in Chicago, and except for brief forays to summer camp and college has always lived in the area. She was graduated from Maine Township High School East and Loyola University of Chicago, where she majored in Communications and English, and was an active member of the theater groups, the student radio stations, and the speech team (original comedy and oratorical declamation).

Jody has worked as a file clerk, bookkeeper at a small publishing house, freelance journalist and photographer, accounting assistant, and costume maker. Before breaking away to write full-time, she spent four years on the technical operations staff of a local Chicago television station, the last year as Technical Operations Manager.

Although she lists her primary career activity as "spoiling cats," since 1985 she has published twenty-two books and over fifty short stories. Among the novels Jody has written are her epic fantasy series, The Dreamland, beginning with *Waking in Dreamland*, four contemporary fantasies, *Mythology 101*, *Mythology Abroad* and *Higher Mythology* (collected as *Applied Mythology*), *The Magic Touch*, and two science-fiction novels, *Taylor's Ark* and *Medicine Show*. Jody also wrote *The Dragonlover's Guide to Pern*, a non-fiction-style guide to the world of internationally best-selling author Anne McCaffrey's popular world. She has collaborated with Anne McCaffrey on four science fiction novels, *The Death of Sleep*, *Crisis on Doona*, *Treaty at Doona* and *The Ship Who Won*. She also wrote a solo sequel to *The Ship Who Won* entitled *The Ship Errant*. Jody co-authored the *Visual Guide to Xanth* with best-selling fantasy author Piers Anthony, and edited an anthology of stories about mothers in science fiction, fantasy, myth and legend, entitled *Don't Forget Your Spacesuit, Dear!* She wrote an episode produced for the animated series *Dinosaucers*, "Tyrannosaurus Store Wars."

Her newest book is *The Grand Tour*, third in the Dreamland series. Due out in 2001 is a contemporary fantasy co-authored with Robert Lynn Asprin, *License Invoked*, and a fourth in the Mythology series, Advanced Mythology.

Jody lives in the northwest suburbs of Chicago, with her husband Bill Fawcett, a writer, game designer, and book packager, and two cats, Lila and Cassandra. Anyone wishing to get in touch with her can write to her at P.O. Box 776, Lake Zurich, IL 60047, USA, or e-mail her at: jodynye@poboxes.com, or visit her website at: http://www.sff.net/people/jodynye.

Jody says:

> "Night Hawks" was inspired mainly by the setting. We have a large backyard, two thirds of which has been allowed to go wild for the sake of the local animal population. Walking in it by moonlight feels mysterious and inviting...even a little dangerous (we have coyotes—and skunks). I'm fascinated by hunting birds. We see red-tailed hawks all summer long, and there are peregrines living on skyscrapers in the city. They aren't alone in their hunting. You have only to read the daily newspaper to know that there are other predators out there besides raptors, and other prey than mice and shrews.

Jody's books include:

The Dragonlover's Guide to Pern. Del Rey, 1989; trade paper, 1992; 2nd ed., 1996.

Visual Guide to Xanth, co-authored with Piers Anthony. Avon Books, 1989.

Mythology 101. Warner Books, 1990.

The Death of Sleep, co-authored with Anne McCaffrey. Baen Books, 1990.

Mythology Abroad. Warner Books, 1991.

Crisis on Doona, co-authored with Anne McCaffre. Ace Books, 1992.

Higher Mythology. Warner Books, 1993.

Taylor's Ark. Ace Books, 1993.

The Ship Who Won, co-authored with Anne McCaffrey. Baen Books, 1994.

Medicine Show (Taylor's Ark II). Ace Books, 1994.

Treaty at Doona, co-authored with Anne McCaffrey. Ace Books, 1994.

The Magic Touch. Warner Books, June 1996.

Don't Forget Your Spacesuit, Dear. Editor. Baen Books, 1996.

The Ship Errant (The Ship Who Won II). Baen Books, 1996.

Waking in Dreamland (Dreamland I). Baen Books, 1998.

School of Light (Dreamland II). Baen Books, 1999.

The Grand Tour (Dreamland III). Baen Books, 2000.

Applied Mythology (Omnibus of books 1, 2 ,3). Meisha Merlin Publishing, 2000.

100 Crafty Little Cat Crimes, "Land Rush." Barnes & Noble, 2000.

Dracula's London, "Everything to Order." Ace Books, 2000.

Warrior Fantastic, "Conscript." DAW Books, 2000.

Forthcoming works:

Oceans of Space, "Pyrats." DAW Books, 2001.

License Invoked, co-authored with Robert L. Asprin. Baen Books, 2001.

Advanced Mythology (Mythology IV). Meisha Merlin Publishing, 2001.

The Lady and The Tiger (Taylor's Ark III). Ace Books, 2002.

⚵ ⚵ ⚵

Laura Resnick, a *cum laude* graduate of Georgetown University, where she studied French and Italian, began her career by selling a romance novel to Silhouette Books; it was released in 1989 under the pseudonym Laura Leone. She has won several awards as a romance writer and has sold more than a dozen romance novels to three different publishing houses.

After establishing herself as a romance writer, Laura also began writing science fiction/fantasy short stories under her own name. By 1993, she won the John W. Campbell Award (best new science fiction/fantasy writer) in recognition of her work. Currently under contract to Tor Books, a major publisher of science fiction and fantasy, she now devotes most of her time to writing epic fantasy novels. Her next major release will be *In Fire Forged* (the sequel to her 1998 hardcover, *In Legend Born*, which is currently available in paperback).

In addition, Laura is the author of the award-winning 1997 release *A Blonde In Africa*, the non-fiction account of her seven-month overland journey across Africa. She has also written several short travel pieces, as well as numerous articles about the publishing business; she currently writes a monthly opinion column, "The Comely Curmudgeon," for *Nink*, the newsletter of Novelists, Inc.

You can find her on the Web at www.sff.net./people/laresnick.

Kristine Kathryn Rusch is an award-winning fiction writer. Her novella, *The Gallery of His Dreams*, won the Locus Award for best short fiction. Her body of fiction work won her the John W. Campbell Award, given in 1991 in Europe. She has been nominated for several dozen fiction awards, and her short work has been reprinted in six Year's Best collections.

In 1999, her story "Echea" was nominated for the Locus, Nebula, Hugo, and Sturgeon awards. It won the Homer Award and the Asimov's Reader's Choice Award. In 1999, she also won the Ellery Queen Reader's Choice Award and the Science Fiction Age Reader's Choice Award, making her the first writer to win three different reader's choice awards for three different stories in two different genres in the same year.

She has published twenty novels under her own name. She has sold forty-one total, including pseudonymous books. Her novels have been published in seven languages, and have spent several weeks on the *USA Today* bestseller list and the *Wall Street Journal* bestseller list. She has written a number of Star Trek novels with her husband, Dean Wesley Smith, including a book in this summer's crossover series called New Earth.

Her most recent novel is *Utterly Charming*, a lighthearted romance (with magic) written under the name Kristine Grayson. Her most recent fantasy novel is *The Black King*, the last book in her Black Throne Series. She has written a science fiction series, The Tenth Planet, with her husband, Dean Wesley Smith. She has also published a mainstream crime novel, *Hitler's Angel*, which was called "a great story, well told," by the *Oregonian* and received a full-page review in the *New York Times*. Her next book will be the second book in her Black Throne series, *The Black King*.

Under the name Kris Nelscott, she has sold two mystery novels set in 1968 to St. Martin's Press.

She is the former editor of the prestigious *Magazine of Fantasy and Science Fiction*. She won a Hugo for her work there. Before that, she and Dean Wesley Smith started and ran Pulphouse Publishing, a science fiction and mystery press in Eugene.

She lives and works on the Oregon coast.

Susan Sizemore lives in the Midwest and spends most of her time writing. Some of her other favorite things are coffee, dogs, travel, movies, hiking, history, farmers markets, art glass, and basketball—you'll find mention of quite a few of these things inside the pages of her stories. She works in many genres, from contemporary romance to epic fantasy and horror. She's the winner of the Romance Writers of America's Golden Heart award, and a nominee for the 2000 Rita Award in historical romance. Her available books include historical romance novels from Avon; a dark fantasy series, The Laws of the Blood, from Ace Science Fiction; science fiction from Speculation Press; and several electronically published books and short stories. One of her electronic books, the epic fantasy *Moons' Dreaming*, written with Marguerite Krause, is a nominee for the Eppie, the e-publishing industries writing award.

Though "Dizzy and the Biker" is technically the first mystery story she's written, she's actually had the idea for Franciscan Place in the back of her head for several years. It's the sort of place she'd like to live if she lived in a city and kept pets. She'd had visions of Dizzy and Harley and their companion people for quite some time, but she had no idea for a mystery plot for them to solve until she started taking her own dog to a fenced-in dog park out in the country. The story that appears in this anthology fell into place while following her own very active greyhound-mix pooch around the paths in this wooded park, so she included the park as part of the setting for Franciscan Place. Only she took it out of an 800-acre forest preserve and put it in the heart of a city where it became the site of a murder and the beginning of a romance—between a pair of dogs, and their owners. According to Susan, "It was a great pleasure writing this story, and I hope to return to Franciscan Place again."

Susan's e-mail address is Ssizemore@aol.com and her web page address is: http://members.aol.com/Ssizemore/storm/home.htm

Early in life, **Deb Stover** discovered a passion for writing and an unwavering respect for honor and fairness. She left a journalism career to pursue her dream of writing romance, and editor Denise Little played a dual role as faerie godmother.

Stover's novels and short stories often include characters with disabilities. She believes strongly that individuals with disabilities must be included in society and fiction as people first, and her belief is reflected both in her writing and in her life. She strives to create characters readers will love and knows imperfection is a fact of life. A reviewer once said that "Ms. Stover's characters are so real—even the ghosts."

In "Keeper of the Well," readers meet Annie Campbell—a little girl with Down syndrome. One of Stover's own children has Down syndrome and served in some ways as a model for Annie. Deb also drew on her experience as an adoptive mother while plotting this story.

Stover is active in many writers' organizations, and has served as director of the Pikes Peak Writers Conference, held annually under the umbrella of the Kennedy Center Imagination Celebration. She has recently completed a two-year term on the Romance Writers of America's National Board of Directors.

Since publication of her first novel in 1995, Stover has received five award nominations from *Romantic Times*, including one for Career Achievement in Innovative Historical Romance. *Another Dawn* has also received the Dorothy Parker Award of Excellence from Reviewers International Organization, and was a finalist for the Colorado Award of Excellence. In 1999 and 1997, she was chosen as Pikes Peak Romance Writers' Author of the Year. She has been a finalist for the Heart of Romance Reader's Choice Award twice, and won in 1998 with *Some Like It Hotter*, which was also a finalist for the Colorado Award of Excellence. *Almost an Angel* was voted Best Time Travel of the Year by Romance Readers Anonymous, and *Some Like It Hotter* was nominated for *Affaire de Coeur*'s Romance Novel of the Year and Best Time Travel. *Almost an Angel* was a finalist for Best Paranormal Romance, and Stover was a favorite author of the year. In 1996, her second novel, *A Willing Spirit*, was voted Romance Novel of the Year by readers of *Affaire de Coeur*.

Deb Stover is a native of Wichita, Kansas, but now lives near Colorado Springs with her husband, their three children, and a mutant dachshund.

For more information, visit her web page: http://www.debstover.com/.

Novels by Deb Stover include:
No Place For A Lady. Zebra Books, September 2001.
A Moment in Time. Zebra Books, 2000.
A Matter of Trust. Zebra Books, 2000.
Stolen Wishes. Zebra Books, 1999.
Another Dawn, Zebra Books, 1999.
Almost an Angel. Pinnacle Books, Denise Little Presents, 1997.
Some Like It Hotter. Pinnacle Books, Denise Little Presents, 1997.
A Willing Spirit. Pinnacle Books, Denise Little Presents, 1996.
Shades of Rose. Pinnacle Books, Denise Little Presents, 1995.

Novellas and Short Stories:
A Dangerous Magic, "The Enchanted Garden." DAW Books, 1999.

Diane A. S. Stuckart, who also writes historical romance as Alexa Smart and Anna Gerard, is a member of that proud breed, the native Texan. The oldest of five children, she was born in the West Texas town of Lubbock and raised in Dallas. She admits to crossing the Red River just long enough to obtain her degree in Journalism from the University of Oklahoma before returning home for good to the Lone Star State. Now settled in a North Dallas suburb, she has worked as a purchasing agent in the electronics, aviation, and medical fields while writing fiction at night.

Diane's historical romances have been published in multiple languages and have garnered rave reviews from critics and fans alike. Her first book, *Masquerade*—written under the name Alexa Smart— was a finalist in the Romance Writers of America's Golden Heart competition. Pinnacle Books published that novel in December of 1994 as part of its popular Denise Little Presents line. Three other historical romances from DLP and Pinnacle soon followed: *Shadows of the Heart*, *A Touch of Paradise*, and *Roses at Midnight*. Diane's most recent novel, *Desert Hearts*, was a September 1999 release from Zebra Books penned under the name Anna Gerard. She has also made a foray into historical romantic fantasy. Writing as Diane A. S. Stuckart, she was one of several authors contributing to the DAW Books anthology, *A Dangerous Magic*. Now, with this book, she is taking her first step into contemporary romantic fiction.

Diane is a firm believer in research and visits her fictional settings whenever possible. She made three trips to New Orleans for *Masquerade*, prowling the French Quarter and old cemeteries, talking to convent groundskeepers and voodoo shop owners. For *A Touch of Paradise*, she journeyed to Bimini in the Bahamas, snorkeling to the underwater site of the "Atlantis Road" that some claim is a remnant of that legendary place. She also traveled the deserts and mountains of Arizona while researching for *Desert Hearts*, stopping in the town of Tombstone, once home to Wyatt Earp and Doc Holliday. Her most recent trip was to Colorado's cloud-high city of Leadville, where she explored silver mining and gold panning for a future historical romance. She was relieved, however, to realize she could do all her research for www.gonnahavekelly.com from the comfort of her own computer.

A fan of good books, bad movies, and '70s rock-and-roll, Diane is a longtime member of Romance Writers of America and a founding member of the Dallas Area Romance Authors. When not working on her next book, she is practicing Tae Kwon Do or yoga, or else wasting precious writing time surfing the Net. She shares her home with her husband, Gerry, and various other motley critters.

Mary Watson worked at a variety of jobs before selling her first romance novel to Harlequin Books in 1983—as patient-advocate at a large hospital, as a weekly newspaper columnist, a bank teller, a reading teacher for learning-disabled elementary school students, and a creative writing teacher.

Since that first book sale, Mary has had thirteen novels published under her Lynn Turner pseudonym, eleven series romances for Harlequin/Mills & Boon, and two single-title books published by the Denise Little Presents line of Pinnacle Books. *Forever*, her first book for Mills & Boon, received the 1986 Romantic Times Reviewer's Choice Award for best Presents. That same year, *Mystery Train* was a finalist for *Romantic Times*'s best Harlequin Intrigue title.

Mary's writing has focused primarily on romantic mystery/suspense. Her most recent books have also incorporated an element of the paranormal. *Race Against Time* was a time travel–romantic mystery story and a finalist for Romance Writers of America's RITA award, while *Dreamer's Heart* featured a psychic heroine targeted by a psychotic serial bomber. Lynn describes herself as a plot-driven reader and writer and loves stories that contain complex, tightly woven plots and lots of surprises. She describes "Hostage to Love" as a trial run for a few of the characters who will populate a novel presently in the outlining stage.

Mary and her husband of thirty-three years live in the southwestern corner of Indiana. Readers can send e-mail to marywatson@email.com.

Murder Most Medieval

Noble Tales of Ignoble Demises

Contents

Introduction   277
John Helfers

Like a Dog Returning . . . A Sister Fidelma Mystery   283
Peter Tremayne

The Country of the Blind   301
Doug Allyn

Cold as Fire   343
Lillian Stewart Carl

A Horse for My Kingdom   363
Gillian Linscott

The Simple Logic of It   379
Margaret Frazer

Plucking a Mandrake   399
Clayton Emery

A Gift from God   421
Edward Marston

The Queen's Chastity   441
Tony Geraghty

The Reiving of Bonville Keep   457
Kathy Lynn Emerson

For the Love of Old Bones   479
Michael Jecks

The Wizard of Lindsay Woods   501
Brendan DuBois

Improvements   529
Kristine Kathryn Rusch

A Light on the Road to Woodstock   541
Ellis Peters

Authors' Biographies   567

Copyrights and Permissions   573

Introduction

John Helfers

There's no doubt that the medieval period (A.D. 750–1500) was a time of great hardship. After the fall of the Roman Empire, most of Europe and the British Isles remained mired in the Dark Ages. Nobles controlled the land, the Catholic Church attempted to rule the royalty, and the peasants owned nothing. Add to this the human devastation caused by the Black Plague, which killed as much as one-third of the population of Europe, and the outlook for humanity appeared very grim. Would Europe fall apart as nobles bickered and battled for lands and crowns? Not likely. The aristocracy and the Church made sure no one overstepped their bounds. Would the continent remain stuck in these medieval ways forever? No. In the fifteenth century, Johann Gutenberg and the Renaissance put an end to the Middle Ages.

During this era mankind continued doing what it had always done: living and dying. The former was difficult (one of every three babies died within six months of birth), and the latter was all too easy (because of plague, starvation, and war, among other factors). But humanity, like the cockroach, is exceedingly easy to kill but very difficult to exterminate. Even with plagues, starvation, and war, mankind was growing, expanding, even learning. One lesson people learned very well was how to survive.

Survival was what everyone fought for in one form or another. Everybody struggled to survive: from kings and queens, who fought to hold their crowns and their countries; to the Church, which fought to maintain control over the masses; to the nobles, who fought to retain their lands and way of life; to the merchants, who fought for trade routes and business; to the peasants, who fought simply to stay alive. Most people would do anything to ensure their survival, to keep what was theirs and perhaps gain a little bit more when the opportunity presented itself. They would conspire for it. They would lie for it. They would steal for it. They would even kill for it.

Which brings us to the theme for this anthology. Of the crimes man commits against his fellow man, murder is the basest one of all. Depriving another human being of life simply to gain what they have, to protect what the murderer has, or to protect one's reputation, is an act that shocks and appalls society, regardless of motive. Even in cases of self-defense, no matter how justifiable, there is a certain amount of wonder about the person who can be pushed no farther, believing that the only way to save themselves is by committing murder.

It is certainly conceivable that there would be people who lived in the Middle Ages who felt this way. Peasant women, subject to a lord's whim if he fancied one, were sometimes treated as badly or worse by their own husbands. Lords spent their whole lives scrabbling for a piece of land and the tenants to make it profitable, or at least livable. Kings did not know which to fear more—their enemies abroad or the ones in their own court—so they hid their treachery behind false smiles and promises of allegiance.

The following stories examine the medieval world—a world of dirt and struggle—and the men and women who lived and died in it. Murder is committed in these stories for many of the same reasons that murder is committed today. And, as always, there were men and women in medieval times who crusaded against the lawlessness that, at times, threatened to overwhelm the land. Peter Tremayne's Celtic detective Sister Fidelma makes an appearance here, solving a twenty-year-old crime of passion. The noble highwayman Robin Hood, as written by Clayton Emery, is also found within these pages, solving a mystery of witchcraft and heresy, with the help of the indomitable Marian. And, of course, what collection of medieval murder mysteries would be complete without a tale from the late, lamented grande dame of historical mystery, Ellis Peters, and her soldier-turned-sleuthing-monk, Brother Cadfael?

From Gillian Linscott's tale of a lord whose survival needs necessitate starting a war, to Margaret Frazer's story of political intrigue and deception at King Henry's court, we are pleased to bring you thirteen tales of murder most foul, murder most malicious, murder most malevolent. So turn the page and prepare to be swept back through time into a world of intrigue, danger, and history—to a time when death was all too common, and murder was a crime committed by everyone from kings to peasants—a time of murder most medieval.

Murder Most Medieval

Like a Dog Returning... A Sister Fidelma Mystery

Peter Tremayne

I t's very beautiful," Sister Fidelma said softly.

"Beautiful?" Abbot Ogán's voice was an expression of disbelief. "Beautiful? It is beyond compare. Worth a High King's honor price and even more."

Fidelma frowned slightly and turned toward the enthusiastic speaker, a question forming on her lips. Then she realized that the middle-aged abbot was not looking at the small marble statuette of the young girl in the robes of a religieuse, which had caught her eye as she had entered the chapel of the abbey. Instead, he was looking beyond the statuette, which stood at the entrance to a small alcove. In the recess, on a small altar, stood an ornate reliquary box worked in precious metals and gemstones.

Fidelma regarded the reliquary critically for a moment.

"It is, indeed, a valuable object," she admitted. But the reliquary box was not unusual in her experience. She had seen many such boxes in her travels, all equally as valuable.

"Valuable? It is breathtaking, and inside it is the original *Confessio* penned in the hand of Patrick himself." Abbot Ogán was clearly annoyed at her lack of homage before the reliquary.

Fidelma was unimpressed and not bothered at all by his look of disfavor.

"Who is the young girl whose statuette guards the entrance to the alcove?" she demanded, turning the conversation to what she considered to be the object of greater interest. Somehow the artist had brought the young religieuse to life, endowing her with a vibrancy that burst through the lines of the cold stone: It seemed that she would leap from the pedestal and greet the worshippers in the tiny abbey church with outstretched hands.

The abbot reluctantly turned from his contemplation of his community's most famous treasure—the reliquary of Saint Patrick. His face darkened slightly.

"That is a likeness of Sister Una," he said shortly.

Fidelma put her head to one side to examine it from every angle. She could not get over the extraordinary vitality of the piece. It was almost as if the artist had been in love with his model and only thus able to draw forth some inner feeling into the cold marble.

"Who was the sculptor?" she asked.

The abbot sniffed, clearly not approving of the interest she was showing.

"One of our brethren, Duarcán."

"And why is her statuette in this chapel? I thought only the holy saints could achieve such honor?"

The corner of Abbot Ogán's mouth turned down. He hesitated and then, observing the determination on Fidelma's face, asked, "Have you not heard of the story of Sister Una?"

Fidelma grimaced irritably. It was surely obvious that she would not be asking the question had she heard the story. The abbot continued: "She was killed on this very spot some twenty years ago."

"What happened?" Fidelma's eyes had widened with greater interest.

"Sister Una entered the chapel when someone was attempting to steal the holy reliquary. The thief struck her down and fled but without the reliquary."

"Was the thief caught?"

"He was overtaken."

"How did the Brehons judge him?"

"Sister Una was very beloved by our local community." The abbot's features were set in deep lines, and there appeared a defensive note in his voice. "Before the culprit could be secured and taken before a Brehon for judgment, the people hanged him from a tree. This small marble statuette was erected in the chapel in Una's honor to guard the reliquary for all eternity."

"Who was the thief and murderer?"

The abbot again hesitated. He clearly was unhappy at her interest.

"A man who worked in the abbey gardens. Not one of our community."

"A sad tale."

"Sad enough," the abbot agreed shortly.

"Did you know Sister Una?"

"I was a young novitiate in the abbey at the time, but I hardly knew her." The abbot turned, clearing his throat as if in dismissal of the memories. "And now . . . I believe that you are staying with us until the morning?"

"I will be continuing my journey back to Cashel in the morning," Fidelma confirmed.

"Stay here then and I will send Brother Liag, our hostel keeper, to you. He will show you to the dormitory of the religieuse. We eat after Vespers. You will forgive me leaving you here. There are matters I must now attend to."

Fidelma watched as he hurried along the aisle and vanished beyond the doors of the chapel. As they banged shut behind him, her eyes were drawn back once again to the extraordinary statuette. It held a curious fascination for her. The artist had, indeed, given the poor Sister Una life and, for a while, she was lost in examining the lines of the fine workmanship.

There was a sound behind her: a shuffle of sandals and an exaggerated cough.

She turned. A religieux had entered and stood a little distance off with his arms folded inside his robe. He was balding and wore a doleful expression.

"Sister Fidelma? I am the hostel keeper, Brother Liag."

Fidelma inclined her head toward him. Yet her gaze was still reluctant to leave the intriguing statuette. The newcomer had observed her interest.

"I knew her."

Brother Liag spoke softly and yet there was a curious emotion in his voice that caught her attention immediately.

"Yes?" she encouraged after a pause.

"She was so full of life and love for everyone. The community worshipped her."

"As did you?" Fidelma interpreted the controlled emotion of his voice.

"As did I," Brother Liag confirmed sadly.

"It is an unhappy story. I have heard it from your abbot."

Did a curious expression flit across his features? She was not sure in the gloomy light.

"Did you also know the man who killed her?" she pressed when it seemed that he was saying no more.

"I did."

"I gather he worked in the gardens of the abbey?"

"Tanaí?"

"Was that his name?"

"That was the man who was lynched by the community for the crime," Brother Liag affirmed.

Fidelma exhaled softly as she gazed at the marble face of the young girl.

"What a miserable waste," she observed, almost to herself.

"Grievous."

"What sort of man was this Tanaí? How did he think that he, a gardener, could steal that precious reliquary and sell it—for presumably he did it for mercenary gain?"

"That was the theory."

Fidelma glanced quickly at him.

"You do not agree?"

Brother Liag returned her gaze and his expression had not changed. It was still mournful.

"I think that we share the same thought, Sister. The only way such an object could be sold for gain is by its destruction. Where and to whom could such a priceless treasure be sold? The selling of jewels pried from the box might be sold individually. The value of the box itself and the greater value of that which is contained in it would be entirely lost. There would be no market for anything so invaluable. Who would purchase such a treasure?"

"Yet if Tanaí was merely a laborer in the garden here, he might not have considered that aspect of the theft. He might simply have seen a precious jeweled box and been overcome by greed."

The hostel keeper smiled for the first time, more a motion of his facial muscles than indicative of any feeling.

"It is true that Tanaí worked here as a gardener. He was an intelligent man. He had been an apothecary and herbalist. One day he mixed a wrong prescription and one of his patients died. He answered before the Brehons for manslaughter and was fined. The Brehons said it was an accident, and there was no guilt of intent involved—only the guilt of error. But Tanaí was conscientious and, although he could have continued to practice as a herbalist, he withdrew here to the abbey and did penance by returning to study the plants and herbs, living a life of penury and self-sacrifice."

Fidelma glanced at Liag cynically.

"Until he coveted the reliquary; for what you are telling me is that he was intelligent enough to know its real value. Maybe he thought he would find someone who would endanger their immortal soul for possession of it?"

Brother Liag sighed deeply.

"That is what everyone has thought these last twenty years."

"You sound as though you still do not agree?" she commented quickly.

Brother Liag was hesitant, and then he sighed reflectively: "The point that I was making is that he was intelligent enough to know that he could never sell the reliquary, if that was his motive.

There are some questions to which I have never found satisfactory answers. Tanaí had removed himself to the monastery with his wife and young daughter because he felt he must do penance for a mistake. That strikes me as the action of a man of moral principle. He worked in the abbey gardens in a position of trust for five years. Never had there been a whisper of anyone's distrusting him. He could have been appointed apothecary of the abbey for the old abbot—he died many years ago now—who had several times urged him to take the position, saying that he had paid for his mistake more than enough.

"Why did he have such a sudden mental aberration? For over five years he was in a position in which he could have stolen the reliquary or, indeed, any one of the several treasures of the abbey. Why did he attempt the theft at that point? And to kill Una! He was never a violent man, in spite of the mistake that led to the manslaughter charge. The killing of poor Sister Una was so out of character."

"What actually connected him with the attempted theft in the first place?" Fidelma asked. "The abbot said that he fled without the reliquary."

Brother Liag inclined his head.

"The reliquary was untouched. Sister Una had disturbed the thief before he could touch it, and she was killed while trying to raise the alarm."

"Where was Tanaí caught?"

"Trying to enter the abbot's rooms." Brother Liag shot her a keen glance. "The community caught up with him at the entrance and dragged him to the nearest tree. God forgive all of us. But Sister Una was so beloved by all of the community that common sense was displaced by rage."

"The abbot's rooms? That is a strange place for a man to run to when he has apparently just committed murder," murmured Fidelma.

"A question that was raised afterward. Abbot Ogán, who was one of the community, a young brother at the time, pointed out that Tanaí must have known that he would be caught and was trying to throw himself on the old abbot's mercy and seek sanctuary."

"I suppose that it is plausible," Fidelma conceded. "What happened to Tanaí's family?"

"His wife died of shock soon after, and his young daughter was raised by the Sisters of the abbey out of charity."

Fidelma was perplexed.

"There is something here that I do not understand. If Tanaí was found at the abbot's rooms, if the only witness was killed and the reliquary had not been touched, and there was no eyewitness, what was there to link Tanaí with the crime? Indeed, how do you know that theft was even the motive for the murder?"

Brother Liag shrugged.

"What else could have been the motive for killing poor Sister Una? Anyway, everyone was crying that it was Tanaí who did the deed and that he had been seen running from the chapel. I presumed that this was without question since everyone was shouting it."

"How much time had passed between the time the crime was committed and when Tanaí was found?"

Brother Liag shifted his weight as he thought over the matter, trying to stretch his memory back two decades.

"I can't really recall. I know it was some amount of time."

"An hour?"

"No, well under an hour."

"A few minutes?"

"More than that. Perhaps fifteen minutes."

"So who identified Tanaí as the culprit?"

Brother Liag gestured helplessly.

"But everyone was shouting that . . . I saw Brother Ogán, the abbot as he now is. In fact, it was Ogán who was foremost in the hue and cry; but there was Brother Librén, the *rechtaire* . . . the steward of the abbey. Everyone was shouting and looking for Tanaí . . . I have no idea who identified him first."

"I see," Fidelma replied with a sigh. "Why do you now have doubts of Tanaí's guilt?"

Brother Liag appeared slightly uncomfortable.

"I know that this community has his death on its conscience because he was unjustly killed by the anger of the mob and not by legal process. That is enough to lay the burden of guilt on us.

There is always doubt if a man has not had a proper chance to defend himself."

Fidelma thought for a moment.

"Well, on the facts as you relate them, you have a right to be suspicious of the guilt of Tanaí. Had I been judging him at the time, I would have acquitted him on grounds that there was insufficient evidence. Unless other witnesses could have been produced. However, there is little one can do after twenty years."

Brother Liag gave a troubled sigh.

"I know. But it is frightening to consider that if Tanaí was not guilty, then all this time the real murderer of Sister Una has dwelt within these walls nursing this dark secret."

"We all live cheek by jowl with people who nurse dark secrets," Fidelma pointed out. "Now, perhaps you'll show me to my room?"

After the evening Angelus bell and a frugal meal in the refectory of the abbey, Fidelma found herself almost automatically making her way to the chapel to once again examine the marble statuette of Sister Una. She disliked unsolved mysteries; they kept nagging at her mind until she had made some resolution of the problem. The face of Sister Una, alive in the marble, seemed to be pleading, as if demanding a resolution to this now-ancient murder.

Fidelma was standing before the statuette when, for the second time, a voice interrupted her meditation.

"He didn't do it, you know."

The voice was a soft feminine one. Fidelma quickly glanced around and saw a religieuse standing nearby. She was, so far as Fidelma could place her, somewhere in her thirties. The face could have been attractive, but even in the softening candlelight it seemed bitter and careworn.

"To whom do you refer?" Fidelma asked.

"To Tanaí, my father. My name is Muiríol."

Fidelma turned to her and examined the woman carefully.

"So you are the daughter of the gardener who was hanged for the killing of Sister Una." It was a statement rather than a question.

"Unjustly so, for, as I say, he did not do it."

"How can you be so sure?"

"Because I was here at the time and he was my father."

"Daughters are not the best witnesses to their father's deeds. I would need more than a statement of belief. You were surely young at that time?"

"I was twelve years old. Do you think that day is not impressed on my mind? I was with him in the abbey gardens, for I used to often play there. I remember seeing Sister Una passing to the chapel. She greeted us and asked my father a question about his work. Then she passed on into the chapel."

Muiríol paused and swallowed slightly. Her dark eyes never left Fidelma's face. There was a haunted look in them as if again seeing the scene—a vivid scene that appeared to torment her.

"Go on," Fidelma encouraged softly.

"A few minutes after she passed into the chapel, there came a scream. My father told me to remain where I was and ran to the chapel. He disappeared inside. Others of the community had heard the scream, and some came into the garden to inquire what it portended. There came shouting from the chapel, a man's voice was raised."

"Was it your father's voice?"

"I did not think so at the time. But time often confuses some details."

"Your memory appears clear enough."

"It is the truth, I tell you," she replied defensively.

"What happened then?"

"I saw my father emerge from the chapel. A voice was crying—'Tanaí has murdered Una!'—or words to that effect. I saw my father running. Later I realized that he was running to the abbot's rooms in fear for his life. But there was an outcry, and the people were angry. I did not know what had happened. I was taken to our rooms by one of the religieuse and remained there until my mother, prostrate with grief, was carried inside. She had seen my father being . . ." Her voice caught and she paused a second before continuing. "She had seen my father being lynched outside the abbot's rooms. She never recovered and died soon afterward."

There was a silence between them for a while.

"From what you tell me, your father could not have killed Una," Fidelma finally observed. "Did you never tell your story?"

Muiríol nodded.

"I told it to the old abbot, but I was not believed."

"But did you tell it to the Brehon who investigated the matter?"

"The matter was kept secret within the abbey for years until the old abbot died. The abbot felt guilty that the lynching had taken place with members of the community involved, and he wished to conceal it. So it was not reported to the Brehons. That was why the religious here were kind to me and raised me as one of the community. After the old abbot had died, no one bothered about the story of Una and my father."

"Knowing this, why did you remain in the abbey?"

The girl shrugged.

"One day, so I hoped, I would find the guilty one. Someone in this abbey killed Sister Una and was also responsible for my father's death."

"So you wished your father's name to be cleared?"

Muiríol grimaced.

"That was my original purpose. Twenty years have passed. Is anyone still interested?"

"Justice is always interested in justice."

"Isn't there a saying that there is little difference between justice and injustice?"

"If I believed that I would not be an advocate of the courts," Fidelma returned.

FIDELMA WAS IRRITATED. SHE could not sleep. Her mind was filled with the thoughts of young Sister Una's death. She turned and twisted for an age, but sleep would not come to her. She sat up and judged it was long past midnight.

Finally, she rose from her bed, put on her robe, and decided to go down to the abbey gardens to walk in the cool of the summer night. The only way to the garden that she knew of led through the chapel.

She heard the sound almost immediately as she opened the door into the chapel—a low groaning sound followed by a thwack as if of leather on a soft substance. The groan rose in a new note of pain.

Then she heard a voice: *"Mea culpa, mea culpa, mea maxima culpa!"*

Her eyes narrowed at familiarity of the masculine voice. She peered into the gloom to seek out the penitent.

A figure was kneeling before the marble statuette of Sister Una, head almost to the ground. The back was bare where the robe was stripped down to the waist. In one hand was a broad leather belt that, every so often, the figure would strike his back with, drawing blood, as she saw by the candlelight. Then the groan would issue a second or so after the impact of the leather on the flesh. The words of contrition were mumbled in Latin.

Fidelma strode forward.

"Explain this, Abbot Ogán!" she demanded coldly.

The abbot froze for a moment and then slowly straightened himself up, still kneeling on the chapel floor.

"This is a private penitence," he replied harshly, trying to summon anger to disguise his shock at being thus discovered. "You have no right to be here."

Fidelma was unperturbed at his animosity.

"On the contrary. As a *dálaigh* of the Brehon courts, no doors are barred to me, Abbot Ogán, especially when it is deemed that a crime has been committed."

The abbot rose from his knees, pulling his robe around his shoulders. Fidelma had noticed that his back was scarred. It was of no concern to her that the abbot practiced flagellation: many mystics of the Church did, although she found such practices distasteful in the extreme. The scars, obvious even in the candlelight, indicated that the abbot had practiced the self-abuse for many years.

Ogán was defensive before her hard scrutiny.

"What crime?" he blustered.

With a slight forward motion of her head, Fidelma indicated the statuette of Sister Una.

"You seem to be expressing some guilt for her death. Were you guilty of it?"

The last sentence was suddenly sharp.

Abbot Ogán blinked rapidly at the tone.

"I was responsible, for had I been in the chapel at that time she would not have been alone to confront Tanaí."

Fidelma's brows came together.

"I do not follow."

"It was my task on the day she was killed to clean the chapel. I had delayed my task out of simple sloth and indolence."

"I see. So you were not here when you should have been. If you feel guilt then that is within you. So when did you become involved in leading the hue and cry after Tanaí?"

A frown passed the abbot's face.

"Who said I did?" he asked cautiously.

"Are you saying that you did not?"

"I . . . I came on the crowd as he escaped across the garden. Everyone was shouting. They caught and hanged Tanaí from the tree outside the old abbot's quarters. That was when I first knew about her death and realized my guilt, for if I had been here . . ."

"An 'if' will empty the oceans," Fidelma snapped. "So you did not witness the event? You did not identify Tanaí as the murderer and would-be thief?"

Abbot Ogán shook his head.

"Everyone was proclaiming that Tanaí was the guilty one."

"But someone must have done so first. Who first identified Tanaí as the culprit?"

The abbot again shook his head in bewilderment.

"Perhaps a few of those who were there that day and who have remained in the abbey might recall more than I do."

"Who might they be?"

"Brother Liag, Brother Librén, Brother Duarcán, and Brother Donngal. Everyone else who was here at the time has either died or moved on."

"You have neglected to mention Tanaí's daughter, Sister Muiríol," observed Fidelma.

The abbot shrugged.

"*And* Sister Muiríol. But she was only twelve years old at the time. No one took any notice of her, for like any loyal daughter, she swore her father was innocent."

Fidelma paused for a moment and looked once again at the vibrant features on the statuette. An idea suddenly occurred to her.

"Tell me, Ogán, were any of the community in love with Una?"

The abbot looked bewildered and then pursed his lips sourly.

"I suppose that we all were," he said shortly.

"I think you know what I mean."

Celibacy was not forbidden among the religious of the Church in Ireland. Most houses, like this abbey, were often mixed communities in which the religious, male and female, lived and brought up their children in the service of the new religion.

Fidelma noted that Ogán's chin jutted out a little more.

"I believe that some of the brethren were emotionally and physically enamored of her. She was a very attractive woman, as you may have noticed, because this statuette is an excellent likeness."

"Were you, yourself, in love with her?"

The abbot scowled.

"I was not alone in my feelings."

"That was not my question."

"I admit it. There was a time when I thought we could have been together under God's holy ordinances. Why are you asking such questions? It has nothing to do with her murder."

"Does it not?"

Abbot Ogán's eyes narrowed at her tone.

"What are you accusing me of?"

"You will know when I am accusing you. At the moment I am simply asking questions."

"Una was killed protecting the holy reliquary when Tanaí attempted to steal it. There is nothing else to consider."

"How can you be so sure? There were no witnesses. The reliquary was not even stolen."

"I do not understand," frowned the abbot.

"You mentioned that you were not alone in your love for Una," she went on, ignoring his implied question. "Is there anyone else in the abbey today who fell into that category?"

The abbot thought for a moment.

"Liag, of course. And Duarcán."

"Did Una show particular affection for any one person?"

Ogán scowled for a moment, and then he shrugged in dismissive fashion.

"It was rumored that she and Liag would be married. I thought they were going to leave the abbey and set up a school together."

"And you mentioned Brother Duarcán. Is that the same Duarcán who sculpted this statuette? You mentioned that name when I asked you earlier who the artist was."

The abbot nodded reluctantly.

"It is the same man," he confirmed. "I think he was very jealous of Liag. After he sculpted the statuette, he refused to undertake any more work of a similar nature. A waste of a great talent."

"It is late," Fidelma sighed. "Before I leave the abbey tomorrow morning, I would like to speak with Brother Duarcán. Where will I find him?"

"He will be in the abbey kitchens. He now works cleaning and cooking for the community."

The next morning, Fidelma found Duarcán, a tall dark man, washing kitchen utensils. He glanced up as she approached him and paused in his task. He smiled nervously.

"You are Fidelma of Cashel. I have heard of you."

Fidelma inclined her head in acknowledgment.

"Then you will have also heard, perhaps, that I am an advocate of the Brehon Court?"

"I have."

"I understand that you were in love with Sister Una."

The man flushed. He laid down the pot he was cleaning and turned to her, clasping his hands loosely before him.

"I'll not deny it," he said quietly.

"I am given to understand that she did not return your sentiments?"

Duarcán's mouth tightened at the corners.

"That is not so. We were going to be married."

Fidelma raised an eyebrow.

"What of the story that she was going to marry Liag and set up a school with him?"

"Brother Liag is a liar to tell you that. It is not so. That was *our* plan; mine and Una's."

Fidelma examined his expression carefully. His eyes met hers with a frankness that she found hard to doubt.

"I am told that you were a good sculptor once and that you executed the exquisite statuette of Una in the chapel. Is that so?"

"It is."

"Why are you now wasting your talent?"

"Wasting? My talent died after I had given Una life in marble. I have nothing else to give. I exist, waiting for the time that I can rejoin Una in spirit."

The dramatic words were rendered without drama, offhanded, as someone speaks of a mere statement of fact about the condition of the weather.

"Do you recall where you were when Una was killed?" pressed Fidelma.

"Do you think that I would forget the events of that day?" There was a controlled passion in his voice. "Yes, I recall. I was in my studio that overlooked the gardens. I was the abbey's stone-mason and sculptor. Una had been with me that morning, and we were planning to see the old abbot—he is now dead—to tell him of our decision to marry and leave the abbey. When Una left me, I saw her walk toward the chapel."

"So you saw her cross abbey gardens?"

Duarcán nodded.

"And you saw her go to the door of the chapel?"

"No. Not as far as that. The door was obscured by the shrubs and trees of the garden."

"What did you see then?"

"Tanaí and his daughter were in the garden. Tanaí was doing some work. I saw Una pass by, pausing momentarily to speak with them. Then she went on. A few moments later, I was looking out, and I saw Tanaí rise and move off rapidly after Una.

There was something suspicious about the way he moved. Rapidly, I mean, purposefully."

"Did you hear anything?"

"Hear anything?" He frowned and shook his head. "I was intent on cutting some stone at the time. I do not even know what made me glance out the window. It was the sight, shortly afterward, of people running through the garden that caught my attention rather than the noise. It caused me to go to the door, and that was when I was told that Una had been killed; that Tanaí had tried to steal the reliquary and had killed her."

"Who told you that?"

"Brother Liag."

Fidelma looked thoughtfully at him for a while.

"Did it ever occur to you that if Tanaí was going to steal the reliquary, he would hardly have waited for Una to pass by on her way to the chapel and then attempt to steal it while she was actually there?"

Duarcán stared at her as if he had difficulty following her logic.

"But, Brother Liag said . . ."

Fidelma raised an eyebrow.

"Yes? What did he say?"

"Well, it became common knowledge that is what happened."

"Was it at your instigation that the statuette was placed in the chapel?"

Duarcán frowned.

"Not exactly. In those long, lonely days and nights that followed, I felt compelled to recreate her likeness in marble from fear that it would be lost in the mists of receding memories. One day, Brother Ogán, as he then was, came to my studio and saw the finished statuette. It was he who persuaded the old abbot that it should be placed in the chapel where it has stood ever since. After that, I did no more work as a stonemason nor sculptor. I now merely work in the kitchens."

Sister Fidelma drew a deep sigh.

"I think I am beginning to understand now," she said.

Duarcán looked at her suspiciously.

"Understand? What?"

"The cause of Una's death and the person responsible. Where can I find Brother Liag?"

Duarcán's face filled with surprise.

"I saw him pass on his way to the chapel a moment or so ago . . . Are you saying . . . ?"

But Fidelma was gone, hurrying toward the chapel. Inside, she saw Brother Liag talking with the abbot.

"Sister Fidelma," Brother Liag seemed surprised to see her. "I thought that you had already started your journey back to Cashel."

"There was some unfinished business. Just one question. Cast your mind back twenty years to the events surrounding Una and Tanaí's death. There was tumult in the abbey gardens, shouting and so forth. You passed by the door of Duarcán's studio, and he came out to see what was amiss. You told him what had happened. That Una had been killed; that Tanaí had committed the deed, and you also told him the reason—that Tanaí had attempted to steal the reliquary and was prevented by Una."

Brother Liag frowned, trying to recall, and then he slowly and reluctantly nodded.

"I seem to recollect that I did so."

"This was before Tanaí had been caught. It was a short time after the community had heard Una's last scream, and Tanaí was even then being chased across the gardens. How did you know so soon, all these details?"

Brother Liag stared at her, his face going suddenly pale.

Abbot Ogán exhaled loudly.

"Liag, did you . . . ?"

He left the question unfinished, for Liag was returning the abbot's look in horror as a further recollection came to him.

Fidelma's lips compressed for a moment in satisfaction as she turned to the abbot.

"You told Liag your version in the garden. You were heard to cry that Tanaí was the murderer. Your and Liag's versions differ so much that one of you was lying.

"The truth, Ogán, was that you were in love with Una, not Liag. When you found that Una was going away with Duarcán, that love turned to hatred. Sometimes what is thought as love is merely the desire to possess, and thus it and hate become two sides of the same coin. Was it here, in this chapel, that Una told you of her love and her decision to leave the abbey? Did you then strike her down in your jealous rage? Her scream of terror as you struck was heard by Tanaí, who came rushing into the chapel . . . too late. He was not running to the abbot for sanctuary, but to tell the abbot what he had seen. You raised the alarm, denouncing Tanaí as the murderer, and the first person you told was Liag. The death of both Una and Tanaí are your responsibility, Ogán."

The abbot stood, head bowed.

When he spoke it was in a dull, expressionless tone.

"Do you not think that I haven't wished for this moment over the years? I loved Una. Truly loved her. I was overcome with a mad rage that I instantly regretted. Once Duarcán's statuette had been placed here, I returned each night to seek her forgiveness . . ."

"Your contrition could have been more readily believed had you made this confession twenty years ago. I would place yourself in the hands of Brother Liag; prepare to answer for your crimes."

Brother Liag was regarding the abbot in disgust.

"Some of us knew that you were secretly flagellating yourself before her statuette. Little did we realize you were merely as a dog, as the Book of Proverbs says; a dog returning to its own vomit. There is no pity for you."

The Country of the Blind

Doug Allyn

I've never much cared for my own singing. Oh, I carry a tune well enough, and my tenor won't scare hogs from a trough, but as a minstrel, I would rate my talent as slightly above adequate. Which is a pity, since I sing for my living nowadays.

As a young soldier I sang for fun, bellowing ballads with my mates on battlements or around war fires, amusing each other and showing our bravery, though I usually sang loudest when I was most afraid.

The minstrel who taught me the finer points of the singer's art had a truly fine voice, dark and rich as brown ale. Arnim O'Beck was no barracks room balladeer; he was a Meistersinger, honored with a medallion by the Minstrel Guild at York.

An amiable charmer, Arnim could easily have won a permanent position in a noble house, but he preferred the itinerant life of the road, trading doggerel tunes in taverns for wine and the favors of women.

My friend ended dead in a cage of iron, dangling above the village gate of Grahmsby-on-Tweed with ravens picking his poor bones. I hadn't bawled since my old ma died, but I shed tears for Arnim, though I knew damned well he would have laughed to see it. In truth, he ended as we'd both known he would.

But it wasn't only for my friend that I cried. I was a soldier long years before I became a singer. Death has brushed past me many times to hack down my friends or brothers-in-arms.

I mourned them, but I never felt their passing had dimmed the light of the world. A soldier's life counts for little, even in battle. His place in the line will be filled.

But when a minstrel like Arnim dies, we lose his voice and all the songs in his memory. And in these dark times, with the Lionheart abroad, Prince John on his throne, and the Five Kings contending in Scotland, this sorry world needs songs to remind us of ancient honor all the more.

My friend the Meistersinger knew more ballads of love and sagas of heroes than any minstrel I've ever known.

But even he was not the best singer I ever heard. . . .

I'D BEEN WAITING OUT a gray week of Scottish drizzle, singing for sausages in a God-cursed log hovel of an alehouse at the rim of the Bewcastle wastes. If the muddy little village had a name, I never heard it nor did I inquire. I was more concerned with getting out of it alive.

The tumbledown tavern had too many customers. Clearly there was no work to be found in the few seedy wattle and daub huts of the town, yet a half dozen hard-bitten road wolves were drinking ale in the corner away from the fire. They claimed to be a crew of thatchers, but their battle scars and poorly hidden dirks revealed them for what they were: soldiers who'd lost their positions. Or deserted them. Men whose only skill was killing.

Bandits.

Ordinarily, outlaws pose no problem for me. Everyone knows singers seldom have a penny, and brigands enjoy a good song as readily as honest folk. If I culled the gallows-bait from my audiences, I'd sing to damned skimpy crowds indeed. But along the Scottish borderlands, thieves are more desperate. And as ill luck would have it, I had some money. And they knew it.

I'd earned a small purse of silver performing at a fest in the previous town. One of the border rats jostled me, purposely I think. Hearing the clink of coins, he hastily turned away. But not before I glimpsed my death in his eyes.

And so we played a game of patience, whiling away the hours, waiting for the rain to end. And with it, my life and possibly the innkeeper's. Cutthroats like this lot would leave no witness to sing them to a gallows tree.

My best hope was sleep. Theirs. And so I strummed my lute softly, murmuring every soothing lullaby I could remember. And praying they would nod off long enough to give me a running start.

And then I heard it. I was humming a wordless tune when an angel's voice joined my own in perfect harmony, singing high and clear as any Gregorian gelding.

Startled, I stopped playing, but the melody continued. For a moment I thought it was a voice from heaven calling me to my final journey. Then the innkeeper, a burly oaf with a black bush of a beard, cursed sharply and ended the song.

"Who was that singing?" I asked.

"My evil luck," he groused. "A nun."

"A nun? In this place?"

"Well, an apprentice nun anyway, a novice or whatever they're called. There were a fire at the abbey at Lachlan Cul, twenty mile north. Most died, but one aud bitch nun stumbled here with her charge before death took her, saddling me with yon useless girl."

"She has a wonderful voice."

"It's nought to me. I've no ear for song, and my customers don't care much for hymns. She's heaven's curse on me, I swear. She's blind, no good for work, nor much inclined to it neither."

"Bring her out, I would like to hear her sing more."

"Nay," he muttered, glancing sidelong at the louts in the corner. "That's a bad lot there. I'll not risk harm coming to a nun under my roof. My luck's foul enough as 'tis."

"I'm sure you're wrong about those fellows," I said a bit louder. "I have plenty of money, and they've not troubled me. Buy them an ale, and bring the girl out to sing for us. I'll pay." I tossed a coin on the counter, snapping the thieves to full alert.

The innkeeper eyed me as though I'd grown a second head, but he snatched up the coin readily enough. Brushing aside the ratty blanket that separated his quarters from the tavern, he thrust a scrawny sparrow of a girl into the room. Sixteen or so, she was clad in a grimy peasant's shift, slender as a riding crop with a narrow face, her eyes wrapped in a gauze bandage.

"What's your name, girl?"

"Noelle," she said, turning her face to the sound of my voice. The landlord was right to worry. She was no beauty, but she'd pass for fair with the grime wiped away.

"Noelle? You're French?"

"No, the sisters told me I was born at Yuletide."

"Ah, and so you were named Noelle for Christmas, and your holiday gift was your lovely voice."

"You're the singer, aren't you?" she asked with surprising directness. She hadn't the mousy manner of a nun. "What are you called?"

"Tallifer, miss. Of Shrewsbury and York; minstrel, poet, and storyteller."

"I've been listening to you. You seem to know a great many songs."

"I've picked up a tune or two in my travels. Most aren't fit for the ears of a nun, I'm afraid. Nor is it proper for you to stay at an alehouse. There is an abbey a few days to the west. I'll escort you there if you like."

"Hold on," the innkeeper began, "I shan't let—"

"Come now, friend, the girl can't remain here, and I need a good deed to redeem my misspent life. I'll pay for the privilege." Pulling the purse from beneath my jerkin, I spilled the coins in a heap on the table. "Consider this as heaven's reward for your kindness to this poor waif. Have we a bargain?"

Stunned, the innkeeper stared at me, than hastily glanced at the crew in the corner. Their eyes were locked on the silver like hounds pointing a hare.

"There's no point in haggling," I continued. "Search me if you like, but I haven't one penny more. Come girl, we'd best be going."

"But it's still raining," the innkeeper protested, eyeing the outlaws, afraid of being left alone with them. "Surely you'll wait for better weather?"

"Nay, I've no money to pay for your hospitality now, and I wouldn't dream of imposing further. Has she any belongings?"

"Belongings? Nay, she—"

"This will do for a cloak then," I said, ripping the blanket from the doorway, draping it about her. Snatching up my lute, I paused at the door long enough for a 'God bless all here,' then I dragged the girl out into the drizzle. But after a few paces she pulled free of my grasp, whirling to face me, her narrow jaw thrust forward.

"Kill me here. Please."

"What?"

"If you mean to dishonor me, then kill me now where I can be buried decently. Sister Adela warned me about men like you."

"And rightly so, but I'm no one to fear. I'm old enough to be your father, girl. I was a soldier once, and I swear my oath to God I mean you no harm. Unfortunately, I can't swear the same for that lot back there. We've got to get away from here and quickly, or we'll both be dead."

"Then stop pulling me along like a puppy. I can walk. Fetch me a slender stick."

Cursing, I hastily cut an alder limb, and she used it as a cane to feel for obstructions in her path. Though she stumbled occasionally, she had no trouble maintaining my pace. Coltish legs, young and supple.

We marched steadily through the afternoon, moving north on a rutted cart track through the forest. Tiring as dusk approached, I began casting about for shelter.

"Why are we slowing?" Noelle asked.

"It'll be dark soon."

"Darkness is nothing to me. Continue on if you like."

"No need. The rain will wash out our tracks, and they may not follow us at all. If I can find a copse of cedar—"

"That way." She pointed off to our left. "There's a cedar grove over there."

She was right. Peering through the misty drizzle, I spied a stand of cedars some twenty yards off the path.

"How could you know that?"

"Scent. We've passed cedars several times in the last hour, though the wood around us is mostly alder, yew, and ash. Each has their own savor. Gathering osier wands for baskets was my task at the abbey. I often did it alone."

Taking her hand, I threaded my way through the brush to a cedar copse with a soft bed of leaves beneath and heavy boughs above that kept it relatively dry. I cut a few fronds to make our beds, then used flint and steel to kindle a small fire.

Leaving Noelle to warm herself, I scouted about and found a dead ash tree with a straight limb as thick as my wrist. Twenty minutes whittling with my dirk produced a usable quarterstaff, a peasant's pike.

Returning to the fire, I was greeted by the heavenly scent of roasting meat. Noelle was holding two thick blood sausages over the fire on the end of a stick, sizzling fat dripping into the flames.

"You came well prepared," I observed, sliding a sausage off the spit, blowing on it til it cooled enough to chew.

"In the country of the blind, one learns to cope."

"But surely you were well treated at the convent?"

"They were kind, but their lives were so . . . stifling. I was always pestering new novitiates for songs they knew and news of the outside world. Have you traveled far?"

"Too far. From London to Skye and back again many times, first as a soldier, now a singer."

"Would you sing something for me? A song of some faraway place?"

"Is France distant enough?" Sliding my lute from its sheepskin bag, I tuned it and began the "Song of Roland," a war ballad from the days of mighty Charlemagne. In the streets or a stronghold, I sing it lustily, but huddled near the fire as dusk settled on the wood, I sang softly. For Noelle only.

A dozen verses into the ballad, she raised her hand.

"Stop a moment, please." And then she sang it back to me, echoing my every word, every inflection in her crystalline angel's voice, ending the refrain at the same place I had.

"Sing on, girl. Your voice does wonders for that song."

"I can't. I've ne'er heard that tune before, and I can only memorize a dozen or so verses at a time. But at the end I'll remember it all."

"Truly? You can learn an entire ballad with one hearing?"

"There are no books or signposts in my country. Memory is everything. Sister Adela said Homer was blind, yet he sang ballads of ten thousand verses."

"Homer?"

"A poet, a Greek I think."

"I know who Homer was. I was bodyguard to the young Duke of York during his schooldays at London. I'm just surprised that nuns study Homer."

"I'm not a nun. I was a ward of the convent, a lodger. I had my own quarters and Sister Adela to teach me and help me get about."

"How long were you there?"

"Always," she said simply. "My whole life."

"But no bairns are born in convents. Where are your parents? Your home?"

"The convent was my home," she said, with a flash of anger. "They had other guests, an idiot girl and a boy so deformed he had to be wheeled about in a barrow. If I had parents, I know nothing of them, nor care to. In the country of the blind all men are handsome, all ladies lovely."

"But all is in darkness?"

"Not all, I can see the changes 'tween day and night readily enough and some colors and shapes, though not clearly. I wear this ribbon to spare confusion and let my other senses compensate. That's how I knew the cedar was near. And that someone is coming now."

"What? Where?"

"Behind us, on the track we left."

"I hear nothing."

"Sight is no help in the dark. He's on horseback, moving slowly."

"I hadn't counted on horses," I said, rising, seizing my cudgel. "The louts from the inn—"

"No," Noelle said positively. "There were no horses at that place. And I hear only one animal now."

And then I heard it as well, the soft *tlot, tlot* of hooves on the muddy trail. Then they stopped.

Silence. Only the drip of the rain.

"Hellooo, the fire," a voice called. "I'm a traveler, wet and in need of direction. I have food to share. May I approach?"

"Come ahead, and welcome," I replied, moving into the shadows.

He walked in warily, leading his animal, a plowhorse from the look of it. Our visitor had much the same look. Heavily built, stooped from farm work, his face was obscured by the cowl of his rough woolen cloak. He appeared to be unarmed, though with his cloak pulled tight I couldn't be sure. I stepped out to face him, quarterstaff in hand.

"God bless all here," he said, glancing about. "I'm John of Menteith, a reeve for Lord Duart. No need for that stick, friend. I mean no man harm."

"You're far from Menteith," I said.

"Aye," he nodded, warming his hands at the fire, "I'm bound for the fair at Grahmsby. Hope to trade this sorry nag for a bullock and a few cups of ale. Who might you folk be?"

"Tallifer of York," I said. "Traveling to Strathclyde with my daughter."

"A blind girl, by chance?"

Sweeping off his cloak, he revealed a sword, a crude blade, standard issue at any barracks.

His bush of a beard split in a gap-toothed grin. "Drop the stick, fellow, or I'll cleave you in two."

If he expected me to wet myself or scamper off, he was disappointed. I've seen blades before; I've even faced one or two with nought in my hand but sweat. I had a stout cudgel and Menteith had the look of a farmer, big but clumsy. I waited.

So did he. His eyes flicked from me to Noelle and back again. He licked his lips, unnerved by our stillness, gathering himself. Then with a roar, he lunged at me, swinging his blade like a field sickle.

He'd have done better with a sickle. Jabbing the cudgel butt between his shins, I sent him sprawling into the fire. He moved quickly for a big man, though. Rolling with the fall, he scrambled clear of the flames, crouching on the far side, panting.

Unable to tell what was amiss, Noelle stood frozen as Menteith began sidling around the fire toward her. I thought he meant to seize her as a shield. I was wrong. Eyes wild, he charged again, this time at Noelle!

He was almost on her, blade raised high to hack her down, when I rammed the pole hard into his gut, doubling him over. Gasping, he staggered back, slashing at me. A mistake. Blocking a blow with one end of my staff, I swept the other around full force, catching him squarely on his bull neck just below the ear.

He stared at me a moment, surprised. Then his eyes rolled up like a hog on a hook, and he toppled backward into the fire. I stood over him, taut as a drawn bow, ready to finish him if he moved. But even the flames couldn't rouse him.

Kicking the blade out of his fist, I prodded him out of the fire with my staff.

"Tallifer? What's happened?"

"Our guest had no manners, and it worked out poorly for him. Do you have any idea who he might be?"

"I've ne'er heard his voice before. Why?"

"He seems an unlikely thief. He was armed with a yeoman's blade, but he was no soldier."

"He said he was a reeve, perhaps he spoke true. He smells of cattle."

"He fought like one, all bull, no skill. He was definitely seeking us, though. He knew you were blind though he could see neither of us clearly."

"I don't understand."

"Nor do I, yet. I'll persuade him to explain when he wakes."

But he didn't wake. As I stripped off his belt to tie his hands, his head flopped unnaturally. I checked his pupils. Dead as a goose on Saint Margaret's Day.

"God's bodkin," I said softly.

"What is it?"

"The bastard's dead. Damn me, I didn't think I hit him that hard. And damn him for an inconsiderate lout. Not only does he keep his secrets, I'll have to haul his useless carcass into the wood. We don't want him found near our camp."

After dragging his dead weight for what seemed like a mile, I used his sword to dig a shallow grave, rolled the reeve in it, and threw his blade in after him. Weapons are outlawed for common folk in Scotland and the sword surely hadn't done the reeve much good. His purse held a few shillings, fair payment for a burial.

I slept poorly, restless from the fight and the death of the reeve. As a soldier I was no hero. I fought for my life and my friends, killed when I had to but took no satisfaction in it. In battle I was always afraid. And afterward, though I survived, I knew how easily it could have been me bleeding out while my enemies divided my gear and had a drink on my luck.

The reeve's death was doubly troubling, though. He was no vagrant bandit. Only a fool travels this country at night, yet he'd arrived at our camp well after dark. He must have been hunting us though I couldn't imagine why.

Had the cutthroats from the inn set him on us? Unlikely. Why hire out work they could easily do themselves?

Odder still, in the midst of the fight, he'd lunged at Noelle when she was clearly no threat. It made no sense. Unless she was the one he came for, and I was just in his way. But who would kill a blind nun?

"Tallifer? Are you awake?"

"Yes."

The fire had burned to embers, and her face was only a vague shape in the shadows. As all faces were in her world.

"I've been thinking. You can't leave me at an abbey."

"Why not?"

"Without money to pay for my lodging, they won't accept me."

"How were your expenses paid before?"

"I don't know, by a kinsman, I suppose. It was a private arrangement with the abbess and she was lost in the fire. I have an idea, though."

"Such as?"

"Take me with you," she said in a rush. "I can earn my way. I sing fairly well and you can teach me to—"

"It's out of the question. Life on the road is too hard; it's nothing for a girl."

"All roads are hard in the country of the blind. I heard you breathing heavily this afternoon, when I could have walked another day without tiring. I can carry burdens, wash clothes. I'll be your woman if you want."

"My what? Good lord, Noelle, what do you know of being a woman?"

"The novitiates seldom talked of anything else, and I know a few songs of love."

"I know songs about dragons, girl, but I can't breathe fire. And I'm much too old for you anyway."

"I wouldn't know."

"Yes, you would. Trust me on that."

"You don't want me? Am I too plain, then? Or does my blindness offend you?"

"Neither, but—"

"Then what is it? You've saved my life twice. Why did you bother if you mean to cast me off?"

"Noelle—"

"A minstrel came to the abbey once. He had a little dog who danced when he played the fife. I can't dance, but I can sing a bit. And I promise to be no more trouble than a little dog. Please, Tallifer."

"Enough!" I said, throwing up my hands. "The sun is rising and we'd best be away from here. We'll talk more of this later."

But we didn't talk. We sang instead. We took turns riding the reeve's mount, entertaining each other, with Noelle memorizing each ballad I sang, then vastly improving it with her marvelous voice.

I skirted the next few hamlets, afraid the reeve's horse might be recognized. But in the first town of any size, I found a tailor and squandered our inheritance to buy Noelle a decent traveling garment.

After the measurements, Noelle and the tailor's wife disappeared into the family quarters for a final fitting. I waited with the tailor, exchanging news of the road and the town. And then Noelle stepped out.

The dress wasn't fancy. It had no need to be. In pale blue woolsey, and with her face scrubbed and shining, my grimy foundling was transformed. And I was lost.

The tailor's wife had replaced her blindfold with a blue ribbon that matched the dress. She was a vision as lovely as the damsels of a thousand ballads. But no mirror could ever tell her so.

My throat swelled and I could not speak. Mistaking my silence for displeasure, the tailor's wife frowned.

"If the color is too dark—"

"No," I managed. "It's perfect. Wonderful. No man ever had a more lovely—daughter."

And so it seemed. Born restless, I've never had a family of my own nor much felt the lack. Yet after a few weeks with Noelle I could scarce remember life without her.

As summer faded into autumn, we worked our way southwest toward the border, singing for our supper. And prospering.

My performances have always been well received, but Noelle brought freshness and sparkle to songs I'd sung half my life, her youth and zest a sprightly contrast to my darker presence.

Audiences responded to her and she to them, basking in the applause like a blossom in the sun. The waif from the convent was fast becoming an assured young beauty. And though she never raised the subject of being more than a daughter to me again, neither was she interested in the young bloods who lingered after our performances to chat her up.

She was always courteous but never a whit more than polite as she dismissed them. When I asked why she showed no curiosity about boys, she replied that they were exactly that. Boys. For now, the music and freedom of her new life were more than enough. She'd never been happier.

Nor had I. The last large town we worked was Strathclyde, a performance in the laird's manor house for his family and kinsmen that was well received. Afterward, his steward offered us a year's position in his household as resident artists.

A month earlier I'd have leapt at the chance, but no more.

I've always felt comfortable amongst Scots. Their rough humor and love of battle songs suits both my art and my temperament, but Noelle was changing that.

As her talent and skills improved, I noted the magical effect her singing had on village folk and was certain she could charm larger, more worldly audiences south of the Roman walls just as easily. Newcastle, York, perhaps even in London itself.

For the first time in years I allowed myself to consider the future. We could become master minstrels, winning acclaim and moving in finer circles than either of us had known before.

But to reach that future, we'd have to survive the present. There are always rumors of war in the Scottish hills, but I was seeing more combatants than usual, not only Scots and their Irish cousins, but also hard-bitten mercenaries from France and Flanders.

In earlier years I would have been pleased at the chance to entertain soldiers far from home with fat purses and dim futures. Lonely troops are an amiable audience, easily pleased and generous with applause and coins.

But I had a daughter to worry about now. So after politely declining the steward's offer, we began working our way south toward the border and England. Perhaps we could even journey to my family home at Shrewsbury after long years.

Traveling was a pure pleasure now, singing through the lowlands, describing the folk and the scenery to a girl who savored every phrase like fine wine. My sole regret was that Noelle remained in her country of the blind and I could do nothing to light her way out.

But there is little difference between a lass born sightless and a fool befuddled by dreams. Though I recall those days as the happiest I've ever known, in some ways I was more blind than my newfound daughter.

THE FIRST FROSTS OF autumn found us moving steadily south and into trouble. We were entering the country of the true border lords now, nobles with holdings and kinsmen on both sides of the river Tweed and loyalties as changeable as the lowland winds. Arnim once described the Scottish border as a smudged line drawn in blood that never dries.

Perhaps someone was preparing to alter the mark once again.

As we neared the Liddesdale, traveling from one small hamlet to another, we often took to the wood to avoid troops, well mounted and heavily armed. Skirmishes between Norman knights on the Tyne or the Rede and restive Scots along the Liddel Water are common in a land where cattle raids are lauded in song. Still, with war in the air, crossing the border would be dangerous. We might be hanged as spies by one side or another.

But our luck held. As we approached Redheugh, I spotted a familiar wagon in a camp outside the town wall, a bright crimson cart with a Welsh dragon painted boldly on its sides.

After changing from our traveling garments into performing clothes, I led Noelle on our mount into a world unfamiliar to most folk, a traveling circus.

Most minstrels, especially in the north, ply their trade alone or in small family groups. But a few singers earn enough renown to gather a larger assemblage, a troupe of musicians, jugglers, and acrobats whose appearance at a town is reason enough to declare a feast day.

One such is Owyn Phyffe, Bard of Wales and the Western World as he calls himself. A small, compactly built dandy, blond-bearded and handsome as the devil's cousin, Owyn is a famed performer on both sides of the border and on the continent as well. A son and grandson of Welsh minstrels, he's a master of the craft. And well aware of it.

His camp was a hive of activity, cookfires being doused and horses hitched for travel. I found Owyn strolling about, noting every detail of the preparation without actually soiling his hands. He dressed more like a young lord than a singer, in a claret velvet doublet and breeches of fine doeskin. His muslin shirt had loose Italian sleeves. And not just for fashion.

Owyn carries a dirk up one sleeve or the other, perhaps both, and I once saw him slit a man's throat so deftly that the rogue's soul was in hell before his heart knew it was dead. Owyn dresses like a popinjay, but he's not a man to take lightly.

Our paths had crossed a number of times over the years, usually on friendly terms. Or so I hoped, because I needed him now.

He scowled theatrically as I approached leading the mount.

"God's eyes, I believe I spy Tallifer, the croaking frog of York. I can't tell which is uglier, you or that broken-down horse. Here to beg a crust of bread, I suppose."

"Not at all. In the last town, folk told me of a perky little Welsh girl who dresses like a fop and calls herself Owyn Phyffe the poet. Is she about?"

"Aye, she's about, about to thrash you for your loud mouth," Owyn said, grinning, seizing my arm in a grip of surprising strength for a small man. "How are you, Tallifer?"

"Not as well as you. The years have been kind to you."

"You were always a poor liar. How goes the road?"

"We've been doing quite handsomely. We've played Ormiston, Stobs, and a half dozen rat-bitten hamlets between, to very good response."

"We?"

"May I introduce my daughter, Noelle, the finest singer in this land or any other."

"I'm sure she is," Owyn snorted, then read the danger in my eyes and hastily amended his tone. "Because, as I said, your father is an inept liar, my dear. Honest to a fault."

Taking her hand, he kissed it with a casual grace I could only envy, favoring her with the smile that melted hearts on two continents. If he noted her blindness, he gave no sign. Owyn is nought if not nimble-witted.

"I would gladly offer you the hospitality of my camp, Tallifer, but we're making ready to leave."

"I see that. Well, there's no point in our playing yon town now. A performance by Owyn the Bard is impossible for lesser minstrels to follow."

"Even shameless flattery is sometimes a Gospel truth," Owyn grinned wryly. "Do we meet by chance, Tallifer, or can I be of some service to you and your . . . daughter?"

"We meet by God's own grace, Welshman. Over the past weeks the roads have grown crowded with soldiers. I'm hoping we can travel with your troupe across the border. I can pay."

"Don't be an ass, come with us and be welcome. We're not bound directly for the border, though. I've an agreement to perform

in Garriston for Lord DuBoyne on All Saints Day. Do you still want
to come?"

"Why shouldn't we?"

"Because the soldiers you've been seeing likely belong to
DuBoyne or his enemies. Whatever the trouble is, we're wandering merrily into the heart of it, singing all the way."

"We're still safer traveling with you than on our own."

"That may be," Owyn conceded grimly. "But I wouldn't take
much comfort in it. The sooner we're south of the Tweed, the
happier I'll be, and devil take the hindmost."

Owyn's company traveled steadily for the next few days,
stopping only at night to rest the animals. If anything, we
encountered more soldiers than before, but with wagons, we
couldn't cede the road. Troops simply marched around us.

Owyn's fame is such that even warriors who hadn't seen him
perform greeted us cheerfully. After chatting with one grizzled
guards' captain at length, though, the Welshman's gloom was
palpable.

"What's wrong?" I asked, goading my mount to match pace
with Owyn's. Noelle was riding on one of the wagons with
Owyn's wife, or perhaps his mistress. His two companions looked
much alike to me, small, dark women, with raven hair. Sisters perhaps? Some things you don't ask.

"Everything's wrong," Owyn said glumly. "You were a soldier
once, Tallifer, have you noted anything odd about the troops
we've encountered?"

"Mostly Scots, supplemented by a few mercenaries. Why?"

"I was talking about their direction."

I considered that a moment. "We haven't met any for the
past few days," I said. "They've all been overtaking us."

"Exactly," Owyn sighed. "They're traveling the same way we
are, and the only holding on this road is Lord DuBoyne's. But
when I offered to buy the captain of that last lot an ale at the fes-
tivities, he declined. He said he wouldn't be there."

"So?"

"So there's nowhere else for him to be, you dolt, only Garriston. And if he's not bound for Garriston to celebrate . . ." He left
the thought dangling.

"Sweet Jesus," I said softly.

"Exactly so," Owyn agreed.

"Perhaps they'll delay the bloodletting until after the holiday."

"That would be Christian of them," Owyn grunted, "though I'm told good Christian crusaders in the Holy Land disembowel children then rummage in their guts for swallowed gems."

"You're growing gloomy with age, Owyn."

"Even trees grow wiser with time. And I wouldn't worry much about old age, Tallifer. We're neither of us likely to see it."

Arriving at Garriston on the fourth day did little to lift Phyffe's spirits. It was a raw border town on a branch of the Tweed, surrounded by a high earthen wall braced with logs. Its gate was open but well guarded. Noelle was riding at the front of the train with Owyn as I trudged along beside.

"What do you think, Tallifer?" he asked, leaning on his pommel, looking over the town.

"It seems a small place to hire such a large troupe."

"So it does. The DuBoyne family steward paid us a handsome advance without a quibble, though."

"Is it a pretty town?" Noelle asked. "It feels lucky to me."

Owyn shot a quizzical glance at me, then shook his head.

"Oh, to live in the country of the blind, where every swamp's an Eden. Aye, girl, it's a fine town with gilded towers and flags on every parapet. But perhaps you'd better stay in the camp, while your father and I taste the stew we've got ourselves into."

Leaving instructions with his wives to camp upstream from Garriston near a wood, Owyn, myself, and Piers LeDoux, the leader of the Flemish jugglers, rode in together. In such a backwater, well-dressed mounted men are seen so rarely we were treated like gentry. The gate guards passed us through with a salute, saying the manor's steward could be found in the marketplace.

An old town, Garriston was probably a hamlet centuries before the Norman conquest. Houses were wattle and daub, set at haphazard angles to the mud streets. It was a market day and the air was abustle with the shouts of tinkers and peddlers, the squeal of hogs at butchering, hammers ringing at a smithy, and, beneath it all, the thunderous grumbling of a mill wheel.

A month earlier I wouldn't have noted the noise, but after traveling with Noelle I found myself listening more, trying to savor the world as she did.

A stronghold loomed over the north end of the town. Crude, but stoutly built in the Norman style, the square blockhouse sat atop a hill with corners outset so archers could sweep its walls. And even in peaceful daylight, sentries manned its towers.

The street wound into an open-air market in the town square, with kiosks for pottery, hides, and leatherwork, an alehouse, and a crude stone chapel. Owyn spied the DuBoyne family steward, Gillespie Kenedi, looking over beeves for the feast day.

Heavyset, with a pig's narrow eyes and a face ruddy from too much food, too little labor, Kenedi wore the fur-trimmed finery of his station and its airs as well. He was trailed by a rat-faced bailiff who bobbed his head in agreement whenever his master spoke. Or farted, probably.

Kenedi talked only with Owyn, considering the Fleming and myself beneath notice. But as the haggling progressed, he kept glancing my way, as though he might know me from somewhere.

When their bargain was struck, Owyn and the steward shook hands on it, then Kenedi beckoned to me.

"You there! Where did you get that horse you're holding?"

"From a crofter north of Orniston."

"And how did the crofter come by it?"

"As I recall, he said he traded a bullock for it. Why?"

"It resembles one of our plowhorses that went missing some time ago."

"I'm sure Tallifer acquired the horse fairly," Owyn put in. "If you have a problem, it's with the man who took it from you."

"Unless you believe I'm that man," I said, facing Kenedi squarely, waiting. But he was more beef than spirit.

"Perhaps I'm mistaken," he said, glancing away. "One spavined nag looks much like another. I'll let it pass, for now." He turned and bustled off with his bailiff scurrying after.

"Nicely done," Owyn sighed. "It's always good business to antagonize one's host before getting paid. So? Did you really get the horse at Orniston?"

I didn't answer. Which was answer enough.

AS DUSK SETTLED ON our camp like a warm cloak, townsfolk and crofters from nearby farms began gathering to us. Dressed in what passed for their best, carrying candles in hollowed gourds or rutabaga hulls to light their way, they brought whatever small gifts they could afford, a flask of ale, bread or a few pickled eggs, walnuts, even a fowl or two.

Drawn by the noise, Noelle came out of the women's tent. I led her to a place near the fire as Owyn entertained the gathering throng, singing in Italian love songs to folk who barely understood English. And winning their hearts.

"What's afoot, Tallifer?" Noelle whispered. "What is all this?"

"We were hired to perform tomorrow at the DuBoyne castle for All Saints Day. But among Celtic peoples, tonight is a much older celebration called All Hallomas Eve, or Samhain, the festival of the dead."

"The dead? But I hear laughter and the music is gay."

"Life is so hard for borderland peasants that death isn't much feared. For the rest of us, Samhain is for remembering those who are gone. And to celebrate that we're not among them yet."

"Owyn is a fine singer, isn't he?"

"Aye, he's very good. He's an attractive man, too, don't you think?"

"Owyn?" she snorted. "You must be joking. He's a snake. His glib tongue and smooth hands put me in mind of the serpent of Eden. And you should hear what his wives say about his lovemaking."

"You shouldn't listen to such things."

"What do you think women talk about when we're alone? They asked me about you as well. About what we really are to each other. They noted we bear little resemblance."

"What did you tell them?"

"The absolute truth, of course. That you are the only father I've ever known and that you never speak of my poor mother."

"Very poetic. And ever so slightly misleading."

"Thank you. I have a good teacher. What's happening now?"

"Piers and the Flemish acrobats are putting on a tumbling show. It's not so fine as they will do for the nobility, but it suits this lot. Some of the women are cracking walnuts to read the future."

"Can they foresee it? Truly?"

"Certainly. A peasant's future is his past, and any fool who trusts a walnut has no future at all."

The crowd continued to swell with folk from the town, tradesmen, manor servants, even a fat priest who mingled with his flock quaffing ale as heartily as the rest. The steward too made an appearance with his rat-shadow of a bailiff, standing apart from the rest, aloof.

"Horses," Noelle said quietly.

"What?"

"I hear horsemen coming. Many. Moving slowly."

For a moment I thought she was mistaken, but then I saw them, moving out of the woods in a body toward our fires. A mounted troop, battle-weary from fighting by the look of them. Their horses were lathered and played out, and the men weren't much better, slumped in their saddles, exhausted, some wounded.

Their leader was young, less than twenty, but he was no boy. Dressed in mail with a black breastplate, he sat on his horse like a centaur. His armor was spattered with blood, not his own, and a broken arrow was stuck in his saddle.

A shaggy mane of dark hair obscured his eyes, but as he scanned the camp, I doubt he missed a thing. Including Noelle. His glance lingered only a moment, but I've seen the look before. In battle. We'd been marked.

"God's eyes," Owyn said, sidling over to us. "Here's trouble if I ever saw it."

"Who are they?"

"Milord DuBoyne's men. That's his eldest son, Logan. Black Logan he's called, both for his look and his sins."

"What sins?"

"Cattle raiding's a national sport in Scotland, but instead of beating or ransoming the thieves Logan hangs them, then guts them to make easy feeding for the ravens."

"I can see why he'd be unpopular with cattle thieves, but that's hardly cause for sackcloth and ashes."

"He's a hotspur, gives battle or extracts a tax from anyone found on DuBoyne lands, even neighbors. He's killed three men in single combat and God knows how many more in frays. There's already a ballad about him."

"He seems a bit young for a song."

"The legend is that after two babes were stillborn, his mother made a Christmas wish for a healthy son. Instead, the devil sent a demon child who sprang full-grown from the womb, called for his armor, and rode off to fight the Ramsays. Villagers hide their children when he passes."

"They hide from thunder as well." I spoke lightly, but in truth I was growing concerned. Black Logan was conferring with Kenedi, and both of them were glancing our way.

"Perhaps you'd better take Noelle . . ." I began. Too late. The steward was bustling toward us, looking altogether too pleased.

"I'm told this girl is with you, minstrel," he said without preamble. "How much for her?"

"What?"

"The girl. Young DuBoyne wishes to buy her for the night. He's willing to pay, but don't think you can—"

And then he was on the ground, stunned, his lip split open. It happened so quickly I didn't even realize I'd hit him.

"Damn," Owyn said softly. "Now we're in for it."

Logan strode angrily to us, his hand on his sword. "What madness is this? You struck my father's steward!"

"He asked my daughter's price and paid a small part of it. Are you here for the rest?"

He blinked, eyeing me more in surprise than anger. "Are you offering me a challenge, commoner?"

"He asked the price, I'm simply telling you what it is. Your life. Or mine. Is that plain enough?"

It was a near thing. Young or not, he was a warrior chief with a small army at his back. I was but a cat's whisker from death. He cocked his head, reading my eyes.

"Do you know who I am?" he asked quietly.

"I only know I'm not your man, nor do I owe that hog on the ground any fealty."

"I'm Sir Logan DuBoyne—"

"He's lying!" Noelle snapped, pulling free of Owyn's grasp.

"What?" DuBoyne and I said together.

"Any DuBoyne would be noble," she continued coldly. "At the convent they said I could tell the nobility by their scent and fine manners. You smell like a horse and show your breeding by insulting my father who was a soldier before you were born. Yet you claim to be a knight? I think not."

For a moment, I thought he might butcher us both. His eyes darkened, and I could see why the villagers hid their children. But the rage passed. He shook his head slowly, as if waking from a dream.

"You were convent raised, miss? Then clearly I've . . . misunderstood this situation. I apologize. I've fought two skirmishes today, and I'm not as young as I used to be. I meant no offense to you. But as for you," he said, turning to me, "if you ever lay hands on a man of mine again, I'll see your head on a pike."

Reaching down, he hauled Kenedi to his feet. "Come on, Gillespie, let's find some ale."

"The bastard struck me!" Kenedi said, outraged.

"He saved your life," DuBoyne said, leading him off. "The girl would have cut our hearts out."

"You idiot," Owyn said angrily, spinning me around. "You could have gotten us all killed!"

"And if she were yours? Would you have sold her?"

For a moment I thought I'd pushed him too far. But Owyn is nothing if not agile. "Sweet Jesus, Tallifer. You may not be the world's greatest singer, but by God you're never dull. And you, girl, you've enjoyed my hospitality long enough. It's time to earn your keep. Come, sing for us. If I'm to be slaughtered defending your honor, you'd better be worth it."

I wanted to fetch my lute to accompany her but I was afraid to risk letting her out of my sight, even for a moment. Black Logan was prowling the camp, talking with pedlars and travelers. And glancing my way from time to time.

It didn't bode well. Most men with black reputations have earned them. His own people shied from him as if he wore a leper's bell and I knew that if he snatched up Noelle, none but me would oppose him.

And so I watched tensely as Owyn led Noelle into the ring of firelight, introduced her, then stepped back. It was an impossible situation. Drunken revelers were bellowing jests, laughing, groping their women. A clown troupe juggling lions with their manes ablaze wouldn't satisfy this lot.

Yet, as that slip of a girl began to sing, the crowd gradually fell silent, listening. She sang a simple French lullaby in a voice so pure and true that my heart swelled with longing, not for Noelle but for all I'd lost in my life. And would lose.

When she finished there was a long moment of stone silence, then the crowd erupted with a roar of applause and cheers. They called for more and she gave it, singing a rousing Irish war ballad I'd taught her and then a love song that would have misted the eyes of a bronze idol.

I was as transfixed as the rest, until I realized that Black Logan was standing a few paces to my left. He was eyeing Noelle like a lion at mealtime, but if her song moved him he gave no sign, not even applauding when she finished. He turned to me instead.

"I didn't know the girl was blind."

"What difference does it make?"

"I don't know. But it does. I've asked around the camp. Folk say you truly were a soldier once. Whom did you serve?"

"I was a yeoman for the Duke of York, bodyguard to his son for a time. Later I fought for Sir Ranaulf de Picard."

"At Aln Ford?"

"I was there, and at a hundred other scuffles you've never heard of."

"Then you must know troops. Whose men did you pass on the road here? How were they armed?"

"I was a soldier once and now I'm a singer. But a spy? That I've never been."

"Minstrel, you're trying my patience at a bad time. My father's health is failing, and his neighbors and enemies have begun raiding our stock and gouging taxes from our people. When I answer their aggression with my own they whine to Edinburgh, branding me an outlaw. My father has invited some of those same neighbors to the feast in hopes of a truce, but I know they've brought troops with them. Perhaps they fear treachery. Perhaps they plan it. Either way, you'd best tell me what you've seen."

"Suppose we compromise, and I tell you what I didn't see instead? We saw no heavy cavalry on the road, nor any siege engines, nor did we encounter any supply trains. The soldiers were carrying a few days' provisions, no more."

"Then they aren't planning a siege; they're escort troops only. Good. How many men did you see, and whose were they?"

"I took no count, and I don't know the liveries of this land well enough to identify them."

"And wouldn't if you could?"

"They did us no harm, DuBoyne. We've no quarrel with them."

"Nor with me. Yet." The camp erupted in a roar as Noelle finished her song, with Owyn standing beside her leading the cheers.

"Your daughter sings well."

"Yes, she does."

He started to say something else but his voice was drowned by the throng as Owyn led Noelle back to me. DuBoyne turned and stalked off to rejoin his men.

"Tallifer, did you hear?" Noelle's face was shining and Owyn's grin was as broad as the Rede.

"You were in wonderful voice, Noelle, and they knew it. What was that French lullaby? I've never heard it before."

"A woman sang it to me when I was small. I don't know why it came back to me tonight. Was I foolish to sing it?"

"*Au contraire, cherie*, it was brilliant," Owyn countered. "By singing softly, you made them quiet down to hear. You won many hearts tonight, little Noelle, including mine."

"All of it?" she asked sweetly. "Or just the parts your wives aren't using at the moment?"

"Get back to your tent, imp," Owyn snorted. "I swear, if you weren't so pretty I might believe you really are Tallifer's child.

Your tongue's as sharp as his." Laughing, Noelle set off, but Owyn grasped my arm before I could follow.

"What did Black Logan want? More trouble?"

"He has trouble of his own." I quickly sketched the situation DuBoyne had described.

"I've heard the old laird's mind is failing," Owyn nodded. "And vultures gather early along the borders. Do you think there will be quarreling at the feast?"

"I hope not. That boy may be young, but he's already a seasoned fighter. I half believe that nonsense about him leaping from his mother's womb to his saddle and riding off to fight the Ramsays."

"He won't have far to ride tomorrow," Owyn sighed. "The Ramsays are among the honored guests. A baker's dozen of them. And that captain I spoke to yesterday, the one who's probably watching us from the hills at this moment? He was a Ramsay man."

"Damn it, you should have warned me away from this, Owyn."

"I tried to, remember? Besides, Noelle likes it here. Thinks the blasted place is lucky."

"She may be right. But good luck or bad, I wonder?"

THE EVENING FEAST OF All Saints Day was a rich one, probably to atone for the carousing and deviltry of the night before. It was also a display of wealth and power by the laird of Garriston, Alisdair DuBoyne. Food and drink were laid on with a will, steaming platters of venison and hare and partridge, wooden bowls of savory bean porridge spiced with leeks and garlic; mulled wine, ale, or mead, depending on the station of the guest.

The great hall, though, was great in name only, a rude barn of a room, smoky from the sconces and cooking fires, its walls draped with faded tapestries probably hung when the DuBoynes first came to this fief a generation ago.

Seated at the center of the linen-draped high table, flanked by his wife and two sons, Laird DuBoyne was even older than I'd expected, seventy or beyond, I guessed. Tall and skeletal with a scanty gray beard, it was said he'd once been a formidable warrior, but his dueling days were long past. He seemed apathetic, as though the juice of life had already bled from him and only the husk remained.

His wife was at least a generation younger. Dressed in green velvet, she was willowy as a doe, a striking woman with aquiline features and chestnut hair beneath a white silken cap. Her youngest son, Godfrey, nine or so, had her fairness and fine features, while his brother, Black Logan, with his dark beard and burning eyes, sat like a chained wolf at the table, seeing everything, equally ready for a toast or a fight.

Kenedi, the stocky steward, and his wife sat at the far end of the high table beside the chubby priest I'd seen at the Samhain fest. Father Fennan, someone had said, was a local man who'd risen from the peasantry to become both parish priest and chaplain to the DuBoynes.

Two lower tables, also decked in fine linen, extended from the corners of the high table to form a rough horseshoe shape, which was appropriate since the guests were probably more familiar with war saddles than silver forks.

Three family groups of DuBoyne's neighbors, the Ramsays, Duarts, and Harden clans, nearly thirty of them, were seated in declining order of status. A hard-eyed crew, wary as bandits, they'd brought no women or children with them. Nor had they worn finery to honor their hosts, dressing in coarse woolens instead, clothes more suited to battle than a banquet.

Randal Ramsay was senior among them. A red-bearded descendent of Norse raiders, Ramsay conversed courteously with his host and the other guests but kept a watchful eye on Logan, an attention the younger man returned.

In England, strict protocols of station would have been observed, but along the borders the Scots and their English cousins act more like soldiers in allied armies, jests and jibes flying back and forth between high and low tables. But I noted the exchanges were surprisingly mild and politely offered, lest harmless banter explode into bloodshed.

Owyn delayed beginning the entertainment as long as he dared. Scots at table can be a damned surly audience, and the tension in DuBoyne's hall was as thick as the scent of roasting meat. Later, with full bellies and well oiled with ale, DuBoyne's guests might be more receptive.

Not so. When Piers LeDoux and his troupe of Flemish acrobats opened the performance, their energetic efforts received the barest modicum of applause.

After a juggler and a Gypsy woman who ate fire fared equally poorly, Owyn took the bull by the horns and strode to the center of the room. He stood silently for a bit, commanding attention by his presence alone. Then, instead of singing, he began to recite a faerie story of Wales and then ghostly doings in the Highlands and Ireland, delivering the tales with such verve and drama that even the bloodthirsty warriors at the low table leaned forward to hear.

It was a masterful performance. Owyn entranced the DuBoynes and their restive neighbors alike, holding them spellbound for the better part of an hour. He finished to rousing cheers and applause, the first enthusiastic response of the night.

"Match that if you can," Owyn whispered with a grin as he passed us in the doorway.

The minstrelsy is a free-spirited life, but it has protocols of its own. As Noelle and I had joined Owyn's troupe last, we were scheduled to perform last, the toughest position of all.

Ordinarily, I warmed up a crowd with a few rowdy ballads before bringing on Noelle, but after the way she won over the revelers at the Samhain, I simply introduced her and began strumming my lute, softly, softly, hoping the crowd would quiet.

Facing her unseen audience, Noelle sang the French lullaby, even more beautifully than the previous night. And with the same wondrous effect. The room fell utterly silent, every eye fixed on Noelle as she poured all the pain and longing of her blighted life and our own into that song. Angels on high couldn't have sung it one whit better. My eyes grew misty as I played the accompaniment, and I wasn't alone.

As I glanced about, reading the room, I noted Randal Ramsay's fierceness had softened, Lady DuBoyne was crying silently, while her husband . . . was up and moving. Laird DuBoyne was shuffling past the low table, coming toward us.

Unaware of his approach, Noelle sang on. I couldn't guess his intentions, but he seemed anguished and angry. Brushing past me, the old man seized Noelle's arm, startling her to silence.

"My dear, this is not fitting. You sing as beautifully as ever, but it's not proper for my lady wife to—"

"Let go of me!" Noelle shouted, pulling away. "Tallifer!"

"Come back to the table, milady, we'll—"

"Milord Alisdair!" Lady DuBoyne's voice snapped like a whip, cutting off her husband's ramblings. He stared up at her, shocked, then turned back to Noelle, eyeing her in wonder.

"I . . . but you're not my lady," he said slowly. "I thought . . . Your voice sounds much like hers did. Long ago. I'm sorry. I've ruined your song . . . "

And then Black Logan was at his father's side. Firmly disengaging his hand from Noelle's arm, he led Laird DuBoyne from the room. But at the door, the old man stopped, turning back to stare at Noelle in confusion.

"Who are you?" he asked, his voice barely a whisper. "Who are you?"

With surprising gentleness, Logan ushered him out, leaving us in stunned silence.

"What was all that?" Lord Ramsay said, rising. "Is our host going mad, then?"

"He had a bit too much wine, that's all," Lady DuBoyne said coldly. "It's a celebration, Ramsay, and you're falling behind. Continue the music, minstrel. Play on!"

And I did. Striking up a merry Scottish reel on my lute, I played as though the strings were on fire. To no avail. The spell of Noelle's song was shattered, and the guests were only interested in discussing their host's behavior with one another.

Owyn led Noelle quietly out of the hall, then after letting me twist in the wind alone for a time, he called the rest of the company back for a final song and bow before we all beat a hasty retreat to a smattering of applause.

Noelle was waiting for us in the outer hall. "Tallifer, what happened? Who was that man?"

"Our host, my lark," Owyn said. "The man who is supposed to pay me tomorrow. Assuming he doesn't mistake me for a tree and have me cut down."

"Is that what happened?" I asked. "He mistook her for someone else?"

"For his lady, I believe. There's a vague resemblance, and a man addled by age could mistake them. Still, if DuBoyne's neighbors came to take his measure, they just saw the ghost of a man who's still alive, but only barely. I don't like the feel of this a damned bit. We're breaking camp at first light, I—"

"Good sirs, hold a moment, please." It was the pudgy priest, red-faced and puffing as he hurried after us. "I'm Father Fennan, Mr. Phyffe, chaplain to the DuBoyne family. Milady DuBoyne would like a word. And with these other two as well, the blind girl and her father."

"It's late," I said. "Noelle should—"

"It's not that late and I want to be ten miles south of here tomorrow," Owyn interrupted. "Lead on, Father."

"You must be a busy man," Noelle said, as we followed the friar. "From what I hear of Black Logan, he badly needs a priest. Or is it already too late for him?"

"It's never too late for salvation, miss," Father Fennan said, eyeing her curiously. "You sang in French very well. Where did you learn?"

"I know only the one song. I grew up in the convent at Lachlan Cul and must have heard it there."

"I see," Fennan said curtly. Too curtly, I thought. Either the song or the mention of the convent seemed to trouble him. I knew the feeling. Everything about this place was worrying me.

We followed the priest down a shadowed corridor lit by guttering sconces, arriving at a windowless room at the west corner of the fortress. Vellum scrolls and ledgers filled pigeonhole racks against the walls.

"A library?" Noelle asked. "Linseed and charcoal. I love the ink scent. It smells like knowledge."

"Nay, it's a counting room," I whispered. Though such a place was normally a steward's lair, Lady DuBoyne was seated alone at his desk with a ledger open before her.

"According to Kenedi's accounts, this was the sum agreed on," she said brusquely, pushing a purse of coins toward Owyn. "Count it if you like."

"That won't be necessary, milady," Owyn said, touching his forelock. "I'm only sorry that—"

"Our business is concluded, Mr. Phyffe. Wait outside with Father Fennan, please. I want a private word with these two."

"As you say, milady." Giving a perfunctory bow, Owyn followed the priest out. Fennan swung the oaken door closed as he left.

Lady DuBoyne eyed me a moment, lips pursed, then pushed a small purse toward me. "This is for you, minstrel. And your daughter."

"I don't understand."

"It's money for travel, the farther the better. And for your silence. My husband is no longer young and has no head for wine, but he's still my husband. I will not have him ridiculed."

"I saw nothing to laugh at, milady, and Noelle saw nothing at all. You need not pay us."

"The girl is truly blind then? I thought the ribbon might be an artifice. Come closer, child. You have a beautiful voice."

"Thank you. Do you know me, lady?"

"I beg your pardon?"

"Have we met? You seem . . . familiar to me, though I can't say why. Have you ever visited the convent at Lachlan Cul?"

"No, and I'm sure we've never met. You're very lovely. I'd remember."

"I must be mistaken, then. Forgive me, the country where I live is a land of shadows. It's confusing sometimes. But Tallifer is right, there's no need to buy our silence."

"Then consider it a payment for your song."

"The song was for any who listened, not for you alone. You needn't pay for it and you have nothing to fear from us. We'll not trouble you again."

She turned and started for the door so hastily I had to grab her arm to save her from injury. I glanced back to make our good-byes, but Lady DuBoyne didn't notice. She was leaning forward on the desk, her face buried in her hands.

"Well?" Owyn said when we joined him in the hall. "What did she want?"

"Not much," I said. "She asked us to be discreet."

"Discretion is always wise," Father Fennan agreed. "We live in fearsome times."

"That lady has nought to fear," Noelle said sharply. "Her son has a ballad of his own already. Tell me, Father, did Logan fight those battles or just bribe minstrels to praise his name?"

"Hardly," the priest said, surprised. "As his confessor, I assure you the song doesn't tell half the carnage he's wrought, and he despises it. He once struck a guardsman unconscious for singing it."

"I'm surprised he didn't hang the poor devil," Noelle snapped. "This is an unlucky town for singing, gentlemen. We'd best be away from here."

Owyn glanced at me, arching an eyebrow. I shrugged. I had no idea why Noelle was so angry. Or why Lady DuBoyne had broken down. Women have always been an alien race to me, as fascinating as cats and no more predictable.

Noelle was right about one thing, though: Garriston was unlucky for us. The sooner we saw the back of it, the better.

Pleading the lateness of the hour, the priest led us to the chapel, which had its own exit through the town wall. He seemed uneasy, eager to have us gone.

"Good luck and Godspeed," he called, as he strained at the heavy door. "And remember, discretion!" The armored door clanged shut like the gates of hell.

"Paid to the last penny," Owyn said somberly, hefting his purse. "A successful engagement, I suppose. At least we finished with a profit."

But we weren't finished with Garriston, nor it with us. We'd scarcely retired to our tents when a commotion arose from behind the city walls. Shouting, men running. A raid? Trouble between the DuBoynes and their guests?

I was pulling on my boots when horsemen thundered into our camp followed by foot soldiers on the run, shouting for us to come out, tearing open the tents and wagons. My first thought was to reach Noelle, but I was seized as soon as I showed myself.

"Hold him! He's one of them!" The rat-eyed bailiff who'd been with Kenedi the first day was on horseback, armed with a poniard, directing the search. Owyn stalked boldly out to demand an explanation, but the bailiff ordered him seized as well. Then they dragged Noelle out and marched the three of us back to the stronghold under guard, directly to the great hall.

The linens were gone now and the high table was occupied by the steward, Kenedi, Black Logan, his younger brother Godfrey, and the heads of the guest families, Randal Ramsay, Nicol Duart, and Ian Harden. Red-eyed, disheveled, and still half-drunk from the feast, they were in an evil mood, eyeing us like wolves 'round a wounded calf.

Armed guards ringed the room and blood was in the air, real blood. A body was laid out on a trestle table in the center of the room covered by a sodden sheet, bleeding gore onto the flagstones.

"What is the meaning of this?" Owyn said coldly. "Why have we been unlawfully seized?"

"You've been brought to answer, Mr. Phyffe," Randal Ramsay said coldly. "For murder."

"Whose murder?"

"See for yourself." The squat soldier holding Noelle thrust her forward, banging her into the corpse. She recoiled, and as he reached for her again, I pulled free and tackled the lout from behind, slamming his face into the floor! Once, twice, and then the others were on me, dragging me off him, kicking me down.

"Enough!" Black Logan's bark stopped the beating instantly. "This is a court, not a damned alehouse brawl!"

"What kind of court?" Owyn said coolly. "I see no townsmen here to act as a jury."

"This isn't a hallmote hearing for selling bad ale, Phyffe," Ramsay said. "As the crime is against a peer of the realm, only his equals can sit as judges."

Jerking his arm free of his guard, Owyn strode boldly to the table with the corpse. Noelle helped me to stand as Owyn drew the sheet back. His mouth narrowed, but he gave no other sign.

"Who's been killed?" Noelle whispered to me. "Is it the steward?"

"God rest him," Owyn said quietly, gazing at the corpse. "Father Fennan seemed a good man, but he was only a parish priest, unlettered and coarse of speech. I doubt he was of noble birth."

"Fennan was not the only one attacked," Ramsay said. "The laird of Garriston also lies wounded and is unlikely to—"

"He's not dead yet," Logan snapped. "He's survived worse."

"When he was younger, perhaps," Ramsay countered, "but he's been failing for some time. No one of sound mind would have loosed you to ravage the countryside!"

"Gentlemen, please," Owyn interrupted. "Could you save your private quarrel for a more convenient time? My friends and I have been hauled from our beds to no good purpose I can discern. There are any number of folk here with cause to harm Laird Alisdair while we have none. If you wish us to testify, let's get on with it."

His sheer audacity stunned the room to silence.

"Testify?" Gillespie Kenedi sputtered. "You are charged with the crime!"

"On what basis?"

"You are the only strangers here, and you were last seen with the priest. Money was found in your tent."

"Money paid to me by the lady of the manor for the night's performance," Owyn replied. "As to the priest, when last we saw him he was alive and well. He saw us out through a portal at the rear of the chapel and bolted it behind us. Once outside the walls, we could not return, and since you found me abed with my wife who will swear I never left once I'd arrived—"

"Your *wife* will swear," Kenedi sneered.

For a moment Owyn stood silent, his eyes locked on the steward's until Kenedi looked away. "Gentlemen, I have been falsely charged with murder. I have answered that charge with truth. I can have six free men in this room in half an hour to vouch for my word. But there is a simpler way. You have impugned my wife's honor, Mr. Kenedi. Suppose we put the question to the test in the courtyard? With any weapons you choose."

It was a bold move, and pure bluff. Owyn was a lover, not a fighter. Though lightning quick with a dirk, he had no real skill with weapons. But he was a master at reading audiences. The Scottish lords, tired and surly, brightened at the idea of a trial by combat. And he read Kenedi correctly as well. The steward had the arrogance of his high office, but no belly for a fight.

"No offense was intended to your wife," Kenedi muttered.

"Then you accept my word and my explanation?" Owyn pressed.

"Yours, yes. But what about the other minstrel? Who was he abed with? His daughter?"

Owyn glanced at me, warning me with his eyes to control my anger. But he wasn't the only one who could read people. Owyn was about to lie for me and I couldn't let him. Nothing but the truth could save us now.

"My daughter was with Owyn's family," I said. "I was quite alone."

"Then you could have returned," Kenedi said intently. "The gate guard has admitted he drowsed off. You could easily have passed by him to commit the crime."

"To what end? I have no quarrel with anyone here."

"You were sent by Lord Alisdair's enemies," Kenedi countered. "You arrived on a stolen horse. My bailiff can testify that the horse came from Garriston."

"No need. I accept your word that the horse came from Garriston. Was the reeve who rode it a Garriston man also?"

The question surprised him. It surprised me as well, but there was no turning back now. Murder had been done, and someone would pay for it before first light. Denials were useless. I had neither witnesses nor friends to vouchsafe my word. I had only my road-weary wits and the glimmer of an idea.

"Aye," Kenedi conceded, "the reeve was from Garriston. Why?"

"Because he attacked me in a wood on the way to Orniston. I buried him there." That woke them up.

"You admit you killed the reeve?" Kenedi said.

"In self-defense, yes."

"Why would a reeve attack you?" Black Logan asked. "Did you quarrel?"

"No, we hardly spoke. And he seemed more interested in killing Noelle than me."

"Same question: Why would he attack your daughter?"

"Much as it pains me to admit it, Noelle is not my daughter. She was a resident at the convent at Lachlan Cul until recently, when it burned."

"All was lost," Noelle put in. "A sister was taking me to her family when she died of injuries. Tallifer saved me."

"A touching tale but irrelevant," Kenedi sneered. "After killing the reeve, you likely came to Garriston for revenge."

"If I'd known the lout came from Garriston, I would hardly have ridden his horse here. Chance brought us to this place, or perhaps fate."

"An ill fate," Kenedi snorted. "You rode here on the horse of a murdered man yet claim you know nothing of the attacks on our laird and his chaplain?"

"I didn't say that. I had no part in what happened tonight, but I believe we may have caused it."

"Don't bandy words, minstrel," Randal Ramsay demanded. "What are you saying?"

"I think what happened tonight was the echo of another crime, one that occurred many years ago."

"What crime?" Logan asked.

"Before I answer, I have a question of my own." Turning to Noelle, I quietly asked her something that had troubled me. Then I turned back to the court. "Gentlemen, I believe the explanation lies in a ballad I heard when I came to this town—"

"What nonsense is this?" Kenedi sputtered. "You stand accused of murder—"

"Let him talk," Randal Ramsay interrupted. "His life is in the balance. But bear in mind, minstrel, if we don't care for your tale, you'll never tell another. Go on."

"The song is one you all know, the "Ballad of Black Logan," the boy warrior. Like most songs, it's part fancy, part truth.

"For example, it speaks of his birth at Christmas. Is this true? Was he born at Yuletide?"

"What difference—?" Kenedi began.

"Aye, it's true enough," Nicol Duart offered. The lanky clan chief had a buzzard's hook nose, and the same implacable eyes. "It was a damned black Christmas for this country. But the rest is a lie. Young Logan never leapt from his crib to raid Lord Randal's lands. He were at least a year old before he turned outlaw." The third lord, Ian Harden, guffawed. Neither Logan nor Ramsay smiled.

"Then the ballad is partly true. And the rest of it, the myth of a bairn riding off to war, is to explain a thing seen but not understood."

"What was seen?" Logan demanded.

"Here is what I believe happened. Seventeen years ago, a young wife who'd lost two stillborn children feared she might be put aside if she didn't deliver her lord an heir. So when she was expecting again, she arranged to obtain a male child. When her own child came, a frail girl born blind, she replaced it with the other and sent her true daughter off to a convent. At Lachlan Cul.

"The boy became a fearsome warrior. But his size at birth did not go unremarked, and a local legend sprang up to explain it. A ballad that grew with his exploits."

"You lying dog," Logan said coldly. "You dare insult my family by—"

"Hold, hold, young Logan," Ramsay said, his face split by a broad grin. "Perhaps you haven't fully grasped the implications. If the minstrel's tale is a lie, his life is forfeit. But at least part of his story *is* true. And if the rest is, then you have no right to threaten anyone, nor even to a seat at this table. Any fool can see you don't favor your father, and the girl looks so like Lady DuBoyne that her own husband mistook her earlier tonight."

"My father is not well—"

"*If* he is your father."

"By God, Ramsay, step into the courtyard, and we'll see which of us doesn't know his father!"

"I don't brawl in the street with common louts, boy. We'll hear the rest of this before I consider your offer. What of it, minstrel? Have you any proof of your tale?"

"Lady DuBoyne knows the truth of it," I said.

"My mother is keeping vigil with her dying husband," Logan snarled. "Anyone who dares disturb her grief for this nonsense will deal with me first."

"I admit it's inconsiderate to trouble the lady now, but neither is it fair to condemn me without asking the one person who knows the truth."

"We needn't hear any more," Kenedi snapped. "The minstrel has admitted to killing a reeve from this town. As steward of Garriston and head of this court, I say we condemn him for that murder and dismiss the rest of this nonsense as a pack of lies told to save himself. We can hang him straightaway unless . . . any of you gentlemen truly wish to dispute the birthright of Lord DuBoyne's son and heir?"

The Scottish lords exchanged glances, and I read my fate in their eyes. Death. They couldn't risk challenging Logan in his own hall with his men about. They might raise the matter another time but that would be far too late for me.

"Well, gentlemen?" Kenedi said. "Shall we put it to a vote?"

"No," Logan said, his face carved from oak, unreadable. "We've gathered to resolve the murder of a priest and assault on my . . . on the laird of Garriston, not the death of a reeve many miles away. If we condemn the minstrel for killing the reeve, the rest remains unresolved and I will not have any stain on my name nor any question of my rights of inheritance. But I see a way to settle this. We'll send my younger brother Godfrey to ask Lady DuBoyne the truth of the minstrel's tale. If she denies it, he stands condemned out of his own mouth. Unless any man here doubts the lady's honor?"

"The minstrel's the one who'll be dancing the hangman's hornpipe if she misleads us," Ramsay noted dryly. "He may have a misgiving or two."

I considered that a moment. "No, as it stands, only a few know the truth of what happened, and the lady is the one most likely to tell it. I agree to the test. Send the boy."

"So be it," Ramsay said, eyeing me curiously. "Duart will accompany the lad to vouch that all is done properly."

"Agreed," Logan nodded, "with one stipulation. If my mother denies Tallifer's lies, he will not hang. One of you will loan him a blade, and we'll settle our differences in the courtyard. If he kills me, you can hang him afterward."

"Or gift him with silver and a fast horse," Ramsay growled. "Duart, take the boy to speak with his mother. And listen well to her answer."

The whey-faced youth and the burly border lord exited, and I resigned myself to wait. Perhaps for the rest of my life.

The reply came sooner than I expected. A stir arose at the back of the room, which grew to an uproar. Logan bolted to his feet, his face ashen. "Help him to a chair, forgodsake!"

I turned. Lord Alisdair had tottered into the hall, supported by Godfrey and Duart. He looked even more ancient than before, as though he might fade to smoke any moment. His muslin night-shirt was bloodstained, hanging loosely over a poultice.

A servant fetched him a chair and Alisdair eased painfully down, but as he looked about him, his eyes were bright and alert.

"Milord," Logan said, "you should not be here."

"Miss a trial for my own murder?" Alisdair asked, his voice barely a whisper. "Not likely. Is this the man accused of the attack?" He gestured weakly at me. "Well, sir, speak up. What have you to say for yourself?"

"Me? Nothing!" I said, dumbfounded. "You know damned well I didn't attack you!"

"I fear not. I sleep like the dead nowadays, especially after wine. Someone jammed a pillow over my face, and when I struggled against it I was stabbed. And woke in the arms of my wife. A most agreeable surprise. I expected to wake in hell."

"Sir," Ramsay said, "perhaps your lady can better answer our questions. You should be resting."

"I'll be at rest soon enough, Ramsay," DuBoyne said. "And my lady is at chapel, praying for my soul. Prematurely, I hope. I've survived cuts before; God willing, I'll survive this. Nothing like a good bleeding to clear a man's senses. And his wife's as well. As I lay a-dying, my lady confessed to a deception long ago, a wondrous tale of a child put aside and another put in its place."

"My God, it is true then?" Ramsay breathed. "Black Logan is not your son?"

"My family tree is no concern of yours, Ramsay, only the murder of my priest."

"But surely they are related!"

"Perhaps, but . . ." DuBoyne winced, swallowing. "It is the minstrel's life and his tale. Let him finish it. If he can."

"As you say, lord," I said. "The exchange of the children took place years ago. But when word came of the fire at Lachlan Cul, a reeve was sent to end the threat the girl represented. He failed. Later, when we arrived, someone realized who she was."

"Who?" Ramsay asked.

"The priest knew, for one. As milady's confessor, he would have heard the tale long since. But only one person stood to lose everything if the truth came out. Not the lady. Her deception was done for love of her husband, and she has borne him a second son since."

"Only Logan stood to lose all," Ramsay said, turning to the youth. Black Logan met his stare but made no reply.

"True, Logan had everything to lose," I agreed, "and he's surely capable of any slaughter necessary to protect himself or his family. But only if he knew the truth of his birth. And he didn't."

"How can you know that?" Ramsay countered.

"Because I'm still alive. A moment ago, the steward could have hanged me for the death of the reeve. Logan prevented it, something a guilty man would never have done."

"Who then?" Ramsay demanded.

"Only one other person had everything to lose if the truth came out. The one who arranged the original substitution. A foundling child couldn't come from this village, too many would know. Who can travel his lord's lands at will to deal with peasants who might sell a babe? And later, when word of the fire came, who could send a reeve to do murder?"

Ramsay swiveled slowly in his seat, to face Kenedi.

"It's a lie," Kenedi breathed.

"Is it? If Lord Alisdair learned the truth he might forgive his wife, and even the foundling boy who came here through no fault of his own. But he would never forgive the man who betrayed him for money by arranging the deception. His steward."

"But killing his lord wouldn't save his position," Logan said coolly. "Surely the lady would guess what happened and confess the truth."

"Only if she knew there'd been a murder. Lord Alisdair said he woke beneath a pillow. If he'd smothered, everyone would believe he died in his sleep. But when the priest surprised him, Kenedi lashed out in desperation."

"All lies," Kenedi said, "a tale told at bedtime. There's not one shred of proof."

"Actually, there is," I said. "When Noelle and I were first brought into this room, she asked if you'd been killed, Kenedi. Tell him why, girl."

"When the soldier pushed me against the body, I smelled linseed and charcoal. Ink," Noelle said, stepping forward. "The scent was unmistakable."

"And the priest was unlettered," I finished. "As are most of us here. Only you have the gift of literacy, Kenedi. And the smell of ink on your hands. Only you."

"It's not true."

"Do you dare say my daughter lies?" Lord Alisdair asked weakly. "If I were hale I'd kill for that alone. But as things are. . . . Logan, see to him."

"Wait," Ramsay interjected. "If Logan is not your blood, he has no standing in this court, no right to be here at all."

"Sir," Alisdair said, rising unsteadily, "the offense was against me and mine in my own hall, so the justice will be mine as well. Gentlemen, I invited you here to celebrate All Saints Day in a spirit of fellowship. The banquet and the . . . entertainment are finished now. And I am very tired."

Ramsay started to object, but a glance at Logan changed his mind. We were still in DuBoyne's hall, surrounded by DuBoyne's men.

"As you wish, milord," Ramsay said, rising. "My friends and I thank you for the fest and pray for your speedy recovery. For all our sakes."

Ramsay stalked from the hall with Harden and Duart close behind, joined by their clansmen at the rear. At Logan's nod, a guardsman led the steward away.

Their departure sapped the fire from DuBoyne. Wincing, he sagged back in the chair. Logan eyed him but didn't approach.

"Where is the girl?" DuBoyne asked quietly. "The one who claims to be my daughter?"

Warily, Noelle stepped forward. DuBoyne raised his head to observe her, then nodded slowly.

"So it is true. You look very like my lady wife did once. A great, great relief."

"Relief?" Logan echoed.

"Aye, that I wasn't completely bereft of my senses last night when I mistook them. And a relief that so late in my life, my daughter has been returned to me."

"And relief that I am no son of yours?"

"That too, in a way. In truth, a part of me has always known you weren't mine, Logan. My young wife lost two sickly babes before the miraculous birth of a strapping lad the size of a yearling colt, a boy who looked not at all like me. I feared she'd taken a lover to get the son I couldn't give her. I'm relieved to be wrong.

"But if you're not my blood, you're still my creation, the son I wanted. And needed. My daughter's birthright will be worthless if our land is lost. Fiefs are bestowed in Edinburgh or London, but they can only be held by arms. Your arms, Logan. You remain lord here in all but name, and for now that is enough. I'm tired, boy. Help me to my bed. Perhaps my daughter can join us later. We have much to talk of, lost years to make up for."

As Logan led the old man out, I touched Noelle's hand.

"I must be going as well, Owyn will be breaking camp. But you needn't stay here unless you choose to. We'll find a way to—"

"No," she said, stopping my lips with her fingertips. "I have always known I belonged somewhere and for good or ill, I've found that place. In the country of the blind, places are much alike, only people are different. Besides, if I go with you, I may end up as Owyn's third wife."

"There are worse fates. It won't take long for that young border wolf to realize he can reclaim his inheritance by marrying the lord's newfound daughter."

"And is he truly such a monster?"

"No, but . . . why are you smiling? My God, Noelle. You've thought through this already, haven't you?"

"At the convent, the young girls talked of little but love, love, love. I can never have love at first sight, but I know Logan wanted me before he knew who I was."

"He wanted to *buy* you! And you said he smelled of horses."

"I suspect he will always smell of horses. I like horses."

"The poor devil," I said, shaking my head in wonder. "He has no chance."

"Perhaps I'm his fate. He may only own his armor now, but he has a song. And you've said I'm a fair singer."

"You have the loveliest voice I've ever heard, Noelle, on my honor. I shall miss you greatly."

"We'll sing together again, whenever the wind or the road bring you to me. Perhaps one day we can sing to my children."

"We will. I promise."

We said our good-byes in the great hall, and I took to the road, leaving my foundling child with strangers. And yet I did not fear for her. She grew up in a harsher land than any can imagine and flourished there. She would have no trouble coping with her new situation, of that I was certain.

And she would have Black Logan. But not because of her family or position. Love at first sight is more than a legend or a girlish fancy. It happens rarely, but it does happen.

I'd seen Logan's face at the Samhain as he listened to Noelle's wondrous voice. He had the look of a starving wolf at a feast, a turmoil of hunger, love, and lust.

I remember that terrible yearning all too well. I felt it for a woman once myself, long years ago.

But that is another tale . . .

Cold as Fire

Lillian Stewart Carl

Geoffrey knew only too well what happened to a bearer of bad news. Nevertheless, he had bad news to bear. The sergeant-at-arms spat sympathetically onto the mucky cobblestones before the castle gate. "So you're off to tell the archbishop the sheriff's arrested one of his men, eh?"

"Yes," Geoffrey replied.

"The archbishop thinks his men are above the law of the land, I'm thinking."

"Whatever I'm thinking, I know enough to keep to myself." Geoffrey wrapped his cloak around his body as though it were armor and trudged down from the castle into the town.

The towers of the cathedral looked like blunted swords against the frost-gray November sky, dominating the rooftops of Canterbury as its archbishop dominated the political squabbles of England. Geoffrey didn't know and refused to guess whether Thomas of London was defending the honor of God or his own pride. Posts as archiepiscopal clerks weren't that easy to come by, but Geoffrey's merchant father had found him one, just as Gilbert Becket had done for his Thomas some twenty-odd years before. With discretion, Geoffrey could rise high—not that he had ambitions toward an archbishopric.

But then, Thomas had had no ambitions toward an archbishopric either. It was his friendship with King Henry that caused his

343

swift if controversial rise in power, and his sudden transition—his sudden conversion—from secular to sacred.

Geoffrey made his way along Castle Street, skirting the foulest of the puddles. Merchants flocked toward the well-dressed young man. Beggars called piteously. A woman brushed against him, her loosely draped cloak affording him a glimpse of her wares. Normally, he'd have gaped at her, but not today. Waving them away like flies, he walked on past the gate of the bishop's palace, through the yard, beneath the portico, and into the great hall.

The air was warm and close, filled with the scents of meats, peas, beans, and bread. Smoke eddied between the carved beams that braced the ceiling. There was Thomas, just rising from his dinner. He was surrounded by clerks and scholars as usual and yet, as usual, he stood aloof, set apart as much by height and bearing as by rank. His profile was as sharp as a hunting bird's, and his golden-brown eyes as keen.

Geoffrey shoved his way through the gathered men. "My lord, I bring news from the castle."

"Yes?"

Geoffrey felt like a field mouse beneath that gaze. "Johanna Frelonde of Estursete, a tenant on your manor, has been found dead."

"Johanna," Thomas repeated. "A widow. She paid five marks a year for the privilege of remaining single. Edward, find out whether she had children who will inherit and then arrange a mass for her soul."

One of the other clerks nodded. Servants began to clear the tables. Geoffrey quickly seized half a loaf of bread.

"Give the extra food to the poor," the archbishop directed.

Geoffrey, remembering the outstretched hands and empty eyes he'd ignored on Castle Street, put the bread back down. "There's more, my lord. Johanna was murdered."

"Murdered? By whom?"

"Some say by Father Baldwin de Lucy."

"What?"

The word was so short and sharp Geoffrey fell back a step. Everyone else fell back two. "He and Johanna were heard arguing.

Within the hour Wulfstan, the village smith, found Baldwin kneeling over her body."

"Where is Baldwin now?"

"The sheriff had him taken to the castle, to be held there until the king's justiciar arrives in two days' time."

A gasp ran around the circle of men. Thomas's face went hard and tight, but his eyes blazed. "Baldwin de Lucy is a priest. It is for us, his peers, to judge him and, if necessary, punish him. He must not—he will not—be tried in a secular court."

It was for just such words and more that Henry had stripped Thomas of his secular honors last month, and the two former friends were now enemies. Was it fortune or choice, Geoffrey asked himself, that drew such a fine line between love and hate? "I just came from Baldwin, my lord. He—he's not sensible. He's babbling of *Dies Irae*, the day of wrath. Judgment day."

"He said nothing of Johanna?"

"He muttered of witchcraft, of *maleficium*, and said Johanna will be consumed by fire for her sins."

"So shall we all," Prior Wibert muttered from the edge of the group, "unless we beg for forgiveness."

"Baldwin's gone mad," Edward offered. "He's been possessed by a demon. He can't be held accountable."

Thomas's mouth crooked upward. "Madness is in the definition, isn't it? Perhaps it's Johanna who was mad. And to dismiss Baldwin's crime—if indeed he committed one—by saying it's the work of madness is much too easy."

"I reminded Baldwin that he can take an oath he's innocent," Geoffrey said. "But he refused, rambling on about innocence and guilt and how the two are different sides of the same coin."

"An oath, no matter who supports Baldwin when he makes it, might not be enough to satisfy the justiciar," Wibert added.

"Nor the king." Thomas set his jaw and Geoffrey remembered he'd once been a warrior, too. "But we mustn't sing the Magnificat at Matins. You, Geoffrey, find out whether Baldwin is indeed the murderer. If he is, well then, I shall deal with him. And the king's justiciar."

"Me?" asked Geoffrey, and added belatedly, "Yes, my lord." But the archbishop had already turned away.

Men said that when Thomas of London was making his way up the social ladder, and even when he'd reached the pinnacle of Chancellor of England, he was known for charm and grace. But now he was an archbishop, on Henry's no doubt much-regretted whim, true, but an archbishop still. Now his charm was abrading to haughtiness. As archbishop of Canterbury, he no longer had to court his betters. He had no betters—save only God Himself.

A CHILL SPRINKLING OF rain wetted Geoffrey's head as he left the palace and turned toward the northwestern part of the town. Evening came on quickly this time of year, and with the thick, heavy clouds, the night would be dark. But he already had reason to hurry.

In the dim, dank interior of Saint Peter's church, the candles standing to either side of the bier and its cloth-covered body seemed bright as bonfires. Beyond them the shadows were so thick that Geoffrey didn't see the old woman crouching by a pillar until she moved and spoke. "You've come to see Johanna, have you?"

"Oh—ah, yes, mother, I have. Geoffrey of Norwich, on the archbishop's business."

"And I'm Edith, Johanna's godmother." The old woman shuffled forward and turned back the cloth. "There she is, then. Poor soul, I remember her as a lass gathering reeds by the Stour in the spring. Odd, isn't it, how when you look back it always seems to be spring."

Geoffrey had so few years to look back on he had yet to assign them a season. He bent over Johanna Frelonde's body.

Even in the uncertain light it was horribly clear how she'd died. Her face was swollen, her tongue protruded from her lips, and all, face, tongue, lips, was the color of a winter storm, an evil purplish black.

"She was a lovely lass," murmured Edith. "You should have seen her on her wedding day, fresh as the flowers she wore in her hair."

It is the spirit that quickens, Geoffrey told himself sadly, and the flesh profits nothing. Grimacing, he pulled one of the candlesticks closer so that the light fell on her neck. Yes, Johanna's skin was bruised and torn, all the way from the angle of her jaw down to the hollow in her throat. She must've fought and fought hard, causing her murderer to loose and tighten his grip repeatedly.

"She was a fine wife and a good mother to her son and her daughter, in happy times and sad as well."

"Of all things God has given for human use, nothing is more beautiful or better than a good woman." Geoffrey bowed politely to the corpse. "But what of Father Baldwin? Do you think he killed her?"

Edith's dried-apple face wrinkled even more. "Baldwin says the words of the sacraments well enough, but I doubt if he listens as he speaks them."

Well, no, Baldwin's kiss of peace had always tended to be a peck of condemnation. "He was—ah—said something about witchcraft."

"Witchcraft? Johanna could see beyond this world is all. So could her mother. She used her sight to help others. There was nothing in it that went against Holy Scripture."

But her sight must've discomforted the other villagers even so. Enough for one of them to kill her? Geoffrey lifted the cloth that covered the rest of Johanna's body, hoping to find some clue.

She'd been well into her years, but not yet old, and even in death looked strong and sturdy. Her hands were callused, the nails cracked and broken off short. She'd labored long and hard, but then as a widow she'd worked the land she inherited from her husband. . . . He looked closer. The nail on the forefinger of her right hand was a bit longer than the others, the end torn and dangling loose. She'd have taken the rest of it off herself, if she'd torn it in life.

And Geoffrey saw as clearly as he saw the body in front of him the pendulous cheeks of Baldwin de Lucy, hanging like empty saddlebags. On the left one was a raw red scratch extending from cheekbone to jawline—made perhaps by a fingernail whose owner had had no other defense.

"Thank you, mother." Geoffrey replaced the cloth over Johanna's bloated and discolored face. He genuflected before the altar cross, hastened outside, and stood in the church porch exhaling the scent of mildew and candle wax, incense and death. His duty demanded that he find and tell the truth, but if Baldwin had done the murder, there would be hell to pay. Not only for Baldwin in the hereafter but for everyone in this life caught between the hammer of the archbishop and the anvil of the king. A day of wrath indeed. . . .

The smith. The smith had discovered Baldwin bending over Johanna's body, yes, but there had to be another explanation.

Geoffrey plodded through the west gate in Canterbury's encircling walls and across the bridge over the river Stour. Another spattering of rain pocked the dull pewter surface of the water. The roofs of Estursete were colorless lumps bunched between the willow-choked bank of the river and the gates of the archbishop's manor house. A cow lowed mournfully. Geoffrey thought of the palace hall, a fire leaping in the fireplace and the table lined with trenchers, and his stomach rumbled.

A sudden rhythmic clanging sent blackbirds whirling into the sky. Ah, Wulfstan Smith himself. Geoffrey ducked beneath the thatched eave of the smithy.

Wulfstan's fire was a sullen lump of red, barely warm. The man himself was short but broad, hair and beard bristling like a boar's. He dipped an iron rod hissing and steaming into a bucket of water, then placed it in the fire. "What do you want?" he asked, his massive right hand tapping his hammer against his vast left palm.

"My name is Geoffrey of Norwich. I'm here on the archbishop's business. The murder of Johanna Frelonde."

"She was murdered all right. By that prig of a priest. I saw."

"What did you see?"

Wulfstan eyed Geoffrey's clothes, then peered beyond his shoulder, as though checking to see if he'd brought reinforcements. "Baldwin was shouting at Johanna, wasn't he? Calling her a witch and telling her to hold her tongue. She told him where to get off, she did. And not an hour later, I looked in her window and there she was, flat on the floor, him bending over her with his hands on her face."

"Her face? Not her throat?"

"He'd already done his worst, hadn't he? When he saw me looking at him, he rolled his eyes like a horse about to bolt and started babbling. In Latin, I warrant, but none of his fine words could take away what he did. And him always going on at us about sin and damnation."

"Baldwin called her a witch?" Geoffrey asked.

Wulfstan stirred the fire with the iron rod. Sparks flew upward and vanished into the cold air. "Johanna was simple, if you ask me. For all that, she was good with herbs. If you had a running sore or a pain in your belly she'd bring you a tonic or a poultice and you'd soon be right as rain. But she'd go on about things she oughtn't to know, things that were said and done in private, and things that were going to happen—I think she listened at windows, myself, although there're those here in Estursete who said she could see beyond this world. But then, some folk will believe anything."

The smith hadn't cared for Johanna, Geoffrey told himself. "Did she get on well with everyone? Except Baldwin, I suppose."

"No one gets on with Father Baldwin. He sees to that. As for Johanna, there're those who'd ask her help when they were in trouble and laugh at her when they healed. Godeswell, for one, he flattered her and Alice and got what he wanted, didn't he? Or Grene, he plowed for her and always praised her cooking to get himself a second helping. Neither of them had much use for her, though. Maybe old Edith treated Johanna like her own daughter, thought she could do no wrong. But I say Johanna stirred up trouble. I'll give that to Baldwin, he was right telling her to hold her tongue."

"Maybe you should try holding yours," said a smooth voice behind Geoffrey's back. He spun around.

A man and a woman stood watching him. Her face within the soft folds of her coverchief was pinched and pale, her shoulders rounded as though she carried a heavy weight. The man was of a good height, his chest beneath its fine linen tunic thrust as far forward as his chin. His eyes were the same color and temperature as the river.

Wulfstan jerked his head toward Geoffrey. "Archbishop's clerk. Asking after your mother. This here's Theoric Frelonde and his wife Alice," he added, his voice acid.

Geoffrey bowed. "I'm very sorry to disturb you, Master and Mistress Frelonde, but with Father Baldwin confined by the sheriff . . ."

"The archbishop's looking for an example, is that it?" Theoric took a step forward. "All he'd do is strip Baldwin of his holy orders, maybe shut him up in a monastery. Is that punishment for taking Mother away from us? For murdering her, and her with years yet to live, God willing?"

"My brother drowned before we were married and now Mother's gone, too," Alice said with a sniffle. "There's no one left but us. I don't understand why . . . "

". . . my lord the archbishop thinks there should be one law for the clergy and another for us," Theoric finished. "Aren't the priests supposed to be caring for us, not lording it over us like Norman nobles?"

"Baldwin's proud as any nobleman," Wulfstan muttered, "always making up to his betters."

"The ancient customs of England must be subject to God's will," Geoffrey pointed out.

"God's will?" asked Theoric. "Or Thomas Becket's will?"

"But the archbishop's a holy man," Alice murmured. "He won't stand for the buying and selling of offices. There's never been a hint of scandal with women or boys either, and he washes the feet of the poor every morning, just as Our Lord washed the feet of His apostles on Maundy Thursday."

Ostentatious humility, Geoffrey said to himself.

Theoric snorted skepticism. "That's as may be. What matters is whether Mother's murderer escapes justice. We have our pride, don't we?"

"But is Baldwin guilty of her murder?" Geoffrey asked.

"Who else?" demanded Theoric. "He was kneeling beside her body!"

Alice added, her voice barely above a whisper, "Mother may have been a bit simple, but she was a good woman. She meant to help folk with her warnings."

"Did she warn herself about her own death?" muttered Wulfstan. He picked up his hammer and the rod from the fire. Its tip was red hot. Geoffrey could feel its heat from where he stood.

"And you, master clerk," Theoric concluded, "can tell the archbishop he has no right to shelter a murderer from what he deserves, no matter how badly he wants to get up the king's nose!"

That was one message Geoffrey wasn't going to deliver. He contented himself by observing, "It's for God to say what we deserve, don't you think?"

"And when He does, some folk will find this little fire of mine as cool as spring water." Wulfstan began hammering, the muscles bulging beneath his sleeve.

Geoffrey's ears rang. He turned away from the shed to see Theoric and Alice also retreating, the man's hand resting comfortingly in the small of her back but his shoulders still square. Proud, yes, Geoffrey thought. As were most prosperous folk. Johanna had done well with her inheritance.

The day was failing, the already fragile light thinning further and further as the shadows streamed out from wall and tree. Rain began pattering down in earnest. Exhaling a long vaporous breath, Geoffrey set his face toward the town.

So the day ended in darkness and confusion. All he'd accomplished was to put Baldwin's head further into the noose. And to bring the sheriff and the justiciar and maybe even the sergeant closer to excommunication. Which was worse, to be stripped of one's life or one's immortal soul?

He dodged from eave to overhanging story to merchant's booth, but still he was cold and wet by the time he returned to the palace. And hungry. He had just enough time to pay a quick visit to Ivo in the kitchen.

Ivo waved him toward the fire blazing merrily on the great hearth. "Well, now—you're a sight, aren't you? Bread? Beef? Mutton?"

"Beef, thank you." Geoffrey took the strip of meat, bit, and chewed. Again he heard the cow lowing in the field at Estursete. Johanna's cow, probably, which now belonged to her son and his wife. "It's a cow when it's alive, isn't it, but *beouf* when it comes to the nobleman's table."

"And a sheep becomes *mouton*. The Normans brought England more than arms and armor. New names for old." Ivo dumped a bowlful of bread dough onto the table and began pummeling it.

Geoffrey remembered Johanna's doughy face and set the meat down. Outside the bells rang for Compline. In the heavy air, the notes sounded like the clang of Wulfstan's hammer.

Wulfstan had enormous hands and arms. He could have strangled Johanna. Accidentally, perhaps, intending only to quiet what he saw as her gossiping tongue. But why would the smith turn murderous—had Johanna "seen" something about him?

And what of Baldwin? Had he witnessed the murder? Then why not say so? And that scratch on his face needed an explanation.

Wiping his hands and mouth, Geoffrey thanked Ivo again. He hurried into the cathedral and took his place beside Edward. The monks were still filing into their seats in the choir. Thomas of London stood before them all, in pride of place, gazing at the high altar. The plain dark robes he wore made his fair skin look like alabaster. His hair was dark, too, if streaked lightly with silver. But his eyes weren't dark at all. In the light of the altar lamp they glowed like embers.

Just which truth, Geoffrey wondered, did Thomas want him to find? Not an easy one, he knew that much.

"How are you getting on?" whispered Edward.

"I'm not getting on," Geoffrey returned.

"The justiciar will be here soon, and the king behind him, breathing fire like a dragon." Edward nodded toward Thomas, his face sculpted like one of the effigies hidden in the side aisles. "And him cold as ice. Who'll give way first, do you think?"

"I'm not thinking, either," repeated Geoffrey. But he was, turning over images of Johanna's broken fingernail, Baldwin's scarred face, Wulfstan's big hands. Of well-dressed Theoric and Alice—*there's no one left but us*, she'd said. And who were Godeswell and Grene? Men who'd courted Johanna for their own purposes, it seemed, as Baldwin courted the prelates at the archbishop's table, as Thomas himself had once courted the king.

The voices of the monks soared into the far reaches of the cathedral. Harmony layered upon harmony until the great stone pillars and the rounded arches above trembled. It was in the fullness of word and sound that mortals praised the king of kings, Geoffrey thought, so that they might be heirs of His everlasting kingdom.

He looked curiously at the archbishop, who looked up to heaven, his face intense with a deep blistering hunger not of the flesh.

A CHILL MORNING FOG hung over Canterbury. The upper stories of the houses leaned like watching ghosts over the street. Even the voices of the merchants crying their goods were muffled. People materialized suddenly out of the street before him, and Geoffrey had to dodge again and again as he walked resolutely toward the castle.

There was the gateway, a dark-toothed rectangle in the expanse of the wall. It took Geoffrey only a moment to state his business and another to find himself in Baldwin's cell. At least the priest hadn't been imprisoned in the dungeon. And compared to the morning outside, the tiny chamber was warm, if redolent of a nearby latrine.

Baldwin huddled on a filthy pallet, a pitiful broken man. Hard to believe he'd ever sat proudly at the archbishop's right hand. He looked up at Geoffrey but said nothing.

His silence was reassuring. The scratch, a coarse red furrow on his unshaven cheek, was not. Geoffrey hunkered down beside him and asked, "How did you come by that scratch on your face? A willow branch, as you walked by the river?"

Baldwin's red-rimmed eyes turned toward the runnels of moisture on the opposite wall. "Guilt and sin will out," he said.

"Yes," Geoffrey prodded.

"I went to talk to Johanna about the fees due the archbishop. She was in one of her fey moods, chattering on about the son who drowned and her husband's death long years ago and Alice's pregnancy."

"Alice is expecting a child?"

"So Johanna said," Baldwin shrugged. "And then, and then— she started spouting nonsense about the archbishop himself."

"Did she?"

"I told her to watch her tongue before she strayed into heresy. But she went on like one possessed. Possessed of the demon who holds her soul now, I expect. She was a witch. How else could she foresee the future, unless she sold herself to an evil spirit?"

"But could she foresee accurately? If not, then she was only speaking idle gossip. If so—well, we won't know until the future comes, will we?"

"Maybe so," Baldwin conceded. "Maybe she was only a gossip making trouble for men, as Eve brought us all to the Fall. What is a woman, after all? Glittering mud, a stinking rose, sweet venom . . ."

"Virgin mother?" Geoffrey asked dryly. "What did Johanna say about the archbishop?"

The priest shook his head so quickly his jowls flapped. "I told you. Lunacies. Heresies. She holds her land from him, she mustn't say such things about him, she owes him respect and veneration and—and . . ."

Geoffrey almost asked, "Flattery?" but said instead, "Warnings?"

"Warnings, yes. Warnings of evil to come."

"There's not a soul in England who doesn't question the archbishop's present path."

"You don't understand!" Baldwin insisted, his eyes bulging. "I had no choice. I had to stop her. I had to shut her up. What if a demon heard her words and carried them out? I wrapped my hands around her throat and squeezed—be it on my head come the day of reckoning—but when she scratched my face it burned like a brand of shame, and I let her go. She was doubled over, choking, no longer speaking, but she was alive when I left her."

"You actually. . . ." Geoffrey's heart sank into his stomach and he grasped at a straw. "You're sure she was still alive when you left her?"

"Yes, as God is my witness, yes. It was when I came back to my senses and went back to her house that I found her dead. I touched her, hoping I could rouse her enough to make her last confession and save her soul, but she was already growing cold." Baldwin leaned back against the wall, shrinking like a deflated bladder. "She mustn't say such things about the archbishop. He's our lord and master. I had no choice but to shut her mouth."

No, thought Geoffrey, Thomas of London wasn't their lord and master, merely his representative. And he could imagine what Johanna's warnings were—Henry was quite capable of bringing Thomas to trial on some charge dating back to his days as Chancellor, simply to break his power as archbishop.

Groaning like an old man, Geoffrey stood, called for the jailer, and wended his way through the castle's corridors back to the street. Today he couldn't see the towers of the cathedral, only a few uncertain rooftops in the smoke-tinged fog. Although whether the fog was inside or outside his own mind he couldn't say.

No wonder Baldwin didn't want to take an oath that he hadn't harmed Johanna. He had. And Geoffrey had only the priest's word he hadn't killed her. He had to find someone else in the village—a human being, not a demon—who might want to see her dead. Who'd chanced upon Johanna weakened by Baldwin and who'd seized his opportunity, adding new bruises to those already on her throat.

What if Theoric, for example, wanted to hasten his inheritance? But as Johanna's son he already had use of the land and its income—why commit matricide? And with a child on the way who would in turn inherit. . . .

The thud of hooves and the jangling of armor shattered Geoffrey's deliberations. Four horses and their riders loomed over him. He skipped sideways. Ah, Hugh de Morville and his retainers. The nobleman was on his way to the bishop's palace, no doubt, there to contest his rank against Thomas's. At least the king and the archbishop—and Theoric Frelonde—agreed on one thing, that the arrogance of the nobles needed to be curbed. If the meek would inherit the earth, what would the proud inherit?

And Geoffrey answered cynically, large estates, entire counties, countries, and their crowns. "Sir Hugh," he called.

De Morville's craggy face peered down at him. "Gervase," he returned, his slight nod bracketing Geoffrey's rank between a bow and a push into the gutter.

"I'm Geoffrey. Geoffrey of Norwich . . ." The knight and his men disappeared creaking and clanking into the fog.

Rolling his eyes, Geoffrey strode on toward Estursete. Gervase, Geoffrey, it was all the same to de Morville. But then, what was a name? Some called the archbishop "Thomas Becket" after his father. And Wulfstan's children might well be "Smith" whether they were smiths or not. New names for old, as Ivo had said.

There was Saint Peter's church. This afternoon Johanna would be laid to rest beside its walls. What a shame that the entire family was gone, with Alice's brother drowned in the river before she and Theoric were married. . . .

Geoffrey stopped dead beside the church gate. Wait a minute. What would it matter to the Frelonde family if Alice's brother had drowned? A sad occurrence, yes, but—but . . . Edith said Johanna had a son and a daughter. Baldwin said Johanna was chattering about her son who drowned. Wulfstan said, *Godeswell, for one, he flattered her and Alice and got what he wanted, didn't he?*

Geoffrey bolted through the gate and wrenched open the heavy oaken door. Edith stood just inside, her hand extended as though she were about to push it open herself. "Well then, young man, you've come to see Johanna again. No hurry, she's not going anywhere."

"I beg your pardon, mother," Geoffrey blurted, "but I need to know which is the child of Johanna's body, Alice or Theoric Frelonde?"

"Why, Alice, of course. Theoric was born Godeswell in Suffolk."

"But since Alice is Johanna's only heir, Theoric took her name."

"Yes." The old woman nodded. "I never thought it was a love match—Alice needed someone to work the land, and since Theoric's people were merchants, he had no land. But he's been properly respectful of them, for all his talk of selling up and buying land in Suffolk. First Johanna and now Alice will have none of that, though. The farm at Estursete's belonged to the family since before the Conquest."

For one short second, Geoffrey was elated by his own cleverness. Then his elation plunged into cold water and steamed
away. "Has Alice been here today?"

"No, only Theoric. He said Alice was dreadfully upset about
Johanna, so much so she insisted on walking beside the river
where her brother died. He's gone to fetch her for the funeral."

"Oh, no. No." Geoffrey grasped Edith's shoulders. Her
frail bones felt like kindling. "Send someone to the castle. Give
the sergeant my respects and ask him to bring his men to
Estursete. Now."

"What?"

"Theoric killed Johanna. Finished killing her. . . ." He shook
his head. But Baldwin had never been as important as he believed
himself to be. "If both Johanna and Alice are dead—if Alice dies
without issue—then Theoric can sell the land. And Alice is pregnant. I don't think she's gone for a walk by the river at all."

"Blessed Saint Peter," gasped Edith. She brushed past Geoffrey and hobbled down the walk. "Blessed Saint Dunstan . . . You,
boy! Come here! I have an errand for you!"

Geoffrey sprinted the other way, caroming off passersby,
and burst out of the city onto the bridge. The fog was thinning
into mist. The roofs of Estursete solidified from nothingness even
as he looked. Black birds circled overhead, like letters incised on
the pallid sky.

He ran faster, the air icy against his feverish face. What did
his own ambitions matter when a living soul—two souls—were at
risk? He could see the scene, Theoric's hand resting on Alice's
back, the smooth voice saying, "Look there, my dear, what's that
in the water?" Then a splash, and Theoric crying to the village
that he'd found his wife's body in the river, drowned just like her
brother—of course she didn't take her own life in despair over
her mother's death, not a good Christian woman like Alice.

Geoffrey burst into the smithy. "Smith. Come with me.
Now."

"What the . . . ?" But Wulfstan was curious enough to follow.
So were several other villagers. Geoffrey could hear their laughter
behind him—an archbishop's clerk lurching clumsily through the

mud was the best joke they'd seen in days. Normally, he'd cringe at the laughter, but not now.

A thin silvery mist hung over the river, veiling the tangled limbs of the willows. A path, yes, and there, the river rimmed with ice, the tips of the willow branches just etching the smooth surface of the water.

From the mist resolved the shapes of Alice and Theoric, standing on a bank above a still, dark pool. Even as Geoffrey inhaled to shout, the cold air burning his laboring lungs, Alice fell. Slowly, slowly, her coverchief waving like the wings of a butterfly, and Theoric's hand extended not to help her but to push.

Her body shattered the water. Droplets sparked in a sudden gleam of sun. "Theoric!" she shouted, but the name disappeared in a gulp. Theoric folded his arms and watched.

"God help us," gasped Geoffrey, and leaped.

The water was so cold it scalded his skin. The current pulled him under. He was powerless against it. His sight blurred, fog above, fog below—water plants waving and—Alice, billowing cloth, staring eyes, and open mouth still screaming, silently now.

No, she'd been cruelly used, but her mortal life wasn't yet over. Neither was his. And he had the strength of his youth, the stubbornness, the anger. . . . Geoffrey thrust himself toward Alice. Grasping her cold white hand, he struggled toward the distant glow of the sky.

His ears thrummed hollowly. A searing pain filled his chest and throat. The day of wrath, he thought, might just as well be cold as hot, frost instead of flame. His foot touched something solid. He heaved himself upward and his head broke through into air and light.

He heard Theoric's voice, ragged now, shouting, "The Normans took my family's land. I deserve my land. Back home in Suffolk, where it's always been. I deserve land."

Beside Geoffrey, Alice gasped and coughed. Wrapping his arm around her waist, he struck out for the bank. She was so slightly built it was hard to believe she'd soon be great with child. A child who would never know its father.

Wulfstan had Theoric's arms pinned behind his back. The man struggled and cursed but couldn't break free. And here came

the sergeant and his men, the now sober crowd of villagers parting before their weapons.

Geoffrey carried Alice out of the water and gave her up to
the other women. Again the sun came out, warm against his icy
skin, and the air he breathed seemed suddenly sweet.

BALDWIN BLINKED UP AT the clear blue sky like a mole. Gingerly,
he stepped across the mucky cobblestones at the castle gate. "So
it was Theoric?"

"Yes," Geoffrey replied. "It was Theoric who took advantage
of your weakness. I didn't tell the sheriff about your assault on
Johanna, but I shall certainly tell the archbishop."

"And I'll be lucky to spend the rest of my life in a monastery
in the wilds of Yorkshire," moaned Baldwin. "But better that than
a dungeon. Thank you, Geoffrey."

"I'm the archbishop's man, aren't I?" For now, Geoffrey added
to himself. His knees were wobbling, for all that he'd dried himself at the sheriff's fire waiting for Baldwin to be released. Impatiently, he urged the priest up Castle Street. A quiet daily round
of prayer and devotion sounded very appealing just now. But even
in a remote monastery there'd probably be those who had ambitions. Geoffrey was beginning to think that simply doing right
was the greatest ambition of all.

And that's probably what Johanna thought she was doing.
"What did Johanna say to you, Baldwin? What did she foresee for
the archbishop?"

Baldwin shook his head. "Swords rising and falling in the red
light of the altar lamp like tongues of flame. The archbishop
hewed to the pavement and his blood a red pool around him. A
new and powerful saint elevated before the high altar."

My God, Geoffrey thought, and he stumbled over the cobbles. But he forced a laugh. "There you are. She was mad, wasn't
she? Not a witch at all, but one of God's most pitiable creatures."

"Yes. Yes, I'm sure you're right."

Am I? Geoffrey asked himself. If Henry was capable of bringing charges against Thomas, his all-too-powerful followers, eager to court his favor, might . . . No. Surely Johanna's vision was only symbolic.

They walked through the gates of the bishop's palace and parted, Baldwin trudging toward the monks' dormitory, Geoffrey to the archbishop's chamber. Over the roof of the cathedral peeked the scaffolding around Prior Wibert's new tower. Each man had to leave his legacy. And Theoric's legacy was a scaffold in the marketplace: an ugly and petty ending for a man who despite all his airs was just as ugly and petty.

Geoffrey found the archbishop alone, seated close beside his fireplace, a book open in his hands. He looked up from beneath his brows, and again Geoffrey felt small and weak in the heat of his scrutiny. "Well, then, Norwich, I hear you've acquitted yourself well."

"Yes, my lord," Geoffrey replied, and told the entire tale, concluding, "Theoric wanted the land. He thought he deserved it."

"So it was all a matter of greed for property and position," Thomas said. "But what is a man profited, if he gains the whole world and loses his soul?"

Had he found the truth Thomas wanted him to find? Geoffrey asked himself. Had the archbishop wanted to confront the king? Did he, too, feel himself carried away by currents beyond his control?

Truth seemed damnably elusive at the moment. "I wonder, my lord, if Theoric's crime was in not aiming high enough. How many noblemen have murdered their way into property and position and suffered nothing for their crimes?"

Thomas's brows angled wryly upward. "Many."

"The king's mother and her cousin plunged England into war, contesting property and position. Why do men commit mortal sins to get what they think they deserve? Why do men go to such great lengths to serve their ambitions? Scripture tells us not to lay up treasures upon earth, where moth and rot corrupt and where thieves break through and steal, but to lay up treasures in heaven."

"Not all men," answered Thomas, "have keen enough eyesight to see heaven before them. Thank you, Geoffrey. Oh . . ."

Geoffrey stopped his turn toward the door and turned back, almost losing his balance. "Yes, my lord?"

"Why did Baldwin try to strangle Johanna?"

He'd prepared himself for that question. "She meant to warn you, my lord, that your debate with the king may in time prove dangerous. Baldwin felt she was speaking nonsense verging upon heresy."

Thomas's smile was thin but not humorless. "On the contrary. She appears to have been quite clever and articulate. A pity she died trying to warn me of something I already know. Thank you. You may go."

But even truth was not as elusive as Thomas of London. Bowing, Geoffrey walked to the door, where he paused and glanced back over his shoulder.

Even though the room was dusky with shadow, Thomas himself sat in the circle of firelight, its rosy glow softening his stern, pale features. He gazed into the flames, but his eyes saw farther, beyond fire, beyond ice, to a place where fire and ice, dark and light, life and death themselves were as one.

With something between a chill and a thrill down his spine, Geoffrey shut the door and asked himself just how long before Johanna's vision came to pass.

Author's Note

In 1164 Thomas Becket was forced into exile in France. A few weeks after his return, on December 29, 1170, he was murdered in Canterbury Cathedral by four of Henry II's knights—including Hugh de Morville. None of them suffered any secular penalty. For almost four hundred years, until the reign of another Henry, the eighth, Thomas was England's greatest saint.

A Horse for My Kingdom

Gillian Linscott

Author's Note

Nobody kills a herald. No matter how hot the hatred or how fierce the fight, the herald is sacred. He goes from one army to the other to challenge, to parley, to arrange a truce or exchange of prisoners. Nobody—king, noble, or common soldier—raises a hand against him any more than they would against a priest. And yet at Mortimer's Cross, not far from the border where England becomes Wales, on a freezing cold morning the day after Candlemas in 1461, Bluemantle, the herald, was killed. England got a new king that day at the Battle of Mortimer's Cross, Edward, the fourth of that name, as anybody may read in the histories. But how and why Bluemantle died has not been told—until now.

Even in the muck and the cold, with night coming on and the enemy so close you could smell the wood smoke from their fires, men turned to watch as she went past. The ground was a paste of red-brown mud with a crust of frost over it just hard enough to take the start of a foot's pressure then crack and sink you ankle-deep in ooze. Yet she walked so cleverly her feet were hardly mired. The winter sun was down level with the tree trunks, with no warmth in it, and the cold river curling round their camp smoked vapor into the colder air. When a man pissed, the heat went out of it in the time it took to splash against the toe of his boot. But she glowed in the cold air as if she'd found the trick of keeping her own private midsummer. Wherever she walked, there was metal whirring and clattering, swords and axes spluttering sparks on grindstones, scythes witter-wattering on whetstones. She only paused for a moment, curious, eyes wide. A man, feeling her sweet breath against the back of his neck, stopped what he was doing and turned, smiling. But before he could touch her, she moved on with that precise delicate walk, haunches swaying.

"Fine horse," he said.

"Yuh."

"What's her name, then?"

"Flut."

Fillette was the chestnut's name to the young man who owned her, but for the more-or-less man-shaped clod of rags and mud that held the end of her halter rope, Flut did well enough. Some names are made to travel a long way. Names like Edward Plantagenet, Duke of York, and Earl of March. That one had to ring out tomorrow in the herald's challenge across the frozen fields to where the enemy, Pembroke's men, were waiting and beyond that to the palace at Westminster where the mad king lived. The name of the clod holding the end of the halter rope only had to travel the length of a small stable yard at the most. Because he went with the horse and if anybody called for him it was because they wanted her, he answered to his version of her name, Flut.

"Who does she belong to, then?"

"Master Thomas."

Which pretty well exhausted the few words Flut knew. He and Fillette turned toward the corner of the field where their camp was, but before they'd taken more than a step or two they had to pull up to let a more important group pass in the opposite direction. At the center of it was a man riding a good bay, surrounded by four servants on foot. He rode like somebody with authority and wore a tabard quartered in Edward's colors of blue and red embroidered in gold thread with lions and fleur-de-lys, with a blue mantle hanging from his shoulders and spread out over the horse's hindquarters. He had no armor or helmet and carried no weapons apart from a short hunting dagger at his belt. His face was stern, giving nothing away. When they saw him, the men went quiet and the whirr of weapon sharpening stopped until he'd gone past. The man who'd admired Fillette spoke in an undertone.

"Been sent for, Bluemantle has. Edward wants to tell him what to say tomorrow."

"Not much doubt about that, is there? Run back to King Henry and tell him to shift his arse and make way for young Edward."

"He won't put it like that."

"That's what he'll mean, though."

Somebody noticed Flut gaping after Bluemantle and explained.

"You never seen a herald, boyo? Nobody can't start fighting until he says so."

Flut's gape shifted from middle distance to the man speaking.

"Wasting your breath explaining it to him," somebody else said. "Stargazy, he is."

"He'll ride out there tomorrow, soon as it's light, through those trees and over the field to where they are, then out comes their herald and they sling words at each other for a bit, then off we all go."

The man flourished his pike. Flut and Fillette jumped backward and everybody laughed.

"Mares is no good for fighting," someone said.

Fillette and Flut ambled on, moving at exactly the same pace. Fillette was eight summers old. Flut, if anybody had been interested enough to ask, could have worked out that he must be quite a bit older because he'd been almost a full-grown man when she was born, but his existence, such as it was, dated from the spring morning when she slid out of her mother's womb onto a bed of dry bracken and he was told, "Lift her up boy. Get her round so the mare can lick at her." At night, he was ordered to sleep in the stable to make sure the wolves from the hills didn't come and get her. He couched in the bracken among the droppings and the sticky afterbirth, exchanging his smell for hers. It was a step up in life for him, who'd never slept between walls before. The dried peas and nuts the foal's mother dropped while she was feeding and he snatched up before the rats could get them were the sweetest things he'd ever eaten. The milk he sucked from her teats when the foal had finished was the warmest thing that ever went down his throat. Since then, the only times he and Fillette had been apart was when the master took her out hunting, and even then he'd follow mile after mile in bare feet over rocks and through brambles to be there when the riders drew rein and then attach himself to her bridle. He was as much a part of the horse as her tail and hooves.

THEIR BILLET WAS IN the far corner of the field because, apart from the beauty of Fillette, they were some of the least important in the whole of the army. The camp was arranged with Edward's pavilion in the middle with his standard hanging from a lance outside, men coming and going all the time, straw packed into the mud around it to make the path easier, but mud still oozed through. Next to it was the tent of his second in command, Sir William Herbert, then of the other great men who'd brought forces of hundreds, archers, foot soldiers, their own armorers. The men were grouped round fires of logs dragged from the wooded slopes behind the camp, cooking mutton and venison in cauldrons, checking weapons. A stallion whinnied at the scent of Fillette. She and Flut stepped out faster, got back to the patch of muddy grass that had been home for three cold days of waiting.

"Stand."

The voice of Thomas Hindwell, owner of Fillette, so owner of Flut, too. As they stood, an arrow swished past them and twanged in a wooden target fixed to a willow. Then three more, striking the target so close together that the feathers of their flights touched. Thomas and his archers practicing, showing that at least they could shoot as well as anybody else there, though in this far corner there was nobody to watch. Thomas gestured to the horse to walk on. He was young and tense, every gesture larger than necessary, as if commanding a whole army instead of a

handful of men. Thomas Hindwell was a remote kinsman of Sir
William Herbert, so when the call had come he'd burnished his
father's sword and helmet, left his estate of a hundred rocky acres,
and marched the twenty miles to Mortimer's Cross with his entire
male household—nine all told. Three good archers, five servants
with pikes or axes, untried in war, a farm lad too young to be
much use, who might pass as a squire. That wasn't counting Flut.
Nobody counted Flut. He settled the horse in her shelter of
branches, fetched hay for her from the wagon, and stood by the
fire, watching as the archers unstrung their bows and checked
their arrow flights. They were in good humor. There was more
meat and ale, even in their small part of camp, than they'd seen in
three Christmases.

"You ready for the fight then, Flut boy?"

"A slummuck like 'im? When meat pasties grow on thorn
trees."

Flut just grinned and went to sit alongside the horse, cross-
legged on the cold ground.

"Thomas Hindwell."

A call from the edge of their trodden patch. A young man
waited, a few years older than Thomas and a head taller, warmly
wrapped in a cloak of russet-colored wool, a big white hound
beside him.

"Ralph."

Thomas gave his bow hastily to one of the archers, wishing
his rich cousin had found him with a sword, a gentleman's
weapon.

"Comfortable here, cousin?"

Ralph and his hound came to the fire without waiting to be
invited. A smoldering branch fell and smoke from damp wood
came pouring out like juices from a pudding. The household men
drew back from the fire, leaving their betters to talk.

"More comfortable tomorrow."

"After the battle."

"After the victory."

Six hours they'd have, at most. Six hours of winter daylight
to win all that Ralph had as a right, and Thomas had only learned
the lack of in a few bitter days in camp. Ralph had arrived leading

fifty men with helmets and good weapons, dressed in their master's livery, a wagon of silver plate to gleam in the firelight and make even a muddy field a feasting place. Above all, with a smile of greeting from Edward himself like the sun coming from behind a cloud: "Rejoiced to see you, Ralph, my cousin." Then an invitation to drink wine in the ducal, almost royal, pavilion. If Edward was declared king on the battlefield tomorrow, Ralph would rise with him. And Thomas? If everything went well in those few hours, then Thomas would rise, too. There'd be no need to trail back to the sheep-nibbled, furze-spiked acres, no need to waste life as his father had, not much better than a border farmer with sword and helmet rusting on the chimney breast and fingers curled inward from the joint-rot of the rainy borderlands.

"They're talking in there."

Ralph gestured over to Edward's pavilion, glowing in the dusk from the candles inside.

"Planning the battle."

Thomas said it like a man of the world, but his stomach lurched. Ralph gave him a sideways look.

"You think so?"

"What are they talking about then, if it's not the battle?"

Ralph smiled, teeth as white in the firelight as his hound's pelt.

"Peace, my dear cousin. Peace."

Thomas thought at first he was being told to keep quiet, hold his peace, but there was more than that in Ralph's smile.

"How can it be peace? Edward won't give way, not after what they did to his father."

"So the father's head is hacked off and the son has to bowl his own after it? Will that really seem a good game to him, do you think?"

"Edward can't give up his claim and march away, not after bringing us all here."

"Depends what the king's side's offering. If they were to promise to make him regent, say, declare him Henry's rightful heir, we might be laughing and drinking with those over there tomorrow night."

"You believe that?"

Ralph shrugged. "Pembroke's no fool. Winning or losing will hang on a hair tomorrow. Buy time. Bargain with us. That's what he'll try."

"And would Edward accept?"

Another shrug.

"Then what would we do?"

"Back to our fields, cousin, and keep our peaceful sheep."

Ralph could joke. He had friends, a fortune, a world before him. And yet Thomas sensed there was a purpose in the joke, a question he was supposed to ask.

"Is that what you wish for, cousin?"

"It is not. There are no reputations or fortunes to be won in peace, eating buttermilk cakes by the fire, and watching your old mother spinning."

They both laughed, and yet Thomas felt a cold hollow round his heart and a sudden wish to taste the warm doughy crumbs on his tongue and know that the whirring sound was his mother's spinning wheel, not blades on grindstones. He crushed it down.

"If he makes peace now, it's a mockery of us all."

Ralph's hand came down on his shoulder, warm through cloth and leather.

"Well said, Thomas. And yet when Bluemantle rides out tomorrow, it's quite likely a truce offer he'll be carrying. Think about that."

A horse whinnied from the other side of the field. Fillette replied, high and sharp. Ralph glanced toward her.

"Has that mare seen a battle before?"

Thomas shook his head.

"I thought not. Your Fillette's too fine and bright for work like this. I'll buy her off you now and breed from her back home."

"No." She was his only horse.

"Just as you wish. To tomorrow then, Thomas."

"To tomorrow." Ralph strode away, the hound at his heels, and Thomas stood so deep in thought that when the guest was gone and his men could move in to roast their collops of meat at the fire, they kept to the other side so as not to disturb him. Flut would get the rags of fat and gristle left when the other men had finished eating so he kept his distance, squatting on the dry bracken under the shelter of branches he'd built for the mare, listening to the men's talk as they waited for their meat to cook.

"Doesn't look too glad, does 'e?"

"Thinking about tomorrow?"

"What else?"

"Never been in a battle, 'e 'asn't."

"You neither."

"Tell us what it's like then."

"Not much."

"Not much what?"

"Not much to tell about. You wins, you walks away. You don't, you runs away."

"If you're lucky."

Fillette stirred and pawed at her bedding. Flut ran a soothing hand down her foreleg. Fighting he knew about, not battles. Fighting was men punching and wrestling over a woman or a stolen sheep, knocking teeth out or breaking bones. When they'd arrived at the field by the river and seen more people than he'd ever seen in his life before, more than he even knew existed, he'd pictured them all wrestling and writhing in the mud like rats in a rain barrel. Slowly, watching them at practice with their swords, axes, and arrows, he realized he'd been wrong.

"They've got Irish," one of the bowmen said, pointing with his chin over to the enemy fires. "Want looking out for, they do. Not as much armor between the lot of 'em as would cover a flea's arse but fight as if God had given 'em all ten lives to waste."

"About running . . . ," one of the untried men said.

"Don't think about it before you have to."

"If you don't think about it, 'ow do you know when you 'ave to?"

"You'll know."

"It's not our lot'll do the running tomorrow," an older bowmen said. "Pembroke's foreigners'll run so fast even she couldn't catch them."

He looked at Fillette, quietly nosing her hay.

"Wish I 'ad 'er. Safer up there on a 'orse with a good sharp gisarme."

The untried man mimed a blow downward with a battle-ax.

"That's not what it will be tomorrow. They'll ride up to the front line, just—then get off and fight on foot like all the rest of us."

"Where's the sense in that?"

"More sense than sitting up there making yourself a target for arrows."

The archer took up the mime, drawing a bow toward Fillette's heedless chest. Flut made a noise of protest, unregarded.

"Proper target she'll make, that bright in the sun. Won't last an eye-blink."

The archer squinted toward her, released his imaginary arrow. Another, sharper noise came from Flut. He jumped in front of the horse, running his hands over her chest where the arrow would have hit, glaring at the archer. The other men laughed.

"Gone and scared the poor gawby, you 'ave."

Flut, still glaring, squatted back in the bracken and didn't take his eyes off them. They ate their meat, heated dagger blades in the fire, and plunged them hissing into leather cups of ale, heating it so that it soothed throats aching from the damp and stored a little warmth to comfort the stomach in the night. The stars came out and the frost came down so cold you could hear the twigs and grass blades crackling as it caught them. The men arranged small branches near the fire, spread baggage sacks over them, and lay down wrapped in their cloaks. Fires across the camp died to a red glow, but the lights in Edward's pavilion glowed as bright as ever. Fillette finished her hay, sighed, and folded herself down for the night. She rested neatly as a cat on her side, long legs tucked up and Flut curled against her, letting her warmth flow into him and his heartbeat and breathing slow until they were indistinguishable from hers. One hand was still on her chest at the point where the archer had aimed his imaginary arrow. He slept and woke like that through hours of darkness. He knew now that he'd die the next day. The proper men, who knew battles, were sure that an arrow would let the warm life out of her, so the life would go out of him, too. It wasn't grief or loyalty—he didn't know about those—but simply a matter of fact, like a trout dying when you took it away from the water. It was, after all, an insecure bundle of warmth that a man carried round inside his own skin. Just an arrow or lance prick would send it spilling into all that cold waiting outside. All he could do was lie there looking up at the stars through the branches of the shelter, hug her warmth while the night lasted, before the man they called Bluemantle rode out in the frosty morning and said the magic words that would start arrows flying.

Then, for the first time in his life, something started growing in his head that troubled him more than the thought of being dead. It was the thought that he might be able to do something about it. Things were done to Flut, not by Flut. The possibility that it might be otherwise turned the world upside down—as upside down as it would look to a trout flipped onto the bank and looking down at the water. And yet the trout twitches and tries with every fiber of its body to live. In the darkest hour of the night a twitch much like the fish's brought Flut upright and shivering. The horse stirred in protest. He bent just long enough to stroke her neck to quiet her then trotted away, feeling the warmth of her still on his hand, raising his fingers to his nostrils to sniff her comforting smell as his cloth-wrapped feet padded over frozen grass.

FILLETTE WITHOUT FLUT SLEPT uneasily, starting at the slightest noise. Then, with the sky deep black and even the voices of the watchmen gone silent, she untucked her legs and was on her feet in a moment, quivering.

"Easy girl, easy Fillette."

A man's leather gloved hand was on her neck, stroking and calming. She gave a little snuffling sound, quivering her lips, pushing against his chest. A hand came out from under his cloak and unclasped to offer her hazelnuts.

"Easy girl. Good girl." She ate and allowed herself to be led softly past the sleeping men and outside the enclosure to a willow tree by the river. A saddle and bridle were waiting there and although the man fumbled, fitting them with frozen fingers in the dark, she stood patiently. He got her to stand beside the tree so that he could mount from a knot in its trunk, then guided her along the river that ran black against the white grass. They followed it until they were past the watchmen's fire, then struck out over the pastureland toward where the enemy's fires glowed no more than a mile away across the fields, like a reflection of the camp they'd left. About halfway between the two lines, the rider made her stop behind a tangle of bushes and brambles on a bank overlooking three bare oak trees. They waited. Twice the noise of something moving near the oak trees made her prick her ears and tremble, but the man's hand calmed her, and she stood quietly until there was the faint stirring in the air that comes before daylight, and the eastern edge of the sky began to turn the same color as the frozen land.

As the light broadened, mist rose up from the river so that men moved in it as if wading, with only heads and upper bodies visible. They beat frozen hands against thighs or nursed them under armpits to supple them enough to cope with buckles, gulped bitter mouthfuls of ale from beakers that had necklets of jagged ice inside the rim. It was some time before Thomas's household realized that both their master and his horse had gone.

"Gone out already, 'e 'as. Wouldn't wait for us."

"Don't be a dunny. How would he go on his own with nobody to fettle the mare for him?"

"Where's 'e gone then?"

"Somewhere around he'll be. Just go and look for him."

Some of them looked all round the camp, but found no sign of him, and with the light growing everybody was too occupied with his own business to worry about an obscure man and his handful of followers. When the men who had gone to look came back to report failure to the others, even the battle veterans looked sick. You had to have a leader, somebody to fight around. Without that, it wasn't a battle, only a confusion. Thomas's men stood and stared at each other and at the Fillette's shelter, empty except for droppings and scattered bracken. As they stared, the sound of a trumpet drifted over from Edward's pavilion. Bluemantle was on his horse and had started his short and lonely ride toward the enemy lines.

MOVING IN THE DARK, moving near the ground were natural to Flut, who never expected to be far away from either. His chapped and callused fingers had never been nimble, so the cold was less of a clog to them than the fingers of quicker men. He did what needed to be done doggedly and slowly in the dark, by feel rather than sight, then huddled up between the tree roots, waiting. When he heard the bugle note drifting over from the camp, he got up, tightened the rags round his feet, and jumped for a low branch of the nearest oak. It took a lot of ungainly scrabbling, but at last he managed to wedge himself with his back against the trunk and his legs astride the branch, watching. Up on the bank, Fillette stirred again, hearing scrabblings from the oak tree.

"Easy, girl, easy. Only a pigeon waking up."

But the rider's voice was strained. He looped the reins over the pommel of the saddle, unhitched the longbow that was slung at his knee, thumbed the bowstring into its slot. It was morning now. Although the sun was not up, the sky above the mist was white and taut like the silk of a banner, and a man could have seen colors if there were any to see in the white and black landscape of rime and river. Then there was color, one patch of it coming quite slowly at easy walking pace, shining out against the black and white. Quarterings of blue and red, a gleam of gold, a blue plume on a hat, and the fall of a blue mantle. The rider took an arrow from the quiver on his back, notched it into the bowstring.

BLUEMANTLE'S BAY WENT AT a collected walk. It was against a herald's dignity to hurry, and nobody would want or expect fighting to start until the sun was well clear in the sky. For the next hour both armies would be waiting on the word of the heralds and, whether for war or peace, the thing must be done in proper order. The bay hardly needed guiding because there was only one sensible way between the battle lines—a causeway at

some distance from the muddy ground closer to the river, passing between oak trees. For most of the journey he kept his eyes
straight ahead to the line of pavilions and white and gold standards that marked the enemy camp of the Earls of Pembroke and
Wiltshire. Then at the last moment a gash of color much closer
and to his right caught his eye. Against the mist and standing on
ground a little higher than he was, Fillette seemed a gleaming
giant horse from legend, a horse out of the sun. Bluemantle
gasped in surprise, raised a hand. At that moment, the arrow
struck his throat, tumbling him backward out of the saddle with
the weight of the mantle pulling him to the ground.

THOMAS, DESPERATE WITH ANGER and humiliation, saw Bluemantle fall and the bay standing with the stolid puzzlement of a
horse that has unexpectedly lost its rider. Then, as his mind
tried to catch up with what was happening, he heard a whinny
that didn't come from the bay and looked up to see what Bluemantle had seen in the last moment of his life: a bright chestnut
horse gleaming against the mist. Fillette. He'd been looking for
her for hours, since he woke in the dark to find her gone and
faced the disgrace of being the only gentleman in the morning
who'd have to go into battle on foot. Without even rousing his
men, he'd rushed out to look for her all round the camp and, as
day broke, into the fields round the camp. Now there she was,
half a mile away from where she should have been, but with a
rider on her back and—unbelievably—Bluemantle on the
ground. Thomas shouted something, not knowing what. The
rider turned his face toward him then yanked the reins and
spurred Fillette at a canter down to the causeway. She almost
trampled the body of Bluemantle and tried to rear up, but the
rider dragged her head down and pointed her between the oak
trees at the enemy lines. Thomas gave chase, but before he
could even shout again or form any idea of what was happening,
there was a twanging sound, the rider was falling, and Fillette
was galloping on alone. Thomas tried to grab for her rein but

missed and fell sprawling over the obstacle in the path that was cousin Ralph's body.

FILLETTE CAME BACK. THE fact that she came back with Flut holding the end of the reins surprised nobody and wasn't even commented on, because that was where anybody would expect him to be. After a few panicking yards she'd stopped, seen him sliding down from the tree, and come to him questioning and trembling. Though he couldn't answer her questions, he could soothe her at least. Thomas couldn't help because he was facing angrier and more urgent questions from Sir William Herbert. Every eye in Edward's camp had been on Bluemantle as he rode out, everybody had seen his fall, and the army was buzzing with speculation and anger. Sir William had gone galloping down and found not only Bluemantle dead but his own kinsman Ralph dead, too, a few paces away, his head half off like a clumsily slaughtered hen in a poultry yard, and a more remote kinsman, Thomas, looking like a man who'd seen the devil.

"B . . . bowstring," Thomas stuttered. "There." He pointed to where the thin line was stretched across the causeway between two oak trees. "He rode into it. Ralph rode into it."

"Who put it there?"

"I . . . I think, sir, Ralph himself did. To kill Bluemantle in case he missed with the arrow."

"You are saying my kinsman killed the herald?"

"He was afraid, sir. Afraid Bluemantle was going to offer peace."

Sir William blinked then looked at Thomas for a long time. "Should I believe you?"

"On my soul's peril, sir. He stole my horse. She's well known in the camp. He wanted it to be thought it was my crime."

From Pembroke's camp a bugle sounded, then another. They were mocking sounds. The herald should have arrived by now and his lateness suggested Edward's side had no stomach for fighting. Sir William made up his mind.

"If you're innocent of these crimes, then prove it by giving every drop of blood in your body for Edward today. If not, you'll go to your God a perjured man."

"I'm innocent, sir."

Sir William nodded, more to indicate an end to discussion than belief and beckoned a servant to help him back on his horse. He looked down at Thomas.

"Say nothing of this. Bluemantle was treacherously butchered by enemy scouts who have no respect for heralds. Ralph was killed trying to save him. Do you understand?"

"Yes sir, I understand."

Flut held the rein as Thomas was helped into Fillette's saddle, then padded after them as they cantered back to their own lines. He'd have liked to get his bowstring back from the oak trees, since he'd stolen it from the pouch of one of the archers, but one of Sir William's men had taken it already.

THE NEWS THAT THEIR herald had been treacherously killed by the enemy infuriated Edward's men. They fought that day as if every man had a kingdom to win and by the time the mists curled back in the evening, the mud in the flat fields was even more red than nature had made it, the river was full of the bodies of Pembroke's soldiers, and every clump of bushes or dead bracken for miles around hid shivering, half-naked men hunted like rabbits at the end of harvest. There were men to bury on the winning side, too, but seven of Thomas's nine followers survived, and although Thomas himself couldn't have said with honesty whether he'd acquitted himself well or badly, he seemed to have done enough to be included in the general rejoicing. He'd shed some blood for Edward from a gash in his arm, although far from every drop as instructed, and when, as evening fell, Sir William came up to his fireside with a tall young man beside him, Thomas's heart dropped. It took him a few moments to recognize the tall young man with his plain cloak and muddied face, but when he did his heart seemed to slip further down, right to his stomach. He bowed and stammered "sir," then "sire."

Sir William said, "I have been telling the king." His voice caressed the last word like a man buffing a helmet. He turned to Edward. "If Thomas is telling the truth, then my kinsman Ralph was a horse thief as well as a murderer."

"If the penalty for stealing a horse is hanging, then he's paid that already."

Edward's voice was light, almost joking, but Thomas wasn't deceived by that and he knew that standing here by his fire he was nearer death than at any time in the battle. Edward had respected Bluemantle. If he believed Thomas had killed him there'd be just one more corpse to bury. Softly, desperately, he said, "Sire, it is the truth."

Fillette, still excited from the battle, whinnied from her shelter. Edward looked toward the noise.

"That's the horse, is it?"

"Yes, sire."

Edward strolled toward her, as if looking at her would decide the case.

"A fine mare."

At that point Thomas made his great decision, the one which not only saved his life but changed the fortunes of his family for generations to come. He stood at Fillette's head and looked straight into the face of Edward who, king or not, was much his own age.

"Yes, sire. Fine enough for a king to ride, if you'd accept her."

A little later, Edward sent his servant to lead Fillette over to his own pavilion. As usual Flut went too and stayed with her, as little noticed in the new king's stables as he was missed from his old yard, but aware that the quality of the hay was better.

The Simple Logic of It

Margaret Frazer

The April rain fell in a straight, soft veil from low clouds, sheening the lead-dull, slate-dark roofs of Westminster Palace and setting a cleansing gleam to the cobbles of the narrow back alleyway between the south gate and the blank rear wall of the Exchequer. It beaded finely on the dead man's face, turned open-eyed and unheeding upward, where he lay in a loose sprawl on his back, though the blood smeared on the stones near the foot of the wall and runneled between the cobbles showed where he had lain before someone turned him over. Probably the guard standing apart from his fellows, York guessed.

He guessed, too, from the guard's clay-colored, queasy face, that he must never have been to the wars in Normandy where dead men were a too-familiar sight for this one to have unsettled him, killed by what looked to have been simply a straight thrust through the body from behind and probably dead before he hit the stones.

"He's one of yours, isn't he?" Master Babthorpe demanded across the body.

"Yes." There was enough dawnlight now that York did not need the paling light from the guard-held torch hissing quietly to extinction in the rain to answer. "He's one of mine."

"He's not part of your London household, is he? What's he doing here?"

Being dead, York almost said but didn't; said instead, level-voiced, "He's one of my couriers between here and Normandy. Why he's here in particular, I don't know."

"Probably looking for you, though?" Master Babthorpe pressed and only belatedly added, without any particular courtesy, "your grace."

York brought his gaze up from Davydd's dead face to meet Master Babthorpe's hard stare, with several equally uncourteous answers coming to mind; but Babthorpe, as an officer of the royal household, had authority if not for his rudeness, then at least for his questions and, for that reason only, York answered his curtness with simply, "Yes. Very probably." Even though admitting it felt like walking by his own will into a trap.

But then he had had that sense of a trap waiting ever since he'd been asked from his breakfast to come here, because it was hardly necessary for the Duke of York to stand in a back alleyway in a drizzling rain identifying a dead man any number of other men could have named as well and apparently had, since someone had known to come for him with word he was wanted to view the body. It was when he'd seen that, besides the expected guards, there were a half dozen of the Earl of Suffolk's men to watch him acknowledge the man as his, that his unease had deepened to something more, because Suffolk had been main among those who had lately tried to bring him down with slanders he had misused his power as the king's governor of Normandy.

York wasn't supposed to know where the slanders had come from but he did, even if they had been so subtle—no open accusations against him, only a quiet, determined undermining of his reputation—that he'd not been able to name names with any proof, but been able only to demand he be vindicated publicly, in Parliament. The slanders had faded away then and Parliament been dismissed without the matter becoming officially open. He had thought—hoped—the thing was finished. But now . . .

"There was a letter found on him," Master Babthorpe said. "To you. From Normandy."

Already more chilled than the early hour and the rain justified, York chilled more deeply but only said, making it seem it hardly mattered to him, "May I have it?"

"After my lord of Suffolk has." An effort not to smirk marred Master Babthorpe's dignity. "This whole matter—and the letter, too—must needs be put into his hands. You know that." Because while York was abroad, trying to keep England's hold on Normandy from disaster and going into debt while doing it, because somehow the garrisons had to be paid whether or not money for it came from England, and mostly the money had not, Suffolk had kept close to King Henry, gathering a great deal of power and a number of offices to himself, including Steward of the Royal Household, so that he had not only control over nearly everything that happened around the king but ready access to King Henry for himself and a strong say in who did or didn't come near the royal person.

York, despite—or because—he was the king's cousin and near enough in royal blood to be possibly King Henry's heir if King Henry died without issue of his own, was among those Suffolk preferred King Henry not to see often, and now Suffolk was who would have this letter and determine what to do about it, and York said, "Later then," as if it did not matter, while the questions ran behind his carefully blank face, beginning with why Davydd had been here in this back alleyway at all. As York's man, he had every right to come the main way into the palace, and if he'd come in the middle of the night, as he must have, a guard would have escorted him from the gate. So why had he been here in the black hour before dawn? Because it looked to be no longer ago than that that he was killed; his blood on the cobbles had started to dry before he had been rolled off of it, opening it to the rain, but had so far darkened only around the edges, enough to tell he had not lain here long. "Secret" and "urgent" were among the words coming to mind, seeing him here like this, but York, in the same, seeming-uncaring tone as before, asked, "Was he robbed?"

"His belt-pouch was empty except for the letter," Master Babthorpe answered.

York looked down at the pouch that hung from Davydd's belt. "Odd. You'd think a cutpurse, having killed him, would simply cut that loose and go."

Master Babthorpe shrugged. "Who knows how those kind of men's minds work?"

Usually more cleverly than that, York thought but did not say.

"My lord of York? Master Babthorpe?" asked a black-robed priest, come almost unnoticed to the fore of Suffolk's men behind Master Babthorpe. "I understand there's a man dead here and in need of prayers."

Belatedly, York realized that the man was no mere priest, despite his plain black gown and the bent shoulders of someone who spent more of his time over books than at anything else. He was the Bishop of Saint Asaph's, unlikely though that seemed, because even bishops of so slight a bishopric as Saint Asaph's were rarely as diffident as this man appeared to be.

But Master Babthorpe was making him a deep bow from the waist, saying hurriedly, "My lord bishop, there's no need of you here. A plain priest will suffice . . ."

Past him Bishop Pecock met York's slight bow of the head with one of his own, they being close enough to each other in rank as royal duke and God's bishop to exchange equal courtesies, and said, ignoring Master Babthorpe, "My lord of York."

"My lord bishop," York returned.

Raynold Pecock had been an Oxford scholar and then warden of Whittington College in London, nothing more, before he was made Bishop of Saint Asaph's for reasons unknown to York, abroad in Normandy at the time. Nor, since his return, had he ever had occasion to more than barely speak to this least of the bishops and never enough to build any thought of what sort of man he might be. Now, as he started toward Davydd's body, Master Babthorpe made to step into his way, saying with somewhat more impatience than respect, "My lord, I was shortly going to send for a priest. There's no need for you . . ."

Bishop Pecock did not pause, merely made a backward beckon of one hand to move Master Babthorpe out of his way, saying as he went past him, "Man dead by murder, gone without proper rites to judgment, is a man with his soul imperiled. A priest should have been sent for before anyone else."

Quietly, York revised his opinion of the Bishop of Saint Asaph's upward: he was not diffident at all, simply so confident of himself that he had no need to assert his place to anyone—unless they were in his way like Master Babthorpe, now out of it and standing in tight-lipped, disapproving silence while Bishop Pecock stood looking down into Davydd's dead face before finally shaking his head and saying, "This was evilly done." With another sad shake of his head, he made the sign of the cross over the body and raised his gaze to York. "I heard he was a Welshman, and being perhaps his bishop, I thought it well to come myself. His name?"

Keeping to himself the thought that there seemed to be a surprising amount known about Davydd to a surprising number of people so soon after his death, York said, "He was Davydd ap Rhys." Giving the name its Welsh form and sound. "Of Neath."

"Not of my diocese then, but Welsh nonetheless and in need of prayers." And, even though the cobbles were both rain-wet and back-alley dirty, Bishop Pecock knelt down and began a low murmuring of the Office of the Dead.

Over his bent head York said at Master Bapthorpe, "I hope you've at least had sense enough to send for the crowner," and left without waiting for an answer, his own three men who had come with him parting from his way, then falling in behind him, their presence at his back more of a comfort than it should need have been, here in the palace where even to draw a weapon made a man liable to arrest.

But here in the palace were his worst enemies, Suffolk and the other lords of the royal privy council. What they wanted for him was nothing so simple as his death, though he suspected they'd not have minded if it came, so long as they could escape any blame for it. Short of that convenience, what they most intended was to cut off any chance of him having influence with the king. Young King Henry VI reigned, but his royal privy council ruled, telling him what his decisions should be in most matters; and King Henry—being more given to piety than kingship—mostly followed their bidding. York, too powerful in his own royal right and too openly opposed to their ways, knew himself to be a risk of which they wanted to be rid. They had tried to cripple his governorship of Normandy when his success in governing both the war and the uneasy peace had roused too many discontented men's claims that he should have more hand in England's government, presently troubled as it was under the royal privy council's rule with increasing disorders and ceaselessly rising debt.

And as surely as he knew all that, York knew that in some way Davydd's death and the letter he had carried was going to be used against him. But how? Who was it from and what was in it?

And how could he find out before too late?

TOO LATE, AS IT happened, came too soon, within two hours, before any of the men he had sent out with questions had returned with any answers. In the outer chamber of the rooms given to him in the palace, trying to pay heed to a bundle of account papers one of his clerks was showing him, he heard Bishop Pecock's Welsh-softened voice at the outer door asking a servant to ask if he might see the Duke of York. More than willingly giving over the accounts he had not been following anyway, York bade him enter and the clerk and other men to withdraw to the room's far end, then led Bishop Pecock to the room's other end, to the narrow window deep-set in the thickness of the stone wall with its sight over rooftops to Westminster Abbey, reared pale and huge against the washed blue of the clearing April sky and wind-drifting clouds. Even now, distracted as he was, the changeful play of sun and cloud shadows over its stonework and flaring buttresses gave him pleasure, but Bishop Pecock gave it not even a glance, and noting the red, curved marks on his cheek and over the bridge of his nose where the heavy wooden rims of glasses must have been setting until lately, York wondered if maybe that was simply because the bishop could not see it. But if Bishop Pecock's sight was poorly, it was quickly clear his wits were not as he began, directly to the point, "My lord of York, I've seen the letter that was found with your man."

"How?"

"There's been a meeting of the king's council." Bishop Pecock amended that. "Of some of the king's council." Then amended again. "Not really of the council but of those my lord of Suffolk thought would be of most use in dealing with the matters raised by the letter, as well as a few others of us to make the matter more credible, we being not suspect of being on one side more than another but expected to follow what we were told concerning conclusions to be drawn from the letter, you understand . . ."

With the suspicion that time would run out long before Bishop Pecock did, York interrupted, "What did it say?" Then more formally, to soften that rudeness, "I pray you, what was in it?"

Not seeming bothered to be interrupted, probably used to it, Bishop Pecock promptly shut his eyes and quoted, frowning at the words to make sure he had them, " 'Moleyns has the answers he sought. All is known. Do what you can.' "

The chill that had come on York beside Davydd's body deepened. A warning to him that "all is known" left far too many directions from which he might be attacked, beginning surely with whatever "answers" Moleyns had been seeking. Bishop Adam Moleyns of Chichester, Keeper of the King's Privy Seal, was Suffolk's creature first and last and always, and whatever he had been seeking would not be to York's good. Now, with this letter in hand, Moleyns could charge anything against him, and Suffolk would claim the letter as proof that the charges, whatever they were, were true.

"Is it signed?" York asked, annoyed to hear that his voice was trying to twist along with his stomach.

Bishop Pecock looked at him reproachfully. "Of course it's not signed. Put name to it of someone who could be asked and would not only deny it but maybe be able to prove the falsehood? Best to leave it with only your name and your denials to be dealt with."

The shape of the trap was becoming clearer by the moment and as yet York saw no way out of it. Who had been fool enough to send him such a letter?

"Except, of course, that everything about the letter is false," Bishop Pecock said as if stating an openly obvious truth.

York stared at him, then said, sharp with disbelief, "Why do you say that? How do you know? You have proof?"

"Assuredly." Bishop Pecock sounded surprised even to be asked.

"What?"

With the open pleasure of a scholar only too happy to present his thoughts, Bishop Pecock said readily, "To begin. I came to pray over your man because I heard Bishop Ayscough say as the household was coming out of morning mass that there was a murdered Welshman behind the Exchequer. Afterward, with thought upon that, it seems to me a strange thing for my lord bishop of Salisbury to know and be commenting upon there and at that hour. You see, even though it was something known, obviously, it was not widely known, the hour being still very early, or others would have been talking of it, too, and no one was, only my lord bishop, and why would he know of it before anyone else since, on the face of it, it was no matter that should come to him at all, let alone be first thing in the day, before even mass, yes?"

"Yes," York granted, having kept pace with that fairly well.

Bishop Pecock nodded, happy they were still together in it, and went on, "Now, if the premise is accepted that Reason governs all that happens—and we can surely accept that it does—then if a thing seems without Reason, there is nonetheless surely Reason behind it, and if one follows by Reason from what is presently known toward what is presently unknown, if, in other words, one follows with Logic the way that Reason leads, we can come to the understanding of anything, even of God, who surely gave us the gift of Reason for exactly that purpose."

Afraid there was little time left before Suffolk moved openly against him and remembering that one of the few things he had heard of Bishop Pecock was that he talked a great deal about things no one wanted to listen to, York cut short the explanation—if that was what it was—with, "Bishop Pecock . . ."

"Raynold," he said absently, his mind still mainly elsewhere. " 'Pecock' is a rather unlikely name, on the whole, don't you think? I like it better that my friends call me Raynold."

Letting it go by that he was disconcerted to be thought a friend, York asked, "How does Reason reckon in this?"

"Ah. Yes." Bishop Pecock veered easily back to where he had been. "Given the premise that it was unreasonable for Bishop Ayscough to take interest in this dead Welshman—or rather, that it seemed unreasonable but must not have been—I took closer look than I might otherwise have at this whole matter of your man being dead and the letter and found that there are certain things to be noted about both, but to begin with the letter . . ."

York held up a hand, stopping him because across the room Master Babthorpe had appeared in the doorway and was asking the servant there for leave to enter. York nodded permission and Master Babthorpe crossed the room and made a bow that included them both but with a curious look at Bishop Pecock, so that York said smoothly, unwilling for him to know anything he need not, "My lord of Saint Asaph's has just come to tell me what disposition is being made for my man's body. And you're here . . . ?"

He left the question hanging, bringing Master Babthorpe to answer, "My lord of Suffolk asks that you come to him in the lesser council chamber, if you would be so good, your grace. And you also, my lord," he added to Bishop Pecock.

"Only my lord of Suffolk?" York demanded.

"And a few others. They're presently there, so if you would come as soon as may be . . ."

"You mean now," York said bluntly.

Master Babthorpe agreed with another slight bow. "If you would be so good."

Be so good as to come and not so foolish as to refuse, York thought, but aloud said evenly, letting himself show nothing but confidence, "I pray you tell my lord of Suffolk and the others that I'm on my way."

THE LESSER COUNCIL CHAMBER was a room meant to impress, not large but well-proportioned, with a mullioned window looking out on the king's garden and the walls hung with painted tapestries showing the Judgment of Paris over the Golden Apple—perhaps not the best of choices for somewhere wise decisions were supposed to be made, York always thought—and the ceiling beams painted with patterns and mottoes concerning Justice and Truth—neither of which, York suspected, would have much place here today.

As expected, Suffolk, Bishop Ayscough, and Bishop Moleyns were there: Suffolk at the head of the council table, facing the door, the other two on the sides immediately to his right and left. It was who else was there that mattered, and York was not displeased to find, ranged down Bishop Ayscough's side of the table, the Duke of Buckingham, Lord Cromwell, and Lord Stourton. They were men who could, as Bishop Pecock had said, be expected to follow what conclusions they were led to about the letter, but they were also men who would be swayed by facts rather than partisanship with Suffolk, and that gave York at least a hope of fairness. It was a small hope but illogically somewhat grown because of Bishop Pecock, who had probably been included as a make-weight. Three bishops and three lords to judge between York and whatever Suffolk came up with against him.

Now, as York crossed toward the table, one of Suffolk's men pulled out the chair set by itself across from Buckingham, Cromwell, and Stourton. To sit there would leave York facing them much like a felon before a jury, with Suffolk, Ayscough, and Moleyns as his "judges" at the table's head. Making no haste and allowing no sign of unease, York made a small bow of his head to his peers, then went deliberately to the high-backed chair at the near end of the table, pulled it out for himself, and sat down to face Suffolk along the table's length.

Coming in behind him, Bishop Pecock went to sit in the pulled-out chair, thanked the man for it, and settled himself comfortably, resting his clasped hands on the tabletop in front of him.

Suffolk gave the briefest of frowns, then quickly smoothed it away, returned to his usual gloss of good manners and ingrained satisfaction with himself. He was a well-featured man and knew it and used it and had charm enough and a sufficient degree of wit to keep the king pleased with him and work other lords around to seeing things his way. He would have willingly worked York around, too, but York could not get past his own belief that Suffolk, regardless of charm and excellent good manners, was dangerously shortsighted concerning the long-term consequences of what he did.

In return Suffolk chose to consider him an enemy, to be shoved and kept from power as far as possible, and said at him now, "Well, York, we've a problem on our hands, it seems," without bothering to hide it was a problem that pleased him.

"Indeed?" York returned evenly. "I'm sorry to hear it."

Suffolk waited for more but was forced to go on without it, saying somewhat tersely, "It seems a man of yours has been found murdered . . ."

"Seems?" York cut in with mild surprise. "I thought it certain that he's found and equally certain that he was murdered."

Thrown out of his course, Suffolk fumbled, "Yes. Well. Be that as it may . . ." and lost track of where he was, and Bishop Ayscough put in sharply, "The point is that there was a letter on your man addressed to you with matter in it that raises troublesome questions."

York turned a cool look his way. The Bishop of Salisbury was a gray-featured, thrusting man, said to be more bane than blessing to his bishopric, and with no reason to expect his good will in any case, York said at him peremptorily, holding out a hand, "Let me see this letter I keep hearing about."

As quick looks and hesitation passed between Suffolk and Ayscough, Buckingham reached to take a paper lying open in front of Suffolk, saying, "Show it to him. It won't change anything," and shoved it down the table.

York took his time reading it despite there was only what Bishop Pecock had quoted: *Moleyns has the answers he sought. All is known. Do what you can.*

"Read the superscription, too," Bishop Ayscough said, and York turned the paper over to what had been the outside when the page had been thrice folded on itself and sealed. There, in dark ink and a firm hand, was written, *For the Duke of York, from Normandy, to be read in all haste.*

York looked at Suffolk, said, "Well?" and shoved the letter back along the table.

It was Bishop Pecock who put out a hand and took it. No one objected, probably no one heeded because, as Buckingham had said, it said what it said, no matter who had it.

"You see the difficulty?" Suffolk said, his course recovered. "Someone has seen fit to send you a strong warning that 'all is known.' Now, as to the answers Bishop Moleyns has been seeking . . ."

York shifted his look coldly to the Bishop of Chichester. "We all know what he's been seeking. We all know he had his nose in places last year when he was in Normandy. And didn't find anything." But that had been when York first understood how deep Suffolk's distrust of him ran. No sooner had he come back to England, than Moleyns had been off to Normandy, seeking some evidence of York's ill-doing in either his governing or his finances or preferably in both, to the point of offering to pay the travel-price of anyone willing to come to England and give evidence. No one had come.

"Questions have continued," Moleyns said with high-nosed dignity. Small-built, he carried himself large and was beginning to be the same around his middle, too, from deeply indulged rich living. "Just of late we've had answers and not ones you'll like."

"Such as?" York asked.

"Such as testimony . . ."

"Suborned," York said.

". . . and witnesses . . ."

"Bought."

". . . and documents . . ."

"Forged."

Moleyns's voice rose a little. ". . . . of your abuse of the moneys entrusted to you, your favoring of some men—Scales, Oldhall, Ogaard, to be precise—over others in the matter of payments for no reason but your whim, your mishandling of both men and funds to the point where presently Normandy is in danger of being destroyed and lost by your doing!"

York could have told them exactly why Normandy was in danger of being lost, and it had more to do with malfeasance here than anything he had or had not done there. First and foremost was the council's failure to send him promised funds to pay anybody anything, followed by the support Suffolk and the others had given to John of Somerset's harebrained, useless campaign into Anjou when it was all English troops could do to hold the frontier as it was and forcing York to hold the Normandy garrisons from revolt by draining his own coffers to pay them at least something now and again . . .

"All this against you has been laid before the king," Suffolk said.

Damn, thought York, careful that his face showed nothing. He had hoped it wasn't gone that far yet.

". . . with promise that Bishop Moleyns' evidence to your wrongdoing will shortly be in his hands," Suffolk went on.

"Not that much in the way of evidence will be needed, what with this letter out of Normandy warning you of your danger," Bishop Ayscough said, arching a finger in disdainful point across the table to the paper lying under Bishop Pecock's hand. "What greater condemnation could there be than a secretly sent warning that all is known, do what you can?"

Especially when what they wanted to find out was not the truth but his supposed guilt, and a brief look at Buckingham, Cromwell, and Stourton's accusing looks back at him was enough to show how other men, even those more interested in fairness, would as easily believe what the letter "proved."

"Yes," Bishop Pecock sighed, paused, and then said, sounding regretful, "But then there's the trouble that this letter never came from Normandy, did it?"

Silence sharp as across a hawk-shadowed meadow fell the length of the table, and York doubted it was Bishop Pecock's poor eyesight that made him seem unaware that everyone was looking at him as he went on, holding the letter up, "It can't have. You see? There's no sign to it having been anywhere very long, in Davydd ap Rhys's belt-pouch or anywhere else. Though it's a little crumpled, the folds are fresh, nor is it marred as if long carried in bag or pouch or however, such as it must needs have been if it had indeed come from Normandy as it purports to. You see?" He turned the letter this way and that for everyone to view but seemed not to notice Suffolk thrusting out a demanding hand for it but instead laid it down again, his own hand firmly on it, and went on, "Therefore it follows that the paper was neither long-folded nor long-carried and therefore could not have been brought from Normandy, not by Davydd ap Rhys or anyone else. Yes?"

He asked the question generally. It was Buckingham, leaning forward over the table who answered, "Yes, but . . ."

"By your leave, my lord, if I might continue?" Bishop Pecock asked mildly and did so without pause for Buckingham's reply. "Therefore the letter must be from here, in England, not Normandy at all, and therefore at the very least the superscription is a lie."

"To mislead us," Bishop Ayscough said sharply, "into not realizing York has a secret ally here who passes word to him received from Normandy some other way."

"That's a little more complicated than need be, don't you think, my lord?" Bishop Pecock asked. "Though possible, I suppose," he granted. "But still, why shouldn't this ally simply speak to him directly rather than commit the matter to paper?"

"Because, whoever he is, he couldn't come to Westminster himself," Bishop Ayscough said. "The letter was his only way . . ."

"But the letter was written here in Westminster," Bishop Pecock said.

"That's a guess," said Suffolk.

"But it's not, my lord." Bishop Pecock sounded faintly scandalized by the thought. "It's a fact, proven by the fact that the paper bears a mark on its edge showing it came from the privy seal office, here in the palace."

York did not move but all his attention was sharply at alert now as Bishop Pecock held the paper edge on to them, turned it from Buckingham to Cromwell to Stourton to Bishop Ayscough to Suffolk to Moleyns and finally to him, saying, "You see here. That black mark on its edge. The privy seal office uses a great deal of paper which, while not so costly as parchment of course, nonetheless is costly enough not to be wasted or lost, which happens when people in need of paper sometimes take it for their own uses. To keep from such wastage, when paper is new-delivered to the privy seal's use, there is a black ink line drawn down the side of the stack, leaving a small black mark on the edge of every sheet, if you see what I mean."

Lord Cromwell demanded, "How do you come to know so much about the privy seal's paper?"

Bishop Pecock made a small, almost deprecating shrug. "One notices things, such as black marks on the edges of papers, and asks questions. I can't help it."

York, whose mind had been racing toward conclusions, said thoughtfully, as if to himself, "And Bishop Moleyns who 'has the answers he sought' is Keeper of the Privy Seal."

"Yes, indeed," Bishop Pecock said, as if that were a mildly interesting observation. "With access to as much privy seal paper as he wants, I suppose. But to return to where I was—if the letter shows no sign of having traveled far and was, in fact, written here in Westminster, it therefore did not come from Normandy. You see? Nor was it written by someone who would have to go so roundabout as to use one of York's couriers out of Normandy." He looked around the table earnestly. "You see how simple it is? Once a premise is granted—in this case, two premises, the first being that the paper is not far-traveled and the second, that it's from here—then a third premise derived from those must be granted—that the letter did not come from Normandy. Besides which, it would seem fair to consider the possibility that it was not meant for York at all, especially if no greater evidence to the contrary can be brought and I doubt that in this matter it can, so . . ."

York doubted he was the only one lost among premises, but it was Moleyns who protested, "That paper could have been stolen at anytime. Months ago even. There's no saying when or where that letter was written."

Bishop Pecock turned a benign gaze on him. "Is every stack of paper marked in the same place, time after time?"

"What? No. No one tries to do that. We just want them marked, is all."

"The mark on this sheet matches the mark on the supply presently on your head clerk's desk, to be given out as he deems necessary."

Bishop Moleyns gaped slightly, then demanded, "How do you know that?"

"I went to see, after our first meeting this morning."

"The mark proves nothing!" Bishop Ayscough said. "Not either way. Not any way. Not . . ."

He broke off, apparently well lost among Bishop Pecock's premises, but, "It raises doubts, though, where there weren't any," said Buckingham. He had a heavy-paced intelligence rather than quick, but he was fair-minded when he could manage it. For him, doubts were doubts and not to be ignored once they were raised, and York felt a stirring toward hope that this wasn't going to go all Suffolk's way after all.

"And then, of course, there's the trouble with how York's man died," Bishop Pecock said.

"There's no trouble there," Suffolk answered. "He was stabbed from behind by a thief who then robbed him and fled."

"Ah, yes. Well. I went with his body, you know, when it was taken for the crowner to view it because I thought it might be best to go on praying over him closely a while longer, his death being sudden and all. The crowner, of course, verified the cause of his death."

"It not taking much to verify a dagger-thrust from behind," York said bitterly.

"But there was more than that, you see," Bishop Pecock said. "There was also the large lump on the side of his head. The crowner commented on that, and I felt of it myself. He'd been struck very hard, I'd judge. And when he was stripped, there were large bruises to be seen around both his upper arms . . ." Bishop Pecock held up a hand, curving it as if around an arm, ". . . that large, as well as raw places rubbed into his wrists and both corners of his mouth. You see?"

At least some of them saw very clearly: Lord Stourton began swearing under his breath and York, sickened and angry, said harshly, "You're saying that the stabbing was only the last thing done to him. Before then, he was sometime hit on the head, maybe knocked unconscious, was also sometime gagged and his wrists tied. He fought against that hard enough to leave raw sores, and the bruises on his arms you're saying look as if they were made by someone holding roughly onto him."

"Or it might have been by two someones, one on either side," Lord Cromwell said.

Though he was holding it, York's anger tightened his voice. "Davydd was killed where he was found. That's certain, because of the blood. And the dagger-thrust looks to have come level at his back, as if he were standing when he was stabbed. But those other marks didn't come from any thief creeping up behind him to kill him. He'd been brought there, maybe unconscious, maybe only still gagged and bound and knowing what was happening, held up between probably two men while a third one ran him through from behind." York rose to his feet and leaned forward with fists braced on the table toward Suffolk. "His death was no chance killing. It was murder, for the sake of that letter supposedly for me being found on him here, where it could do the most damage to me."

Into the taut silence after that almost accusation, with Suffolk all too clearly naked of any reply, Bishop Pecock said mildly, "Judging by the facts as we have them, it would seem within the reaches of Reason to say so."

"Damnably right it does," Lord Stourton said forcefully. Lord Cromwell was nodding frowning agreement, his look along with Buckingham's glare turning toward Suffolk as Bishop Pecock went on, "The question then becomes . . ."

But Suffolk had regrouped enough to interrupt him warningly, "My lord bishop."

As if he suffered from deafness as well as poor eyesight, though York doubted it, Bishop Pecock went blandly on, ". . . how to close the whole matter with his grace of York cleared of the charges that I believe have already begun to spread through the palace, without making obvious what truly occurred?"

He ended on a question spread with seeming innocence among Suffolk, Ayscough, Moleyns, and the other lords, leaving it for Ayscough to say with forceful calm, "An excellent point, well taken. I think we should adjourn, though, for a time and take it up later, when we've all had time to think on it. Agreed?" he added at Suffolk, who said quickly, "Yes. Yes, I think so. This is definitely something we should take time to think on. My lords, until later?"

He was rising as he said it and on his own way out before anyone else was fully on their feet. Less hurriedly but no less firmly closing off the possibility of further talk, Ayscough and Moleyns followed him, and shortly, after a brief exchange of words with Buckingham, Cromwell, and Stourton to no particular purpose, York was alone with the Bishop of Saint Asaph's, the two of them still seated, regarding each other along the table in a full silence that finally ended with Bishop Pecock saying with soft, apologizing sadness, "There's nothing to tie them decisively to your man's death. You understand that, yes?"

"Yes," York agreed. While there was enough in all that Bishop Pecock had brought forward to discredit the letter, there was no way at all to bring Davydd's murder home to anyone— neither those who had planned it nor the men who had done it for them.

"It's your name must needs be fully cleared now, my lord, lest the taint of Moleyns's charges against you stick despite the facts being disproved. Not that they're actually Moleyns's charges against you. My lords of Suffolk and Salisbury have a large or larger hand in them, no doubt. It was simply that Moleyns has been most lately in Normandy, making it most reasonable to use his name in this, here and now. Therefore it's for him to refute what's said against you in his name, and from what little I've known of him, being myself but these two years a bishop and of the royal council but never of the most inner circles . . ."

"Raynold," York said.

Bishop Pecock broke off, blinked, gathered himself, and said, admirably to the point for a change, "Moleyns has no courage in himself. Present his charges against you in writing to King Henry. Forced to face you openly, Moleyns will dodge like a hunted hare."

York slowly nodded, seeing his point and that Suffolk and Bishop Ayscough would not say anything for risk of showing their own part in the matter too openly.

"But Davydd's death . . ." York said and stopped, frustrated.

"There's no way to bring anyone to trial for it that I can see," Bishop Pecock said with the clear feeling that if he could not see a way, there must not be one. "Countering their intents against you is the most retribution there can be."

Again York slowly nodded agreement. As vengeance went, it wasn't enough but it would have to be. They were stopped and he was safe.

For now.
Until they moved against him again.
Or he moved against them.

Author's Note

Of the named characters here, only Davydd ap Rhys is imagined. Both York's challenge to Bishop Moleyns and Moleyns's gibbered protest of innocence are on record. It was very few years afterward that Suffolk, Moleyns, and Ayscough were all murdered within a few months of each other. It was seven years more before Bishop Pecock proved too clever for other men's good and was brought down by the court faction who replaced them. Three years after that the Duke of York was killed in battle.

Plucking a Mandrake

Clayton Emery

The hunter's ears pricked to the gabble of ducks and bate of wings. From under an old blanket stuck full of sweet flag and canary grass, he watched the flock jitter across the sunset: teals, mallards, pintails, and fat graylag geese.

All afternoon Robin Hood had lain sopping wet amid tussocks of reeking marsh under his blind. With the caution of a hungry man, he nocked a bird arrow with steel spines like a hedgehog's. As he'd guessed, the weary ducks dropped toward this pond, for it was sheltered from the north wind, removed from foxes and badgers, and warmed by the southern sun. Slowly, Robin shrugged the itchy blanket from his shoulders, came to one knee, drew as he rose—

—and jumped at a cry of *"Yah yah yah!"*

Ducks exploded off the water, groping for sky, colliding and dodging and quacking. With his eye on the graylags, the outlaw loosed. Steel tines ripped the female's breast and she tumbled. Within seconds he dropped five more birds, but he'd hoped for twice that.

Cursing, Robin pushed through reeds. What bastardly fool blackguard had rousted his birds with that idiot croak?

He stopped. Dying ducks and feathers dotted the pond. Amidst them sloshed a bedraggled stick-man in a filthy smock and matted hair and beard. He seized a dying duck, stretched the neck, and bit to suck heart's blood.

Shocked, angered, and disgusted, Robin shouted, "Drop that, varlet! 'Tis mine!"

The man crouched, cringing, his mouth smeared with blood and feathers, eyes vacant. Robin saw a rude cross stitched to his smock: a cure for madness. The fool swatted water at Robin, hooting, "*Yah, yah!*" Clutching the duck, he floundered out of the pond and scuttled up the wooded slope toward the village.

Swearing, teeth chattering, Robin slogged through icy water to retrieve his ducks. Piercing the webbing on a string, he trudged up a twisted path between trees. He'd lay a few stripes on that madman. Even a dog knew better than to steal a man's game.

But shooting ducks was foolish, he decided: gigging hooks or drowning nets would gather more sooner. He needed many ducks. With Easter past and May Day looming, winter apples and rye and salt pork and herring were all eaten, and famine stalked the land. Food was so scarce in the Greenwood, he'd dispersed his band until fatter times. Not that that was why he hunted so far from home.

Muttering, dodging branches, stumbling over roots as dusk fell, absorbed, Robin bumped into a pair of dangling feet. In horror he snatched a handful of grass to scrub his face, then crossed himself repeatedly.

The dead man hung from an elm. Shrunken to a skeleton, neck stretched like a sausage, skin curdled a moldy gray, his lips were cracked, and his eyes picked out by crows and sparrows. The sockets glared at Robin in accusation.

Snatching his bow and birds, Robin Hood dashed up the trail toward the village.

SKEGBY MOOR WAS PONDS and fingers and rills and marsh and tall grass and brambles. Above the moor on low mounds rambled the village of Skegby, thirty cottages linked by muddy tracks and bridges of fallen trees. A fief of Tevershalt, a manor in the north, Skegby was old, squirreled away like a motte-and-bailey castle in the dark days of raids by blue-painted demons. The occupants spoke in canted words and archaic idioms and had gaped at Robin and Marian as if they were elephants from Egypt.

Yet the wattle-and-daub cottages were neat, the gardens and patchwork fields tended. The air was ripe from privies and pigs, yeast from the alehouse, coal smoke from the smithy, and incense from the chapel. On the outskirts stood the cottage of a wise woman, or witch. Robin Hood stopped running at her door.

The cottage was buried under vines and rosebushes, lapped on all sides by a garden like a spring tide. Bees bumbled at a hive, two brown goats rooted through chaff, and chickens scratched for weevils. Indoors was just as crowded. Robin ducked hanging herbs. The only furniture was a plank table crowded with pestles and bowls and pots, a pair of stools, and a pallet that unrolled for a bed. A white cat licked its paws by the hearth.

Fitful rushlight surrounded Marian's dark head like a halo. She was dressed like Robin in winter-brown shirt and trousers and greased deerhide boots. The witch was barrel-round in a faded red gown and kirtle. A headscarf made her chapped cheeks rounder. Her name was Rocana, an old name Robin had never heard before.

"What's wrong, Rob?" Marian asked. "Why do you pant so?"

"Dead man." The outlaw gulped air. "On the path at the bottom of the hill. Hanged. Walked right into him."

"Aye, a sad place to hang a man." Rocana's eyes crinkled in sympathy. At the fireplace, she turned turnips buried in dock leaves and ashes. "But that elm is traditional. I'm sorry, I should have warned you. Ducks and a goose! Lovely!"

Robin shucked his sopping clothes and hung them near the fire, then cleared a spot on the table for the ducks. Fingering a diamond on a hen mallard's wing, Marian recited, " 'Touch blue and your wish will come true.' "

They lopped off heads and winkled out innards while Robin got his breath back. "What was he hanged for? Who is he—or was he?"

"Ingram. Our local rake. Fathered half the bastards in the parish. A poacher of sheep. The hills are full of deer and the moor of ducks and eels, but Ingram wanted mutton. And I'd cook it for him!" Rocana hooted. "But that half-Irish beast, Fedelm, the bailiff, finally caught him. He always danced the Jack in the Green, too. Don't know who'll do't this year."

"It's almost May Day, isn't it?" Robin said. The first of May meant festivity, when a man donned the Jack in the Green, a cone of wicker and leaves for the forest spirit, the mythical tree man. Escorted by Green Men in face paint and leaves, and Morris dancers with sticks, and cloggers with swords, the Jack would caper while people danced after it, till the Jack was felled with swords to die and rise again, to show spring had arrived. It was Robin's favorite holiday, and he was suddenly homesick for the Greenwood.

Marian asked, "How long must he hang there?"

"Till he's ripe and falls. Like a pheasant."

"We'll have to tell our cousin, Will Scarlett. He's gallows fodder, too."

Robin carried guts to the back door to pitch them on the midden. A snuffling at the stoop jarred him. "What the hell?"

On hands and knees, the madman from the pond lapped from a wooden bowl.

"That's just Serle," Rocana called. "He drinks the milk we put out for the wee folk. They don't seem to mind."

Robin stepped around the madman, pitched the guts, and wiped his hands on mint leaves. Serle scuttled off. The outlaw huffed. Every village had an idiot: even he had Much the Miller's Son. Returning to pluck ducks, he asked, "What was Serle's offense, that God punished him so?"

Rocana seared duck breasts in a kettle, then added water from a red clay ewer. "I'll stew 'em to go farther. Serle abused his family. After a pot of ale he'd see in his poor wife and children all the demons of Hell. He pickled his brain. Now he's one with the beasts, and may God bless us all, I say."

"Beasts," Robin groused. "Better we lived like beasts. They follow God's will without questioning. Or meddling."

Marian sniffed. "Rocana says we needs stay a few days more."

"As you wish, honey," Robin sighed. "T'will let me lay in more ducks. If we can keep—Serle?—clear of the marshes."

"We can." The witch plucked herbs from the sheaves overhead and crumbled them in the stew. "I have a special way with him."

LONG AFTER DARK, THE cat lifted her head. Robin, an outlaw since boyhood, felt for his knife and checked the back exit. Something scratched at the door like a small dog.

Rocana admitted a young woman in faded brown. Her belly was swollen and her gown damp at the breasts. She carried a big baby, almost a toddler. She gasped at the witch's company and, timid as a deer, had to be coaxed inside. She sagged on a stool and relinquished her toddler to Marian, confessed that her child had stopped kicking, and was that right? While Rocana asked questions and ground herbs and seeds in a pestle, Marian cooed and kissed the baby's blonde head, inhaling its milky fragrance. Robin sat by the fire and fletched an arrow with a gray goose quill.

"Such a beautiful child." Marian touched the woman's swollen belly. "And another on the way. You're lucky."

The young woman smiled vacantly and touched her stomach. "This one's father is an angel."

"What?" Marian bobbled the infant.

The simple woman was sincere. "His father's an angel that comes in the night. He's tall and dark. This child will be doubly blessed."

"Yes . . ." Marian stroked the ash-blonde head. "I see . . ."

The cat picked up her head and scooted behind a sheaf of woodruff. Robin Hood laid his arrow on the hearth.

The door rattled and banged as a priest barged in. "Willa! You're not to come here! I've forbidden it!"

The young woman upset her stool, but Marian caught her. The priest offered no help. His dark cassock bore buttons from throat to hem and was girdled by a rosary with a wooden cross that banged his knee. His high brow, eagle's nose, and sharp cheekbones recalled a talking skull.

"And you, interloper," he snarled at Marian, "you'll not talk to this woman either!"

Robin Hood rose. "How is that your business?"

"Everything that transpires in this village is my business!"

The outlaw stifled a rising temper. Robin took clerics as he found them. Friar Tuck was poor as dirt, dedicated, and honest. The greedy Bishop of Hereford had been forced to dance in the Greenwood at arrow-point. Robin kept his voice level. "Not today."

Snorting, the priest grabbed Willa's arm. Robin Hood seized his, and the priest gasped. "Father, pray contain your zeal. The women discuss women's affairs. Men are not needed."

The priest could not wriggle free. "It's a sin to manhandle a cleric!"

Up close, Robin was distracted, for the glitter in the priest's deep eyes was somehow familiar. He brushed the thought aside. "It's man's nature to sin. I but do my part." Robin pitched the priest out the door. The man just missed rapping his head on the lintel. Robin shut the door.

Rocana swept her mix into a clay cup, then instructed Willa how to brew a tea. It took three tries. Marian surrendered the baby and Willa slipped into the night, tears of fear in her eyes. Fletching again, Robin asked, "Does the priest visit often?"

Smiling, crinkly, Rocana tidied her work table. "Alwyn's forbidden the women to come for my curings. They come anyway."

Robin licked a split feather. "What does he dislike?"

"Competition. We wrestle like boars for the same wallow. He's got his Latin and holy water and incense, I my Gaelic and magic water and herbs." She banged vessels as she worked. "We villagers are partial to harelips and webbed fingers, living on rabbits and ducks as we do, but you won't see Alwyn wield a needle or a knife! Yet he rails that I defy God's will with blasphemous magic! So when Young Gerald slashed his palm with a knife, Alwyn could only pray. I drew the blood poisoning with a sage and apple poultice and saved his arm and his life, thus defying God's will!"

The wise woman sighed. The cat rubbed against her hairy leg. "But it happens all over. Witches bein' driven out by churchmen. There're more of them, and better organized, with their bishops and councils and diets and edicts, while we're a handful of old women who pass on secrets from mother to daughter. And men are hungry as wolves. You know't, don't you, Marian? Men rule this world and women endure it."

Neither the Fox nor the Vixen of Sherwood denied it. Marian asked, "Why does Willa think her husband is an angel?"

"I let her think that. Her true husband is Serle, who's been mad more than a year. Better she's visited by an angel."

Robin Hood cleared his throat. "Rocana, if this village ever drove you out, you'd find a home in Sherwood."

The witch cocked her head like a girl. "Would I? That's very kind. But," she peered around at leaves and vines and flowers, "you can't grow a garden in the forest. And I'm rooted here the same way. Whate'er others may think, I'm part of this village."

FOR DAYS, THE WOMEN worked on Marian's "problem." Married more than a year, she had yet to conceive. Word was Rocana had cures. "Don't fret, dear. We can fix't. A good marriage is a prolific marriage."

The witch suggested many things. "Like cured like," so Robin set braided snares around clover patches, and Marian ate rabbit until she swore her ears grew. She drank tea of mugwort picked in May. For lovemaking, husband and wife slept outdoors under a rose arbor and the moon, yet with faces covered lest the moonshine drive them mad. Around their bed of blankets they scratched a six-pointed Seal of Solomon. Before and after making love, they prayed to Saint Anne. Rocana joked she had no pearls, or she'd grind one into Marian's food. And they eschewed green as unlucky for lovers.

Robin Hood chafed at probing questions. Did they have relations twice a week? Did he shed enough seed to fill the hollow of her palm? What of their families? Marian listed brothers and sisters while Robin had none, living or dead. Yes, it had taken his mother years to conceive, but how could that matter?

By day, unneeded, Robin hunted alone. Yet Marian was hopeful. One night, dreaming at the sky, she piped, "Look, Rob, a falling star! The soul of a child coming to be born! Maybe ours!"

ONE NIGHT, ROCANA WOKE Marian from their pallet, bid her dress, and gave her a knife and basket. The witch carried a frayed rope. Marian pressed her husband's shoulder to keep him abed. "Rob, stay and watch here, please?" Pleading and apologizing at the same time. Her husband neither nodded nor shook his head.

A full moon etched the world with silver light. The earth seemed blown of milky glass lit from below. The two women bustled to the dark garden, where the witch slipped the rope around the neck of a brown goat. Then the three hobbled off into the dark.

Catching up his bow and quiver, Robin followed the witch's creaking knees and wheezing. He couldn't hear Marian. They trod the path down the hill. Robin guessed their destination and muttered charms of protection, but wondered what they planned.

Like a lost scarecrow, the dead poacher Ingram hung from the elm. Under his dangling feet, Marian dug as Rocana instructed. Pressing alongside an oak, Robin watched and listened.

"I didn't think it grew in England," the young woman said. She grubbed in the soil some time. "I don't find it."

"Oh, dear. My memory's not what it used to be. . . . No, it don't grow in England. I planted it here before they hanged him. Ah, got it? Careful! Just uncover it, don't disturb it!" Rocana nickered to the goat and fumbled with the rope. "My rheumatism hates this spring damp. Slip the bight under a stub of it."

Robin hissed. Were they both mad?

"Stay! Stay! Move up the slope, dear. Stay!" Leaving the goat under the hanged man, the women backed past Robin's post without seeing him. A hundred feet up the slope, the witch warned, "Cover your ears."

Robin Hood clamped both hands to his head. Dark against dark in silver-splintered light, the goat tugged, then plodded up the slope toward its mistress. Gingerly, Robin uncovered his ears. He heard the witch reward the goat with a treat. She untied the rope and stuffed their prize into her basket.

"*Yah yah yah!*" The raucous blat split the night.

"There they are!" boomed a voice. Golden torchlight banished the silver moonlight.

Rocana muttered in Gaelic. Marian trilled, "Shall we run?"

"No, child. Stay put."

Through the trees came the priest, Alwyn, and three villagers, alike as stalks of wheat. They carried torches. Leading the pack like a dog shambled Serle, the madman. The priest's cassock and rosary flapped about his knees. Catching Serle's arm, he called, "Rocana! You dare defile the dead? You'll bring down the wrath of God with your doubly-damned blasphemy!"

"I've touched not the dead, Alwyn." The witch waved a crooked hand. "The lord's tree still bears fruit."

The priest ordered a torch held near the grotesque body. "If you don't trifle with the dead—and we may've interrupted your grisly work—what do you do at this witching hour?"

"It's none of your business," the witch snapped, "but we harvest by moonlight. Oak buds and cuckoo's pintle and such oddments."

Hidden in the dark, Robin Hood grunted. Those innocent plants were not what the goat plucked from the ground.

Unsatisfied, Alwyn refused to leave the women alone with the corpse. "Seize her! Drag her to the chapel! We'll see if she's innocent or not! Go on, grab her!"

Robin Hood startled everyone when he slipped to Rocana and planted his feet. The villagers balked, but the witch muttered, "No, let us go. We'll get this over with, once and for all."

Nonplussed, Robin didn't move. Marian tugged him away. "Watch and wait, darling. We'll make sure she suffers no harm."

The three men caught Rocana's elbows, gently, reluctantly, and avoided the basket on her arm. They escorted her up the slope after Alwyn.

Robin waggled his useless bow and squeezed his wife's hand. "I'm sorry I broke faith, honey, and spied. It's hard, but—"

His wife sniffled in the darkness. "We need help for me to conceive, Rob."

"Not that. I won't let you do it."

"Hush. We'll discuss it later."

Torchlight ringed the village chapel and common like fairy fire. Barefoot villagers streamed from their cottages, rubbing their eyes. Alwyn waved a Bible as he exhorted the crowd in a high singsong. The three men held Rocana, who waited, resigned and hardly terrified. Beside her stood the pregnant and confused Willa, wife of Serle. Beyond the crowd, in a disused byre, Robin saw the Jack, an eight-foot cone woven of wicker and thatched with prickly holly leaves for the dance on May Day.

Alwyn ranted against sin, and the villagers attended. A few men hollered agreement, some women vexed, but most just listened. This was neither sermon nor trial by ordeal but entertainment, another round in an ancient village feud. Robin Hood had seen grimmer football matches.

". . . Too long, witch, has this village tolerated your heathen interfering ways! Like the Witch of Endor, you've urged our women to wickedness! You've dealt out potions and salves that keep wives from conceiving even when visited by their husbands! You've dazzled the minds of good women and made them like drunks so men might ravish them in the fields! You've caused father to lie with daughter, brother with sister, and son with mother! You've stolen the bowels and members of babies to conjure flying potions . . ."

Rocana clucked her tongue. "Stop this rubbish, Alwyn! Everyone knows my healings, and everyone's profited by them . . ."

"Why not mount her on a horse again? Perry, fetch your cob!" a man joked. "Touch her brow with an iron knife!" jibed another. "Float her in the pond!" a woman shrilled. Even the jests were ancient.

The priest ranted, fulfilling his duty if not moving his audience. Robin Hood wondered if he were drunk. Or partly mad. Madness ran deep in this isolated hamlet . . . Suddenly, Robin gawked, realizing why the priest seemed familiar. "Marian, Alwyn is Serle's brother!"

"Yes, yes, Rob. Listen."

Robin Hood pouted. "Why do women always know these things first?"

"It demands in Exodus, 'Suffer not a witch to live!' Yet this village harbors a viper at our bosoms!" The priest raised a Bible as if he'd squash a fly, then thumped Rocana's brow. "Be condemned! Feel the fire of the holy word! Know the burning pits of Hell beckon!"

Rocana pushed at the book with feeble hands. "Get that thing off me!" As she struggled, her basket upended. A knife and a dirty root thumped at the priest's feet. Alwyn pounced on the root, holding it up to catch the light. It resembled a triply forked carrot crusted with dirt.

Silence fell hard on peoples' ears. Alwyn's eyes grew feverish in the torchlight. "*This* you harvested under the gallows tree? You've done worse than *defile* the dead! You *use* them for purposes too foul to bespeak! You'll *burn* for this!"

Rocana bleated. The villagers murmured as the game took an ugly and unfamiliar turn. The priest wrung Rocana's shoulder. "There is no pit deep enough! No damnation strong enough—"

"Stop!" Rocana writhed in the priest's grip. "Unhand me, you rake! Must you paw every woman in this village—"

Quickly, Alwyn slapped her, then raised his hand again.

Quicker, Robin Hood's bow snagged the priest's wrist. "I'll break your arm, you black-bearded bastard! Don't you *dare* strike a woman!" Marian tugged her Irish knife loose in its sheath.

Maddened by his own ranting, Alwyn pointed at Marian. "You outlaw interloper! You'll suffer torments unimaginable when your wife conceives a *demon's child!*"

Growling, Robin Hood gripped the man's throat. The priest struggled as he waved the root in the air. Everyone saw it, and knew it.

Mandrake was the most ancient and mysterious of herbs. Its manlike shape let it breathe beneath the ground, where it stored up power for fertility and prophecy. Dangerous and jealous, a mandrake hugged the earth and hated to leave, so if carelessly plucked it screamed, loud and harsh to drive men mad. To harvest it, a witch tied the root to a dog or a goat, then whistled the animal from out of earshot to yank it from the ground.

"See you this?" rapped the priest. "A mandragon! A denial of God! She buried it under a dying man to soak up his seed that spilt upon strangling! And she'll compel *your* wife to purge *your* seed and insert *this* instead! Thus do *Christian* women birth devils—"

"Oh, no! *Oh, no, no, no!*" A soul-wrenching cry cut through even Alwyn's bellowing.

The deluded Willa pushed at her swollen belly with clumsy hands. "No, no! She said t'would make the child strong, t'would ward off the madness! Oh, get it away! Help me, Mother Mary! Get the devil child out of me!"

Villagers surged back as if from a mad dog. Rocana reached, but Willa lurched around the firelit circle, grasping at people, pleading. "Get it away, please, sweet Christ, get it away!"

No one could help, she saw. Her hand snatched at a man's belt for a knife. The blade flashed yellow in the torchlight.

"Stop her!" screamed Marian, and shoved at the crowd. Robin tangled with a man backing up. Rocana swiped at the young mother's hands.

All too late. Willa drove the blade into her low-slung belly. Transported by passion, unmindful of pain, she stabbed until blood and water gushed red and white and splashed in the dirt. She stabbed until she stumbled and fell. People screamed and howled and prayed as if the world ended.

Rocana flopped on her knees, clutched the dying woman's head, and wept. Willa's bloody hand floated toward Heaven.

Robin Hood hoicked Alwyn in the air by his cassock. "You—"

A man howled in the darkness. A woman screamed. "The Jack! It lives! It's Ingram come back! God have mercy!"

People shouted, screamed, pushed, ran. Robin fought to see and remember. What about the Jack? And who was Ingram? Then he saw.

Jerking and jigging, the Jack in the Green, a living dancing tree, thrashed and shivered as it dashed amidst the shrieking villagers. The cone's shiny leaves shimmered in the wild light as torchbearers ran hither and thither. Only Rocana kept her place, cradling the dying woman's head.

Alwyn squirmed from Robin's grasp. He fumbled his cross high to banish the evil apparition, then his nerve broke and he ran.

The crowd melted like a breaking sea wave. Despite fear and superstition boiling in his brain, Robin noticed bare feet stamped the turf under the green cone.

Sensing that the outlaws stood fast, the Jack rushed.

Shoving Marian aside, Robin snaked an arrow from his quiver, pulled to his cheek, and loosed.

The arrow slapped into the Jack, parting leaves at the height of a man's breast.

The spirit kept coming.

Superstition conquered reason. Robin hollered, "Run, Marian!" His wife had already bolted for sanctuary. Robin loped after. Marian dove into the chapel like a quail into a hedge. Robin grabbed the door and slammed it shut. In black stillness, their rasping breath was loud.

Visions whirled in Marian's mind: ghosts and fire and blood and wonder. But one picture stood out starker than the rest. "Robin—you missed!"

"What? No! I never miss!"

"He didn't go down!"

"*I never miss!*"

IT WAS HOURS BEFORE the outlaws dared peek. The moon was down, the common deserted, even the dead woman gone. The night was still, as if God had called home every man, woman, and child.

Close together and casting every which way, Robin and Marian crept down the path to Rocana's cottage. They had only starlight to see by, but they walked fast because they argued. They'd fought ever since coming to Skegby Moor, Robin reflected. What prompted all the anger in this village?

Robin's bow sliced the air as he whispered, "It's necromancy! I'll not have it, not mandrake! It goes against God's plan! It's criminal to put that—root up your—insides—"

"Women have used mandrake for centuries! It's in the Bible! Jacob's wife Rachel was barren until she asked Leah to borrow her mandrakes—"

"But plucking it under a corpse by the full moon!"

Marian hissed, "This is our only hope! Maybe the old ways—"

"You want the seed of a *dead man*? A living ghost? So you birth an imp or a changeling?"

"That's a man's help for you! Forbid everything and offer nothing in its place!"

"It's dangerous! You could go mad from the mandrake's scream! That priest was right about one thing! God's wrath has descended on us! You saw that poor woman kill herself—"

"That fool priest killed Willa, surely as if he plunged in the knife himself! Him and his wild accusations!"

"It wasn't the father, it was the witch! She duped that poor woman and the devil seized her! Retribution comes from crossing God's ways!"

"Oh, hush! You sound like these other ignorant sots! Men know more about breeding dogs than women!"

"That witch causes harm! She has a goat for a familiar—"

"A goat can't be a familiar!"

"Satan takes the form of a goat! Cloven hooves, a beard—"

"Satan's form is a *man!*"

"Oho! So it's *men* who—*Whoa!*"

Robin Hood spilled headlong over an obstacle across the path: a round springy mass of rustling leaves. Robin felt pricks along his arms and legs. "What the—These are holly—"

"It's the Jack!" Marian breathed. Now they could make out the shape, a long cone interwoven with leaves.

Robin huddled close to Marian. "Christ, look where it lies!"

Here the path split, one fork leading to Rocana's cottage, the other down the hill toward the marsh, passing under the gallows elm.

"Oh, Mother Mary . . ." squeaked Marian.

Both were reluctant to touch the fallen icon, but Robin's curiosity goaded. In the dark, he fumbled inside the wicker frame. "Nothing. Neither body nor blood. Nor arrow."

"It'd go through a ghost."

"A ghost couldn't lift this frame."

"A dead man, then."

"Then the arrow would stick him! Let's not talk of such things . . ." Robin sucked wind. "I'm going down the hill."

"I'll go with you."

"No. See if Rocana's returned. She might need guarding."

"Be careful."

"Oh, yes."

Crossing his breast, holding his bow foremost, Robin Hood wafted like a ghost down the path. In dead quiet, no night birds sang, no owls hooted. Robin crossed fingers on both hands.

Straining, he recognized the widened spot under the elm tree. The noose still dangled in place. Ingram was gone.

With a knife, the outlaw cut the rope's shank and tugged it down. The hangman's noose of thirteen turns was yanked almost closed. Robin Hood shuddered.

Noose in hand, he dashed up the slope.

The door of the witch's cottage hung open. A rush lamp flickered on the worktable, and he was grateful for the light and life. But something made him stumble at the threshold, a bad sign, and he snapped his fingers to dispel ill luck.

The place stank, he realized, rank and cold and brassy.

The worktable was bare. Pottery shards and herbs littered the floor. Ashes were scattered like snow. The stools were knocked over. The back door hung at an angle. Marian sat on the hearth, tears on her cheeks. Hard by the fireplace lay the squat shape of Rocana. Deep blue fingerprints marred her throat.

Wordlessly, the outlaw held up the noose. By rushlight they saw the tiny noose was foul with grime and sloughed skin.

"So it's true!" Marian breathed. "Ingram came back—"

"Hist! Don't say his name! You'll call him hither!"

Marian rose to shrink against her husband's chest. "The hanged man, then, the poacher! He got down off one tree and climbed into another! He donned the Jack to dance again! To take revenge on the village! The dead taunting the living! Oh, sweet Lord!"

Reaching under Robin's arms, Marian made the sign of the cross at the doors. "So much death in this village. It's in the air, like contagion. Maybe we should leave."

"Yes. With the dawn."

YET THEY STAYED, FOR with the sun came work to be done.

Father Alwyn refused to administer last rites for Rocana, or to hold a vigil, or to bury her in the chapel graveyard. Pagans could rot, he said, as offal for dogs. And he had Willa's funeral to minister. So Robin and Marian sank Rocana in the garden she'd loved, and entwined a wooden cross with yellow cowslips.

Warned off by the priest, most villagers stayed away. The few women who came crossed themselves as they talked. They'd all seen the abandoned Jack. They guessed dead Ingram murdered Rocana because she'd berated him for fathering bastards. And the dead resented the living. Ingram killed Rocana the same as he'd died, by strangling. At every Mass, Alwyn preached that "one sinner had fetched away another." No one, they reported, ventured out after dark.

Each night, as Robin barred the doors, he cut a fresh cross in the wood.

Ducks winged in, and Robin needed meat, so for days the archer netted and hooked and shot birds, then dressed them, smoked their breasts over a low fire, and packed them. The birds' numbers dwindled as the flocks nested in summer grounds farther north.

In spare moments, Robin returned to the common, to sight, pace, and crawl with his nose to the ground. Finally, he discovered his arrow buried in dirt lengthwise. It lay yards from where he'd shot it. When he plucked it free, he learned why. It lacked a red hen feather.

Back at the cottage, he showed Marian. "See? I didn't miss. This arrow passed through something that skinned off this fletch. That made it hook sharp to the right."

Marian pricked a chicken strung over the fire. "I see, Rob. I was wrong to think you'd missed. Yet the villain inside the Jack was dead. No arrow could stop him." She crossed her breast.

Robin grunted, but added, "Still, I didn't miss."

"Here. I've found something queer, too. I tried sorting herbs and seeds, but without Rocana's knowledge, they might as well be oak leaves. Yet I discovered this." She fetched a small stone crock that held a pale yellow dust. "Mandrake root."

"So?"

"Mandrake's rare, Rob. It only grows in the Holy Land. Rocana, may she find peace, claimed to have only a single whole root that she never cut. Yet here's a handful ground fine."

"Why would she lie?"

"I don't know. We all have secrets. Wash your hands."

They sat down to chicken roasted with sage and onions and a pitcher of goat's milk. "Drink up. It's the last. The bailiff collected the heriot and the mortuary, the death taxes. The best goat went to the lord and the second-best to the priest. We get the cat."

"She'll hardly make a meal."

"At least we don't need the milk. Serle hasn't returned for his bowlful since the witch died. He must scent death, like a dog."

"Or else he misstepped in the marsh and sank. Or was also killed by the vengeful dead man." Robin stopped chewing. "Do you suppose Serle might've killed Rocana, may she rest in peace? A madman can do anything."

"Why should he harm her? She fed him milk every night at the stoop. Even mad, he'd remember kindness."

"Poor dead Willa, may she rest easy, was his wife. She must have fed him when they were wed, but that didn't spare her beatings."

"I'd offer that Alwyn, the priest, killed her out of spite!" Marian threw chicken skin to the cat. " 'Like people, like priest,' and he's the most hateful man in the village!"

"Why should Alwyn kill her?" The outlaw plied his knife. "They feuded, but that went back years. And Alwyn wouldn't have wrecked the cottage."

"He's almost mad as his brother. The whole family's cursed by bad blood. And Alwyn has a temper. Once he saw that mandrake root, he turned vicious as a mad dog! He struck Rocana and bellowed about women birthing demons! The filthy hypocrite! Remember how he accused Rocana of bedazing women to be ravished?"

"I think so." Robin scratched his beard with a knife point. "He ranted about many things."

"What do you always say? 'A man accuses others of what he practices? A thief is quickest to say he's robbed, a cheat to say he's cheated'?"

"So . . . you think the priest bewitches women and ravishes them?"

"No, I think he promises Heaven and threatens Hell until they lie down."

"A woman shouldn't listen to a man," the husband mumbled. "Some reckon it's no sin to sleep with a priest. Some women think it's lucky!"

"How long has Serle been afflicted mad?"

"Hunh?" Robin's mouth was stuffed with chicken.

"More than a year, according to Rocana." Marian waved a drumstick. "Yet Willa bore only seven months. Serle didn't get her with child. And neither did mandrake root."

"So . . . wait. The *priest* bedded Willa? Christ on the cross, he can't do that! She's his brother's wife! That's incest!"

Marian nodded. "Another sin that he laid at Rocana's feet. He accused her of luring father to lay with daughter, and brother with sister, and mother with son."

"While Father Alwyn was lying with his sister-in-law!" Robin shook his head. "Pitiful Jesus, an incestuous priest! What would a bishop do? Castrate him?"

"Nothing. No one would tell. This village is like a family. It keeps it secrets close."

"Hang on. *Everyone* knows Alwyn fathered his brother's wife's child?"

"All the women know. 'Who's the father?' is the first question a woman would ask."

"*Incest?*"

"It's thick as fleas in this village, Rob. See you, how they all look alike? See the harelips and webbed toes and simple minds? Poor Willa, may she rest in peace, thought a dark angel visited her by night. Rocana, may she lie quiet, let her believe it."

"Still," Robin sighed, "men need a priest, same as they need a king."

"Men, yes. Women, no."

"Marian!"

"It's true! Men need a priest to absolve them of sins, but what can they do for women? When a woman's screaming in child-birth, can a priest put a knife under the bed to cut the pain or brew a broth of asparagus and chestnuts and fennel? Men work women harder than oxen. They kill them slowly with too many babies. The graveyards are full of three wives for every dead husband. Women cherish the old ways, because women don't need God! They need other women!"

"Jesus, Marian, you'll draw down lightning! I'll agree if you wish't. But a priest should tend spiritual matters and the witch secular ones. A wise woman shouldn't interfere in God's plans—"

"It was God who made me barren! And with Rocana dead, I'll stay that way!" Suddenly, Marian was sobbing. Robin reached to comfort, but she pulled away. "Just . . . leave me alone . . ."

Robin took his bow outside. The moonlit sky was strung with wisps blown from the north. "One way or another, we each dig our own grave."

DAYS LATER ROBIN SLOGGED knee-deep through tea-colored water after a dropped pintail. He stumbled against something lodged in duckweed.

A dead man bubbled up, gurgled, and belched gas. He had no head, just a gnawed stump tipped with the white dice of a spine.

Retching, Robin Hood slopped from the water and stumbled up the hill. The hell with ducks. He wanted out of this ghastly village. He and Marian had sought new life and found only death.

And nightmares that repeated. In back of the cottage, the madman Serle raided his smoking racks. The outlaw barked, "Hoy, get away!"

The madman clawed hair from his eyes and croaked, "I'm hungry! A man's got a right to eat!"

Robin stopped cold. Serle was filthy and ragged, but upright, pouty, and arrogant. His old self. "You're sane!"

"What of 't?"

Marian came to the doorway. Serle turned. Robin plucked a fleck of red from his coarse smock. "My hen feather! It was *you* in the Jack! You bent over and ran with it, so my arrow skinned your back! Why'd you do it?"

"The Jack saved Rocana from the trial by ordeal!" Marian was breathless. "Was that why, Serle? Because she'd been kind to you?"

"Hardly!" retorted Robin. "He dumped the Jack on the path to her cottage! My, God! *You* killed her!"

"I din't kill no one!" Dizzy and dazed, Serle sputtered. "I din't—"

Something flickered on the path to the gallows tree that caught Robin's eye. He saw Alwyn drop a sack and run. Wondering, Robin fetched the sack and found bread, cheese, and a jug of ale.

" 'The guilty flee where none pursueth.' " Robin ran after the priest. Marian caught up, loping like a deer.

Robin yelled, "That Alwyn is a two-faced lying hypocrite! That night, when everyone scattered before the Jack, he went searching for Serle and found he'd strangled the witch! He couldn't let his brother take the blame, so he dragged the Jack across the path to the gallows tree. He ripped down Ingram's body—popped the head right off!—and stuffed him in the pond to make him disappear! Then he shooed Serle into the marsh to hide! He's been taking him food, which is why Serle doesn't come sniffing for milk at the stoop. Alwyn blamed Rocana's murder on a dead man!"

They found the chapel barred and shuttered. Villagers clustered around twittering. Marian nodded at the door. "Break it down."

"What? A church?"

"Quickly, Rob."

Robin Hood handed Marian his bow. "Some men put faith in God, others in their wives." He ran shoulder-first and smashed the door, backed and bashed again until the bracket tore free.

Inside, Robin and Marian gasped. Another hanged man dangled, but this one wriggled and writhed.

Marian thrust the longbow at Robin. "Shoot him down!"

Alwyn, parish priest of Skegby Moor, swung by his neck. His hands clawed at a hemp rope sunk deep into his throat. A wooden cross lay tumbled on the dirt floor where he'd jumped off the altar.

The greatest archer in the England nocked, drew, and loosed. The arrow sliced the jerking rope. The priest crashed with a bone-jangling jolt. Robin and Marian knelt and tugged loose the noose, yet Alwyn remained blue. His hands flapped. Robin cursed. "His windpipe's crushed. He's finished."

"Strangled same as Ingram, same as Rocana." Marian called loudly, "Alwyn! You're dying! You needs confess! You killed Rocana, didn't you?"

The priest's eyes bugged at the ceiling, or Heaven beyond. He nodded.

"What?" Robin barked. "*He* killed Rocana?"

"And has hanged himself as punishment. Serle could tell the truth now. Alwyn made Serle hide in the marsh because Serle witnessed *Alwyn* strangle Rocana! But why did you kill her?"

"She drove—" a harsh whisper "—my brother—mad with—her witchments! Plucked—mandrake—when he was—nearby! The scream—drove him mad!"

"But now he's sane again!"

"I—saw."

From the doorway where villagers gaped, the scruffy brother shuffled up. Crying, he said, "Wyn . . ."

The childhood name tugged tears from the priest. His lips formed the word. "How?"

Marian began to cry. "It *was* mandrake root that drove Serle mad, but *not* by its scream. By milk. Women sip drams of mandrake when birthing because it fogs the mind and dulls pain. Rocana ground some root fine and fed it to Serle in goat's milk. One strong taste masks another. The potion banished Serle's reason."

"But *why* did she?" asked Robin.

Marian flung out a hand. "Serle terrorized his poor wife! He beat Willa without mercy! But he was shielded from justice by his brother's office. Rocana was just an old woman, but she had potions, so dosed him daily at her stoop. It rendered him harmless as a dog. But since Rocana's been dead these nine days, Serle's mind has cleared. You killed Rocana for the wrong reason, Alwyn, but it brought your brother back, damn him."

The priest sagged. "God—forgives."

Half-dazed by events, Robin Hood fetched a bowl of holy water. He knelt over the priest and dipped his finger to absolve the man—

Hissing, Marian slapped the bowl away. Holy water splashed and soaked into the dirt floor.

"Marian!" Robin was shocked. "He'll die unshriven!"

"Let him!"

"He confessed!"

"It's not enough! Look at him!" Tears spilled down Marian's cheeks. "He has no remorse! Never a word for poor Willa, his own sister-in-law, raped and deceived and degraded! Not a word for his bastard child, killed by his own words that made a deluded mother rip open her belly! No regrets for a harmless witch strangled! No regrets for the child I'll never have! Let him burn in Hell!"

Robin Hood stood tall over his wife, the back of his hand to his mouth. "God help us all, then."

A Gift from God

Edward Marston

England, 1371.

Nobody had told him how beautiful she was. When he
heard about her reputation as a weaver of spells, he
imagined that she would be an ugly old crone who lived
in some hovel, with only a mangy cat or a flea-bitten dog for
company. Instead, much to his astonishment and pleasure,
Catherine Teale was a handsome woman in her late twenties,
alert, bright-eyed, and glowing with health. Her attire was serviceable rather than costly, but it enhanced her shapely figure.
Hugh Costaine was duly impressed. As he reined in his horse, he
gave her a smirk of admiration.

"*You* are the sorceress?" he said in surprise.

"No, sir," she replied with a polite shake of her head. "There
is no sorcery involved in what I do. I have a gift, that is all."

"You have many gifts, as I can see."

Costaine leered at her. He was a tall, sharp-featured man,
little above her own age but coarsened by debauchery that added
a greyness to his beard and a decade to his appearance. As befitted the eldest son of Sir Richard Costaine, lord of the manor of
Headcorn, he was wearing the finest array and riding a spirited
black stallion. Catherine was about to go into the house when he
accosted her. She had just returned from a walk across the fields
to gather herbs. Costaine feasted his eyes on her.

"I need your help," he said at length.

"It is yours to command, sir."

"Prepare me a flask of poison. Something swift and venomous. Our stables are overrun with rats, and I would be rid of them."

"Then you must look elsewhere," Catherine suggested. "I do not make potions to end life, only to preserve it. I medicine the sick. That is my calling."

"If you can cure, you can also kill," he insisted. "I'll not be balked. Now, get into the house and mix what I require."

"I do not know how to, sir."

"Hurry, woman!"

"There is no point."

Costaine angered. "You deny my request?"

"It has been brought to the wrong person."

"But I heard many tales about you. They say that you practice sorcery. That you conjure spirits out of the air to help you."

"Idle gossip. Do not believe it."

"Too many mouths praise your skills."

"Skills of healing. Nothing more."

"Unnatural skills. Deeds of wonder. Magic. No more of this evasion," he ordered, dismounting to confront her. "I have ridden five miles on this errand. I need that poison forthwith. Fetch it at once."

He was close enough to appreciate her charms even more now. Her face was gorgeous, her skin luminous. Catherine exuded a scent that was almost intoxicating. Costaine inhaled deeply. Lust stirring, he gave her an oily grin and took a step nearer.

"You will be well-paid," he promised her. "Give me what I seek, and I will reward you with a kiss. A hundred of them." He reached out, but she eluded his grasp. He chuckled. "Do you find me so repellent?"

"No, sir."

"Then why keep me at bay? Is it to whet my appetite?"

"I would never do that."

"Not even to please me?"

"Not even then, sir."

"Do you know who I am?" he boasted. "And what I am?"

"Yes, sir."

"Well?"

"You are the son of Sir Richard Costaine, an honest gentleman and a courteous knight who would never show such a lack of gallantry."

"To hell with gallantry!" he retorted, snatching her by the arm. "You dare to refuse me? I'll have more than a kiss from you for that. When you have made my flask of poison, I'll have a sweeter potion from you in a bedchamber."

"But I am married, sir," she protested.

"What does that matter? So am I."

"You would take me against my will?"

"Of course not, lady," he said with a snigger. "I will woo you like any lovesick swain. Now, do as I tell you, and be swift about it."

As Costaine released her arm, a figure emerged from the house. Adam Teale was a big, broad-shouldered man in his thirties. He ambled across to them with an easy smile, but his eyes were watchful.

"What is the trouble, sir?" he asked. "I heard raised voices. Has my dear wife upset you in any way?"

"Yes," snarled the other. "She is trying to thwart me."

"Catherine would not do that without cause, sir. I am Adam Teale, the vintner, and I can vouch for my wife's good temper. There never was a gentler or kinder woman." He loomed over Costaine. "What is it that you want, sir? Perhaps I can help you."

"It's not wine that I'm after, vintner. It's poison."

"Then you've wasted your journey, sir. Only wholesome liquid is on sale here. Your father has been pleased to buy it from me on occasion."

"Enough of my father!"

"Does he know why you have come?"

"That is nothing to do with you," said the visitor, dismissively. He turned back to Catherine. "Will you obey me or will you not?"

She gave a shrug. "I have told you, sir. I do not concoct poison."

"It is true," her husband added. "Such gifts as my wife possesses are put to the relief of pain and sickness. You must search elsewhere."

Hand on the hilt of his sword, Costaine squared up to him, but Adam Teale met his gaze without flinching. He was not afraid of his belligerent visitor. Costaine was livid. Not only was he being turned away without the potion he sought, he was being deprived of the joys of ravishing the comely wife. They were two good reasons for his hatred to smolder. He vowed to exact revenge.

"A vintner, are you, Master Teale?" he sneered.

"And proud of my trade," Adam said.

"Take care your wine is not tainted by this sorceress you married."

"Catherine is a devout Christian."

Hugh Costaine let out a sudden laugh and mounted his horse.

"We shall see about that!" he cried.

As the visitor rode away, Adam put a protective arm around Catherine's shoulders. She planted a grateful kiss on his cheek.

"Did I arrive at the right moment?" he said.

"Oh, yes," she answered, fondly. "You always do."

AGNES HUCKVALE SAT DUTIFULLY beside her husband throughout the meal. He was in an expansive mood, loud, laughing, boastful, generous with his hospitality, and flushed with wine to the point where he kept shooting sly and meaningful glances at his wife. Agnes could no longer remember if she had ever loved Walter Huckvale. She had been struck by his wealth and impressed by his military feats, but she could not recall if her heart had really opened to him. It seemed so long ago. Agnes had been barely sixteen when she married a man who was well over twice her age. The gap between them had steadily widened and it was not only measured in years. Walter Huckvale pounded the table with his one remaining hand.

"More wine!" he called.

"You have already drunk more than your fill," warned his wife.

"I could never do that, Agnes." He looked around the empty tables through bleary eyes. "Where are our guests?"

"They retired to bed."

"So soon? Why did they not bid their host adieu?"

Agnes sighed. "They did, Walter, but you were too caught up in your memories to listen to them. When our guests took their leave, you were still fighting the Battle of Poitiers."

"And Crècy," he reminded her. "I won true renown at Crècy. It was at Poitiers that I lost my arm."

"You told us the story. Several times."

"It bears repetition."

The grizzled old warrior jutted out his chin with pride. A servant arrived with a jug of wine and poured some into his goblet. He did not offer any to Agnes. The servant bowed and left the room. Husband and wife sat amid the remains of the banquet, their faces lit by the flames of a hundred candles. Walter Huckvale sipped his wine and became playful.

"Let them go," he said. "I would be alone with my wife."

"I am tired."

"Then let me rouse you from your tiredness."

"It is too late an hour."

"Nonsense!" he announced, taking a long swig from his goblet. "I'll soon rekindle your spirits. Have you ever known me to fail, Agnes?"

He thrust his face close to her, and she caught the stink of his breath. There was no point in trying to contradict him. She had pledged obedience at the altar, and there was only one escape from that dread commitment. Agnes was doomed to suffer his bad breath, his coarse manners, his drunkenness, his bursts of rage, and his interminable reminiscences of military campaigns. Worst of all, she had to enjoy the random brutality of his love-making. It was an ordeal.

Huckvale remembered something, and an accusatory stare came into his eyes. Putting down his goblet, he reached out for her wrist.

"Where have you been all day?" he asked, sternly.

"Here."

"That's not true. I wanted you this afternoon, and you could not be found. You sneaked off somewhere, didn't you?"

"No, Walter."

"Yes, you did. Where was it?"

"You're hurting my wrist," she complained.

He tightened his grip. "Tell me, Agnes."

"I was in the garden, that is all."

"Where *were* you?" he roared.

But the question went unanswered. As the words left his tongue, they were followed by a gasp of sheer agony. Releasing her wrist, he went into a series of convulsions, his eyes bulging, his face purple, his whole body wracked with pain. Walter Huckvale put a hand to his stomach and looked appealingly at his wife. Then he pitched forward on to the bare wooden table, knocking his goblet to the floor with a clatter. Agnes drew back in horror. It was minutes before she was able to cry for help.

THE SHERIFF CAME TO arrest her with four armed men at his back, a show of strength that was quite unnecessary but which deterred her husband from any intervention. Catherine Teale was bewildered.

"What is my crime?" she wondered.

"Witchcraft," the Sheriff said.

"I am no witch, my lord."

"That remains to be proved, Mistress Teale."

"Who laid the charges against me?"

"Hugh Costaine. He traces the murder to your door."

"Murder?" echoed Catherine in alarm.

"Walter Huckvale was poisoned to death last night. It is alleged that you slew him by means of a venomous brew in his wine."

"How can that be, my lord sheriff?" Adam Teale asked. "I do not provide the wine for Walter Huckvale's table."

The Sheriff was sarcastic. "And why might that be?"

"He and I fell out over an unpaid bill."

"Yes, Master Teale. Harsh words were exchanged between you and Walter Huckvale. There were many witnesses. I can understand why you wanted to get back at him, but you lacked the means to do so." He turned to Catherine. "Your wife, however, did not. Because he refused to buy from you, she cast a spell on the wine he got elsewhere. She made him pay in the most dreadful way. He suffered the torments of Hell."

"That is a monstrous allegation!" Adam exclaimed.

"It is one that Mistress Teale must face. Be grateful that I do not arrest you on a charge of complicity. If I did not know you to be so upright and decent a man, I would suspect you had some part in this."

"No!" Catherine said firmly. "Take me alone, my lord. My husband is not implicated in any way."

"You confess your guilt, then?" demanded the Sheriff.

"I protest my innocence!"

"You will be examined by Bishop Nigel."

"So be it."

Catherine silenced her husband's protests with a patient smile. There was no point in incurring the sheriff's anger. Adam was as baffled by the charge as she was, but it was important that one of them remained at liberty. Catherine submitted to the indignity of having her hands tied then she was lifted onto the spare horse that had been brought for her. As the little cavalcade pulled away from him, Adam Teale bit his lip in exasperation. He remembered the parting words of Hugh Costaine. Evidently, their unwelcome visitor had spread his own brand of poison.

BISHOP NIGEL WAS A wiry little man in his sixties with a bald head that was covered with a network of blue veins and a pair of watery eyes. His voice was quiet but tinged with irritation. Several hours of interrogation had produced nothing but calm answers from the prisoner. Nigel was annoyed that he had not yet broken her spirit. They were alone together in a fetid cell, but it was the manacled Catherine Teale who bore herself with equanimity in the foul conditions. Perspiration glistened on the prelate's brow. He resumed his examination.

"Are you in league with the Devil?" he hissed.

"No, my lord bishop. I am married to the best man alive."

"Then your husband is part of this conspiracy."

"There *is* no conspiracy," she assured him.

"Adam Teale had a disagreement with Walter Huckvale."

"My husband has a disagreement with anyone who does not pay his bill. That is only right and proper. I seem to remember that he once had a mild altercation with your own steward when an account was left unsettled, but he did not wish to poison you, my lord bishop."

"Heaven forbid!"

"Adam had no *reason* to strike at Walter Huckvale."

"That is why you took retribution upon yourself. Do not deny it, Mistress Teale. Worrying reports about you have been coming in to me for several months now. I can no longer ignore them. You have been covertly engaged in sorcery." Bishop Nigel consulted the document in his hand, angling it to catch the light from the candle. "I have a full record of your nefarious activities here."

"Has anyone laid a complaint against me?"

"I lay a complaint," he snapped. "On behalf of the Church. I am enjoined by God to drive out the Devil."

"A worthy purpose but hardly relevant here."

"Is it not true that you cured an old woman from Pluckley of an ague that threatened to kill her? Is it not true that you brought a stillborn baby back to life in Marden by laying-on of hands? And is it not true that you helped to trace a man who had been missing from his home in Staplehurst for over a week?"

"I willingly admit all these things."

"Then your witchcraft is established!" he said, triumphantly.

"How?" she challenged. "A herbal compound cured the old woman in Pluckley. Such a mixture as any physician would pre-scribe. As for the stillborn child, it had never really been dead. It needed only some love and prayer to bring it fully to life. Most midwives would have done exactly as I did."

"And the man from Staplehurst?"

"He was a woodcutter, dazed when the bough of a tree chanced to fall on him. He wandered off, lost his bearings, and could not find his way back. I sensed that he had found his way to Maidstone."

"*Sensed?*"

"Yes, my lord bishop."

"What evil powers enabled you to do that?"

"They are not evil, or the result would not have been so good."

"Do not bandy words with me!"

"When people come to me for help, I give it to them."

"By means of sorcery."

"By means of my gift."

"And from whom does that come?"

"From the same source as your own—from God Almighty."

Her voice was so earnest and her manner so sincere that he was checked for an instant. Bishop Nigel had to remind himself that he was in the presence of a witch, clever enough to dissemble, cunning enough to assume whatever shape she wished. He was engaged in a tussle with the Devil and must not relax his hold.

"Hugh Costaine alleges that you know how to mix poison."

"My whole life is dedicated to healing."

"Unless you wish to strike at your husband's enemies."

"Adam has no enemies. Just one or two awkward customers. As it happens, your own steward was far more of a nuisance than Walter Huckvale. He claimed that the bill had been paid. And much more wine was sent to your palace than to—"

"Forget my steward!" barked the other. "He is immaterial."

"The point still holds."

"The only thing that holds in my view is the allegation from Hugh Costaine that you boasted about your skill in concocting vile poisons. You claimed that you could turn fine wine to foul simply by casting a spell. Why gainsay it? Hugh Costaine has sworn as much on the Bible."

"Bring that same Bible here and I will swear on Holy Scripture that I am innocent of this charge. I have nothing to do with this murder."

"But you do admit that you saw Hugh Costaine recently?"

"Yes, my lord bishop. He called at the house."

"And you discussed poison?"

"I made it clear to him that I had no means of making it."

"That is not what he says."

"Then it is a question of my word against his."

"His allegation is buttressed by this list of your crimes," said the Bishop, waving the document at her. "I have mentioned only three cases of your witchcraft so far. Over two dozen are recorded here."

"Have any of the people I helped spoken against me?"

"They dare not."

"Because they have no cause."

"Because you put the fear of death into them."

Bishop Nigel took a deep breath. He was about to launch into a recital of her alleged misdeeds, when a key grated in the lock and the oak door swung back heavily on its hinges. A tall, stately figure entered. Sir Richard Costaine was an older version of his son, but he had none of the latter's arrogance or marks of dissipation. Instead, he was a symbol of nobility, a distinguished soldier who had fought beside the Black Prince and a man who was renowned for his fair-mindedness. He glanced at Catherine with a mixture of apology and apprehension, not knowing whether to release her or accuse her of further villainy.

"Has your examination been completed?" he asked.

"Not yet, Sir Richard," said Bishop Nigel, airily. "The creature was on the point of capitulation when you interrupted us. Why have you come? Is something amiss?"

"I'm afraid that it is, Bishop Nigel. My son has disappeared."

"Disappeared?"

"He has not been seen all day. Nobody has any idea where he can be. A search has been organized, but there is no sign of Hugh." His eye traveled to Catherine. "I hope that this is not your doing, Mistress."

She was adamant. "I give you my word that it is not, Sir Richard."

"Do not be misled," warned the prelate, wagging a finger. "If she is capable of casting a spell on Walter Huckvale's wine, she has the power to work her evil on your son."

"When my hands are manacled?" she said, reasonably. "What sorcery can I practice when I am locked up here? You have been with me since this morning, my lord bishop. Your holiness would quell any evil spirits. Though, in truth, there are none here to quell."

Bishop Nigel snorted. "I beg leave to doubt that."

"How did Hugh mysteriously vanish?" Sir Richard asked.

"Not by any sorcery," returned Catherine.

"He should have been here hours ago. It is my wife's birthday. Nothing would keep him away from the celebrations. Hugh has his faults, but he loves his mother dearly. I suspect foul play."

"So do I," decided the bishop. "Hatched in this very cell."

Catherine Teale shook her head and gave a gentle smile.

"No evil has befallen your son, Sir Richard," she announced. "That I can tell you. Hugh Costaine is alive and well."

"Then where is he?" said the anxious father.

"I do not know. But I could help you to find him."

"How?"

"By using my gift."

"Do not trust her, Sir Richard!" warned the bishop. "The only gifts she possesses are for witchcraft and dissimulation."

"I find it difficult to accept that, Bishop Nigel."

"Look at the facts. Her husband argues with a customer, and the man's wine is poisoned. Your son accuses her, and she casts a spell on him. There are clear connections here. We are dealing with cause and effect."

"Are we?" Sir Richard said doubtfully. "I am not so sure. Could we not simply be looking at two coincidences?" He regarded Catherine with a mixture of curiosity and embarrassment. "I am sorry that you have been treated so harshly, Mistress Teale. When a serious charge is laid against you, it must be answered but I would have thought this interrogation could have been conducted in better surroundings than these." He wrinkled his nose in disgust. "You say that you can find my son."

"I can try, Sir Richard."

"By what means?"

"By sensing where he might be."

"Sensing?"

"That word again!" exclaimed the bishop.

"Let me touch something belonging to your son," she said. "A garment, a weapon, a personal item of some kind. It will help me in my search. Could you bring such a thing to me, Sir Richard?"

"I will do more than that, Mistress Teale. I will take you to my house and let you examine all of Hugh's wardrobe."

"But she is being held as a prisoner," complained Bishop Nigel.

"The sheriff will release her into my care when he understands the situation. We are in extremity here, Bishop Nigel. My wife is beside herself with fear. So is Hugh's own wife. They are both certain that he has met a dreadful fate. We want him back to celebrate what should be a happy occasion for the whole family. Hugh is missing. If Mistress Teale can find him for us," he added, soulfully, "we will believe that she really does have a gift from God."

GLAD TO BE RESCUED from her imprisonment, Catherine rode the short distance to Headcorn with Sir Richard Costaine at her side. The house was in a state of mild uproar when they arrived. Everyone was firmly convinced that Hugh was the victim of some attack. It was felt that he was such a strong and capable man that only violence could prevent his return. It was the hapless wife for whom Catherine felt most sympathy. The tearful Isabella Costaine still loved her husband enough to be blinded to his blatant shortcomings. When she heard that the visitor was there to aid the search, she begged Catherine to find her missing spouse soon.

Sir Richard calmed the household then led his companion off to the private apartments used by his son and his wife. Catherine was given ready access to Hugh Costaine's wardrobe. When she saw the apparel he was wearing at the time of his confrontation with her, she gave a mild shudder. Then she reached out to take the rich material in her hands. Closing her eyes, she let her fingers play with the mantle until she felt a distinctive tingle. She raised her lids once more.

"We must ride toward Sutton Valence," she said.

"But what would Hugh be doing there?" wondered Sir Richard.

"I do not know, but that is where I am being guided."

"By what? A voice? A sign?"

"By instinct."

Within a few minutes, their horses were cantering out of the courtyard. Four men-at-arms acted as an escort. Catherine was a good horsewoman, and they covered the ground at a steady pace. It was only when they reached the woods that she raised a hand to bring them to a halt. After looking all around, she elected to strike off to the right, nudging her mount forward so that it could pick its way through the trees. Sir Richard was directly behind her, trying to control a growing skepticism. Could a vintner's wife really have divine gifts? Or was he being led on a wild-goose chase?

When they came to a clearing, Sir Richard's doubts fled at once. Tethered to a bush was a black stallion, cropping the grass contentedly.

"It is my son's horse!" he said, dismounting.

Catherine nodded. "I expected to find a clue of some sort here."

"But what about Hugh himself?"

"We still have some way to go before we reach him," she said. "This is only the start. The first signpost, so to speak. But it shows that we are on the right track."

"Where do we go next, Mistress Teale?"

Catherine closed her eyes and was lost in meditation for a few minutes. When she came out of her trance, she spoke with certainty.

"We must continue on the road to Sutton Valence."

"How far?"

"I will know when we reach the spot, Sir Richard."

"And will Hugh be there?"

"Not this time."

Sir Richard Costaine mounted his horse then went back to rejoin his men, towing his son's stallion behind him by its rein.

Catherine paused in the clearing long enough to notice the little
wine flagon that was all but concealed behind a bush. It was the
sign she wanted.

The six of them rode on until they came to a fork in the
road. Without hesitation, Catherine struck off to the left and followed a twisting track down a steep hill and on through a stand
of elms. When they emerged from the trees, the track petered out
beside a stream. Catherine indicated a tall pile of brushwood, a
short distance away on the opposite bank.

"The trail leads to that dwelling," she explained.

"What dwelling? I see nothing but a heap of old wood."

"That is where he lives, Sir Richard."

"Who?"

"Thomas Legge."

"What manner of man would live in such a place?"

"A strange one."

"You know the fellow?"

"Only by repute."

They crossed the stream and headed along the opposite
bank. As they got closer, they could see a thin wisp of smoke
emerging from the top of the brushwood. A small dog suddenly
leaped out and yapped at them. The noise brought Thomas
Legge out of his lair. The entrance to his little home was so low
that he had to crawl out on his hands and knees. The newcomers
looked down at the bedraggled old man who peered up at them
with suspicion. Thomas Legge seemed to be more animal than
human, a misshapen creature with white beard and hair that were
grimed with filth. He scrambled to his feet and kicked his dog
into silence. His speech was slurred, his tone unwelcome.

"What do you want?" he growled.

"We need your help," Catherine explained. "This is Sir
Richard Costaine, and we have come in search of his son."

"He's not here," Legge said. "Nobody's here but me."

"But I believe he came here." She pointed to the black stallion. "On that horse. Do you recognize the animal?" Legge gave a
reluctant nod. "I thought so. He came in search of something,
didn't he?"

"That's private," grunted the old man.

"Not if it concerns my son," Sir Richard said sharply. "Keep a civil tongue in your head, or you'll feel the flat of my sword. We want answers."

"I think I can give you one of them," Catherine ventured. "Your son came here to buy some rat poison. True or false, Thomas Legge?"

"True," Legge mumbled.

"He told you that his stables were overrun with rats, didn't he?"

"But they're not," Sir Richard said. "We keep too many dogs to have any trouble with vermin. Hugh knows that." He glared at the old man. "Is that what my son told you? We were plagued by rats?"

"Yes," agreed Legge.

"Did you give him the poison there and then?" Catherine asked.

"No. It took a long time to mix."

"So what happened?"

"He told me a man would come to fetch the poison that same afternoon. I had it ready. The man paid me."

"Who was the man?" said Sir Richard.

Legge gave a shrug. "No idea."

"Which direction did he come from?"

"I can tell you that, Sir Richard," Catherine said. "We have learned all that we can here. Follow me." She swung her horse around and led the party away.

Watching the group leave, Thomas Legge scratched his head in surprise. Why was he so popular all of a sudden? He could go for weeks without seeing anyone, yet he had had two visits already that day. He did not much care for the lady with her armed escort. His first visitor was much more preferable. Climbing back into his lair, he reached for the flagon of wine that the man had left him by way of reward. He took a long, satisfying swig.

IT TOOK THEM ONLY a short time to identify the man they sought. When they arrived at the house, they found it deep in mourning.

The body of Walter Huckvale still lay in the mortuary at the family chapel. His wife, the lovely Agnes, was bearing up well under her grief and was able to give her unexpected visitors a welcome. She was puzzled by their request.

"You wish to talk to my servants, Sir Richard?" she said.

"That is so," he replied, softly. "We have reason to believe that one of them may be able to help us. I was shocked to learn of your husband's untimely death. He and I fought together at Crècy and at Poitiers. Walter Huckvale deserved a hero's end."

Agnes nodded, showing a loyalty she did not really feel. She was clearly discomfited by Sir Richard's presence. Catherine believed that she could guess why.

"Let us get on with it," Sir Richard suggested briskly. "Perhaps you could have the servants sent into us one by one so that we can question them. We hope to throw new light on your husband's murder."

But the examination proved unnecessary. When the word spread among the servants, one of them took fright and bolted. Sir Richard's men had to ride for a mile before they ran him to ground. The man was dragged unceremoniously back to the house. He was squirming with guilt. Sir Richard was merciless.

"You helped poison your master," he accused.

"No, Sir Richard!" bleated the other.

"Do not lie to me!" A blow to the face knocked the man to the ground. "You served him that fatal draught of wine, didn't you?" The man shook his head. A kick made him groan. "Didn't you, you rogue?"

"Yes," confessed the servant.

"On whose orders?"

"I cannot tell you, Sir Richard."

"Do I have to beat the truth out of you, man?"

The servant looked up with a mixture of pleading and defiance.

"I wouldn't do that, if I were you," he said with a hollow laugh. "You might hear something that you wish you hadn't."

It was Catherine who once again led them with unerring accuracy to the right place. The cottage was on the edge of the Huckvale estate, small, comfortable, isolated, and well hidden by woodland. They found Hugh Costaine in the bedchamber,

securely bound, gagged, and blindfolded. When he heard them
enter the house, he kicked violently on the floor to attract their
attention. Sir Richard was the first person to see him. He gazed
down at his son with contempt before removing the blindfold
and the gag. Hugh Costaine squinted in the light. He recognized
the figure who towered over him.

"Father!" he exclaimed. "Thank heaven you came!"

"I can find no reason for thanks," the other said, grimly.

"Untie me so that I may pursue the rogue who attacked me."

"The only rogue I see is the one who lies at my feet. Whoever delivered you to me like this deserves a rich reward for he
has solved the murder of Walter Huckvale."

"I did that!" ranted his son, nodding at Catherine. "There's
the villain, standing beside you. That black-hearted witch put a
spell on Walter Huckvale and struck him down with poison."

"Be quiet!" his father ordered. "We have caught the wretch
who bought and administered the poison at your behest. He is
under arrest and will hang for his crime. It shames me that my
own son will hang beside him. What kind of birthday present is
this for your mother? What kind of reward is it for your dear
wife? You disgust me, Hugh. You and that heartless woman,
Agnes Huckvale. She may have had no part in the murder, but
she was ready to share a bed with you before her husband had
even been consigned to his grave." He turned away. "Take him
out. He offends my sight!"

Two men-at-arms hauled Hugh Costaine to his feet and hustled him out. Catherine ignored the vile taunts that were hurled
at her by the departing prisoner. When Sir Richard looked at her,
his face was ashen with despair. He tried to master his feelings.

"We owe you a huge apology, Mistress Teale," he said. "You
were wrongly accused in order to throw suspicion away from the
true villain. My son is the real sorcerer here. He knew that the
only way to possess Agnes Huckvale was to remove her husband.
You were unwittingly caught up in his evil design. There will be
restitution for the way in which you have been cruelly abused."

"My liberty is restitution enough, Sir Richard."

"You have my heartfelt apology, and I will make sure that
Bishop Nigel offers his words of regret as well. I will also insist on

making some financial reparation. After all," he added with a sad smile, "you did find a missing son for me. I had no idea that you would solve a heinous crime in the process. It is a sorry day for my family."

Catherine put a consoling hand on his arm. She had no quarrel with Sir Richard Costaine. He had behaved honorably toward her and had made no attempt to shift the blame away from his son when the latter's villainy was exposed. The experience had aged him visibly.

"One of my men will take you back home," he offered.

"Thank you, Sir Richard."

"You were right, Mistress Teale. You do have a gift."

ADAM WAS WAITING FOR her in the house. After a warm embrace, he conducted her to the wooden bench and sat beside her with his arm around her shoulders. Catherine gave him a detailed account of all that had happened since her arrest. He listened patiently.

"It was that lie about the rats that betrayed him," he noted. "When you told me that Hugh Costaine came in search of rat poison, I knew that it was a ruse. A man like that would never run his own errands. He wanted that poison for a darker purpose."

"I counted on you working that out, Adam."

"I worked out much more than that, my love. Costaine would only stoop to murder for one reason. Lust. It seeps out of the man. Well, look at the way he tried to molest you. No," reflected Adam, "there had to be a woman involved and Walter Huckvale's wife was the obvious person. Then there was the poison, of course. If you would not provide it, there was only one person who would."

"Thomas Legge."

"I loosened his tongue with a flagon of wine, and he told me all I wanted to know. His testimony pointed me in the direction of the Huckvale estate. Hugh Costaine was not a person to bide his time. He wanted his reward immediately. When I saw his horse outside that cottage, I guessed that he was inside with his prize. Agnes Huckvale. I waited until the young widow slipped out then crept in to overpower Costaine and tie him up. That was how you found him."

"Delivered up to justice," she said. "Bishop Nigel would not believe me when I told him that I could sense things. For that is what I did. I sensed exactly what you would do to prove my innocence. You would go first to Thomas Legge to establish if and when he sold some poison. I knew that you would leave a sign for me and guessed where it would be."

"In a place very dear to both of us, my love."

"That clearing in the woods where you once asked for my hand." She gave a smile. "I did not expect to find a black stallion there, I can tell you. But it satisfied Sir Richard that we were on the right trail."

"Did you see the flagon?"

"Of course. It was certain proof of your success."

"My real success was getting wed to you, Catherine."

"I have been thinking the same about you," she admitted. "It has been a marriage of true minds. When I am being accosted by a foul-mouthed man like Hugh Costaine, you come to my aid at just the right time. When I am falsely accused, you spring to my defense. I love you so much," she said, kissing him on the lips. "You always know when I need you and how best to help me. That is my real gift."

"What is?"

"A husband called Adam Teale."

"Me?" he said with a grin. "Am I really a gift?"

"Oh, yes. A gift from God."

The Queen's Chastity

Tony Geraghty

*"BY THE GRACE OF ALMIGHTY GOD, BE THIS SAD HISTORIE
NOT INCONTINENTLY REVEALED 'TIL YET TWO MILLENNIA
HAVE PAST—requiescat in pace"*

*Queen Eleanor's tomb at Llanthony, with its cryptic inscription, had long been an
object of speculation among scholars. Now that it was opened to reveal the remains
not of one, but three human skeletons, seven centuries after her presumed death,
medievalists revived a long-standing dispute. The matter was of little constitutional
importance now. Yet there was no shortage of academic dinosaurs ready to make
war about it on the Internet, from Honolulu to the London Library in Saint
James's. Both factions believed it was important to know the truth. To express the
matter somewhat indelicately, did the Queen of England cuckold her husband, the
future King Edward I, while he was crusading in the Holy Land from 1270 to
1272? Forensic science could only confirm that one skeleton was that of a woman
in her early forties. The other two—almost identical, apart from differences of
gender—were in their twenties and could have been twins. The skull of one of these
people was missing. In its place was that of a bird of prey. The younger skeletons
were, perhaps, her offspring (the DNA said as much), but to admit that would
have been to concede that the queen was indeed unfaithful, a theory peddled vigorously by the Honolulu Faction and passionately opposed by the London Library
Faction, united by their belief in Eleanor's virtue. The London faction asserts that
Eleanor of Castille was with Edward all the way to the Holy Land and back.*

441

It is late afternoon in autumn. The forest air blends the odors of rutting deer, horse dung, and wood smoke from the charcoal burner, piled up irreverently at the center of a circle of standing stones.

"Did!"

"Didn't."

"Did!"

Two children, a boy and a girl, their faces and bare feet blackened from a life built around the process of burning wood, face one another like quarrelsome cats.

"How, then?" says the girl at last, a nervous finger curled into her long hair. "How did he come back from the dead like you say?"

"It was a manacle," the boy retorts, one tiny fist punching into the palm of the other hand, just as he had seen the priest at Christmas. "Sweet Jesu came back through a manacle after they nailed him to the tree."

"Well, I don't believe you," the girl says. She turns clockwise, pirouetting to show her nakedness beneath the worn dress. "I believe in Green Man. I believe in the Old Religion." Sticking her tongue out for good measure, she adds, "And the Moon Goddess."

"Well, then," the boy shouts at her, his eyes glowing through the smoke-dirt on his face, "you will go to Hell and be damned for ever-and-ever-Amen."

Watching from among the clustered, conspiratorial sessile oaks, a trio of women turn to one another. Two smile indulgently, but the third, a peasant, casts her eyes down, murmuring, "They shame me, Ma'am . . . If you wish to—"

"Not at all, Jenny Blackthorn." The Queen's smile does not conceal her pallor or the deadly shadows beneath her tired eyes. "Here,"—giving her a small bag of jingling coins—"take them to the market and buy shoes for them. Soon it will be Hallowe'en." Her hand shakes, but not because of cold.

Eleanor's companion, the taller of the two, buxom and glowing in a red gown that hampers her on horseback, even riding sidesaddle, whispers, "Ma'am . . .We are far from home. Your escort will wonder . . ." She touches the Royal arm, a breach of protocol permitted only to a trusted lady of the bedchamber. Reluctantly, Eleanor allows herself to be led away, stifling what might be a cough or a sob, or both.

Browne to Long: Dear Long—What do you make of Queen Eleanor's deathbed confession?

—Browne, Honolulu.

Long to Browne: Dear Browne—Just another smear, started by Giraldus Cambrensis, working off his old grudge against Edward. He never forgave the King for refusing to confirm his election as Bishop of Saint David's. His way of hitting back was to tell the world that the King was a cuckold.

—Long, London.

"FATHER, FORGIVE ME, FOR I have sinned a mortal sin, a sin of impurity, and would be shriven now my hour is come."

The candle flickers. The rosary lies inert among the Queen's dying fingers.

"Be at peace, my child. Our Lord God is ever merciful. He died that we may live."

The voice of Bishop Gerald of Wales, lately returned from Ireland with young Prince John and preparing his great recruitment for the Crusade through the Welsh Marches, soothes Eleanor out of this life with a voice that is soft as the silk lining of her coffin. "But make your confession whilst there is yet time."

A little way off, a loose floorboard squeaks. Gerald raises a cautionary finger, silencing the intrusion. Two men—tall Prince John, his hooked nose scarred from jousting, and his inseparable companion and Clerk, Dark John, small and sinuous as a marmoset—strain to hear the words that follow.

"Father this is hard . . . hard. My husband Edward, having taken the Cross, was at Acre. Word came that he had died of a green wound. But it was false, a calumny, the work of the Evil One. I was comforted one night in my grief. Even now I dare not speak his name for it were mortal sin even were I in truth the widow I had thought myself to be."

She coughs. The side of her mouth stains pink bubbles, then smooth crimson as if an invisible artist has her as his paint pallet.

"So much blood there was. I was delivered a month before Edward disembarked at Southampton."

Her eyes roll back into her skull. Prince John, from the other side of the room, hisses: "The name! What is the Bastard's name? Is he a Pretender?"

Bishop Gerald's finger again ordains silence, though he, also, is disturbed by the political implications of this revelation. A Pretender? Where? Supported by what? An army of peasants, perhaps? These are dangerous times and Wales is still untamed.

The Queen's eyes open, fixed on the candle as if she sees hellfire looming.

"My son, my firstborn, was one of two. One son, one daughter, like puppies in a litter. John was later, the true son of his father."

"What became of them, child?"

"Jenny Blackthorn . . ."

The last flicker of life flows away as the candle gutters. Gerald closes her staring eyes, makes the Sign of the Cross on her forehead, and kneels to pray for her departing soul.

Browne, Honolulu, to Long, London: But Gerald wrote of twins, with the superstitious horror surrounding the phenomenon at that time. Why would he complicate a false story without cause?

Long, London, to Browne, Honolulu: Further evidence, in itself, that the Queen—and by extension, Edward—was cursed. He even hints at incest and suggests that the boy carried the "Mark of Cain" on his face (a single, linked eyebrow). All nonsense, of course.

THE MOURNING BELL TOLLS on a biting winter morning at Llanthony Priory, that huge, grey, graven emptiness that not even a host of gargoyles, nor even the gaping sheila-na-gig, can populate: a place that shudders under the perpetual storms that rage on the Black Mountain just above it. The choir sings its requiem for Eleanor. An angry Prince, his nose red with cold, his chain mail heavy with ice after the long ride from Gloucester, stamps stone flags either from frustration or cold, or both, ignoring the burial service.

The service over, he summons Bishop Gerald.

"Your Grace, lookie-here. Before our period of mourning is done, certes before our coronation, we will have the Bastard found."

Gerald notes with disquiet, but not surprise, that Prince John has already adopted the royal "We" instead of the humble, human "I."

"What is your advice?"

"This is not a matter for spiritual counsel, Sire. Perhaps"—he nods in his shrewd, political fashion toward Black John—"perhaps your loyal Clerk would know where to find Jenny Blackthorn if she yet live? Black John knew the Forest of Dean well as a boy, before the seminarians sent him to study in France to remove him from that sinister place of Devil worship where all who enter do so at risk to their immortal souls." Crossing himself, he continues: "In Gloucester it is rumored that one of that name succored twins: a boy and a girl, and that the same Jenny Blackthorn, the wife of a charcoal burner, was once visited by a fine gentlewoman who gave her money."

Browne, Honolulu, to Long, London: And what are we to make of "Black John," the Prince's confidant?

Long, London, to Browne, Honolulu: The Prince's creature, no more. European history is replete with witch-finders.

THE TUMBLED HAMLETS CLING to the edge of the Forest, as if afraid to venture far from it or enter the dark, unmarked green ways known only to the furtive people of the interior, the aboriginal

Celts. Doors shudder beneath blows of mailed fists. Dogs bark
and babies scream and puke as the gnomic Black John and his
posse storm like Norman centaurs into the huddled settlements.
The villeins are arranged along one stone wall—or hawthorn
hedge if no stone stands—the women at another. They face the
wall to be kicked, pushed, or lashed if they complain.

"Where is Jenny Blackthorn?"

"Dead, sire, these ten years an' more."

"What of her brats?"

"The boy was taken by the Bishop's people to be priested,
just before Jenny died of the red mushroom."

"And the girl?"

The villagers are silent, as if waiting. The posse turns, sensing something, as if stalked by a wood nymph. A slight, graceful
woman dressed in faded green, her black hair wantonly about her
shoulders, approaches them on bare feet. Her eyes are grey and
the dark eyebrows meet above them. About her neck she wears a
torque of gold. There are other marvels. On her left, gloved wrist
rests a fine goshawk, its talons held in leathern jesses, the eyes
masked by a hood.

"I am Cerridwen, daughter of Jenny Blackthorn."

The voice is surprisingly low. It carves patterns of sound that
could make a man—and some women—drunk with the melody,
most particularly the name, in which each syllable is spoken separately, like a drumbeat: "Cer-rid-wen."

"What would you want of me?"

Now the eyes are grey-green, changing, chameleonlike, with
the shifting patterns of illusory light in an enchanted land. And
they flash toward Black John with dangerous recognition. "T'were
not love potions, I ween. Not twixt us."

Her laughter saws at the sinews of the centaurs about her.
Black John, fear his companion, taps the arm of his giant escort.
"Take her."

As they close on her, she slips off the hawk's hood and lofts
the bird into the air. It circles over the posse, shrieking, and she
responds: "Fly! Fly, my beauty!" With a last unearthly call, the
sound of the very soul ascending, it soars, still circling, leather
jesses still dangling from its legs, into invisibility. Later, they said

this was no ordinary bird of prey, nor even a falcon of the hunting sort, trained by man, but one of her familiars. Certainly, she had a way with animals.

Browne, Honolulu, to Long, London: The real mystery here is the identity of this woman and what it was that made her so important. She was no possible threat to Prince John or his spurious claim to the throne.

Long, London, to Browne: Bread and circuses perhaps? As you say, there was no Pretender only the fear of one. But once the hunt was up and running, there had to be a quarry, even if it was some poor superstitious hag hauled out of her bed of cabbages to be hanged for the fun of it.

THE INQUIRY BEGINS. NO lack of witnesses this Beltane eve to attest that dark things have happened the year past in the gloomy Forest of Dean: babies stillborn and beasts aborting; agues and boils and the falling sickness afflicting the innocent; curdled milk and chimneys blocked by jackdaws. The procession of hard-luck stories through the echoing hall of Hereford Castle, beside the salmonful Wye, is a jolly romp, with mead and bread for all; a fair, my dear, with the hope of more entertainment to come and the start of better things after. Would they use the ducking stool? Or even swim the witch? Not yet, for no witness was found who had seen Cerridwen at her exercise . . . Not yet. Besides, she is here present, and who would denounce her to her face, she who has cured so many with her magic? What might befall if we did?

"I cannot swear on my oath it was her doing, Sire."

Black John twists restlessly in his seat. It is a fine wooden seat, almost like a throne, that elevates him above the common people. "Tell it to me again, your history," he orders the witness. Cerridwen, her wrists bound before her and legs tied likewise, squats with her back to a pillar behind him, out of his eye. The witness repeats his story as he faces her, avoiding her gaze.

Long, London, to Browne: There was also a genuine fear of "Sathan" and his works including sorcery, heresy, and what the writer Perkins described later as "the damned Art of Witchcraft." Witchcraft was tolerated through much of Christendom until Rome linked it to heresy for internal, political reasons at about the time this trial took place.

Browne to Long, London: Or even earlier in some places. Remember the "Canon Episcopy"? All that stuff about "some wicked women are perverted by the Devil so they believe they ride out at night on beasts with Diana, the pagan goddess and a horde of women." That was A.D. 900.

ON THE FOURTH DAY, the Ecclesiastical Court hears the testimony of one Symonds, wheelwright, red of hair and quick of temper. Symonds for years past has sought to bed Cerridwen, and always did she stifle his lust with laughter. Now comes his revenge.

"I have heard the woman say to others of her persuasion, 'May the injured Lucifer greet thee.' I have seen her at full moon trip naked and consort with things not of this world."

Consort? How, "consort"?—"In her body. Couple with Sathan in the form of a black dog, sire."

A sigh of horror mixed with satisfaction—a catharsis—overcomes those present. They cross themselves piously even as they revel in its sinfulness. Black John's "Hah!" breaks the silence that follows. Then, turning to face Cerridwen, he puts the Question:

"Art thou a witch?"

She, looking him in the eye, replies, "I am thy mother's childe, John."

What's this? A buzz of interest fills the room like the drone of a blowfly on the King's meat before it be covered with tansy.

Black John touches the crucifix that rests upon his chest. "You talk in riddles, woman. The demon within you it is that speaks. You are possessed of the Evil One."

Why yes, of course . . . The congregation nods its assent. Only the Prince, watching from a high place, out of sight of them all, does not nod. His grip tightens on the dagger at his waist, the knuckles white with sudden anger.

"Put her down," Black John says. "Let her see the instruments. Return her to us tomorrow, and we shall examine her body for the customary marks." With that, he sweeps out of the room, almost invisible behind his screen of armed men.

THAT NIGHT, UNDER A waning moon, three figures in the habit of the Brown Monks, their faces in the obscurity of their cowls, unlock the door and enter her cell. Without ado, two of them suppress her struggles whilst the third opens a leathern vessel, enters his hand therein, and, like unto a boy taking eggs from a plover's nest, plucks forth a small sponge. She feels the finger enter her privy parts. Her last, living experience on this plane is a spreading warmth from her arse, from where the sponge passeth its deadly, drowsing benison into her very vitals.

Browne, Honolulu, to Long, London: The record is unclear at this point. The woman they called "Cerridwen" is found dead on the fifth day of her trial, her body unmarked. There is no sign of violence, no evidence of poisoning. She leaves a long, written confession in good Latin, although it seems unlikely she was literate in any language, including her own.

"THE CONFESSION IS QUITE clear, Sire," says Black John.

The Prince, whittling a cross-stave with his knife, spits.

"How do I know that? Am I a Clerk? Am I to spend my time learning letters? I script my name. That is enough. But show me the document."

The Prince touches the manuscript with his fingers as if willing the symbols to obey his will and answer to him, yet they remain inert on the page like the closed eyes of Cerridwen.

"I will read it again, Sire," Black John says.

" 'I, Cerridwen, natural-born daughter of Jenny Blackthorn of Crabtree Hill within the Forest of Dean in the County of Gloucester, doe declare on my dying breath and in the full knowledge I am about to face my maker the Lord God Jesus Christ, and doe confess as follows:

'This night the Angel of Death appeared unto me and called upon me to repent my life of wicked apostasy, to renounce Satan and all his works and that I did. I die a Christian.

'In my infancy a Great Ladie visited my mother and brought with her a baby she must conceal because of some great shame. The baby died of a fever and was buried eftsoons in unconsecrated ground in the deepest part of the Forest. The grave was uncovered by hogges and the body eaten by the said hogges and other carnivorous beasts. Jenny Blackthorn, fearful of the Great Ladie's wrath and hoping for preferment, adopted a male child of the same age, her sister's tenth-born, her sister now being out of her wits. The Great Ladie did visit us once and was persuaded that the son of my mother's sister was in truth her own beloved infant. She sent us many a groat to keep us fed, and may she be blessed for her Christian charity.

'I was seduced by Satan when young and was his bride 'til taken by the Clerk they call "Black John." The son of my mother's sister I called "Jack," that some also say is known to be "John." I know not what was his fate after he sailed to France from the port of Gloucester with John of Salisbury, but 'twas malice and the Anti-Christ that spoke when I told to the congregation here at Hereford that we were kin, Black John the Clerk and I.

'Signed in her own blood . . . Cerridwen, daughter of Jenny Blackthorn. The sixth day of June 1290.' "

The Prince, a very Apollo, shines upon Black John and embraces him. "So ends our search for the Bastard. You did well, coz." Yet his eye, over the shoulder of his Clerk, meets the eye of Bishop Gerald and things unsaid pass between them.

"How shall we end this business, dear heart?" the Prince asks Black John. "Shall we bury the witch and have done? What says our good Bishop?"

"Sire, if she be truly a disciple of Satan, she may not be laid in consecrated earth for 'twould be blasphemy. Nor if she be a suicide, for 'twould be the only sin without release, it being the sin of despair and therefore renunciation of Our Lord's grace."

"Why then, Bishop, do you and your physicians and herbals examine the woman's body forthwith for the usual blemishes, the teats, the suckling-marks, the strawberries and hirsute moles, and the rest? Now to horse! The deer run and my hounds have need of exercise and I be no Acteon for turning from hunter into hunted stag even by the sorcery of a dead Diana."

Roaring with laughter at his own wit, he exits the castle.

Long, London, to Browne, Honolulu: Yet it is clear that something happened as a result of this woman's death that had considerable implications for the main players in the drama. What is your theory?

Browne, Honolulu, to Long, London: I believe she knew too much. But who was at risk from the knowledge she concealed?

IN AN UNCONSECRATED BELL tower that stands alongside but detached from the Church of Saint Dubricius at Pembridge, beyond the spite-filled eyes of the Forest and the wagging tongues of Hereford City, they bare the corpse of Cerridwen and seek signs of the incubus . . . without success. The skin upon this form is so white as to be transparent; the body hairless as a childe's. Black John, ordered to attend the hunt, is not present. Gerald, his hirsute hands and arms bare, still wears his ecclesiastical ring and Holy Cross for his soul's sake. His eyes seek heaven but see only the oaken beams above and the bell they call Big Tom . . . and perched upon one of the beams, a goshawk with loose jesses about its legs, an unnatural bird that gazes contumaciously upon him with human intelligence through lambent yellow eye.

"The privy parts," he says. His assistants, heads covered, open the legs. And turn their backs. Gerald's fingers delve and probe as they have done many times before to uncover the signs, the guilty teats and warts but always 'til this day upon a still-living body. He

reflects that he must write a careful treatise concerning this matter
for the scholars of the Holy See . . . But what is this? Inside the
rear orifice, like a fledgling within the nest, a sponge which, when
removed from its place of concealment, exudes an essence the
herbalist knows is not Self-heal nor Saint John's Wort but tincture
of mandrake, hemlock, and poppy contained within that tiny
angel of oblivion favored by midwives and called by some "the
soporific sponge." And there is something more: monkshood, that
seductive blue-and-white flower shaped exactly like its sacerdotal
namesake. It is a delight to behold on a fine summer's day in the
hedgerow yet, like wolfbane, the most perfect poison.

The herbalist has a sad mien, like a dog that be kicked daily
or the oft-whipped Ass that Apuleius became when bewitched.
His nose affrighted, the herbalist says: "Your Grace, this poor
creature did not die naturally nor of her own hand, but incontinently at the hand of another. Never have I seen the sponge thus
used against a mortal body. This be the Devil's work."

*Long, London, to Browne, Honolulu: The end of Black John was equally enig-
matic. One fragment attributed to John Dee quotes an earlier source, now lost,
to suggest that in this case the body was discovered in a gown that had been
worn by Cerridwen and that so dressed, he was her very double.*

*Browne, Honolulu, to Long, London: This fragment I had not traced. Could it
be that there are still some significant manuscripts to be found in England rather
than more safely in the air-conditioned libraries of Texas? It is an interesting
anecdote. We know for sure only that Dark John disappeared from the history
at this point.*

THE HUNT RETURNS, SPATTERED with gore but not yet sated with
blood. Bishop Gerald waits at the Keep. He has a secret for the
Prince's ear alone that cannot wait the morrow. The Prince's eyes
darken at the disclosure. That night, they banquet on venison and
nightingale, the Prince and his bosom companion Black John. Also
here present are the Bishop, the hunt, the Master of Hounds, and

sundry others. Last to enter is the bearded Penhebogyd, Master of the Hawks, for whom even the Prince must needs rise to welcome, by ancient custom, as he takes his place at table, the fourth in precedence. But not even Penhebogyd observes the jessed goshawk that perches patiently upon a windowsill high above the room.

The feast nears its end. The lutenists make musicke, and the Prince murmurs to Black John, "I would entertain Lady Katherine in my bedchamber this night, when the last candle be out."

Black John makes his preparations: doth paint his face like a girl's; color his lips cherry; adorn his head with a wig of rich hair that touches his shoulders; his body with sweet oils and a gown that transforms him from man to woman as if Circe herself were his wardrobe mistress. The Court well knows of Lady Katherine but speaks not of the matter. This night, for the last time, though she wit it not, she walks the long, silent gallery to the Prince's bedchamber, lifting her skirts delicately as she steps daintily over the Irish wolfhound that guards the door.

Next morning she is discovered facedown in the castle moat, still gowned, a green ribbon that was in her hair now about her neck, her eyes and tongue protuberant. The court jester capers. Others do likewise. But only he dare lampoon that Black John was privily impaled even before they removed the head for treason. "Forsooth!" he rejoices. "Treason in the head without doubt but otherwise, and otherwhere, faithful unto death, ah-hah!"

The head of Black John upon its pole faces down the rebellious West from the city walls of Hereford through a long, dry summer but no carrion molest it, for it is guarded night and day by a goshawk. The skull shrinks, desiccates, and when the wind blows it shifts and moves on its pole, and the lower jaw snaps open and shut as if to speak. Undevout, superstitious country folk say it has a secret message for them that the Prince would keep from their ears as he increases their tithes most cruelly.

Browne, Honolulu, to Long, London: We do know, however, that some six months after the death, the Forest of Dean rebelled.

Long, London, to Browne, Honolulu: That was a pathetic protest by a rag-tag rabble. According to Giraldus, the Prince suspected that his Clerk was financially corrupt. So, arbitrarily, he doubled local taxes to generate the income he believed was on tap already. That was a serious mistake.

THE REBEL ARMY HAS straw for armor and a few Welsh mountain cobs for cavalry; bows and slings for skirmishing; pikes, sickles, and even scythes for the combat. The Prince laughs, his visor raised carelessly, battle-ax honed to a glittering niceness. The first head he will take is the rebel leader's. The leader is an inconsequential, moonstruck baker. The Prince spurs his horse forward, without waiting for his escort, into the narrow forest trail, where the uncommitted spectators mock him with arses exposed and turned in his way. His ax swings in his right hand and in rhythm to the canter of the horse as he closes on his opponent. The baker, riding a cob, flinches and endeavors to turn away, but he is no horseman and gives the wrong aid. His animal swings into the Prince's thundering path; rears up in fright, hurling him to the ground where he lies gasping for breath. The Prince turns back, comes in for the kill, still smiling as a pair of goshawk talons lash his face, blinding him with his own blood.

The hawk, shrieking vengeance like a banshee forewarning of death, flies off a short way, returns, and attacks again. Now its beak removes first one eye, then a second. The newly blind Prince spurs his horse, holding his seat, but crashes into an overhanging branch in his sightlessness. The peasants with their pikes finish what the bird has miraculously begun, then melt like kernes or sprites into the green gloom among mocking crickets as the Prince's men carry home the corpse of their leader.

Browne, Honolulu, to Long, London: Did the Prince die as Gerald suggests, pursued by some demon or familiar owing its allegiance to Cerridwen?

Long, London: I think not, unless you count his own folly as something that was supernaturally inspired. If that be so, we are all bewitched at some point in our lives. But dare we admit that?

The Reiving of Bonville Keep

Kathy Lynn Emerson

Bonville Keep lay two days' ride from Edinburgh. Driven by his desire for revenge, Sir Gavin Dunnett and his men made the journey in one. Only the temporary truce between England and Scotland prevented them from laying siege to the castle. An act of war against an English baron would have angered the king of Scots, to whom Gavin now owed allegiance. He was obliged to employ more devious means to gain entry.

At dusk, he donned the full, black gown of a Benedictine and entered enemy territory alone. What he found inside the curtain wall astonished him. The place was ripe for reiving. Guards lazed at their posts. Half the servants were far gone in drink. Even the steward seemed lax in his duties. New to the Borders, Gavin decided. From the bleary look in his watery blue eyes, the fellow had also imbibed a considerable quantity of ale.

"We are about to sup," the steward said. "Will you join us, brother?"

Careful to keep his hood raised to hide his lack of a tonsure, since a full head of black hair on a monk would raise far too many questions, Gavin accepted the invitation.

"A pity monks cannot perform marriage ceremonies."

"You wish to wed?" Gavin asked as they entered the great hall. "Who is the lucky woman?"

The steward gestured toward the raised dais at the far end of the room. "Lady Bonville is a new-made widow and ripe for the plucking."

It was as well the steward did not have all his wits about him, for Gavin could not control his start of surprise. Lord Bonville was dead? Then who had sent him word of Isabella's death?

The logical answer to his question sat in regal splendor at the table on the dais. Beatrice Bonville, Gavin's old nemesis. His eyes narrowed as he stared at her. Seven years had passed since he'd last seen her, but she still possessed an exotic beauty. Sleek, glossy, raven locks contrasted with milk-white skin. For a woman whose husband had recently died, she seemed most merry. In spite of losing him? Or because he was no longer alive?

As Gavin watched from a place at a lower table, Lady Bonville smiled and flirted with her flaxen-haired steward and with the black-avised man who seemed to be the husband of one of her stepdaughters. Three of them shared the dais. With their distinctive Bonville hair, its color so pale a shade of yellow that it was nearly white, Gavin had no difficulty picking them out. Two of them looked enough alike to be twins.

A waiting gentlewoman, small of stature with a plain face and drab brown tresses, stood just behind Lady Bonville. Without warning, her mistress turned and boxed her ears. She had been too slow to refill a goblet with wine. The pockmarked servant lad, who stumbled and sloshed the sauce as he set a platter full of steaming food on the table, received a hard pinch on the forearm for his carelessness.

"Heartless bitch," muttered the burly halberdier seated to Gavin's right.

"What has Lady Bonville done to you?"

"Refused to pay our quarterly stipend. Says there is no money at all. None to pay her servants. None to attract husbands for Bonville's three youngest daughters. There's talk she means to send them to be brides of Christ at Holystone Priory."

Gavin had a hard time believing Lord Bonville had died penniless. There must be some gold left. Some of *his* gold. He had sent enough of it here over the years, he thought bitterly.

"There is the child to be dowried, too," the halberdier said.

Gavin dipped his venison in pepper sauce. "What child is that?"

"The half-Scots wench. The old lord's granddaughter. Just seven years old is Mistress Isabella, but they do say she's been ill, nigh unto death, mayhap." He crossed himself piously before draining another mazer of ale.

Gavin scarce noticed if the taste of the sauce on his tongue was fierce or merely pungent. He felt his heart contract. His breathing became labored. His daughter was still alive? What trick was this?

"From what illness does she suffer?" he asked cautiously.

"No one knows."

"How long has she been ill?"

After a moment's computation, something which seemed to tax the fellow's inebriated brain, he answered. "Nearly a month now. 'Twas shortly after Lord Bonville's death. To keep any possible contagion from spreading, the widow had her moved to the north tower."

Gavin scowled at the dais. Beatrice Bonville had exiled a sick child. Left her to die alone. He drank deeply of his own ale and tried to make sense of what he'd just heard.

Two days earlier, after he'd sent word to Bonville Keep that he intended to reclaim Isabella, he'd received a missive, signed by Lord Bonville, telling him that his daughter, his only child, had died in infancy.

But it was Bonville who was dead. That meant Lady Bonville must have dispatched the messenger. Gavin frowned. Even if she'd expected Isabella to die before he arrived, he could not imagine why she'd lie about the matter.

Far from keeping him away, the widow's callous message had spurred Gavin into action. He'd jumped to the conclusion that Lord Bonville had robbed him, taking under false pretenses the generous sums Gavin had sent to England to defray the cost of Isabella's upbringing.

His daughter had been a newborn when Gavin had last seen her. He'd left England the same day he'd buried Mariotta Bonville, his beautiful young English wife. Since then, he'd gained fame and fortune fighting in tournaments on the Continent and hiring out as a mercenary. He'd given little thought to Isabella. Indeed, when he'd heard the child was dead, and had been all along, he'd felt more anger than grief. Enraged at what he'd seen as Bonville's duplicity, Gavin had vowed to reive Bonville Keep and take back all that hard-earned gold from the man who'd dared deceive him.

He should have known, Gavin thought, that Beatrice would be the real villain in this. She was the one who had objected, eight years earlier, when he'd asked Lord Bonville for his daughter's hand in marriage. Beatrice had told her husband that Gavin was not worthy to wed Mariotta. She'd denounced him for being a Scot and called undue attention to his poverty. At the same time, behind her husband's back, she'd tried to get Gavin into her bed.

When he'd declined this dubious honor and threatened to expose her wanton ways if she did not withdraw her objections, Beatrice had been furious. They'd avoided each other throughout his brief marriage to Mariotta. Afterward, blinded by his grief for the wife who'd died in childbirth, Gavin had accepted Beatrice's show of sympathy at face value.

What a fool he'd been to leave his daughter here! A belated sense of guilt fanned the flames of Gavin's resentment toward Beatrice, even though he knew he'd had little choice. In truth, he'd have been no fit caretaker for an infant.

Lord Bonville, on the other hand, had seemed an ideal person to look after the child. Mariotta's father had possessed more experience than any man in England when it came to raising up young gentlewomen. In hope of a son to inherit after him, he'd married four times. The first three wives had been fertile but had produced only girls. Twelve in all. The last Lady Bonville, Beatrice, had been barren.

Staring at the woman on the dais, Gavin felt his anger at her intensify until a red haze seemed to form in front of his eyes. He blinked hard to regain control of his emotions, but his desire for revenge did not dissipate. The monk whose robes he'd borrowed would have advised him to forgive Beatrice. Gavin was more inclined to make the wicked woman pay for her sins.

Supper and the revelry that followed continued deep into the night. During those long hours, Gavin bided his time, listening and learning as much as he could from the conversations around him. It seemed to be the popular belief that Lord Bonville had spent all his money marrying off the first nine of his daughters.

Most people also knew that the steward, Michael Barlow, was Beatrice Bonville's lover. So was James Maplett, her step-daughter Marion's husband, the dark-haired man on the dais. No one said much about the other Bonville sisters, or about Isabella.

Gavin waited until Beatrice retired for the night, then slipped quietly out of the great hall. He started toward the north tower, then stopped. He had time, he realized, to carry out part of his original plan. He could still assuage his desire for revenge.

Afterward, he would reclaim Isabella.

EXHAUSTION DULLED ALISON BONVILLE'S usually sharp reflexes. Despite her best efforts to stay awake, she'd fallen into a fitful doze and was slow to realize the significance of a rush of cooler air into the tower chamber.

A faint shuffling sound—leather-shod feet on the rush-covered floor—had her eyes popping open in alarm. At the same time, she caught a whiff of spilled ale and damp wool. Almost too late, a sense of imminent danger engulfed her.

Alison sat bolt upright on the window seat, reaching for the knife that hung from her belt as she searched the dimly lit room for an intruder. Rage and fear in equal parts filled her heart, when she saw a dark shape bending over her niece's bed. Her only thought to protect the defenseless child, she launched herself at this threatening figure.

She attacked just as he started to lift Isabella into his arms, but some small, inadvertent sound on her part was enough to warn him of another presence in the chamber. At the last possible moment, he released his burden and started to turn. Instead of finding its target in his back, where Alison had hoped to damage some vital organ, her blade struck his shoulder and stuck there as he turned to face her fully.

Heedless of the danger of reaching across the breadth of his massive chest to grasp at the hilt of the knife, she tried to retrieve her weapon. Her fingers barely grazed it before he seized her wrist in a crushing grip. To cut off any outcry, his free arm clamped down with bruising force across her back, pressing her face into the muffling folds of his robe.

Instinctively, she struggled, but it was impossible to break free. Even breathing became difficult once her nose and mouth were tight against his chest. She dimly realized, too late for it to matter, that even had her aim been true, she'd have done little damage. She could feel the thick padding of a quilted gambeson beneath an outer covering of wool. Her small, sharp blade was imbedded in naught but cloth.

A child's whimper penetrated the haze of Alison's desperation when her captor's soft-spoken command to be still could not. The moment she stopped fighting, he loosened his grip sufficiently to allow her to gulp in much-needed air.

"Isabella," she whispered in a hoarse croak she scarce recognized as her own voice.

His hesitation lasted no more than an instant. As soon as his hold on her eased, Alison dashed to the girl's side, all thought of calling for help banished by her need to assure herself that Isabella was no worse.

The forehead beneath her palm was cool and dry. Isabella responded to the familiar touch with a little sigh and sank once more into drugged sleep. With loving fingers, Alison brushed a wisp of hair away from her niece's face. Only then did she realize that the intruder had moved silently to the other side of the bed. Belatedly, she recognized his outer garb as that of a monk.

Confusion held her motionless as he knelt, his attention fixed on the child's pale face. The man was no Benedictine, no matter how he was dressed. Only moments earlier, she had been certain that he was a murderer bent on killing Isabella, but watching him now, Alison experienced an odd sense of familiarity. Inexplicably, she no longer feared him.

Without looking at her, he spoke in a soft, deadly voice. "If you cry out, I will kill you."

"At this hour of the night, the servants are all asleep and what guards may have been posted are most likely deep in their cups, their wits addled." Even sober, they'd have been loath to bestir themselves. None of them felt much loyalty to the Bonvilles these days. Why should they when they had not been paid for months?

As if surprised by her comment, the man lifted his head. For the first time, Alison saw the face of the man she'd tried to kill.

Recognition sent her reeling.

She had been right. This was no monk. Nor was he a brigand or a border reiver, as she had supposed. He was no stranger, either. The man kneeling opposite her was Isabella's father. It might have been years since she'd last seen him, but she'd never forgotten his eyes. They were the color of a stormy sea at dusk.

"What is wrong with her?" He indicated his daughter.

"Lady Bonville tried to kill her."

The moment the words were out, her hands flew to her lips. Even if this was Isabella's father, it had been passing foolish of her to make such a claim.

He stared at her without speaking, the angry flare of his nostrils the only indication of his feelings. Then he reached again for the sleeping child, lifting her into his arms as he stood. "She will never hurt Isabella again." He started toward the door.

"Wait."

"Silence, woman, or I'll bind and gag you."

His tone made Alison realize that he had taken her for a servant. It was an understandable error. To nurse Isabella, she had put off the trappings of a noblewoman. The cote-hardie she wore over her linen chemise, its full skirt short enough to clear the ground but long enough to hide her flat, leather slippers, was made of plain russet-colored wool, bereft of decoration save for the belt that held the now empty sheath for her knife and an undecorated leather bag.

Gavin Dunnett had no reason to think her one of his wife's little sisters. She'd been a child of eleven when he'd last seen her. Moreover, Alison's distinctive Bonville hair, of the pale blonde color some poets called "silver-gilt," was covered by a simple linen coif.

"Isabella is my daughter," he said.

Alison had no wish to challenge his rights. The girl would be far better off with him.

So would she.

"She needs warm clothing," Alison told him. "And someone to look after her. Give me but a moment, and I will pack her belongings and mine, too."

It was the perfect solution, Alison thought. She could not bear the idea of being separated from Isabella, to whom she had long been more mother than aunt. And after what had happened earlier tonight in Beatrice's chamber, escaping across the border into Scotland had undeniable appeal.

She had been dreading the new day, but until Gavin Dunnett appeared, she'd given no consideration to flight. She'd had no place to go. Now, in spite of all the unknown danger that might lie ahead, she felt like a condemned prisoner who'd just been offered a pardon.

"Make haste," he said.

Within minutes, Alison had Isabella bundled into layers of wool and camlet and had retrieved her own warm outerwear. The child was stirring when Gavin once again lifted her.

"Who are you?" she asked in a sleepy voice.

"I am your father."

Isabella looked around for Alison.

"He is your father, Isabella. We are going to go with him now. We must be very quiet."

Her eyes wide and solemn, Isabella nodded.

Alison followed Gavin Dunnett down the narrow, winding steps cut into the thickness of the wall and along the passageway that led to the cavernous, vaulted kitchen that occupied the ground floor of the north tower. They passed through, mere shadows, unseen by any of the servants sleeping there, and exited by way of a heavy wooden door. Gavin paused just outside, at the top of a flight of worn stone stairs. Below them was the inner bailey, an open space they'd have to cross in order to reach the postern gate.

Nothing seemed to be stirring. No one challenged their progress as they went past the kitchen garden and the fish pond stocked with trout and pike. They made it safely across a small wooden bridge and reached the high stone wall without mishap.

"I've a currach hidden a short way downstream," Gavin whispered as he unbarred and opened the oaken gate. Just on the other side, a path descended to the riverbank.

Alison turned to take one last look at her home. To her horror, she saw armed men streaming toward her across the little bridge.

"Stop her!" one shouted. "Do not let her escape!"

Alison pushed hard at the door in the wall, slamming the postern gate closed before the rapidly approaching guards could catch sight of Gavin or Isabella. She turned back toward the castle, calling out, "I have no intention of going anywhere. Can a lady not enjoy a moonlit walk in her own garden without causing such a to-do?"

Rough hands seized her. Alison recognized Michael Barlow, the steward. The others were men-at-arms under his command.

"Release me, sirrah! What have I done to warrant such treatment?"

"Murder," Barlow said.

"Who has been murdered?"

"You know the answer to that question, Mistress Alison, else why would you try to run away? Your stepmother is dead. Stabbed through the heart."

He shoved her into the arms of one of his men.

"Lock her up for the crowner to question! No one is to talk to her until he arrives."

MISTRESS ALISON?

FROM HIS place of concealment on the other side of the postern gate, Gavin Dunnett absorbed the shock of this revelation. The young woman who'd fought him to protect Isabella was no mere nursemaid. She was Alison Bonville. One of Mariotta's sisters. Isabella's aunt.

She could not have killed Beatrice.

In spite of the fury with which she had attacked him, he did not believe her capable of murder, but his opinion, Gavin realized, would not save her. She had been in the wrong place at the wrong time. Now that she'd been taken into custody while trying to escape, no one at Bonville Keep would trouble to look elsewhere for a killer.

She'd gone quietly so he and Isabella could get away.

There could be no other explanation for her silence.

When the tramp of boots had receded and it was safe to move, he set Isabella on her feet and hunkered down until their eyes were level. "Who cares for you, Isabella? Who looks after your needs."

"Mine Aunt Alison."

He was not surprised by the answer. "Not some servant?"

Isabella shook her head. "Is it true you are my father?"

"Aye."

"Mine Aunt Alison has told me stories about you. She said you are a brave and honorable knight."

Gavin had men and horses waiting at an encampment only a short distance downstream. He could take Isabella there and set out for Scotland at first light. Once she was certain Isabella had time to get safely away, Alison could accuse him of the murder, thus regaining her own freedom.

But would she? And would they believe her if she did? Gavin frowned.

With Beatrice dead, he supposed there was no need to kidnap his daughter. As long as no one learned of this visit to the castle, he could return in daylight and claim her openly. If he did so, he would also be able to help Alison, who out of love for his child had sacrificed herself.

He sighed.

A brave and honorable knight, she'd called him.

She had been listening to too many ballads, tales of knights with pure hearts and noble intentions. What she'd seen here on the Border should have given the lie to such fancies. Real knights served whatever man paid for their services. They cared little for honor and less about those who got in their way. No matter who won any of the wars between England and Scotland, the folk who lived in the Debatable Land were the worse for it. Man, beast, and crops, all were trampled under the hooves of knights' horses and the bootheels of foot soldiers.

After seven years, Gavin had grown tired of fighting, tired of killing. He'd had no interest in finding employment in another endless, futile war. He'd had enough of innocent people dying. He'd returned home to Scotland to purchase a modest and remote estate. There he'd hoped to settle down, raise his daughter, and with God's blessing find a new wife to give him more children.

In a quiet voice, he told Isabella what they must do.

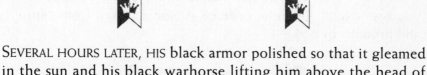

SEVERAL HOURS LATER, HIS black armor polished so that it gleamed in the sun and his black warhorse lifting him above the head of his squire, who rode upon a mule, Sir Gavin Dunnett once again entered Bonville Keep. This time the steward came out to greet him with a wary look upon his face.

"We are in mourning here," he announced. "We cannot offer hospitality."

"And you are?"

"He is Michael Barlow, Lady Bonville's *former* steward," another voice interrupted. "Now that she is dead, I am the one who will decide who is welcome here."

Although Gavin recognized the speaker as James Maplett, husband to Marion Bonville, he inquired as to his identity. When he received the answer he expected, he asked by what authority James laid claim to the castle.

"I am the husband of the eldest of Lord Bonville's heiresses."

"Is that all it takes, then? To be the eldest daughter's husband? You would yield your authority to the husband of an older sister?"

Caught off guard by the question, Maplett conceded that he would. "But there are none here," he pointed out.

"In that you are mistaken. I am Sir Gavin Dunnett. My wife, Mariotta, was older by a year than your Marion."

The smug look on Maplett's face was replaced by one of chagrin. Barlow gaped at Gavin in shocked disbelief.

Ignoring them both, he caught the eye of the halberdier with whom he'd supped and tossed the fellow a pouch heavy with coins. "Use that to pay back wages," he commanded.

His generosity stilled any protests guards or servants might have made. The arrival of the rest of his men silenced belated objections from Barlow and Maplett.

Once he had control of Bonville Keep, Gavin closeted himself with his daughter, who had done as he bade her in the wee hours of the morning and returned to her bed, saying nothing to anyone of her father's nocturnal visit. After reassuring her that all would be well, he entrusted her to the keeping of Alison's two younger sisters. Then he ordered Alison released from captivity and brought to him.

GAVIN DUNNETT REMINDED ALISON of a caged beast as he paced back and forth in the tower chamber. At last he turned on her. "Did you kill Beatrice Bonville?"

"I was about to ask you the same thing. You have certainly profited by her death."

"I did not kill her, either. Oh, I thought about it." In a few pithy words, he told her of Beatrice's claim that Isabella had died in infancy and his intent, when he'd believed that lie, to reive the castle. "I deemed it a just revenge to liberate a few of Beatrice's favorite pieces of jewelry before coming for Isabella."

So, Alison thought, he'd broken into the castle treasury. She did not begrudge him any of the trinkets he'd taken. Indeed, she would not have blamed him if he *bad* killed Beatrice.

"Does it matter who stabbed my stepmother?" she asked. "I can think of no one here who mourns her passing."

"It rests with me, as temporary caretaker of this castle, to discover who killed Lady Bonville, if only because the crowner has already been sent for. In search of the king's share of the criminal's estate, he'll want someone to blame. Being English, he'd delight in finding evidence against a Scot."

"So you propose to give me to him instead?"

"I propose that you help me discover the real killer. If you did not murder her and I did not, then it only makes sense that we work together to find the truth." Taking Alison's agreement for granted, he barked another question at her. "You accused Beatrice of poisoning Isabella. What did you mean?"

"Why, what I said. Two days ago, I returned early from an errand on which Beatrice had sent me and caught her dosing Isabella with a substance I did not recognize. Soon after, Isabella suffered a relapse. She became violently ill. I feared she would die, even though I treated her with nettle, and goat's milk, and honey water, and even mustard seed. All the antidotes I knew of."

"She first sickened hard upon her grandfather's death, or so I have been told. Was that the result of poison, too?"

"I think so. When she fell ill, no one knew the cause, just as no one knew what caused my father's sudden demise."

"Do you mean to say Lord Bonville was murdered?"

"I cannot prove it. He was not a young man, nor in the best of health."

Gavin seemed to read her mind. "You think Isabella saw something . . . heard something . . . but would she not have told you?"

"Not if Beatrice threatened her. I think she did. And then, to make sure of Isabella's silence, she tried to kill her, too. There is henbane missing from the stillroom."

"A poison?"

"Aye. Oh, there was reason for it to be there. My father suffered from gout. Henbane leaves, stamped with populeon ointment, are used in its treatment. But the juice, if enough be taken internally, can kill in a matter of minutes."

"A dangerous poison, then."

"Aye. Just smelling the flowers can make one drowsy. A small dose cures insomnia. A larger one causes an unquiet sleep that ends in death." She did not add that some superstitious folk believed the plant could also be used as a love charm—if it were gathered in the early morning by a naked man standing on one foot.

"Did you tell anyone of your suspicions?"

"Only my sisters."

"Which sisters?"

"The two who are younger than I am. I was born tenth, Tertia eleventh, and Ysende twelfth."

"The three Beatrice meant to send to Holystone to be nuns."

Alison bristled. "If you think that would be reason enough for one of us to kill her—"

"Can you account for their whereabouts every minute of last night? For that matter, can you prove you were here with Isabella when Beatrice was murdered?"

Alison was unable to school her features in time. One look at the expression on her face and his suspicions about her returned. "What is it you have not told me, Alison?"

"Nothing to do with murder." She sighed. Better Gavin hear the truth from her than wonder if she'd committed a much greater crime. "I searched my stepmother's chamber while she was still at supper. I was looking for the missing container of poison. I found nothing. I dreaded the morrow—today—when Beatrice would take me to task for my actions, but I did not kill her to prevent being scolded."

"How would she know you'd been in her chamber?"

"Christiana saw me creeping away."

"Christiana?"

"Beatrice's waiting gentlewoman. I was certain she would tell Beatrice, but I meant to brazen it out. It is not as if I stole anything." She sent him a pointed look. "But then you came, and I did not want to lose Isabella, and I saw a chance to get away from Beatrice's wrath, besides."

"Or a chance to escape punishment."

It hurt to think he still did not trust her. And angered her. Hands on her hips, Alison glared at her accuser. "Ask Christiana. She can swear nobody was in Beatrice's chamber, dead or alive, when I left it."

Where else, she wondered suddenly, had Gavin gone before he came to the north tower for Isabella? He'd been in the great hall, disguised as a Benedictine monk. That much she'd surmised. But that left several hours unaccounted for. *Could* Gavin have killed Beatrice? The possibility turned her almost as cold as her fear that he would continue to suspect her of the crime.

Gavin heaved a gusty sigh. "I believe you, Alison. I need no confirmation. Let us go, together, and talk to Isabella."

IN THE INNER CHAMBER in which his daughter had slept before her banishment to the north tower, a room she'd shared with Lord Bonville's three unmarried daughters, Tertia and Ysende kept their niece company. So did Christiana Talbot. Gavin did not notice her at first. It was easy to overlook the plain-faced waiting gentlewoman when she was in the company of a flock of tall, slender, fair-haired Bonvilles.

"This chamber adjoins the one where Beatrice was struck down," he said to Alison's sisters. "Did you hear anything?"

"We slept soundly," one of the sisters told him. They looked too much alike for him to tell which one she was.

"I heard naught until Christiana screamed," the other said.

"You found the body?" He turned to stare at the gentlewoman. His intense gaze seemed to fluster her.

Before he could pose his next question, Alison asked one of her own. "Did you see anyone near Beatrice's chamber after I left it?"

"Only Lady Bonville herself," Christiana replied. "She'd ordered me to sleep on the truckle bed, in case she wanted something fetched in the night."

Gavin lowered his voice in deference to his daughter's presence, although the child seemed intent on a piece of embroidery and was paying no attention to their conversation. "She slept alone?"

"Aye, Sir Gavin. For once."

Gavin frowned. "But if you were in the room, how did the killer reach her without waking you?"

"I went out to use the privy," Christiana mumbled. "I was only gone a few minutes. When I came back, I noticed that the bedcurtains were askew. Then I saw the blood."

"Could one of her lovers have killed her? For jealousy? For revenge? Because she rejected him?"

"She never rejected anyone," Alison muttered.

Christina looked discomfited, but after a moment her face brightened. "I have remembered something! She did have a falling-out with one of them. A Scots emissary visited here a month ago. Lady Bonville seemed most taken with him at first, but he left in anger."

Another lover? "Before or after Lord Bonville's death?"

"He left the day after. But he might have come back!"

Clearly, she hoped he had. Better, to her mind, that the killer be an outsider.

"I thank you for this intelligence, mistress. It may be most significant."

Christiana bobbed a curtsy and fled the chamber.

Gavin let her go, but he could not so easily dismiss the disturbing possibility she had raised. If Bonville's death, or Beatrice's, had been motivated by some political intrigue between England and Scotland, then he might never discover the truth.

After a few more questions, which yielded no new information, Gavin sent Alison's sisters away. Then, in a gentle, coaxing voice, he spoke to his daughter. "Lady Bonville can no longer harm you, Isabella," he said. "She is dead."

The child looked up from her embroidery, her small, pinched face too somber for her years. "Dead? Like Grandfather?"

He nodded.

"Is the man dead, too?"

"What man, Isabella?"

Although she stabbed her needle into the cloth with more force than necessary, Isabella did not answer. She was stitching a rose, Gavin saw, in blood red silk.

Alison knelt beside the girl's low stool. "Your father speaks true, sweeting. No one will hurt you ever again. But you must tell us everything you know."

A single tear dropped onto the fabric. "I wanted to keep Grandfather company."

Gavin settled himself on the floor, tailor-fashion, the better to hear his daughter's soft-spoken words. With one hand, he reached out to her. The other sought Alison's fingers until, with the kneeling woman and the seated child, he had formed a circle. He could not be certain how the others felt, but the contact rendered him calmer and more hopeful.

"You did nothing wrong, Isabella," he said.

"Lady Bonville told me to stay away."

"She banned you from your grandfather's sickroom?"

Isabella nodded.

"And you disobeyed?" Alison dried Isabella's tears.

"Yes."

"Tell us, sweeting. What happened then?"

With a final sniff, Isabella glanced at Gavin, then set aside her embroidery and turned to her aunt to confess. "I crept back to sit with him. He did not wake up, but I think he knew I was there."

"I am sure that comforted him," Alison said.

"Then I heard someone coming, so I hid myself behind the screen."

"What screen?" Gavin asked.

"It conceals the close stool," Alison told him. "Go on, Isabella. What did you hear?"

"Lady Bonville. She said—" Isabella broke off and looked about to weep again.

"What did she say?" Alison now held both of Isabella's hands in hers. Their eyes were locked.

"Hold him down while I make him swallow it."

Alison's gaze shifted to meet Gavin's, then away. Even though they had suspected as much, it was a shock to hear Beatrice's guilt so clearly revealed. He could only imagine how his daughter had felt.

"Did the man say anything?" Gavin hated to force Isabella to go on reliving that terrible day, but there was no choice. Beatrice might be dead, but her accomplice was not.

"I heard noises," Isabella whispered. "Choking and sputtering."

Her grandfather's death throes.

"And the man? Did he say anything when the noises stopped?"

"He said all this would be his now that Bonville was dead."

"Did you recognize his voice? Think, Isabella. Had you ever heard it before?"

"He whispered."

Alison wrapped the girl tight in an embrace. It seemed the most natural thing in the world for Gavin to shift his position so that he, too, could fling one comforting arm around their shoulders. Neither of them objected. Alison even managed a faint smile of approval.

"What happened after Beatrice and the man left?" he asked.

Isabella's eyes filled once more. "I came out of hiding and I saw him. Dead." A choked sob all but obscured the word. "I ran away, back to mine own chamber, but she saw me."

"Beatrice saw you leave the room?"

"She caught me and shook me till my teeth rattled. She said if I ever said a word about what went on in Grandfather's chamber, she'd kill me. I promised not to tell anyone, ever." Isabella turned wide, confused eyes to Gavin. "Why did she still hurt me when I promised not to tell?"

If Beatrice had not been dead already, Gavin thought, he'd kill her now for what she'd done to his daughter. He rose stiffly when Isabella dissolved once more into tears, and went to stand by the chamber window, while Alison calmed her.

He was still there some time later when, exhausted by her weeping, Isabella finally fell asleep.

"She is not yet out of danger," Alison whispered as she came up beside him.

"Aye. It stands to reason that the same person who helped Beatrice murder Lord Bonville also killed Beatrice."

"A falling-out among criminals?"

He nodded. "And if he knows what Isabella overheard, if he believes there is any chance she can identify him, he will try to silence her."

"Then we must discover who he is," Alison said. "One of Beatrice's recent lovers, that much seems certain. That narrows the field to three."

"Two, unless you think the Scots emissary returned to the castle in disguise."

She sent him a speaking glance. If Gavin had done so, someone else could have. Aloud, she asked, "Which one seems more likely? Michael Barlow or James Maplett?"

"Barlow wanted to marry Beatrice. It is not unheard-of for a steward to wed his . . . mistress. In that way he'd have gained power and, perhaps, wealth. *All this would be his*. But if that was his goal, why kill her? With Beatrice dead, he'd have nothing."

"A lover's quarrel?" Alison suggested. "A crime of passion?"

"Maplett had a better motive. He expected by Beatrice's death to gain the Bonville estates, by virtue of being the husband of your sister Marion. But any fool should have known his reasoning was faulty. He is no more the Bonville heir than I am."

Alison looked thoughtful, but she had no more to contribute. She went off to question the servants while Gavin talked to the Bonville men-at-arms.

A FEW HOURS LATER, they were no closer to a solution. Gavin swallowed the last of the ale in his mazer and contemplated the dregs. Would that he could read the truth in their pattern. 'Twas as good a method as any.

Word had come just before they sat down to sup that the crowner would arrive on the morrow. Gavin was determined to present him with a murderer and be on his way soon after. Truce or no, it was dangerous for a Scot to linger long on the English side of the border.

Old Lord Bonville had known that. It had been, in truth, his only objection to Gavin's marriage with Mariotta. Kinship, he'd said, made for a strong bond, but an outsider would always find acceptance hard to come by. A pity, he'd joked, that Gavin did not have the look of a Bonville.

Gavin blinked. Could the answer be that obvious?

He turned to Alison, with whom he shared a trencher, and whispered a question in her ear.

After giving him a startled look, she nodded. "There has scarce been time for word of my father's death to reach the cadet branch of the family. They settled in Cornwall generations ago."

"Motive for murder." He started to rise.

Her hand on his forearm stayed him. "Which murder?"

"Both."

But she shook her head. "I do not think so, for I have remembered something, too. And yet, I do think that if you accuse my father's poisoner of murdering Beatrice, you might just startle her killer into speaking."

Gavin did not ask for an explanation. He trusted Alison's instincts. Abruptly, he stood, scattering the remains of his meal, and called for more light.

When every sconce boasted a torch, every candlestick a taper, Gavin's gaze went first to Maplett, then moved on to Michael Barlow. "You are an impostor," he said to the latter, "and a murderer. You will hang for your crimes."

Before he could enumerate his reasons for accusing Barlow, Christiana Talbot cried out in distress. Everyone turned to look at her.

"You must not harm him. He did not kill Lady Bonville!"

"How can you be so certain?"

Christiana sent Barlow a glance filled with painful longing, then squared her shoulders and faced Gavin. "Because I killed her."

"Did you, by God?" In spite of Alison's prediction, Gavin had not expected this. "Why?"

"To keep Michael from marrying her." As if that confession sapped all her bravado, she dissolved into tears.

It was some time before Gavin could extract a coherent story. Details emerged in fits and starts, punctuated by much wailing and many loud lamentations.

Michael Barlow had promised to marry Christiana, but when Lord Bonville died, he'd told her he intended to wed the widow instead. He'd have it all, he'd bragged. Desperate to win him away from Beatrice, Christiana had confronted the other woman in her bedchamber.

"I told her she could not have him." Tears flowed freely down Christiana's pale cheeks. "He was mine! But she laughed at me. Made sport of me. Said I was too plain of face to take him away from her."

In a moment of overwhelming rage, Christiana Talbot had used the knife with which she cut her meat to stab Lady Bonville to death.

Gavin felt sorry for the woman, even as he ordered her taken into custody. "Seize Barlow, too," he added.

"You cannot arrest me," Barlow protested. "She's just told you she acted alone. She killed the woman I meant to marry. I had naught to do with it."

"But you had everything to do with another crime. You helped Beatrice Bonville kill her husband."

Barlow began to sputter a denial. Gavin held up one hand to silence him, then told the gathered company what Isabella had overheard.

"Arrant nonsense," Barlow declared. "You say yourself that the child did not recognize the voice of Lady Bonville's accomplice. He could have been anyone. That Scots emissary—"

"There might be more than one man willing to kill at Lady Bonville's bidding," Gavin interrupted, "but only one had an inheritance to gain. By law, the Bonville title and much of the estate goes to the last baron's closest male relative. A distant cousin, I believe. Distant enough that church and state would permit him to marry the widow if he chose to."

"No. No, I—"

"You carry the proof of your inheritance with you, Master Barlow. If that is your name. You are the only man here who could be the Bonville heir, for you are the only man here who has the Bonville hair."

At a signal from Gavin, the men-at-arms pulled Barlow out of the shadows. His flaxen locks shone silver-gilt in the candle-light, rendering futile any further denials.

As the prisoners were led away, Gavin turned to Alison. "How did you guess Christiana was guilty?"

"She slept that night in the same chamber with Beatrice, the same chamber where my father died. That meant there was no reason for her to leave the room to visit the privy. That chamber is furnished with a perfectly good close stool, behind the screen where Isabella hid."

"But why did you think she'd confess to save Barlow?"

Alison looked surprised he should ask. "Everyone in the castle knew about Christiana's unrequited passion for my step-mother's lover."

THE NEXT MORNING, AFTER the crowner had accepted Gavin's evidence and ridden away with two murderers in custody, Gavin came to collect his daughter and her belongings. Alison was waiting with the girl, her own possessions packed and ready.

"I will accompany Isabella to Scotland," she informed him. "I am certain that whatever distant male cousin is next in line to inherit cares not a whit what I do or where I go."

To her surprise, Gavin did not argue. He merely pointed out, lest she have any false hopes, that under English law a man could not marry his deceased wife's sister without a papal dispensation.

"I am not interested in marriage," she informed him in a haughty voice. "I am content to be Isabella's companion."

"Better than life in a nunnery," he agreed.

Dusk was falling by the time they crossed the border. Gavin turned to Alison and smiled down at her through the open visor of his helmet.

"Then again," he said in a conversational tone of voice, as if there had been mere minutes instead of most of a day's ride between his last remark on the subject and this one, "Scots law on marriage differs from the English."

"In what way?" she asked.

His smile widened into a grin as he produced the Bonville betrothal ring, the one piece of jewelry he'd not returned to the castle treasury. "In Scotland it is a much simpler matter for a widower to marry the sister of his late wife."

She smiled back at him, a twinkle in her bright blue eyes.

"I know," she said, and extended her hand.

For the Love of Old Bones

Michael Jecks

The sudden violence was a shock: swift and devastating. They came at us from all sides, and what were we supposed to do? We couldn't run; we couldn't hide. There was nowhere to conceal ourselves on that desolate damned moor.

I was struck down early. When I came to, it was to find my head being cradled in the lap of a rough countryman, a shepherd from the rank smell of him, holding a leather bottle of sour-tasting water to my lips that I drank with gratitude. All about me, when I felt able to gaze around, were my companions: resting, holding broken heads, or wincing as their bruised limbs gave them pain. It was all I could do to pull away and kneel, fingering my rosary as I offered my thanks to God for delivering us from our attackers.

"The Abbot is dead!"

The cry broke in upon my devotions and I had to stifle my gasp of horror. I saw Brother Charles at the side of Abbot Bertrand's slumped figure and hurried over to them as fast as my wounded head would allow.

Abbot Bertrand de Surgères, my lord, lay dead; stabbed in his back.

479

IT IS DIFFICULT ALWAYS to try to recall small details after a horrible event. I and my English brethren have suffered much in the years since the great famine of 1315 to 1316. As peasants lost their food, so there was less for us monks; the murrain of sheep and cattle that followed devastated our meager flocks and herds, and now, late in the year of our Lord thirteen hundred and twenty-one, I had myself taken my fill of despair.

With the pain in my head from the crushing blow, I was in no state to assist my brothers in tidying the body of our Abbot. I sat resting while they unclothed him and redressed him in fresh linen and tunic; others walked a mile or more northward to a wood, from where they fetched sturdy boughs to fashion a stretcher. The horses had gone, of course. For my part, I could not help them. I knew only pain and sadness as I watched them work.

It was a cold, quiet place, this. The sun was watery this late in the year, and its radiance failed to warm. We were on the side of a hill, with a small stream gurgling at our feet. A few warped and twisted trees stood about, but all were distorted, grotesque imitations of the strong oaks and elms I knew. The grass itself looked scrubby and unwholesome, while the ground held a thick scattering of rocks and large stones, giving the scene a feeling of devastation, as if a battle had raged over it all. It felt to me like a place blasted with God's rage. As it should, I thought, with one of His Abbots lying murdered on the ground.

The shepherd disappeared soon after I awoke, but while my companions set the Abbot's body on the stretcher and began gathering together the few belongings that the robbers had scattered, I sat quietly. I saw Brother Humphrey pick up the Abbot's silver crucifix. He saw my quick look and smiled weakly. In our little convent there have been occasions when odd bits and pieces have gone missing, and he knows I suspect him. The cord of the cross was broken, although the cross and tiny figure were fine; nearby, Abbot Bertrand's purse lay on the ground. Humphrey picked up both and passed them to me with a puzzled expression.

As he stood there, I heard hoofs. Looking up, I saw three men at the brow of the hill. One was the shepherd, the other two were on horseback. They were unknown to me; indeed, I could hardly make out their features for the low, autumnal sun was behind them, and it was hard to see more than a vague shadow. Now, of course, I know Bailiff Puttock of Lydford and his friend Sir Baldwin of Furnshill near Cadbury, but then they were only strange, intimidating figures on their horses, staring down at us intently while the shepherd leaned on his staff.

At the sight of them Humphrey let out a cry of despair, fearing a fresh attack; a pair of servants grabbed their staffs and advanced, determined to protect us. The three remaining brothers began reciting the *paternoster;* me, I simply fell to my knees and prayed.

THE MEN RODE DOWN the incline and I could make them out. It was soon obvious that one of them was a knight—his sword belt and golden spurs gleamed as the sun caught them. His slow approach was reassuring, too. It gave me the impression that we were safe: he hardly looked like one of the predatory knights who might conceal robbery by making demands in courtly language. In any event, such a one would have brought a strong party of men-at-arms to steal what they wanted.

"Brothers, please don't fear us," the other man said as he neared the staffman. "I'm Bailiff Puttock under Abbot Champeaux of Tavistock Abbey and my friend is Sir Baldwin, the Keeper of the King's Peace in Crediton. This shepherd told us of the attack and we have already sent for the Coroner to view the body. May we help you?"

I heaved a sigh of relief. There was no fearing men such as these. "Godspeed, gentlemen! It is an enormous relief to meet you. Now at least we need fear no footpads while on the moors."

It was the knight who spoke first, studying me with an oddly intense expression, like one who has no liking for monks. He was tall, with heavy shoulders and a flat belly to prove that he practiced regularly with his sword. Intelligent dark eyes glittered in a square face with a thin beard that followed the line of his jaw. One scar marred his features, twisting his mouth. "Your name, Brother?"

"I am Brother Peter, from Launceston Abbey. My Abbot sent me to help our brethren on their arduous journey to France and back. We were on our way to Launceston when this happened."

"It's a long way to go without horses, Brother," the other man pointed out.

"We had horses until last night, when they were taken."

"You were robbed? God's teeth! The thieving bastards!" Bailiff Puttock burst out. "How many were there? And which way did they go?"

"I was knocked down early on," I grimaced, gingerly feeling the back of my tonsure. The skin was broken slightly and there was a large lump forming that persuaded me not to prod or probe too hard.

"There were six of them. They appeared like devils as the sun faded, running straight at us . . ."

As I spoke I could recall the horror. Screaming, shrieking men, all wielding staves or clubs, springing down from the surrounding rocks, belaboring us, holding us off while two young lads, scarcely more than boys, took our horses. And a short while later, nothing: they had clubbed me.

The knight was silent, but the Bailiff cocked his head. "None of them had a knife?"

"I don't recall. My head—I was unconscious."

"What was their leader like?"

"Heavyset, bearded, with long dark hair."

"I have heard of him."

"They took most of our provisions as well as our mounts."

Sir Baldwin walked off a few yards, bending and studying the ground. He went to the stream and followed its bank a short distance, then round the curve of the hill, disappearing from sight.

His friend appeared confused. "You say these men attacked and took your horses—but only your Abbot was stabbed? It seems odd. . . ."

He would likely have added more, but then his friend called, "They went this way. Their prints are all over the mud at the side of the stream. It looks like they have gone westward."

"Which is where we should go as well," Bailiff Puttock said. "If there are thieves on the moors we should warn the abbey. We can send a second messenger to the Coroner explaining where we have gone."

"And it would be a good place for these good brothers to recover from their ordeal," Sir Baldwin agreed.

"IT SEEMS CURIOUS THAT the thieves should have left such wealth behind."

We were resting in a hollow on the old track to Tavistock. All of us were tired after our ordeal and needed plenty of breaks. The knight was squatting, studying the crucifix and purse.

The Bailiff shrugged unconcernedly. "They grabbed what they could."

"But they killed an Abbot."

"So? In the dark they probably didn't realize he was an Abbot, nor that they had killed him. It was a short, sharp scuffle in the gloom."

"Hmm."

I could see that the knight wasn't convinced. The Bailiff, too, for all his vaunted confidence, scarcely seemed more certain. Both stared down at the items. I cleared my throat and held up the cold meat in my hand. "Could one of you lend me a knife? My own was still on the packhorse."

With a grunt the knight pulled a small blade from his boot and passed it to me.

"I've known thieves leave behind goods after being scared off," Bailiff Puttock continued after a while.

"And I have known Bailiffs who have left wine in the jug after a feast—but that does not mean I have ever seen you behaving abstemiously. No, these robbers planned their raid. Two things are curious: first, that they bothered to kill the man; second, that they left his wealth at his side."

"Who were these robbers, Sir Baldwin?" I interjected.

"We may never catch them, Brother," he said with a smile. "There are so many who have been displaced since the recent wars in Wales. They have swollen the ranks of the poor devils who lost everything during the famine."

"Poor devils, my arse!" Puttock growled. "They should have remained at their homes and helped rebuild their vills and towns, not become outlaw and run for the hills."

"Some had little choice," Sir Baldwin said.

"Some didn't, no, but this gang sounds like Hamo's lot again."

"They've never killed before," Sir Baldwin said slowly.

"True, but the leader sounds like Hamo and the theft of the horses is just like his mob."

Sir Baldwin rose. "This is not helping us. You saw nothing of the death of your Abbot, Brother Peter?" I shook my head. "Then let us ask your friends. Could you introduce us?"

I nodded. "Brother Humphrey is another Englishman like me, but Brother Charles comes from France. He is the shorter of the three. The third, the handsome young one, is Brother Roger, who is also French. He comes from the Abbot's own convent."

"What was the reason for their visit?" the Bailiff asked.

"There has been debate for many years about where certain relics should be stored. The fingerbone of Saint Peter is held at Launceston and I was sent to the Abbot to explain why we felt it should remain," I told him sadly.

My head throbbed again with the recollection of that dreadful meeting. It was held by Abbot Bertrand in his chapter house, and the place reeked. The fire's logs hadn't been properly dried and the hearth in the middle of the room smoked foully, filling the place with an acrid stench; censers competed with it, with the result that all of us were coughing by the end of the meeting—if it could be so termed. We discussed the ins and outs of sites for the bones, but the decision had already been made. That was made abundantly clear. Our carefully thought-out arguments were overruled or ignored.

"They could think of taking such a relic back to France?" Sir Baldwin asked with frank astonishment.

I allowed a little acid into my voice. "It's the way of the French. Now that they have installed the Pope in Avignon they feel that they can win any argument they wish."

"But to take the bones from a place like Launceston! It is not as if there is much else for the people to venerate there!"

"No, indeed. Launceston is far from civilization. It is an out-post on the fringes of society; without the few items we have, how can we hope for God's grace to protect us?"

Bailiff Puttock watched the men. "And you say that this Brother Charles is French? Let's ask him about last night."

MY FRIEND BROTHER CHARLES was a short, thickset man of maybe five-and-twenty years. Originally from the southern provinces of France, near the border with Toulouse, his tonsure was fringed with sandy colored hair. Upon being called to meet with the knight and his comrade, Brother Charles appeared nervous, as if he feared their presence.

Bailiff Puttock spoke first. "I hear you're from a French Abbey, come here to remove English relics?"

Brother Charles threw me a helpless look. "I was com-manded to join my Abbot, it is true."

"To take away bones from Launceston?"

"That was the plan. The mother-abbey has need of them."

"So does Launceston," the Bailiff snarled gruffly.

"My Abbot decided. I was ordered to join him together with my friend Brother Roger and these other good monks, Humphrey and Peter, from the monastery of Launceston."

"Very well. What happened last night?"

"My Lord, I was preparing some pottage for our evening meal when I heard a shout. It was one of the grooms. I looked up and saw him toppling over. A great bear of a man stood behind him, grasping a heavy staff. It was awful! I was about to rush to help the groom when I realized there were more attack-ers. I thought it better to go to the Abbot's side and help defend the camp."

"Where was everyone else?" Sir Baldwin asked.

"I can hardly recall, Sir Baldwin. It is all so confused in my mind. The men attacked so swiftly . . . I was at the fire when I heard the first scream. When I turned I saw Brother Peter crum-ple. Abbot Bertrand still had Brother Humphrey and Brother

Roger with him. There was so much shouting—so many cries and screams. One of our servants was felled and then I realized a man was near me, the same gross fellow who had hurt Brother Peter. I avoided his club and went to my Lord Abbot's side.

"But when I got there, two men rushed at us, and I only had time to grab a stick and thrust at them, but missed, I fear. I was knocked back, driven toward the fire again, fearing all the time that the big man who had knocked Brother Peter down could strike me from behind. The Abbot fell. I saw him, I think. It was all so confused! Then they were pulling away, and we heard the sound of our horses cantering away. The men laughed as they scurried off. And I saw my Abbot on the ground."

"Did he say anything?"

"No. He was dead. The blade that struck him down killed him instantly. He made no sound."

"How close was he to you?"

"He was only a few yards from me." Brother Charles belatedly realized that the questioning was focusing unpleasantly upon him. "But we had all gathered close to each other!"

Sir Baldwin held up his hand. "Do not worry yourself. We only wish to see the place through your eyes. Tell me, what was the Abbot like?"

Brother Charles threw me a confused, desperate look, and I interjected, "Sir Baldwin, what has this to do with his death? Surely, it would be better for us to continue on our way and warn others of these thieves before they can harm other travelers?"

"Yes, but please humor us. This Abbot of yours—was he a generous, kindly fellow?"

I gave a brittle smile. One should hardly speak ill of the dead, but . . . I chose the path of least trouble. "He was deeply religious and devoted to his abbey."

Sir Baldwin eyed me with a faint grin. "He was not your friend, then."

There was no need for me to say anything. I merely hung my head.

"Was it the bones?"

I met his eye with stern resolution. "Sir Baldwin, I feel that your questions are bordering upon the impertinent. You are questioning me about a matter that is of little, if any, concern of yours. An Abbot has been murdered and that offense falls under Canon Law. It is not within your jurisdiction. However, we do have a responsibility to others to see to their protection. For that reason I should like to hurry to Tavistock. In addition, I have to take the good Abbot's body to the abbey for burial. Should we not continue on our way?"

THE WAY WAS HARD. Devonshire has few good roads. All of them involve climbing hills and dropping into rock-strewn valleys with few good bridges over the chilly, fast streams. It was a miracle that none of us broke an ankle on the treacherous soil or fell into one of the foul-smelling bogs.

The knight and his friend were good enough to lend their horses, one to me, one to poor Brother Roger. He, too, had been struck down in the attack, and he rode slumped, his head rocking as if he were dozing. Once I had to hurry to his side and hold him upright when he all but fell from the saddle.

After that I felt I had little option but to accede when the Bailiff suggested that we should stop again. It led to my feeling fretful and irritable, but I could see no alternative.

We had come to a pleasant space in which strange buildings of stone abounded. They might have been ancient huts for shepherds like the man who had helped us and who now traipsed along gloomily. He had been told that he should join us so that his evidence could also be given alongside our own.

Many men worked the moors, I reflected. Miners scrabbled for tin, copper, and arsenic on the wildlands; farmers raised their sheep and cattle; builders dug quarries. All lived out there, in the inhospitable waste.

Yet none could be seen from here. The moor stretched five leagues, maybe, north and south of this point, and was at least four leagues wide. That was why gangs of thieves and outlaws could easily lose themselves. Even now they could be up there watching us, laughing as they sat astride our own ponies.

The thought made me shiver with anger. Knaves like them deserved to die!

THE BAILIFF AND THE knight approached Humphrey almost as soon as we had stopped, and I pursed my lips with annoyance. It was obvious that they intended to question him as they had Brother Charles, and I wasn't going to have it. Instead, I called Brother Humphrey to me, asking him to join me in prayer.

He did so with alacrity, and I smiled, glad to have rescued him. I also caught sight of the speculative expression on the knight's face. It was suspicious, as if he thought I was behaving oddly, but I didn't care. I took Humphrey's hand and led him away, sitting with him on a stone and murmuring the prayers for the office of Sext. It was surely about noon.

While we prayed and offered ourselves once more to God, I saw Brother Roger walking away to fetch water. It was a relief, for I was sure that as soon as they could, the knight and the Bailiff would be after him as well with their questions.

Finishing our prayers, I patted Humphrey's arm and he gave me an anxious smile in return. Poor Humphrey was plainly scared. His pale grey eyes were fearful, darting hither and thither like those of a hunted animal. The affair was taking its toll on the nineteen-year-old, and I gave him a reassuring grin.

I was about to offer him some advice when he stopped me. "Last night—I have to tell someone . . ."

"Shh!" I hissed. I could sense the two pests approaching. Their shadows loomed.

"Brother Humphrey, we'd like to ask you what you saw last night," Bailiff Puttock said.

The knight hunkered down beside us. "It's hard to understand why the Abbot should have died. Especially since he had money on him, money that was not taken but was instead left at his side. Did you see him stabbed?"

"No, Sir Baldwin. I could scarcely see anything."

"You weren't knocked unconscious?" the Bailiff asked.

"No."

"You came from Launceston with Brother Peter here, didn't you?"

"Yes. We were both sent to persuade the Abbot against taking our relics."

"But he decided to in any case?"

"They wouldn't listen to us!" Humphrey stormed. "It wasn't fair! They'd already decided to steal our . . ."

I interrupted hastily. "This was no theft, Humphrey. It was their right and their decision."

"The relics are ours! They should remain in Cornwall!"

"Did you like the Abbot?" Sir Baldwin asked.

Humphrey looked at me, and I glanced at the knight with an annoyed coldness. "Sir Baldwin, what has this to do with anything? The Abbot—God bless his soul!—is dead. What good can raking over other people's feelings for him achieve?"

"Brother, you were unconscious and couldn't have seen much," Bailiff Puttock said easily, "but we have to find out as much about these robbers as we can because we have to catch them. All we want is to gain a good idea of exactly what happened last night."

Before Humphrey could answer, I peered over my shoulder. Brother Roger had not returned. "Go and seek Brother Roger. I fear he could have become lost. God forbid that he should be swallowed in a mire."

When he was gone, I faced the two once more. They exchanged a look.

"Brother Humphrey is well known to me, and I would prefer that you didn't question him too deeply. It could harm him."

"What's that supposed to mean?" the Bailiff demanded. "The man's fine, but you seem determined to protect him from our questions. *Why?*"

"Because he is not well," I told him harshly. "Good God! Can't you see? The fellow is a wreck."

"Because of the attack?"

I took a deep breath. "No, because his father was a clerk in Holy Orders who raped a nun. Humphrey is convinced that his whole existence is an affront to God."

"Christ's bones!" the Bailiff gasped. "The poor bastard!"

"So I would be most grateful if you could leave the poor fellow alone. He needs peace, and the attack itself has severely upset him. I should have thought that you would have been able to see that!"

The two apologized handsomely. It was plain that the Bailiff was shocked by what he had heard. And who wouldn't be? The story was one to chill the blood—being born as a result of the rape of one of Christ's own brides was hideous. It had marked out poor Humphrey from early on: the product of a heretical union.

"Did the Abbot know of his past?" Sir Baldwin asked.

"Yes. Naturally. Abbot Bertrand knew about all of us."

I saw the knight's attention move behind me and turned in time to see Humphrey leading Brother Roger back into the makeshift camp. The Frenchman looked confused and happily took his seat on a satchel, while Humphrey solicitously spread a blanket over his knees and patted his hand. I called to him sharply and asked him to fetch a wineskin. We could all do with some refreshment.

Only a few moments after the knight and Bailiff had risen, they began to move in the direction of Brother Roger. I followed them, pointing out that the poor lad was dazed still from his wound.

"I understand that, but I would still like to ask him a little about the attack," the knight stated in what I can only call a curt manner. He was growing testy.

"There seems little need. I have told you what I saw, and you know who the killer is."

"You have told us that you did not see anyone stab him," the Bailiff said. "We still have to see whether anyone might have seen who actually did."

"Good God above! I told you about our attackers—what more do you want?"

"A witness who saw him shove a knife into your Abbot's back," he said shortly.

I could feel the anger twisting my features as I trailed after them toward the sitting monk, and I was forced to pray for patience in the face of what felt like overwhelming provocation.

Brother Roger was young, only perhaps twenty-two. Looking up with a mild squint against the brightness of the day, he had to keep closing his eyes as we spoke, as though the sun's light was too powerful for him.

"My friend, these men wish to ask you about the attack last night to find out whether you saw the leader of the outlaws stab . . ."

The knight interrupted me. "Brother Roger, you were yourself knocked on the head. When did you waken?"

"This morning. I was unconscious for some hours. And my head!" He winced. "It was worse than the headache after an evening drinking strong wine!"

"What do you remember of the attack?"

"I was near the Abbot, and when the first cry came to us, he was on his feet and rushing for the horses, but he was stopped. A group of the felons appeared, and we ran to the Abbot's side to protect him. I was there at his right hand," he added with a hint of self-consciousness.

"Did you see anyone stab him?"

"No."

Brother Charles had approached and now he interrupted. "I saw him crumple like an axed pig. One moment up and fighting, the next, collapsed in a heap. It was as if he had been struck by a rock."

"You are sure of this?" the knight pressed him.

"Oh, yes," Charles said emphatically. "He fell because he was struck on the head."

"One of the outlaws could have heaved a stone at him," the Bailiff said pensively.

"Perhaps," Sir Baldwin said. "Tell me, Brother Roger: the Abbot, was he always a bold man?"

"Very brave and courageous. He would always leap to the front of any battle. He had been a knight, you see. He was Sir Bertrand de Toulouse before he took Holy Orders."

Now Baldwin's brow eased. The frown that had wrinkled his forehead faded. "So that is why he was so keen to be at the forefront of the fighting!"

"Yes. He would always go to a fight to protect his own. And, of course, he saw a man attacking Humphrey," he added with a faintly sneering tone to his voice.

"Humphrey was sorely pressed?" Bailiff Puttock asked.

I shot the loathsome Frenchman a look of warning but he met it with sneering complacency. "No, Bailiff. Abbot Bertrand was a sodomite; he wished to preserve the life of the man he adored."

AFTER HE HAD LET it out, there was little more for me to say. I walked away and left the knight and his friend still talking to the Frenchman, but I wished to hear no more of their inquiry. If they wanted more, they could come and find me.

I left the camp, seeking the stream that Roger had apparently discovered. It was a short distance away. Some twenty yards farther up was the corpse of a sheep, and as I drank I saw that it had horns still attached to its skull. As soon as I had drunk my fill, I walked up and pulled them off. They would decorate a walking stick.

It was relaxing here, listening to the chuckle and gurgle of the water. I rested upon a rock and stared at the water for a time, considering. So much had happened recently: There was the horror of finding that the Abbot wanted our relics, to help him persuade gullible peasants and townspeople to give him more money in exchange for prayers said within the church. The shock of learning that he had made up his mind before the arguments could be put before him. And last there was the terror in Humphrey's eyes when the Abbot had fondled and caressed him after the meeting, promising him wealth and advancement should he agree to share the Abbot's bed.

Humphrey had lost the veneer of calmness he had developed over such a long period. It had been appalling to him to discover that the Abbot was corrupt—*perverted!* How could he respond, he asked, and I told him: simply refuse and walk from the Abbot if he tried it again.

But now I had to cover my face in my hands at the result.

I AROSE, PREPARING TO return to the camp, when I heard the scream. Eerie, it seemed to shiver on the air as a gust wafted it toward me. It was as if a hand of ice had clutched at my heart. A trickle of freezing liquid washed down my spine, and I felt the hairs of my head stand erect.

All at once I remembered the stories of ghosts and demons on the moors. This grim wasteland was home to devils of all kinds who hunted fresh souls with their packs of baying wishhounds. This shriek sounded like that of a soul in torment, and my hand grabbed at my crucifix even as I mouthed the *paternoster* with a shocked dread.

Before I could finish, Sir Baldwin was at my side, his sword in his hand. "Where did it come from?" he rasped, staring northward from us.

For the second time that day, I was glad to see him, and for the second time I could tell him little. "Up there somewhere."

He gave me a twisted little grin. "This is hardly what a monk should be used to."

"I'm not!" I said grimly. The sight of his unsheathed sword had recovered a little of my courage. The blade was beautiful, fashioned from bright peacock-blue steel.

He motioned with it. "Shall we see what caused that noise?"

"Very well."

I had no desire to see this, but equally I had no wish to appear a coward. Also, if it were a human or mortal beast creating that unholy row, I would be safe enough with the knight; while if it were the noise of a devil seeking a soul, I should be as safe out in the moors as I was in the camp. Either way, I knew that however strong my faith *should* have been, I would feel happier with this armed man at my side.

"I've told the servants to guard the camp," Bailiff Puttock said, striding toward us. He carried a coil of rope over one shoulder.

"Good," Sir Baldwin said absently. "Brother Peter thinks the noise came from over there."

The Bailiff chuckled. "I'm afraid not. The wind can do odd things to sounds out here. No, it would have come from there." He pointed, and soon was leading the way.

THE SCREAM CAME AGAIN as we clambered over rocks and tussocks of
loose grass. It was also damp. "What could that noise be?" I asked.

Bailiff Puttock cast me a smiling glance. "Haven't you got
bogs near Launceston? It's the sound of a desperate man bellowing for help after falling in one of our mires. Not a nice way to
die, that."

I realized then what my eyes and feet had been telling me.
The ground here trembled underfoot as I placed my feet upon it,
and the grasses each carried an odd, white pennant at the tip of
their stems: this was no grass, it was a field of rushes.

"Watch my feet and step only in my own footprints," the
Bailiff commanded.

I was happy to obey him. When I lost concentration for a
moment, my leg slipped up to the shin in foul, evil-looking mud. I
muttered a curse, and as I pulled my foot free, there came another
cry. It scarcely sounded human.

We scrambled up to the top of a ridge, and upon the other
side we had a clear view for some miles. There, at the edge of a
field of white rush flowers, we saw a man's head. His arms were
outspread and one gripped at something, a bush or twig.

"He's further gone than I'd thought," the Bailiff muttered
before springing down the gentle incline, the knight, his sword
now sheathed, and I stumbling along as best we could. At the base
of the hill was a kind of path made of stepping-stones and we had
to hop from one to another until we came close to the mire.

"Christ Jesus; praise the saints! Thank you, thank you, thank
you!"

"My God!" I said. "It's him!"

The Bailiff grinned. "Meet Hamo!"

It took time to persuade the moor to give up its victim.
When we finally hauled him from the filthy mud, he lay
sprawled like a drowned cat rescued from a rain butt, as if he
were already dead. Bailiff Puttock bound his arms with his rope.
Soon Hamo gave a convulsive gasp, almost a sob, his face red
and fierce after his struggle.

"The *bastards*," he wheezed. "They threw me there to die, God rot their guts!"

"You," Sir Baldwin said mildly, "are arrested."

"What for?" the man demanded suspiciously.

"The murder of Abbot Bertrand," Bailiff Puttock said, firmly binding his hands. "You stole his horses last night and stabbed the Abbot when he lay on the ground."

Hamo shrugged expansively. "I'll hang for the horses, and you can only hang a man the once, but I never killed him. That was why my gang threw me in the mire to die, the bastards! Because they heard a rumor that an Abbot had been killed, but it wasn't me. I saw him fall like he'd been struck dead while we fought, but then there were two other men to worry about. I didn't have time to stab him. Do you know where the gang lives? I can take you there if you want to kill them." He shivered, casting a glance back at the mire.

"We'll think about it. Do you swear on your soul that you didn't kill the Abbot?" the Bailiff asked.

"I swear it on my soul and on my mother's soul. I never hurt the man. He fell before I could strike him."

IT WAS CLEAR THAT the two were impressed by his assertions. Sir Baldwin prodded him with his sword while the Bailiff gripped the rope's end, and I wandered along cautiously in their wake.

Returning we took a longer path, one which was, I am glad to say, less soggy than the one we had taken on the way to find this barbarous fellow. Before long we had got back to the camp and had bound our captive to a tree. He nodded and grinned to the men gathered there, but he was refused any wine or water from our stores. Since he had stolen our stocks, we reasoned it was hardly reasonable that he should take a share in what was left us.

"Why didn't you take the Abbot's crucifix?" the Bailiff asked.

"I didn't even see it. Look, there was a fight, right? I waded in quickly so that our boys could cut the horses free and lead them away. I stood against the Abbot, but he suddenly fell, when

he did, I was beset by two more men." He grudgingly nodded
toward Roger and Charles. "I didn't have time to feel the man's
body. Almost as soon as he fell there was a shout and we withdrew. That's all I know."

"What of these others?" Sir Baldwin said, indicating
Humphrey and me.

"I saw that one," he said, nodding toward me. "I hit him
early on. Not hard, but he dropped. The other one—I don't
remember."

"So you, Brother Humphrey, are the only one who is not
accounted for," Sir Baldwin said softly.

"Sir Baldwin, that is outrageous!" I roared. "Dare you suggest . . ."

"Quiet, father, let me . . ."

The Bailiff's jaw dropped. "You . . . *you* are his father?"

I sank wearily to a rock and passed a hand over my forehead.
"Yes," I admitted. "I was the evil fool who raped his mother, may
God forgive me! And I murdered the Abbot."

"Father, no! It was me he insulted!"

"Bailiff, I know what I am saying," I said again. In truth, it
was a relief to end the anticipation. "My son was in danger from
the Abbot. I had to protect him. The Abbot wanted him to go
to his bedchamber. He told me, and I sought to defend him as
best I could." I stood and patted my son's shoulder. "When I saw
the fight, it was as if I saw the means. I threw a stone at the
Abbot hoping that he would falter and be struck down, killed.
He fell, and I then went and stabbed him when no one else was
watching."

"Interesting," Sir Baldwin said. "Yet you were yourself unconscious during the attack."

"I fell, but I was only bewildered for a moment. As soon as I
came to, I saw what was happening. There was a rock by my hand
and I hurled it at him."

"And?" Bailiff Puttock asked.

"What do you mean, 'and'?"

"You threw the stone at him, jumped to your feet, and hurled
yourself across the camp to stab him?"

"Yes," I said.

"Where is your knife?"

His words made me blink. I hadn't thought of that. I don't wear a knife. My eating knife was on the packhorse. I had already told them that. "My knife . . . I dropped it after—"

"Father, stop it!"

I couldn't restrain him, my boy threw himself at my feet. "I didn't kill him and neither did you! You never threw a rock. You had collapsed! I saw you."

"So who *did* kill him?" I asked, and now, I confess, I was too astonished to be more than a little bemused by the course of events.

"*Him!*" Humphrey spat, pointing at Brother Roger. "When I saw you had fallen, I cried out. The Abbot thought I had been hurt and leapt to my side. Roger knocked the Abbot down in a fit of jealousy, and I think he stabbed the Abbot later when no one was watching."

"Me? Why should I do this?"

"Because the Abbot had thrown you over. He thought you pretty when you were a choirboy, and I suppose he loved you in a way, but then he wanted me instead, and you couldn't cope with that, could you?"

"I was fighting with *him*, and I fell, just as did your father."

"My father has blood on his head and a lump—what do you have?" Humphrey sneered.

It was with a sense of—I confess it—disbelief that I realized what my son had noticed. The Frenchman had said that he was dreadfully knocked, had taken a horse because of his supposed pain, and yet he had no bruise, no lump, no blood. And he could stand and debate with Humphrey.

As the thought came to me, I saw him stand, white-faced with rage. Suddenly, he whipped a hand beneath his robe and pulled out a knife. He launched himself on my boy.

I suppose I didn't think of the danger. All I knew was that my boy was at risk. Did I realize I was risking my own life? I don't know. Perhaps there was an awareness, but no matter. I would do it again if I had the opportunity.

You see, all my son's life I had seen him walk in shame, paying the debt that I had created for him. This at least I could do for him: I could protect him, and hopefully prove that his father was himself forgiven by God for his great sin.

Yes, I jumped forward and threw my arms about Brother Roger. The first stab was nothing, a thud against my breast as if he had clenched a fist and thumped me with it; the second made a huge pain which is with me still, and my left arm was made useless. Still, I could hold on with my right, and this I did. I held him until Bailiff Puttock struck him smartly with the pommel of his sword, and Brother Roger collapsed with me on top of him.

This is the truth, as I believe in the life to come. Oh, Holy Lady, take me and heal me from the sins and pain of this world!

My son, farewell!

SIR BALDWIN WATCHED AS Brother Humphrey finished the dictation and set the paper aside, sniveling, dropping his reed. The knight's attention went to the frankly bemused expression on the face of the outlaw. Near him lay the knife that had fallen from Brother Roger's hand. Baldwin stared at it a long moment, then at the felon. Slowly, he turned away and faced the group again.

"We must take the body of Brother Peter with us. Perhaps we could put it on the stretcher with the Abbot," he said, walking around the group.

Simon kicked the unconscious Brother Roger. "We have to get this shit back to town as well. And then organize a posse to get the rest of the outlaws."

"They'll be long gone by now," Sir Baldwin said. He looked toward the outlaw. There was a profoundly innocent expression on Hamo's face. "You! Where will your gang be tonight, do you think?"

"They said they were going to head down toward Dartmouth. There're always women to be bought in a sailor's town."

"There you are," Baldwin said. "Now, I know it is not within our jurisdiction to arrest a monk because he falls under Canon Law, but do you think we could tie this fellow and ensure he doesn't try to run away?"

Bailiff Puttock was about to answer when a scrabbling of feet and a gasp made him turn. Where the felon had squatted bound to a tree, there remained only a coil of rope. Hamo was pelting away over the coarse grass.

As the Bailiff made to chase after him, Sir Baldwin put a hand to his arm. "Leave him, friend. There have been enough deaths already. Let's allow one man to remain alive."

"But he and his gang started all this!"

"Yes, I know. But under Canon Law no monk or cleric can be hanged. This man murdered his Abbot, an act of treachery as well as homicide, but can't swing; that felon didn't kill anyone, but he would be hanged as soon as he appeared in a town. Is that justice? Let him go."

The Bailiff watched the man disappear among the thick rocks of the moors. "So long as the damned cretin doesn't fall into another mire again," he said with resignation. "I'll be buggered before I save him a second time!"

The Wizard of Lindsay Woods

Brendan DuBois

I n the year of our Lord 1296 and in the fourteenth year of the reign of Edward the First, in the village of Bromley, the parish priest of the village, one Father Stephen, was preparing for his early evening vespers in his tiny home near the church, when there was a pounding on the door. He got up from the stained wooden table and walked over the dirt floor, past the small, smoldering hearth, and called out, "Who be there?"

"If you will, Father, do open up," came the familiar voice. "It is Gawain, of your brother's manor."

Father Stephen undid the door and let the large man in. It was a warm afternoon in April, on the feast day of Saint George, and dusk was approaching. From the door he could make out the small stone church where he serviced the people of this village, and the fields where he did his other work as well, to feed himself and whatever visitors he might have. He had one weak tallow candle burning in the center of the table, and as Gawain took one of the stools, his sword clanking at his side, Father Stephen went to a shelf on the wall and removed a small bottle of ale, a wooden goblet, and a flat piece of bread. He set the food before Gawain, who eagerly began eating. The bearded Gawain was broad in shoulders and in girth and was one of the knights under the guide of Lord Henry, who ruled this village and others in the area.

Lord Henry. Butcher of Isle-sur-la-Sorgue. The man who ruled these villages and fields with a heavy and bloody hand. He had many knights and men in his service, and Father Stephen felt a small bit of comfort at being visited by Gawain. While a rough and crude man, Gawain did not quite share the blood taste that many of his fellow travelers at Lord Henry's manor shared.

Father Stephen sat down across from Gawain and asked, "And how I can be of assistance on this day, Gawain?"

The burly man drew a hand across his face, swallowed the last of the ale. "Two matters have arisen that require your service, Father. The first is the death of Thomas, son of Atwood. He died yesterday and his body needs to be shrived. Tonight, if possible."

Father Stephen nodded, not letting his disquiet show on his face. Thomas had been a bright young lad, son of the local tanner, who had a head for numbers and an interest in Latin. Father Stephen had wanted to see the boy enter the priesthood or the monastery, but Thomas was built like a bull, with wide shoulders and strong arms. So he had been called into knightly service, to put his arms under his lord, and now he was dead. Another young man with such promise, now growing cold. And for what? To be in service of those who kill. Now he is nothing, a body to be shrived, to receive penance.

Aloud, Father Stephen said, "I see. I will be ready to travel shortly. And what is the other matter of which you speak?"

Gawain belched and began picking at bread crumbs along the tabletop, wetting his thumb, picking each crumb up, and noisily sucking the morsel off. "The manner of his death, Father. I saw it myself. He was killed by a wizard, a wizard who lives in Lindsay Woods."

He folded his hands. "A wizard? In Lindsay Woods? And why were you there anyway? Are those woods not the property of Lord Mullen?"

Another satisfied belch and Gawain hooked a thumb in his sword belt. "True, those woods at one time did belong to that drunken fool. But there was a hearing at court, some complex thing that makes my head ache just thinking about it. A dispute between Lord Mullen and Lord Henry. All I know is that those woods now belong to our Lord Henry." He grinned. "Lord Mullen had been boastful, when he last saw Lord Henry. He said you may have those woods, but you will never possess them. A wizard lives there, and he will not let you nor anyone that belongs to Lord Henry pass on through. Any such shall die in those woods, and Lord Henry replied that while Normans no doubt believe in such tales, as a good Saxon he believes in cold iron and nothing else."

Father Stephen nodded. "I see. And Thomas was killed by this magical man yesterday, was he?"

Gawain now looked fearful, as he remembered the day. "Yes. There were three of us. William of deNoucy, myself, and Thomas. The young boy was eager, so I allowed him to ride first. It was late in the morning, almost at the noon sun, and we were riding along the trail. You pass over three streams along the way. The third stream is the boundary to Lindsay Woods. As we were riding up a slight hill, a tall man came out, in black robes bordered with red. The tallest man I had ever seen. He held up his hand and a staff, and said he would not allow us to pass."

Outside there were the sounds of crows, as they circled the fields being worked, seeking to pick at some scrap. "Then what happened?"

Gawain shuddered and crossed himself. "He seemed to be such an old man. I told Thomas to ride ahead and to push the man aside. I told him not to kill the old man, just to show him that Lord Henry was now the ruler of these woods. So Thomas laughed and drew his sword, and rode toward the man. That . . . that's when it happened."

Silence came into the small hut, and the flickering candle made Gawain's features seem to dance. Father Stephen looked into the fear of those eyes and felt a taste of disquiet. Gawain was known as one of the most fearless of all the knights and men at Lord Henry's manor. It was not a good thing to see, to see such a man frightened.

Gawain's voice seemed to tighten. "On my honor, Father, I swear that I am not telling a tale. This is what I truly did see, as did William of deNoucy. As Thomas rode toward the wizard, he raised his staff and uttered some words loudly, words I did not recognize. Then the end of the staff burst into flames and lightning, and Thomas fell from his horse. Our own mounts reared and tossed us both onto the ground, Father. When we got back on our own feet, all three horses had fled back down the trail. The wizard had disappeared. William and I were not severely injured, but Thomas . . . he was dead, Father. In an instant."

"I see," he said. "And did the wizard reappear?"

"Nay, he did not."

"And what did you and William do then?"

"We carried Thomas between us, and led him to a small home that belongs to a woodcutter named Harold, just outside of Lindsay Woods. Along the way we found all three of our horses, including Thomas's mount. All three were still shaking and foaming with fear. I then went to Lord Henry, where he then commanded me to retrieve you, to give the Last Rites for Thomas's immortal soul."

Father Stephen got up from the stool and went to another shelf, where he took down a small leather satchel that held his vestments and sacred oils. "For that I will do. And that is all."

Gawain shook his massive head. "I fear not, Father. For Lord Henry also demands that you vanquish the wizard."

He felt his throat tighten up at the thought of Lord Henry. "Our lord did, did he? And did he say how I was to vanquish this wizard?"

Gawain now looked embarrassed. "I know not, Father. Lord Henry said . . . well, he said that you would be able to do so."

Father Stephen returned to the table. "What exactly did our lord say about me?"

The knight said shyly, "He said that Father Stephen is known widely among these lands as a particularly holy man, and if wizards are in the employ of the devil, then Father Stephen should have no difficulty banishing him from Lindsay Woods."

"I see," he said, looking into the man's disturbed face. "Tell me, Gawain. Do you believe in spirits, in witches, in the life of wizards?"

Gawain answered. "I am a simple man, Father, who believes in the end of the sword, and not much else. Yet I have seen and heard things that strike fear into me. Lights in the sky. Screams in the night. Stories from my fellow knights of odd things that have happened in the woods. And this wizard, killing Thomas with a staff, some distance away. I know the legends and the tales. I know not if all of these tales are true. But I do know what I saw with my own eyes. I saw this wizard and what he did." There was a pause, and Gawain spoke again. "And you, Father? What do you believe in?"

Father Stephen said, "I believe in our Lord God and nothing else. Let us depart."

GAWAIN RODE ON HIS black horse, called Shadow, while Father Stephen made do with his donkey, called Job, which he kept in a small stall built on the side of his house. Along with his satchel he brought along a simple wool blanket, rolled up. Gawain sighed heavily as he slowed his horse's gait to match the plodding stride of Job.

"Cannot Lord Henry supply you with a horse?" Gawain asked. "One would think a priest of your stature would . . . well, you think he would supply you with a mount better than your donkey."

"A donkey such as Job brought our Lord Jesus into Jerusalem," Father Stephen said, looking out on the fields and woods surrounding his stone church, Saint Agatha's. "I deserve no better. I am just a simple priest."

Gawain kept silent for a half dozen gaits, and said softly, "Father, you know you are more than just a simple priest. A man such as yourself, Oxford learned and the brother of Lord Henry himself, a man who once carried arms, you could do better. You should at least be a bishop."

Father Stephen saw the stooped-over figures of the men and women and children of his church, whom he blessed and married and baptized and buried. His people, his flock, his responsibility. "God's work needs to be done, and I am a better man for doing it here."

"Is it God's will, then?"

"No," he said sharply. "It is mine. And we will speak of it no further."

IT WAS DARK WHEN they reached the hut that belonged to the woodcutter Harold and his family, and the family of the dead knight Thomas was there as well. The man's body was laid out on a table outside, clad only in a shroud, and as the people about him sobbed and cried out, Father Stephen went through the rituals of the Last Rites. *Quid quid delquisti* . . . Though he had not been here at the time of Thomas's death, this was the best he could do, and as he said aloud the Latin phrases, he looked down at the young man's face.

My poor Thomas, he thought, how did you come to this? A chance to inhabit the world of learning and books and knowledge, the true path of God's work, to learn more about you and your world, and you turned it down. You chose the easy path, the path of fame and wealth and honor and death, of course, death all about you. Men with swords and shields and armor, spreading death among the simple people, his flock. Burning homes and fields for coin and honor, bloody swords rising up and down, the stench of smoldering hay and wooden beams, the harsh cries of the men, the screams of the women, and the piercing cries of the children, newly orphaned. . . .

He stopped, his mind awhirl. He could not remember what to say next. In the dim light of the torches, the people looked toward him, looked toward their shepherd in this world to lead them to the light, to lead them from the darkness. For just a moment the old memories came back and he felt like a fraud, an impostor. What was he doing here? What could he possibly do for these people? He was terrified for an instant, at being uncovered for what he was.

But only for a moment. The eyes of some of the children up front were looking at him, trusting in him, knowing that he spoke for God. He went on and completed the services, if for no one else, then at least for the children. *In nomine Patris, et Filii, et Spiritus sancti.* Amen.

LATER HE SPOKE TO Gawain and said, "I have need of you, and a torch, and nobody else."

"What for, Father?"

"I wish to look at Thomas."

Gawain gulped audibly. "In what manner, Father?"

Father Stephen said, "He was killed by a wizard. I wish to see if I can learn how this deed was done. You will agree there is no wizard here among us. I cannot talk to him. But the wizard's work remains. I wish to see it."

"But Father . . . I mean . . ."

He grasped the man's shoulder. "Have no fear, Gawain. For we are doing God's work this evening, and God will not allow us to fall into any harm. Our brother Thomas is gone. Only his body remains. We will not disturb his flesh or bones. We will only look. Do come with me."

They were outside again, and Gawain spoke briefly with the family of Thomas, who all crossed themselves and went into the woodcutter's hut. The night sounds of frogs and crickets filled the cool air and Father Stephen stepped closer. Gawain was behind him, as if seeking comfort from having the priest move in first. "Bring the torch up behind me, if you will," he said, and as Gawain did so, he saw that the features of the young man were beginning to change. He would have to be buried early on the morrow, before the rot set in. He said a brief prayer and then undid the shroud, and the torchlight began to quaver.

He looked back and saw that Gawain's hand was shaking. "Be strong, Gawain," he whispered. "Be strong."

When the shroud was lying aside, he bent over and examined the flesh. There were old marks and scars along the shoulders and wrists and legs, from even such short service as a knight, but there was a fresh wound that intrigued him.

"Here," he said, "bring the torch in closer to the chest."

The light flickered some more, and Father Stephen heard Gawain murmuring a prayer, the Latin words nearly meaningless in the rush to be said. He looked at the wound, which was in the center of the chest. It was almost round in its shape, and about as wide as his thumb.

"Look there," he said. "Gawain, have you ever seen such a wound?"

"Nay, Father, I have not." The knight's voice sounded strained.

"Nor have I." He went around to the side and grasped the dead boy's shoulders, and pulled him to his side. The dead boy's flesh was cold and stiff and he murmured a quick prayer, asking for forgiveness for disturbing him such as this. His view was blocked and Father Stephen said, "Gawain, do you see anything on his back? Another wound?"

"Father, aye, I do. But this one is bigger and has torn his flesh so. Father, please, I am disturbed. Are we finished here?"

He gently lowered the boy's body down and blessed him yet again. "Yes, Gawain, we are."

Dinner was bread and ale and seasoned cold venison, and he and Gawain slept in the rear barn on a pile of hay. The woodcutter had offered to let him sleep in their tiny home, but that would mean putting some of the children out in the barn, and that he would not do. He would not disturb the children. They made their beds as well as they could, as they heard the rustle of rats among them. Gawain extinguished a small oil lamp that they had borrowed from the woodcutter and he rested his head back in his hands, staring up at the darkness.

"Gawain?" Father Stephen asked, resting there in the night.

"Aye, Father."

"Did you know Thomas well, before he died?"

He could hear the crackling of hay as Gawain shifted. "No, not really, Father. I just knew that he was young and eager, and quite strong."

Father Stephen sighed. "Did you know that he had a taste for learning? That for a while he was eager to learn how to read and write? Did you know that?"

"No, Father, I did not."

Of course not, Father Stephen thought. You and your kind, all that matters is the moment, the manner of death and honor, and blood being spilled. Always and always, blood being spilled.

"The day of his death," Father Stephen said.

"Yes?"

"What was he wearing? What kind of armor?"

"Why, none, Father. He was just wearing a cloak, his hose, and a leather jerkin. For we feared not that we would encounter any men of arms on our trip to Lindsay Woods."

"No, just a wizard, am I right? An old man who could be pushed away or killed without much work on your part."

"Aye," came the sad voice. "You are right."

He thought for a moment longer and said, "Gawain, after the burial tomorrow of Thomas, we must travel."

Gawain's voice was troubled. "To Lindsay Woods?"

"No, to Lord Henry's manor. We must see him, and I must talk to him."

The knight's voice was cautionary. "He will not be pleased, to see you without news of the wizard's death."

"His pleasure is not my worry," Father Stephen said. "Now, I bid you a good night's sleep, Gawain."

"And you, too, Father."

Father Stephen pulled his old wool blanket over him and turned over, soon listening to the whistling snore of Gawain and the squeaks and rustles from the rats sharing their quarters.

THE MORNING MEAL WAS old bread, dried apples, and another small piece of venison, and in a cleared area near the path, they laid Thomas's body to rest. It was not a churchyard but it would have to do, and later, Father Stephen would come back to consecrate this ground. The hole had been dug and Thomas's body had been wrapped in the shroud, and as his body was lowered into the ground, Father Stephen said the Latin prayers again, commending Thomas's soul unto the Lord. The boy's family and the family of Harold the woodcutter watched on, and some of the children—bored at what was going on—played in the distance. Life, Father Stephen thought, life does go on. No matter what the men at arms say.

When the services were done and the last of the dirt had been shoveled over the body by Harold and the boy's uncle, Father Stephen got onto his donkey and said to Gawain, "Now, we travel."

"Aye, Father. Whatever you say."

THE MIDDAY MEAL WAS eaten along the way, more dried apples and stale heels of bread, and as they approached the large, cultivated fields around the manor house of Lord Henry, Gawain said, "There are many things that I do not understand, Father."

"Then do not fret," he said. "For that is the way of the world. And what is the matter for which you do not understand?"

Gawain waved a hand about their surroundings. "You could be here, Father. Either at your brother's side or serving your church, but you could be here. In warm quarters, eating meat every day. Meeting with travelers and lords who read and write as you do, and who speak Latin as well. Educated people, traveled people. Yet you stay in Bromley, in a muddy house with a leaky roof, eating food that is no better than what the villains eat. Why is that?"

"Because that is what I have chosen," he said carefully.

Gawain glared at him from his high perch on his saddle. "That is no answer, Father, and you know it."

"Then that is the best answer you can have. Look, we near my brother's manor. Let us not talk of it any more."

As their mounts were led away, Father Stephen looked with a critical eye at the manor, the place where he had been born and had been raised. There were a few happy memories here but not too many. His older brother had been his father's son, and he had been his mother's. While Henry learned the ways of armor and battle and fighting, he had learned to read and write and had memorized the old tales and songs. He had even done some learning at nearby Oxford. They had been brothers but had been rivals, right from the start. Their three sisters—all now married off, and one, Celeste, living in Burgundy—had stayed within their own manors, and he had not seen them for years.

But it had not been a bad life, not until their mother and father had taken ill and had died, within a week of each other. Henry had been thrust into the head of the family, and in some complicated plot to increase his power and his holdings, he had traveled to France, to fight for King Edward, old Longshanks. And Stephen had gone along as well, as a frightened yet eager young knight, to show his older brother that he, too, could fight for their family, even if he was book-learned and knew how to read and write Latin.

He shook his head at the memories, looked again at the manor. Henry had done well. Part of the manor had been expanded, and it looked like some of the windows had been replaced with real glass. The large door to the manor opened and a tall man came out, bowed in their direction. It was Ambrose, Lord Henry's head servant. "Father, Lord Henry bids you welcome, and invites you to join him."

Father Stephen bowed back. "As he wishes."

As they dismounted Gawain said, "And how did Lord Henry know we were approaching?"

"These are my brother's lands," he said. "No doubt we were spotted some distance away, and the news came here quickly. My brother does not like to be surprised by unwelcome guests."

Shortly they were in the manor hall, where tables were set up on the stone flooring. Tapestries hung along the wall and even some music was being played, by a player of the fiddle and a player of a pipe in one corner. Dogs wandered about, snarling and biting at each other over scraps tossed at them by the well-dressed men and women sitting at the long tables. Lord Henry—and my, how his brother had gotten heavy and his beard gray—sat at the table at the head of the room, laughing loud at something. Next to him was a thin girl, Lady Catherine, a young girl not yet thirteen, and who had been betrothed to Henry to settle some land dispute.

Father Stephen murmured a quiet prayer as he advanced across the room. That laughter from his brother brought back memories of their time in France, the laughter as he bounded into battle and slaughtered the inhabitants of a village whose only crime was that they pledged their loyalty to a French king.

"Come, come," his brother yelled out. "Look who approaches." He belched and swayed in his great chair, and Father Stephen realized Lord Henry was drunk. His brother yelled out, "My holy brother comes to greet me. Do you bring me good news, then? Has the wizard been vanquished? Did you bathe him in Holy Water? Did you strike at him with a relic of Saint Agnes? Did you bid him farewell by tossing phrases at him in Latin?"

Lord Henry laughed and the other people in the great hall laughed as well, and dogs barked some more as scraps were tossed to them. Father Stephen thought of the hungry families in his village, who would gladly get on the floor to wrestle the scraps away from the dogs, and he stepped closer to his older brother.

"No," he said, speaking clearly and plainly. "The wizard has not yet been vanquished. And if he is to be vanquished by my services, then I demand payment."

From behind him he listened to the gasp of anguish from Gawain, and then the sudden silence, as the laughter and the jeers from the guests quieted. Even the musicians had silenced themselves. There was snarling from two battling dogs by the doorway and no other sound. Lady Catherine sat very still, her thin hands in her lap. Lord Henry's face grew redder and he said, his voice no longer booming and full of laughter, "What nonsense is this?"

"There is no nonsense," Father Stephen said. "Just fair compensation, for ridding your new possession of Lindsay Woods of a wizard, a wizard who has killed one of your knights."

Lord Henry stared right at him. "You are a servant of the church. You will do your duty."

"Aye, but I am not a servant of you, Lord Henry. I serve a greater master. To fight against a wizard who is not in my village, who has not harmed anyone of my parish, is something that I must be compensated for. It is only fair."

"I shall not pay you, or any other meddlesome priest, by God," he growled. "For I will take care of this matter myself. You can go back to your muddy village and starve for all I care."

"Really?" Father Stephen said, looking about the faces of the men among the guests. "Which one of your knights or compatriots wishes to ride against a wizard, a man who strikes death from afar? I have seen what he has done. I have held Thomas's own body in my hands, have seen the dreadful wound that this wizard has caused. I can vanquish the wizard easily, my Lord, but to do so, I demand payment. It is only fair. You know that well."

Lord Henry stared at him again, and Father Stephen willed his legs not to quake. The look from those eyes was similar to what he had seen in battle in France, when Henry was approaching his enemies, and Father Stephen knew that was what his brother now considered him: an enemy, nothing else.

"A compensation, then," Lord Henry said. "What price does a servant of God place upon destroying a wizard?"

He took a deep breath. "One-third of Lindsay Woods to be given to the Church of Saint Agnes, for service to the poor and our parish. That is all."

"All?" Henry shouted. "That is all? One-third of my property to a useless man of the cloth? One-third of my property to one who will not raise arms against my enemies? Who will not perform his rightly duties for his family?"

By now Henry was on his feet, and his young wife was trembling as she listened to his shouts. Even the dogs had run away from the inside of the hall, and Father Stephen saw how all the guests were now looking away, as if afraid that by looking at Lord Henry, they, too, would incur his wrath.

Father Stephen clasped his hands before him in a prayerful gesture, but one that he knew was only being done to prevent his hands from shaking. Trying to keep his voice level, he called out,

"My lord, my duties are now to the Church and to God. I have taken a sacred oath, one that cannot be broken, even by a man as powerful as you. While I no longer raise arms against your enemies, I am a loyal subject to our king and to you. Yet I am not a slave nor a serf. I ask for compensation fairly, not for my own purse, but to aid the Church and the people whom she serves."

"One-third," Lord Henry muttered, looking around the room. "One-third . . . "

"With all respect and graciousness, my lord, you know as well as I do that with the wizard in those woods, and the death that he can incur in the snap of a finger, that those woods of yours will forever be useless. It is better to have two-thirds of something, my lord, rather than three-thirds of nothing."

A few brave souls at the rear of the manor hall—who could not readily be identified—chuckled in appreciation at his comments, and Lord Henry sat heavily down upon his great chair. Lady Catherine tried to hide a tiny smile with a handkerchief. He pulled up a goblet of ale and emptied it in a few large swallows, and then tossed the empty goblet upon the stone floor.

"Is this how you repay your older brother?" he said. "I called upon you to rid me of this wizard, to bring yourself fame and attention in these parts. Nothing else. And you come to me, filled with impertinence, demanding payment. I think, younger brother, it would have been better for all of us if you had not come back to Bromley from France."

Father Stephen bowed slightly. "I came back from France due to God's will, and nothing else."

Lord Henry raised a hand dismissively. "If the wizard is vanquished, then you will receive your one-third of Lindsay Woods, priest. And may those woods be cursed to you and whoever from your church who gains to profit from them."

A little voice inside of him said, You won, you've actually won, but Father Stephen pressed forward. "There is the matter of two more items, my lord."

Lord Henry managed to smile. "Two more subjects, you slippery toad? And what might they be?"

"When I left this manor years ago, I left behind a trunk of some of my possessions. I wish to examine this trunk."

"What, so you can charge me with theft?"

"No, my lord. It is just a matter that I must attend to."

Lady Catherine stroked her husband's arm and whispered into an ear. He said, "Yes, yes, you may examine the trunk. My servant Ambrose will tell you where it is. And what is the second matter, and be quick about it."

"I plan to ride out and meet with the wizard tomorrow," Father Stephen said. "I wish to be accompanied by one of your knights. Gawain. And none other."

Father Stephen thought he heard the knight's low moan from behind him. His older brother scowled and said, "And what for? So he may kill this wizard if you lose your nerve?"

"No," Father Stephen clearly said. "So that he may come back and tell you if I have failed, and that the wizard has indeed killed me."

Lord Henry's smile was quite wide. "That will indeed be worth the time of one of my knights. So it shall be done. Now, leave me and this room. You bore me, priest."

He nodded and quickly walked out, hoping his legs would not quite give out until he had passed through the door.

THE STALL AT LEAST had some clean hay, and Father Stephen made his bed again among the dry grasses. This barn was large, and there were the grunts and whinnies of some of the lord's horses to keep him company. He knew that as a brother of Lord Henry and a son of the man who had first built this place, that he could have demanded better quarters. But when Lord Henry's head servant Ambrose had directed him to these stables, he had not protested. Nor had he protested when Ambrose had said the kitchen servants were no longer available, so no evening meal could be provided. Father Stephen would give his older brother these tiny victories. He had gained one much greater.

He pulled his wool blanket about him and tried not to think of tomorrow, but only the here and now. He said his evening prayers and ate a dried apple that he had saved from their midday meal, and when he had closed his eyes, he tried to go to sleep.

But sleep would not come. There was someone else in the stable, someone coming in his direction. He could hear the steps upon the stone walkway leading past the main stables. A cold touch of fear stirred in his chest. He knew his brother well. His brother had been bested and humiliated today in front of his peers. Perhaps that was not worth the eventual use of a portion of Lindsay Woods. Perhaps the death of an impertinent younger brother would make Lord Henry a pleased man this evening. There were many knights and men at arms who would come in this stable tonight with a sharp blade, to do their Lord's bidding, as knights did Henry II's bidding in killing Saint Thomas á Becket in Canterbury so many years ago. The flickering light of a small lamp was now visible.

Father Stephen spoke up. "If you mean to see me and do me harm, then do approach now, and waste not either of our evenings."

A familiar voice came to him in reply. "That is an odd thing to say, Father Stephen, to one who is trying to bring you a meal."

From the darkness Gawain emerged and sat down heavily on the hay next to Father Stephen. He held a wooden bowl that he passed over and which Father Stephen bent to. There was a hunk of cheese, some ham, and soft, freshly baked white bread. He ate the feast and offered some to Gawain, who declined.

"No, Father, I've had my fill of the lord's hospitality tonight. When I heard where they had placed you and how they had not fed you, well . . . it did not seem right. So here I am."

"Bless you, Gawain, for your thoughtfulness," he said earnestly.

"Bah," he said. "What kind of blessings have you brought upon me, to demand that I accompany you tomorrow to meet the wizard?"

He finished the last of the bread. "What I said earlier to my brother was true. I do not require your presence to fight the wizard. I will do that on my own. I require you to be a witness, that is all. You need not put yourself in any harm."

Then, Father Stephen was surprised when Gawain grunted in reply and blew out the light. Gawain shifted his weight in the hay and Father Stephen could make him out, lying down next to him.

"Why are you here?" he asked. "Should you not go back to your own quarters?"

"Aye, you are right," the knight said wearily. "I should go back. In fact, there is a new serving girl who has looked at me with interest, and I feel sure that I would not be spending my night alone if I had spoken to her earlier. But still . . . it is not right that you be in the stable alone, Father. I decided to come here and share your quarters, as poor as they are."

"That is noble of you, Gawain."

"Bah, nobility has nothing to do with it," he said. "I wanted to speak to you, Father, about you and your brother. His lordship said something earlier, about your not returning to Bromley from France, and about your not taking arms to defend your family. What was the meaning of those words?"

In the darkness, now, in the dark it was easy to remember. With no light, with nothing to look at but the blackness, it was easy to recall all those memories. Not only the sights of what he had seen in France, but the sounds as well. The creak of leather. The clang of swords against shields. The gurgling cries of the wounded, drowning in their own blood. The dark growls of the horses, riding in fear. The snapping sounds of timber and thatch burning. And the scents, as well. The strong smell of spilt blood. The stench of sweat and tears. The musky odors of villages and bodies being burnt.

"It is no secret," Father Stephen said slowly, "that I was not always a priest. That I once raised arms in defense of my family and for our king. That is all. That is no secret."

"But what happened, then, to change everything?" Gawain asked, pressing on. "What happened?"

And then he surprised himself, by letting go, by telling tales that he had only shared with his confessor. "I was young when I was with my brother in France. It was a glorious adventure, at first. To serve your family, to serve your King, and to serve your God. It all seemed destined, all seemed right. The first few battles, knights against knights, they were desperate battles, but they had a . . . well, a righteousness about them. But later, then, we pressed a siege against a French town. The town belonged to the King of England, but they pledged their loyalties to the King of France. My brother would not let this happen. We laid siege to the village and when we finally broke through their walls, the killing started. The burning of the homes and farms. The slaughter not only of the men at arms, but the women as well. And the old men. And the children."

Oh, the cries of the small children, as the knights chased them along the muddy paths, screaming for their mother, screaming for their father, screaming for the Lord God to save them all. . . .

"When I saw all that happened, I threw away my sword and left the battle," he said. "I could not stand to see what I had done, in aiding my brother and our family and our King. I swore then on that bloody soil, that if I survived getting back to England, that I would enter the priesthood and serve the poor, the people who have no arms nor men to defend them. That is what I swore, and that has angered my brother ever since."

Gawain spoke softly to him. "But you were in the service of your King, and your God, when you were in France. There was nothing wrong in what you did, you must know that."

"Hah," Father Stephen said. "What I do know is that the King of England and the King of France and all the people they rule, they all worship the same God, and that God must shed tears of anger and sorrow at what those Kings do in His name. And when I witnessed this by own eyes, and I saw what I had joined in doing, I knew that I could no longer raise arms, nor support those men who raise arms as well. And that is what I have done."

"And what will you do tomorrow, against the wizard?"

Father Stephen rolled over in the hay. "I will do the bidding of my God, to help my people. Nothing else."

If Gawain said anything in reply, Father Stephen did not hear it. Soon, Gawain was snoring, loud enough to drown out the sounds of the horses in their stalls, and the ever-present rustling of rats in the stored hay.

MORNING DAWNED COLD AND wet, with a heavy mist over the fields of Lord Henry's manor. Today was the feast day of Saint Mark, the Evangelist. Father Stephen had gotten up the earliest and had examined his old trunk, given to him as a young boy by his parents, and where he had stored his old memories and possessions of his previous life. The chest had been in a crowded cellar and when he was done, he had been glad to get out into the morning light.

He had clambered up on his donkey, Job, his chest feeling heavy and slow, and he joined Gawain out in the front of the manor. And to his surprise, they were not alone. Lord Henry was there, in simple clothes, sitting astride a huge white horse, his face scowling yet again.

"Ah, so the priest is still here and has not run away, his bowels and bladder loose with fear," he said, holding the reins of his horse tightly in his beefy hands.

Father Stephen nodded. "I have pledged to you that I will vanquish this wizard today. Just as you have pledged to pass over one-third of Lindsay Woods to my church when this deed is done."

Lord Henry managed a smile. "Ah, priest, but perhaps I do not recall making such a pledge. Perhaps the drink I had last night loosened my tongue and my wits. Perhaps there is no such pledge."

Again, he nodded, in polite deference. "My lord, of course, is correct. Perhaps there is no pledge. Yet I remind him that he uttered such a pledge in front of numerous lords and ladies yesterday in his manor hall. To back away from such a pledge . . . well, my lord knows all too well what would happen to his reputation and standing among his peers and subjects."

His brother's face was glaring again, and even his horse shifted anxiously, stomping one hoof and then another. "Be gone, priest, and be quick. The King has called a council, about a campaign upon Scotland, and I need not to burden my mind with the problems of a wizard and poor priest. Go on and do what must be done."

"So I shall, my brother, so I shall."

But before Lord Henry went to return to the manor, he leaned over his mount and spoke quietly to Gawain, who nodded at the words told to him. Then Gawain moved on, spurring his horse, Shadow, to the open road. When Father Stephen started out to the trail, he looked back, knowing somehow that he would never again see his brother or the manor.

THE TRIP WAS SLOWER this time, as the weight about his chest and shoulders seemed to grow heavier with each passing step. Even his donkey, Job, seemed burdened by all that had occurred, and Father Stephen could sense the frustration of Gawain, riding next to him.

"By God, Father," he growled, "could we at least pick up our pace? I do not want to face this wizard at dusk or at dark. I want this awful job done as soon as possible, in the brightness of noon, if possible."

Father Stephen replied, "We will be there when we get there, and not any sooner. Be patient, Gawain, be patient."

Eventually, they were in the fields near Lindsay Woods, and they crossed the first of the three streams, and then the second. When they approached the third stream, Gawain crossed himself and halted his horse next to Father Stephen. The stream was wide and seemed deep, and it moved with ferocity, raising white-caps and spumes of spray.

"There, Father," he said, his voice lowered. "To the right is a ford, which even your donkey should be able to traverse. Then, the trail goes up this slight hill. Near the top of the hill is where we saw the wizard."

Father Stephen stayed quiet, his chest and back aching with the weight he was carrying. The sounds were of their animals breathing and the rushing of the stream. It seemed like all of the animals of the woods had disappeared, as if the wizard had bade them to run away and not witness what was about to occur. He, too, crossed himself. He was sure earlier of what he was to do and what would happen, but he was no fool. He felt the taste of fear, a taste that was even stronger than when he was in the muddy fields of France, fighting for his life against another swordsman.

He spoke up. "I will go first, Gawain. Please do follow me, but do not be reckless or bold. This is my matter, not yours. I will approach the wizard and face him down, no matter what magic or fiery staff he may possess. God rides with us both, this I promise. Be not afraid."

Gawain pulled out his sword and laid it across the spine of his horse. "I am afraid, this I do admit. But I will follow you, Father. Do lead on."

Father Stephen pulled on the reins, and Job reluctantly stepped into the water. Job was not one to hesitate, no matter how stubborn he could be, and he wondered if perhaps the poor dumb beast could sense the danger that was ahead. The water wet his feet and legs but then he was on the other side, in Lindsay Woods. He turned and saw Gawain splashing across, to join him. Father Stephen smiled at him, then reached into his robes, and took out a small crucifix.

He started saying the Our Father as he went up the hill. *Pater noster qui es in coelis. . . .* As he approached the top of the hill, the fear that had been there earlier returned with a vengeance, like a mid-winter storm. An old man with a white beard was at the top of the hill, clad in robes of red and black, holding up his hand as to halt them both. The man was tall, quite tall, possibly the tallest man he had ever seen. In his other hand, he held a long staff of wood and metal. Just like Gawain had said.

The wizard of Lindsay Woods.

Father Stephen raised up his crucifix and pressed on.

IT WAS THE WIZARD who spoke first. "Get ye away from here. These are my woods, my home. Ye have no right here. Get away before I kill thee all."

His donkey, Job, seemed to start at the sounds of the old man. His voice was raspy and low, as if he had shouted for many days as a young lad.

Father Stephen swallowed, noting how dry his mouth had become. He raised up his crucifix. "I bid you to leave, old man.

These woods belong to Lord Henry. You have no right of owner-
ship. Let us pass and then be on your way, before any harm comes
to you."

The wizard laughed. "A priest, are ye? I have traveled long
and far in this world, priest, to learn that your religion is no more
the true religion than any other. There are many places and
people who have never heard of you and your God. Ye have no
power over me. So leave, now, damn ye, before I smite ye down."

He held up the crucifix again and spurred on Job, who was
breathing hard and struggling against the reins. But move on the
donkey did, and Father Stephen spoke aloud, "Move away,
wizard, before harm befalls you. I command you in the name of
God and Lord Henry to depart this place forever."

As he spoke, he saw something on a rock near the wizard's
lance. Something was smoldering there, a wisp of smoke rising
up. The wizard cackled again and said, "I warned ye, and now ye
shall die!"

The old man moved quickly for one so aged, for he grasped
some smoldering stick and brought it up in his left hand. With his
right hand he held out the staff of metal and wood, and Father
Stephen saw another V-shaped stick there as well, now holding
up the staff. He spurred on Job and then the wizard cackled
again, started shouting in a strange tongue, and he brought the
smoking stick against the side of the staff.

What happened next happened almost as fast as the blink of
an eye, for there was a loud thunderclap, like a sudden appearance of a rainstorm, and the end of the staff spew forth a cloud of
smoke and fire, and then something hammered at his chest, and
Father Stephen fell to the ground, unable to breathe, unable to
move, unable even to pray.

EVERYTHING WAS GRAY, FOR what seemed to be a long time. Then
Father Stephen coughed and sat up. His chest throbbed and
ached, and before him were two figures. He wiped at his eyes
and saw Gawain standing over the figure of the wizard, cursing,

and raising up his sword. Father Stephen shouted, "No, do not kill him, I forbid it!"

With sword raised, Gawain turned to him in astonishment. "By all the saints . . . Father, you are still alive?"

He grabbed at his chest and stumbled to his feet. Job and Shadow were nowhere to be found. "I am. I may be in some pain, but I am alive. Pray to come over here and assist me."

Gawain came to him as Father Stephen removed his outer robe, and Gawain again looked at him in amazement. Underneath the cloak Father Stephen wore a dull-colored breastplate, a piece of armor he had not worn since returning from France during those cold and bloody days, and which had been stored in the trunk back at the manor. The armor still fit him well and was in good shape, save for the deep dent now in the center. Though now aching and dizzy, he felt good at having guessed right about the true nature of the wizard's power. He had no doubt there were witches and wizards in this world. But he found it easier to believe in the actions of man. He undid the straps and let the armor fall to the ground, and then strode uneasily over to the wizard.

Gawain followed, saying, "When he smote you down, Father, I had to come and strike at him, no matter what the consequences. Bad enough that he killed the young Thomas in my presence. I could not allow him to kill you as well without replying in kind."

Father Stephen knelt down to the old man. His staff was on the ground, some distance away. There was a stench in the air, of decay and sulfur. Blood was on the wizard's lips, and soiled the side of his robe. The robe had also fallen across the man's thin legs, and Father Stephen noted the small stilts he had been standing on. Stilts, hidden by his robes, and which made him that much taller.

"He has been injured," Father Stephen said.

"Aye," Gawain said. "I struck him a blow after you fell, and I was to strike again before you stopped me. Yet I believe my first blow may be enough."

The wizard's eyes fluttered open, and he coughed, and smiled again. "The strong man is right, he is, and I fear I am mortally injured."

Father Stephen bent closer. "Who are you, then, old man? A friend or relative?"

"A friend or relative of who, do you ask?"

"Of Lord Mullen, the previous owner of these woods. The tale of the Wizard of Lindsay Woods came to pass only after these woods were taken from him and given to Lord Henry. Not before. The wizard who supposedly haunted these woods has only been here for a short while. So, who are you, then?"

Another cough. "I am his older brother, I am. William."

Gawain shook his head. "That cannot be true. William is believed dead. He left for one of the last Holy Crusades, years ago."

The old man cackled. "That is true, that is true, and here I am, back among our family estates, though everyone thought I had died, years ago. I did go on the Holy Crusade, and the places I went and the things I saw . . . such poor peasants as yourself would never believe what I saw, what I did."

Father Stephen eyed the wizard's staff. "Is that where you got your staff, the one that makes so much noise and propels a stone with such speed that it can kill?"

"No, not stone," William said, his voice growing softer. "A piece of soft metal. I stole the staff from a merchant from Cathay, where I served as a slave for years. I also stole some of the soft metal and a bag of the powder that ignites so easily. . . . Cathay, a place where the men and the women dress in such luxuries, yet their eyes are like cats . . . Cathay . . ."

Gawain said, "So why were you here, playing at being a wizard?"

Father Stephen answered him. "So the woods would be thought to be haunted. So that all travelers would avoid it. So that sometime in the future, Lord Mullen could get it back from Lord Henry, at a pittance. Am I right, William?"

A slow nod, as blood started trickling down into his beard. "You are a smart one, priest. A smart one. You outfoxed me by wearing that armor under your cloak. . . . If I had put more of the fire powder inside the lance, you might not have lived. . . ."

"But I did, William, I did."

Gawain started to say something but Father Stephen held up his hand, as the old man murmured something. Father Stephen bent over and said, "Please speak again, William."

A soft, breathy voice. "I meant not what I said earlier, in insulting you, Father. Would you . . . would you . . . give me the Last Rites? Please?"

Father Stephen nodded. "Of course."

And as he began the prayers, the old man died.

THEY BURIED HIM IN the woods, and when they went out into the open, Gawain picked up the staff and examined it. "Now I can see how it works," he said. "There is a small hole here at the base, where that small stick that was burning was placed. It ignited the powder inside and propelled that metal that killed young Thomas and knocked you from Job."

Gawain looked up. "Yonder is the bag that contains the fire powder. I must bring these back to Lord Henry. His alchemist can determine what is in the powder, and his smithy can see how this fire lance was made. Imagine how powerful his knights will be once they have weapons such as these."

Father Stephen picked up the small bag that contained a black, gritty powder, and lumps of metal. "You are right, of course, Gawain. May I examine the staff, as well?"

Gawain handed over the tube of metal and wood, which felt heavy. There were elaborate carvings along the wooden base, showing dragons and other creatures. He looked up at Gawain and said, "My friend, is that your horse, coming down the hill?"

When Gawain turned Father Stephen tossed the bag with the powder into the stream, and then smashed the fire staff once and then twice against the near boulder. After the metal and wood had been bent and broken, and before the bellowing Gawain could get any closer, he tossed the destroyed lance into the raging waters of the stream as well.

"Father!" Gawain shouted. "What in the name of the Blessed Mary and the Saints did you do that for? Do you know what you've just done?"

Father Stephen's chest ached and his throat still was dry; but he pressed on. "Earlier today, what did my brother tell you, before we left?"

Gawain glared at him. "I cannot say."

"Ah, you cannot say, but I can certainly guess. He told you that if the wizard was just a man, and nothing else, that after I vanquished him you should find out what his weapon was and bring it back to him. Am I right?"

Gawain still looked angry. "The old man was right. You are a smart one. But why, Father?"

Father Stephen felt his chest, felt the tender area that had been hurt by that hurtling piece of metal. "Why? You need to ask me that question, why? It's a weapon of barbarism, that is why. You see how much blood men armed only with swords and bows spill on this good earth, day in and day out. Can you imagine the slaughter that can occur, if each knight, if each man of arms, can kill with such a weapon as this staff? Who can kill from afar? What that can mean to the villages and people of this land?"

Gawain said, "That may be true, Father, but you saw with your own eyes. This weapon exists. It is from Cathay. One of these days it will come back to this island, will come back to men such as Lord Henry."

Father Stephen nodded, and went over and picked up his robe. "Perhaps you are right. Perhaps it will come next year, perhaps next century. And perhaps in that time, men on this island will finally come to listen to the words of God, learn to love each other, and put down the tools of killing."

Gawain sighed and bent down to pick up his sword. "That day may never come, Father."

"True, but only if we let it happen," Father Stephen said. "Only if we let it happen, and I intend to do my best not to see it happen. That is my calling. To work for my people and to work for peace."

LATER, AFTER THEY HAD recovered both Shadow and Job and began riding out of Lindsay Woods, Gawain said, "What do you intend to tell Lord Henry?"

"Me?" Father Stephen said. "I intend to say nothing, and to return to my parish. It is up to you to tell him what happened this day, that we were successful in killing the wizard and freeing Lindsay Woods for his lordship. Two-thirds to him, of course, and one-third to my parish."

Gawain said, "He will complain."

"Aye, he will complain, but he will proceed. He must, to preserve his name among his peers. And it will also be up to you, Gawain, on what you will say—or won't say—about the fire staff."

The knight laughed. "Say? I will say nothing, Father, since I have nothing to show. Who would believe me, that a weapon exists that would allow a serf or slave to kill a knight from afar, without even touching him?"

As they rode away, the image of the old man William bothered him for a while, the older brother, trying to protect the lands of his younger brother. That is all. A sad thing, to die in defense of one's brother, after having traveled across Europe and to Cathay. Yet noble. Father Stephen imagined it must be a pleasurable thing, to have such a brother.

Still, a sad thing, all the same, but Father Stephen soon thought of other things, as well. A new roof for the church. More land for himself, to grow more food to help those families who nearly starved each year. More peace for the people of the village of Bromley, and of course, a future—and if God willed it, not too far off—when men of arms turned their swords into plowshares, so that the villages would no longer burn and that the children would no longer cry.

God willing, he would live long enough to see that day.

Improvements

Kristine Kathryn Rusch

When the strange woman appeared, Maude was in the buttery, speaking with the clerk of the kitchen about his latest round of purchases. He went to market too often, she thought, and was too extravagant for the types of meals he produced. She would, if he did not modify his expenditures, have to fire him.

He would be the first servant she fired since her husband died.

The very idea filled her with dread. She had run the household since her marriage ten years before, but her husband had handled the money, the hiring and firing of servants, and the overall management of the large estate.

Now she managed it in trust for their only child, a son who was still in swaddling. Still, some duties made her hands shake.

The clerk of the kitchen was a large florid man whom her husband had hired shortly before the baby was born. She had had misgivings about him then but had been too tired to speak of them. Then her husband became ill, the baby had been born, and her husband had died, all within half a year's time. She felt as if she woke up only recently to find herself in a life that only resembled the one she had once had.

The buttery was a small room off the kitchen. Beer and candles sat on the shelves. The stairs from the beer cellar descended down one side, and the main door of the buttery opened into the hall. She had sent the yeoman of the buttery—he was such a gossip—into the garden for a brief rest. Not that he needed one. His services were rarely used this early in the day.

The clerk of the kitchen was explaining, in his condescending voice, how some foods tasted poorly without the proper ingredients. She had her hands folded inside her sleeves, her wimple pinching her chin. She had been listening to him for too long, but she didn't know how to make him stop.

And that was when they heard the screams, coming from the kitchen.

The clerk looked at her as if he had never heard such sounds before. She pushed past him into the Hall, through the Court, and into the kitchen.

It stank of grease and smoke and roasting meat. Even though no one was yet cooking the evening meal, the smell from last night's lingered.

The kitchen staff was huddled near the outside door. One of the kitchen maids had her hands over her mouth. She was doubled over away from the door, as if she had seen something horrible.

Maude hurried past the work table to the door. The servants parted as they saw her, all but the chief cook who blocked her way with his large body.

"Milady," he said. "This is not for a lady to see."

"Move aside," she said.

He stared at her a moment, his blue eyes red-streaked from smoke, his lips thin and pursed as if he had tasted something bad. Then he stepped away from the door.

A woman lay on the flagstones leading into the garden. Her ragged clothes were blood-covered as were her face and hair. When she saw Maude, she raised a thin hand as if beseeching her.

"We shall take care of this, Milady," the chief cook said. "It is nothing that should bother you."

But they hadn't taken care of it so far, had they? Besides, how could she leave a creature in such obvious distress?

"It is simply a beggar woman," the chief cook said. "We see many of them at the kitchen. She was probably beset by thieves."

"A beggar woman beset by thieves? That does not seem likely." Maude stepped outside. She knew why the staff was protecting her. The woman wore garments that Maude recognized from the town's stew.

"She is a harlot, Milady," the chief cook hissed. "Please. It is not right for you—"

"Enough!" Maude said. She crossed the flagstones and crouched beside the woman.

The woman smelled of sweat and fear. She was so thin that all the bones in her hand were visible. Her face was swollen and bruised, her teeth blackened and nearly gone. Yet Maude was certain the woman was younger than she.

Her surcoat had once been a rough wool, but time and use had worn it to nothing. There were several tears in it, recent tears, that rendered it nearly useless. She wore nothing underneath, and Maude could see scars beside the fresh bruises.

"Milady," the woman murmured.

Maude put a hand on the woman's forehead. No fever. She could not see where the blood came from. "Who did this to you?"

The woman touched her bloody garment. "Not mine." She spoke so softly that Maude could barely hear her. "Anne's."

Maude felt a shiver run through her. "Where is Anne?"

The woman looked toward the forest beyond, and the road that led back into town. "I could not help her any longer . . ."

It was then that Maude looked at the woman's feet. She wore no hose and no shoes. Her right arm, Maude suddenly realized, was twisted in an unnatural way

"Help me get her inside," Maude said to the chief cook.

"No, Mistress," the woman said, but Maude ignored her.

The chief cook crossed his arms. "Milady, she is—"

"One of God's children," Maude said. "We shall take care of her."

The chief cook sent out scullions and the indoor grooms. Apparently, the cook was too good to help a woman in need.

The men slipped their arms beneath the woman and she moaned. Maude wondered how many other bones had been broken.

"Place her in the servants' quarters and send for the wet nurse," Maude said. Her wet nurse knew potions and herbs and healings. She had cursed the doctors when she saw what they had done to Maude's husband, saying that if Maude had brought her in sooner, she could have saved him.

Considering that she saved the steward, who later fell to the same disease, Maude believed her.

The quarters where she had them take the woman were for the greater servants. They had rooms of their own, with cots stuffed with straw, instead of mattresses on the floor. This room had been empty since her husband died. She had lost a few servants and hadn't had the energy to replace them.

The men laid the woman on the bed. She was paler than she had been before, and her eyes were glassy with pain.

"What are you called?" Maude asked.

"Mistress, your man, he is right about what I am."

"Do not argue," Maude said. "You are here now. What are you called?"

"Joan."

"Joan," Maude said. "Who did this?"

Joan closed her eyes. At that moment, the wet nurse appeared. She held a towel as if she had just left the young lord, and her surcoat was not properly fastened.

When she saw the woman on the bed, her gaze met Maude's. "Milady, you know—"

"I know," Maude said. "See what you can do. She's been badly beaten and her arm is broken."

The wet nurse nodded. She came inside, put a hand on Joan's forehead, and then began to examine her. Maude stood.

The men were still crowded inside the room. It was as if they saw Joan as a curiosity and nothing more.

"Come," Maude said. "We shall find this Anne."

HALFWAY TO TOWN, THEY found what remained of Anne. She lay in a crumpled heap beside the road, her limbs bent at unnatural angles. Her face was bloodied, as if her nose had been broken, but that was not where all of the blood came from.

She had knife wounds on her hands and arms, and another through her belly. The dry road contained a black trail, as if she had lost blood the entire way.

Joan had carried her on a broken leg, until she could come no farther.

Maude turned to the head groom who had accompanied her. She took one of Anne's cold, damaged hands, and held it out to him.

"What do you think of this?" she asked.

He shrugged. He could barely look at her. "This is not your concern, Milady."

"Of course it is," she snapped, startled at the tone that came out of her mouth. Had she ever spoken to anyone so harshly? "This is my land."

He looked at her then, and it seemed as though there was pity in his eyes. It made her bristle.

"What becomes of these women," he said, "is their choice."

"I doubt anyone would choose to die like this," Maude said. She ran her fingers over the deep wounds. The skin had parted so far that she could see muscle. "I believe she was trying to defend herself."

"Be that as it may, Milady," the groom said, "she knew what such a life would bring."

Did she? Did anyone? Maude remembered the day after her marriage, as she rode in her husband's carriage to her new home, the estate she now ran. Had she known that day how many miscarriages she would have? How the first babe born to them would die three days later in so much pain that his little wails broke her heart? Had she known then that she would love her surviving son so much that it hurt?

Of course not. And the greatest surprise of all had been how badly she missed her husband, now that he was gone.

"You know something of these women then?" she asked her groom.

He flushed. "Only what I have overheard in taverns, Milady."

She narrowed her eyes, not believing him. "They are from the stew, are they not?"

He nodded.

"Is such treatment common there?"

His flush grew deeper. "Milady, I am not—"

"I am a woman married and widowed," she said. "I am not unfamiliar with such things."

"There are perversions, Milady, that I cannot speak of to a gentle-born lady."

She raised her eyebrows. "Perversions that would result in this?"

He looked away from her. His skin was the color of dark wine. "There are men who enjoy inflicting pain."

She shuddered once and decided that perhaps he was right; she was not ready to hear such things. Still, a woman had died on her land and another had come to her for help.

"What do you think they were doing here?" she asked. "Where do you think they were going?"

He shook his head. He knew, as well as she, that no one would have taken the women in.

The hand did not feel human. It was too cold, the flesh hard.

"We shall give her a Christian burial," Maude said.

"Milady! She deserves no such treatment."

"Did you know her then?" Maude asked.

He shook his head.

"Then you do not know who and what she was. Like me, you can only guess. And I choose to guess that she was a godly woman. You shall send some men to bring her back to the house. We shall place her in the chapel, find her suitable clothes before the priest arrives, and have him say a few words over her."

"He will not like this, Milady."

"He will not know," she said.

"How will he not learn of it?" the groom asked. "So many have seen her, so many already know."

She raised her head, anger making her feel stronger than she had for almost a year. "If anyone speaks of this," she said firmly, "he will be fired."

The groom's eyes widened. She had never been this cold before.

He nodded once. "As you wish," he said.

BECAUSE OF HER DUTIES to young Henry, the wet nurse enlisted the aid of two kitchen maids and a chambermaid, all of whom, the wet nurse said, also had knowledge of healing.

Maude was amazed that she knew so little of her staff. They bowed to her when she came into the room. It now smelled of wine and camphor. While Maude was gone, Joan's sore feet had been cleaned and bound with cloth, her bruises rubbed with hot stones, and her broken arm set and splinted.

But she was awake, her eyes dark against her pale face.

"Leave us for a moment," Maude said to the servants.

They bowed again and slipped through the door. Maude took Joan's hand. It was fragile as a bird's wing, but at least it felt alive, warm and callused, the bones delicate against her palm.

"Anne is dead," Maude said.

Joan closed her eyes for a moment, and nodded. It was as if Maude's words made the death real.

"I am giving her a Christian funeral," Maude said. "She is in the chapel. If you are well enough, you may attend."

Joan bit her lower lip. "You do not want me there."

"Of course I do," she said.

" 'Tis not a place for me." Joan bowed her head.

"Our Lord did not think so," Maude said. "Mary Magdalene was of your profession, yet she was at his side."

Joan squeezed Maude's hand. "You are a good woman. I did not mean to burden you."

"It is no burden." Maude put her other hand on top of Joan's. "Who did this to you?"

"Milady, it is not for you to hear."

"I am so tired of everyone telling me what I may and may not hear," Maude said. "I have lived more than a score of years, and I know of the stew and the men who frequent it. Now, stop protecting my dainty ears and tell me who did this to you."

"A man," Joan whispered. "I do not know his name."

"Is he the same one who killed Anne?"

A tear eased out of Joan's right eye. "No."

"Yet you left together."

"She would not have been hurt if not for me."

"Tell me," Maude said, and so Joan did.

THE STORY CAME OUT in fits and whispers, sometimes lost beneath the choking sound of Joan's heavily drawn breath. A man—a customer—had ill used her, and Anne, seeing how badly Joan was hurt, went to William, the stewholder, asking him to send for a doctor. He refused and demanded that Joan, who was popular, finish her night's work.

Anne returned to Joan's room and bundled her up, taking bread from the kitchen, and rolled it and some clothing in two blankets. Anne had heard of nunneries that took in Daughters of Eve—the Order of Saint Mary Magdalene—and they would travel until they found such a place.

Anne was helping Joan out of the stew when William found them. He accused Anne of stealing, and he drew a knife. He cut her, and that brought him to a frenzy. He attacked her like a madman, and did not stop. Joan could not help her.

Blood spattered her face, and then his, and that seemed to awaken him from his fit. He left them in the road outside the stew; left them, Joan believed, to die.

She managed to lift Anne over her shoulder, holding her in place with her good hand. Somehow she managed to make it to the middle of the forest before she fell, unable to go on. There she realized that Anne's eyes were open and unseeing, that Anne was not drawing a breath.

She remembered no more.

"I do not even think I saw your manor," she said. "I was just walking because I did not know what else to do."

MAUDE DID NOT KNOW what to do either. She sat in her private chamber, head bowed. But she did not ask for God's aid. Somehow she felt that God's presence was in none of this.

The stewholder, she knew, had rights over his women. He could prevent them from leaving. He could punish them for an obvious theft. But Maude did not believe the theft of bread and blankets was sin enough for this. She did not believe that women who sought to better themselves deserved to die by the side of the road, to be left there like discarded clothes.

It took her an hour to come to her decision.

And then she sent for her steward.

HE WAS A MAN of some years, thin after his illness, his hair gone except for graying tufts at the sides. Her husband had trusted him implicitly and Maude had trusted him as well. His advice had been sound, his care for the estate excellent.

He seemed uncomfortable to be in her private rooms. He waited, with the door open, for her instruction.

"Have the sheriff arrest the stewholder," she said. "His name is William."

"Milady," the steward said. "Since your husband's death, we have had no magistrate."

She nodded. "I will sit in judgment," she said.

He stared at her for a long moment, as if she were not someone he recognized.

"What would be the charge, then?" the steward asked.

"Murder," she said.

SHE HELD THE HEARING the next day. She sat in her hall as the sheriff brought in William the Stewholder. He was a portly man

who   ...s made of an expensive serge and whose
shoes we   ..n fur.

He looked as if he could afford the loss of a blanket or two.

His hands were shackled, but his feet were not.

When he saw her, his face flushed the color of his tunic. "I'll not sit before a woman!" he cried.

"You have no choice," she said in her new voice, the voice that had been born of this experience. "I am the trustee of my husband's lands, and until my son comes of age, I am the one who runs them."

"That means she's the magistrate," the sheriff said, shaking William.

"Did you," she asked, "stab a woman named Anne?"

"She stole from me."

"Enough to warrant two dozen wounds?" Maude asked.

"The price of theft is death!" he shouted, spittle coming from his mouth. Apparently, he felt that she would only understand him if he yelled.

"I determine the price of theft on these lands," Maude said, amazed she could sound so calm. "Those women were injured. They wanted medical care."

"Only one was injured," he said.

"Yet you wanted her to work."

He shrugged. "She'd done it before."

Maude stared at him for a long moment. He stared back, unrepentant.

"I sentence you," she said, "to a pilgrimage. You shall visit holy sites until you learn the meaning of humility."

"How shall that be judged?" the sheriff asked.

"I believe it will take many years," she said. "Perhaps your pilgrimage shall be eternal. I shall think on it and come to that decision by the morrow, when you shall be shipped out."

"You cannot do this," he said.

"We've already established that I can."

"Those whores you're so worried about will have no one to manage them."

She felt cold. She hadn't thought of that. She looked at the sheriff. "You shall bring them here. They shall learn useful work."

"Milady, they may leave, but that will not stop someone else from opening a stew," the sheriff said.

"I am aware of that," she said. "But at least it will not be William here." She waved in dismissal. "Take him away."

THAT EVENING, SHE SAT alone in the chapel as the priest sent Anne's soul on its way. Joan had been too ill to come. It would take many weeks for Joan to heal.

By then, Maude hoped the men she had sent to find the nearest Order of Saint Mary Magdalene would have returned with good news.

For it did not matter how a woman was born, as a daughter of Eve, or a daughter of Mary, she deserved to live a life free of brutality and pain.

Maude lived such a life, but she had not known it until now. And it had taken a sight that most would have shielded her from to teach her that she had strengths she had never expected.

She would hold these lands in trust for her son. And when he came of age, she would give them to him gladly, better than they had been when she came to them.

Better, because she had made them so.

A Light on the Road to Woodstock

Ellis Peters

The King's court was in no hurry to return to England that late autumn of 1120, even though the fighting, somewhat desultory in these last stages, was long over, and the enforced peace sealed by a royal marriage. King Henry had brought to a successful conclusion his sixteen years of patient, cunning, relentless plotting, fighting, and manipulating, and could now sit back in high content, master not only of England but of Normandy, too. What the Conqueror had misguidedly dealt out in two separate parcels to his two elder sons, his youngest son had now put together again and clamped into one. Not without a hand in removing from the light of day, some said, both of his brothers, one of whom had been shoveled into a hasty grave under the tower at Winchester, while the other was now a prisoner in Devizes, and unlikely ever to be seen again by the outer world.

The court could well afford to linger to enjoy victory, while Henry trimmed into neatness the last loose edges still to be made secure. But his fleet was already preparing at Barfleur for the voyage back to England, and he would be home before the month ended. Meantime, many of his barons and knights who had fought his battles were withdrawing their contingents and making for home, among them one Roger Mauduit, who had a young and handsome wife waiting for him, certain legal business on his mind, and twenty-five men to ship back to England, most of them to be paid off on landing.

There were one or two among the miscellaneous riffraff he had recruited here in Normandy on his lord's behalf whom it might be worth keeping on in his own service, along with the few men of his household, at least until he was safely home. The vagabond clerk turned soldier, let him be unfrocked priest or what he might, was an excellent copyist and a sound Latin scholar, and could put legal documents in their best and most presentable form, in good time for the King's court at Woodstock. And the Welsh man-at-arms, blunt and insubordinate as he was, was also experienced and accomplished in arms, a man of his word, once given, and utterly reliable in whatever situation on land or sea, for in both elements he had long practice behind him. Roger was well aware that he was not greatly loved, and he had little faith in either the valor or the loyalty of his own men. But this Welshman from Gwynedd, by way of Antioch and Jerusalem and only God knows where else, had imbibed the code of arms and wore it as a second nature. With or without love, such service as he pledged, that he would provide.

Roger put it to them both as his men were embarking at Barfleur, in the middle of a deceptively placid November, and upon a calm sea.

"I would have you two accompany me to my manor of Sutton Mauduit by Northampton, when we disembark, and stay in my pay until a certain lawsuit I have against the abbey of Shrewsbury is resolved. The King intends to come to Woodstock when he arrives in England and will be there to preside over my case on the twenty-third day of this month. Will you remain in my service until that day?"

The Welshman said that he would, until that day or until the case was resolved. He said it indifferently, as one who has no business of any importance anywhere else in the world to pull him in another direction. As well Northampton as anywhere else. As well Woodstock. And after Woodstock? Why anywhere in

particular? There was no identifiable light beckoning him anywhere, along any road. The world was wide, fair, and full of savor,
but without signposts.

Alard, the tatterdemalion clerk, hesitated, scratched his
thick thatch of grizzled red hair, and finally also said yes, but as if
some vague regret drew him in another direction. It meant pay
for some days more, he could not afford to say no.

"I would have gone with him with better heart," he said later,
when they were leaning on the rail together, watching the low
blue line of the English shore rise out of a placid sea, "if he had
been taking a more westerly road."

"Why that?" asked Cadfael ap Meilyr ap Dafydd. "Have you
kin in the west?"

"I had once. I have not now."

"Dead?"

"I am the one who died." Alard heaved lean shoulders in a
helpless shrug, and grinned. "Fifty-seven brothers I had, and now
I'm brotherless. I begin to miss my kin, now I'm past forty. I never
valued them when I was young." He slanted a rueful glance at his
companion and shook his head. "I was a monk of Evesham, an
oblatus, given to God by my father when I was five years old.
When I was fifteen, I could no longer abide to live my life in one
place, and I ran. Stability is one of the vows we take—to be content in one stay, and go abroad only when ordered. That was not
for me, not then. My sort they call *vagus*—frivolous minds that
must wander. Well, I've wandered far enough, God knows, in my
time. I begin to fear I can never stand still again."

The Welshman drew his cloak about him against the chill of
the wind. "Are you hankering for a return?"

"Even you seamen must drop anchor somewhere at last,"
Alard said. "They'd have my hide if I went back, that I know. But
there's this about penance, it pays all debts, and leaves the record
clear. They'd find a place for me, once I'd paid. But I don't know
. . . I don't know . . . The *vagus* is still in me. I'm torn two ways."

"After twenty-five years," said Cadfael, "a month or two
more for quiet thinking can do no harm. Copy his papers for him
and take your ease until his business is settled."

They were much of an age, though the renegade monk looked the elder by ten years, and much knocked about by the world he had coveted from within the cloister. It had never paid him well in goods or gear, for he went threadbare and thin, but in wisdom he might have got his fair wages. A little soldiering, a little clerking, some horse-tending, any labor that came to hand, until he could turn his hand to almost anything a hale man can do. He had seen, he said, Italy as far south as Rome, served once for a time under the Count of Flanders, crossed the mountains into Spain, never abiding anywhere for long. His feet still served him, but his mind grew weary of the road.

"And you?" he said, eyeing his companion, whom he had known now for a year in this last campaign. "You're something of a *vagus* yourself, by your own account. All those years crusading and battling corsairs in the midland sea, and still you have not enough of it but must cross the sea again to get buffeted about Normandy. Had you no better business of your own, once you got back to England but you must enlist again in this muddled mêlée of a war? No woman to take your mind off fighting?"

"What of yourself? Free of the cloister, free of the vows!"

"Somehow," said Alard, himself puzzled, "I never saw it so. A woman here and there, yes, when the heat was on me, and there was a woman by and willing, but marriage and wiving . . . it never seemed to me I had the right."

The Welshman braced his feet on the gently swaying deck and watched the distant shore draw nearer. A broad-set, sturdy, muscular man in his healthy prime, brown-haired and brown-skinned from eastern suns and outdoor living, well provided in leather coat and good cloth, and well armed with sword and dagger. A comely enough face, strongly featured, with the bold bones of his race—there had been women, in his time, who had found him handsome.

"I had a girl," he said meditatively, "years back, before ever I went crusading. But I left her when I took the Cross; left her for three years and stayed away seventeen. The truth is, in the east I forgot her, and in the west she, thanks be to God, had forgotten me. I did inquire, when I got back. She'd made a better bargain and married a decent, solid man who had nothing of the *vagus* in him. A guildsman and counselor of the town of Shrewsbury, no less. So I shed the load from my conscience and went back to what I knew, soldiering. With no regrets," he said simply. "It was all over and done, years since. I doubt if I should have known her again, or she me." There had been other women's faces in the years between, still vivid in his memory, while hers had faded into mist.

"And what will you do," Alard asked, "now the King's got everything he wanted, married his son to Anjou and Maine, and made an end of fighting? Go back to the east? There's never any want of squabbles there to keep a man busy."

"No," said Cadfael, eyes fixed on the shore that began to show the solidity of land and the undulations of cliff and down. For that, too, was over and done, years since, and not as well done as once he had hoped. This desultory campaigning in Normandy was little more than a postscriptum, an afterthought, a means of filling in the interim between what was past and what was to come, and as yet unrevealed. All he knew of it was that it must be something new and momentous, a door opening into another room. "It seems we have both a few days' grace, you and I, to find out where we are going. We'd best make good use of the time."

There was stir enough before night to keep them from wondering beyond the next moment or troubling their minds about what was past or what was to come. Their ship put into the roads with a steady and favorable wind, and made course into Southampton before the light faded, and there was work for Alard checking the gear as it was unloaded, and for Cadfael disembarking the horses. A night's sleep in lodgings and stables in the town, and they would be on their way with the dawn.

"So the King's due in Woodstock," Alard said, rustling sleepily in his straw in a warm loft over the horses, "in time to sit in judgment on the twenty-third of the month. He makes his forest lodges the hub of his kingdom, there's more statecraft talked at Woodstock, so they say, than ever at Westminster. And he keeps his beasts there—lions and leopards—even camels. Did you ever see camels, Cadfael? There in the east?"

"Saw them and rode them. Common as horses there, hard-working and serviceable, but uncomfortable riding and foul-tempered. Thank God it's horses we'll be mounting in the morning." And after a long silence, on the edge of sleep, he asked curiously into the straw-scented darkness, "If ever you do go back, what is it you want of Evesham?"

"Do I know?" Alard responded drowsily, and followed that with a sudden sharpening sigh, again fully awake. "The silence, it might be . . . or the stillness. To have no more running to do . . . to have arrived, and have no more need to run. The appetite changes. Now I think it would be a beautiful thing to be still."

THE MANOR THAT WAS the head of Roger Mauduit's scattered and substantial honor lay somewhat southeast of Northampton, comfortably under the lee of the long ridge of wooded hills where the King had a chase, and spreading its extensive fields over the rich lowland between. The house was of stone, and ample, over a deep undercroft, and with a low tower providing two small chambers at the eastern end, and the array of sturdy byres, barns, and stables that lined the containing walls was impressive. Someone had proved a good steward while the lord was away about King Henry's business.

The furnishings of the hall were no less eloquent of good management, and the men and maids of the household went about their work with a brisk wariness that showed they went in some awe of whomever presided over their labors. It needed only a single day of watching the Lady Eadwina in action to show who ruled the roost here. Roger Mauduit had married a wife not only handsome but also efficient and masterful. She had had her own way here for three years, and by all the signs had enjoyed her dominance. She might, even, be none too glad to resign her charge now, however glad she might be to have her lord home again.

She was a tall, graceful woman, ten years younger than Roger, with an abundance of fair hair and large blue eyes that went discreetly half-veiled by absurdly long lashes most of the time, but flashed a bright and steely challenge when she opened them fully. Her smile was likewise discreet and almost constant, concealing rather than revealing whatever went on in her mind, and though her welcome to her returning lord left nothing to be desired, but lavished on him every possible tribute of ceremony and affection from the moment his horse entered at the gate, Cadfael could not but wonder whether she was not, at the same time, taking stock of every man he brought in with him, and every article of gear or harness or weaponry in their equipment, as one taking jealous inventory of his goods and resolved to make sure nothing was lacking.

She had her little son by the hand, a boy of about seven years old, and the child had the same fair coloring, the same contained and almost supercilious smile, and was as spruce and fine as his mother.

The lady received Alard with a sweeping glance that deprecated his tatterdemalion appearance and doubted his morality, but nevertheless she was willing to accept and make use of his abilities. The clerk who kept the manor roll and the accounts was efficient enough, but had no Latin, and could not write a good court hand. Alard was whisked away to a small table set in the angle of the great hearth, and kept hard at work copying certain charters and letters, and preparing them for presentation.

"This suit of his is against the abbey of Shrewsbury," said Alard, freed of his labors after supper in hall. "I recall you said that girl of yours had married a merchant in that town. Shrewsbury is a Benedictine house, like mine of Evesham." His, he called it still, after so many years of abandoning it; or his again, after time had brushed away whatever division there had ever been. "You must know it, if you come from there."

"I was born in Trefriw, in Gwynedd," Cadfael said, "but I took service early with an English wool merchant and came to Shrewsbury with his household. Fourteen, I was then—in Wales fourteen is manhood—and as I was a good lad with the short bow, and took kindly to the sword, I suppose I was worth my keep. The best of my following years were spent in Shrewsbury. I know it like my own palm, abbey and all. My master sent me there a year and more, to get my letters. But I quit that service when he died. I'd pledged nothing to the son, and he was a poor shadow of his father. That was when I took the Cross. So did many like me, all afire. I won't say what followed was all ash, but it burned very low at times."

"It's Mauduit who holds this disputed land," Alard said, "and the abbey that sues to recover it, and the thing's been going on four years without a settlement, ever since the old man here died. From what I know of the Benedictines, I'd rate their honesty above our Roger's, I tell you straight. And yet his charters seem to be genuine, as far as I can tell."

"Where is this land they're fighting over?" Cadfael asked.

"It's a manor by the name of Rotesley, near Stretton, demesne, village, advowson of the Church and all. It seems when the great earl was just dead and his abbey still building, Roger's father gave Rotesley to the abbey. No dispute about that, the charter's there to show it. But the abbey granted it back to him as tenant for life, to live out his latter years there undisturbed, Roger being then married and installed here at Sutton. That's where the dispute starts. The abbey claims it was clearly agreed the tenancy ended with the old man's death, that he himself understood it so, and intended it should be restored to the abbey as soon as he was out of it. While Roger says there was no such agreement to restore it unconditionally, but the tenancy was granted to the Mauduits, and ought to be hereditary. And so far he's hung on to it tooth and claw. After several hearings they remitted it to the King himself. And that's why you and I, my friend, will be off with his lordship to Woodstock the day after tomorrow."

"And how do you rate his chances of success? He seems none too sure himself," said Cadfael, "to judge by his short temper and nail-biting this last day or so."

"Why, the charter could have been worded better. It says simply that the village is granted back in tenancy during the old man's lifetime, but fails to say anything about what shall happen afterward, whatever may have been intended. From what I hear, they were on very good terms, Abbot Fulchered and the old lord, agreements between them on other matters in the manor book are worded as between men who trusted each other. The witnesses are all of them dead, as Abbot Fulchered is dead. It's one Godefrid now. But for all I know the abbey may hold letters that have passed between the two, and a letter is witness of intent, no less than a formal charter. All in good time we shall see."

The nobility still sat at the high table, in no haste to retire, Roger brooding over his wine, of which he had already drunk his fair share and more. Cadfael eyed them with interest, seen thus in a family setting. The boy had gone to his bed, hauled away by an elderly nurse, but the Lady Eadwina sat in close attendance at her lord's left hand and kept his cup well filled, smiling her faint, demure smile. On her left sat a very fine young squire of about twenty-five years, deferential and discreet, with a smile somehow the male reflection of her own. The source of both was secret, the spring of their pleasure or amusement, or whatever caused them so to smile, remained private and slightly unnerving, like the carved stone smiles of certain very old statues Cadfael had seen in Greece, long ago. For all his mild, amiable, and ornamental appearance, combed and curled and courtly, he was a big, well-set-up young fellow, with a set to his smooth jaw. Cadfael studied him with interest, for he was plainly privileged here.

"Goscelin," Alard said by way of explanation, following his friend's glance. "Her right-hand man while Roger was away."

Her left-hand man now, by the look of it, thought Cadfael. For her left hand and Goscelin's right were private under the table, while she spoke winningly into her husband's ear; and if those two hands were not paddling palms at this moment Cadfael was very much deceived. Above and below the drapings of the board were two different worlds. "I wonder," he said thoughtfully, "what she's breathing into Roger's ear now."

What the lady was breathing into her husband's ear was, in fact: "You fret over nothing, my lord. What does it matter how strong his proofs, if he never reaches Woodstock in time to present them? You know the law: If one party fails to appear, judgment is given for the other. The assize judges may allow more than one default if they please, but do you think King Henry will? Whoever fails of keeping tryst with him will be felled on the spot. And you know the road by which Prior Heribert must come." Her voice was a silken purr in his ear. "And have you not a hunting lodge in the forest north of Woodstock, through which that road passes?"

Roger's hand had stiffened round the stem of his wine cup. He was not so drunk but he was listening intently.

"Shrewsbury to Woodstock will be a two- or three-day journey to such a rider. All you need do is have a watcher on the road north of you to give warning. The woods are thick enough, masterless men have been known to haunt there. Even if he comes by daylight, your part need never be known. Hide him but a few days, it will be long enough. Then turn him loose by night, and who's ever to know what footpads held and robbed him? You need not even touch his parchments—robbers would count them worthless. Take what common thieves would take, and theirs will be the blame."

Roger opened his tight-shut mouth to say in a doubtful growl, "He'll not be traveling alone."

"Hah! Two or three abbey servants—they'll run like hares. You need not trouble yourself over them. Three stout, silent men of your own will be more than enough."

He brooded, and began to think so, too, and to review in his mind the men of his household, seeking the right hands for such work. Not the Welshman and the clerk, the strangers here; their part was to be the honest onlookers in case there should ever be questions asked.

THEY LEFT SUTTON MAUDUIT on the twentieth day of November, which seemed unnecessarily early, though as Roger had decreed that they should settle in his hunting lodge in the forest close by Woodstock, which meant conveying stores with them to make the house habitable and provision it for a party for, presumably, a stay of three nights at least. It was perhaps a wise precaution. Roger was taking no chances in his suit, he said; he meant to be established on the ground in good time, and have all his proofs in order.

"But so he has," said Alard, pricked in his professional pride, "for I've gone over everything with him, and the case, if open in default of specific instructions, is plain enough and will stand up.

What the abbey can muster, who knows? They say the abbot is not well, which is why his prior comes in his place. My work is done."

He had the faraway look in his eye, as the party rode out and faced westward, of one either penned and longing to be where he could but see, or loose and weary and being drawn home. Either a *vagus* escaping outward, or a penitent flying back in haste before the doors should close against him. There must indeed be something desirable and lovely to cause a man to look toward it with that look on his face.

Three men-at-arms and two grooms accompanied Roger, in addition to Alard and Cadfael, whose term of service would end with the session in court after which they might go where they would, Cadfael horsed, since he owned his own mount, Alard afoot, since the pony he rode belonged to Roger. It came as something of a surprise to Cadfael that the squire Goscelin should also saddle up and ride with the party, very debonair and well armed with sword and dagger.

"I marvel," said Cadfael dryly, "that the lady doesn't need him at home for her own protection, while her lord's absent."

The Lady Eadwina, however, bade farewell to the whole party with the greatest serenity, and to her husband with demonstrative affection, putting forward her little son to be embraced and kissed. Perhaps, thought Cadfael, relenting, I do her wrong, simply because I feel chilled by that smile of hers. For all I know she may be the truest wife living.

They set out early, and before Buckingham made a halt at the small and penurious priory of Bradwell, where Roger elected to spend the night, keeping his three men-at-arms with him, while Goscelin with the rest of the party rode on to the hunting lodge to make all ready for their lord's reception the following day. It was growing dark by the time they arrived, and the bustle of kindling fire and torches, and unloading the bed linen and stores from the sumpter ponies went on into the night. The lodge was small, stockaded, well furnished with stabling and mews, and in thick woodland, a place comfortable enough once they had a roaring fire on the hearth and food on the table.

"The road the prior of Shrewsbury will be coming by," said Alard, warming himself by the fire after supper, "passes through

Evesham. As like as not they'll stay the last night there." With every mile west, Cadfael had seen him straining forward with mounting eagerness. "The road cannot be far away from us here; it passes through this forest."

"It must be nearly thirty miles to Evesham," Cadfael said. "A long day's riding for a clerical party. It will be night by the time they ride past into Woodstock. If you're set on going, stay at least to get your pay, for you'll need it before the thirty miles is done."

They went to their slumber in the warmth of the hall without a word more said. But he would go, Alard, whether he himself knew it yet or not. Cadfael knew it. His friend was a tired horse with the scent of the stable in his nostrils; nothing would stop him now until he reached it.

It was well into the middle of the day when Roger and his escort arrived, and they approached not directly as the advance party had done, but from the woods to the north, as though they had been indulging in a little hunting or hawking by the way, except that they had neither hawk nor hound with them. A fine, clear, cool day for riding, there was no reason in the world why they should not go roundabout for the pure pleasure of it—and indeed, they seemed to come in high content!—but that Roger's mind had been so preoccupied and so anxious concerning his lawsuit that distractions seemed unlikely. Cadfael was given to thinking about unlikely developments, which from old campaigns he knew to prove significant in most cases. Goscelin, who was out at the gate to welcome them in, was apparently oblivious to the direction from which they came. That way lay Alard's highway to his rest. But what meaning ought it to have for Roger Mauduit?

The table was lavish that night, and lord and squire drank well and ate well, and gave no sign of any care, though they might, Cadfael thought, watching them from his lower place, seem a little tight and knife-edged. Well, the King's court could account for that. Shrewsbury's prior was drawing steadily nearer, with whatever weapons he had for the battle. But it seemed rather an exultant tension than an anxious one. Was Roger counting his chickens already?

The morning of the twenty-second of November dawned, and the noon passed, and with every moment Alard's restlessness and abstraction grew, until with evening it possessed him utterly, and he could no longer resist. He presented himself before Roger after supper, when his mood might be mellow from good food and wine.

"My lord, with the morrow my service to you is completed. You need me no longer, and with your goodwill I would set forth now for where I am going. I go afoot and need provision for the road. If you have been content with my work, pay me what is due, and let me go."

It seemed that Roger had been startled out of some equally absorbing preoccupation of his own and was in haste to return to it, for he made no demur but paid at once. To do him justice, he had never been a grudging paymaster. He drove as hard a bargain as he could at the outset, but once the agreement was made, he kept it.

"Go when you please," he said. "Fill your bag from the kitchen for the journey when you leave. You did good work, I give you that."

And he returned to whatever it was that so engrossed his thoughts, and Alard went to collect the proffered largesse and his own meager possessions.

"I am going," he said, meeting Cadfael in the hall doorway. "I must go." There was no more doubt in voice or face. "They will take me back, though in the lowest place. From that there's no falling. The blessed Benedict wrote in the Rule that even to the third time of straying a man may be received again if he promise full amendment."

It was a dark night, without moon or stars but in fleeting moments when the wind ripped apart the cloud covering to let through a brief gleam of moonlight. The weather had grown gusty and wild in the last two days, the King's fleet must have had a rough crossing from Barfleur.

"You'd do better," Cadfael urged, "to wait for morning and go by daylight. Here's a safe bed, and the King's peace, however well enforced, hardly covers every mile of the King's high roads."

But Alard would not wait. The yearning was on him too strongly, and a penniless vagabond who had ventured all the roads of Christendom by day or night was hardly likely to flinch from the last thirty miles of his wanderings.

"Then I'll go with you as far as the road, and see you on your way," Cadfael said.

There was a mile or so of track through thick forest between them and the high road that bore away west-northwest on the upland journey to Evesham. The ribbon of open highway, hemmed on both sides by trees, was hardly less dark than the forest itself. King Henry had fenced in his private park at Woodstock to house his wild beasts, but maintained also his hunting chase here, many miles in extent. At the road they parted, and Cadfael stood to watch his friend march steadily away towardsthe west, eyes fixed ahead, upon his penance and his absolution, a tired man with a rest assured.

Cadfael turned back toward the lodge as soon as the receding shadow had melted into the night. He was in no haste to go in, for the night, though blustery, was not cold, and he was in no mind to seek the company of others of the party now that one best known to him was gone, and gone in so mysteriously rapt a fashion. He walked on among the trees, turning his back on his bed for a while.

The constant thrashing of branches in the wind all but drowned the scuffling and shouting that suddenly broke out behind him, at some distance among the trees, until a horse's shrill whinny brought him about with a jerk and set him running through the underbrush toward the spot where confused voices yelled alarm and broken bushes thrashed. The clamor seemed some little way off, and he was startled as he shouldered his way headlong through a thicket to collide heavily with two entangled bodies, send them spinning apart, and himself fall asprawl upon one of them in the flattened grass. The man under him uttered a scared and angry cry, and the voice was Roger's. The other man had made no sound at all, but slid away very rapidly and lightly to vanish among the trees, a tall shadow swallowed in shadows.

Cadfael drew off in haste, reaching an arm to hoist the winded man. "My lord, are you hurt? What, in God's name, is to do here?" The sleeve he clutched slid warm and wet under his hand. "You're injured! Hold fast, let's see what harm's done before you move . . ."

Then there was the voice of Goscelin, for once loud and vehement in alarm, shouting for his lord and crashing headlong through bush and brake to fall on his knees beside Roger, lamenting and raging.

"My lord, my lord, what happened here? What rogues were those, loose in the woods? Dared they waylay travelers so close to the King's highway? You're hurt—here's blood . . ."

Roger got his breath back and sat up, feeling at his left arm below the shoulder, and wincing. "A scratch. My arm . . . God curse him, whoever he may be, the fellow struck for my heart. Man, if you had not come charging like a bull, I might have been dead. You hurled me off the point of his dagger. Thank God, there's no great harm, but I bleed . . . Help me back home!"

"That a man may not walk by night in his own woods," Goscelin fumed, hoisting his lord carefully to his feet, "without being set upon by outlaws! Help here, you, Cadfael, take his other arm . . . Footpads so close to Woodstock! Tomorrow we must turn out the watch to comb these tracks and hunt them out of cover, before they kill . . ."

"Get me withindoors," snapped Roger, "and have this coat and shirt off me, and let's staunch this bleeding. I'm alive, that's the main!"

They helped him back between them, through the more open ways toward the lodge. It dawned on Cadfael, as they went, that the clamor of furtive battle had ceased completely, even the wind had abated, and somewhere on the road, distantly, he caught the rhythm of galloping hooves, very fast and light, as of a riderless horse in panic flight.

THE GASH IN ROGER Mauduit's left arm, just below the shoulder, was long but not deep and grew shallower as it descended. The stroke that marked him thus could well have been meant for his heart. Cadfael's hurtling impact, at the very moment the attack was launched, had been the means of averting murder. The shadow that had melted into the night had no form, nothing about it rendered it human or recognizable. He had heard an

outcry and run toward it, a projectile to strike attacked and
attacker apart; questioned, that was all he could say.

For which, said Roger, bandaged and resting and warmed
with mulled wine, he was heartily thankful. And indeed, Roger
was behaving with remarkable fortitude and calm for a man who
had just escaped death. By the time he had demonstrated to his
dismayed grooms and men-at-arms that he was alive and not
much the worse, appointed the hour when they should set out for
Woodstock in the morning, and been helped to his bed by
Goscelin, there was even a suggestion of complacency about him,
as though a gash in the arm was a small price to pay for the successful retention of a valuable property and the defeat of his clerical opponents.

IN THE COURT OF the palace of Woodstock the King's chamberlains,
clerks, and judges were fluttering about in a curiously distracted
manner, or so it seemed to Cadfael, standing apart among the com-
moners to observe their antics. They gathered in small groups, con-
versing in low voices and with anxious faces, broke apart to regroup
with others of their kind, hurried in and out among the litigants,
avoiding or brushing off all questions, exchanged documents, hurried to the door to peer out, as if looking for some late arrival. And
there was indeed one litigant who had not kept to his time, for there
was no sign of a Benedictine prior among those assembled nor had
anyone appeared to explain or justify his absence. And Roger
Mauduit, in spite of his stiff and painful arm, continued to relax,
with ever-increasing assurance, into shining complacency.

The appointed hour was already some minutes past when
four agitated fellows, two of them Benedictine brothers, made a
hasty entrance, and accosted the presiding clerk.

"Sir," bleated the leader, loud in nervous dismay, "we here are
come from the abbey of Shrewsbury, escort to our prior, who was
on his way to plead a case at law here. Sir, you must hold him
excused, for it is not his blame nor ours that he cannot appear. In
the forest some two miles north, as we rode hither last night in

the dark, we were attacked by a band of lawless robbers, and they have seized our prior and dragged him away . . ."

The spokesman's voice had risen shrilly in his agitation, he had the attention of every man in the hall by this time. Certainly, he had Cadfael's. Masterless men some two miles out of Woodstock, plying their trade last night, could only be the same who had happened upon Roger Mauduit and all but been the death of him. Any such gang, so close to the court, was astonishing enough; there could hardly be two. The clerk was outraged at the very idea.

"Seized and captured him? And you four were with him? Can this be true? How many were they who attacked you?"

"We could not tell for certain. Three at least—but they were lying in ambush; we had no chance to stand them off. They pulled him from his horse and were off into the trees with him. They knew the woods, and we did not. Sir, we did go after them, but they beat us off."

It was evident they had done their best, for two of them showed bruised and scratched, and all were soiled and torn as to their clothing.

"We have hunted through the night but found no trace, only we caught his horse a mile down the highway as we came hither. So we plead here that our prior's absence be not seen as a default, for indeed he would have been here in the town last night if all had gone as it should."

"Hush, wait!" the clerk said peremptorily.

All heads had turned toward the door of the hall, where a great flurry of officials had suddenly surged into view, cleaving through the press with fixed and ominous haste, to take the center of the floor below the King's empty dais. A chamberlain, elderly and authoritative, struck the floor loudly with his staff and commanded silence. And at sight of his face silence fell like a stone.

"My lords, gentlemen, all who have pleas here this day, and all others present, you are bidden to disperse, for there will be no hearings today. All suits that should be heard here must be postponed three days and will be heard by his Grace's judges. His Grace the King cannot appear."

This time the silence fell again like a heavy curtain, muffling even thought or conjecture.

"The court is in mourning from this hour. We have received news of desolating import. His Grace with the greater part of his fleet made the crossing to England safely, as is known, but the *Blanche Nef,* in which his Grace's son and heir, Prince William, with all his companions and many other noble souls were embarked, put to sea late, and was caught in gales before ever clearing Barfleur. The ship is lost, split upon a rock, foundered with all hands, not a soul is come safe to land. Go hence quietly, and pray for the souls of the flower of this realm."

So that was the end of one man's year of triumph, an empty achievement, a ruinous victory, Normandy won, his enemies routed, and now everything swept aside, broken apart upon an obstinate rock, washed away in a malicious sea. His only lawful son, recently married in splendor, now denied even a coffin and a grave, for if ever they found those royal bodies it would be by the relenting grace of God, for the sea seldom put its winnings ashore by Barfleur. Even some of his unlawful sons, of whom there were many, gone down with their royal brother, no one left but the one legal daughter to inherit a barren empire.

Cadfael walked alone in a corner of the King's park and considered the foolishness of mortal vainglory, that was paid for with such a bitter price. But also he thought of the affairs of little men, to whom even a luckless King owed justice. For somewhere there was still to be sought the lost prior of Shrewsbury, carried off by masterless men in the forest, a litigant who might still be lost three days hence, when his suit came up again for hearing, unless someone in the meantime knew where to look for him.

He was in little doubt now. A lawless gang at liberty so close to a royal palace was in any case unlikely enough, and Cadfael was liable to brood on the unlikely. But that there should be two—no, that was impossible. And if one only, then that same one whose ambush he had overheard at some distance, yet close enough, too close for comfort, to Roger Mauduit's hunting lodge.

Probably the unhappy brothers from Shrewsbury were off beating the wilds of the forest afresh. Cadfael knew better where to look. No doubt Roger was biting his nails in some anxiety over the delay, but he had no reason to suppose that three days would release the captive to appear against him, nor was he paying much attention to what his Welsh man-at-arms was doing with his time.

Cadfael took his horse and rode back without haste toward the hunting lodge. He left in the early dusk, as soon as the evening meal was over in Mauduit's lodging. No one was paying any heed to him by that time of day. All Roger had to do was hold his tongue and keep his wits about him for three days, and the disputed manor would still be adjudged to him. Everything was beautifully in hand, after all.

Two of the men-at-arms and one groom had been left behind at the hunting lodge. Cadfael doubted if the man they guarded was to be found in the house itself, for unless he was blindfolded he would be able to gather far too much knowledge of his surroundings, and the fable of the masterless men would be tossed into the rubbish heap. No, he would be held in darkness, or dim light at best, even during the day, in straw or the rush flooring of a common hut, fed adequately but plainly and roughly, as wild men might keep a prisoner they were too cautious to kill, or too superstitious, until they turned him loose in some remote place, stripped of everything he had of value. On the other hand, he must be somewhere securely inside the boundary fence, otherwise there would be too high a risk of his being found. Between the gate and the house there were trees enough to obscure the large holding of a man of consequence. Somewhere among the stables and barns, or the now-empty kennels, there he must be held.

Cadfael tethered his horse in cover well aside from the lodge and found himself a perch in a tall oak tree, from which vantage point he could see over the fence into the courtyard.

He was in luck. The three within fed themselves at leisure before they fed their prisoner, preferring to wait for dark. By the time the groom emerged from the hall with a pitcher and a bowl in his hands, Cadfael had his night eyes. They were quite easy about their charge, expecting no interference from any man. The groom vanished momentarily between the trees within the enclosure, but appeared again at one of the low buildings tucked under the fence, set down his pitcher for a moment, while he hoisted clear a heavy wooden bar that held the door fast shut, and he vanished within. The door thudded to after him, as though he had slammed it shut with his back braced against it, taking no chances even with an elderly monastic. In a few minutes he emerged again empty-handed, hauled the bar into place again, and returned, whistling, to the hall and the enjoyment of Mauduit's ale.

Not the stables nor the kennels, but a small stout hay store built on short wooden piles raised from the ground. At least the prior would have fairly snug lying.

Cadfael let the last of the light fade before he made a move. The wooden wall was stout and high, but more than one of the old trees outside leaned a branch over it, and it was no great labor to climb without and drop into the deep grass within. He made first for the gate, and quietly unbarred the narrow wicket set into it. Faint threads of torchlight filtered through the chinks in the hall shutters, but nothing else stirred. Cadfael laid hold of the heavy bar of the storehouse door, and eased it silently out of its socket, opening the door by cautious inches, and whispering through the chink: "Father . . . ?"

There was a sharp rustling of hay within, but no immediate reply.

"Father Prior, is it you? Softly . . . Are you bound?"

A hesitant and slightly timorous voice said, "No." And in a moment, with better assurance: "My son, you are not one of these sinful men?"

"Sinful man I am, but not of their company. Hush, quietly now! I have a horse close by. I came from Woodstock to find you. Reach me your hand, Father, and come forth."

A hand came wavering out of the hay-scented darkness to clutch convulsively at Cadfael's hand. The pale patch of a tonsured crown gleamed faintly, and a small, rounded figure crept forth and stepped into the thick grass. He had the wit to waste no breath then on questions, but stood docile and silent while Cadfael rebarred the door on emptiness and, taking him by the hand, led him softly along the fence to the unfastened wicket in the great gate. Only when the door was closed as softly behind them did he heave a great, thankful sigh.

They were out, it was done, and no one would be likely to learn of the escape until morning. Cadfael led the way to where he had left his horse tethered. The forest lay serene and quiet about them.

"You ride, Father, and I'll walk with you. It's no more than two miles into Woodstock. We're safe enough now."

Bewildered and confused by so sudden a reversal, the prior confided and obeyed like a child. Not until they were out on the silent high road did he say sadly, "I have failed of my mission. Son, may God bless you for this kindness that is beyond my understanding. For how *did* you know of me, and how could you divine where to find me? I understand nothing of what has been happening to me. And I am not a very brave man . . . But my failure is no fault of yours, and my blessing I owe you without stint."

"You have not failed, Father," Cadfael said simply. "The suit is still unheard and will be for three days more. All your companions are safe in Woodstock, except that they fret and search for you. And if you know where they will be lodging, I would recommend that you join them now, by night, and stay well out of sight until the day the case is heard. For if this trap was designed to keep you from appearing in the King's court, some further attempt might yet be made. Have you your evidences safe? They did not take them?"

"Brother Orderic, my clerk, was carrying the documents, but he could not conduct the case in court. I only am accredited to represent my abbot. But, my son, how is it that the case still goes unheard? The King keeps strict day and time, it's well known. How comes it that God and you have saved me from disgrace and loss?"

"Father, for all too bitter reason, the King could not be present."

Cadfael told him the whole of it, how half the young chivalry of England had been wiped out in one blow, and the King left without an heir. Prior Heribert, shocked and dismayed, fell to praying in a grieving whisper for both dead and living, and Cadfael walked beside the horse in silence, for what more was there to be said? Except that King Henry, even in this shattering hour, willed that his justice should still prevail, and that was virtue in any monarch. Only when they came into the sleeping town did Cadfael again interrupt the prior's fervent prayers with a strange question.

"Father, was any man of your escort carrying steel? A dagger, or any such weapon?"

"No, no, God forbid!" said the prior, shocked. "We have no use for arms. We trust in God's peace, and after it in the King's."

"So I thought," Cadfael said, nodding. "It is another discipline, for another venture."

BY THE CHANGE IN Mauduit's countenance, Cadfael knew the hour of the following day when the news reached him that his prisoner was flown. All the rest of that day he went about with nerves at stretch and ears pricked for any sensational rumors being bandied around the town, and eyes roving anxiously in dread of the sight of Prior Heribert in court or street, braced to pour out his complaint to the King's officers. But as the hours passed and still there was no sign, he began to be a little eased in his mind, and to hope still for a miraculous deliverance. The Benedictine brothers were seen here and there, mute and somber-faced; surely they could have had no word of their superior. There was nothing to be done but set his teeth, keep his countenance, wait, and hope.

The second day passed, and the third day came, and Mauduit's hopes had soared again, for still there was no word. He made his appearance before the King's judge confidently, his charters in hand. The abbey was the suitor. If all went well, Roger would not even have to state his case, for the plea would fail of itself when the pleader failed to appear.

It came as a shattering shock when a sudden stir at the door, prompt to the hour appointed, blew into the hall a small, round, unimpressive person in the Benedictine habit, hugging to him an armful of vellum rolls and followed by his black-gowned brothers in close attendance. Cadfael, too, was observing him with interest, for it was the first time he had seen him clearly. A modest man of comfortable figure and amiable countenance, rosy and mild. Not so old as that night journey had suggested, perhaps forty-five, with a shining innocence about him. But to Roger Mauduit it might have been a fire-breathing dragon entering the hall.

And who would have expected, from that gentle, even deprecating presence, the clarity and expertise with which that small man deployed his original charter, punctiliously identical to Roger's according to the account Alard had given, and omitting any specific mention of what should follow Arnulf Mauduit's death—how scrupulously he pointed out the omission and the arguments to which it might give rise, and followed it up with two letters written by that same Arnulf Mauduit to Abbot Fulchered, referring in plain terms to the obligatory return of the manor and village after his death, and pledging his son's loyal observance of the obligation.

It might have been want of proofs that caused Roger to make so poor a job of refuting the evidence, or it might have been craven conscience. Whatever the cause, judgment was given for the abbey.

CADFAEL PRESENTED HIMSELF BEFORE the lord he was leaving, barely an hour after the verdict was given.

"My lord, your suit is concluded, and my service with it. I have done what I pledged, here I part from you."

Roger sat sunk in gloom and rage, and lifted upon him a glare that should have felled him, but failed of its impact.

"I misdoubt me," Roger said, smoldering, "how you have observed your loyalty to me. Who else could know . . .' He bit his tongue in time, for as long as it remained unsaid, no accusation had been made, and no rebuttal was needed. He would have liked to ask, How did you know? But he thought better of it. "Go, then, if you have nothing more to say."

"As to that," Cadfael said meaningly, "nothing more need be said. It's over." And that was recognizable as a promise, but with uneasy implications, for plainly on some other matter he still had a thing to say.

"My lord, give some thought to this, for I was until now in your service and wish you no harm. Of those four who attended Prior Heribert on his way here, not one carried arms. There was neither sword nor dagger nor knife of any kind among the five of them."

He saw the significance of that go home, slowly but with bitter force. The masterless men had been nothing but a children's tale, but until now Roger had thought, as he had been meant to think, that that dagger-stroke in the forest had been a bold attempt by an abbey servant to defend his prior. He blinked and swallowed and stared, and began to sweat, beholding a perilous gulf into which he had all but stumbled.

"There were none there who bore arms," said Cadfael, "but your own."

A double-edged ambush that had been, to have him out in the forest by night, all unsuspecting. And there were as many miles between Woodstock and Sutton Mauduit returning as coming, and there would be other nights as dark on the way.

"Who?" asked Roger in a grating whisper. "Which of them? Give him a name!"

"No," Cadfael said simply. "Do your own divining. I am no longer in your service, I have said all I mean to say."

Roger's face had turned grey. He was hearing again the plan unfolded so seductively in his ear. "You cannot leave me so! If you know so much, for God's sake return with me, see me safely home, at least. You I could trust!"

"No," said Cadfael again. "You are warned, now guard yourself."

It was fair, he considered; it was enough. He turned and went away without another word. He went, just as he was, to Vespers in the parish church, for no better reason—or so he thought then—than that the dimness within the open doorway beckoned him as he turned his back on a duty completed, inviting him to quietness and thought, and the bell was just sounding. The little prior was there, ardent in thanksgiving, one more creature who had fumbled his way to the completion of a task and the turning of a leaf in the book of his life.

Cadfael watched out the office and stood mute and still for some time after priest and worshippers had departed. The silence after their going was deeper than the ocean and more secure than the earth. Cadfael breathed and consumed it like new bread. It was the light touch of a small hand on the hilt of his sword that startled him out of that profound isolation. He looked down to see a little acolyte, no higher than his elbow, regarding him gravely from great round eyes of blinding blue, intent and challenging, as solemn as ever was angelic messenger.

"Sir," said the child in stern treble reproof, tapping the hilt with an infant finger, "should not all weapons of war be laid aside here?"

"Sir," said Cadfael hardly less gravely, though he was smiling, "you may very well be right." And slowly he unbuckled the sword from his belt and went and laid it down, flatlings, on the lowest step under the altar. It looked strangely appropriate and at peace there. The hilt, after all, was a cross.

PRIOR HERIBERT WAS AT a frugal supper with his happy brothers in the parish priest's house when Cadfael asked audience with him. The little man came out graciously to welcome a stranger, and knew him for an acquaintance at least and now at a breath certainly a friend.

"You, my son! And surely it was you at Vespers? I felt that I should know the shape of you. You are the most welcome of guests here, and if there is anything I and mine can do to repay you for what you did for us, you need but name it."

"Father," Cadfael said, briskly Welsh in his asking, "do you ride for home tomorrow?"

"Surely, my son, we leave after Prime. Abbot Godefrid will be waiting to hear how we have fared."

"Then, Father, here am I at the turning of my life, free of one master's service, and finished with arms. Take me with you!"

Authors' Biographies

Peter Tremayne is the pseudonym of Peter Beresford Ellis, a professor of law who lives in London, England. He conceived the idea for Sister Fidelma, a seventh-century Celtic lawyer, to demonstrate for his students that women could be legal advocates under the Irish system of law. Sister Fidelma has since appeared in eight novels, the most recent being *The Spider's Web*, and many short stories that have been collected in the anthology *Hemlock at Vespers* and *Other Sister Fidelma Mysteries*. He has also written, under his own name, more than twenty-five books on history, biography, and Irish and Celtic mythology, including *Celtic Women: Women in Celtic Society* and *Literature and Celt and Greek: Celts in the Hellenic World*. A native of Coventry, England, he has written a column for the *Irish Democrat* since 1987.

Doug Allyn is an accomplished author whose short fiction regularly graces a year's best collections. His work has appeared in *Once Upon a Crime*, *Cat Crimes Through Time*, and *The Year's 25 Finest Criman and Mystery Stories*, volumes 3 and 4. His stories of Talifer, the wandering minstrel, have appeared in *Ellery Queen's Mystery Magazine* and *Murder Most Scottish*. His story "The Dancing Bear," a Tallifer tale, won the Edgar Award for short fiction for 1994. His other series character is veterinarian Dr. David Westbrook, whose exploits have recently been collected in the anthology *All Creatures Dark and Dangerous*. He lives with his wife in Montrose, Michigan.

Lillian Stewart Carl writes what she calls "gonzo mythology" fantasy novels, as well as mystery and romantic suspense novels. While growing up in Missouri and Ohio, she began writing at an early age and has continued all her life, even while traveling to Europe, Great Britain, the Middle East, and India, among other places. Her novels include *Dust to Dust*, *Shadow Dancers*, and *Wings of Power*. Her short fiction has appeared in *Alternate Generals* and *Past Lives, Present Tense*. She lives in Carrollton, Texas.

Gillian Linscott lives a few miles from the site of the Battle at Mortimer's Cross, where she took inspiration for her story. Known for her Edwardian novels featuring radical suffragette Nell Bray, she has also written five novels about Bray. A former Parliamentary reporter for the BBC, she has also written a historical mystery set in Alaska as well as a contemporary mystery series featuring ex-policeman-turned-physical-trainer Birdie Linnett. Her short fiction appears in such anthologies as *Murder, They Wrote*. She lives with her husband, nonfiction author Tony Geraghty, in England.

Margaret Frazer is the pseudonym of Gail Frazier, who has been writing mystery novels for years, formerly with Mary Kuhfield. She has since taken the pseudonym of Margaret Frazer to continue the medieval murder mysteries featuring Sister Frevisse, a great-niece of Geoffrey Chaucer. The series spans nine novels, with *The Maidens' Tale* and *The Prioress's Tale*. She lives in Minnesota and is hard at work on more Sister Frevisse mysteries.

Clayton Emery has been a blacksmith, dishwasher, schoolteacher in Australia, carpenter, zookeeper, farmhand, land surveyor, volunteer firefighter, and award-winning technical writer. He's forty-four years old, an umpteenth-generation Yankee, a Navy brat, and an aging hippie. He lives in New Hampshire with his doctor wife and son Hunter, who keeps him apprised of the latest computer games. He spends his spare time restoring a 1763 house, gardens, and stone walls, and reenacting the American revolution in a kilt. He has written in every genre from children's books to mystery to fantasy to science fiction. Other short stories featuring Robin Hood and Marian have been published in *Ellery Queen's Mystery Magazine*. Read more of his stories at www.claytonemery.com.

Edward Marston is the prolific author of plays, short stories, and novels, with his historical mystery *The Roaring Boy* being nominated for the Edgar Award for best novel in 1995. He is currently writing two series, one featuring Nicholas Bracewell, a stage manager for an acting company in Elizabethan England, the other with Ralph Delchard and Gervase Bret, two men who travel England investigating land claims in the eleventh century. His latest novel is *The King's Evil*, another mystery, set in Restoration England. A former chairman of the Crime Writer's Association in the United Kingdom, he lives in rural Kent, England.

Tony Geraghty is the respected author of the nonfiction military books *Who Dares Win*, a history of the British Special Air Services Regiment; *March or Die: A New History of the French Foreign Legion*; and *Brixmis*, the story of England's spying role during the Cold War. A veteran paratrooper, he lives with his wife, fellow author Gillian Linscott, in England.

Kathy Lynn Emerson has enjoyed great success with her Lady Appleton–Face Down series. Her latest, *Face Down Beneath the Eleanor Cross*, has just been released. She has written in just about every genre, including romance, children's fiction and nonfiction, biography, and history. Recently, the Face Down series was optioned for film. She lives and writes in rural Maine with her husband of more than twenty-five years and a large calico cat.

Michael Jecks worked as a computer salesman until 1994, when an industry sales slump forced him to consider a new career. He wrote *The Last Templar*, the first of nine medieval mystery novels, found an agent, and then a publisher who offered him a three-book deal. Of his novels, he says, "I guess I'm like many people who love books—for many years I thought I should try writing, but with a mortgage to support, there never seemed to be time. My stories are based on extensive research, which has persuaded me that people haven't changed at all in seven hundred years. The same motivations lead to murder: jealousy, infidelity, greed, and so on. I try to show where our ancestors were different. How did the law work, how did people generally view government and justice? How did they live? It's not easy to show what life was really like, but it's a challenge I enjoy." Recent novels in his Medieval West County series include *The Abbot's Gibbet* and *Belladonna at Belstone*.

Brendan DuBois, primarily known for making the New England countryside come alive in his novels and short stories, has written several dozen critically acclaimed short stories, and has had his work appear in several best year's anthologies. One of his latest stories, "The Dark Snow," was nominated for the Edgar Award for best short story of 1996. Recent novels include *Shattered Shell*, the third mystery featuring contemporary magazine writer-sleuth Lewis Cole, and *Resurrection Day*, a techno-thriller extrapolating what might have happened if the Cuban Missile Crisis had turned into a full-fledged war. He lives in Exeter, New Hampshire.

Kristine Kathryn Rusch won three Reader's Choice Awards in 1999 for three different stories in three different magazines in two different genres: mystery and science fiction. That same year, her short fiction was nominated for the Hugo, Nebula, and Locus Awards. Since she had just returned to writing short fiction after quitting her short-fiction editing job at *The Magazine of Fantasy and Science Fiction*, she was quite encouraged by this welcome back to writing. She never quit writing novels, and has sold more than forty-five of them, some under pseudonyms, in mystery, science fiction, fantasy, horror, and romance. Her most recent mystery novel is *Hitler's Angel*. Her most recent fantasy novel is *The Black Queen*.

Ellis Peters (1913–1995) wrote more than seventy novels during her forty-year career as an author, but she will always be remembered as the creator of the twelfth-century Benedictine monk Cadfael, arguably the most famous of all medieval sleuths. The Cadfael novels were successful worldwide, eventually translated into twenty languages, and adapted into a BBC series starring Derek Jacobi. The series was also critically lauded, and she won a

Crime Writers Association Silver Dagger for the novel *Monk's Hood* and was nominated for an Agatha Award for the novel *The Potter's Field*. She also won the Edgar Allan Poe Award from the Mystery Writers of America for her novel *Death and the Joyful Woman*, featuring her earlier series characters, George, Bunty, and Dominic Felse, a sleuthing family that lived in Shropshire, England. She was awarded the Order of the British Empire in 1994, just before the last Cadfael novel, *Brother Cadfael's Penance*, was released.

Introduction:
John Helfers is a writer and editor living in Green Bay, Wisconsin. His fiction appears in more than a dozen anthologies, including *Future Net*, *Once Upon a Crime*, *First to Fight*, and *The UFO Files*, among others. His first anthology project, *Black Cats and Broken Mirrors*, was published by DAW Books in 1998, and it contains the Nebula Award–winning short story "Thirteen Ways to Water." Recent books include the published anthologies *Future Crimes* and *Alien Abductions*, as well as a novel in progress. Born in Lombard, Illinois, he moved to Green Bay in 1990, where he attended the University of Wisconsin–Green Bay, graduating in 1995 with a degree in English. Currently, he writes and edits full time.

Copyrights and Permissions

Murder Most Divine

Ecclesiastical Tales of Unholy Crimes

Contents

Introduction / 579
RALPH McINERNY

The Second
Commandment / 587
CHARLOTTE ARMSTRONG

Holy Living and Holy
Dying / 627
ROBERT BARNARD

Mea Culpa / 637
JAN BURKE

The Wrong Shape / 657
G. K. CHESTERTON

Brother Orchid / 675
RICHARD CONNELL

The Monk's Tale / 693
P. C. DOHERTY

When Your Breath
Freezes / 717
KATHLEEN DOUGHERTY

State of Grace / 733
LOREN D. ESTLEMAN

Jemima Shore's First
Case / 743
ANTONIA FRASER

The Witch's Tale / 763
MARGARET FRAZER

Murder Mysteries / 781
NEIL GAIMAN

The Bishop and the Hit
Man / 807
ANDREW GREELEY

The Sweating Statue / 819
EDWARD D. HOCH

The Stripper / 833
H. H. HOLMES

The Base of the
Triangle / 845
RALPH McINERNY

Conventual Spirit / 865
SHARAN NEWMAN

Miss Butterfingers / 881
MONICA QUILL

In the Confessional / 915
ALICE SCANLAN REACH

Author Biographies / 925

Copyrights and
Permissions / 931

Introduction

RALPH McINERNY

No literary genre exhibits art's dependence on a moral point of reference more strikingly than the murder mystery. To take the life of another is wrong; the murderer must be discovered and suitably punished. That is the rock bottom assumption of the murder mystery. In an age when commonly shared moral beliefs are increasingly atrophying, the murder mystery continues in popularity, perhaps as the last refuge of the reader who wants to see good triumph and evil punished, at least on the printed page.

Was G. K. Chesterton's Father Brown the first clerical sleuth? I do not know. Given Chesterton's accomplishment in the five collections of stories featuring his engaging priest, Father Brown might have been the last as well. Few writers would be willing to risk comparison with the works of one of the consummate stylists of the English language. When it was proposed to me that I should launch a series of mysteries featuring a priest, I reacted as one would to any sacrilegious suggestion. Get thou behind me, agent. Presume to rival Chesterton's Father Brown? It is tough enough being compared with lesser lights. But I was young and foolhardy then and overcame my reluctance. I have just finished the twentieth of my Father Dowling mysteries, *Triple Pursuit*. It is not that I survived the comparison with Chesterton—only a few reviewers were irresponsible enough to make it—but that I and many other writers came to see that in a morally disintegrating society, any appeal to what had once been the common morality is more easily made through a clerical or religious figure whose confidence in the moral law was bolstered by their religious faith.

The nun or priest or monk represents right and wrong more dramatically than an officer of the law or ordinary private detective. A master detective need not be a moral paragon; since Sherlock Holmes, it is the convention to invest the great man with flaws, though flaws unrelated to the skills needed for detecting. Severer demands are put on the man of the cloth or cowl and the woman with a veil. Writers, themselves unsympathetic with religious beliefs, are drawn to such figures in order to look for chinks in the armor of representatives of religion. Finding celibacy incredible, a writer's imagination may teem with images of sexual repression. "State of Grace" is one such story; "Holy Living and Holy Dying" another. The former, a hardboiled story in which everyone is corrupt, including the sleuth, displays an unsure grasp of the ins and outs of clerical life, but not only readers who are similarly ill-informed can enjoy it. The bishop's basement is equipped with all the instruments of torture with which Hollywood has furnished the Inquisition; a Bible said to have belonged to Saint Thomas More is sold for a hundred dollars! The latter, "Holy Living and Holy Dying," one of the better written stories in this collection, somehow surmounts its reliance on cliches of this variant on the genre—the confessional, the supposed celibate having recourse to prostitutes—and makes the improbable plausible. There is little detecting done in either—events simply disclose themselves.

The eighteen stories brought together in this collection are not, of course, homogenous. The role of the cleric or religious varies from story to story. There are four stories that have a religious woman as principal figure, but some are modern and some are medieval. In several of the stories, it is the cleric who is the criminal rather than the sleuth. Andrew Greeley's story conveys something of the confusion felt by some clerics as to what it is they represent, but by and large, whether seen as the basis for a charge of hypocrisy or as the filter through which events are assessed, the requirements of Christianity are unambiguously assumed in most of these stories.

† † †

Unlike natural kinds, literary genres and their subdivisions can be shuffled and reorganized in various ways. Thus, the stories in this collection can be divided into the medieval and the modern. They can be separated into those that feature religious women and those that feature male clerics—priests, bishops, monks. They can be divided into those that approach the world of religious belief from the outside and those that move from within. And they could be divided into those that are marked by rather elementary mistakes about Christianity and Church lore and those that are sure. The medieval ones could be divided into those that contain embarrassing ignorance of Latin and those that do not. And the familiar subcategories of the mystery could be invoked—hardboiled vs. softboiled. Two of the stories ascend into almost mystical fantasy.

Given these various possibilities for grouping the stories, any taxonomy chosen would be more or less arbitrary. So it is that the stories are presented in an alphabetic order based on the surnames of the authors. I would like to say at least a word or two about all the stories, but considerably more about some of them. Readers will of course agree or disagree with my preferences, and that is as it should be. The stories were not gathered to represent any *a priori* attitude of my own, and the hope is that those who do not share my predilections will find here ample opportunity to indulge their own delights.

✝ ✝ ✝

Stories set in the Middle Ages inhabit a world where Christian belief is taken to be universal and murder is unlikely to be thought of as just what you would expect from a believer. "The Monk's Tale" is perhaps the most successful use of the medieval setting by the stories in this collection. We are in England in the fourteenth century; the story is told in a chronicle that a penitent friar keeps for his superior—he is under a cloud for having gone off to war despite his clerical status, and for having taken a brother with him who was killed, leaving their parents bereft of children —the problem is the death of an abbot. Our friar is the assistant in such matters of Sir John the coroner, and off they go. The monastic life is described with authority but the story never becomes learned display. The transposition into this setting of the conventions of the detective story is adroitly handled.

Medieval mystery stories seem to have a recurrent component of their own—murder by poisoning, the poison garnered from the monastery herb garden. At least this is true of both "The Witch's Tale" and "The

Monk's Tale." "Conventual Spirit" is set in the convent of the Parclete, founded by Peter Abelard, with Heloise as abbess. Mysterious muddy footprints visible within the walls each morning lead the nuns to sometimes sniggering speculation as to which of them might be having a night visitor. Detection makes clear that one of the nuns is going out at night, and leaving the muddy footprints on her return. In the final scene, the nun whose curiosity has uncovered this much receives sage advice from Heloise the abbess. The sleepwalking nun is espied dancing in the nude on a moonlit hill and Heloise gives the younger nun a quasi-psychiatric explanation. One would have liked more of Heloise, endowed with her historical gifts of high intelligence and self-effacing passion. "When Your Breath Freezes" is written on the assumption that the religious life is somehow pathological. The setting, for unexplained reasons, is Alaska; the narrator's presence in the convent is curiously unjustified, the ending gothic.

"Brother Orchid"—was this made into a movie starring Edward G. Robinson?—is set in the 1930s, its slang is hopelessly dated, but still it somehow engages the reader and holds his interest right through to the surprising and satisfying ending. Of all the authors represented here, Andrew Greeley knows most about the priesthood. His story is adroitly constructed and engagingly narrated by a priest—or is he a bishop? This is never made quite clear—who unsurprisingly holds most of the author's progressive views. In an effort to deal with a penitent who wants absolution before he kills someone, Bishop [or Father] Ryan finally, against his bent, has recourse to the old catechism explanation of mortal sin. A surprising yet perfectly plausible ending puts this story at the head of the class.

"Mea Culpa" will be the favorite of many readers, I think. The character of the narrator is well-rounded, and if the adults, particularly the stepfather, are often grotesques, the story moves with unhurried sureness toward its denouement. The use of the confessional is particularly effective. "The Second Commandment" is a long and subtle story which is in many ways the most religious in this collection. The ending may have the look of a contrivance, but waiving that, the story has the most elaborate architecture of any in this collection.

And so I come to "Murder Mysteries." It would be easy to ridicule the theology of the story—an angel is murdered, its body found with blood all over the floor. Of course angels don't have bodies and they couldn't die if they wanted to, let alone be murdered. Somehow such metaphysical niceties cease to matter. The story begins in the City of the Angels, Los Angeles, and employs the device of a stranger telling a somewhat amoral young man a story involving angels, through the course of which we eventually learn he is one. The narrated story is set in heaven prior to the creation and angels are depicted as busy designing the world God will bring into being. They are trying to get the hang of death, and this is what leads to the murdered angel. The antagonists are God and Satan and the fallen angel on the park bench in Los Angeles, who tells the story,—no mute Milton he, however inglorious—sided with Satan. The revolt against God is based on the charge that He causes everything necessarily and yet holds agents accountable. How revolt would be possible if freedom is absent is a bit of a problem, but the story's imaginative range and success in writing about angels and heaven in juxtaposition with a seedy and decadent Los Angeles, makes this reader forgive all its faults.

† † †

It is sometimes said that Chesterton deliberately created an anti-Sherlock Holmes character with Father Brown. Holmes proceeds with all the impersonal objectivity of the scientific method. Brown steps into the shoes of the unknown perpetrator and is thereby able sympathetically to discern which of the suspects is guilty. "The Wrong Shape" is from the first collection of Father Brown stories, *The Innocence of Father Brown,* and has been chosen in the hope that it is relatively less known than the others. Of my own Father Dowling story, I will say only that my character began to feature in shorter fiction more than a decade after first appearing in print. I write a Father Dowling story for each issue of *Catholic Dossier,* a magazine I edit. This is one of them.

Recently I was in Melbourne at an academic meeting where we speakers were given a dinner by Archbishop Eric D'Arcy, substituting for the ordinary, Archbishop George Pell, who was in Rome. Before we went in to table, a short, bearded priest came up to me and studied me with smiling eyes. "I am Father Dowling," he announced. And so he was. He had an armful of my novels which I was delighted to sign for him. But I had the odd feeling that he was the fictional and my own Father Dowling the real one. Authorial fantasy, of course. But doubtless all the authors of stories in this collection harbor a similar certainty. Our common hope is that the reader will share it, if only for an hour or two.

Murder Most Divine

THE SECOND COMMANDMENT

CHARLOTTE ARMSTRONG

HALLEY WAS SURE GLAD THE damn fog had rolled up and was billowing off over the mountains. Hey, if you looked southwest, you could even see a couple of stars. Lucky. They might have to hang around, maybe till morning.

And it was a little too quiet out here. Not much traffic on California Route 1; on a night like this there had better not be. The sea kept booming; it always did. The men shouted once in a while at their work, but they knew their business. They'd have her up on the road, and pretty quick.

Hey, here's my chance, thought Halley, to get all the stuff down, like they keep telling me. So the young sheriff's deputy opened the back door of his official car and leaned over to let the dome light fall on his paperwork. The husband was sitting inside, and quiet.

"May I please have your name again, sir?" Halley used the polite official drone.

"Hugh Macroy." The other's voice, even in exhaustion, had a timbre and a promise of richness. A singer, maybe? Young Halley's ear had caught this possibility when he had first answered the call. He never had seen the man—at least, not too well. Now the lighting was weird—red lights flashing on the equipment, for instance.

"Address?" Halley asked, after he had checked the spelling.

"382 Scott—no, I'm sorry. 1501 South Columbo."

"That's in Santa Carla, sir? Right out of L.A?

"Yes." The man was holding his head at the temples, between thumb and two middle fingers. Poor old guy, he didn't hardly remember where he lived. But Halley, who knew better than to indulge in emotions of his own over one of these routine tragedies, figured himself lucky the fellow wasn't cracking up.

"Your age, sir?"

"Forty-five."

(Check. Kind of an old-looking guy.) "Occupation?"

"I am the pastor at St. Andrew's."

Halley became a little more respectful, if possible, because—well, hell, you were supposed to be. "Just you and your wife in the car, sir? En route from Carmel, didn't you say? To Santa Carla?

"We had expected to stay the night in San Luis Obispo."

"I see. Your wife's name, please?"

"Sarah. Sarah Bright."

Halley wrote down *Sara.* "Her age, please?"

"Fifty-five."

(Huh!) "Housewife, sir, would you say?"

"I suppose so." The man was very calm—too beat, probably, thought Halley, to be anything else. Although Halley had heard some who carried on and cried and sometimes words kept coming out of them like a damn broken faucet.

"And how long you been married?" the deputy sheriff continued politely.

"I think it has been two days, if today is Wednesday." Now, in the syllables, the voice keened softly.

"Any chil—"(Oh oh!) "Excuse me, sir."

"There is Sarah's daughter in San Luis Obispo. Mrs. Geoffrey Minter. She should be told about this as soon as may be. She will have been worrying."

"Yes, sir," said Halley, reacting a little crisply, not only to the tone but to the grammar. "If you've got her address or phone, I can get her notified right now."

The man dictated an address and a phone number as if he were reading them from a list he could see. Halley could tell his attention had gone away from what he was saying.

Halley thanked him and called in from the front seat. "Okay. They'll call her, sir. We probably won't be here too long now," he told the silent figure and drew himself away, shutting the car doors gently.

He strolled on strong legs to the brink. He could hear the heavy water slamming into rock forty feet below. (Always did.) The night sky was clearing all the way overhead now. There was even a pale moon.

Some honeymoon, thought Halley. But he wasn't going to say anything. It had occurred to him that this one might not be routine, not exactly, and that Halley had better watch his step, and be at all times absolutely correct.

"How's it going?" be inquired cheerfully of the toilers.

† † †

They had a strong light playing on her as she came up in the basket. She was dead, all right.

Macroy got out of the car and looked down at her and maybe he prayed or something. Halley didn't wait too long before he touched the clergyman's arm.

"They'll take her now, sir. If you'll just come with me?"

The man turned obediently.

Halley put him into the back seat of the official car and got in to drive.

As the deputy steered skillfully onto the pavement, Macroy said, "You're very kind. I don't think I could drive—not just now." His voice sounded shaky, but it was still singsongy.

"That's all right, sir," said Halley. But he thought, Don't he know his car's got to stay put and get checked out, for godsake? That kind of voice—Halley didn't exactly trust it. Sounded old-timey to him. Or some kind of phony.

On the highway, that narrow stretch along the curving cliffs, Halley scooted along steadily and safely toward the place where this man must go. By the book. And that was how Halley was going, you bet—by the book. It might not be a routine case at all.

So forget the sight of Sarah Bright Macroy, aged fifty-five, in her final stillness. And how she'd looked as if she had about four chins where the crepey skin fell off her jawbone. And thick in the waist, but with those puny legs some old biddies get, sticking out like sticks, with knots in them, and her shoes gone so that the feet turned outward like a couple of fins, all gnarled and bunioned. Um boy, some honeymoon! Halley couldn't figure it.

So swiftly, decisively, youthfully, he drove the official car, watching the guy from the back of his head in case he got excited or anything. But he didn't.

He just sat there, quiet, stunned.

† † †

Sheriff's Captain Horace Burns was a sharp-nosed man of forty-seven and there was a universal opinion (which included his own) that you had to get up early in the morning to fool him. His office had seen about as much wear as he had, but Burns kept it in stern order, and it was a place where people behaved themselves.

Burns had felt satisfied with Halley, who sat up straight in the hard chair by the door with his young face poker-smooth. His report had been clear and concise. His mien was proper. The Captain's attention was on this preacher. He saw a good-looking man, about his own age, lean and well set up, his face aquiline but rugged enough not to be "pretty." He also saw the pallor on the skin and the glaze of shock in the dark eyes—which, of course, were to be expected.

Macroy, as invited, was telling the story in his own words, and the Captain, listening, didn't fiddle with anything. His hands were at rest. He listened like a cat.

"So we left Carmel early this afternoon," Macroy was saying. "We had driven up on 101. We thought we'd come down along the ocean, having no idea that the fog was going to roll in the way it did."

Behind him a clerk was taking it down. Macroy didn't seem to be aware of that.

"But it did," said that voice, and woe was in it. "As thick a fog as I've ever experienced. We had passed Big Sur. You can't, you know, get through the mountains and change routes."

"You're stuck with it," the Captain said agreeably.

"Yes. Well, it was very slow going and very tiring. We were so much delayed that the sun went down, although you could hardly tell."

"You stopped," Burns prodded, thinking that the voice sounded like a preacher's, all right. "About what time?"

"I don't know. There was a sudden rift and I was able to see the wide place to our right. On the ocean side. A scenic point, I imagine." The Captain nodded. "Well, it looked possible to take the car off the highway there, so I—so I did. I had been so tense for such a long time that I was very glad to stop driving. Then Sarah wished to get out of the car, and I—"

"Why?"

"Beg pardon?"

"Why did she wish to get out of the car?" The Captain used the official drone. When the minister didn't answer, Burns said, "It has to be included in your statement."

"Yes," said Macroy. He glanced at the clerk. "She needed to—"

When he got stuck, Halley's face was careful not to ripple.

"Answer a call of nature," droned the Captain. "Has to be on record. That's right, Reverend?"

Macroy said with sober sadness, "Yes. I took the flashlight and got out to make sure there was enough margin between us and the edge." He stared over the Captain's head, seeing visions. "The light didn't accomplish much," he went on, "except to create a kind of blank white wall, about three feet before me. But I could check the ground. So I helped her out. I gave her the light and cautioned her. She promised not to go too far. I, of course, got back behind the wheel."

He hesitated.

The Captain said, "Car lights on, were they?"

"Yes.

"She went around behind the car?"

"Yes."

"Go on. Full details, please. You're doing fine."

"I was comforting my right shoulder with a little massage," said the minister with a touch of bitterness, "when I thought I heard her cry out."

"Motor off, was it?" The Captain's calm insistence held him.

"Yes. It was very quiet. Except for the surf. When I heard, or thought I heard—I listened, but there was no other cry. In a short while, I called to her. There was no answer. I couldn't—couldn't, of course, see anything. I called again. And again. Finally, I got out."

"And what did you do?" said the Captain.

"The flashlight," he said, "was there."

"Oh, was it? The light on, I mean?"

"Yes." Macroy seemed to wait for and rely on these questions. "It was lying on the ground, pointing to sea. I picked it up. I began to call and range the whole—the whole—well, it was a sort of platform, you might say, a sort of triangular plateau. I shuffled over all of it—between the pavement and the brink—and she wasn't—"

"Take your time," said the Captain.

But the minister lifted his head and spoke more rapidly. "At last, and I don't know when, a car came along. Mercifully it stopped. The driver offered me a ride. But I couldn't leave her." The anguished music was back in the voice. "How could I leave her?"

"He didn't get out? The driver of the car?" said Burns, again coming to the rescue.

"No. No. I begged him to send some help. Then I just kept on ranging and calling and—hoping and waiting, until help came." Macroy sank back.

"He called in, all right," Burns said in his flat tone. "Hung up without giving his name. But he can be found, I think, any time we need him."

Macroy was staring at the Captain with total incomprehension. He said, "I would like to thank him—yes, I would like to someday." Not now, wept his voice. Not yet.

"Can be arranged." Burns leaned back. "Just a couple of questions, Mr. Macroy. Was it your wife's suggestion that you stop the car?"

"I beg your pardon?"

"Did she ask you to stop? Or was it your idea?"

"Oh, I'm sorry. I wasn't following. No, it was my—well, you see, I knew she was in distress. But it was I who saw the opportunity."

"I see," said the Captain. "And you got back in the car for reasons of—er—privacy?"

"Values," said Macroy with sudden hollowness. "How ridiculous! In that dangerous spot. I knew how dangerous it was. I shouldn't have let her. I shouldn't."

The Captain, had he been a cat, would have had his ears up, and his tail, curled, would have stirred lazily.

"I will always—" Macroy was as good as weeping now. "Always regret." His eyes closed.

"You were only a few miles from low ground," said the Captain calmly. "You didn't know that?"

Macroy had his face in his hands and he rocked his whole body in the negative.

The Captain, when his continued listening was obviously proving unprofitable, said for the record, "You didn't know. Well, sir, I guess that's about all, for now."

"Where have they brought her?" Macroy dropped his hands.

"I—er—wouldn't go over to the funeral parlor. No point. You realize there's got to be an autopsy?" Macroy said nothing. "Now, we aren't holding you, but you're a lot of miles from home, so I think what you'd better do, Reverend, is go over to the motel and rest there for the night. We'll need your signature on your statement, for one thing. In the morning will do." The Captain stood up.

"Thank you," said Macroy. "Yes. I couldn't leave."

"Did you push your wife?" said the Captain conversationally.

Macroy's face could be no paler. "No," he said with wondering restraint. "I told you."

"The motel," said the Captain in exactly the same conversational manner, "is almost straight across the highway, a little to your left."

Macroy ducked his head in farewell, said nothing, and walked to the door. Halley jumped up and politely opened it for him.

"Halley." Burns was mild but Halley turned quickly and let the door close itself behind the minister.

"Yes, sir."

"This one is going to splash," said Burns glumly. "So watch yourself."

"Yes, sir. Did he do it, sir?" My master will know, of course, Halley's face said.

"Whether he did or not, we're going to be able to say we went looking for every damn crumb of evidence there ain't going to be." This was, however crossly said, a palsy-walsy kind of thing for Burns to be saying.

"You saw the woman, sir?" The Captain stared sourly but Halley went on. It bubbled out of him. "I can't help thinking—some honeymoon! I mean—"

The Captain grunted, "Yeah, and he's a pretty good-looking Joe. Well," he added with a warning glare, "keep your little old baby face *shut*."

"Yes, *sir.*"

"Thing of it is," said the Captain less belligerently, "there was this opportunity. But if he did it, he don't *know* why. And he can't believe it, so he don't really know it at all. Don't think that can't happen."

Halley marveled respectfully.

"You get on over to the funeral parlor, and when the daughter shows bring her by."

Burns turned to instruct the clerk. Damn vultures, he thought. The damn press was out there. Well, *they* didn't have to go by the book, but they'd get precious little out of him.

✝ ✝ ✝

Saul Zeigler, aged twenty-two, was standing with Carstairs in the hallway of the low building. Zeigler was a local, just out of college, working for peanuts and green as grass. He deferred to the older man, who was semi-retired these days but still picked up occasional plums for the big L.A. paper. Carstairs, with his connections, had already been on the phone to Santa Carla. Zeigler was impressed.

When they saw a man come out of the Captain's office alone, Carstairs moved in before Zeigler could get his own wits going. The hall was a barren length, with institutional green walls, a worn linoleum floor, and three naked light bulbs strung in a line overhead. The tall thin man looked ghastly.

"Reverend Macroy?" Carstairs was saying. "Excuse me. Terrible tragedy. Could we talk a minute?" Carstairs did not wait for permission. "Your bride was Sarah Bright? That's right, isn't it, sir?"

"Yes."

"My name is Carstairs," said Carstairs, forcing the manly handshake. "I'm that necessary evil, the newspaperman. But it's always best to get the facts from the ones who were there. Better all around."

Smooth, thought Zeigler, as Carstairs kept boring in.

"Sarah Bright was the widow of Herman Bright? Bright Electronics?"

"Yes.

"A very successful enterprise, I understand."

"Yes, I—yes."

"I understand you'd moved into her mansion on South Columbo?" Carstairs was chatty-sounding.

"Her house," said Macroy wearily.

"About how long had you two been courting, Reverend?" Carstairs became the old buddy.

Zeigler thought the drawn face winced, but the man said quietly, "We met about six months ago."

"She was an older woman?"

"Older than I," said Macroy. "If you would excuse me, please, I am not feeling up to an interview. I would like to get over to the motel now and be alone."

Carstairs brushed this off as if it had never been spoken. "Bright died four years ago, wasn't it? And your first wife died when?"

The minister put out one hand and braced himself on the wall. "Nine years ago," he said patiently.

"You and Sarah Bright got married Monday?"

"Yes. In the morning."

"And took off for a honeymoon trip?" Carstairs had shouldered around to face Macroy, who seemed driven closer to the wall.

"Yes. Yes. May I please—" Macroy pleaded.

"I'm very sorry," said Carstairs, "I know this is a very bad time." But his feet in their battered alligator shoes didn't move. "If you could just run over what happened, just briefly? I certainly want to get it absolutely straight, absolutely correct."

"We left Carmel early this afternoon." The minister put his free palm over one eye. "I took the scenic route because I thought she would enjoy—"

"Bum choice this time of year, wasn't it?" said Carstairs in a genial way.

The minister took his hand down and moved until his shoulders touched the wall. He was blinking, as if there was something going on that he couldn't understand. His silence was thunderous.

Zeigler found himself pushing in to say respectfully, "I understand, sir, that the whole coastline was closed in tight. Worst fog in years. Pretty bad, was it?"

"Yes," said Macroy, but he was looking at the older man and a hostility had sprung up, as invisible but as unmistakable as a gust of wind. The dazed look was beginning to lift from the dark eyes, like mist being blown away.

Carstairs said blandly, "Now, you stopped, sir? Why was that?"

Macroy didn't answer.

"I'm trying to find out how this terrible thing could have happened," said Carstairs, all innocent patience. "Why you stopped, for instance? What I mean, there couldn't have been a whole lot of scenery to see, not in that fog and after dark." Now his innocence was cruel and he was defensively hostile. Zeigler could feel it on his own skin.

Macroy said, "No." His voice had gone flat.

"Why did you get out of the car? Or, I should say, why did the lady get out? By herself, did she? Didn't have a little lover's spat, I'm sure. Then why did she get out?"

Carstairs was bullying now, and young Zeigler discovered that *he* couldn't take it. So he tugged at the bigger man. "She hadda go," he said deep in his skinny young throat, "and you know it, so why badger the poor guy? Lay off!"

"So okay," said Carstairs, "but you tell me how in hell she could have *fallen* off that damn cliff?"

"Maybe you don't understand women," said Zeigler fiercely.

Carstairs laughed. Then Zeigler saw the minister's face. He stood there, leaning against the wall, having made no move to escape. On his face there was such a look of loathing and sorrow and bewilderment—

"People are always interested," said Carstairs cheerily, turning back on his prey. "Do you happen to know what Mrs. Bright—excuse me, Mrs. Macroy—was worth?"

Macroy shook his head slightly. His lips were drawn back. He looked like a death's-head. Abruptly he thrust himself from the wall. "Let me pass."

"Why, certainly. Certainly." Carstairs played surprise that his courtesy could possibly be questioned. "Thank you very much, sir," he called after Macroy, who walked away from them. Then he said to Zeigler, "And how do you like them velvet tonsils? I'll *bet* he knows. The merry widow was worth millions, kiddo. So maybe she *did* have to go. Right?"

Zeigler didn't dare open his mouth.

Then, at the far end of the hall, the street doors burst open and a woman and two men entered. The woman came first, weeping violently, her head down, a handkerchief over her mouth.

Macroy saw her and said, "Eunice. I'm so sorry, my dear. So sorry." The music was back in his voice.

But the woman dropped the handkerchief and lifted red-rimmed furious eyes. She was about thirty, already thickening at the middle, no beauty at best, and now ugly in hysteria. "I don't want to talk to you!" she shrieked, recoiling. "I never want to see you again, ever!"

A dapper man with dark-rimmed eyeglasses put his arm around her. "Come now, Eunice. Hush up, sweetheart."

"All *I* know," the woman screamed, "is that my darling mother was just fine until she had to marry *him*, and now she's all smashed up and dead and broken!" She wailed and hit out at the air.

Captain Burns was there as if he had flown in. He didn't care for scenes. He and Halley took hold of the woman between them, but she cried out to her husband, "You *tell* him. He's *not* going to live in my mother's house and have all my mother's lovely things."

Burns said, "You'll come with me now, Mrs. Minter." And she went.

But Geoffrey Minter lingered to say to Macroy in a high, cold, uninflected voice, "You'd better not try to talk to Eunice just now. She's very upset."

The understatement of the year, thought Zeigler.

Macroy said, "Geoffrey, believe me—"

But Geoffrey said, "By the way, Eunice wants *me* to take charge of the funeral. I certainly hope you aren't going to raise any objections."

"No," said Macroy, staggering. "No. None at all." He walked away, curving erratically to brace himself against the wall at every few strides.

Zeigler said, "He's never going to make it across the damn road."

"So be his guide," said Carstairs. "You and your bleeding heart. But what you get you bring back to Papa. I'll cover the loved ones."

Young Zeigler went sailing after the minister. Carstairs was waylaying the son-in-law. Zeigler heard Minter's high voice saying, "I don't know the legal position. No new will has been drawn, not since the marriage. We'll find out." He, too, seemed furious in his own tight way.

Zeigler took the Reverend Macroy's arm and began to lead him.

✝   ✝   ✝

The arm he held was tense and deeply trembling and it accepted his hand only by default, but Zeigler got them safely across the highway and into the motel office. Zeigler explained to the woman there—"tragic accident"—"no luggage"—"Sheriff's Captain suggested—"

The woman was awed and a little frightened. It was Zeigler who took the key. He knew the place and guided Macroy into the inner court, found the numbered door, unlocked it, switched on a light, glanced around at the lifeless luxury.

He didn't know whether he was now alone with a heartbroken bridegroom or with a murderer. It was his job to find out, if he could. He said, "Looks all right, sir. Now how about I call up and have somebody bring some hot coffee? Maybe a sandwich? You probably ought to eat."

A funny thing was happening to Zeigler's voice. It was getting musical. Damn it, whichever this man was, he was suffering, or Zeigler was a monkey's uncle.

But the minister rejected music. "No, thank you. Nothing." He remained motionless, outside the room. There were hooded lights close to the ground along the flowered borders of this courtyard and they sent shadows upward to patch that stony face with black. Zeigler looked where the man was looking—at three high, scraggly palm tops, grotesque against the clearing sky—between them and the stars, some wispy remembrances of that deadly fog still scudded.

"Come in," coaxed Zeigler. "I'll be glad to stick around a little bit if you'd like—"

"I'd rather be alone."

It was time for Zeigler to insist solicitously. But he heard himself. Saying, "Okay. I don't blame you." As he turned away, Zeigler said to himself in disgust, and almost audibly, "But I'm one hell of a newspaperman."

Macroy said, "And I'm one hell of a clergyman."

He didn't seem to know that he had spoken. He was standing perfectly still, his hands clenched at his sides. Up there the palm fronds against that ambiguous sky were like a witch's hands, bent at the knuckles, with too many taloned fingers dripping down.

The moment had an eerie importance, as if this were some kind of rite. To placate the evil mist now departing? Or a rite of passage?

A goose walked over Zeigler's grave.

Then the Reverend Macroy went into the room and closed the door.

✝   ✝   ✝

Carstairs pounced. "What did you get?"

"Nothing. Not a word," said Zeigler, lying instinctively. "Shocked stupid, poor guy."

"How stupid can you get for more than a million bucks?" said Carstairs. "Especially if you're untouchable."

"What?" said Zeigler.

"I just got off the phone with his Bishop." Carstairs looked disgusted. "Whaddaya know? Your buddy is a Lamb of God or something and pure as the driven snow."

"What did he ever do to you?" asked Zeigler curiously.

"What did I do to him, for God's sake?" Carstairs' eyes looked hot. "So I don't live in the Dark Ages! I got to get back on the phone."

Zeigler wondered who was guilty of what. He honestly didn't know.

✝   ✝   ✝

The Bishop, whose name was Roger Everard, came as soon as he could, which was at about ten o'clock the following morning. "I don't think it's wise, Hugh," he said soothingly as he pulled up his trouser legs to sit down and gazed compassionately at this unshaven face, so drawn with suffering. "I don't think you should make any such decision, and certainly not so precipitously. It's not wise at this time."

"But I *cannot*—" said Macroy.

"Surely you understand," said Everard, who often had a brisk executive way of speaking, "that these people are only doing what is their obligation according to law. Nobody seriously imagines, my dear fellow, that this was anything but an accident. And you must not feel abandoned, either. After all, you should realize that the members of your congregation can scarcely rally around when they don't even know where you are. Now, now—" the Bishop didn't pat him on the head, but he might has well have "—there are certain things that must be done and I'm here to do them."

"I am not—" said Macroy "—good enough for the job."

"You have had a terrible shock," said the Bishop didactically, "a grievous loss, and a very bad night. I beg you to be guided by me. Will you be guided by me?"

The Bishop had already tried praying aloud, but when he had seen that the praying was only increasing Macroy's distress he had cut it short. "You know," he continued, leaving God temporarily unmentioned, "that I am perfectly sure of your complete innocence, that I entirely understand, that I mourn your dear wife with you, and that I want only to be helpful and do what is best. You know that, do you not?"

"I know," groaned Macroy.

"Well, now. Here is what I advise. First, you must make yourself presentable. I believe that your suitcase is now available. Then, since you are not to be in charge—and after all, Hugh, Sarah *isn't here*—you must come home."

"Where is home?" Macroy said. "I gave up the apartment. And I cannot go to Sarah's house."

"Home with me, of course," said the Bishop triumphantly. "Now, I have brought along young Price. His father used to do my legal work and the son has more or less inherited. Freddy may not be the churchman his father was, but he is trained and intelligent and surely he can be helpful in this unfamiliar thicket. There must be an inquest, you see. I want you to talk to him, and then you must talk to the Sheriff's man, but I should imagine only briefly. And, Hugh, I want you to brace yourself to your tasks. I shall drive you by your church and you will go to your office long enough to cancel or rearrange your appointments and delegate your responsibilities. You must be strong and you must not be afraid, for remember—" and the Bishop went into scripture.

When he had finished, the face was looking somewhat less strained. The Bishop patted Macroy on a shoulder and then trotted back across the road to see whether there was any other way in which he could be helpful. A very busy man himself, the Bishop had had to cancel several appointments but he didn't begrudge his time and effort in this emergency. Obviously, poor Macroy was devastated, and the Bishop must and would take over.

† † †

Frederick Price, a busy young man in his middle thirties, ready and willing to be useful, came swinging into the court of the motel carrying the Reverend Macroy's suitcase, which had been taken from Macroy's car. The car was now parked behind the Sheriff's office, still subject to examinations of some technical kind.

Price knocked on the proper door and went in, introduced himself, and offered the minister his possessions. He saw the strain and the fatigue, of course, and was not surprised. He didn't believe this man was guilty of any crime. He guessed him to be a sensitive type and thought the whole thing, especially the red tape, was a rotten shame under the circumstances. But Price was well acquainted with red tape.

As Macroy opened the suitcase and took out his shaving kit and a clean shirt, Price said, "I've been talking to Burns and the others. The inquest is set for Friday morning. I don't think we'll have any trouble at all, sir. I'll be with you. You'll be all right, sir, so don't worry. It's only a formality. As a matter of fact, there is no evidence of *any* kind."

"Evidence?" said Macroy vaguely. He went into the bathroom to shave, leaving the door open.

"Oh, by the way," sang out Price loudly enough to be heard over the buzz of the electric shaver, "they found that motorist. The one who came by?" Price was practicing lay psychology. He'd better not pour it on too thick or too soon—not all that he had found out. Chat a little. Engage the mind. Distract the sorrow. Un-numb the man, if he could. "Captain Burns was pretty clever," he continued. "As soon as that call came in last night, he guessed from where. So right away he calls a man—Robbins is his name—the man who runs the first all-night gas station you hit once you're off the cliffs. He asked this Robbins to take a look and see if anyone had just been using the phone booth, and if possible to get the license number on his car. But the gas-station man did even better, because the fellow had used his credit card."

Price got up and ambled toward the bathroom, not sure he was being heard. Macroy seemed to be avoiding the sight of himself in the mirror while he shaved. "Name was Mitchell Simmons."

"I beg your pardon?"

"The man who stopped out there on California One." Price understood Macroy's fragmented attention.

"He was very kind," murmured Macroy.

"What he was," said Price, "was very drunk. Oh, he corroborates what you say, of course. He's a salesman. Admits he was in high spirits, to coin a pun, and in the mood to pick up waifs and strays. Which is a risk, you know."

"It is?"

"Matter of fact," said Price cheerily, "it was one of his strays who phoned the Sheriffs office. Your kind friend was in no condition to dial, I guess."

The minister turned his clean-shaven face and it was full of pain.

Price said quietly, "I'm sorry. Didn't mean to say he wasn't kind. Look, I've got some further details. I suppose you'll want to know—er—just how she died. Burns will tell you. Or I can, if you like."

"Thank you," said Macroy. He came back into the bedroom and started to unbutton his rumpled shirt. "Yes?"

She broke her neck on the rocks," said Price. "So it was instantaneous, if that's any comfort. No pain at all."

Macroy's face was still.

"She—well, you see—" Price was remembering uncomfortably that it may have taken very little time to fall forty feet, but it had taken some. "She was washed to and fro until she was—" Price didn't have the heart to say how battered. "Well, soaking wet, for one thing. The coroner says that her bladder was empty, but that has no meaning. With death—"

Macroy sat down abruptly and put his hands over his, face. "Go on, he said.

"That—part of it," said Price. "It's a little unfortunate that it has to be brought out, but I think I can assure you that it will all be handled in good taste. I think, by the way—" he changed the subject gladly "—that Minter has cooled off considerably. He made a few poorly chosen remarks last night—about her estate, I mean—but he's thought twice about it and he'll be more circumspect in the future."

Macroy was shaking his head. "I don't want her money. I won't have anything to do with Sarah's money. That wasn't what she was worth."

Price was unable to keep from sighing his relief "That's fine," he said innocently. "Now please don't worry about Friday's inquest, sir. I'll be there, right by your side all the time. The thing is to give your testimony as quietly as possible and try to—I could coach you a little, perhaps. I've been through this before, you know."

"Thank you. Have they—finished with her?" Macroy took his hands down and seemed stiffly controlled. He didn't look at Freddy Price.

"The body will be released in time to be flown to Santa Carla for services on Saturday. Mrs. Minter wants the services there—because of her mother's friends. I'm sure—" Price stuck. The fact was, he couldn't be sure that Macroy was going to be welcome at his wife's funeral.

Macroy stood up and reached for his clean shirt.

"As for this inquest, that has to be, you know—" said the young man "—it *will* be an ordeal. Why should I lie to you?"

Macroy looked at him curiously.

"But there's nothing to worry about, really," said Price heartily. "The important thing is to get you completely in the clear."

"Is it?" said Macroy monotonously.

✝   ✝   ✝

In the car later on, the Bishop excused himself and began to work on some papers. Price was riding next to the Bishop's driver. Macroy sat silent in a rear corner.

When they pulled up before St. Andrew's the Bishop noticed that Macroy was looking at it as if he had never seen it before. "Come," said Everard briskly, "run in. Your secretary will be there, I assume. Just make your arrangements as quickly as possible."

Price looked around. "You clergymen sound as if you're in the old ratrace, just like everybody else."

"Too true," sighed the Bishop.

Macroy got out and walked through the arch and across the flagstones and then into his office. Miss Maria Pinero, aged forty, leaped up and cried out, "Oh, Mr. Macroy! Oh, Mr. Macroy!" She had heard all about it on the air.

✝   ✝   ✝

In the car, Price said to the Bishop, "It's still a little hard to figure how she could have fallen. They didn't find a thing, sir. They can't even be sure just where she went over. Too many people messed around out there while they were getting her up the cliff. But there's nothing for *him* to worry about, that's for sure."

"I see," said the Bishop, looking sternly over the tops of his spectacles. "Guide him, Freddy, will you? He's in a sad state, I'm afraid."

"Do you think, sir," said Freddy Price, "I could possibly ask him to tone down his voice? It might sound—well, just a bit theatrical."

The Bishop's brows moved. "Bring it to his attention. That is, if you can get his attention." The Bishop sighed deeply. "No relatives. Nobody who can reach him on that needed human level. Well—"

✝   ✝   ✝

"I'll take care of everything," Miss Pinero was saying. "Of course I will. I understand just how you feel. It seems so cruel. To get out, just to stretch her legs after a long, long drive—" She began to weep.

Miss Pinero was not an unhandsome woman, but something about her did not appeal to men. As a matter of fact, Miss Pinero did not like men, either. But the Reverend Macroy was different. So kind, so clean and gentle—and so distant. She would do almost anything for him. She had been so happy that he wouldn't be lonely any more.

"But God knows, doesn't He," she wept, "and we must believe that it is, somehow, for the best?" Carried away by her own noble piety—for it was her loss, too—she snatched up his right hand. Macroy snatched it away.

She looked up at him with tear-dimmed vision. She had never so much as touched him before, but surely he must know that taking his hand would have been like kissing the hem of his garment.

"I must leave now." He sounded strange.

"I'll be here," she cried, "and whatever you ask—"

"Forgive me," he said hoarsely.

He walked away. She knew that he staggered as he turned a corner, and her heart skipped. He sounded as if he couldn't bear to think of what she had almost done. Neither could she. Miss Pinero trembled. She wished it hadn't happened. She wished that Sarah Bright was still alive. Maria had felt so deliciously safe, and free to go on worshiping him.

✝   ✝   ✝

The newspapers gave the story considerable space. After all, it had everything. They cautiously asked no questions, but they inevitably raised
them. How could the elderly bride have fallen? There were some blithe
spirits in the city who took to collecting the assorted circumlocutions
having to do with the poor woman's reason for going off alone into the
foggy dark. There was one columnist, based in the East, who—supposing
that, of course, there was no such thing in Southern California as a religious group that was *not* led by some crackpot—was open to a suit at law.
The Bishop considered it wiser to ignore him.

Macroy did not read the newspapers.

✝ ✝ ✝

On Friday the inquest came rather crisply to the verdict of Death from
Accidental Causes.

Halley, telling how he had been the first to see a body down below,
was a model of professional objectivity. The medical part was couched in
decently euphemistic language. Eunice Minter had not attended at all.
Geoffrey Minter said that, as far as he knew, Mrs. Sarah Bright Macroy had
been a happy bride. He exuded honorable fairness. Freddy Price was
pleased on the whole with Macroy's behavior.

The minister, however, looked beaten and crushed. His voice was low
and sad and tired. Everything droned along properly. When the coroner,
who was a straightforward country type, said bluntly, "You got back into
the car for reasons of leaving her alone to do what she had to do?" Macroy
answered, his voice dead against the dead silence of the room, "I thought,
at the time, that it was the courteous thing to do."

A soft sigh ran across the ranks of those present.

"So you have no idea how she came to fall?" pressed the coroner.

"No, sir."

And the coroner thought to himself, Well, the truth is, me neither.

But when Price spoke finally, to inform the world in a quiet and matter-of-fact manner that the Reverend Macroy firmly and irrevocably
refused to have any part of the Bright money, that did it.

Price got the minister through the swarming cameras and away with
an air of "Aw, come on, boys, knock it off" jaunty enough to arouse
nobody's aggressions. But afterward, as they drove back to the Bishop's
house, young Price for the life of him could think of nothing to chatter
about. Freddy would have enjoyed hashing it all over; he'd done his job.

But this man was a type he didn't understand. So Freddy made do with the car radio.

✝ ✝ ✝

The Bishop's spacious residence was well staffed—Macroy had every creature comfort. But the Bishop was simply too busy to spend many hours or even an adequate number of minutes with his haunted guest, who from time to time renewed his plea for a release from his vocation.

The Bishop, refusing to consider this, continued to advise patience, pending a future clarity. But, he said, obviously someone else would have to take over the Sunday services at St. Andrew's. The Bishop had resolved to do it himself.

But he did think that if Macroy, with the help of God, could find the fortitude, he also ought to be there. This martyred innocence, thought the Bishop (who *had* read the papers), had its rights, but also its duties. A man, he mused, must stand up to adversity.

✝ ✝ ✝

On Saturday, at two o'clock, the funeral of Sarah Bright Macroy was well attended. The Minters and their two teenage children sat invisibly in a veiled alcove. But those of Macroy's congregation who had had the temerity to come spotted him and nudged each other when he arrived a trifle late and sat down quietly at the very back of the chapel.

He did not join the family at any time, even afterward. Nor did he speak to any of his own people. When it was over, he vanished.

He had looked like a ghost. It was a little—well, odd.

✝ ✝ ✝

On Sunday the Bishop, at the last minute, found himself unable to conduct the nine-thirty service, which had to be canceled. (Although the organist played.) In consequence, at eleven o'clock, St. Andrew's had all its folding chairs in its aisles.

Macroy, in his robe, was up there, inconspicuously, at the congregation's right or contra-pulpit side, where, when he was sitting down, he was actually invisible to most. When they all stood, it was noticed that he did not sing the hymns. But he did repeat with them the Lord's Prayer, although his voice, which they were accustomed to hear leading, so richly and musically, the recitation of the ancient words, seemed much subdued.

Then the Bishop, who had never himself dwelt on some of the circumstances, and did not for one instant suppose that anyone *here* could do less than understand their essential pathos, made an unfortunate choice of words in the pastoral prayer.

"Oh, God," he prayed in his slight rasp, "Who, even in fog and darkness, seest all, be Thou his comfort; station him upon the rocks of his faith and Thy loving kindness, that he may stand up—"

The ripple ran, gasping from some of the listeners, yet not so much sound as movement, swinging the whole congregation like grass, before it ceased and all sat stiffly in a silence like plush.

The Bishop sat down, a bit pinkly. He could not see Macroy very well. Macroy did not seem to have taken any notice. In fact, Macroy had been moving, looking, acting like an automaton. The Bishop was very much worried about him, and he now bemoaned his own innocence, which had tripped him up, on occasion, before. When it was time, he preached an old sermon that was sound, although perhaps a little less than electrifying.

Then there they were, standing together in the narthex, as was the custom at St. Andrew's, Macroy a tall black pole beside the little black-robed beetle-bodied Bishop.

Now the people split into two groups, sheep from goats. Half of them simply went scurrying away, the women contriving to look harassed, as if they were concerned for a child or had something on the stove at home, the men just getting out of there. The other half lined up, to speak first to the Bishop and gush over the honor of his appearance in their pulpit. Then they each turned righteously to Macroy and said phrases like "So sorry to hear" and "Deepest sympathy" or a hearty "Anything I can do."

About twenty of them had gone by, like a series of coded Western Union messages, when Macroy put both hands over his face and burst into loud and anguished sobs.

The Bishop rallied around immediately and some of the older men shouldered through to his assistance. They took—almost carried—Macroy to his own office, where, Macroy having been put down in his chair, the Bishop firmly shut the door on everybody else. He sat down himself, and used his handkerchief, struggling to conquer his disapproval of a public exhibition of this sort. By the time the Bishop had recovered his normal attitude of compassionate understanding, Macroy had stopped making those distressing and unmanly noises.

"Well, I was wrong," the Bishop announced good-naturedly. "I ought not to have urged you to come here and I am sorry for that. You are still in shock. But I want you to remember that *they* are also in shock, in a way."

The Bishop was thinking of the reaction to his boner. He was not going to quote what he had inadvertently said, since if Macroy had missed it the Bishop would accept this mercy. Still, he felt that he ought to be somewhat blunt—it might be helpful.

"I'll tell you something, Macroy," he said. "You've got a fat-cat suburban bunch in this church, with economic status and—may the Lord help them all—middle-class notions of propriety. My dear fellow, they can't help it if they don't know what to say to you, when it has probably never crossed their minds that the minister or his wife might sometimes have to go to the bathroom."

Then the Bishop sighed. "This is especially difficult for them, but they'll stand by you—you'll see. I'm sure that you can understand them as well or better than I."

"It's not that I don't understand them," said Macroy. "It's that I can't love them." He had put his head down on his desk like a child.

"Oh, come now—"

"I cannot," said Macroy. "So I must give it up. Because I cannot do it."

"I think," said the Bishop in a moment, "that you most certainly can't—that is, not yet. You must have time. You must have rest. Now, I shall arrange for substitutes here. Don't worry about it."

"Don't you still understand?" said Macroy drearily.

"Of course I do! Of course I do! It was simply too much for you."

"Yes. Yes, if you say so."

"Then, if the coast is clear, we had better go home." The Bishop thought that this might become a serious breakdown. Poor tortured soul.

✝ ✝ ✝

That evening the Bishop bustled from his study into his living room, where Macroy was sitting disconsolately idle.

"Now," the Bishop said in his raspy voice, "you know that you are very welcome in this house. There is plenty of room. The cooking is not bad. Everything here is yours. However, I'm afraid that I shall have to be out of town for a day or two beginning tomorrow and I don't like to leave you all alone in your present state, so I'm going to ask you to do something for me, Hugh. Will you promise?"

"Yes," said Macroy listlessly.

"Will you talk to a Dr. Leone tomorrow?"

"A doctor?"

"He's a psychiatrist whom I've known for years. There have been occasions— He is excellent in his profession. He can give you a full hour tomorrow, beginning at one o'clock. I have set up the appointment and I think it is wise—very wise—that you keep it. He can help you through this very bad time."

"What?" said Macroy strangely. "Isn't God enough?"

"Ah ah," said the Bishop, shaking a finger, "you must not despise the scientist. In his own way he is also a seeker after the truth. And God knows that you need some human help. That's why I simply cannot leave you here alone—don't you see? Yet I should go, I must. So will you please be guided by me and do as I suggest?"

"Yes, I will," said Macroy apathetically.

† † †

"She died when you were twenty-five?" Doctor Leone said. He had observed the harsh lines on this face relax in memories of childhood, and he began to forgive himself for his own faulty technique. Well, he had to push this one. Otherwise the man would still be sitting as an owl by day, and there wasn't time. The doctor already knew that he would never see this man again.

"You were the only child?" he continued. "You must have adored her."

"I didn't pray to her, if that's what you mean," said Macroy with a faint touch of humor. "I loved my mother very much. But she wasn't perfect."

"How not?"

"Oh, she wasn't always—well, she didn't love everyone. She had a sharp tongue sometimes." But the voice was as tender as a smile.

"Didn't always love you, for instance?" the doctor said lightly.

"Of course she loved me. Always. I was her son." This was unimpassioned.

"Tell me about your father."

"He was a machinist, a hard-working man. A reader and a student by night. Very solid and kind and encouraging."

"You were how old when he died?"

"He died when I was twenty-seven—suddenly and afar."

The doctor listened closely to the way the voice caressed a phrase. "He loved you, of course. And you loved him."

"He was my father," the minister said with a faint wonder.

The doctor was beginning to wonder, Is he putting me on? He said with a smile, "Just background—all that we have time for today. Now tell me about your first wife. Was it a happy marriage?"

"It was," said Macroy. "Emily was my young love, very dainty and sweet. A cherishable girl." The doctor heard the thin and singing overtone.

"You had no children?"

"No. We were sad about that. Emily, I suppose, was always frail."

"After she died, what did you do?"

"Went on, of course."

The doctor continued to suspend judgment. "Now, this second marriage. What did you feel for Sarah?"

"She was a lovely, lively spirit," said the minister. "We could talk. Oh, how we could talk." He fell silent.

"And you loved her?"

"Not with the same kind of love," said Macroy, faintly chiding, "since we weren't young any more. We were very—compatible I believe is the accepted word."

Putting me on? He must be, thought the doctor. "And her money was no object," he said cheerily.

"The love of money is the root, Doctor."

"All right. I know my questions may sound stupid to you," said Leone. "They sound pretty stupid to me, as a matter of fact." He leaned back. Leone never took notes. He was trained to dictate, in ten minutes, the gist of fifty. "Now, I'm going to become rather inquisitive," he announced, "unless you know that you not only can but should speak frankly to me."

Macroy said gently, "I understand." But he said no more.

Going to make me push, thought the doctor. All right. "Tell me about your honeymoon."

"I see," said Macroy. "You want to know—whether the marriage was consummated? Will that phrase do?"

"It will do."

"No, it was not," said Macroy. "Although it would have been sooner or later, I think. She was—so warm-hearted and so lovable a presence. But you see, we had understood, quite well."

"You had both understood," said the doctor, more statement than question.

"I told you that we could talk," said Macroy, catching the latent doubt. "And that meant about anything and everything. That was our joy. As for—after all, in my case, Doctor, it had been nine years. I was a Minister of the Gospel."

"Did you try with Sarah and fail?" the doctor said easily.

"No."

"There wasn't a disillusion of any kind in the intimacy?"

"No. No. We enjoyed. We enjoyed. I can't be the only man in the world to have known that kind of joy." Macroy's face contorted and he became silent.

"Which you have lost," the doctor said softly.

"Which I have lost. Yes. Thank you." The man's head bent.

"So the very suggestion that you—yourself—might have thrown all this violently away. It must have been very painful to you."

"Yes."

"Knowing that you wouldn't, couldn't, didn't—there's still that sense of guilt, isn't there?"

"Yes."

"Surely you recognize that very common reaction to sudden death— to any death, in fact." The doctor wasn't having any more nonsense. "You have surely seen it, in your field, many times. People who compulsively wish that they had done what they had not done and so on?"

"Oh, yes, of course. But am I not guilty for letting her venture alone on that cliff?"

"It was the natural thing."

"It is the human convention." The voice was dreary and again it ceased.

The doctor waited, but time flew. So he said, "Every one of us must take his time to mourn his dead. But Bishop Everard tells me that you wish to give up the ministry, *now*. Why, Mr. Macroy?"

Macroy sighed deeply. "I am thinking about the silly but seemingly inevitable snickering, because of the circumstances."

The doctor hesitated. "The—er—circumstances do make an anecdote for thoughtless people. That must be very hard for you to endure."

"Oh, my poor Sarah."

"Then is this a factor?"

"I will say," said Macroy, "that I don't altogether understand that snickering. And why is it inevitable? If I may speak frankly to you, Doctor—"

Leone thought that there was a glint of life and challenge in the eyes.

"Surely," said Macroy, "every one of us knows his body's necessities, and furthermore knows that the rest of us have them, too. Yet all of man's necessities are not as funny as all that. Men don't think it funny, for instance, that they must eat."

"The whole toilet thing," said the doctor, "is too ancient and deep-rooted to be fully understood. It may be that the unpleasantness is too plain a reminder of our animal status."

"We laugh at what we hate so much to admit?" Macroy said quickly.

"Possibly." The doctor blinked.

"'Tis a pity," Macroy said in mourning.

"Why," said the doctor, who was beginning to feel that *he* had fallen into some trap, "is it that a man like you, who can look with this much detachment at human inconsistencies, cannot transcend an unimportant and temporary embarrassment? Surely you ought not to be driven out of a life's work just because of—"

"I didn't say those were my reasons."

"I'm sorry. Of course you didn't. What are your reasons?" The doctor was sunny.

"I cannot continue," said Macroy slowly, "because there are too many people I cannot love."

"Could you—er—amplify?"

"I mean that I felt so much anger. Fury. I hated them. I despised them. I wanted to hit them, shake them, scream at them, even hurt them back."

"In particular?"

"It began—" said Macroy. "No, I think that when the police officer asked me whether I had pushed Sarah to her death—oh, it hurt, of course it did, but I remembered that he might be compelled by the nature of his duties to ask me such a thing. But then there was a newspaperman. And when to him Sarah's death meant somewhat less than the death of a dog would have meant to a man who never cared for dogs, that's when I found myself so angry. I hated and I still do hate that man. From then on, I have seemed to be hating, hating—"

The doctor was lying low, rejoicing in this flow.

"Sarah's own child, for instance," Macroy went on, "who was so cruel in her own pain. Oh, I know she was not herself. But I had better not go near her. I would want to make her suffer. Don't you see? Of all the contemptible—I want revenge. Yes, I do. That young lawyer who missed the point. I know he meant no harm, but I just couldn't—I even loathe my poor secretary for making some kind of idol out of me. But I'd known and understood and borne that for years. Even if she is wrong to do that, I shouldn't suddenly loathe her for it. Yet I find I do. And I loathe the cowards and the hypocrites and the snickerers—they all disgust me. There seems to be no way that I can bring myself to love them. I simply cannot do it."

"You cannot love?" droned the doctor hypnotically.

"Even the Bishop, who is a good man. When he refuses—oh, in all good heart—to hear the truth I keep trying to tell him, sometimes I must hang on desperately to keep from shouting at him. Isn't that a dreadful thing?"

"That you can't love?" said the doctor. "Of course it is a dreadful thing. When your young love died so many years ago, perhaps—"

"No. *No!*" Macroy groaned. "You don't seem to understand. Listen to me. I was commanded to love. I was committed to love. And I thought I could, I thought I did. But if I *cannot do it,* then I have no business preaching in His Name."

"I beg your pardon?" The doctor's thoughts were jolted.

"In the Name of Jesus Christ."

"Oh, yes. I see."

"No, you don't! You don't even know what I'm talking about!"

The doctor got his breath and said gently, "I see this. You have a very deep conviction of having failed."

"Indeed," said Macroy, "and I am failing right now. I would like, for instance, to hit you in the mouth—although I *know* you are only trying to help me." The minister put both hands over his face and began to cry bitterly.

The doctor waited it out, and then he said that they wouldn't talk about it any more today.

✝ ✝ ✝

When the Bishop returned to town, he had a conference with Dr. Leone.

"He's had a traumatic experience," the doctor said, "that has stirred up some very deep guilt feelings, and, in projection, an almost unmanageable hostility that he never knew was there. I doubt he is as sophisticated as he thinks he is—in his understanding of the human psyche, I mean. He does need help, sir. He isn't really aware of the demons we all harbor. It's going to take a lot of digging to get at the root."

"Hm. A lot of digging, you say?"

"And I am not the man," said Leone. "I doubt that he and I can ever establish the necessary rapport. Furthermore, my fees—"

"I know." The Bishop was much distressed. "But what is to be done, I wonder. He isn't fit, you imply, to go on with his tasks?"

"You know he isn't."

"Oh, me," the Bishop sighed. "And he has nobody, nowhere to be taken in. Since I—" the Bishop shook his head sadly "—am not the man, either. You don't think this—this disturbance will simply go away? If he has shelter? And time to himself?"

"May I suggest," said Leone smoothly, "that the state hospitals are excellent? Very high-class in this state. And even the maximum fee is not too high."

"Well, as to that, there is what amounts to a Disability Fund. I should also suppose that the Minters, who are very rich people—" the Bishop was thinking out loud "—even if the marriage has to be declared invalid. But wouldn't it be cruel?" The Bishop blinked his eyes, hard. "Am I old-fashioned to think it would be cruel?"

"Yes, you are," said the doctor kindly. "He needs exactly what he can get in such a place—the shelter, the time, the trained attention. As far as time goes, it may be the quickest way to restore him."

"I see. I see." The Bishop sighed again. "How could it be done?"

"He would have to commit himself," said Leone gently.

"He would do so, I think," said the Bishop, "if I were to advise him to. It is a fearful—yet if there is no better alternative—"

"The truth is," said Leone fondly, "you have neither the free time nor the training, sir."

"We shall see," said the Bishop, who intended to wrestle it out in prayer. "We shall see."

✝ ✝ ✝

Two years later, Saul Zeigler approached the entrance with due caution. He had stuck a card reading PRESS in his windshield, anticipating argument since he wasn't expected, but to his surprise there was no gate, no guard, and no questions were asked. He drove slowly into the spacious grounds, found the administration building, parked, locked his car, and hunted down a certain Dr. Norman.

"Nope," said the doctor, a sandy-colored man who constantly smoked a pipe, "there is no story. And you won't write any. Absolutely not. Otherwise, how've you been?"

"Fine, fine," said Zeigler, who was up-and-coming these days and gambling that he could become a highly paid feature writer. He'd had some bylines. "Just insane, eh?"

The doctor grinned cheerfully. "Not my terminology."

"Put it this way: you're not letting him out?"

"Uh uh."

"Will you ever?"

"We hope so."

"When?"

The doctor shrugged.

"Well, I suppose I can always make do with what I've heard," said Zeigler impudently.

"Saul," said the doctor, "your dad was my old buddy and if I'd been the dandling type I probably would have dandled you. So you won't do this to me. Skip it. Go see Milly. She'll have a fit if you don't drop in to say hello."

"So would I," Zeigler said absent-mindedly. "Tell me, *did* he murder his wife?" There was no answer. "What set him off, then?"

"I'm not going to discuss a case with you or anybody else but the staff," said the doctor, "and you know it. So come on, boy, forget it."

"So how come I hear what I hear?" coaxed Zeigler.

"What do you hear?"

"You mean this is an instance of smoke without even one itty-bitty spark of fire? Not even one *semi*-miraculous cure?"

The doctor snorted. "Miraculous! Rubbish! And you're not going to work up any sensational story about him or this hospital. I can't help it if millions of idiots still want to believe in miraculous cures. But they're not coming down on us like a swarm of locusts. So forget it."

"I've met Macroy before, you know," said Zeigler, leaning back.

"Is that so?"

"Yep. On the night it happened."

"And what was your impression?"

"If I tell you," said Zeigler, "will you, just for the hell of it and off the record, tell *me* what goes on here?"

The doctor smoked contemplatively.

"Religion and psychiatry," said Zeigler, letting out his vocabulary and speaking solemnly, "have been approaching each other recently, wouldn't you agree, Doctor—in at least an exploratory manner? Supposing that you had, here, a clue to that growing relationship. Is that necessarily a 'sensational' story?"

"Oh no, you don't," said the doctor. "For one thing, he isn't preaching religion."

"How do you know?"

"I know."

Zeigler said, "You won't even let me talk to him, I take it."

"I didn't say so. If we understand each other—"

"Well, it was a long drive and it shouldn't be a total loss. Besides, I'm personally dying of curiosity. My impression, you want? Okay. I felt sorry for him, bleeding heart that I am. He was in shock and he sure had been pushed around that night. If he didn't always make plain sense, all I can say is that I wouldn't have made sense, either." Zeigler waited.

"I will admit," said the doctor between puffs, "that there have been some instances of sudden catharsis." He cocked a sandy eyebrow.

"Don't bother to translate," said Zeigler, crossing the trouser legs of his good suit, because the reporter got around these days and needed front. "I dig. How many instances?"

"A few."

"Quite a few? But no miracles. Didn't do a bit of good, eh?"

"Sometimes treatment was expedited." The doctor grinned at his own verbiage. "We *are* aware of a running undercurrent. One patient advises another, 'All right, you can go and talk to him.'"

"So if he doesn't preach, what does he do?"

"I don't know. They talk their hearts to him."

"Why don't you find out?" said Zeigler in astonishment.

"Tell me this, Saul. On that night, was he annoyed with *you* in any way?"

"Might have been." Zeigler frowned. "He sure brushed me off. But he had taken quite a beating. I didn't blame him."

"Why don't you go and see him?" the doctor said. "I'd be interested in the reaction. Afterward, come by and we'll make Milly feed us a bite of lunch."

"Where can I find him?" Zeigler was out of the chair.

"How should I know?" said the doctor. "Ask around."

Zeigler went to the door, turned back. "I don't want to hurt him, Doc. How shall I—"

"Just be yourself," the doctor said.

†   †   †

Zeigler came out into the sunshine of the lovely day. He had never been to this place before and it astonished him. He had expected a grim building with barred windows, and here he was on what looked like the sleepy campus of some charming little college, set between hills and sprawling fields, with the air freshened by the not-too-distant sea. There were green lawns and big trees and some mellow-looking buildings of Spanish design. There was even ivy.

It was very warm in the sun. He unlocked his car, tossed his jacket inside, and snatched the PRESS card away from the windshield. He locked the car again and began to walk. Ask around, eh? There were lots of people around, ambling on the broad walks, sitting on the grass, going in and out of buildings. Zeigler realized that he couldn't tell the patients from the staff. What a place!

The fourth person he asked was able to direct him.

The Reverend Hugh Macroy was sitting on a bench along the wide mall under one of the huge pepper trees. He was wearing wash trousers and a short-sleeved white shirt without a tie. He seemed at ease—just a handsome, well tanned, middle-aged gentleman growing quietly older in the shade.

Zeigler had begun to feel, although he couldn't tell who was who around here, that *they* could and were watching him. He approached the man with some nervousness.

"Mr. Macroy?"

"Yes?"

"Do you remember me, sir? Saul Zeigler."

"I don't believe I do, Mr. Zeigler. I'm sorry."

Zeigler remembered the voice well. But the face was not the old mask of agony and strain. The mouth was smiling, the dark eyes were friendly.

Zeigler said smoothly, "I'm not surprised you don't remember. I met you only once, a long time ago, and very briefly. Is it all right if I sit down?"

"Of course." The minister made a token shifting to give him more welcoming room on the bench and Zeigler sat down. "This place is sure a surprise to me," said Zeigler.

The minister began to chat amiably about the place. He seemed in every way perfectly rational. Zeigler felt as if he were involved in a gentle rambling conversation with a pleasant stranger. But it wasn't getting him anywhere.

He was pondering how to begin again when Macroy said, "But you are not a patient, Mr. Zeigler. Did you come especially to see me?"

"Yes, I did," said Zeigler, becoming bold. "I'm a writer. I was going to write a story about you but I'm not allowed to. Well, I wanted to see you, anyway."

"A story?"

"A story about all the good you do here."

"The good *I* do?" said the man.

"I've heard rumors about the good you've done some of these—er—patients."

"That isn't any story." Macroy seemed amused.

"So I'm told. And even if it is, I'm not going to be permitted to write it. I've given my word. Honestly, I won't write it."

The minister was looking at him with a pleasant smile. "I believe you," he said.

Zeigler found himself relaxing. "The truth is, I want in the worst way," he admitted, "to know what it is that you do here. Do you—well, preach to them? I know you're a minister."

"No, sir. I'm not. Not any more. And so, of course, I don't preach."

"Then what?"

"Oh, I listen to them. Some of them. Sometimes."

"But that's what the doctors do, isn't it? Do you listen *better*?"

Macroy said, as if to correct him gently, "The doctors here, and all the staff, are just as kind and understanding as they can be."

"Yes. But maybe you listen *differently*?"

Macroy looked thoughtful.

"The point is," pressed Zeigler, "if there's some kind of valuable insight that you have, shouldn't it be told to the world?"

"I'm not saving the world, Mr. Zeigler," said Macroy drily. "I'm not *that* crazy. Or that good, either." He was smiling.

Ziegler, who had momentarily forgotten that this man was supposed to be insane, said, "Just a mystery, eh? You don't know yourself?"

"It may be," said Macroy melodiously, "because I'm one of them. For I understand some of these sheep."

"In what way do you understand them, sir? I'm asking only for myself. Last time I saw you—Well, it's bothered me. I've wished I could understand." Zeigler really meant this.

Macroy was looking far away at the pleasant hills beyond the grounds. Then, as if he had reached into some pigeonhole and plucked this out, he murmured, "One hell of a newspaperman."

"Yes, sir," said Zeigler, suddenly feeling a little scared.

But Macroy didn't seem perturbed. In a moment he went on pleasantly, "Some of them don't speak, you know. Some, if they do, are not coherent. What man can really understand them? But there are others whom I recognize and I know that I love them."

"That's the secret?" Zeigler tried not to sound disappointed. "Love?"

Macroy went on trying to explain. "They've fallen out of mesh—out of pattern, you know. When they've lost too many of their connections and have split off from the world's ways too far, they can't function in the world at all."

Elementary, my dear Watson, thought Zeigler.

"But it seems to me," Macroy continued, "that quite a few of them didn't do what they were pressured to do, didn't depart from the patterns, because they could sense—oh, they couldn't say how, they couldn't express it. Yet they simply knew that somehow the mark was being missed, and what the world kept pressuring them to do and be just wasn't good enough. Some, poor seekers, not knowing where there was any clue, have made dreadful mistakes, have done dreadful things, wicked things. And yet—" He seemed to muse.

Zeigler was scarcely breathing. Wicked things? Like murdering your wife, for instance? "In what way," he asked quietly, "are you one of *them*, sir?"

"Oh." The minister was smiling. "*I* always wanted to be good, too. I was born yearning to be good. I can't remember not listening, beyond and through all the other voices, for the voice of God to speak to me, His child."

He smiled at Zeigler, who was feeling stunned. "I don't mean to preach. I only say that, because I have it—this yearning, this listening, this *hearing*—"

In a moment Zeigler said, rather vehemently, "I don't want to upset you. I don't want to trouble you in any way. But I just don't see—I can't understand why you're not back in the pulpit, sir. Of course, maybe you're expecting to leave here someday soon?"

"I really don't know," said Macroy. "I cannot return to the ministry, of course. Or certainly I don't expect to. I must wait—as I would put it—on the Lord. And it may be that I belong here."

He caught Zeigler's unsatisfied expression. "Excuse me. The obvious trouble is, Mr. Zeigler, that every time they take me into town, as on occasion they do, sooner or later I stop in my tracks and burst into tears. Which wouldn't make me very useful in the pulpit, I'm afraid."

"I guess," said Zeigler, "you've had a pretty rough deal. In fact, I know you've had, but—"

"No, no," said Macroy. "That's not the point. It isn't what anyone did to me. It's what I couldn't do. And still can't. Of course, here it is much easier. I can love these people, almost all of them."

"And you can't help trying to help them, can you?" Zeigler said, finding himself irresistibly involved. "Why do you say you don't expect to return to the ministry?"

"Oh, that's very simple." Macroy smiled a little ruefully. "I've explained, it seems to me, to a great many people." He sighed.

"I wish you'd explain it to me," said Zeigler earnestly.

"Then of course I'll try," said Macroy. "But I hope you'll understand that, while I must use certain terms, I don't mean to exhort you to become a Christian, for instance."

"I understand," said Zeigler.

"Christians were given two commandments," Macroy began slowly. "You, too, were given much the same ones, I believe, although in a different form."

"Go on," said Zeigler eagerly.

"The first is to love God, which God knows I do. But I was also committed to the second commandment and that one I could not obey. Oh, I longed to—I even thought that I was obeying. But it isn't, I discovered, a thing that you can force yourself to do. And when that Grace—I mean, when it didn't come to me and I simply was not able—"

"To do what, sir?"

"To love them all."

"*All!*" Zeigler's hair stirred.

"That's what He said." Macroy was calm and sure. The voice was beautiful. "Thy neighbor? Thy enemy?"

And suddenly Zeigler saw it. "You took it literally!" he burst out.

"Yes."

"But, listen," said Zeigler in agitation, "that's just too hard. I mean, that's just about impossible!"

"It was certainly too hard for me," said Macroy sadly, yet smiling.

"But—" Zeigler squirmed. "But that's asking too much of *any* human being. How *can* you love all the rotten people in the whole damn world— excuse me, sir. But surely you realize you were expecting too much of yourself."

"So they keep telling me," said Macroy, still smiling. "And since that's my point, too, I know it very well. What I don't feel they quite understand, and is so perfectly plain to me—" He turned to Zeigler, mind-to-mind. "Suppose you're committed to follow Him, to feed His sheep, to feed His lambs, to be His disciple—which is a discipline, isn't it?—and suppose you cannot make the grade? Then, when you see that you cannot, mustn't you leave the ministry? How could I be a hypocrite when He said not to be?

"Let me put it in analogy," Macroy continued, warming to argument. "Some young men who wish to become airplane pilots wash out. Isn't that the term? They just can't make the grade. So they may not be pilots. They would endanger people. They may, of course, work on the ground."

Zeigler was appalled. He couldn't speak.

"So if I have necessarily left the ministry," said Macroy, "that doesn't mean that I may not love as *many* as I can."

Zeigler saw the image of a ray of light that came straight down, vertical and one-to-one. Suddenly there was a cross-piece, horizontal, like loving arms spread out—but it had broken. Zeigler's heart seemed to have opened and out of it flooded a torrent of such pity, such affectionate pity, that he thought he was going to cry.

A thousand schemes began to whirl in his brain. Something should be done. This man should be understood. Zeigler would storm into the doctor's office. Or he *would* write a story, after all.

He said, his voice shaking, "Thanks, Mr. Macroy, for talking to me. And may the Lord lift up His countenance upon you and shine upon you and give you peace."

Macroy looked up. His look made Zeigler turn and almost run away.

Speeding along the walk, he was glad no one else had heard him sounding off in singing scripture, like some old rabbi, for God's sake! Okay, he'd felt like doing it and he'd done it and what was it with the human race that you'd better not sound as if you felt something like that?

Maybe that man *is* crazy! But I love him!

Just the same, Zeigler wasn't going back to Doctor Norman's office—not right now. There'd been a reaction, all right, but he didn't care to have it seen all over his face. He'd go see Milly Norman, who would give him some coffee and gossip. She always did. He'd take time to cool it. Or figure out how to translate it—

No, let the man alone, let him stay where he was. Why should Zeigler say one word to help get Hugh Macroy back into the stinking world, which would kill him. Sure as hell, it would.

Zeigler was blind and ran slambang into a man and murmured an apology.

"Hey," said the man, moving to impede him further, "hey, Press, you get any good news outta the nutty preacher?"

"Nothing I can use," said Zeigler bitterly. He started off, but he thought, Love them *all*?

So he stopped and looked experimentally at this stranger. Here was a patient. Zeigler didn't doubt it. A middle-aged, foxy-faced, shambling man with salted red hair, little beady eyes, and soft, repellent lips. A more unlovable sight Zeigler had seldom seen.

Just the same, he said aloud and heartily, "Hey, don't you worry about a thing, old-timer," and then—with his eyes stinging but telling himself to stop being so much the way he was, because he'd never make it, anyhow—suddenly it was too much for him and Zeigler sprinted to his car.

✝ ✝ ✝

In a little while a man shambled up to where Macroy still sat on the bench under the pepper tree.

"Hey, you the Reverend Macroy?"

"I'm Hugh Macroy. Not a Reverend."

"Well—er—my name's Leroy Chase."

"How do you do, Mr. Chase?"

"Glad to meetcha. Say, listen, there's something I guess I gotta tell you."

"Sit down," said Macroy cordially.

The man sat down. He put his unkempt hands through his greying red hair. "I'm kinda nervous."

"You needn't tell me anything."

"Yeah, but I wish—I mean, I want to."

"Well, I'm listening."

"It's a kinda long story."

"Go ahead."

"Well, see, I was up Salinas this time and I was hitching back down to L.A."

Macroy had turned his body slightly toward his companion.

"Well," the man said, "I guess you know that hitchers can't be choosers. Hah! So I get this ride and this stupe, he takes California One." Chase's little eyes shifted nervously.

Macroy said, "I see."

"So he dumps me in Big Sur, which is nowhere. So when I finally get another hitch south, I figure I'm lucky. Only trouble is, I find out this bird is juiced up pretty strong, and when the fog starts rolling in, believe me, I'm scared. So I want out. So I *get* out. So there I am."

The man was speaking in short bursts. "In that fog, what am I? A ghost or something? Who can see a thumb? Nobody's going to take his eye off the white line to look, even. And it gets dark. And what can I do?"

Macroy was listening intently, but he kept silent.

The red-headed man chewed on his mouth for a moment before he went on. "Well, I got my blanket-roll on me, so I figure I'll just bed down and wait out the fog. Why not? So I find this big rock and I nest myself down behind it, where no car is going to plow into me, see? And there I am, dozing and all that. Then there's this car pulls off the road and stops right ten, fifteen feet in front of me."

The man leaned suddenly away to blow his nose. Macroy looked away, flexed one ankle, then let it relax. He said nothing.

"So I wonder, should I jump up and beg a ride? But it's all so kinda weird, see—white air, you could say?" Chase was gesturing now, making slashes in the air for emphasis. "A man gets out with a flashlight. It's like a halo. And the other party gets out, see. Well, I dunno what's up. I can't see too good. I know they can't see me. I got a grey blanket. I'm practically another rock. And I'm lying low and thinking, why bother? What's the matter with where I am? It's kinda wild out there that night—the white air and all. And I can hear the sea. I always liked listening to the sea, especially by myself, you know?"

Macroy nodded. His eyes were fixed on the man's face.

"Listen, you know what I'm trying to—"

"I'm listening."

"So when this person starts coming along with the flash, I turn my face, so it won't show—"

"Yes" said Macroy, with a strange placidity.

"Then the light goes down on the ground. It don't fall, see? It's just pointing down. And I'm wondering what the hell—excuse me—when—" The voice was getting shrill. "My God, I know what she's gonna do! Listen, no man can take a thing like that, for God's sake!"

The man was crying now. "So I think, Oh, no, you don't—not on *me*, you don't!" So I just give a big heave and, holy God, it's too close and over she goes! Oh, I never meant—I never—but who could take a thing like that?"

Chase was now on the edge of the bench. "Before I know what I'm doing, I drag my roll and I'm running up the edgy side, north. My life is in my feet, brother, but I gotta get out of there. It's just instinct, see? I could hear you calling—"

"You heard me?" Macroy was looking at the sky.

"'Listen. Listen. So I'm about half, three-quarters of a mile away and now here comes this car going south. So I figure to look like I been going south the whole while. That way, I never *was* there. And damned if this guy don't stop in the fog and pick me up. Well, I soon find out *he* ain't exactly cold sober, but by this time I don't care. Then what does he have to do but stop for you? But you tell him to send help and we just—we just went on by."

Chase slumped.

"If you had told me then—" Macroy had shut his eyes.

"Oh, listen, maybe you're some kind of saint or something, but I didn't know, not then. Didn't even know you was a preacher."

"And you had two chances."

"Well, I had—well, three really. But look, nobody coulda said I'd done that on purpose. Maybe manslaughter. Who knows? What I couldn't take was the—was the *motive*. See, it's too damned hilarious. What I couldn't take was the big ha-ha. I mean, I knew she never saw me, I know that—she wouldn't have done a thing like that. But all I thought at the time was, Hey, this I don't have to take. If I would have stopped for one second—but here it comes, outta the night, you could say—who's going to understand? Because what a screaming howl, right?"

Chase was sobbing. He wasn't looking at Macroy. He sobbed into the crook of his own elbow.

Macroy said musingly, "Yes, it is supposed to be quite funny."

"Listen, what I did do." Chase gathered voice. "This happy-boy, he finally gets to that gas station, and he don't even know what day it is. The message is long gone from his mind. So I made the call to the Sheriff. That was the third chance. But I chickened out. I hung up. And I say 'so long' to this happy character and go in the cafe. When I see the cop car I figure I done all I could and maybe she's okay. I'm praying she's okay. It was the best that I could do."

They were silent then, in the sunshine that had crept around the tree.

Macroy said in a moment or two, "Why are you here?"

Chase mopped his face with his sleeve. "Oh, I fall apart, see?" he said rather cheerfully. "I practically never been what they'd call 'together.' You talk about chances. I had plenty chances. But not me, I wouldn't stay in school. I coulda even gone to college. But I wouldn't go. So I'm forty years old and I'm crying in my wine, when I can get any, like a baby whining after a shining star, too far—" The man controlled his wailing rhyme abruptly. "Well. So now they don't know what else to do with me. So I'm a nut. That's okay."

He relaxed against the back of the bench with a thump. "So now," he spoke quietly, "I'll do anything. I mean, clear your name if you want. What can they do to me?"

Macroy didn't speak.

"I wish—" said Chase. "Well, anyhow, now you know it wasn't your fault and it wasn't her fault, either. And it wasn't—" He stopped and seemed to listen, anxiously.

"Excuse me," said Macroy. "I was wondering what I would have done. I'm no saint." He turned his face. "And never was."

"But I didn't know you, Mr. Macroy." Chase began to be agitated again. "You got to remember, for all I knew you mighta killed me."

Macroy said, "I might have. I *think* not. But I wouldn't have laughed."

Chase drew in breath, an in-going sob. "Ah, you don't know me, either. All I *ever* been is a bum, all my life. I never did no good or been no good."

"But you wish you had? You wish you could?"

"God knows!" The cry came out of him, astonished.

"Yes. And I believe you." Macroy bent his head. "I'm sorry. I'm sorry. That woman was very dear to me. Very dear."

"Don't I believe it?" cried Chase as if his heart had split. "Oh God, don't I *know*! I heard you calling her. I knew it in your voice." Chase was sobbing. "I remember a thing—what they say in church—I remember.

Don't tell me it was good enough, the best I could do. Because it wasn't, and that's what I know."

Chase was on his knees, hanging onto the minister's knees and sobbing. "Oh, listen, listen. I'm sorry. I got a broken heart. Believe me? Please believe me!"

✝

Holy Living and Holy Dying

Robert Barnard

W HEN THE ACT OF LOVE was over, or the act of intimacy, or whatever lying euphemism you cared to call it by, Gordon Chitterling rolled over on to his back, stared at the off-brown ceiling, and sighed. The girl, who had said her name was Jackie (didn't they all?) reached over for her cigarettes on the bedside table, took one as if this was an invariable habit, and lit it.

"Come a bit quick, didn't you?" she said, in her horrible Midlands accent. "You can have another go for an extra twenty. I've nothing fixed till half past eight."

"I'm not made of money," said Gordon irritably. "I'm a journalist."

"Shouldn't have thought journalists went short," said Jackie. "There's a gentleman on the *Sun* has me regular on expenses."

"That doesn't happen with the *Catholic Weekly*."

"Is that religious?" Jackie asked, blowing out smoke. Gordon immediately regretted having told her.

"Not really. It means we are Catholic in our interests. Wide-ranging," Gordon lied.

Jackie frowned, trying to understand, but soon gave it up.

"Fifteen," she said. "I can't say fairer than that, can I? It'll save me the hassle of going out again."

Gordon raised his eyebrows to heaven. This was beginning to resemble a street bazaar in Cairo. At any moment she'd be throwing in Green Shield stamps. He jumped off the bed and began pulling on his clothes.

"Some other time," he said, buttoning his flies. Gordon was one of the few men in London who still had button-up flies. There was an all-or-nothing quality about zips that he distrusted. "Duty calls," he added, in his tight-lipped way.

He grabbed at his attaché case, but either because he was clumsy, or because he hadn't shut it properly before, it fell open and spilled its contents on to the linoleumed floor.

"Damn and blast."

"There, I told you you shouldn't rush away, all excited like that."

About as worked up as Calvin Coolidge on a wet Monday, thought Gordon, as he bent down to retrieve his papers. Jackie had idly rolled over on the bed to have a look.

"Coo, look at that. It's old Mossy. One of my regulars."

She was pointing to a large, glossy photograph of a distinguished gentleman in his fifties. Gordon snatched it up.

"You are quite mistaken."

"'Course I'm not. Comes regular. Real old sport. I think he's something in the world of finance."

"You certainly are mistaken. He was a Bishop."

"Go on! Well, he never lets on. Dirty old Bish!"

"I mean you are altogether mistaken in the man," said Gordon, shutting his briefcase with an irritable click. "You must have confused him with another . . . client. Bishop Bannerman was a highly respected figure in the Catholic Church. In addition to which he is dead."

"I didn't say he'd been recently."

"He was a very fine man. Highly respected. Unimpeachable character. Almost saintly."

He was shutting the door when Jackie shouted:

"And he had a strawberry birthmark the shape of Australia on his left shoulder."

Gordon gave the game away by his pause after he had shut the door. Jackie must have registered that it was a full ten seconds before he clattered down the bare floorboards on the stairs and out into Wardour

Street. In fact, he knew she had registered, because he heard her hideous shrill laugh as he descended.

Gordon Chitterling walked through Soho in the direction of Victoria Street, a frown on his rather insignificant face.

The first thing that concerned him was that Bishop Bannerman might become a subject for scandal and concern—or, rather, that *he* might be the cause of his so becoming. If he hadn't spilled that damned attaché case . . . If he hadn't gone to her straight from work. But somehow it was straight after work that he most felt like it.

His profile of Bishop Bannerman, who had died two months previously, was already fully researched and was only waiting to be written up. The outlines of his career were clear. Born in 1930 into a middle-class family in Warwick, where his father had been a chartered accountant, Anthony Bannerman had begun the process of conversion to Catholicism at the early age of seventeen. Many such early enthusiasms were to be put down to the powerful tug of religion working on the impressionable adolescent mind, but Bannerman's had held, and had stuck with him through university, so that by the time he had his BA, his aim of then studying for the priesthood had been accepted both by the church into which he had been received, and by his family.

After that it had been onwards and upwards: exemplary parish priest, much-loved broadcaster on *Lift Up Your Hearts* and *Thought for the Day,* eventually Bishop of West Ham, and strongly tipped for the Westminster job, when or if it became vacant. That was not to be: he had been struck down by a heart attack while attending a conference in Venice . . . Death in Venice . . . Well, at least he had not been *that* way inclined.

Gordon Chitterling let himself into the *Catholic Weekly* offices, and went along to his own neat little cubicle. There was nobody much about, and he switched on his desk light and sat there thinking. Imagine! that much-loved pastor, that fearless campaigner against apartheid, that helper among AIDS sufferers, that tireless worker for peace and reconciliation in Northern Ireland—to patronize a common prostitute. Regularly. But then, to patronize one regularly would be safer than picking up just anyone off the streets. Safer too to choose an ignorant little tart like Jackie.

Ah well, that was one aspect of the Bishop that would not get into the Profile.

Yet everything else, *everything,* had been so positive, so enthusiastic, so admiring. He opened his bottom drawer, and pulled out the thick sheaf of transcribed interviews. He leafed through them: "caring pastor"

. . . "concerned, committed crusader" . . . It had all seemed of a piece. Here was the interview with his brother, where he'd talked about the birthmark the shape of Australia: "He always said it meant he would end up Archbishop of Sydney, but actually he never even went there . . ."

A phrase caught his eye: "He was essentially a man of the people, among people, at home with people." He stopped and read on. It was an interview with Father O'Hara, a parish priest in the borough of Camden. It went on:

"I once saw him in a pub in my parish. I'd been visiting the wife of the publican. It was the Duck and Whistle—*not* an up-market pub, in fact rather a dubious place, with a lot of dubious characters among the regulars. Bishop Bannerman was in 'civvies,' talking and laughing with Snobby Noakes, a petty crook who'd been in and out of jail. They were completely man-to-man. I even saw money changing hands. I expect he was putting a bet on a horse—something he loved to do now and then. When he saw me he came over, and he talked to me just as naturally as he'd been talking to Snobby. You got the feeling that he'd chat with the Queen in exactly the same way he'd chat with a housewife in a block of council flats. That was the kind of man he was . . ."

It had seemed admirable at the time. The man of God who was at home in all worlds. Now it made Gordon wonder. There was no reason why it should: bishops went into pubs: bishops talked to criminals. The fact that, apparently, on occasion he used a prostitute did not mean there was anything less than innocent about his talking in a pub with a petty criminal.

And yet . . . and yet . . . That money changing hands. Gordon Chitterling did not like that at all.

The next day, when he sat down to write the Profile, his pen seemed to be weighted with lead. Not that his words were normally winged. Gordon was a reliable, competent journalist rather than an inspired one. Yet it was that very reliability that prevented the clichés of his pen-picture attaining any sort of conviction. Words and phrases like "saintly humility," "committed campaigner," "a man of God who was also a man among men" seemed to snicker back at him from the page. "You don't believe that, do you?" they seemed to say. It is not easy to work for a religious newspaper. You have to believe what you write. So much simpler to work for Murdoch.

To light upon a Bishop who broke his vows worried Gordon. His own sins worried him only a little, but then—he had taken no vows as a reporter on the *Catholic Weekly*. He knew he was going to have to go to the Duck and Whistle. What he was going to do when he got there he did not know, but he knew he was going to have to go.

In the event the Duck and Whistle, over the next two or three weeks, came to know him quite well. It was, as Father O'Hara had said, a decidedly down-market pub, with men doing dubious deals in nooks and corner. There was a juke-box, the blare from which was used to cover muttered conversations. The first evening Gordon spent there Snobby Noakes simply breezed in, downed a whisky and water, and breezed out again. Gordon did no more than identify him, from the landlord's greeting, and the talk of other customers. Snobby was a thin, perky character, rather better or more flashily dressed than the others in the bar. These mostly had a look that was decidedly seedy, and as his visits became regular Gordon—for his was the outlook and talents of the chameleon—came to merge with his surroundings and become seedier: he resurrected an old raincoat, made sure he wore a shirt with frayed cuffs.

His first talk with Snobby was innocuous—about horses and dogs, the kind you bet on, of course. Snobby was man-of-the-world, and rather condescending to Gordon's shabbiness. Snobby had once worked as a bookie's runner, and was adept at the smart disappearance when a big pay-out was due. What Snobby loved, it became apparent in later conversations, was a "wheeze"—a smart idea for a quick financial killing. Any other kind of killing was way outside his territory, for his heroes were shysters and con men. Where others might hero-worship Cromwell or Napoleon, Snobby saved his admiration for an Horatio Bottomley or a Maundy Gregory.

Gordon he accepted as a small-time con artist, rather on his own level, though less prosperous. "Though you've got a touch of class in the voice," he once said, flatteringly. "You could sell encyclopaedias, you could."

"The best cons," Snobby would say expansively over a drink, especially if Gordon bought it for him, "are the simple cons. Look at the South Sea Bubble. Learnt about that at school—always stayed with me. Simple, effective, beautiful!"

Gordon nodded wisely. He was never quite sure when Snobby was being humorous. Snobby had a sense of humour, where Gordon had very little.

"The other thing about your simple con is, it's them that clean up the biggest," Snobby went on. "Take the bloke that thought up the wheeze that Venice is sinking. Brilliant. He must have pulled in millions over the years."

"You're not suggesting Lord Norwich—"

"Whoever he was. Some smart little Mafia con I'd've thought. A real little beauty. Because bleedin' Venice isn't sinking, any more than Southend is. All high and dry and dandy. Mind you the bloke who thought of building it there in the first place was something of an artist too. Did you ever see a more obvious tourist trap? A man ahead of his time he must have been."

Snobby winked. Quite unprompted by Gordon, the conversation had begun to take a turn he liked.

"You seem taken with Venice," he said casually.

"Oh, I was. Lovely little place. Only drawback that I could see was you couldn't do a good snatch there, because the getaway presents problems."

"Been there often?"

"Just the once. A church conference."

Gordon's heart rose.

"Well!" he said. "I wouldn't have thought of you as a Christian."

Snobby laughed.

"That's why I was there, though. The Fourth Ecumenical Conference. You know: Catholic and C. of E. clergymen holding hands in gondolas. *That* was a right occasion. Tell you about it some day."

He didn't, though, not over the next two evenings spent chewing over the great cons, past and present. In the end Gordon had the brainwave of bringing the conversation round to clergymen.

"I don't know about you," he said, with the air of long and disreputable experience, "but I never found there was much to be got out of the clergy. They're supposed to be so bloody other-worldly, but somehow there's never anything much to be got there. Maybe they're too hard up."

Snobby's face assumed a relishing smile.

"True. Most of them are that. Church of England, anyhow." He leaned forward confidingly. "But I'll tell you this, me boy: there's money to be got not *from* the Church, but *by* the Church. That's for sure."

"What do you mean? Collection boxes, appeals, that kind of thing?" asked Gordon innocently.

"No, I do not mean that at all. Let me put it to you like this: if a man wants to lead a comfortable life, and enjoys tacking over to the windy side of the law, what better trade to enter than the Church? And here I'm talking about the Catholic Church, me boy. Very comfortable life, especially

the higher you go. The celibacy rule doesn't bother you, because you've
no intention of abiding by it. And as a way into the criminal life it has one
great, glorious advantage."

"What's that?"

"Who hears most secrets? A bank manager? A politician? A social
worker? No—it's a priest."

Gordon's heart almost stopped beating.

"My God—you don't mean—?"

"Right. The confessional. That's where the really interesting secrets are
poured out." Snobby grinned. "I can see you're shocked, laddie.
Supposed to be secret, isn't it? But think of it like this: there's this man—
I have one in mind, but don't think you'll ever learn who—who goes into
the Church purely and simply for what he can get out of it. Purely, simply and solely. Not an ounce of religious feeling in his whole make-up. He
likes the good things of life, and this is his way of getting them—and a
nice little bit of power to boot. From the beginning he knows that one of
his ways will be using the confessional. I tell you, it's the most brilliant
wheeze I ever knew."

"You mean—blackmail?" Gordon stuttered.

"'Course I mean blackmail. Used very, very discriminatingly. Which
means it's a slow starter. When you're parish priest of Little Wittering-on-
the-Wallop you don't try to blackmail Mary Sykes because she's sleeping
with the local publican. Oh no—you take it slowly, get the notice of your
superiors, emphasize that for you it's the *urban* parishes that present the
real challenges to Christianity in the modern world, take up all the fash-
ionable causes—famine, apartheid, battered wives. And little by little you
get to the sort of parish, the sort of position, where you've got the real villains, and the people with things in their lives that are worth hiding."

"Say London," said Gordon.

"Say London," agreed Snobby, "though you needn't think you're
going to get any more out of me than that."

"But what's the point? What's all the blackmail money going to be
spent on?"

"High living, indulged in very discreetly, and in out-of-the-way
places: the Azores, Curaçao, the Æolian islands."

Again there was that tiny click, as something fell into place.
Somewhere in his notes there was a reference to a "tiny community" of
religious brothers in the Azores, to which Bishop Bannerman had often
gone in retreat. Also to periods of solitary prayer, on Lipari . . .

"What was your 'in' on all this?" Gordon asked, in his con-man-of-the-world manner. "How do you come to know so much about it?"

"Oh, I was the collector. I wasn't one of the faith—that wouldn't have done at all—but he'd got something on me, never mind what, from someone who was. I collected the dibs, handed it over intact, and collected my percentage. Miserable little percentage it was too, but it all added up. No, it was a beautiful scheme, and I was proud of my part in it—profitable and risk-free. Or so I thought."

"Not?"

"Well, my part was safe enough. You don't catch me taking any risks in a simple matter of picking up a parcel of ten-pound notes. Piece of cake, as I'm sure you know. On the other hand, the Bish—my religious friend—well, I'm afraid he overplayed his hand."

"Went for the really big villains?"

"Something like that, though not quite in the way you mean. Now, in this bloke's parish—we'll call it a parish—there were all sorts of villains, big, medium and small, from pimps to company directors, but naturally among the ones he knew best were the Mafia mob."

"Of course. But would they come to Confession?"

"Some of 'em. Very devout little shysters, some of 'em. So he'd hear all about the rackets involving the Iti restaurants, the fruit and veg markets, not to mention some of the fall-out from the Calvi affair, and the Banco Ambrosi-how's-yer-father. All very intriguing and profitable. And in among the rest, another little tit-bit. What that was precisely, I don't claim to know. Mostly I never *did* know. But the Mafia guy he got it from was a hard little pimp in Hackney, and I'd guess he'd been a hard little pimp in Palermo before that, so whatever it was, it was probably sexual. If it'd been something bigger he might have twigged . . ."

"So there was an Italian connection, was there? Hence Venice."

"Oh, there was an Italian connection all right. Though of course at Venice, at this 'ere conference I attended in an unofficial capacity, there were holy-rollers from all over, as well as C. of E., Methodists, Baptists, everything except the Reverend Ian Paisley, all making out they were matey as hell and brothers in Christ. It was all very affecting, if you didn't listen to what they was saying behind each other's backs. O' course, I was just there on a package tour—"

"To collect the loot."

"That's it. The trouble was, in Italy I was a bit of a fish out of water." Snobby shook his head. "Or so the B—so my reverend bloke thought. He made a plan for picking up the loot, made it himself, and I was too bleeding ignorant to argue against it. If I'd known about gondoliers . . ."

"Gondoliers?"

"I mean, all I knew about was honeymoon couples steered through the canals by a bloke with a pole who needed a shave and sang 'O Sole mio.' I didn't know they were the biggest pimps and petty crooks in the business, and had been going back centuries, ever since they built that place on stilts."

"I suppose it was asking for a double-cross."

"Too right it was. Added to the fact that Mario, the punter *my* bloke employed, had a mother from Messina, and contacts with all the underworld characters in Venice and on the mainland, all the way down to sunny Sicily."

"What went wrong?"

"Everything. Every-bloody-thing. Oh, the Iti Bishop came along—"

"Italian Bishop?"

"That's right. Him that my bloke had got the juicy little piece of information about, from the hard little crook in Hackney. He came along with his packet of ten-thousand-lira notes, and left it under the seat at the gondolier's end, just as he'd been told to in the note, and as I'd arranged with this Mario. Then I took my romantic little trip round the back canals, feeling a right berk, since I hadn't got anyone to hold 'ands with, not even a gay vicar. And then we went out into the lagoon and I transferred the package to my little briefcase—all as ordered, though somehow I didn't feel happy about it even then."

"I suppose you were followed when you got back to dry land?"

"Must've been. And very cleverly too, because I know all the wheezes an English follerer will get up to. Naturally I didn't go straight to my bloke and say 'Here's the loot.' I went up and down these dark little streets and alleyways, stopped for a cappucino, stopped for a plate of spaghetti, though I got most of it down my shirt-front. Must've been pretty conspicuous, looking back on it, because I'm not the type to carry a briefcase. Eventually, as per arrangement, I went into this scruffy bar, went to make a phone call, and dropped the parcel. My bloke, in civvies, went in immediately after, and hey presto it went into *his* brief-case. Trouble was, I wasn't followed any longer. He was. Then it was child's play to find out which hotel room he was in, and who he was. So from then on his fate was sealed."

"His . . . fate?"

"Well, it's obvious, isn't it? Mind you, he made it easier for them him-self. He'd palled up with his victim, him who was Bishop of this big town in Sicily which shall be nameless. Oh, right palsy-walsy they were, swapping jokes in Latin and I don't know what. Gave my bloke a good laugh, and that nice little feeling of power to boot—for as long as it lasted. He was in this Iti Bishop's room when he died."

"When he had his heart attack?"

Snobby, well launched into his story, was oblivious to Gordon's mistake: so far he had not mentioned any such thing as a heart attack.

"Whatever you care to call it. Sharing a bottle of Corvo they was, a nice thick Sicilian red, in the Italian Bish's hotel room. And what does he do, this Bish, when my bloke falls down and starts eating the carpet? Does he ring the hotel Reception and say "Get me the hotel doctor"? Oh no he does not. He rings a buddy-pal, practising in Venice, brought up in the same little village on the slopes of Mount Etna. No problems about a certificate from *him*. What's the betting he was alerted in advance, eh?"

"You're not saying this bishop . . . *murdered* your man?" said Gordon, aghast. Snobby sat back in his chair and looked at him pityingly.

"You haven't understood a word I've been saying, have you? That's the whole point—they were two of a kind. They'd both gone into the Church for the same reason. That Bish was the Mafia's spiritual arm back in their home island. Confessions heard daily and passed straight on. Once he knew that his blackmailer was a priest, he knew exactly how he'd got on to him, and exactly what to do." Snobby pushed his beer-mug away and felt for his scarf. "Which leads me to my final words of advice to you tonight there's no con so brilliant that two people can't think it up. And if two people running the same con bump into each other—wait for the explosion."

He pushed back his chair and got up, but as he did so he caught sight of Gordon's troubled expression, and seemed as if he was seeing the real man for the first time. He sat down again and looked at him seriously.

"It's fair bowled you over, hasn't it?" he said. "You're a serious chap at heart, aren't you? Sympathetic too. People must talk to you, I shouldn't mind betting. You ever thought of going in for the Church?"

✝

MEA CULPA

JAN BURKE

IT WAS GOING TO BE my turn next, and I should have been thinking about my sins, but I never could concentrate on my own sins—big as they were—once Harvey started his confession. I tried not to listen, but Harvey was a loud talker, and there was just no way that one wooden door was going to keep me from hearing him. There are lots of things I'm not good at anymore, but my hearing is pretty sharp. I wasn't trying to listen in on him, though. He was just talking loud. I tried praying, I tried humming "Ave Maria" to myself, but nothing worked. Maybe it was because Harvey was talking about wanting to divorce my mother.

It was only me and Father O'Brien and Harvey in the church then, anyway. Just like always. Harvey said he was embarrassed about me, on account of me being a cripple, and that's why he always waited until confessions were almost over. That way, none of his buddies on the parish council or in the Knights of Columbus would see him with me. But later, I figured it was because Harvey didn't want anybody to know he had sins.

Whatever the reason, on most Saturday nights, we'd get into his black Chrysler Imperial—a brand-spanking-new soft-seated car, with big fins on the back, push-button automatic transmission and purple dashlights.

We'd drive to church late and wait in the parking lot. When almost all the other cars were gone, he'd tell me to get out, to go on in and check on things.

I would get my crutches and go up the steps and struggle to get one of the big doors open and get myself inside the church. (That part was okay. Lots of other folks would try to do things for me, but Harvey let me do them on my own. I try to think of good things to say about Harvey. There aren't many, but that is one.)

I'd bless myself with holy water, then take a peek along the side aisle. Usually, only a few people were standing in line for confession by then. I'd go on up into the choir loft. I learned this way of going up the stairs real quietly. The stairs were old and wooden and creaked, but I figured out which ones groaned the loudest and where to step just right, so that I could do it without making much noise. I'd cross the choir loft and stand near one of the stained glass windows that faced the parking lot and wait to give Harvey the signal.

I always liked this time the best, the waiting time. It was dark up in the loft, and until the last people in line went into the confessional, I was in a secret world of my own. I could move closer to the railing and watch the faces of the people who waited in line. Sometimes, I'd time the people who had gone into the confessionals. If they were in there for a while, I would imagine what sins they were taking so long to tell. If they just went in and came out quick, I'd wonder if they were really good or just big liars.

Sometimes I would pray and do the kind of stuff you're supposed to do in a church. But I'm trying to tell the truth here, and the truth is that most often, my time up in that choir loft was spent thinking about Mary Theresa Mills. Her name was on the stained glass window I was supposed to signal from. It was a window of Jesus and the little children, and at the bottom it said it was "In memory of my beloved daughter, Mary Theresa Mills, 1902–1909." If the moon was bright, the light would come in through the window. It was so beautiful then, it always made me feel like I was in a holy place.

Sometimes I'd sit up there and think about her like a word problem in arithmetic: *Mary Theresa Mills died fifty years ago. She died when she was seven. If she had lived, how old would she be today, in 1959?* Answer: Fifty-seven; except if she hasn't had her birthday yet, so maybe fifty-six. (That kind of answer always gets me in trouble with my teacher, who would say it should just be fifty-seven. Period.)

I thought about her in other ways, too. I figured she must have been a good kid, not rotten like me. No one will ever make a window like that in my memory. It was kind of sad, thinking that someone good had died young like that, and for the past fifty years, there had been no Mary Theresa Mills.

There was a lamp near the Mary Theresa Mills window. The lamp was on top of the case where they kept the choir music, and that case was just below the window. When the last person went into the confessional, I'd turn the lamp on, and Harvey'd know he could come on in without seeing any of his friends. I'd wait until I saw him come in, then I'd turn out the lamp and head downstairs.

Once, I didn't wait, and I reached the bottom of the stairs when Harvey came into the church. A lady came down the aisle just then, and when she saw me she said, "Oh, you poor dear!" I really hate it when people act like that. She turned to Harvey, who was getting all red in the face and said, "Polio?"

I said, "No," just as Harvey said, "Yes." That just made him angrier. The lady looked confused, but Harvey was staring at me and not saying anything, so I just stared back. The lady said, "Oh dear!" and I guess that snapped Harvey out of it. He smiled real big and laughed this fake laugh of his and patted me on the head. Right then, I knew I was going to get it. Harvey only acts smiley like that when he has a certain kind of plan in mind. It fooled the lady, but it didn't fool me. Sure enough, as soon as she was out the door, I caught it from Harvey, right there in the church. He's no shrimp, and even openhanded, he packs a wallop.

Later, I listened, but he didn't confess the lie. He didn't confess smacking me, either, but Harvey told me a long time ago that nowhere in the Ten Commandments does it say, "Thou shalt not smack thy kid or thy wife." I wish it did, but then he'd probably just say that it didn't say anything about smacking thy stepkid. That's why, after that, I waited until Harvey had walked in and was on his way down the aisle before I came down the stairs.

So Harvey had been in the confessional for a little while before I made my way to stand outside of it. I could have gone into the other confessional, and I would, just as soon as I heard Harvey start the Act of Contrition—the last prayer a person says in confession. You can tell when someone's in a confessional because the kneeler has a gizmo on it that turns a light on over the door. When the person is finished, and gets up off the kneeler, the light goes out. But I knew Harvey's timing and I waited for that prayer instead, because, since the accident, I can't kneel so good. And once I get down on my knees. I have a hard time getting up again. Father O'Brien once told me I didn't have to kneel, but it doesn't seem right to me, so now he waits for me to get situated.

Like I said, I was trying not to eavesdrop, but Harvey was going on and on about my mom, saying she was the reason he drank and swore and committed sins, and how he would be a better Catholic if there was just some way he could have the marriage annulled. I was getting angrier and angrier, and I knew that was a sin, too. I couldn't hear Father O'Brien's side of it, but it was obvious that Harvey wasn't getting the answer he wanted. Harvey started complaining about me, and that wasn't so bad, but then he got going about Mom again.

I was so mad, I almost forgot to hurry up and get into the confessional when he started the Act of Contrition. Once inside, I made myself calm down, and started my confession. It wasn't hard for me to feel truly sorry, for the first sin I confessed weighed down on me more than anything I have ever done.

"Bless me, Father, for I have sinned. I killed my father."

I heard a sigh from the other side of the screen.

"My son," Father O'Brien began, "have you ever confessed this sin before?"

"Yes, Father."

"And received absolution?"

"Yes, Father."

"And have you done the penance asked of you?"

"Yes, Father."

"You don't believe in the power of the Sacrament of Penance, of the forgiveness of sins?"

I didn't want to make him mad, but I had to tell him the truth. "If God has forgiven me, Father, why do I still feel so bad about it?"

"I don't think God ever blamed you in the first place," he said, but now he didn't sound frustrated, just kind of sad. "I think you've blamed yourself. The reason you feel bad isn't because God hasn't forgiven you. It's because you haven't forgiven yourself."

"But if I hadn't asked—"

"—for the Davy Crockett hat for your seventh birthday, he wouldn't have driven in the rain," Father O'Brien finished for me. "Yes, I know. He loved you, and he wanted to give you something that would bring you joy. You didn't kill your father by asking for a hat."

"It's not just that," I said.

"I know. You made him laugh."

I didn't say anything for a long time. I was seeing my dad, sitting next to me in the car three years ago, the day gray and wet, but me hardly noticing, because I was so excited about that stupid cap. We were going somewhere together, just me and my dad, and that was exciting, too. The radio was on, and there was something about Dwight D. Eisenhower on the news. I asked my dad why we didn't like Ike.

"We like him fine," my father said.

"Then why are we voting for Yodelai Stevenson?" I asked him.

See how dumb I was? I didn't even know that the man's name was Adlai. Called him Yodelai, like he was some guy singing in the Alps.

My dad started laughing. Hard. I started laughing, too, just because he's laughing so hard. So stupid, I don't even know what's so funny. But then suddenly, he's trying to stop the car and it's skidding, skidding, skidding and he's reaching over, he's putting his arm across my chest, trying to keep me from getting hurt. There was a loud, low noise—a bang—and a high, jingling sound—glass flying. I've tried, but I can't remember anything else that happened that day.

My father died. I ended up crippled. The car was totaled. Adlai Stevenson lost the election. My mom married Harvey. And just in case you're wondering, no, I never got that dumb cap, and I don't want one. Ever.

Father O'Brien was giving me my penance, so I stopped thinking about the accident. I made a good Act of Contrition and went to work on standing up again. I knew Harvey watched for the light to go off over the confessional door, used it as a signal that I would be coming out soon. I could hear his footsteps. He'd always go back to the car before I could manage to get myself out of the confessional.

On the drive home, Harvey was quiet. He didn't lecture to me or brag on himself. When I was slow getting out of the car, he didn't yell at me or cuff my ear. That's not like him, and it worried me. He was thinking hard about something, and I had a creepy feeling that it couldn't be good.

The next day was a Sunday. Harvey and my mom went over to the parish hall after Mass. There was a meeting about the money the parish needed to raise to make some repairs. I asked my mom if I could stay in the church for a while. Harvey was always happy to get rid of me, so he said okay, even though he wasn't the one I was asking. My mom just nodded.

The reason I wanted to stay behind was because in the announce-
ments that Sunday, Father O'Brien had said something about the choir
loft being closed the next week, so that the stairs could be fixed. I wanted
to see the window before they closed the loft. I had never gone up there
in the daylight, but this might be my only chance to visit it for a while.
As I made my way up the stairs, out of habit I was quiet. I avoided the
stairs that creaked and groaned the most. I guess that's why I scared the
old lady who was sitting up there in the choir loft. At first, she scared me,
too.

She was wearing a long, old-fashioned black dress and a big black hat
with a black veil, which made her look spooky. She was thin and really,
really old. She had lifted the veil away from her face, and I could see it
was all wrinkled. She probably had bony hands, but she was wearing
gloves, so that's just a guess.

I almost left, but then I saw the window. It made me stop breathing for
a minute. Colors filled the choir loft, like a rainbow had decided to come
inside for a while. The window itself was bright, and I could see details in
the picture that I had never seen before. I started moving closer to it, kind
of hypnotized. Before I knew it, I was standing near the old lady, and now
I could see she had been crying. Even though she still looked ancient, she
didn't seem so scary. I was going to ask her if she was okay, but before I
could say anything, she said, "What are you doing here?"

Her voice was kind of snooty, so I almost said, "It's a free country," but
being in church on a Sunday, I decided against it. "I like this window," I
said.

"Do you?" She seemed surprised.

"Yes. It's the Mary Theresa Mills window. She died when she was little, a long time ago," I said. For some reason, I felt like I had to prove to
this lady that I had a real reason to be up there, that I wasn't just some
kid who had climbed up to the choir loft to hide or to throw spitballs
down on the pews. I told her everything I had figured out about Mary
Theresa Mills's age, including the birthday part. "So if she had lived, she'd
be old now, like you."

The lady frowned a little.

"She was really good," I went on. "She was practically perfect. Her
mother and father loved her so much, they paid a lot of money and put
this window up here, so that no one would ever forget her."

The old lady started crying again. "She wasn't perfect," she said. "She
was a little mischievous. But I did love her."

"You knew her?"

"I'm her mother," the lady said.

I sat down. I couldn't think of anything to say, even though I had a lot of questions about Mary Theresa. It just didn't seem right to ask them.

The lady reached into her purse and got a fancy handkerchief out. "She was killed in an automobile accident," she said. "It was my fault."

I guess I looked a little sick or something when she said that, because she asked me if I was all right.

"My dad died in a car accident."

She just tilted her head a little, and something seemed different about her eyes, the way she looked at me. She didn't say, "I'm so sorry," or any of the other things people say just to be saying something. And the look wasn't a pity look; she just studied me.

I rubbed my bad knee a little. I was pretty sure there was rain on the way, but I decided I wouldn't give her a weather report.

"Is there much pain?" she asked, watching me.

I shrugged. "I'm okay."

We sat there in silence for a time. I started doing some figuring in my head, and realized that I had been in my car accident at the same age her daughter died in one.

"Were you driving?" I asked.

"Pardon?"

"You said it was your fault she died. Were you driving?"

"No," she said. "Her father was driving." She hesitated, then added, "We were separated at the time. He asked if he could take her for a ride in the car. Cars were just coming into their own then, you know."

"You mean you rode horses?" I asked.

"Sometimes. Mostly I rode in a carriage or a buggy. My parents were well-to-do, and I was living with them at the time. I don't think they trusted automobiles much. Cars were becoming more and more popular, though. My husband bought one."

"I thought you were divorced."

"No, not divorced, separated. We were both Catholics. We weren't even legally separated. In fact, the day they died, I thought we might be reconciling."

"What's that?"

"Getting back together. I thought he had changed, you see. He stopped drinking, got a job, spoke to me sweetly. He pulled up in a shiny new motor car, and offered to take Mary Theresa for a ride. They never came back. He abducted her—kidnapped her, you might say. She was his daughter, there was no divorce, and nothing legally barring him from doing exactly what he did."

"How did the accident happen?"

"My husband tried to put a great distance between us by driving all night. He fell asleep at the wheel. The car went off the road and down an embankment. They were both killed instantly, I was told. I've always prayed that was true."

I didn't say anything. She was crying again. I pulled out a couple of tissues I had in my pocket and held them out to her, figuring that lace hankie was probably soaked already.

She thanked me and took one of them from me. After a minute, she said, "I should have known! I should have known that a leopard doesn't change his spots! I entrusted the safety of my child to a man whom I knew to be unworthy of that trust."

I started to tell her that it wasn't her fault, that she shouldn't blame herself, but before the words were out of my mouth, I knew I had no business saying anything like that to her. I knew how she was feeling. It bothered me to see her so upset. Without really thinking much about what I was doing, I started telling her about the day my father died.

Since I'm being completely honest here, I've got to tell you that I had to use that other tissue. She waited for me to blow my nose, then said, "Have you ever talked to your mother about how you feel?"

I shook my head. "She wanted me to, but since the accident—we aren't as close as we used to be, I guess. I think that's why she got together with Harvey. I think she got lonely."

About then, my mother came into the church, and called up to me. I told her I'd be right down. She said they'd be waiting in the car.

As I got up, the old lady put a hand on me. "Promise me that you will talk to your mother tonight."

"About what?"

"Anything. A boy should be able to talk to his mother about anything. Tell her what we talked about, if you like. I won't mind."

"Okay, I will," I said, "but who will you talk to when you start feeling bad about Mary Theresa?"

She didn't answer. She just looked sad again. Just before I left, I told her which steps to watch out for. I also told her to carry an umbrella if she went out that evening, because it was going to rain. I don't know if she took any of my good advice.

In the car, I got worried again. I was expecting Harvey to be mad because I kept them waiting. But he didn't say anything to me, and when he talked to my mom, he was sweet as pie. I don't talk when I'm in a car anymore, or I might have said something about that.

Harvey went out not long after we got home. My mother said we'd be eating Sunday dinner by ourselves, that Harvey had a business meeting he had to go to. I don't think she really believed he had a business meeting on a Sunday afternoon. I sure didn't believe it. My mom and I don't get to be by ourselves too much, though, so I was too happy about that to complain about Harvey.

My promise to Mary Theresa's mother was on my mind, so when my mother asked me what I was doing up there in the choir loft, I took it as a sign. I told her the whole story, about the window and Mary Theresa and even about the accident. It was the second time I had told it in one day, so it wasn't so rough on me, but I think it was hard on her. She didn't seem to mind, and I even let her hug me.

It rained that night, just like my knee said it would. My mom came in to check on me, saying she knew that the rain sometimes bothered me. I was feeling all right, though, and I told her I thought I would sleep fine. We smiled at each other, like we had a secret, a good secret. It was the first time in a few years that we had been happy at the same time.

I woke up when Harvey came home. When I heard him put the Imperial in the garage, I got out of bed and peeked from behind my bedroom door. I knew he had lied to my mom, and if he was drunk or started to get mean with her, I decided I was gonna bash him with one of my crutches.

He came in the front door. He was wet. I had to clamp my hand over my mouth to keep from laughing, because I realized that he had gone out without his umbrella. He looked silly. The rain and wind had messed up his hair, so that his long side—the side he tries to comb over his bald spot—was hanging straight down. He closed the front door, really carefully, then he went into the bathroom near my bedroom, instead of the one off of his room. At first I thought he was just sneaking in and trying not to wake up my mom, but he was in there a long time. When he came out, he was in his underwear. I almost busted a gut trying not to laugh. He tiptoed past me and went to bed. The clock was striking three.

I waited until I thought he might be asleep, then I went into the bathroom. There was water all over the place. He hadn't mopped up after himself, so I took a towel and dried the floor and counter. It was while I was drying the floor that I saw the book of matches. It had a red cover on it, and it came from a place called Topper's, an all-night restaurant down on South Street. I picked up the matchbook. A few of the matches had been used. The name "Mackie" was written on the inside, and just below that, "1417 A-3." I closed the cover and looked at the address for Topper's. 1400 South Street. I knew Harvey's handwriting well enough to know that he had written that name and address.

What was he doing with matches? Harvey didn't smoke. He hated smoke. I knew, because he had made a big speech about it on the day he threw away my dad's pipes. I had gone into the trash and taken them back out. I put them in a little wooden box, the same one where I kept a photo of my dad. I never looked at the photo or the pipes, but I kept them anyway. I thought my mom might have found the place I hid them, but so far, she hadn't ratted on me.

I opened the laundry hamper. Harvey's wet clothes were in there. I reached in and pulled out his shirt. No lipstick stains, and even without lifting it close to my nose, I could tell it didn't have perfume on it. It could have used some. It smelled like smoke, a real strong kind of smoke. Not like a fire or anything, but stronger than a cigarette. A cigar, maybe. I had just put the shirt back in the hamper when the door flew open.

"What are you doing?" Harvey asked.

I should have said something like, "Ever heard of knocking?" or made some wisecrack, but I was too scared. I could feel the matchbook in my hand, hot, as if I had lit all the matches in it at once.

Luckily, my mom woke up. "Harvey?" I heard her call. It sounded like she was standing in the hall.

"Oh, did I wake you up, sweetheart?" he said.

My jaw dropped open. Harvey never talked to her like that after they got married.

"What's wrong?" she asked.

"I was just checking on the boy," he said, He looked at me and asked, "Are you okay, son?"

Son. That made me sick to my stomach. I swallowed and said, "Just came in to get some aspirin."

"Your leg bothering you because of this rain?" he asked, like he cared.

"I'll be all right. Sorry I woke you up."

My mom was at the door then, so I said, "Okay if I close the door? Now that I'm up . . . well, you know . . ."

Harvey laughed his fake laugh and put an arm around my mom. He closed the door.

I pulled a paper cup out of the dispenser in the bathroom. I turned the cup over and scratched the street numbers for Mackie and Topper's, then put the matchbook back where I found it. By now, I was so scared I really did have to go, so I didn't have to fake that. I flushed the toilet, then washed my hands. Finally, I put a little water in the cup. I opened the door. I turned to pick up the cup, and once again thought to myself that one of the things that stinks about crutches is that they take up your hands. I was going to try to carry the cup in my teeth, since it wasn't very full, but my mom is great about seeing when I'm having trouble, so she said, "Would you like to have that cup of water on your nightstand?"

I nodded.

Harvey watched us go into my bedroom. He went into the bathroom again. My mom started fussing over me, talking about maybe taking me to a new doctor. I tried to pay attention to what she was saying, but the whole time, I was worrying about what Harvey was thinking. Could he tell that I saw the matchbook? After a few minutes he came back out, and he had this smile on his face. I knew the matches wouldn't be on the floor now, that he had figured out where he had dropped them and that he had picked them up. He felt safe. I didn't. I drank the water and saved the bottom of the cup.

† † †

The next morning I got up early and went into the laundry room. Harvey's clothes were still in the bathroom, but I wasn't interested in them anyway. I put a load of his wash in the washing machine, checking his trouser pockets before I put them in. I made sixty cents just by collecting his change. I put it in my own pocket, right next to the waxy paper from the cup.

I had just started the washer when my mom and Harvey came into the kitchen. My mom got the percolator and the toaster going. Harvey glared at me while I straightened up the laundry room and put the soap away.

"You're gonna turn him into a pansy, lettin' him do little girl's work like that," he said to my mom when she brought him his coffee and toast.

"I like being able to help." I said, before she could answer.

We both waited for him to come over and cuff me one for arguing

with him first thing in the morning, but he just grunted and stirred a
bunch of sugar into his coffee. He always put about half the sugar bowl
into his coffee. You'd think it would have made him sweeter.

That morning, it seemed like it did. Once he woke up a little more,
he started talking to her like a guy in a movie talks to a girl just before he
kisses her. I left the house as soon as I could.

Before I left, I told my mom that I might be home late from school. I
told her that I might catch a matinee with some of the other kids. I never
do anything with other kids, and she seemed excited when I told her that
lie. I felt bad about lying, even if it made her happy.

All day, I was a terrible student. I just kept thinking about the matchbook and about Mary Theresa's father and Harvey and leopards that don't
change their spots.

After school, I took the city bus downtown. I got off at South Street,
right in front of Topper's.

The buildings are tall in that part of town. There wasn't much sunlight, but up above the street, there were clotheslines between the buildings. The day was cloudy, so nobody had any clothes out, although I
could have told them it wasn't going to rain that afternoon. Not that there
was anything to rain on—nothing was growing there. The sidewalks and
street were still damp, though, and not many people were around. I was
a little nervous.

I thought about going into Topper's and asking if anybody knew a guy
named Mackie, but decided that wouldn't be too smart. I started down
the street. 1405 was the next address. Linden's Tobacco Shop. I had
already noticed that sometimes they skip numbers downtown. I stopped,
thinking maybe that was where Harvey got the smoke on his clothes. Just
then a man came out of the door and didn't close it behind him as he left
the shop. As I stood in the doorway, a sweet, familiar smell came to me,
and I felt an ache in my chest. It was pipe tobacco. It made me think of
my father, and how he always smelled like tobacco and Old Spice After-
Shave. A sourpussed man came to the door, said, "No minors," and shut
it in my face. The shop's hours were painted on the door. It was closed on
Sundays.

I moved down the sidewalk, reading signs, looking in windows.
"Buzzy's Newsstand—Out-of-Town Papers," "South Street Sweets—
Handmade Chocolates," "Moore's Hardware—Everything for Home and
Garden," "Suds-O-Mat—Coin-Operated Laundry." Finally, I came to "The

Coronet—Apartments to Let." The address was 1417 South Street. The building looked older than Mary Theresa's mother.

Inside, the Coronet was dark and smelled like a mixture of old b.o. and cooked cabbage. There was a thin, worn carpet in the hallway. A-3 was the second apartment on the left-hand side. I put my ear to the door. It was quiet. I moved back from the door and was trying to decide what to do when a man came into the building. I turned and pretended to be waiting for someone to answer the door of A-4.

The man was carrying a paper sack and smoking a cigar. The cigar not only smelled better than the hallway, it smelled exactly like the smoke on Harvey's clothes. It had to be Mackie.

Mackie's face was an okay face, except that his nose looked like he had run into a wall and stayed there for a while. He was big, but he didn't look clumsy or dumb. I saw that the paper sack was from the hardware store. When he unlocked his door, I caught a glimpse of a shoulder holster. As he pulled the door open, he saw me watching him and gave me a mean look.

"Whaddaya want?" he said.

I swallowed hard and said, "I'm collecting donations for the Crippled Children's Society."

His eyes narrowed. "Oh yeah? Where's your little collection can?"

"I can't carry it and move around on the crutches," I said.

"Hmpf. You won't get anything there," he said, nodding toward the other apartment. "The place is empty."

"Oh. I guess I'll be going then."

I tried to move past him, but he pushed me hard against the wall, making me drop one of my crutches. "No hurry, is there?" he said. "Let's see if you're really a cripple."

That was easy. I dropped the other crutch, then reached down and pulled my right pant leg up. He did what anybody does when they see my bad leg. They stare at it, and not because it's beautiful.

I used this chance to look past him into his apartment. From what I could see of it, it was small and neat. There was a table with two things on it: a flat, rectangular box and the part of a shot they call a syringe. It didn't have a needle on it yet. You might think I'm showing off, but I knew it was called a syringe because I've spent a lot of time getting stuck by the full works, and sooner or later some nurse tells you more than you want to know about anything they do to you.

Mackie picked up my crutches. I was trying to see into the paper sack, but all I could make out was that it was some kind of can. When Mackie straightened up again, his neck and ears were turning red. Maybe that's what made me bold enough to say, "I lied."

His eyes narrowed again.

"I'm not collecting for Crippled Children. I was just trying to raise some movie money."

He started laughing. He reached in his pocket and pulled out a silver dollar. He dropped it into my shirt pocket. "Kid, you earned it," he said and went into his apartment.

I leaned against the wall for another minute, my heart thumping hard against that silver dollar. Then I left and made my way to the hardware store.

No other customers were in there. The old man behind the counter was reading a newspaper. I cleared my throat. "Excuse me, sir, but Mackie sent me over to pick up another can."

"Another one? You can tell Mackie he's got to come here himself." He looked up at me and then looked away really fast. I'm used to it. "Look," he said, talking into the newspaper, "I'm not selling weed killer to any kid, crippled or no. The stuff's poisonous." That's the way he said it: "crippled or no." Like I had come in there asking for special treatment.

I had too much on my mind to worry about it. I was thinking about why a guy who lived in a place like the Coronet would need weed killer. "What's weed killer got in it, anyway?" I asked.

He folded his newspaper down and looked at me like my brain was as lame as my leg. "Arsenic. Eat a little of that and you're a goner."

✝   ✝   ✝

At home that night, I kept an eye on Harvey. I noticed that even though he was still laying it on thick with my mom, he was nervous. He kept watching the clock on the mantle. My mom was in the kitchen, making lunches, and he kept looking between the kitchen and the clock. When the phone rang at eight, he jumped up to answer it, yelling. "I got it." To the person on the phone, he said, "Just a sec." He turned to me and said, "Get ready for bed."

I thought of arguing, but changed my mind. I went into the hallway, and waited just out of sight. I hoped he'd talk as loud as he usually did.

He tried to speak softly, but I could still hear him.

"No, no, that's too soon. I have some arrangements to make." He paused, then said, "Saturday, then. Good."

† † †

That night, when my mom came in to say good night, I told her not to let Harvey fix her anything to eat, or take anything from him that came in a rectangular box. "He wants to poison you, Mom," I whispered.

She laughed and said, "That matinee must have been a detective movie. I was waiting for you to tell me about your afternoon. Did you have a good time?"

It wasn't easy, but I told her the truth. "I didn't go to a movie," I said. "But I thought . . ."

"I went downtown. To South Street."

She looked more scared than when I told her that her husband wanted to poison her.

"Please don't tell Harvey!" I said.

"Don't tell Harvey what?" I heard a voice say. He was standing in my bedroom door.

"Oh, that he got a bad grade on a spelling test," my mom said. "But you wouldn't get angry with him over a little thing like that, would you, dear?"

"No, of course not, sweetheart," he said to her. He faked another laugh and walked off.

Although I don't think Harvey knew it, she hadn't meant it when she called him "dear." And she had lied to him for my sake. Just when I had decided that meant she believed me about the poison, she said, "You and I will have a serious talk very soon, young man. Good night." She kissed me, but I could tell she was mad.

† † †

That was a terrible week. Harvey was nervous, I was nervous, and my mom put me on restriction. I had to come straight home after school every day. I never got far enough in the story to tell her what happened when I went downtown; she just said that where Harvey went at night was his business, not mine, and that I should never lie to her again about where I was going.

We didn't say much to one another. On Friday night, when she came in to say good night, I couldn't even make myself say good night back. She stayed there at my bedside and said, "We were off to such a good start this week. I had hoped . . . well, that doesn't matter now." I know you're angry with me for putting you on restriction, but you gave me a scare. You're all I have now, and I couldn't bear to lose you."

"You're all I have, too." I said, "I don't mind the restriction. It's just that you don't believe anything I say."

No, that's not it. It's just that I think Harvey is trying to be a better husband. Maybe Father O'Brien has talked to him, I don't know."

"A leopard doesn't change his spots," I said.

"Harvey's not a leopard."

"He's a snake."

She sighed again. She kept sitting there.

All of a sudden, I remembered that Harvey had mentioned Saturday, which was the next day, and I sat up. I hugged her hard. "Please believe me," I said. "Just this once."

She was startled at first, probably because that was two hugs in one week, which was two more than I'd given her since she married Harvey. She hugged back, and said, "You really are scared, aren't, you?"

I nodded against her shoulder.

"Okay. I won't let Harvey fix any meals for me or give me anything in a rectangular box. At least not until you get over this." She sounded like she thought it was kind of funny. "I hope it will be soon, though."

"Maybe as early as tomorrow," I whispered, but I don't think she heard me.

I hardly slept at all that night.

✝ ✝ ✝

The next morning, Harvey left the house and didn't come back until just before dinner. He wasn't carrying anything with him when he came in the house, just went in and washed up. I watched every move he made, and he never went near any food.

"C'mon," he said to me after dinner, "let's go on down to the church."

A new thought hit me. What if the weed killer was for someone else? What if Harvey had hired Mackie to shoot my mom? "I don't want to go," I said.

"No more back talk out of you, buster. Let's go. Confessions will be over if we don't get down there."

I looked at my mom.

"Go on," she said. "I'll be fine."

As Harvey walked with me to the car, I kept trying to think up some way to stay home. I knew what Mackie looked like. I knew he carried his gun in a shoulder holster. I knew he liked silver dollars, because I had one of his in my pocket. I knew—

I looked up, because Harvey was saying something to me. He had opened the car door for me, which was more than he usually did. "Pardon?"

"I said, get yourself situated. I've got a surprise for your mother."

Before I could think of anything to say, he was opening the back door and picking up a package. A rectangular package. As he walked past me, I saw there was a label on it. South Street Sweets.

My mother took it from him, smiling and thanking him. "You know I can't resist chocolates," she said.

"Have one now," he said.

I was about to yell out "No!", thinking she'd forgotten everything I said, but she looked at me over his shoulder, and something in her eyes made me keep my mouth shut.

Harvey followed her glance, but before he could yell at me, she said, "Oh Harvey, his knee must be bothering him. Be a dear and help him. I'm going to go right in and put my feet up and eat about a dozen of these." To me, she said, "Remember what we talked about last night. You be careful."

All the way to the church, Harvey was quiet. When we got there, he sent me in first, as usual.

"But the choir loft is closed," I said.

"It hasn't fallen apart in a week. They haven't even started work on it. Go on."

I went inside. He was right. Even though there was a velvet rope and a sign that said, "Closed," it didn't look like any work had started. I wanted to be near Mary Theresa's window anyway. But as I got near the top of the stairs, I noticed they sounded different beneath my crutches. Some of the ones that were usually quiet were groaning now.

I waited until almost everyone was gone. By that time I had done more thinking. I figured Harvey wouldn't give up trying to kill my mom, even if I had wrecked his chocolate plan. He wanted the house and the money that came with my mom, but not her or her kid. I couldn't keep watching him all the time.

I turned the lamp on and waited for him to come into the church. As usual, he didn't even look toward me. He went into the confessional. I took one last look at the window and started to turn the lamp off, when I got an idea. I left the lamp on.

I knew the fourth step from the top was especially creaky. I went down to the sixth step from the top, then turned around. I held on to the rail, and then pressed one of my crutches down on the fourth step. It creaked. I leaned most of my weight on it. I felt it give. I stopped before it broke.

I went on down the stairs. I could hear Harvey, not talking about my mom this time, but not admitting he was hoping she was already dead. I went into the other confessional, but I didn't kneel down.

I heard Harvey finish up and step outside his confessional. Then I heard him take a couple of steps and stand outside my confessional door.

For a minute, I was afraid he'd open the door and look 'nside. He didn't. He took a couple of steps away, and then stopped again. I waited. He walked toward the back of the church, and I could tell by the sound of his steps that he was mad. I knocked on the wall between me and Father O'Brien, "All right if I don't kneel this time, Father?" I asked.

"Certainly, my son," he said.

"Bless me, Father, for I have sinned. I lied three times, I stole sixty cents, and . . ."

I waited a moment.

"And?" the priest said.

There was a loud groaning sound, a yell, and a crash.

"And I just killed my stepfather."

✝   ✝   ✝

He didn't die, he just broke both of his legs and knocked himself out. A policeman showed up, but not because Father O'Brien had told anyone my confession. Turned out my mother had called the police, showed them the candy, and finally convinced them they had to hurry to the church and arrest her husband before he harmed her son.

The police talked to me and then went down to South Street and arrested Mackie. At the hospital, a detective went in with me to see Harvey when Harvey woke up. I got to offer Harvey some of the chocolates he had given my mom. Instead of taking any candy, he made another confession that night. Before we left, the detective asked him why he had gone up into the choir loft. He said I had left a light on up there. The detective asked me if that was true, and of course I said, "Yes."

The next time I was in church, I put Mackie's silver dollar in the donation box near the candles and lit three candles: one for my father, one for Mary Theresa Mills, and one for the guy who made up the rule that says priests can't rat on you.

After I lit the candles, I went home and took out my wooden box. I put my father's pipes on the mantle, next to his photo. My mom saw me staring at the photo and came over and stood next to me. Instead of thinking of him being off in heaven, a long way away, I imagined him being right there with us, looking back at us from that picture. I imagined him knowing that I had tried to save her from Harvey. I thought he would have liked that.

My mom reached out and touched one of the pipes very carefully. "It wasn't your fault," she said.

You know what? I believed her.

✝

The Wrong Shape

G. K. Chesterton

Certain of the great roads going north out of London continue far into the country a sort of attenuated and interrupted spectre of a street, with great gaps in the building, but preserving the line. Here will be a group of shops, followed by a fenced field or paddock, and then a famous public-house, and then perhaps a market garden or a nursery garden, and then one large private house, and then another field and another inn, and so on. If anyone walks along one of these roads he will pass a house which will probably catch his eye, though he may not be able to explain its attraction. It is a long, low house, running parallel with the road, painted mostly white and pale green, with a veranda and sunblinds, and porches capped with those quaint sort of cupolas like wooden umbrellas that one sees in some old-fashioned houses. In fact, it is an old-fashioned house, very English and very suburban in the good old wealthy Clapham sense. And yet the house has a look of having been built chiefly for the hot weather. Looking at its white paint and sun blinds one thinks vaguely of pugarees and even of palm trees. I cannot trace the feeling to its root; perhaps the place was built by an Anglo-Indian.

Anyone passing this house, I say, would be namelessly fascinated by it; would feel that it was a place about which some story was to be told.

And he would have been right, as you shall shortly hear. For this is the story—the story of the strange things that did really happen in it in the Whitsuntide of the year 18—:

Anyone passing the house on the Thursday before Whit-Sunday at about half-past four P.M. would have seen the front door open, and Father Brown, of the small church of St. Mungo, come out smoking a large pipe in company with a very tall French friend of his called Flambeau, who was smoking a very small cigarette. These persons may or may not be of interest to the reader, but the truth is that they were not the only interesting things that were displayed when the front door of the white-and-green house was opened. There are further peculiarities about this house, which must be described to start with, not only that the reader may understand this tragic tale, but also that he may realize what it was that the opening of the door revealed.

The whole house was built upon the plan of a T, but a T with a very long cross piece and a very short tail piece The long cross piece was the frontage that ran along in face of the street with the front door in the middle; it was two stories high, and contained nearly all the important rooms. The short tail piece, which ran out at the back immediately opposite the front door, was one story high, and consisted only of two long rooms, the one leading into the other. The first of these two rooms was the study in which the celebrated Mr. Quinton wrote his wild Oriental poems and romances. The farther room was a glass conservatory full of tropical blossoms of quite unique and almost monstrous beauty, and on such afternoons as these was glowing with gorgeous sunlight. Thus when the hall door was open, many a passerby literally stopped to stare and gasp; for he looked down a perspective of rich apartments to something really like a transformation scene in a fairy play: purple clouds and golden suns and crimson stars that were at once scorchingly vivid and yet transparent and far away.

Leonard Quinton, the poet, had himself most carefully arranged this effect; and it is doubtful whether he so perfectly expressed his personality in any of his poems. For he was a man who drank and bathed in colours, who indulged his lust for colour somewhat to the neglect of form—even of good form. Thus it was that he had turned his genius so wholly to eastern art and imagery; to those bewildering carpets or blinding embroideries in which all the colours seem fallen into a fortunate chaos, having nothing to typify or to teach. He had attempted, not perhaps with complete artistic success, but with acknowledged imagination and invention, to compose epics and love stories reflecting the riot of violent and even cruel colour; tales of tropical heavens of burning gold or blood-red copper; of eastern heroes who rode with twelve-turbaned mitres upon elephants painted purple or peacock green; of gigantic jewels that a hundred negroes could not carry, but which burned with ancient and strange-hued fires.

In short (to put the matter from the more common point of view), he dealt much in eastern heavens, rather worse than most western hells; in eastern monarchs, whom we might possibly call maniacs; and in eastern jewels which a Bond Street jeweller (if the hundred staggering negroes brought them into his shop) might possibly not regard as genuine. Quinton was a genius, if a morbid one; and even his morbidity appeared more in his life than in his work. In temperament he was weak and waspish, and his health had suffered heavily from oriental experiments with opium. His wife—a handsome, hard-working, and, indeed, overworked woman—objected to the opium, but objected much more to a live Indian hermit in white and yellow robes, whom her husband had insisted on entertaining for months together, a Virgil to guide his spirit through the heavens and the hells of the east.

It was out of this artistic household that Father Brown and his friend stepped on to the door-step; and to judge from their faces, they stepped out of it with much relief. Flambeau had known Quinton in wild student days in Paris, and they had renewed the acquaintance for a week-end; but apart from Flambeau's more responsible developments of late, he did not get on well with the poet now. Choking oneself with opium and writing little erotic verses on vellum was not his notion of how a gentleman should go to the devil. As the two paused on the doorstep, before taking a turn in the garden, the front garden gate was thrown open with violence, and a young man with a billycock hat on the back of his head tumbled up the steps in his eagerness. He was a dissipated-looking youth with a gorgeous red necktie all awry, as if he had slept in it, and he kept fidgeting and lashing about with one of those little jointed canes.

"I say," he said breathlessly, "I want to see old Quinton. I must see him. Has he gone?"

"Mr. Quinton is in, I believe," said Father Brown, cleaning his pipe, "but I do not know if you can see him. The doctor is with him at present."

The young man, who seemed not to be perfectly sober, stumbled into the hall; and at the same moment the doctor came out of Quinton's study, shutting the door and beginning to put on his gloves.

"See Mr. Quinton?" said the doctor coolly. "No, I'm afraid you can't. In fact, you mustn't on any account. Nobody must see him; I've just given him his sleeping draught."

"No, but look here, old chap," said the youth in the red tie, trying affectionately to capture the doctor by the lapels of his coat. "Look here. I'm simply sewn up, I tell you. I—"

"It's no good, Mr. Atkinson," said the doctor, forcing him to fall back; "when you can alter the effects of a drug I'll alter my decision," and, settling on his hat, he stepped out into the sunlight with the other two. He was a bull-necked, good-tempered little man with a small moustache, inexpressibly ordinary, yet giving an impression of capability.

The young man in the billycock, who did not seem to be gifted with any tact in dealing with people beyond the general idea of clutching hold of their coats, stood outside the door, as dazed as if he had been thrown out bodily, and silently watched the other three walk away together through the garden.

"That was a sound, spanking lie I told just now," remarked the medical man, laughing. "In point of fact, poor Quinton doesn't have his sleeping draught for nearly half an hour. But I'm not going to have him bothered with that little beast, who only wants to borrow money that he wouldn't pay back if he could. He's a dirty little scamp, though he is Mrs. Quinton's brother, and she's as fine a woman as ever walked."

"Yes," said Father Brown. "She's a good woman."

"So I propose to hang about the garden till the creature has cleared off," went on the doctor, "and then I'll go in to Quinton with the medicine. Atkinson can't get in, because I locked the door."

"In that case, Dr. Harris," said Flambeau, "we might as well walk round at the back by the end of the conservatory. There's no entrance to it that way but it's worth seeing, even from the outside."

"Yes, and I might get a squint at my patient," laughed the doctor, "for he prefers to lie on an ottoman right at the end of the conservatory amid all those blood-red poinsettias; it would give me the creeps. But what are you doing?"

Father Brown had stopped for a moment, and picked up out of the long grass, where it had almost been wholly hidden, a queer, crooked Oriental knife, inlaid exquisitely in coloured stones and metals.

"What is this?" asked Father Brown, regarding it with some disfavour.

"Oh, Quinton's, I suppose," said Dr. Harris carelessly; "he has all sorts of Chinese knick-knacks about the place. Or perhaps it belongs to the mild Hindoo of his whom he keeps on a string."

"What Hindoo?" asked Father Brown, still staring at the dagger in his hand.

"Oh, some Indian conjurer," said the doctor lightly; "a fraud, of course.

"You don't believe in magic?" asked Father Brown without looking up.

"Oh crikey! magic!" said the doctor.

"It's very beautiful," said the priest in a low, dreaming voice; "the colours are very beautiful. But it's the wrong shape."

"What for?" asked Flambeau, staring.

"For anything. It's the wrong shape in the abstract. Don't you ever feel that about Eastern art? The colours are intoxicatingly lovely; but the shapes are mean and bad—deliberately mean and bad. I have seen wicked things in a Turkey carpet."

"*Mon Dieu!*" cried Flambeau, laughing.

"They are letters and symbols in a language I don't know; but I know they stand for evil words," went on the priest, his voice growing lower and lower. "The lines go wrong on purpose—like serpents doubling to escape."

"What the devil are you talking about?" said the doctor with a loud laugh.

Flambeau spoke quietly to him in answer. "The Father sometimes gets this mystic's cloud on him, " he said; "but I give you fair warning that I have never known him have it except when there was some evil quite near."

"Oh, rats!" said the scientist.

"Why, look at it," cried Father Brown, holding out the crooked knife at arm's length, as if it were some glittering snake. "Don't you see it is the wrong shape? Don't you see that it has no hearty and plain purpose? It does not point like a spear. It does not sweep like a scythe. It does not *look* like a weapon. It looks like an instrument of torture."

"Well, as you don't seem to like it," said the jolly Harris, "it had better be taken back to its owner. Haven't we come to the end of this confounded conservatory yet? This house is the wrong shape, if you like."

"You don't understand," said Father Brown, shaking his head. "The shape of this house is quaint—it is even laughable. But there is nothing *wrong* about it."

As they spoke they came round the curve of glass that ended the conservatory, an uninterrupted curve, for there was neither door nor window by which to enter at that end. The glass, however, was clear, and the sun still bright, though beginning to set; and they could see not only the flamboyant blossoms inside, but the frail figure of the poet in a brown velvet coat lying languidly on the sofa, having, apparently, fallen half asleep over a book. He was a pale, slight man, with loose, chestnut hair and a fringe of beard that was the paradox of his face, for the beard made him look less manly. These traits were well known to all three of them; but even had it not been so, it may be doubted whether they would have looked at Quinton just then. Their eyes were riveted on another object.

Exactly in their path, immediately outside the round end of the glass building, was standing a tall man, whose drapery fell to his feet in faultless white, and whose bare, brown skull, face, and neck gleamed in the setting sun like splendid bronze. He was looking through the glass at the sleeper, and he was more motionless than a mountain.

"Who is that?" cried Father Brown, stepping back with a hissing intake of his breath.

"Oh, it is only that Hindoo humbug," growled Harris; "but I don't know what the deuce he's doing here."

"It looks like hypnotism," said Flambeau, biting his black moustache.

"Why are you unmedical fellows always talking bosh about hypnotism?" cried the doctor. "It looks a deal more like burglary."

"Well, we will speak to it, at any rate," said Flambeau, who was always for action. One long stride took him to the place where the Indian stood. Bowing from his great height, which overtopped even the Oriental's, he said with placid impudence:

"Good evening, sir. Do you want anything?"

Quite slowly, like a great ship turning into a harbour, the great yellow face turned, and looked at last over its white shoulder. They were startled to see that its yellow eyelids were quite sealed, as in sleep. "Thank you," said the face in excellent English. "I want nothing." Then, half opening the lids, so as to show a slit of opalescent eyeball, he repeated, "I want nothing." Then he opened his eyes wide with a startling stare, said, "I want nothing," and went rustling away into the rapidly darkening garden.

"The Christian is more modest," muttered Father Brown; "he wants something."

"What on earth was he doing?" asked Flambeau, knitting his black brows and lowering his voice.

"I should like to talk to you later," said Father Brown.

The sunlight was still a reality, but it was the red light of evening, and the bulk of the garden trees and bushes grew blacker and blacker against it. They turned round the end of the conservatory, and walked in silence down the other side to get round to the front door. As they went they seemed to wake something, as one startles a bird, in the deeper corner between the study and the main building; and again they saw the white-robed fakir slide out of the shadow, and slip round towards the front door. To their surprise, however, he had not been alone. They found themselves abruptly pulled up and forced to banish their bewilderment by the appearance of Mrs. Quinton, with her heavy golden hair and square pale face, advancing on them out of the twilight. She looked a little stern, but was entirely courteous.

"Good evening, Dr. Harris," was all she said.

"Good evening, Mrs. Quinton," said the little doctor heartily. "I am just going to give your husband his sleeping draught."

"Yes," she said in a clear voice. "I think it is quite time." And she smiled at them, and went sweeping into the house.

"That woman's over-driven," said Father Brown; "that's the kind of woman that does her duty for twenty years, and then does something dreadful."

The little doctor looked at him for the first time with an eye of interest. "Did you ever study medicine?" he asked.

"You have to know something of the mind as well as the body," answered the priest; "we have to know something of the body as well as the mind."

"Well," said the doctor, "I think I'll go and give Quinton his stuff."

They had turned the corner of the front façade, and were approaching the front doorway. As they turned into it they saw the man in the white robe for the third time. He came so straight towards the front door that it seemed quite incredible that he had not just come out of the study opposite to it. Yet they knew that the study door was locked.

Father Brown and Flambeau, however, kept this weird contradiction to themselves, and Dr. Harris was not a man to waste his thoughts on the impossible. He permitted the omnipresent Asiatic to make his exit, and then stepped briskly into the hall. There he found a figure which he had already forgotten. The inane Atkinson was still hanging about, humming and poking things with his knobby cane. The doctor's face had a spasm of disgust and decision, and he whispered rapidly to his companion: "I must lock the door again, or this rat will get in. But I shall be out again in two minutes."

He rapidly unlocked the door and locked it again behind him, just balking a blundering charge from the young man in the billycock. The young man threw himself impatiently on a hall chair. Flambeau looked at a Persian illumination on the wall; Father Brown, who seemed in a sort of daze, dully eyed the door. In about four minutes the door was opened again. Atkinson was quicker this time. He sprang forward, held the door open for an instant, and called out: "Oh, I say, Quinton, I want—"

From the other end of the study came the clear voice of Quinton, in something between a yawn and a yell of weary laughter.

"Oh, I know what you want. Take it, and leave me in peace. I'm writing a song about peacocks."

Before the door closed half a sovereign came flying through the aperture and Atkinson, stumbling forward, caught it with singular dexterity.

"So that's settled," said the doctor, and, locking the door savagely, he led the way out into the garden.

"Poor Leonard can get a little peace now," he added to Father Brown; "he's locked in all by himself for an hour or two."

"Yes," answered the priest; "and his voice sounded jolly enough when we left him." Then he looked gravely round the garden, and saw the loose figure of Atkinson standing and jingling the half-sovereign in his pocket, and beyond, in the purple twilight, the figure of the Indian sitting bolt upright upon a bank of grass with his face turned towards the setting sun. Then he said abruptly: "Where is Mrs. Quinton?"

"She has gone up to her room," said the doctor. "That is her shadow on the blind."

Father Brown looked up, and frowningly scrutinized a dark outline at the gas-lit window.

"Yes," he said, "that is her shadow," and he walked a yard or two and threw himself upon a garden seat.

Flambeau sat down beside him; but the doctor was one of those energetic people who live naturally on their legs. He walked away, smoking, into the twilight, and the two friends were left together.

"My father," said Flambeau in French, "what is the matter with you?"

Father Brown was silent and motionless for half a minute then he said: "Superstition is irreligious, but there is something in the air of this place. I think it's that Indian—at least, partly."

He sank into silence, and watched the distant outline of the Indian,

who still sat rigid as if in prayer. At first sight he seemed motionless, but
as Father Brown watched him he saw that the man swayed ever so slightly
with a rhythmic movement, just as the dark tree-tops swayed ever so
slightly in the little wind that was creeping up the dim garden paths and
shuffling the fallen leaves a little.

The landscape was growing rapidly dark, as if for a storm, but they
could still see all the figures in their various places. Atkinson was leaning
against a tree, with a listless face; Quinton's wife was still at her window;
the doctor had gone strolling round the end of the conservatory; they
could see his cigar like a will-o'-the-wisp; and the fakir still sat rigid and
yet rocking, while the trees above him began to rock and almost to roar.
Storm was certainly coming.

"When that Indian spoke to us," went on Brown in a conversational
undertone, "I had a sort of vision, a vision of him and all his universe. Yet
he only said the same thing three times. When first he said, 'I want nothing,' it meant only that he was impenetrable, that Asia does not give itself
away. Then he said again, 'I want nothing,' and I knew that be meant that
he was sufficient to himself, like a cosmos, that he needed no God, neither admitted any sins. And when he said the third time, 'I want nothing,'
he said it with blazing eyes. And I knew that he meant literally what he
said; that nothing was his desire and his home; that he was weary for
nothing as for wine; that annihilation, the mere destruction of everything
or anything—"

Two drops of rair. fell; and for some reason Flambeau started and
looked up, as if they had stung him. And the same instant the doctor
down by the end of the conservatory began running towards them, calling out something as he ran.

As he came among them like a bombshell the restless Atkinson happened to be taking a turn nearer to the house front; and the doctor
clutched him by the collar in a convulsive grip. "Foul play!" he cried;
"what have you been doing to him, you dog?"

The priest had sprung erect, and had the voice of steel of a soldier in
command.

"No fighting," he cried coolly; "we are enough to hold anyone we
want to. What is the matter, doctor?"

"Things are not right with Quinton," said the doctor, quite white. "I
could just see him through the glass, and I don't like the way he's lying.
It's not as I left him, anyhow."

"Let us go in to him," said Father Brown shortly. "You can leave Mr.

Atkinson alone. I have had him in sight since we heard Quinton's voice."

"I will stop here and watch him," said Flambeau hurriedly. "You go in and see."

The doctor and the priest flew to the study door, unlocked it, and fell into the room. In doing so they nearly fell over the large mahogany table in the centre at which the poet usually wrote; for the place was lit only by a small fire kept for the invalid. In the middle of this table lay a single sheet of paper, evidently left there on purpose. The doctor snatched it up, glanced at it, handed it to Father Brown, and crying, "Good God, look at that!" plunged towards the glass room beyond, where the terrible tropic flowers still seemed to keep a crimson memory of the sunset.

Father Brown read the words three times before he put down the paper. The words were: "I die by my own hand; yet I die murdered!" They were in the quite inimitable, not to say illegible, handwriting of Leonard Quinton.

Then Father Brown, still keeping the paper in his hand, strode towards the conservatory, only to meet his medical friend coming back with a face of assurance and collapse. "He's done it," said Harris.

They went together through the gorgeous unnatural beauty of cactus and azalea and found Leonard Quinton, poet and romancer, with his head hanging downward off his ottoman and his red curls sweeping the ground. Inside his left side was thrust the queer dagger that they had picked up in the garden, and his limp hand still rested on the hilt.

Outside, the storm had come at one stride, like the night in Coleridge, and garden and glass roof were darkening with driving rain. Father Brown seemed to be studying the paper more than the corpse; he held it close to his eyes; and seemed trying to read it in the twilight. Then he held it up against the faint light, and, as he did so, lightning stared at them for an instant so white that the paper looked black against it.

Darkness full of thunder followed, and after the thunder Father Brown's voice said out of the dark: "Doctor, this paper is the wrong shape."

"What do you mean?" asked Doctor Harris, with a frowning stare.

"It isn't square," answered Brown. "It has a sort of edge snipped off at the corner. What does it mean?"

"How the deuce should I know?" growled the doctor. "Shall we move this poor chap, do you think? He's quite dead."

"No," answered the priest; "we must leave him as he lies and send for the police." But he was still scrutinizing the paper.

As they went back through the study he stopped by the table and picked up a small pair of nail scissors. "Ah," he said with a sort of relief; "this is what he did it with. But yet—" And he knitted his brows.

"Oh, stop fooling with that scrap of paper," said the doctor emphatically. "It was a fad of his. He had hundreds of them. He cut all his paper like that," as he pointed to a stack of sermon paper still unused on another and smaller table. Father Brown went up to it and held up a sheet. It was the same irregular shape.

"Quite so," he said. "And here I see the corners that were snipped off." And to the indignation of his colleague he began to count them.

"That's all right," he said, with an apologetic smile. "Twenty-three sheets cut and twenty-two corners cut off them. And as I see you are impatient we will rejoin the others."

"Who is to tell his wife?" asked Dr. Harris. "Will you go and tell her now, while I send a servant for the police?"

"As you will," said Father Brown indifferently. And he went out to the hall door.

Here also he found a drama, though of a more grotesque sort. It showed nothing less than his big friend Flambeau in an attitude to which he had long been unaccustomed, while upon the pathway at the bottom of the steps was sprawling with his boots in the air the amiable Atkinson, his billycock hat and walking-cane sent flying in opposite directions along the path. Atkinson had at length wearied of Flambeau's almost paternal custody, and had endeavoured to knock him down, which was by no means a smooth game to play with the Roi des Apaches, even after that monarch's abdication.

Flambeau was about to leap upon his enemy and secure him once more, when the priest patted him easily on the shoulder.

"Make it up with Mr. Atkinson, my friend," he said. "Beg a mutual pardon and say 'Good night.' We need not detain him any longer." Then, as Atkinson rose somewhat doubtfully and gathered his hat and stick and went towards the garden gate, Father Brown said in a more serious voice: "Where is that Indian?"

They all three (for the doctor had joined them) turned involuntarily towards the dim grassy bank amid the tossing trees, purple with twilight, where they had last seen the brown man swaying in his strange prayers. The Indian was gone.

"Confound him," said the doctor, stamping furiously. "Now I know that it was that nigger that did it."

"I thought you didn't believe in magic," said Father Brown quietly.

"No more I did," said the doctor, rolling his eyes. "I only know that I loathed that yellow devil when I thought he was a sham wizard. And I shall loathe him more if I come to think he was a real one."

"Well, his having escaped is nothing," said Flambeau. "For we could have proved nothing and done nothing against him. One hardly goes to the parish constable with a story of suicide imposed by witchcraft or auto-suggestion."

Meanwhile Father Brown had made his way into the house, and now went to break the news to the wife of the dead man.

When he came out again he looked a little pale and tragic; but what passed between them in that interview was never known, even when all was known.

Flambeau, who was talking quietly with the doctor, was surprised to see his friend reappear so soon at his elbow; but Brown took no notice, and merely drew the doctor apart. "You have sent for the police, haven't you?" he asked.

"Yes," answered Harris. "They ought to be here in ten minutes."

"Will you do me a favour?" said the priest quietly. "The truth is, I make a collection of these curious stories, which often contain, as in the case of our Hindoo friend, elements which can hardly be put into a police report. Now, I want you to write out a report of this case for my private use. Yours is a clever trade," he said, looking at the doctor gravely and steadily in the face. "I sometimes think that you know some details of this matter which you have not thought fit to mention. Mine is a confidential trade like yours, and I will treat anything you write for me in strict confidence. But write the whole."

The doctor, who had been listening thoughtfully with his head a little on one side, looked the priest in the face for an instant, and said: "All right," and went into the study, closing the door behind him.

"Flambeau," said Father Brown, "there is a long seat there under the veranda, where we can smoke, out of the rain. You are my only friend in the world, and I want to talk to you. Or, perhaps, be silent with you."

They established themselves comfortably in the veranda seat; Father Brown, against his common habit, accepted a good cigar and smoked it steadily in silence, while the rain shrieked and rattled on the roof of the veranda.

"My friend," he said at length, "this is a very queer case. A very queer case."

"I should think it was," said Flambeau, with something like a shudder.

"You call it queer, and I call it queer," said the other, "and yet we mean quite opposite things. The modern mind always mixes up two different ideas: mystery in the sense of what is marvellous, and mystery in the sense of what is complicated. That is half its difficulty about miracles. A miracle is startling; but it is simple. It is simple because it *is* a miracle. It is power coming directly from God (or the devil) instead of indirectly through nature or human wills. Now you mean that this business is marvellous because it is miraculous, because it is witchcraft worked by a wicked Indian. Understand, I do not say that it was not spiritual or diabolic. Heaven and hell only know by what surrounding influences strange sins come into the lives of men. But for the present my point is this: If it was pure magic, as you think, then it is marvellous; but it is not mysterious—that is, it is not complicated. The quality of a miracle is mysterious, but its manner is simple. Now, the manner of this business has been the reverse of simple."

The storm that had slackened for a little seemed to be swelling again, and there came heavy movements as of faint thunder. Father Brown let fall the ash of his cigar and went on:

"There has been in this incident," he said, "a twisted, ugly, complex quality that does not belong to the straight bolts either of heaven or hell. As one knows the crooked track of a snail, I know the crooked track of a man."

The white lightning opened its enormous eye in one wink, the sky shut up again, and the priest went on:

"Of all these crooked things, the crookedest was the shape of that piece of paper. It was crookeder than the dagger that killed him."

"You mean the paper on which Quinton confessed his suicide," said Flambeau.

"I mean the paper on which Quinton wrote, 'I die by my own hand,'" answered Father Brown. "The shape of that paper, my friend, was the wrong shape; the wrong shape, if ever I have seen it in this wicked world."

"It only had a corner snipped off," said Flambeau, "and I understand that all Quinton's paper was cut that way."

"It was a very odd way," said the other, "and a very bad way, to my taste and fancy. Look here, Flambeau, this Quinton—God receive his soul!—was perhaps a bit of a cur in some ways, but he really was an artist, with the pencil as well as the pen. His handwriting, though hard to read, was bold and beautiful. I can't prove what I say; I can't prove anything. But I tell you with the full force of conviction that he could never have cut that mean little piece off a sheet of paper. If he had wanted to cut down paper for some purpose of fitting in, or binding up, or what not, he would have made quite a different slash with the scissors. Do you remember the shape? It was a mean shape. It was a wrong shape. Like this. Don't you remember?"

And he waved his burning cigar before him in the darkness, making irregular squares so rapidly that Flambeau really seemed to see them as fiery hieroglyphics upon the darkness—hieroglyphics such as his friend had spoken of, which are undecipherable, yet can have no good meaning.

"But," said Flambeau, as the priest put his cigar in his mouth again and leaned back, staring at the roof. "Suppose somebody else did use the scissors. Why should somebody else, cutting pieces off his sermon paper, make Quinton commit suicide?"

Father Brown was still leaning back and staring at the room, but he took his cigar out of his mouth and said: "Quinton never did commit suicide."

Flambeau stared at him. "Why, confound it all," he cried; "then why did he confess to suicide?"

The priest leaned forward again, settled his elbows on his knees, looked at the ground, and said in a low distinct voice: "He never did confess to suicide."

Flambeau laid his cigar down. "You mean," he said, "that the writing was forged?"

"No," said Father Brown; "Quinton wrote it all right."

"Well, there you are," said the aggravated Flambeau; "Quinton wrote: 'I die by my own hand,' with his own hand on a plain piece of paper."

"Of the wrong shape," said the priest calmly.

"Oh, the shape be damned!" cried Flambeau. "What has the shape to do with it?"

"There were twenty-three snipped papers," resumed Brown unmoved, "and only twenty-two pieces snipped off. Therefore one of the pieces had been destroyed, probably that from the written paper. Does that suggest anything to you?"

A light dawned on Flambeau's face, and he said: "There was something else written by Quinton, some other words. 'They will tell you I die by my own hand,' or 'Do not believe that—'"

"Hotter, as the children say," said his friend. "But the piece was hardly half an inch across; there was no room for one word, let alone five. Can you think of anything hardly bigger than a comma which the man with hell in his heart had to tear away as a testimony against him?"

"I can think of nothing," said Flambeau at last.

"What about quotation marks?" said the priest, and flung his cigar far into the darkness like a shooting star.

All words had left the other man's mouth, and Father Brown said, like one going back to fundamentals:

"Leonard Quinton was a romancer, and was writing an Oriental romance about wizardry and hypnotism. He—"

At this moment the door opened briskly behind them and the doctor came out with his hat on. He put a long envelope into the priest's hands.

"That's the document you wanted," he said, "and I must be getting home. Good night."

"Good night," said Father Brown, as the doctor walked briskly to the gate. He had left the front door open, so that a shaft of gaslight fell upon them. In the light of this Brown opened the envelope and read the following words:

"DEAR FATHER BROWN—*Vicisti, Galilæe!* Otherwise, damn your eyes, which are very penetrating ones. Can it be possible that there is something in all that stuff of yours after all?

"I am a man who has ever since boyhood believed in Nature and in all natural functions and instincts, whether men called them moral or immoral. Long before I became a doctor, when I was a schoolboy keeping mice and spiders, I believed that to be a good animal is the best thing in the world. But just now I am shaken; I have believed in Nature; but it seems as if Nature could betray a man. Can there be anything in your bosh? I am really getting morbid.

"I loved Quinton's wife. What was there wrong in that? Nature told me to, and it's love that makes the world go round. I also thought, quite sincerely, that she would be happier with a clean animal like me than with that tormenting little lunatic. What was there wrong in that? I was only facing facts, like a man of science. She would have been happier.

"According to my own creed I was quite free to kill Quinton, which was the best thing for everybody, even himself.

But as a healthy animal I had no notion of killing myself. I resolved, therefore, that I would never do it until I saw a chance that would leave me scot free. I saw that chance this morning.

"I have been three times, all told, into Quinton's study to-day. The first time I went in he would talk about nothing but the weird tale, called 'The Curse of a Saint,' which he was writing, which was all about how some Indian hermit made an English colonel kill himself by thinking about him. He showed me the last sheets, and even read me the last paragraph, which was something like this: 'The conqueror of the Punjab, a mere yellow skeleton, but still gigantic, managed to lift himself on his elbow and gasp in his nephew's ear: "I die by my own hand, yet I die murdered!"' It so happened, by one chance out of a hundred, that those last words were written at the top of a new sheet of paper. I left the room, and went out into the garden intoxicated with a frightful opportunity.

"We walked round the house, and two more things happened in my favour. You suspected an Indian, and you found a dagger which the Indian might most probably use. Taking the opportunity to stuff it in my pocket I went back to Quinton's study, locked the door, and gave him his sleeping draught. He was against answering Atkinson at all, but I urged him to call out and quiet the fellow, because I wanted a clear proof that Quinton was alive when I left the room for the second time. Quinton lay down in the conservatory, and I came through the study. I am a quick man with my hands, and in a minute and a half I had done what I wanted to do. I had emptied all the first part of Quinton's romance into the fireplace, where it burnt to ashes. Then I saw that the quotation marks wouldn't do, so I snipped them off, and to make it seem likelier, snipped the whole quire to match. Then I came out with the knowledge that Quinton's confession of suicide lay on the front table, while Quinton lay alive, but asleep, in the conservatory beyond.

"The last act was a desperate one; you can guess it: I pretended to have seen Quinton dead and rushed to his room. I delayed you with the paper; and, being a quick man with my hands, killed Quinton while you were looking at his confession of suicide. He was half-asleep, being drugged, and I put his own hand on the knife and drove it into his body. The knife was of so queer a shape that no one but an operator could have calculated the angle that would reach his heart. I wonder if you noticed this.

"When I had done it the extraordinary thing happened. Nature deserted me. I felt ill. I felt just as if I had done something wrong. I think my brain is breaking up; I feel some sort of desperate pleasure in thinking I have told the thing to somebody; that I shall not have to be alone with it if I marry and have children. What is the matter with me? . . . Madness . . . or can one have remorse, just as if one were in Byron's poems! I cannot write any more.

—JAMES ERSKINE HARRIS."

Father Brown carefully folded up the letter and put it in his breast pocket just as there came a loud peal at the gate bell, and the wet waterproofs of several policeman gleamed in the road outside.

✝

Brother Orchid

Richard Connell

"Be smart," the warden said. "Go straight."

A grin creased the leather face of Little John Sarto.

"I *am* goin' straight," he said. "Straight to Chi."

"I wouldn't if I were you, Sarto."

"Why not? I owned that burg once. I'll own it again."

"Things have changed in ten years."

"But not me," said Little John. "I still got what it takes to be on top."

"You didn't stay there," the warden observed.

"I got framed," Sarto said. "Imagine shovin' me on the rock on a sissy income tax rap!"

"It was the only charge they could make stick," the warden said. "You were always pretty slick, Sarto."

"I was, and I am," said Little John.

The warden frowned. "Now look here, Sarto. When a man has done his time and I'm turning him loose, I'm supposed to give him some friendly advice. I do it, though I know that in most cases it's a farce. You'd think men who'd done a stretch here in Alcatraz ought to have a sneaking notion that crime does not pay, but while I'm preaching my little sermon I see a faraway look in their eyes and I know they're figuring out their next bank job or snatch."

"Don't class me with them small-time heisters and petty-larceny yeggs," said Little John. "I'm a born big shot."

"You're apt to die the same way," said the warden dryly.

"That's okay, net, by me," said Little John. "When I peg out I want to go with fireworks, flowers and bands; but you'll have a beard to your knees before they get out the last extra on Little John Sarto. I got a lot of livin' to do first: I got to wash out the taste of slum with a lakeful of champagne, and it'll take half the blondes in the Loop to make me forget them nights in solitary. But most of all I got to be myself again, not just a number. For every order I've took here on the rock, I'm goin' to give two. I'm goin' to see guys shiver and jump when I speak. I've played mouse long enough. Watch me be a lion again."

The warden sighed. "Sarto," he said, "why don't you play it safe? Stay away from Chicago. Settle in some new part of the country. Go into business. You've got brains and a real gift for organization. You ran a big business once—"

"Million a month, net," put in Sarto.

"And you're only forty-six and full of health," the warden went on. "You can still make a fresh start."

"Using what for wampum?" asked Little John.

"You've got plenty salted away."

Sarto laughed a wry laugh.

"I got the ten bucks, and the ticket back to Chi, and this frowsy suit the prison gimme, and that's all I got," he said.

"Don't tell me you're broke!"

"Flat as a mat," said Little John. "I spent it like I made it—fast. A king's got to live like a king, ain't he? When I give a dame flowers, it was always orchids. My free-chow bill ran to a grand a week. They called me a public enemy but they treated me like a year-round Sandy Claws. . . . But I ain't worryin'. I was born broke. I got over it."

✝ ✝ ✝

A prison guard came in to say that the launch was ready to take Sarto to the mainland.

"Well, goodbye, Warden," said Sarto jauntily. "If you ever get to Chi gimme a buzz. I'll throw a party for you."

"Wait a minute," said the warden. "I can't let you go till I make one last attempt to start you on the right track. I know a man who'll give you a job. He runs a big truck farm and—"

He stopped, for Sarto was shaking with hoarse laughter.

"Me a rube?" Little John got out. "Me a bodyguard to squashes? Warden, the stir-bugs has got you."

"It's a chance to make an honest living."

"Save it for some cluck that would feel right at home livin' with turnips," Sarto said. "I got other plans."

The siren on the launch gave an impatient belch.

"So long, Warden," said Little John. "I won't be seein' you."

"You're right there," the warden said.

Sarto's face darkened at the words.

"Meanin' Chi might be bad for my health?"

"I've heard rumors to that effect," replied the warden.

"I've heard 'em for years," said Little John. "They're a lotta rat spit. Plenty guys has talked about what they was goin' to do to me. I always sent flowers to their funerals—you heard about that."

He chuckled.

"A big heart of forget-me-nots with 'Sorry, Pal' in white orchids on it."

"All right, wise guy," the warden said. "Go to Chicago. The sooner you get rubbed out, the better for everybody. You're no good and you never will be."

"Atta clown," said Little John Sarto. "Always leave 'em laughin' when you say goodbye."

Laughing, he started out toward the big gray gate.

† † †

Deep in the woods in an out-of-the-world corner of Michigan, squat, unkempt Twin Pine Inn hides itself. It was silent that summer night, and dark save for a single window in the taproom. Behind the customerless bar, Fat Dutchy was drinking his fourth rock-and-rye.

"Stick 'em up. This is a heist."

The voice, low and with a snarl in it, came from the doorway behind him. Up went Fat Dutchy's hands.

"Easy with the rod," he whimpered. "There ain't a sawbuck in the joint."

"Not like the good old days," the voice said.

Dutchy turned his head. Little John Sarto was standing there with nothing more lethal in his hand than a big cigar. Dutchy blinked and goggled.

"Well, greaseball, do I look funny?" Sarto demanded.

"No—no—boss, you ain't changed a bit."

"I don't change," Sarto said. "Gimme a slug of bourbon."

Fat Dutchy sloshed four fingers of whisky into a glass. His hand trembled. Liquor splashed on the bar.

"What you got the jits about?" asked Sarto.

"You gimme a turn comin' in like you was a ghost or sumpin'," said Fat Dutchy. He wiped sweat from his mottled jowls with the bar rag. Sarto gulped his drink.

"Business bad, eh?"

"It ain't even bad, boss. It just ain't."

"Cheer up, big puss. You'll soon be scoffin' filly miggnons smothered with century notes," Sarto said. "I'm back."

✝   ✝   ✝

Fat Dutchy rubbed his paunch and looked unhappily at the floor. "Things is different," he said.

Sarto banged his glass down on the bar.

"If one more lug tells me that, I'll kick his gizzard out," he said. "Now, listen. I'm holin' up here till I get my bearin's. Soon as I get things set, I'm goin' to town. But first I gotta contact some of the boys."

Fat Dutchy played nervously with the bar rag.

"Gimme another slug," Sarto ordered. "I got a ten-year thirst."

Fat Dutchy poured out the drink. Again his shaking hands made him spill some of it.

"Here's to me," said Sarto, and drank. "Now, listen: I want you to pass the office along to certain parties that I'm here and want to see 'em, pronto. For a starter, get in touch with Philly Powell, Ike Gelbert, Ouch O'Day, Willie the Knife, Benny Maletta, French Frank, Hop Latzo, Al Muller and that fresh kid that was so handy with a tommy gun—"

"Jack Buck?"

"Yeah. I may need a torpedo. When I fell out, he had the makin's of a good dropper. So get that phone workin', lard head—you know where they hang out."

"Sure," said Fat Dutchy. He held up his hand and ticked off names on his thick fingers.

"Ike Gelbert and Al Muller is in the jug doin' life jolts," he said. "Philly Powell and French Frank was crossed out right at this bar. Ouch O'Day threw an ing-bing and was took to the fit house; the G-boys filled Benny Maletta with slugs and sent Willie the Knife to the hot squat; I dunno just where Hop Latzo is but I've heard talk he's at the bottom of Lake Mich in a barrel of concrete. So outa that lot there's only Jack Buck left and I don't guess you wanna see him—"

"Why not?"

"He's growed up," said Fat Dutchy. "He's the loud noise now. What rackets there is, Jack Buck's got 'em in his pocket."

"I'll whittle him down to his right size," said Sarto.

"Jack's in strong. He's waitin' for you, boss, and he ain't foolin'. The boys tell me it's worth three G's to the guy that settles you."

Sarto snorted. "Only three grand!" he said indignantly.

"That's serious sugar nowadays," said Fat Dutchy. "I'm tellin' you times is sour. Jack Buck has cornered the few grafts that still pay. He's got a mob of muzzlers that was in reform school when you was head man. You ain't nothin' fo'em but a name and a chance to earn three thousand fish."

Sarto sipped his drink. Lines of thought furrowed his face.

"I'll stay here till I figure out an angle," he announced.

"Boss," said Fat Dutchy, "I don't wanna speak outa turn, but wouldn't it be a smart play to take it on the lam for a while?"

"Where to?"

Fat Dutchy shrugged his stout shoulders.

"I wouldn't know, boss," he said. "When the heat's on—"

"Yeah, I know," cut in Sarto. "You're smoked wherever you go."

"What are you goin' to do, boss?"

"I'm goin' to hit the sheets and dream I'm out," said Little John.

Dog-tired though he was, he could not get to sleep. His mind yanked him away from dreams, back to prison, to the death-house, where men were lying in the dark, as he was, trying to sleep.

"They got the bulge on me, at that," he thought. "They *know* when they're goin' to get it."

He felt like a man reading his own obituary, complete but for two facts: where and when.

He knew he was safe where he was, but not for long. They'd comb all the known hideouts. He tried to think of some friend he could trust to hide him. Name after name he considered and rejected. He had come to the ninety-sixth name and found no one he could count on when he fell asleep.

† † †

A light in his eyes and a voice in his ear jerked him awake.

A man was bending over him, smiling and saying:

"Wake up, dear. You'll be late for school."

He was a huge, soft-looking young man with a jovial freckled face. His suit was bottle-green and expensive. Sarto had never seen him before.

"Up, up, pet," he said, and waved at Sarto a big blue-black automatic.

A second man watched from the other side of the bed. He was younger and smaller than the first man, and his flour-white face was perfectly blank. Sarto did not know him either.

Sarto sat up in bed.

"Listen, fellas," he said, "if I get a break you get five grand."

"Got it on you, darling?" asked the freckled man.

"Nope. But I can dig it up inside a week."

"Sorry. We do a strictly cash business," the freckled man said.

"I'll make it ten grand," said Little John. He addressed the pallid man. "Wadda you say, bud? Ten G's."

The freckled man chuckled.

"He'd say 'no' if he could say anything," he said. "He doesn't hear, either. His eyes are good, though. His name is Harold, but we call him Dummy."

Sarto held his naked, flabby body very stiff and straight.

"Do your stuff," he said.

Dummy took his hand from his pocket. There was a pistol in it. The freckled man brushed the gun aside.

"We don't want to give this charming place a bad name," he explained to Sarto. "For Dutchy's sake."

"So that fat rat tipped you," said Sarto.

"Yes," said the freckled man. "For a modest fee. Come along, baby."

† † †

They were speeding through open farm country. The speedometer hit seventy-five. Sarto closed his mouth and his eyes.

"Praying?" asked the freckled man.

"Naw!"

"Better start, toots."

"I know nuttin' can help me."

"That's right," said the freckled man cheerfully. "Nothing but a miracle. But you might pray for your soul."

"Aw, go to hell."

They turned into a rutty, weed-grown road. As they bumped along through a tunnel of trees, suddenly, silently Little John Sarto began to pray.

"Listen! This is Little John Sarto of Chicago, Illinois, U.S.A. I know I got no right to ask any favors. I guess I got a bad rep up there. Well, I ain't goin' to try to lie away my record. Everything on the blotter is true. I don't claim I rate a break. All I say is I need one bad and I'll pay for it. I don't know how; but look me up in the big book. It ought to say that when I make a deal I never run out on it. If I'm talkin' out of turn, forget it. But I won't forget if—"

"Last stop. All out," sang out the freckled man. He halted the car by a thicket of thigh-high brush.

Sarto got out of the car. Dummy got out, too. He kept his gun against Little John's backbone.

"Goodbye, now," said the freckled man, and lit a cigarette.

Dummy marched Sarto off the road and into the thicket. Abruptly, like a spotlight, the moon came out. Dummy spun Sarto around. Sarto could see his face. It held neither hate nor pity. Dummy raised his pistol. As he brought it up on a level with Sarto's forehead, the breeze whipped a straggling branch of a wild rosebush across the back of his hand, and the thorns cut a wet, red line. For part of a second Dummy dropped his eyes to his bleeding hand. Sarto wheeled and dove into the underbrush. Dummy fired three quick shots. One missed. One raked across Sarto's skull. One seared his shoulder. He staggered, but kept plunging on. Dummy darted after him. Then the moon went out.

As Sarto floundered on he could hear Dummy crashing through the brush behind him. But Dummy could not hear his quarry. Dizzy and weak, the wounded man fought his frantic way through tar-black brush. Thorns stabbed him, briers clawed. A low branch smashed him on the nose, and he reeled and nearly went down. Bending double, he churned on. Then his head hit something hard, and he dropped, stunned for a moment. He reached out an unsteady hand and felt an ivy-covered wall. No sound of pursuit came to his ears.

Painfully he dragged himself up to the top of the wall. Not a sob of breath was left in him. He straddled the wall and clung to it. Then he fainted.

✝   ✝   ✝

In the monastery of the Floratines, today was like yesterday and yesterday was like a day in the ninth century when the order was founded. Neither time nor war nor the hate of kings had changed their humble habits or their simple creed. Over the door this creed was carved: "Be poor in purse, pure in heart, kind in word and deed and beautify the lives of men with flowers."

These were the words of the Blessed Edric, their founder, and, ever since his day, Floratines in every land had lived by them, harming no one, helping man, raising flowers.

When King Henry VIII set his face against other monks, he let no hostile hand be laid on the few Floratines.

"They do much good," the monarch said, "and, in sooth, they have nothing worth the taking, these Little Brothers of the Flowers."

They kept the name, and it gave rise to a custom. When a man left the world behind to enter their ranks, he left his name, too, and took the name of a flower.

In the first light of a new day they sat in their refectory, forty-four men in snuff-hued robes, most of them growing old. Their tonsured polls were brown from the sun, their faces serene from inner peace.

"Brother Geranium is late with the milk," observed Brother Tulip, eyeing his dry porridge.

"Perhaps the cow kicked him," suggested Brother Hollyhock.

"She wouldn't. She's fond of him," said Brother Nasturtium. "I'll go down to the dairy and see if anything has happened to him," volunteered Brother Nasturtium. But as he rose from his bench, Brother Geranium, popeyed and panting, burst into the room.

"There's a naked man lying in the petunia bed," he gasped out. "I think he's dead."

✝   ✝   ✝

Little John Sarto thought he was dead, too, when he opened his eyes in the infirmary and saw Abbot Jonquil and Brother Nasturtium at his bedside.

"I made it," he exclaimed huskily. "I beat the rap."

"Take it easy, son," said the abbot. "You've been badly hurt."

"But I ain't in hell," said Little John. Then he added, "Or if I am what are you guys doing here?"

"You're alive and in a safe place."

Sarto stared at him.

"Say, do you know who I am?" he asked.

"No."

"You musta seen my mug in the papers."

"We don't see newspapers here," the abbot said. "And we don't ask who a man is if he needs help."

Sarto touched his bandaged head.

"How long am I in for?" he inquired.

"Until you are well and strong again."

"I got no money."

"Neither have we," said the abbot. "So that makes you one of us, doesn't it?"

"That's one for the book, mister," said Little John.

"I'm Abbot Jonquil. This is Brother Nasturtium, your nurse. If you wish us to notify your friends—"

"I got no friends," grunted Little John.

"You have now," said the abbot.

"I tell you I'm broke."

"You poor fellow," said the abbot gently "What a life you must have led!"

"I been round long enough to know you never get sumpin' for nuttin'."

"I think you have talked enough for the present," the abbot said. "Try to rest and try not to worry—about anything. You may stay here as long as you wish, as our guest."

He went to the door.

"I'll look in again this evening," the abbot said. "Meantime, if you need anything, tell Brother Nasturtium."

His sandals shuffled softly away down the stone corridor.

Sarto squinted at the bulky monk.

"Get me a slug of bourbon, Nasty," he said.

"If you don't mind, I'd rather be called Brother Nasturtium," said the other mildly.

"Whatever you say, only gimme a snort."

Brother Nasturtium brought him a glass of water.

"Try it," he said. "'Twill give you strength."

"Water?" said Sarto disdainfully.

"Look at lions and tigers," said Brother Nasturtium.

As he drank the water, Little John studied the man. He noted the dented nose, gnarled ears, lumpy knuckles and the jaw like an anvil.

"You was a fighter, wasn't you?" said Sarto.

"We don't ask questions like that," said Brother Nasturtium. "What we were, rich or poor, big or small, good or bad, does not matter here."

"That's double jake by me, " said Little John. "I think I'm going to like it here."

"I hope so."

"Say, tell me sumpin', big boy. What's your graft?"

Brother Nasturtium's eyes twinkled.

"'Tis twenty years and more since I've heard such talk," he said. "We raise flowers and sell them in the city."

"There's a good gelt in that," said Sarto. "You boys must be cuttin' up a nice profit."

"What we clear, and it isn't much, goes to the poor."

"That's a nutsy way to run a business," observed Little John.

✝   ✝   ✝

He closed his eyes. Presently he said:

"How does a guy join up with this outfit?"

"It's fairly easy," Brother Nasturtium told him, "if a man wants to be a lay brother—"

"A which?"

"Lay brother. I'm one. They don't take holy orders. They have few religious duties, chiefly saying their prayers. They are not permitted to go outside the walls, and they must obey their superiors. The discipline is rather severe. Some men say it's like being in prison—"

"They do, do they?" said Little John.

"Except that there are no bars."

"That might make a slight difference," conceded Little John. "What are the other catches?"

"Before a man can take his first vow as a lay brother, he must be on probation for a year. That means—"

"I know about probation," said Little John. "Where do I sign?"

"You'll have to talk to the abbot."

"Shoo him in."

"Lay brothers do not shoo abbots."

"Then tell him I wanta proposition him."

"If you're in earnest about this," Brother Nasturtium said, "you might be choosing the name we are to call you."

"Just call me 'Lucky.'"

"It must be the name of a flower."

Little John thought a moment.

"I've picked my new tag," he announced.

"What is it?"

"Brother Orchid."

✝ ✝ ✝

At dusk Brother Nasturtium left the sickroom to get his patient's supper.

When he had gone, Little John began to laugh. It hurt him to laugh, but he couldn't help it.

"Boy, oh, boy!" he said. "What a hideout!"

✝ ✝ ✝

As he weeded the rose garden Brother Orchid sang softly:

> *Johnny saw Frankie a-coming,*
> *Out the back door he did scoot.*
> *Frankie took aim with her pistol,*
> *And the gun went rooty-toot-toot.*
> *He was her man—*

He turned the tune deftly into "Abide with Me" as he saw Brother Nasturtium come out of the greenhouse and head toward him.

Three nights before he had taken the vows that made him a full-fledged lay brother. As he flicked a ladybug from a leaf, he reflected that it hadn't been such a tough year. The routine didn't bother him; he was used to one far more rigid; but he was not used to men like Abbot Jonquil, Brother Nasturtium and the rest. At first he felt sure that some sly, dark purpose lay behind their kindness to him. He watched, warily, for the trap. No trap was sprung. Always they were thoughtful, patient, pleasant with him and with one another.

"Maybe I've got into a high-class whacky house," he thought.

Whatever it was, he decided, it was perfect for his plans. There he could bide his time, snug and safe, ready to strike. He was old enough to know the wonders time can work. And he was wise enough to know that while Jack Buck reigned as czar he must remain in exile. If he ventured back to his old kingdom now, he might just as well go straight to the morgue and book a slab. But czars slip, and czars fall, sometimes suddenly in this violent world. He'd wait and be ready.

"Well, Brother Orchid, your roses are doing well," said Brother Nasturtium as he came up.

"Lay you three to one they bring more than your lilies," said Brother Orchid.

"It's a hundred to one they won't bring anything," said Brother Nasturtium, somberly. Brother Orchid looked up and saw that the face, usually so benign, was grave.

"What's the gag?" he asked.

"Our market is gone."

"How come?"

"They won't handle our flowers."

"Who won't?"

"The wholesalers. We don't belong to the association."

"Why don't we join it?"

"They won't let us. Not a flower can be sold in the city that isn't grown in their own nurseries."

"I get it," said Brother Orchid. "The old chisel. Who's the wheels in this shakedown?"

"A man named Buck is behind it, I believe. So Abbot Jonquil learned when he was in town. He tried to see this Mr. Buck to plead with him not to take away our only means of livelihood. One of Buck's ruffians kicked him downstairs."

"I suppose the abbot was sucker enough to go to the coppers," said Brother Orchid.

"He did go to the police."

"What did *they* do—slug him?"

"No. They were polite enough. But they said that so far as they knew the Floral Protective Association was a legitimate business concern."

"The bulls still know the answers," said Brother Orchid. "And the D.A. said he'd like to do sumpin', but his hands is tied, because you gotta have evidence, and all the witnesses is scared to talk."

"You seem to know all about it."

"I seen movies," said Brother Orchid.

He weeded away, deep in thought.

"Have we got any jack in the old sack?" he asked suddenly.

"About four hundred dollars, the abbot told me."

"Peanuts," said Brother Orchid. "But enough for a couple of secondhand choppers. You and me could handle 'em. We'd need roscoes for the rest of the boys. But I know an armory that's a soft touch. You and me and Geranium and Lilac could charge out tonight, hustle a hot short, and knock it off. Once we was heeled we could move in on Buck and his gorillas and—"

"Man alive, what sort of talk is that?" demanded the scandalized Brother Nasturtium.

"Forget it, pal," said Brother Orchid. "I guess this sun has made me slap-happy. What are we goin' to do?"

"Be patient and pray."

"And eat what?"

"Heaven knows."

"Yeah, and they claim it helps guys that help themselves."

"Maybe Mr. Buck will see the light."

Brother Orchid plucked up a clump of sour grass.

"Maybe this weed'll turn into an American Beauty," he said. He wrung the weed's neck and hurled it into his basket.

"That's the only way to treat weed," he said.

"But is it?" said Brother Nasturtium. "Wasn't everything put into the world for some good use, if man had the sense to find out what that use is?"

"That's a lot of words," said Brother Orchid. "Weeds is weeds."

"No," said Brother Nasturtium, as he turned away, "weeds are flowers out of place."

✝   ✝   ✝

Hungry after their day of work, the Little Brothers of the Flowers waited in the refectory for their abbot to come in and say grace. They tried to make light talk of events in their small world. But there was a shadow over them.

Abbot Jonquil entered, walking slowly. It came to them for the first time that he was a very old man.

"I'm afraid I have more bad news," he said. "Our funds have been taken from my safe. Of course none of us took them—"

He stopped and looked down the long table.

"Where is Brother Orchid?" he asked.

"Maybe he's in his cell, praying," said Brother Nasturtium. "Shall I fetch him?"

"Yes, please."

Brother Nasturtium came back alone. His big ruddy face was twisted with trouble.

"Maybe I was wrong about weeds," he said.

† † †

In his office, Thomas Jefferson Brownlow, special prosecutor of rackets, was talking to the press. The reporters liked him. He was so earnest and so green.

"Same old story, boys," he said. "All I can tell you is that men are selfish animals, and that's not news. I know Buck is back of all these new rackets. So do you. But I can't prove it in a court of law. The men who can simply will not go before the grand jury and tell their stories. They put their skins before their civic duty. I'm not blaming them. But the fact remains I can't force them to testify. They're not afraid of *me*. I wish they were. That's all today, gentlemen."

The reporters filed out. Brownlow bent morosely over the indictment of a jobless man who had stolen a peck of potatoes.

Swerling, his assistant, bustled in. He was excited.

"Chief," he said, "they're back."

"Who?"

"Those florists and laundrymen and fruit peddlers. And they're ready to talk."

"The devil you say!"

"Better grab 'em while they're hot, Chief," urged Swerling.

"But what's got into 'em?"

"You have me there."

"It doesn't matter," said Brownlow, "if they'll talk. Send 'em in and lock all the doors."

Once they started to talk Thomas Jefferson Brownlow had a hard job to stop them. The Grand Jury was back before its seats in the box had cooled off, and shortly thereafter Jack Buck and three of his top aides were passengers on a special train that would not stop till it had

carried them to a station near a big, gray gate. Most of his lesser lieu-
tenants also took trips, accompanied by large, official-looking men,
who returned alone. A few escaped, some by taking to their heels, others by wriggling through loopholes in the law.

Mr. Brownlow was walking toward his office, debating whether he
should run for governor or the Senate, when he bumped into Mr. Chris
Poppadoppalous, emerging from the room where witnesses are paid
their fees. Mr. Poppadoppalous beamed, bowed, and handed Mr.
Brownlow a large box.

"Gardenias," he said. "I brink dem for you."

"Thanks," said Brownlow. "And there's one more thing you can do
for me."

"Anythink," said Mr. Poppadoppalous with another bow.

"One day you boys were afraid to talk. The next day you talked. Why?"

"We were afraid not to," said Mr. Poppadoppalous.

"Afraid of me?" asked Brownlow, rather pleased.

Mr. Poppadoppalous tittered apologetically.

"Oh, no, sir," he said. "You're a nice man. You don't say, 'Talk, you
Greek so-and-so, or I'll tear out your heart and eat it before your eyes.'"

"Did somebody say that to you?"

"Yes, sir. To all us boys."

"Who?"

"The little fellow," said Mr. Poppadoppalous, and bowed, and scurried away.

✝   ✝   ✝

From his hotel window Little John Sarto looked out over the lighted city
spread at his feet. Somebody knocked on his door.

"Come in," said Sarto.

The freckled young man came in. He had on a new suit, mossgreen
this time, and he was still jovial.

"Hello, sweetheart," he said.

"Hello, Eddie," said Sarto.

"You know why I'm here."

"Sure," said Sarto. "Have a drink?"

"Why not?" said Eddie, and poured out a drink from a bottle of
bourbon on the table. Sarto took one, too.

"Nice going, boss," said Eddie, raising his glass. "We'll run this town right."

"We?"

"You will, I mean," said Eddie. "I'll be glad to work under a man with your brains. Poor Jack didn't have many. Nerve, yes. But he never looked ahead. You do. Well, what do you say, boss? Dummy and some of the boys are waiting downstairs for the answer. They're solid for you, boss. Anything you say goes."

Sarto didn't say anything. He went to the window and looked out over the city.

"Of course, things are rather ragged right now," said Eddie. "We'll have to take it slow and easy for a while. But the boys are counting on you to work out some nice, new, juicy angles. The town's yours."

"I don't want it," said Little John.

"What do you mean?" Eddie was not jovial now.

"I got other plans."

"You can't run out on us."

"I'm walking out," said Sarto. "Right now."

"The boys won't like that."

"I'm doing what *I* like."

"That's always expensive," said Eddie.

"I know all about that."

Eddie shrugged his shoulders.

"Okay," he said, and sauntered out of the room.

Hurriedly, Little John Sarto began to strip off his loud, plaid suit.

✝ ✝ ✝

"I'm right," said the warden to the chaplain, laying down the morning paper. "You say all men have some good in them. I say some men are all bad and nothing can change them. Take this fellow, Sarto. Last night in Chicago, as he was getting on a bus, he was filled full of lead."

"That hardly proves your point." The chaplain smiled. "Bullets are very democratic. They'll kill good men as well as bad, you know."

"There was nothing good about Sarto. Just listen to this: 'The police say Sarto plotted to return to power in the underworld. They are at a loss to explain why, at the time of his death, he was disguised as a monk.' Why, the scheming wolf! Whether there's any good whatsoever in such a man, I leave it to you to judge."

"He does sound pretty bad, I grant you," the chaplain said. "But. even so, I hate to condemn him or any man. I might be reversed by a higher Judge."

✝

The Monk's Tale

P. C. Doherty

The Feast of the Assumption 1376
(15th August)

I have begun this journal because my Prior has asked me. I received his letter and, I say this in the spirit of obedience, his remarks about my past cut like barbs. I know I have sinned before God and man but here in the parish of St. Erkonwald in Southwark I daily atone for my sins. I observe most strictly the rule of St. Dominic and spend both day and night in the care of souls. God knows, the harvest here is great; the filthy alleyways, piss-strewn runnels and poor hovels shelter broken people whose minds and souls have been bruised and poisoned by grinding poverty. The great fat ones of the land do not care but hide behind empty words, false promises and a lack of compassion which even Dives would have blushed at.

My house is no more than a white-washed shed with two rooms and a wooden door and casement which do not fit. My horse, an aged destrier, whom I call Philomel, eats as if there is no tomorrow but can go no faster than a shuffling cat. He drains my purse of money. I simply mention these matters to remind myself of my present state and to advise my Prior that his strictures are not necessary. As I have said, my purse is empty, shrivelled up and tight as a usurer's soul. My collection boxes have been stolen, the chancel screen is in disrepair, the altar is marked and stained and the nave of the church is often covered with huge pools of water, for our roof serves as more of a colander than a covering.

God knows I atone for my sins. I seem to be steeped in murder, bloody and awful, it taxes my mind and reminds me of my own great crime. I have served the people here six months now. I have also taken on those duties assigned by my Prior as clerk and scrivener to Sir John Cranston, coroner of the city. Time and again he takes me with him to sit over the body of some man, woman or child pitifully slain. "Is it murder, suicide or an accident?" he asks. And so the dreadful stories begin. Of stupidity, a woman who forgets how dangerous it is for a child to play out on the cobbled streets, dancing between the hooves of iron-shod horses or the creaking wheels of huge carts as they bring their produce up from the river. Still, a child is slain, the little body flung bruised and marked while the young soul goes out to meet its Christ. But there are more dreadful deaths. Men drunk in taverns, their bellies awash with cheap ale; their souls dead and black as the deepest night as they lurch at each other with sword, dagger or club. When the wound is made and the soul fled, Cranston and I arrive. I mean no offence for Sir John, despite his portly frame, plum red face, balding pate and watery eyes is, I think, in heart a good man. An honest official. A rare man indeed, who does not take bribes, searches for the truth, ever patient before declaring the true cause of death and I am always with him. I and my writing trays, my pens and inkpots, transcribing the lies, the deceits, the stories which flourish like weeds about any death.

I always keep a faithful record and every word I hear, every sentence I write, every time I visit the scene of the murder, I am back on that bloody field fighting for Edward, the Black Prince. I, a novice monk who has broken his vows and taken his younger brother off to war. Every night I dream of that battle: the press of steel men, the lowered pikes, the screams and shouts. Each time the nightmare goes like a mist clearing above the river, leaving only me kneeling beside the corpse of my dead brother, screaming into the darkness for his soul to return, I know it never will.

However, I beg Christ's pardon for I wander from the story. I was in my church long before dawn on the eve of the feast of St. John saying my office, quietly kneeling before the chancel screen, the only light being that of a taper lit before the statue of the Madonna. I confess I had not slept that night. Instead, I had climbed to the top of the church tower to observe the stars for I do admit that the movements of the heavens still have the same fascination for me as they did when I studied at Oxford in Friar Bacon's observatory on Folly Bridge. I was tired and slightly fearful for Godric, a well known murderer and assassin, had begged for sanctuary in the church and while I prayed he lay, curled up like a dog, in the corner. He had eaten my supper, pronounced himself well satisfied and settled down to a good night's sleep. How is it, I ask, that such men can sleep so well? Godric had slain a man, struck him down in the market place, taken his purse and fled. He hoped to escape but had the misfortune to encounter a group of city officials and their retainers, who raised the hue and cry and pursued him here. I was attempting to repair the chancel screen and let him in after he hammered on the door. Godric brushed by me, gasping, waving the dagger, still bloody from his crime, and ran up the nave breathlessly shouting,

"Sanctuary! Sanctuary!"

The officials did not come into church though they expected me, as clerk to Sir John Cranston, to have handed him over but I could not.

"This is God's house!" I shouted, "Protected by Holy Mother Church and the King's decree!"

So they left him alone though they placed a guard on the door and swore they would kill him if he attempted to escape. Godric will either have to give himself up or abjure the realm.

Anyway, I digress, my prayers were again disturbed by a commotion outside the church and I thought the city authorities had sent armed retainers to take Godric, for we live in turbulent times. Our present King, Edward III, God bless him, is past his prime and the mighty men of war have their own way in most matters. I took the taper and hurried down the church, splashing through the puddles as there had been a violent thunderstorm, you may remember it, two days previously. Outside, the city guards had been disturbed from their sleep and were locked in fierce argument with Sir John Cranston, who bellowed as soon as he saw me,

"For God's sake, Father, tell these oafs who I am!" He patted the neck of his horse and glared around. "We have work to do, priest, another death murder at Bermondsey, one of the great ones of the land. Come! Ignore these dolts!"

"They did not know who you are, Sir John." I replied, "Because you are muffled in robe and hood worse than any monk."

I then explained to the men that Sir John Cranston was coroner of the

City of London and had business with me. They backed off like beaten
mastiffs, their dark faces glowering with a mixture of anger and fear.

"Leave Godric be!" I warned. "You are not to enter the church!"

They nodded, I locked the church door and went over to my own
house. I stuffed my panniers with parchment, quills and ink, saddled
Philomel and rejoined Sir John. The coroner was in good spirits, thoroughly enjoying his altercation with the city guard for Sir John hates offi-
cialdom, damns them loudly along with goldsmiths, priests and even, he
looked slyly at me and grinned, Dominican monks who study the stars!

"Ever heavenwards," I quipped in reply, "We must look up at the sky
and study the stars."

"Why?" Cranston replied brusquely. "Surely you do not believe in that
nonsense about planets and heavenly bodies governing our lives? Even
the church fathers condemn it."

"In which case," I answered. "They condemn the Star of Bethlehem."

Sir John belched, grabbed the wineskin slung over his saddle horn,
took one deep gulp and, raising his bottom, farted as loudly as he could.
I decided to ignore Sir John's sentiments, verbal or otherwise. He means
well and his wine is always the best that Gascony can grow.

"What business takes us to Bermondsey?" I asked.

"Abbot Hugo," he replied. "Or rather Hugo who was once Abbot.
Now he is as dead as that cat over there." He pointed to a pile of refuse,
a mixture of animal and human excrement, broken pots and, lying on
top, a mangy cat, its white and russet body now swollen with corruption.

"So, an Abbot has died?"

"No, murdered! Apparently Abbot Hugo was not beloved by his
brethren. After Prime this morning he had his customary daily meeting
with the leading officials of the Abbey and, as usual, infringed the rule of
St. Benedict by breaking his fast in his own private chamber, a jug of
Malmesy wine and the best bread the abbey ovens can bake. His door was
locked. Some time later, when he did not attend Divine Service, the
brothers came and found his door still barred. When they forced it open,
Hugo was lying dead at his table. At first they thought it was apoplexy, a
stroke or the falling sickness but the Infirmarian, a Brother Stephen, smelt
the wine cup and said it contained Belladonna. So," Sir John looked sideways at me, "We hunt murder in a monastery. Priests who kill. Tut! Tut!
What is the world coming to?"

"God only knows!" I replied. "When coroners drink and fart, and
make cutting remarks about men who are still men with all their failings,

be they priest or prelate!" Sir John laughed, pushing his horse near mine, slapping me affectionately on the shoulder.

"I like you, Brother Athelstan!" he bellowed. "But God knows," he mimicked my words, "Though God knows why your order sent you to Southwark and your Prior ordered you to be a coroner's clerk."

We have had this conversation before. Sir John probing whilst I defended. Some day I will tell him the full truth though I think he surmises it already.

"Is it reparation?" he queried.

"Curiosity," I replied, "Can be a grave sin, Sir John." But the coroner laughed and deftly turned the conversation to other matters.

We rode along the river bank arriving at Bermondsey shortly before noon. I was glad to be free of the city, the stinking streets, the shoving and pushing in the market place, the houses which rear up and block the sun. The great swaggering lords who ride through on their fierce, iron-shod destriers in a blaze of silks and furs, their heads held high, proud, arrogant and as ruthless as the hawks they carry. The women are no better with their plucked eyebrows and white pasted faces: their soft, sensuous bodies are clothed in lawn and samite, their heads covered by a profusion of lacy veils; while only a coin's throw away a woman, pale and skeletal, sits crooning over her dying baby, begging for a crust to eat. God should send fire on the city or a leader to raise up the poor, but there again I preach sedition and remember my vow to keep silent.

At Bermondsey the great door to the abbey was kept fast. Sir John had to clang the bell as if raising the "Hue and Cry," before the gates squeaked open and we were led into the abbey forecourt by a most anxious-looking lay brother. The abbey was a great facade of stone, carved and sculptured, soaring up into the heavens, man's ladder to God. The place was subdued and quiet. The cloisters were empty, the hollowed stone passageways ghostly, even menacing. I felt I was entering a house of shadows. The lay brother took us to the Prior's office, a large comfortable room, the floor, so polished it could serve as a mirror, was covered here and there by thick woollen rugs. The black granite walls were draped and decorated with cloths of gold. The Prior was waiting for us; like all his kind, a tall, severe man, completely bald, with features as sharp as any knife and grey eyes as hard as flint. He greeted Sir John Cranston with forced warmth but, when I introduced myself and described my office, he smiled chillingly, dismissing me with a flicker of his eyes.

"Most uncommon," he murmured, "For a friar to be free of his order and serving in such a lowly office." Sir John snorted rudely and would have intervened if I had not.

"Prior Wakefield," I replied. "My business is my own. Like you, I am a priest, a man as learned as yourself, who now wonders why murder should be committed in a Benedictine monastery."

"Who said it was murder?"

"The Infirmarian who sent the message," Sir John interrupted. "He told us the Abbot had been poisoned, even naming the substance found in the cup." The Prior shrugged.

"You are correct," he murmured. "Evil news seems to have wings of its own."

"We are here to see the body!" Cranston bluntly reminded him.

The Prior led us out into the cloisters which lay to the south side of the abbey church. Its centre or garth had been carefully cultivated, laid out with raised vegetable beds, herb gardens and the sweet-smelling roses now in full bloom under a hot mid-day sun. As the rule of Benedict laid down, there was silence, except for the scratching of pens from carrels where monks studied or pored over painted manuscripts. The doors of their cells were wide open because of the oppressive heat.

The Prior led us down more passageways and out to the Abbot's personal residence, a large, spacious, two-storied building. The ground floor was the Abbot's own refectory. We passed through it, up some wooden stairs into what the Prior termed the Abbot's private chambers: a large study sumptuously decorated, the walls painted red with golden stars, thick rugs on the floor and a huge oaken desk and table. There were cupboards full of books, the rich, leather coverings exuding their own special perfume so my fingers itched to open them. Behind this lay the Abbot's bedroom and I was struck by its austerity, no glazed or coloured windows here and the walls were just white, freshly painted with lime. The only furniture were a stool, a small table and a huge four-poster bed now stripped of any coverings, it bore the Abbot's corpse, rigid, silent, accusing under its linen sheet.

Cranston did not wait for the Prior but pulled back the linen cloth to expose a skull-like head and skeletal features made even uglier by the rictus of death. Abbot Hugo had been an old man, well past his sixtieth summer. Cranston pulled the sheet down further, revealing how the Abbot had been laid out for burial in the thick, brown smock of his order with coarse sandals strapped round the bare feet. The Abbot's face, like the features of any murdered victim, fascinated me; the slight purplish tinge in his face and sunken cheeks. The monks had attempted to close his eyes in death and, unable to, had placed a coin over each of his eyes, one of these had slipped off and the Abbot glared sightlessly at the ceiling. Cranston indicated I should examine the body more closely, not that he is squeamish, I just think he enjoys making me pore over some corpse, the more revolting the better.

"I must open the robe." I said turning to the Prior. The fellow nodded angrily.

"Get on with it!"

Taking the hem of the Abbot's robe, I lifted it and pushed it right up to his neck to expose a thin, emaciated body, a dirty white, like the underbelly of a rat. There were no contusions or bruises and the same was true of the neck and chest; the only marks were the ink stains on two fingers of his left hand.

"Nothing unusual about that," the Prior remarked, "Abbot Hugo was a great writer." I nodded and looked closer. The ink seemed to be stained permanently but there was no cut on the fingers and, when I raised the cold hand, I detected nothing untoward. I re-arranged the Abbot's robe and, muttering the Requiem, pulled the linen sheet back up to his chin before examining the half-open mouth. The Infirmarian was right, even the most stupid of physicians would have detected poison. I gently prised open the lips, still not yet fully rigid in death, revealing yellow stumps of teeth. The gums, tongue and palate, however, were now stained black and, when I leant down and smelt, I detected the sour sweet tang of a powerful poison.

"How do we know," I asked, "that the Abbot died alone?"

Wakefield shrugged.

"Quite easily. Two lay brothers always stayed at the foot of the stairs leading to his chambers. They would sit there, pray, meditate or be on call when the Abbot rang a small bell on his desk."

"That could be heard at the foot of the stairs?"

"Yes."

"And these two lay brothers maintain no one went up?" The Prior smiled thinly.

"I didn't say that. They did allow the servant through with a tray bearing wine and bread, as well as the Abbot's Secretarius, Brother Christopher."

"Ah, yes, Brother Christopher." I replied. "And how long was he in there?"

"A very short while."

Cranston slumped on the foot of the bed.

"Abbot Hugo, you liked him?" he barked.

The Prior nodded.

"I respected him deeply."

"And your brethren?"

"Abbot Hugo was a hard man but a holy one. He was a zealot who upheld the rule but could be capable of great compassion."

"When was the meal served?" I asked him.

"I asked the servant. He said the cellarer had laid the bread and wine out during the fourth hour after midnight. That was customary. Abbot Hugo's instructions were always to bring it when the hour candle had burnt mid-way between five and six."

The Prior looked down at the floor. He was embarrassed, uneasy.

"There is something else?" I asked.

"What do you mean?"

"Oh, you know full well what I mean." I said curtly.

The Prior coughed nervously.

"You are right," he answered after a while. "The Infirmarian, he has kept the Abbot's wine and bread locked away but he went down to the kitchen to inspect the jug of wine which the Cellarer had used. He found a large stain on the table. It smelt of Belladonna."

"Ah!" Cranston let out a long sigh.

I watched the Prior closely.

"Did anything happen in the days leading up to Abbot Hugo's death?"

The Prior was silent.

"Answer the question!" Cranston snapped.

The Prior rubbed his eyes with the back of his hand and glanced up. He looked grey and exhausted.

"Yes, today is. . . ."

"Wednesday!" Cranston interjected.

"On Sunday evening after Compline, the Abbot met us here in his own quarters. He announced he was going to resign, retire."

"Why?"

"He claimed he was too old to continue as Abbot and wished to go into retreat. Go to another house, revert to being a simple monk and so prepare for his death."

"What was the reaction to this?"

"We were all horror-struck. We had our differences with the Abbot.

That is only natural in an enclosed community but we did revere him."

There was a pause as Cranston and I eyed each other. We both knew what question we would like to ask next.

"If the Abbot had retired," I began slowly. "Who would have been elected as his successor?"

The Prior's face softened as if he was preparing me for what came next.

"I think I would have been." His face flushed as he looked at both of us. "I know what you're thinking, what you're hinting at." He got up. "To slay someone is an abominable act, a mortal sin. To be guilty of the murder of a man like Abbot Hugo would be nothing more than blasphemous sacrilege."

"Tush, Prior Wakefield," Cranston said softly. "We did not say that."

The Prior flung a look of hate at me.

"He did!" he said.

"My Lord Prior," I replied. "I did not. Before God I did not!" I looked at Cranston. "Sir John, we must interview the lay brothers. My Lord Prior, Sir John will use the Abbot's study. First, we would like to question the lay brothers; the servant who brought the bread and wine as well as the two who stood guard at the foot of the stairs."

The Prior nodded and, giving a hasty bow to Sir John Cranston, stalked out of the room. Once he was gone I closed the door, opened one of my panniers and, bringing out a sharp needle which I use to sew parchment together, went over to the corpse and pulled back the shroud. Abbot Hugo's face, still stared, transfixed by death. I pressed the lower jaw down and, using the needle, scraped between the yellow teeth.

"What is it?" Cranston asked.

I went over to the casement window and opened the wooden shutter to look more carefully at what the needle had dug out for me. A soft, greyish, pulpy mass. Cranston came over to stand by me, a look of disgust on his face.

"What do you think it is?" he asked.

I grimaced.

"The remains of a meal the night before or even the bread. God knows!"

Cranston, apparently bored by my mysterious attitude, pulled the shroud back over Abbot Hugo and told me to join him in the Abbot's study where he slumped unceremoniously into the great chair behind the table. He waved me to a small stool which stood alongside, gripping the side of the desk as he studied it carefully. A book of hours in one corner, the clasp broken, allowing us a glimpse of the golds and blues of the illuminated writing. Rolls of parchment, a writing tray similar to the one I used, bearing an ink pot, a long quill pen and a small battered, wooden cross which the Abbot must have used when meditating. Nothing remarkable but Cranston told me to list it. After all, it is quite common after such inquisitions for the coroner to be accused of filching the dead man's goods.

After this, the Prior returned with the lay brothers whom Cranston wished to question. They were all old, rather venerable men, who had been taken into the abbey for good services performed in the King's wars or in some nobleman's household. Cranston questioned them carefully, tolerating their garrulous replies but dismissed them, for what they said corroborated the Prior's story.

During the afternoon Cranston and I pieced together the events leading up to the Abbot's sudden death, only the distant booming of the abbey bell or the soft patter of sandalled feet in the corridor outside interrupted our deliberations. For once in his long, hard-drinking life, Sir John refrained from downing goblet after goblet of rich red wine. Perhaps it was his concentration and sober attitude which made me guess that Sir John had been directed here by some powerful personage at court.

"Look, Athelstan," he said, using his fat, stubby fingers to list events. "Abbot Hugo was a holy but strict man; he rises and sings the morning office with his brethren. He then returns to his room. In the kitchen the cellarer pours a goblet of wine and lays out a dish of freshly baked bread. These are brought up by a lay brother who leaves it outside the room on a bench: the staircase is guarded by two lay brothers: the Abbot's Secretarius brings the bread and wine in and leaves. No one else comes up but later Abbot Hugo cannot be roused. The next thing is that the Abbot's door has been broken down and the Prior, who had been talking to the Sub-Prior, Brother Paul, at the time, comes into the room. The Sub-Prior is with him." Cranston paused and looked at me. "What then?"

I sighed and shrugged.

"According to Prior Wakefield and the lay brothers," I replied, "Wakefield and Brother Paul found the Abbot slouched back in his chair. The Prior removes the body himself and lays it on the ground. A few minutes later the Infirmarian arrives. It is he who smells the wine and detects the poison."

"Had the Abbot eaten or drunk anything?" Cranston queried.

"According to Prior Wakefield," I replied, "He had, a little. They found this when they removed the cup of wine and bread. They have kept it under lock and key as evidence." Cranston shook his head and sighed in exasperation.

"I see," he said despondently, "no solution in this."

"Who wants a solution?" I asked Sir John abruptly. The coroner looked at me slyly.

"News was sent immediately to the court and, within an hour, the order to come here had arrived at my house." He chewed his lip thoughtfully. "But what answer can I give? Was the bread and wine poisoned in the kitchen and, if so, by whom? Or did Brother Christopher or one of the lay servants perpetrate the crime?"

I shook my head, unable to offer Cranston any solution.

The day drew on. Cranston asked for food and this was brought; a jug of ale, some small white loaves and two bowls of rich broth stew, garnished with onions and leeks and heavily seasoned. Cranston, eating noisily, slurped from his bowl, using the special pewter spoon he always carried with him. As he ate he summarised what we knew.

"We have an old Abbot who intends to resign. He attends the first part of the Divine Office just after midnight and retires here to his chamber, though he is expected back in the abbey church about six to sing Prime. He locks himself in his room, the only visitor is his Secretarius, Brother Christopher, who brings in the bread and wine brought up by one of the servants. Brother Christopher," he continued, "is only there for a few minutes. But the cup he has brought in is poisoned." Cranston rose and, after stretching himself, walked round the room. "The solution is quite simple. The murderer either must be one of the following: the Cellarer, for there was a poison stain found in the kitchen, the old servant who brought it up or, more likely, Brother Christopher. No one else could have done it for the stairs were guarded."

I agreed and was about to make my own suggestion when the great bell of the abbey began to toll for Vespers.

"Sir John," I asked, "What shall we do now?"

"What do you mean?"

"Are we to return to the city or to stay here?"

"We have come so far we might as well see the matter through," he replied.

"Then, if you don't mind," I retorted. "I would like to join my brothers in Christ in church," Cranston shrugged.

"Do what you like."

I left Cranston in the Abbot's study and went quickly down to the church. The great west door was open. I went inside. Torches had been lit which only increased the sense of watchful silence, making the shadows dance and slither across the great pillars. The sunlight still streamed through the coloured glass windows but I thought the church must always be dark. I went up through the heavily ornamented rood screen, past the pulpit and into the sanctuary, a small chapel in itself with choir stalls of carved wood on either side. Each stall had a richly decorated canopy at the back with a desk in front. The monks were now filing in from another door; ghostly figures with their hoods pulled up. They looked indistinguishable, despite the fire of the torches and the light of the huge beeswax candles placed on the altar. A dark figure loomed over me, pulling his cowl back. I recognised Prior Wakefield.

"You wish to join us?" he whispered.

"Yes, Father."

He waved me to an empty stool.

"Brother Anselm is sick, we would be only too pleased for you to help us with our singing."

I could not decide if he was being helpful or sarcastic but I murmured my thanks and took my place, waiting for the other monks to join us. I caught the faint, fragrant smell of incense but my soul sensed something else. The figures lining up in their stalls were quiet, calm, possessed of one intent, to use all their energy in the praise of God. Nevertheless, I caught the awful smell of fear and knew that each man must be wondering which of their brethren had committed the horrible crime of murder. The Abbot's empty seat, which stood at the west end of the choir, dominated the gathering, its very emptiness turning it into an accusatory finger as if the Abbot was stretching his hand out beyond death, seeking his killer here, at the very foot of God's throne.

I leaned against the stall seat and waited until the leading cantor moved up to the lectern, a huge brass stand in the shape of an eagle with outstretched wings. In a clear angelic voice he began the chant.

"Oh, Lord, arise in haste to help me!"

The monks thundered their reply, answering each verse with the response. I joined in, forgetful of sin, blasphemy and sacrilege, only too pleased to be back amongst my fellow priests, singing the beautiful plain chant of the church.

After the service I joined the monks as they filed back across the darkening cloister into the refectory or frater, a long, well lit room roofed in timber and generously served by huge windows; some filled with horn, others with beautiful decorated glass. The high table on the dais at the end was empty except for the Prior who stood there intoning the "Benedicite." The monks sat down, pulling back their cowls, sitting patiently while the lay brothers served them and a young monk, standing at a pulpit built in the refectory wall, read from the writings of Jerome. Apart from the reading, the meal was ate in complete silence. No one seemed concerned by my presence, though I sensed an atmosphere of menace and I knew their very detachment masked close scrutiny, indeed resentment at my presence. So intense was this feeling that I gulped my food and, forgetting all etiquette, hastily rose, bowed to the great crucifix which hung above the dais and gratefully fled back to the cloisters.

Cranston was waiting for me in the Abbot's chamber, noisily eating a better meal than I had been served in the refectory and taking great gulps of wine from a shallow bowl.

"Did you enjoy yourself, Brother?" he asked his mouth full.

"An interesting experience," I replied. "Though one I would not like to repeat."

Whilst Cranston gobbled his meal I went over and picked up the book of hours, trying to calm myself by studying the beautiful paintings, a feast of colour and light. Cranston announced he had finished eating by noisily smacking his lips, slouching back in the Abbot's great chair and belching as loudly as a trumpet blast.

"And what has my Lord Coroner decided to do now?" I said sarcastically.

Cranston shrugged.

"I have told that whey-faced Prior I wish to see the following: himself, the Sub-Prior, the Infirmarian, the Cellarer and, of course, dear Brother Christopher. We shall question these to throw some light on our dark mystery."

He had hardly finished speaking when there was a knock at the door and Prior Wakefield entered, a file of monks behind him. Cranston, now full of his own importance as well as good wine, made no attempt at welcome. He imperiously waved them in front of the desk and, after instructing me to light candles, ordered me to take careful note of what was said.

The young man who had been the leading cantor in the church helped me find a tinder and light the branched candlestick bringing the room to life.

"Good" murmured Sir John, revelling in his authority. "Those things that were done in the dark," he added, misquoting scripture, "shall be examined on the mountain top."

"There is no need to treat us like errant scholars, Sir John." Prior Wakefield insisted.

"I am not," Cranston replied brusquely. "But I am the King's Coroner."

"You have no jurisdiction in this abbey." Wakefield interrupted.

"I have every jurisdiction. The King's writ rules here as it does anywhere else. So, my Lord Prior, please introduce me to your brethren."

Wakefield, swallowing his pride, gestured towards his fellow monks. The Sub-Prior Brother Paul, small, chubby-faced and great bellied, he could have taken the part in any mummer's play as Robin Hood's Friar Tuck. The Infirmarian, Brother Stephen, tall, scholarly looking, a man full of his own importance with a great nose and arrogant eyes. If I had not known better I would have sworn he was the Prior. Brother Ambrose, the Cellarer, surprisingly lean, sallow-faced, a look of constant worry souring his mouth. Finally, Brother Christopher the Secretarius, the young man with the voice of an angel.

Once the introductions were over, Cranston went through what we had learnt so far and no one demurred.

"Right!" Sir John barked, using his stubby fingers to score points. "We know you, the Cellarer, poured the drink and prepared the bread during the fourth hour after midnight. It stood in the monastery kitchens until taken up by the lay brother, who placed it outside the Abbot's lodging on the same bench later used to break the door down. The only visitor was you, Brother Christopher." The young man nodded, a look of intense fear in his eyes as he nervously ran his fingers through his close cropped, blond hair. "You did take the wine in?" Again Brother Christopher nodded. "Speak up, man." Prior Wakefield was about to intervene but Cranston stopped him with a warning glance. "You have a tongue, Brother Christopher?"

"Yes, I have a tongue," he answered softly. "I took the tray in, as usual Abbot Hugo was kneeling on his *prie dieu*." He nodded towards the far corner before pointing to the book of hours on the table. "I placed the tray on the table."

"Did the Abbot say anything?"

"He whispered 'Gratias.'"

"What then?" I interrupted. "After you left, what would Abbot Hugo do?"

The young man spread his hands.

"As customary, he would sit where you are and write letters whilst breaking his fast. A few minutes before Prime he would leave his chamber and join us in the abbey church."

"Did the Abbot write anything the night he died?" I asked.

"No," the Cellarer, interrupted, "He simply checked my accounts. The roll was found on his desk."

"Who has it now?"

"Brother Christopher later gave it over to me," the Prior answered. "I have looked at it. There's nothing untoward."

Sir John grimaced.

"Are you hinting that Brother Christopher did anything wrong?" Wakefield asked peevishly.

"Oh, no, Brother Christopher would not do anything untoward!"

Cranston and I looked in surprise at Brother Paul's clever mimicry of the Prior's words. Wakefield, his face flushed with anger, turned on the Sub-Prior.

"Brother Paul, I suggest you keep your mouth shut!" Wakefield smiled at the Secretarius. "Do not worry, Christopher, we know you did nothing wrong."

"How do you know?" the Sub-Prior interrupted, "He was the last man to see the Abbot alive. He did carry the wine in."

Brother Christopher fell to his knees, sobbing into his upraised hands. Cranston and I were both transfixed by this tableau. The calm composure of these monks now broken by the child-like weeping of Brother Christopher and the look of hatred exchanged between the Prior and Brother Paul. I was about to intervene but Cranston waved me to silence.

"We both know how you looked after your darling Christopher!" the Sub-Prior spat spitefully.

"What are you hinting at, Brother?"

Wakefield drew himself up to his full height and I was surprised at the way that the small Sub-Prior, his smiling face now hard and impassive, stood his ground.

"Oh, we know how you interceded with the Abbot," he commented, throwing a knowing look at Cranston, "To beg for mercy when this young man was found stealing from the monastery at night, dressed in multi-coloured hose, red shoes and velvet jacket, to enjoy the pleasures of the city."

"That was years ago," Brother Christopher sobbed.

"We are forgetting one thing," Brother Stephen, the Infirmarian interrupted. "Traces of the Belladonna poison were found in the kitchen."

"What are you implying?" the Cellarer shouted. "You are the Infirmarian, you had access to poisons!"

The Infirmarian was about to yell back when Cranston clapped his hands.

"Enough is enough is enough!" he bellowed. "Prior Wakefield," he continued evenly as the brothers regained some composure. "I suggest we interview each of you separately and I will begin with you. The rest should wait outside."

He was about to continue when he was interrupted by a knock on the door and the lay brother who had earlier admitted to bringing the wine and bread from the kitchen shuffled in, head down, hands hanging dejectedly on either side of him. He went over to Prior Wakefield and knelt at his feet.

"Peccavi," the old man whispered, "I have sinned."

"What is it, Brother Wulfstan?"

"It is true," the old man whispered in a now still room. "I brought up the wine as usual and, as usual, I drank from it." There was a few moments silence, shattered by the uproar the lay brother's words caused.

"See!" the Cellarer shouted. "I am innocent!"

"It must have been poisoned later," the Infirmarian added gleefully, "And the only person who touched it was our darling Brother Christopher."

The young monk, unable to accept this, howled in protest and, before anyone could stop him, fled from the room.

Cranston rose to his feet.

"Prior Wakefield, you will wait on me now. Brother Ambrose," he indicated to where the lay brother still lay sobbing at the Prior's feet. "Take this man away and, Brother Stephen," he turned to the Infirmarian, "Bring back the Secretarius. Now! Go, all of you!"

Once the room was cleared, Cranston sat down and turned to me, a look of complete surprise on his face.

"So, my dear Athelstan, Chaucer's words are true, the cowl doesn't make the monk."

"No more than the robe makes the judge or armour the knight." I replied, "Though I agree, we have uncovered a filthy plot of passions here."

Cranston grimaced.

"The murderer must be Christopher. We must find out why."

I shook my head.

"Too easy," I replied.

But Cranston just shrugged, shouting for Prior Wakefield to come back into the room.

The Prior had regained his composure and, not waiting for Cranston's invitation, pushed across a small stool to sit opposite him. He did not even bother to stare at me but sat fingering the tassel of his cord, waiting for Cranston to begin. The coroner smiled.

"Prior Wakefield, your relations with Brother Paul, the Sub-Prior, are not what they should be?"

"What do you mean?"

"There is very little charity between two brother priests."

"I do not like Brother Paul." Wakefield replied evenly. "Read your Aquinas, Sir John, one can draw distinctions between loving and liking. I do not like Brother Paul because he is arrogant, with great ambition but not the talent to match."

"Nor," continued Cranston drily, "does he like your protégé, Brother Christopher."

"Brother Christopher is a weak vessel, he fell from grace some years ago. I recommended him to the post of Secretarius so both I and Father Abbot could keep an eye on him."

"Your Sub-Prior is hinting at something else."

Wakefield's sallow face flushed.

"Brother Paul will have to atone for his sin," he answered. "He hints at an unnatural love between Brother Christopher and myself. That is not true."

"Who sent the messenger to me?" Cranston interrupted.

"I believe it was the Infirmarian, Brother Stephen." Cranston nodded.

"Then we will see him next."

"He has brought the Abbot's wine and bread with him."

"Good." Cranston replied.

Brother Stephen entered the room as soon as Wakefield left, placing the bread and wine triumphantly on the table before Cranston as if laying an altar for Mass. Cranston sniffed at both before handing them to me. There was a tinge of mould on the bread so I snapped it in two and held it close against my nose but I could detect nothing. The wine cup was a different matter. A silver chased goblet, it was still half-full of wine but reeked of that sour-sweet stench I detected from Abbot Hugo's lips. Cranston watched me pull a face.

"What made you think of poison?" he asked Brother Stephen abruptly.

"What do you mean?" the Infirmarian snapped back.

"Well," Cranston smiled. "Abbot Hugo was an old man. You found him dead over his desk?"

"I did not find him."

"Agreed, your Prior did, but you came into the room and immediately checked the cup. Was it spilled?"

"Of course not."

"So why examine it?"

"I do not know," Brother Stephen replied crossly. "Perhaps I am naturally suspicious. I looked around, everything was in order."

"Everything?" I interjected. A slow doubt began to form in my mind, "You are sure about that, Brother Stephen?"

"Yes. I simply picked up the cup out of curiosity. But the smell of Belladonna was so strong I knew immediately it was drugged."

"Are you so proficient in poisons?" Cranston asked, "That you can detect it even when it's laced with wine?" Brother Stephen looked at him arrogantly.

"Of course. I am a specialist in poisons: Nightshade, Belladonna, the juice of the foxglove. Not that," he looked at us both in one sweeping glance, "Not that I am the only person with access to them. We use poison in keeping our beehives, to get rid of rats and mice and in the garden. Indeed, any of the brothers could mix poisons from the herbs we grow."

"So, why did you send for Sir John?" I asked. "Why the King's coroner?"

"Sir John knows that himself," Brother Stephen replied artfully and, before I could intervene, Cranston smoothly dismissed the Infirmarian, telling him to send Brother Christopher in.

After a short while the young monk entered, escorted by Prior Wakefield. He was white-faced, red-eyed, his cheeks stained by tears.

"Sit down," Cranston said kindly. "We have no need for you, Prior Wakefield."

The Prior seemed reluctant to move.

"I repeat myself, my Lord Prior, there is no need for you to stay."

Once Wakefield was gone, Cranston leaned across the table.

"Brother Christopher, let us be brief. We know when the wine left the kitchen it was not poisoned or the lay brother who drank from it would have died. We have also learnt that no one approached the wine whilst it was outside Abbot Hugo's study. The only conclusion we can draw is that you must have poisoned the cup before bringing it in and stained the kitchen table to spread confusion. Well, what do you have to say?"

The young monk, looking totally crestfallen, shook his head.

"I am innocent!" he stuttered, "Completely in this matter!"

"Oh, no, you're not!" Cranston snapped. "My Lord Prior!" he bellowed.

Wakefield, waiting outside, re-entered immediately.

"I would be grateful," Cranston declared and broke off yawning, "If Brother Christopher could be taken and locked in some cell. I believe you have armed retainers?"

The Prior nodded and, before he could object, Cranston rose.

"By the King's authority, I order this and I do not wish my orders questioned."

Wakefield took the young Secretarius by the arm as if he was some small boy and led him out of the room. Cranston stretched and turned.

"I would like to be civil, Brother Athelstan but, with all due respect to yourself, I have had enough of monks for one day. So I bid you good-night."

Cranston nodded his head and scurried off whilst I stayed in the Abbot's study and sent for the Infirmarian.

After some time, Brother Stephen arrived, cross-faced and sleep laden.

"What is it, Friar?" he brusquely asked.

"One question, monk!" I snapped back. "And one question only. If you gave me Belladonna in wine, how long would it take for me to die?"

The fellow seemed to find that a pleasant thought.

"No more than a few seconds," he replied.

I gave out a great sigh and grinned.

"Then Brother Stephen, I demand this on the King's authority; you are to rouse Prior Wakefield and tell him to take Brother Christopher from custody and bring him here. Now!" I shouted, seeing the arrogant obstinacy in his face. The monk shrugged, dismissed me with a supercilious glance and padded out of the room. Well over half an hour passed before I heard footfalls in the corridor outside.

"Come in!" I shouted. "Do not let us wait on idle ceremony!" Wakefield entered, holding up a now distraught Christopher, white-faced, wild eyed. I momentarily wondered if he had lost his wits. "Brother

Christopher," I began kindly, "Sit on the stool. Prior Wakefield, please stay outside." I leaned across the table. "Brother Christopher, I do not think you are the murderer." I was pleased to see the look of relief in the young man's eyes. "But you must gather your wits. You put the tray bearing the wine down on the table?"

The young monk nodded.

"Then come!" I rose. "Come here, Brother Christopher, and sit in the Abbot's chair."

The young man did so, slowly like a dream walker, his eyes staring fixedly at the table top.

"Now, Brother, you are the Abbot. You have drunk your wine. What would you do next?"

The young man picked up the quill, dipped it in the inkhorn and, taking a piece of paper, began scratching words upon it. I went round and noted ruefully that the young monk had written the words of the Chief Priest from Christ's trial in the Gospel—"What need we of proof?"

"I need proof," I said quietly. "Now please pretend you are the Abbot, imitate his every mannerism."

I sat on the stool and watched Brother Christopher play-act. As I urged him on, my suspicions firmed into certainty. I asked him a few questions about what had happened on the day before. He answered that he had worked in his office, he told me who had visited him. When he mentioned one name, I remembered something said earlier in the day.

"Thank you, Brother," I said. "Just one final question. You brought the wine and bread into Father Abbot? When did you see him previously? I mean, by yourself?"

"Oh," the young monk answered. "I brought him a letter, sealed by the Prior." He stopped and gazed into the air. "That was the previous evening. Then, just before retiring, I came back with the writing tray."

"The one that is on the desk now?" I asked.

Brother Christopher nodded.

"Yes, it is. Why?"

I shrugged.

"It's of little matter. I thank you, Brother. You may join Prior Wakefield and inform him, on my authority, as well as that of Sir John Cranston, that you may return to your cell on one condition, you are to stay there until we leave."

Early next morning, woken from my sleep in the Abbot's chair by the booming of the bells for Prime, I stretched my aching body and went down to rouse Sir John Cranston. The old coroner was snoring like a pig and I confess I took great joy in waking him. I told him of my conclusions. At first he argued vehemently against me, angry that I had ordered Brother Christopher's release, so I went through my arguments again. Sir John, sitting up in bed, still dressed in the clothes he wore the previous day, reluctantly agreed to what I asked. Cranston rose, washed himself at the Lavararium and followed me round the cloisters back to the Abbot's lodgings. An old lay brother sat dozing on the low cloister wall, half listening to the dawn chant of the monks in the abbey choir. I gently roused him and told him to bring Prior Wakefield and the Sub-Prior to us as soon as the service was over. This time Cranston did not sit in the Abbot's chair but dramatically waved me into it, as if his own presence was no longer necessary. Playing the role he had assigned me, I placed two stools before the table and we waited quietly until Prior Wakefield and Brother Paul entered. I gestured at them to sit.

"Prior Wakefield," I said. "Tell me what you were doing when the news of Abbot Hugo's death was brought to you?"

The Prior, his eyes still red from lack of sleep, yawned as he rubbed his brow, trying to remember.

"Yes, I have told you," he snapped peevishly. "I was in my office talking to Brother Paul. He had asked to see me on some matter. I forget now." Brother Paul nodded in agreement.

"Then what?" I asked.

"The lay brother came down, saying something was wrong, Brother Paul and I ran up here and, once the door was forced, we both entered the room."

"What then?" I asked.

"Abbot Hugo was lying back in his chair. Brother Paul pulled the chair back, I picked the Abbot up. He was no weight and I laid him gently on the floor. I checked his breath and felt for the blood beat in his neck but there was nothing."

"Is that when you changed the pens, Brother Paul?" I asked abruptly, Never have I seen a monk's face go so ashen.

"What do you mean?" he asked hoarsely.

"You know what I mean," I replied. "Like Brother Christopher, you know how the Abbot often sucked the end of a quill whilst writing or preparing to write. So you coated it with poison and, the previous evening, went into Brother Christopher's office and placed the poisoned quill on the Abbot's writing tray. You knew when Abbot Hugo would pick it up and I suggest you kept very close to the Prior, hence your request for a meeting just before Prime on that fatal day. You had no reason to doubt anything would go wrong. Abbot Hugo's routine was established. He was a creature of habit."

"This is. . . ."

"I would be grateful if you did not interrupt me!" I snapped, "and let me finish. You had to be with the Prior so when the body was discovered you gained immediate access to the room. After that it was simple. While Prior Wakefield moved Abbot Hugo's body you poured the poison into the cup and replaced the poisoned quill with an untainted one. A few seconds, the phial of poison and the quill already hidden in the voluminous sleeves of your robe. No one would dream of examining where the writing tray was placed. I am sure if we check the Cellarer's account, we would find places where the Abbot used the quill to tally amounts. He would have then leaned back in the chair, unwittingly drinking the poison as he licked the quill. He would feel ill, place it down and fall back into death." I paused. "Later on, a little poison was dropped on the table down in the kitchen and you successfully spread the seeds of suspicion. Any one of your brothers could have poisoned the Abbot's wine, even when the old lay brother admitted to sipping from the cup, you thought you were safe. For the only possible culprit could be Brother Christopher."

"That is ridiculous!" the Sub-Prior muttered. "You have no proof!"

"Oh, yes I do," I replied. "First, you did visit Brother Christopher's office the night beforehand on some petty errand which engaged the young Secretarius' attention. Secondly, the fresh pen you used to replace the poisoned one. You made sure that it had been dipped in ink and certainly used by yourself. Now you are a right-handed man, when you use a quill the tip is worn away on the right side but Abbot Hugo was left-handed, his quill should have been worn down on the left." I picked up the quill from the writing tray. "This is the untainted quill you brought in." I pointed to the tip. "Look, it is worn down on the right side. When I checked Abbot Hugo's corpse I noticed the ink stain on his left hand. This quill could never have been used by him. Finally, Belladonna is a quick-acting, powerful poison. If the Abbot had raised the cup to his lips he would never have had time to place it back on the table. It would either have fallen on the table or the floor.

"Why?" Prior Wakefield asked, glaring at the Sub-Prior.

"Oh, I think I can answer that," Cranston interrupted. "There is no love lost between you two. If Abbot Hugo had retired; you, Prior Wakefield, could well have replaced him. That's the last thing Brother Paul wanted. So Abbot Hugo dies in mysterious circumstances. A feeling of suspicion is created and your superiors may well have been tempted to place someone else, an outsider, in charge."

"A mummer's tale!" Brother Paul sneered. "A fable, nothing else."

"In which case," I remarked, digging into the pocket of my own robe, "You will not object to placing the tip of this quill in your mouth?" I drew out a battered quill and held it up. "Look, Brother Paul, it's worn on the left side and is still stained with ink. I ask you to put it into your mouth."

"That's not the quill that Abbot Hugo used," Brother Paul snapped back and immediately raised his hand to his lips to bite back his words.

"You are correct! How do you know that, Brother Paul?"

"I don't! I don't!" the Sub-Prior murmured. "I will say no more."

"What are you going to do?" Prior Wakefield asked, for the first time ever looking at me squarely in the face. "I ask you, Brother Athelstan, not Sir John Cranston, for you too are a disgraced monk aren't you?" he smiled thinly. "Oh, I made a few enquiries, a little digging amongst the gossip, Brother Athelstan, who fled his novitiate to join the King's army and took his own younger brother, only to get him killed. A man who not only broke his monastic vows but the hearts of his parents."

God forgive me, I could not stop the tears welling up in my eyes. Wakefield's words stirred my memory and I recalled the tragic, tear-stained faces of my mother and father.

"I have sinned," I replied. "And my sin is always before me and let that be Brother Paul's sentence. You, Prior Wakefield, will be elected Abbot. Brother Paul will resign as Sub-Prior and stay in this monastery for the rest of his life being ruled by a man he hates. I could not think of a worse form of hell. That is," I added crisply, "if Sir John agrees."

Cranston, who had been watching me closely, nodded and rose, not bothering to give the still seated Brother Paul a glance.

"I would be grateful, Lord Prior, if you would ensure that this malignant was locked away until we leave. Of course, he may object to Brother Athelstan's sentence, in which case he can take his chances before the King's Justices in the Guildhall. I suggest he does not do that."

Prior Wakefield nodded and patted Brother Paul on the shoulder, who followed him as meekly as a lamb out of the room.

Once they had left, Cranston came up and nudged me gently on the chest.

"They are bailiffs in cowls," he said, quoting a current proverb about monks. "I don't like monks" he continued evenly. "I am not too sure whether I like you but I do respect you, Athelstan. Now let's be gone from this hell pit!"

Our journey back into London was uneventful but, before we parted, Cranston pulled back his hood and leaned closer to me.

"I agree with your sentence, Athelstan" he said, "But the Infirmarian sent for me because Abbot Hugo had once been spiritual confessor to our dread King, Edward III. I will let the court know what happened. I am sure Brother Paul will meet with an accident before Michaelmas Day."

I left Cranston to go back to my own church. The pools of water were still on the floor and the church door hung loose. Someone had stolen the small statue of the Virgin from its niche. Godric the murderer had been taken, snatched by officials of the Mayor, or so Ranulf the rat-catcher told me when I found him sleeping on the steps of the sanctuary. I gave him a coin and dismissed him. I knelt before the crucifix and said the "De Profundis" for Godric's soul and for that of Abbot Hugo and for my own brother, Francis. Souls sent before their time to stand before the throne of God. So now I have related this story, perhaps I will look once more at the stars, say my Office and go merrily to bed. Pray God Cranston gives me peace.

✝

When Your Breath Freezes

Kathleen Dougherty

There are seven of us.

I am Sister Ellen: the youngest, the ugliest, the least devout, the most fragile. I need the vast silences of northern Alaska and the imposed silence of this cloister. The souls of these women are quiet, their musings as distant as the Chukchi Sea. The nuns have taken me in for the winter, an act of charity, a, charity they might well regret. But they don't know about my special ability, my accursed gift. If they did, they'd shun me as others have. Their unspoken thoughts, though, are safe from me. Nothing could compel me again to peruse the mind of another. What you see there are the ugly shapes of nightmares.

Under my white robes, the color for a novice, are a pair of expeditionweight long johns, the fabric a heat-retaining, sweat-wicking synthetic; then a pair of wind-blocking pile pants. We have no television, no radio, yet we have the latest in underwear.

Off come the sturdy black shoes and on go the insulated knee-high boots. I unpin the white novice's veil from my hair and hang the veil on a wall peg. I slide a black ski mask over my head, position the mouth and eye holes. I like wearing the mask; its blank anonymity hides my facial scars. There is only one mirror here, in the infirmary. I have little use for mirrors.

I wrap my neck with the wool scarf knitted by Sister Gabrielle. I think tenderly of her gnarled hands, twisted by arthritis, the black yarn, and the slow clack of the needles. She had embroidered "Ellen" on a cloth tag. My fingers worked a stretch cap on top of the ski mask, then I shrug on the anorak with its thick pile of yellow fleece lining, its rich fringe of fox fur around the hood. The drawstring snugs the hood low on my forehead and up over my mouth. The fur tickles and has that dusty aroma of animal skin.

Last are the glove liners and the padded mittens with Velcro wrist bands. Even before I open the heavy wooden door, I imagine I hear the cows lowing, though that's not possible. The wind's voice whips away sound and, deceptively, mimics the wail of a cat, a distant locomotive, an unhappy ghost.

I flick on the outdoor lights and step beyond the door, pulling it closed behind me. The frigid air steals my breath. Outside all is the white of an unusually bitter February. Though midmorning, there are hours before dawn bleaches the sky. My teeth chatter. It is colder than death out here.

The north wind pauses in its cold rush. I spit. The saliva crackles, freezing in midair, and shatters like glass on the walkway. Cold, very cold, even by the standards of northern Alaska. More than seventy below. Gusts sweep snow pellets, hard as gravel, across the covered walkway to the barn. That wooden structure, like the convent, appears to sprout from the mountainside.

During the Yukon gold rush, miners hewed these caverns, clawing from granite the shelters that shielded them from brutal winters. The southfacing walls are wood; north-facing walls and much of the ceiling are the smoothed underbelly of the mountain. Snaking into the earth from those north walls are tunnels; a few lead to steaming pools of hot springs, potable—though slightly sulfurous—water. After the Second World War, the exhausted claim was purchased by the Immaculata order, and this remote land, once brimming with the harsh voices and greed of prospectors, became the refuge of silent nuns.

The gale blasts against my long skirts and I cover the walkway in a graceless stagger. The barn door sticks, its hinges cranky with cold. I wrench open the door and step inside to rich aromas: cow hide, dung, hay, bird droppings, wood smoke. The miners had used the large room as a barracks. Humid air fogs a tunnel entrance, one which leads to the hot springs, where the nuns take paying guests during the brief summers.

The barn houses two cows, a mangy good-for-nothing goat, and a chicken-wire enclosure with a dozen hens and an irritable cock. The hens set up a comical squawking and fluttering, shocked to their very cores every few hours when I come to tend the wood stove. The cows regard me with their calm brown eyes, aware that it's morning and hoping for fresh fodder. These are, as far as I've seen, the only cows in Alaska, a gift from a rancher in the lower forty-eight. He'd stayed here last summer, Leonidist said, soaking in the convent's hot sulfur springs, and was convinced he'd been miraculously healed of gout.

Pine logs dropped into the wood stove make the coals flare. The stove stands in an isolated hollow scooped from the mountain. The flue disappears into the rocky ceiling.

I milk the cows and the sullen goat, gather eggs from the hens. I slap the cow's haunches, urging them up and down the center aisle. They don't like the enforced exercise, but their shanks tend to develop abscesses. Sister Fiske, a paramedic and our only source of medical expertise during these frozen months, prescribed aerobics. The cows want only to stare into their food bins and meditate golden hay into existence. Their resistance makes the stroll hard work and I wonder about the medical benefits for any of us. After half an hour, I stop, panting. Their bony heads study me quietly, a pitying look which makes me smile.

I muck out the stalls and coop, spread down fresh straw, and rake the soiled material to the far entrance. I switch on the outdoor lights. This part gets tricky. If drifts have built up in the past hours, a path will have to be cleared. That means shoveling for two minutes, dashing into the warmth of the barn and scaring the heck out of the chickens, shoveling another two minutes, and so on.

To my delight, the door swings open easily and the path to the garden appears clear. I rake the straw outside and drag the mound a few yards when a snow-dusted rock catches my eye. A mound of black, a large stone that hadn't been there before . . . and with awful clarity the form resolves into that of a huddled person. My chest tenses with shock. I am kneeling next to the shape without memory of moving closer.

She is curled into the fetal position. The ebony veil, hard and shiny, has frozen into place, covering most of the profile, but there's enough exposed to see the broad jaw, the deep etch of lines from nose to mouth, the dark brown mole with its two stiff hairs stark against ashen flesh. Frost has made a mask of the features, smoothed out the web of wrinkles on her full cheeks, lessened the downward draw of persimmon lips. It is

Sister Praxades, our cook, who refuses—refused—to bake white bread. In the kitchen with her black sleeves rolled up over dimpled forearms, she taught me to knead whole-grain dough. She smelled of flour and yeast and discontent.

With my right glove and liner off, I touch her throat where, in life, the carotid artery throbs. Her neck is frozen solid, hard and unyielding.

Her pudgy hands and feet are bare, pale as alabaster. How can this be? No one would willingly tromp barefoot in Alaska's winter.

My thoughts are slow lizards, too long in the cold.

My right hand signs the cross over the body. I mentally begin an Act of Contrition, but retreat to the barn when the air hurts my lungs. Chickens cackle and the goat bleats while I finish the prayer for Sister Praxades, an inadequate charity for a woman who had been more than tolerant of a newcomer.

Tears burn my cheeks. I, who have so little opportunity for love, loved her.

There had been seven of us.

Now there are six.

† † †

Reverend Mother thinks in German, a language I don't comprehend. Snatches of words, swirling in her mind-winds, fly out: *schnee, tot, unschuld, verlassen.* She is in her late forties, the youngest except for me, yet authority is a mantle she wears with ease. Her bearing is military, her oval face composed, her gray eyes sharp. Only now her gaze reveals disquiet upon my panicked report of Sister Praxades's death. Reverend Mother's face shutters down; her thoughts whirl. Rosary beads rattle within the folds of her black robes. Her pale lips shape the English words, "Jesus, Mary, Joseph," a favored indulgence of this order. Each nun says this prayer so often that the rhythm becomes one with each inhale and exhale. When the rare words seep from their minds, that is what I sense: JesusMaryJoseph.

Reverend Mother orients on me. Her lapse of control is over. Her fingers sign, *You—lead me—Praxades.* Even now Reverend Mother does not break the quiet meditation.

Her hand halts me as I turn. She shapes sentences fast, too fast, and I shake my head in confusion. She places a long index finger to her lips, then signs, *No tell—others.*

Why not tell the others? They'll know Sister Praxades is missing. I gesture for permission to speak, my sign language inept. Reverend Mother slices her hand in the negative, a command that reminds me of my position here. The shock of finding Sister Praxades has made me exceed my bounds. Flushing, I bow my head in apology, nod compliance, and we exit her office. It is up to Reverend Mother, not the distraught pseudo-novice "Sister" Ellen, to decide when to tell the nuns. If she waits until after the Angelus, before the noon meal when contemplation officially ends, Sister Praxades will not be any less dead for the delay.

In the hall Sister Leonidist, standing on a foot stool, scrapes tallow from a wall sconce. Candle glow highlights the postmenopausal down of her cheeks and chin. Thick red eyebrows shadow her sockets, making her pale blue eyes seem large and black. Leon the Lion, my pet name for her in my head, is the one I'd have gone to first to share the terrible discovery. She performs a modified curtsy from her perch in respect of Reverend Mother as we pass. I look longingly over my shoulder at Leon. She grins and winks, pretends to stick a finger up one wide nostril.

At the side door, before Reverend Mother dons her anorak, she removes her black headdress. Her hair is a flattened, short gray-brown, and its thinness somehow diminishes her authority. I focus on the splintered wood planks, embarrassed. It is disrespectful to see her so. After a moment, she nudges me, not unkindly. It is time to go out into the cold.

† † †

One voice: "*Dominus vobiscum.*" The Lord be with you.

Five voices: "*Et cum spiritu tuo.*" And with your spirit.

It is noon and the hours of silence end. Reverend Mother observes us from the lectern. Her hands clutch the frame on either side of the Bible. Her knuckles whiten. She is, I know, gathering strength to talk about Sister Praxades. The nuns do not speak. Their minds are suspended in a sea of expectation; no gleanings travel from their consciousness to mine, not even the Jesus, Mary, Joseph prayer. Leon catches my attention with a raised bushy eyebrow and looks pointedly at her lap. She signs: *Cook sick?*

The others may think that. We are not allowed in our cells except to sleep or to rest if we're ill. How I wish Sister Praxades were on her pallet, tucked under quilts, resting away a fever instead of curled miserably outside, the door of her mind forever frozen closed. I hope that whatever malady caused her to wander in the snow also prevented the cook from suffering.

My vision blurs and I drop my gaze to the pine table. In front of me and the four seated nuns are blue ceramic bowls of potato soup, our lunch. In the kitchen I simmered the potatoes in chicken stock—no wonder those fowl squawk with such alarm—and added cream, butter, salt, pepper, and a dash of crisp Chardonnay. As Sister Praxades taught, I tasted and added more butter, cream, tasted and added more spices, tasted and added more wine . . . and still the broth seemed bland.

Rich yellow butter dots the soup's surface, my poor attempt to duplicate the dead woman's craft. Only the bread, a thick, sweet rye, can be trusted. The large, round, crusty loaves were baked by the cook yesterday.

Reverend Mother's sharp inhale pulls my attention to the lectern. Her lips pressed together. "Sister Ellen found Sister Praxades outside this morning. Sister Praxades is dead." The bald statements straighten every spine, including my own.

"No," cries Sister Gabrielle, an old friend of the cook, eldest nun, knitter of woolens for the likes of me. Her misshapen hand fists, hits the table, and spoons jump. Her anguish bolts to my heart. She cries again: "No!"

"Sister Gabrielle," comes the cautioning, authoritative voice of Reverend Mother.

The old nun's mouth gapes, showing too-even dentures. Tears diffuse down cheeks as creased as parchment. She hunches over the table, gasping with hushed sobs, and a thread of saliva descends from her lips. Sister Fiske, the medic, sits next to the stricken woman. Her chin lifts, her eyes narrow behind magnified glasses. A sharp, disapproving line creases between her brows and her mouth thins, a compassionless look from a woman who frets about the abscesses of cows.

At a nod from Reverend Mother, Fiske rises, accompanies the crying Gabrielle into the stone corridor. The old woman's voice muffles in decrescendo. After a moment, the thin creak of the chapel door reveals their location. And in this room . . . silence. Leon stares at her lap. Sister Xavier, our housekeeper, an angular woman with a jaw as square as a box, fingers a soup spoon. She rarely speaks even when conversation is allowed.

Reverend Mother sighs deeply and bows her head. She says, "Why did you doubt?" Stress has made her German accent noticeable. Their shared emotion builds critical mass and penetrates my carefully erected barriers.

Each is deeply, piercingly ashamed.

✝   ✝   ✝

Reverend Mother restricts me to the kitchen with my bowl of cooling soup while she conducts a private meeting with the others in the dining room. At the pine counter where Praxades taught me to shape loaves of whole wheat, I force myself to finish my lunch. Food is never wasted. Each tight swallow emphasizes my hurt: grief for the cook and, to my chagrin, the wound of being excluded from the nuns' discussion. I don't belong here, I chide myself. Why should Reverend Mother behave as though I'll stay beyond the spring thaw?

After I eat and feed more coal to the stove, the temptation to eavesdrop wins. I press my ear against the swinging door to the dining room. Not even hushed conversation seeps through the wood. Pushing the door open a crack—my toes still on the kitchen floor so there isn't technical disobedience—I see the five blue bowls on the table, still full. The nuns are gone.

Determined to be a help and to demonstrate a charity I'm not exactly feeling, I busy myself in the pantry, planning dinner. Surveying the shelves, my gaze touches opaque brown vials, medicines that Sister Praxades took on a complicated schedule. The names on the labels don't mean anything to me; once she showed me the collection on her chubby palm, pointing out one for blood pressure, another for cholesterol, and so on.

I pop the cap of one bottle and spill out beautiful azure capsules into my hands. Whatever her medications were supposed to do, they hadn't done their job last night. Sighing, I return the pills to their container and scoop the half-dozen prescriptions into my pocket. Fiske will want these returned to the infirmary.

I decide on tuna casserole, a dish I'm unlikely to ruin. I gather the canned fish, mushroom soup, noodles, and a stale bag of potato chips. The planks squeak under my tread and I see Praxades of last night, after dinner, sashaying and spinning her robes in exaggerated mockery of Sister Fiske, floorboards complaining under her weight. Mimicry was her gift and no one, myself included, was exempt, but Fiske was the cook's specialty.

At the sink I twist the crank of the opener around the tuna can and indulge the sweet sorrow of memories. Oddly enough, Praxades was liberal while the much younger Fiske was conservative. Praxades wanted a satellite dish and television so she could learn recipes from Julia Child; she wanted a subscription to *Gourmet* magazine, deliverable by bush pilot when weather allowed. In the common room, the arguments between Praxades and Fiske were high entertainment. Fiske struggled to control her indignation, I'll give her that. However, Praxades was a master of provocation. The cook's suggestions would become more and more extreme: the nuns should forgo habits and wear fleece slacks and shirts, the L. L. Bean catalogue had them in black.

Last night the cook's trump card, so to speak, enraged Fiske to unusual heights. Praxades suggested that evenings be passed by rousing games of stud poker, using holy cards as chips. The silent Sister Xavier grinned. Leon always looked happy, as though her features were incapable of any other expression. Fiske sprang to her feet, hands clenched by her sides, her complexion red; she'd flung her book to the floor. She sputtered, "You . . . you . . . you sacrilegious old fool, you disgusting—"

"Enough," interrupted Reverend Mother, a regal lift to her chin. "Sister Praxades, hold your tongue. Sister Fiske, you allow the cook to bait you every evening. Both of you must learn control and tolerance." However, Reverend Mother's eyes held a glitter of amusement; not, I'm sure, because of Fiske's fury but because of the cook's inane ideas.

Smug satisfaction brightened Praxades's plump face. Fiske retrieved *The Lives of the Saints,* touched the cover to her lips in apology—to the book, which must have been blessed—and returned to her chair, hands trembling. I felt the heat of her hate for the cook, an emotion as searing as any that had touched me in the cities. It is Lent, weeks of sacrifice in preparation for Easter, but she definitely wasn't offering up her aggravation to the Lord. Fiske even lacked the control to school her expression. She darted a withering, mean look at Reverend Mother, then dropped her gaze to her book. Her face was murderous.

The fork in my hand stops scooping out the tuna. An uneasy resonance jingles in my mind. Had Fiske looked surprised at Reverend Mother's dire announcement? I recall only Fiske's disapproving expression over Gabrielle's outburst.

Perhaps Fiske had nothing to be surprised about.

Fiske, while not a physician, plays the part of one by doling out medications. In my habit's pocket, my fingers clutch the containers of pills.

No one would know if they had been tampered with. No one, that is, except for Fiske.

No, I think, please. Not here.

Not again.

$$\dagger \quad \dagger \quad \dagger$$

Reverend Mother imposes an afternoon of silence in memory of the cook. When I enter her office and request permission to speak, she signs, "later." Minutes afterward, swaddled in my anorak, I tromp through the barn, chickens squawking in terror, and exit by the rear door. If Praxades was disoriented by medication, probably Fiske had to lead her outside. Snow squeaks like plastic pellets under my boots. Wind whips up millions of grains as fine as baby powder, shoving me nearly off my feet. My polarized lenses fog. I push the goggles above my eyes with awkward mittens and squint. The body is gone. While I was sequestered in the kitchen, the nuns moved the cook.

The day's dilute glow is muted by dark-bellied clouds, and though I search, crouching near the ground, crabwalking the path, there's no evidence that anyone has been here: not the dead cook, not the nuns, and—as I look at ground near my boots—not even Sister Ellen. The harsh land of winter has wiped away the traces. A spasm of shivering makes my jaw muscles tremble. I straighten. Abruptly a gale whites out the world and my name floats through the whirl: "*Ellen.*"

I pivot, pulse galloping, half-expecting to see Praxades levitating from the ground. That movement is a dangerous mistake. The wind increases, howling and spinning drifts, shoving so hard that I stagger. The mad swirl of snow is blinding. Panic shoots through my very core, more invasive than the cold. Which way is the barn? How long have I been out here? Two minutes? Three? Already my fingers are deadened, ice freezing together my eyelashes, narrowing my view to thin, blurry slits.

I must move. My feet stumble, forcing my body against the wind, and again I hear my name, swallowed by the squall, but definitely from my left. If I'm hallucinating, if hypothermia is creating a false call, then I'm dead. I fight, moving to my left for an eternity of seconds; finally arms grab and pull me into the thick smell and chicken cackles of the barn. Violent shivers drop me to my knees on the straw. The door latch clunks closed. My rescuer drags me to the heat of the wood stove.

My gloves are pulled off, then the liners, and my frozen fingers are clasped in hands so warm they burn my flesh. When the ice melts from my lashes, I'm staring into the kind, silent face of Sister Xavier. I know her the least, yet I know this: She will perform extra penance for the sin of breaking silence when she called my name.

✝ ✝ ✝

In the infirmary, I proffer Sister Praxades's medicines. Fiske's cold fingers remove the bottles from my palm.

I speak, violating the imposed quiet. "Why would Sister Praxades go outside?"

The woman is still a moment, studying me, and the intensity of her stare and the knowledge of my scars make my cheeks warm. Then she shrugs, a who-knows gesture. That motion is a lie. I feel her dissembling, controlling body language. She walks across the rough brick floor, twirling her robes in the way that Praxades mocked. For a moment the mirrored cabinet bounces her image at me, then her double swings away as she opens the cabinet. I follow. "The cook was fine last night. What would make her do such a thing?"

Fiske ignores me, reads the label on one vial, and places it on a shelf cabinet. In my cell, under my pallet, is a list of the prescriptions and one pill from each container. Feeble evidence. The thought strikes me that if Fiske decides to remove any other thorn in her side, by persisting like this, I'm making Sister Ellen the next likely target. Fiske's pinched face last night rises to mind, her seething fury at the cook . . . and, now I recall, toward Reverend Mother.

Anger, however, isn't an omen of murder. "What do you think caused her odd behavior?" I ask, observing her profile as she shelves the remaining vials. "The mix of drugs she'd been taking?"

Her lips curl slightly in contempt. This impugning of her medical care prompts her to talk. "Not at all."

During the next pause, I expect her to announce that Praxades was befuddled by a stroke or low blood sugar. Instead, she closes the wall cabinet. I'm careful not to look into the mirror. Fiske says, "Separation from God."

"What?"

"That's what killed your precious Sister Praxades."

She turns in a flair of robes and for a moment a silly picture forms, a ballet of nuns in long black habits. I catch her by the arm. With slow disdain, she rotates her head to fix a dark gaze on my hand. I don't let go. "She . . . you're saying she died from, what, weak faith? That's your clinical diagnosis?"

She raises her eyes to meet mine. Behind thick lenses her irises glint as though forged of hard, shiny metal. "No, Sister Ellen. That's my spiritual diagnosis."

Our gazes lock. I almost do the thing that I vowed never to do again under any circumstances: invade the mind of another.

If I forcibly examine her thoughts, she will know. They always knew. The last time I used this accursed ability, I destroyed everyone around me.

Fiske stares, a smirking, superior look. It strikes me that she knows all about me, but that's impossible. Her hands shape the words *Look, Files, Top, Ellen.* With a nod she indicates the tall file cabinet.

I release Fiske. She strides away, footfalls slapping the brick floor, and exits the infirmary. As I look at the file cabinet, my stomach clenches in sudden, inexplicable fear. *I,* of all people, understand that some things are better left alone. Yet minutes later I have scanned the thick files bearing my name. Everything is there: the *Journal of the American Medical Association* study about a woman with provable telepathy; the Duke University professor's interview in *People* magazine and a photo of me hooked to an EEG machine; the *Newsweek* and *Time* articles about my assisting with various murder investigations nationwide; the *New York Times* report about how Gardini the Magician, a debunker of so-called psychics, finally paid a quarter of a million dollars to a bona fide mindreader.

Dozens of newspaper and magazine articles cover the famous psychic's last murder case: Psychic's Husband and Brother Guilty of Business Partner's Murder. Then the same grainy photograph shows up in report after report: my disfigured features after the men my brother hired attacked me with acid. Long before that, though, everyone I came into contact with was leery of me. And weeks before acid ate away my features, I decided never again to snare thoughts from another's mind. After plastic surgeons had done the best they could with flesh that scarred so badly, I sought anonymity, a location where my history and notoriety might be unknown, where I might find, if not peace, at least isolation.

I thought that the nuns hadn't questioned me about my past or my scars due to their otherworldliness. Now I see that they had no need to interview me.

I stand in front of the infirmary mirror, holding the heavy file and gazing at my wretched reflection.

† † †

During dinner, while heads bend over a surprisingly tasty tuna casserole, first Leon, then Reverend Mother read passages from the Bible. Dinners are a time to fortify our bodies and our spirits. Reverend Mother, now at the podium, chooses the verses describing Jesus walking on the sea. The expressions of Leon, Xavier, Reverend Mother, and Gabrielle—especially Gabrielle—are serious and downcast. Fiske, to my eye, appears artificially solemn. I swallow a second helping of casserole, eager for the meal to end so that I can interrogate Leon over the dishes. After a minute, the only sound of fork against plate is my own. I look up. Fiske, Xavier, Gabrielle, and Leon are rapt with attention on Reverend Mother. She reads:

> "But when he saw that the wind was boisterous, he was afraid;
> and beginning to sink he cried out, saying, 'Lord, save me!'
> And immediately Jesus stretched out His hand and caught him,
> and said to him, 'O you of little faith, why did you doubt?'"

Reverend Mother closes the Bible, kisses the gold-embossed cover, and returns to her place at the table. Everyone resumes eating, but something has happened which I've missed. The heavy cloud of their mood has lifted. On a psychological level, the dim dining room is bright.

† † †

In the cavern, Leon and I wear headlamps to light our way to the spring. The earth-generated heat keeps the temperatures from dropping below fifty, yet the high humidity is chilling. The damp mist blurs her shape and when our buckets accidentally clang together as we walk, my pulse jumps. She appears comfortable with how the cook died. She explains that Sister Praxades was moved to a mining shaft north of the barn. After leaving the corpse, they barricaded the entrance. When the ground thaws and, with the approval of the medical examiner—from two-hundred-mile-away Lygon—and Praxades's relatives, a burial plot will be prepared. Until then, her body will remain frozen and will be safe from the occasional arctic fox.

Her chipper tone nonpluses me. She might be discussing the disposal of the goat. We reach the pool and kneel down to draw water. I ask, "Why can't we have a memorial service now?"

"To mourn her would be to question God's will."

I set my full bucket down impatiently; water sloshes over the lip. "Leon, *talk* to me."

The desperation in my voice must have moved her. She sets her pail next to mine and says, "Of course I miss Sister Praxades. She brought this place alive. She made us laugh." Through the steam I see her grin. "Well, everyone except Sister Fiske," Leon amends. "Ellen, look at it this way. If you died, would you want those you love to feel grief, to suffer over losing you?"

I wouldn't. Still, I'm troubled by the acceptance of the cook's death. Even the elderly Gabrielle appears adjusted to her friend's absence, though perhaps that's not true. She might be numb with grief.

Leon places her hand on my shoulder. In the steam, her headlamp creates a bright halo. "Perhaps it's easier for us. Our beliefs treat death as a natural part of the soul's journey. It wouldn't make sense for us to behave as though Sister Praxades is gone forever."

I wish I believed in the immortality of the soul. "What if Fiske messed with Praxades's medication?"

Leon is quiet a moment. I know I've surprised her. "I guarantee that Sister Fiske is innocent of everything except anger. She's devoted to safeguarding our health, not endangering it."

Leon could probably find good in Judas. We trudge back through the tunnel toward the living quarters. An aura radiates from her, and in that aura three words ring over and over: JesusMaryJoseph.

† † †

I assume the duties of the cook, though joy has evaporated for me. The others appear inexplicably cheered, except for Reverend Mother, who wears a preoccupied expression as though straining to hear a faint voice just beyond the audible range. A snowstorm blankets the grounds with one foot, then two feet of powder. I watch Fiske, who ignores me. The weather rages and we turn inward; the times of silence are natural for them. This spiritual hibernation makes me edgy, though my bread-baking improves. Two days pass.

On the third morning, Gabrielle vanishes.

† † †

I sleep. I wake with a start, furious with my failed vigil. Today Leon, Xavier, and I search outside for Gabrielle, but our efforts were thwarted by the storm's bluster. She disappeared in the night, like Praxades. The spirits of the nuns are visibly leadened, even Fiske's. My mind is groggy; confused speculations stick in my skull. Why is everyone so resigned— about Praxades, now Gabrielle? Why does Reverend Mother appear fatigued? She walks hesitantly, as if movement is an effort. Is Fiske poisoning Reverend Mother? Has Fiske killed Gabrielle?

A distant sound travels from the corridor. I sit up. Was that the timbers creaking? I toss off the comforter; chill seeps through my habit, cold slipping like spiders under the thermal underwear. In a few seconds I light the hurricane lamp, pull on my insulated boots, and tiptoe into the dark hall. All but one of the cell doors are closed. I peer into that room and my candlelight glows to an empty pallet. Seeing the tidy vacant room is a blow. I run to the kitchen, the dining room, the infirmary, the sitting room, the chapel, my search as fruitless as I feared. At the entryway door, I yank on anorak, gloves, cap and let myself out into the clear, breezy night, the cold so sharp my lungs inhale reflexively with the shock. It is always like this after a storm, as though fierce weather hones winter to better express its nature. The northerly has swept the entryway clear of all but a half-foot of powder, though drifts smooth the side wall clear up to the eaves. I round the building and find wind and deep snow . . . and heartache.

A figure glows in the frosty moonlight, skin gleaming whitely, a wide sweep of black and jiggling buttocks. "Leon!" I cry. She turns, a statue of salt, merging into the colorless world except for dark thatches of hair at crotch and head. My boots sink deep into the fresh powder as I struggle to her side.

"Please don't worry," Leon said. "I have faith." Syllables slur from frozen lips. "I'm getting warmer. My feet—"

"Leon, for the love of God, *please*." Unshed tears chill my eyes. "You're not getting warmer. You're freezing."

My own face is ice. My stiff fingers won't grip. I loop my arm under hers and guide her toward the building. She resists; her red-lashed eyes blink sleepily under the narcotic of hypothermia.

"Damn you, Leon, *walk*."

Her pale mouth opens in a semblance of a smile, the muscles of her jaw stiff with cold. "I'm walking, Ellen," she mumbles. "I'll come back. Reverend Mother did." Her arm slips like mist from mine and she stumbles away, wading through fresh snow, moving with speed I wouldn't have thought possible. But she is numb. My legs drag through thigh-deep drifts and, trailing her, I fall, flounder deep in powdery whiteness. My freezing arms thrash for purchase in a substance as unstable as flour. Snow blankets my vision. I regain my footing, breathing hard, brushing ice from my face. Every muscle trembles so violently, my body straining to produce heat, that I can barely stand. I am alone in a landscape as pale and barren as the moon, and I suddenly understand who the murderer is.

✝ ✝ ✝

I race through the corridor to Reverend Mother's room and enter without knocking, throat parched from cold and panic. A single candle flickers from the floor. Reverend Mother lies on her bed in full habit, fingers laced at her waist, thick black socks on her feet. The down comforter and blankets have been kicked to the floor. I lean over her. "I don't know what rot you've been telling these women, but Leon's out there and you're going to help me get her inside. If she hears you calling, she'll come in." Part of me says it's already too late for Leon, but I can't listen to that.

Reverend Mother stares at me, eyes glittering as though a fire blazes inside her skull. "It's Lent. The Lord calls her. She's being tested."

I pull her to a sitting position and her heat radiates like a furnace. Fever has glossed her skin with perspiration. "This is not Christ asking the apostles to walk on water, damn it. This is Alaska and she'll die out there. No one can survive that cold."

Her hands clutch my shoulders with a frenzied strength. "I did."

An odor pierces my hysteria, a fetid smell. It isn't a chamberpot stink, but a scent of putrefaction and decay. With horror, I look at her feet, which she suddenly tucks under her skirts, a childlike gesture. I pull back the material. She isn't wearing thick, dark socks; frost-bitten toes and heels have swelled, rotted, and blackened. I slide up the polypro of her long underwear. Dark streaks on the calves disappear under the fabric, infection spreading toward her groin. Sickened, I cover her legs. Reverend Mother lies back against her pallet, and whispers a few words in German, the gist of which I understand. "Yes," I nod sadly, "you have faith."

✝ ✝ ✝

The pilot and I haven't spoken. I'm his only passenger and wear heavy, insulated ear muffs to dull the engine noise; conversation is impossible. I'm also wearing a thin gauze mask that Sister Xavier fashioned at my request before I left the cloister. The pilot didn't ask about it. He probably thinks the mask is a religious garment. Below us is Anchorage, refreshingly green in its springtime mantle.

Xavier and I hunted but never found Leon's body. We speculated that she must have entered an abandoned mine shaft. After the start of the thaw, I found Gabrielle not far from the tunnel where the others had barricaded Praxades, and where we had entombed the corpse of Reverend Mother. I spent the last four months meditating on my own considerable responsibility in these terrible deaths. At first I raged at the twisted beliefs that corralled this small, insular society into suicidal behaviors. After talking awhile with Fiske and Xavier, though, I saw that I could have played a part in bringing a sort of heathen reasoning to their lives. However, my goal was self-protection and isolation, not involvement. Perversely, I managed to neither protect myself nor remain uninvolved. Guilt will always reside within me, a hard, frozen shard of northern Alaska.

After the pilot lands, I step down from the plane, pull the mask below my chin, and walk toward the terminal.

Travelers at the airport stare, but I've taken a gift—and a lesson—from my months in the cloister. In my soul spreads a vast emptiness, images and ideas bright stars with light-years of distance in between.

✝

STATE OF GRACE

Loren D. Estleman

"RALPH? THIS IS LYLA."

"Who the hell is Lyla?"

"Lyla Dane. I live in the apartment above you, for chrissake. We see each other every day."

"The hooker."

"You live over a dirty bookstore. What do you want for a neighbor, a freaking rocket scientist?"

Ralph Poteet sat up in bed and rumpled his mouse-colored hair. He fumbled the alarm clock off the night table and held it very close to his good eye. He laid it face down and scowled at the receiver in his hand. "It's two-thirty ayem."

"Thanks. My watch stopped and I knew if I called you you'd tell me what time it is. Listen, you're like a cop, right?"

"Not at two-thirty ayem."

"I'll give you a hundred dollars to come up here now."

He blew his nose on the sheet. "Ain't that supposed to be the other way around?"

"You coming up or not? You're not the only dick in town. I just called you because you're handy."

"What's the squeal?"

"I got a dead priest in my bed."

He said he was on his way and hung up. A square gin bottle slid off the blanket. He caught it before it hit the floor, but it was empty and he dropped it. He put on his Tyrolean hat with a feather in the band, found his suit pants on the floor half under the bed, and pulled them on over his pajamas. He stuck bare feet into his loafers and because it was October he pulled on his suitcoat, grunting with the effort. He was forty-three years old and forty pounds overweight. He looked for his gun just because it was 2:30 A.M., couldn't find it, and went out.

Lyla Dane was just five feet and ninety pounds in a pink kimono and slippers with carnations on the toes. She wore her black hair in a page-boy like Anna May Wong, but the Oriental effect fell short of her round Occidental face. "You look like crap," she told Ralph at the door.

"That's what two hours' sleep will do for you. Where's the hundred?"

"Don't you want to see the stiff first?"

"What do I look like, a pervert?"

"Yes." She opened a drawer in the telephone stand and counted a hundred in twenties and tens into his palm.

He stuck the money in a pocket and followed her through a small living room decorated by K-Mart into a smaller bedroom containing a Queen Anne bed that had cost twice as much as all the other furniture combined and took up most of the space in the room. The rest of the space was taken up by Monsignor John Breame, pastor of St. Boniface, a cathedral Ralph sometimes used to exchange pictures for money, although not so much lately because the divorce business was on the slide. He recognized the monsignor's pontifical belly under the flesh-colored satin sheet that barely covered it. The Monsignor's face was purple.

"He a regular?" Ralph found a Diamond matchstick in his suitcoat pocket and stuck the end between his teeth.

"Couple of times a month. Tonight I thought he was breathing a little hard after. Then he wasn't."

"What do you want me to do?"

"Get rid of him, what else? Cops find him here the Christers'll run me out on a cross. I got a business to run."

"Cost you another hundred."

"I just gave you a hundred."

"You're lucky I don't charge by the pound. Look at that gut."

"*You* look at it. He liked the missionary position."

"What else would he?"

She got the hundred and gave it to him. He told her to leave. "Where'll I go?"

"There's beds all over town. You probably been in half of them. Or go find an all-night movie if you don't feel like working. Don't come back before dawn."

She dressed and went out after emptying the money drawer into a shoulder bag she took with her. When she was gone Ralph helped himself to a Budweiser from her refrigerator and looked up a number in the city directory and called it from the telephone in the living room. A voice like ground glass answered.

"Bishop Stoneman?" Ralph asked.

"It's three ayem," said the voice.

"Thank you. My name is Ralph Poteet. I'm a private detective. I'm sorry to have to inform you Monsignor Breame is dead."

"Mary Mother of God! What happened?"

"I'm no expert. It looks like a heart attack."

"Mary Mother of God. In bed?"

"Yeah."

"Was he—do you know if he was in a state of grace?"

"That's what I wanted to talk to you about," Ralph said.

† † †

The man Bishop Stoneman sent was tall and gaunt, with a complexion like wet pulp and colorless hair cropped down to stubble. He had on a black coat buttoned to the neck and looked like an early martyr. He said his name was Morgan. Together they wrapped the monsignor in the soiled bedding and carried him down three flights of stairs, stopping a dozen times to rest, and laid him on the backseat of a big Buick Electra parked between streetlamps. Ralph stood guard at the car while Morgan went back up for the monsignor's clothes. It was nearly 4:00 A.M. and their only witness was a skinny cat who lost interest after a few minutes and stuck one leg up in the air to lick itself.

After a long time Morgan came down and threw the bundle onto the front seat and gave Ralph an envelope containing a hundred dollars. He said he'd handle it from there. Ralph watched him drive off and went back up to bed. He was very tired and didn't wake up until the fire sirens were grinding down in front of the building. He hadn't even heard the explosion when Lyla Dane returned to her apartment at dawn.

✝ ✝ ✝

"Go away."

"That's no way to talk to your partner," Ralph said.

"Ex-partner. You got the boot and I did, too. Now I'm giving it to you. Go away."

Dale English was a special investigator with the sheriff's department who kept his office in the City-County Building. He had a monolithic face and fierce black eyebrows like Lincoln's, creating an effect he tried to soften with pink shirts and knobby knitted ties. He and Ralph had shared a city prowl car for two years, until some evidence turned up missing from the property room. Both had been dismissed, English without prejudice because unlike the case with Ralph, none of the incriminating items had been found in English's possession.

"The boot didn't hurt you none," Ralph said.

"No, it just cost me my wife and my kid and seven years' seniority. I'd be a lieutenant now."

Ralph lowered his bulk onto the vinyl-and-aluminum chair in front of English's desk. "I wouldn't hang this on you if I could go to the city cops. Somebody's out to kill me."

"Tell whoever it is I said good luck."

"I ain't kidding."

"Me neither."

"You know that hooker got blown up this morning?"

"The gas explosion? I read about it."

"Yeah, well, it wasn't no accident. I'm betting the arson boys find a circuit breaker in the wall switch. You know what that means."

"Sure. Somebody lets himself in and turns on the gas and puts a breaker in the switch so when the guy comes home the spark blows him to hell. What was the hooker into and what was your angle?"

"It's more like who was into the hooker." Ralph told him the rest.

"This the same Monsignor Breame was found by an altar boy counting angels in his bed at the St. Boniface rectory this morning?" English asked.

"Thanks to me and this bug Morgan."

"So what do you want?"

"Hell, protection. The blowup was meant for me. Morgan thought I'd be going back to that same apartment and set it up while I was waiting for him to come down with Breame's clothes."

"Bishops don't kill people over priests that can't keep their vows in their pants."

Ralph screwed up his good eye. Its mate looked like a sour ball someone had spat out. "What world you living in? Shape the Church is in, he'd do just that to keep it quiet."

"Go away, Ralph."

"Well, pick up Morgan at least. He can't be hard to find. He looks like one of those devout creeps you see skulking around in paintings of the Crucifixion.

"I don't have jurisdiction in the city."

"That ain't why you won't do it. Hey, I told IAD you didn't have nothing to do with what went down in Property."

"It would've carried more weight if you'd submitted to a lie detector test. Mine was inconclusive." He paged through a report on his desk without looking at it. "I'll run the name Morgan and the description you gave me through the computer and see what it coughs up. There won't be anything."

"Thanks, buddy."

"You sure you didn't take pictures? It'd be your style to try and put the squeeze on a bishop."

"I thought about it, but my camera's in hock." Ralph got up. "You can get me at my place. They got the fire out before it reached my floor."

"That was lucky. Gin flames are the hardest to put out."

✝ ✝ ✝

He was driving a brand-new red Riviera he had promised to sell for a lawyer friend who was serving two years for suborning to commit perjury, only he hadn't gotten around to it yet. He parked in a handicapped zone near his building and climbed stairs smelling of smoke and firemen's rubber boots. Inside his apartment, which was also his office, he rewound the tape on his answering machine and played back a threatening call from a loan shark named Zwingman, a reminder from a dentist's receptionist with a Nutra-Sweet voice that last month's root canal was still unpaid for, and a message from a heavy breather that he had to play back three times before deciding it was a man. He was staring toward the door, his attention on the tape, when a square of white paper slithered over the threshold.

That day he was wearing his legal gun, a short-nosed .38 Colt, in a clip on his belt, and an orphan High Standard .22 magnum derringer in an ankle holster. Drawing the Colt, he lunged and tore open the door just in time to hear the street door closing below. He swung around and crossed to the street window. Through it he saw a narrow figure in a long black coat and the back of a closecropped head crossing against traffic to the other side. The man rounded the corner and vanished.

Ralph holstered the revolver and picked up the note. It was addressed to him in a round, shaped hand.

> Mr. Poteet:
> If it is not inconvenient, your presence at my home could prove to your advantage and mine.
>
> > Cordially,
> > Philip Stoneman,
> > Bishop-in-Ordinary

Clipped to it was a hundred-dollar bill.

Bishop Stoneman lived in a refurbished brownstone in a neighborhood that the city had reclaimed from slum by evicting its residents and sandblasting graffiti off the buildings. The bell was answered by a youngish bald man in a dark suit and clerical collar who introduced himself as Brother Edwards and directed Ralph to a curving staircase, then retired to be seen no more. Ralph didn't hear Morgan climbing behind him until something hard probed his right kidney. A hand patted him down and removed the Colt from its clip. "End of the hall."

The bishop was a tall old man, nearly as thin as Morgan, with iron-gray hair and a face that fell away to the white shackle of his collar. He rose from behind a redwood desk to greet his visitor in an old-fashioned black frock that made him look like a crow. The room was large and square and smelled of leather from the books on the built-in shelves and pipe tobacco. Morgan entered behind Ralph and closed the door.

"Thank you for coming, Mr. Poteet. Please sit down."

"Thank Ben Franklin." But he settled into a deep leather chair that gripped his buttocks like a big hand in a soft glove.

"I'm grateful for this chance to thank you in person," Stoneman said, sitting in his big swivel. "I'm very disappointed in Monsignor Breame. I'd hoped that he would take my place at the head of the diocese."

"You bucking for cardinal?"

He smiled. "I suppose you've shown yourself worthy of confidence. Yes, His Holiness has offered me the red hat. The appointment will be announced next month."

"That why you tried to croak me? I guess your right bower cashing in in a hooker's bed would look bad in Rome."

One corner of the desk supported a silver tray containing two long-stemmed glasses and a cut-crystal decanter half full of ruby liquid. Stoneman removed the stopper and filled both glasses. "This is an excellent Madeira. I confess that the austere life allows me two mild vices. The other is tobacco."

"What are we celebrating?" Ralph didn't pick up his glass.

"Your new appointment as chief of diocesan security. The position pays well and the hours are regular."

"In return for which I forget about Monsignor Breame?"

"And entrust all related material to me. You took pictures, of, course." Stoneman sipped from his glass.

Ralph lifted his. "I'd be pretty stupid not to, considering what happened to Lyla Dane."

"I heard about the tragedy. That child's soul could have been saved."

"You should've thought about that before your boy Morgan croaked her," Ralph gulped off half his wine. It tasted bitter.

The bishop laid a bony hand atop an ancient ornate Bible on the desk. His guest thought he was about to swear his innocence. "This belonged to St. Thomas. More, not Aquinas. I have a weakness for religious antiques."

"Thought you only had two vices." The air in the room stirred slightly. Ralph turned to see who had entered, but his vision was thickening. Morgan was a shimmering shadow. The glass dropped from Ralph's hand. He bent to retrieve it and came up with the derringer. Stoneman's shout echoed. Ralph fired twice at the shadow and pitched headfirst into its depths.

† † †

He awoke feeling pretty much the way he did most mornings, with his head throbbing and his stomach turning over. He wanted to turn over with it, but he was stretched out on a hard, flat surface with his ankles strapped down and his arms tied above his head. He was looking up at water-stained tile. His joints ached.

"The sedative was in the stem of your glass," Stoneman was saying. He was out of Ralph's sight and Ralph had the impression he'd been talking for a while. "You've been out for two hours. The unpleasant effect is temporary, rather like a hangover."

"Did I get him'?" Ralph's tongue moved sluggishly.

"No, you missed rather badly. It required persuasion to get Morgan to carry you down here to the basement instead of killing you on the spot. He was quite upset."

Ralph squirmed. There was something familiar about the position he was tied in. For some reason he thought of Mrs. Thornton, his ninth-grade American Lit. teacher. *What is the significance of Poe's "Pit and the Pendulum" to the transcendentalist movement?* His organs shriveled.

"Another antique," said the bishop. "The Inquisition did not end when General Lasalle entered Madrid, but went on for several years in the provinces. This Particular rack was still in use after Torquemada's death. The gears are original. The wheel is new, and of course I had to replace the ropes. Morgan?"

A shoe scraped the floor and a spoked shadow fluttered across Ralph's vision. His arms tightened. He gasped.

"That's enough. We don't want to put Mr. Poteet back under." To Ralph: "Morgan just returned from your apartment. He found neither pictures nor film nor even a camera. Where are they?"

"I was lying. I didn't take no pictures."

"Morgan."

Ralph shrieked.

"Enough! His Holiness is sensitive about scandal, Mr. Poteet. I won't have Monsignor Breame's indiscretions bar me from the Vatican. Who is keeping the pictures for you?"

"There ain't no pictures, honest."

"Morgan!"

A socket started to slip. Ralph screamed and blubbered.

"Enough!" Stoneman's fallen-away face moved into Ralph's vision. His eyes were fanatic. "A few more turns will sever your spine. You could be spoon-fed for the rest of your life. Do you think that after failing to kill you in that apartment I would hesitate to cripple you? Where are the pictures?"

"I didn't take none!"

"Morgan!"

"*No!*" It ended in a howl. His armpits were on fire. The ropes creaked.

"Police! Don't move!"

The bishop's face jerked away. The spoked shadow fluttered. The tension went out of Ralph's arms suddenly, and relief poured into his joints. A shot flattened the air. Two more answered it. Something struck the bench Ralph was lying on and drove a splinter into his back. He thought at first he was shot, but the pain was nothing; he'd just been through worse. He squirmed onto his hip and saw Morgan, one black-clad arm stained and glistening, leveling a heavy automatic at a target behind Ralph's back. Scrambling out of the line of fire, Ralph jerked his bound hands and the rack's wheel, six feet in diameter with handles bristling from it like a ship's helm, spun around. One of the handles slapped the gun from Morgan's hand. Something cracked past Ralph's left ear and Morgan fell back against the tile wall and slid down it. The shooting stopped.

Ralph wriggled onto his other hip. A man he didn't know in a houndstooth coat with a revolver in his hand had Bishop Stoneman spread-eagled against a wall and was groping in his robes for weapons. Dale English came off the stairs with the Luger he had been carrying since Ralph was his partner. He bent over Morgan on the floor, then straightened and holstered the gun. He looked at Ralph. "I guess you're okay."

"I am if you got a pocketknife."

"Arson boys found the circuit breaker in the wall switch just like you said." He cut Ralph's arms free and sawed through the straps on his ankles. "When you didn't answer your telephone I went to your place and found Stoneman's note."

"He confessed to the hooker's murder."

"I know. I heard him."

"How the hell long were you listening?"

"We had to have enough to pin him to it, didn't we?"

"You son of a bitch. You just wanted to hear me holler."

"Couldn't help it. You sure got lungs."

"I got to go to the toilet."

"Stick around after," English said. "I need a statement to hand to the city boys. They won't like County sticking its face in this."

Ralph hobbled upstairs. When he was through in the bathroom he found his hat and coat and headed out. At the front door he turned around and went back into the bishop's study, where he hoisted Thomas More's Bible under one arm. He knew a bookseller who would probably give him at least a hundred for it.

✝

Jemima Shore's First Case

Antonia Fraser

At the sound of the first scream, the girl in bed merely stirred and turned over. The second scream was much louder and the girl sat up abruptly, pushing back the meagre bedclothes. She was wearing a high-necked white cotton nightdress with long sleeves which was too big for her. The girl was thin, almost skinny, with long straight pale-red hair and oddly shaped slanting eyes in a narrow face.

Her name was Jemima Shore and she was fifteen years old.

The screams came again: by now they sounded quite blood-curdling to the girl alone in the small room—or was it that they were getting nearer? It was quite dark. Jemima Shore clambered out of bed and went to the window. She was tall, with long legs sticking out from below the billowing white cotton of the nightie, legs which like the rest of her body were too thin for beauty. Jemima pulled back the curtain which was made of some unlined flowered stuff. Between the curtain and the glass was an iron grille. She could not get out. Or, to put it another way, whatever was outside in the thick darkness, could not get in.

It was the sight of the iron grille which brought Jemima properly to her senses. She remembered at last exactly where she was: sleeping in a ground-floor room at a boarding-school in Sussex called the Convent of the Blessed Eleanor. Normally Jemima was a day-girl at the Catholic boarding-school, an unusual situation which had developed when her mother came to live next door to Blessed Eleanor's in her father's absence abroad. The situation was unusual not only because Jemima was the only day-girl at Blessed Eleanor's but also because Jemima was theoretically at least a Protestant: not that Mrs. Shore's vague ideas of religious upbringing really justified such a positive description.

Now Mrs. Shore had been called abroad to nurse her husband who was recovering from a bad attack of jaundice, and Reverend Mother Ancilla, headmistress of the convent, had agreed to take Jemima as a temporary boarder. Hence the little ground-floor room—all that was free to house her—and hence for that matter the voluminous nightdress, Mrs. Shore's ideas of nightclothes for her teenage daughter hardly according with the regulations at Blessed Eleanor's. To Jemima, still staring uncomprehendingly out into the darkness which lay beyond the grille and the glass, as though she might perceive the answer, none of this explained why she should now suddenly be awakened in the middle of the night by sounds which suggested someone was being murdered or at least badly beaten up: the last sounds you would expect to hear coming out of the tranquil silence which generally fell upon the Blessed Eleanor's after nine o'clock at night.

What *was* the time? It occurred to Jemima that her mother had left behind her own smart little travelling-clock as a solace in the long conventual nights. Squinting at its luminous hands—somehow she did not like to turn on the light and make herself visible through the flimsy curtains to whatever was outside in the night world—Jemima saw it was three o'clock. Jemima was not generally fearful either of solitude or the dark (perhaps because she was an only child) but the total indifference with which the whole convent appeared to be greeting the screams struck her as even more alarming than the noise itself. The big red-brick building, built in the twenties, housed not only a girls' boarding-school but the community of nuns who looked after them; the two areas were divided by the chapel.

The chapel! All of a sudden Jemima realized not only that the screams were coming from that direction but also—another sinister thought—she might conceivably be the only person within earshot. The so-called "girls' guest-room" (generally old girls) was at the very edge of the lay part of the building. Although Jemima had naturally never visited the nuns' quarters on the other side, she had had the tiny windows of their cells pointed out by her best friend Rosabelle Powerstock, an authority on the whole fascinating subject of nuns. The windows were high up, far away from the chapel.

Was it from a sense of duty, or was it simply due to that ineradicable curiosity in her nature to which the nuns periodically drew grim attention suggesting it might be part of her unfortunate Protestant heritage . . . at all events, Jemima felt impelled to open her door a crack. She did so gingerly. There was a small night-light burning in the long corridor before the tall statue of the Foundress of the Order of the Tower of Ivory—Blessed Eleanor, dressed in the black habit the nuns still wore. The statue's arms were outstretched.

Jemima moved warily in the direction of the chapel. The screams had ceased but she did hear some other sound, much fainter, possibly the noise of crying. The night-light cast a dim illumination and once Jemima passed the statue with its long welcoming arms—welcoming, that is, in daylight; they now seemed to be trying to entrap her—Jemima found herself in virtual darkness.

As Jemima cautiously made her way in to the chapel, the lingering smell of incense began to fill her nostrils, lingering from that night's service of benediction, that morning's mass, and fifty other years of masses said to incense in the same place. She entered the chapel itself—the door was open—and perceived a few candles burning in front of a statue to her left. The incense smell was stronger. The little red sanctuary lamp seemed far away. Then Jemima stumbled over something soft and shapeless on the floor of the central aisle.

Jemima gave a sharp cry and at the same time the bundle moved, gave its own anguished shriek and said something which sounded like: "Zeeazmoof, Zeeazmoof." Then the bundle sat up and revealed itself to be not so much a bundle as an Italian girl in Jemima's own form called Sybilla.

At this point Jemima understood that what Sybilla was actually saying between sobs was: "She 'as moved, she 'as moved," in her characteristic strong Italian accent. There was a total contrast between this sobbing creature and the daytime Sybilla, a plump and rather jolly dark-haired girl, who jangled in illicit gold chains and bracelets, and wore more than a hint of equally illicit make-up. Jemima did not know Sybilla particularly well despite sharing classes with her. She pretended to herself that this was because Sybilla (unlike Jemima and her friends) had no interest in art, literature, history or indeed anything very much except Sybilla herself; pleasure, parties and the sort of people you met at parties, principally male. Sybilla was also old for her form—seventeen already—whereas Jemima was young for it, so that there was a considerable age gap between them. But the truth was that Jemima avoided Sybilla because she was a princess (albeit an Italian one, not a genuine British Royal) and Jemima, being middle class and proud of it, had no wish to be accused of snobbery.

The discovery of Sybilla—Princess Maria Sybilla Magdalena Graffo di Santo Stefano to give her her full title—in the chapel only deepened the whole mystery. Knowing Sybilla, religious mania, a sudden insane desire to pray alone in the chapel at night, to make a novena for example, simply could not be the answer to her presence. Sybilla was unashamedly lazy where religion was concerned, having to be dragged out of bed to go to mass even when it was obligatory on Sundays and feast days, protesting plaintively, like a big black cat ejected from the fireside. She regarded the religious fervour of certain other girls, such as Jemima's friend Rosabelle Powerstock, with goodnatured amazement.

"So boring" she was once overheard to say about the Feast of the Immaculate Conception (a holiday of obligation). "Why do we have this thing? I think we don't have this thing in Italy." It was fortunate that Sybilla's theological reflections on this occasion had never come to the ears of Reverend Mother Ancilla who would have quickly set to rights this unworthy descendant of a great Roman family (and even, delicious rumour said, of a Pope or two).

Yes, all in all, religious mania in Princess Sybilla could definitely be ruled out.

"Sybilla," said Jemima, touching her shoulder, "don't cry—"

At that moment came at last the sound for which Jemima had been subconsciously waiting since she first awoke: the characteristic swoosh of a nun in full habit advancing at high speed, rosary at her belt clicking, rubber heels twinkling down the marble corridor.

"Sybilla, *Jemima?*" The rising note of surprise on the last name was evident in the sharp but controlled voice of Sister Veronica, the Infirmarian. Then authority took over and within minutes nun-like phrases such as "To bed at once both of you" and "No more talking till you see Reverend Mother in the morning" had calmed Sybilla's convulsive sobs. The instinctive reaction of nuns in a crisis, Jemima had noted, was to treat teenage girls as children; or perhaps they always mentally treated them as children, it just came to the surface in a crisis. Sybilla after all was nearly grown-up, certainly if her physical appearance was any guide. Jemima sighed; was she to be hustled to bed with her curiosity, now quite rampant, unsatisfied?

It was fortunate for Jemima that before dispatching her charges, Sister Veronica did at least make a quick inspection of the chapel—as though to see what other delinquent pupils might be lurking there in the middle of the night.

"What happened, Sybilla?" Jemima took the opportunity to whisper. "What frightened you? I thought you were being murdered—"

Sybilla extended one smooth brown arm (unlike most of the girls at Blessed Eleanor's, she was perpetually sun-tanned, and unlike Jemima, she had somehow avoided wearing the regulation white nightdress).

"Oh, my God, Jemima!" It came out as "Omigod, Geemima! I am telling you. She 'as moved!"

"Who moved, Sybilla?"

"The statue. You know, the one they call the Holy Nelly. She moved her arms towards me. She 'as touched me, Jemima. It was *miraculo*. How do you say? A mir-a-cul."

Then sister Veronica returned and imposed silence, silence on the whole subject.

But of course it was not to be like that. The next morning at assembly the whole upper school, Jemima realized, was buzzing with excitement in which words like "miracle," "Sybilla's miracle" and "there was a miracle, did you hear" could be easily made out. Compared to the news of Sybilla's miracle—or the Blessed Eleanor's miracle depending on your point of view—the explanation of Sybilla's presence near the chapel in the middle of the night passed almost unnoticed: except by Jemima Shore that is, who definitely did not believe in miracles and was therefore still more avid to hear about Sybilla's experiences than she had been the night before. Jemima decided to tackle her just after Sister Hilary's maths lesson, an experience calculated to leave Sybilla unusually demoralized.

Sybilla smiled at Jemima, showing those dimples in her pinkish-olive cheeks which were her most attractive feature. (Come to think of it, was that pinkish glow due to a discreet application of blush-on? But Jemima, no nun, had other things on her mind.)

"Eet's ridiculous," murmured Sybilla with a heavy sigh; there was a clank as her gold charm bracelet hit the desk; it struck Jemima that the nuns' rosaries and Sybilla's jewellery made roughly the same sound and served the same purpose, to advertise their presence. "But you know these nuns, they won't let me write to my father. So boring. Oh yes, they will let me *write,* but it seems they must read the letter. Mamma made them do that, or maybe they did it, I don't know which. Mamma is so holy, Omigod, she's like a nun . . . Papa"—Sybilla showed her dimples again—"Papa, he is—how do you say—a bit of a bad dog."

"A gay dog," suggested Jemima helpfully. Sybilla ignored the interruption. She was busy speaking affectionately, even yearningly, of Prince Graffo di Santo Stefano's bad (or gay) dog-like tendencies which seemed to include pleasure in many forms. (The Princess being apparently in contrast a model of austere piety, Jemima realized that Sybilla was very much her father's daughter.) The Prince's activities included racing in famous motor cars and escorting famously beautiful women and skiing down famous slopes and holidaying on famous yachts, and other things, amusing things. "Papa he 'ates to be bored, he 'ates it!" These innocuous pursuits had according to Sybilla led the killjoy Princess to forbid her husband access to his daughter: this being Italy there could of course be no divorce either by the laws of the country or for that matter by the laws of Mother Church to which the Princess at least strictly adhered.

"But it's true, Papa, he doesn't want a divorce either," admitted Sybilla. "Then he might have to marry—I don't know who but he might have to marry this woman or that woman. That would be terrible for Papa. So boring. No, he just want some money, poor papa, he has no money, Mama has all the money, I think it's not fair that, she should *give* him the money, si, he is her *marito,* her 'usband, she should give it to him. What do you think, Jemima?"

Jemima, feeling the first stirrings of primitive feminism in her breast at this description of the Santo Stefano family circumstances, remained politely silent on that subject.

Instead: "And the statue, Sybilla?" she probed gently.

"Ah." Sybilla paused. "Well, you see how it is, Jemima. I write to him. I write anything, amusing things. And I put them in a letter but I don't like the nuns to read these things so—" she paused again. "So I am making an arrangement with Gregory," ended Sybilla with a slight but noticeable air of defiance.

"Yes, Gregory," she repeated. "That man. The gardener, the chauffeur, the odd-things man, whatever he is, the taxi-man."

Jemima stared at her. She knew Gregory, the convent's new odd-job man, a surprisingly young fellow to be trusted in this all-female establishment, but all the same—

"And I am placing these letters under the statue of the Holy Nelly in the night," continued Sybilla with more confidence. "To wake up? Omigod, no problem. To go to sleep early, *that* is the problem. They make us go to bed like children here. And he, Gregory, is collecting them when he brings the post in the morning. Later he will leave me an answer which he takes from the post office. That day there will be one red flower in that big vase under the statue. And so we come to the night when I am having my *miraculo*," she announced triumphantly.

But Jemima, who did not believe in miracles, fell silent once more at what followed: Sybilla's vivid description of the statue's waving arms, warm touch just as she was about to hide the letter (which she then retrieved) and so forth and so on—an account which Jemima had a feeling was rapidly growing even as she told it.

"So you see I am flinging myself into the chapel," concluded Sybilla. "And sc-r-r-reaming and sc-r-r-reaming. Till you, Jemima *cara,* have found me. Because you only are near me!"

Well, that at least was true, thought Jemima: because she had formed the strong impression that Sybilla, for all her warmth and confiding charm was not telling her the truth; or not the whole truth. Just as Jemima's reason would not let her believe in miracles, her instinct would not let her believe in Sybilla's story, at any rate not all of it.

Then both Jemima and Sybilla were swirled up in the sheer drama of Sister Elizabeth's lesson on her favourite Wordsworth ("Oh, the lovely man!").

"Once did she hold the gorgeous East in fee," intoned Sister Liz in a sonorous voice before adding rather plaintively: "Sybilla, do wake up; this is *your* Venice after all, as well as dear Wordsworth's." Sybilla raised her head reluctantly from her desk where it had sunk as though under the weight of the thick dark hair, unconfined by any of the bands prescribed by convent rules. It was clear that her thoughts were very far from Venice, "hers" or anyone else's, and even further from Wordsworth.

Another person who did not believe in miracles or at any rate did not believe in this particular miracle was Reverend Mother Ancilla. Whether or not she was convinced by Sybilla's explanation of sleepwalking—"since a child I am doing it"—Mother Ancilla dismissed the mere idea of a moving statue.

"Nonsense child, you were asleep at the time. You've just said so. You dreamt the whole thing. No more talk of miracles please, Sybilla; the ways of Our Lord and indeed of the Blessed Eleanor may be mysterious but they are not as mysterious as *that*," announced Mother Ancilla firmly with the air of one to whom they were not in fact at all that mysterious in the first place. "Early nights for the next fourteen days—no, Sybilla, that is what I said, you need proper rest for your mind which is clearly, contrary to the impression given by your report, over-active . . ."

Even Sybilla dared do no more than look sulky-faced with Mother Ancilla in such a mood. The school as a whole was compelled to take its cue from Sybilla: with no further grist to add to the mill of gossip, gradually talk of Sybilla's miracle died away to be replaced by scandals such as the non-election of the Clitheroe twins Annie and Pettie (short for Annunziata and Perpetua) as Children of Mary. This was on the highly unfair grounds that they had appeared in a glossy magazine in a series called "Cloistered Moppets" wearing some Mary Quantish version of a nun's habit.

Jemima Shore did sometimes wonder whether Sybilla's illicit correspondence still continued. She also gazed from time to time at Gregory as he went about his tasks, all those tasks which could not be performed by the nuns themselves (surprisingly few of them as a matter of fact, picking up and delivering the post being one of them). Gregory was a solid-looking individual in his thirties with nice thick curly hair cut quite short, but otherwise in no way striking; were he not the only man around the convent grounds (with the exception of visiting priests in the morning and evening and parents at weekends) Jemima doubted whether she would have remembered his face. But he was a perfectly pleasant person, if not disposed to chat, not to Jemima Shore at least. The real wonder was, thought Jemima, that Sybilla had managed to corrupt him in the first place.

It was Jemima's turn to sigh. She had better face facts. Sybilla was rich—that much was obvious from her appearance—and she was also voluptuous. Another sigh from Jemima at the thought of Sybilla's figure, so much more like that of an Italian film star—if one fed on dollops of spaghetti—than anything Jemima could achieve. No doubt both factors, money and figure, had played their part in enabling Sybilla to capture Gregory. It was time to concentrate on other things—winning the English Prize for example (which meant beating Rosabelle) or securing the part of Hamlet in the school play (which meant beating everybody).

When Sybilla appeared at benediction on Saturday escorted by a middle-aged woman, and a couple of men in camel-haired coats, one very tall and dark, the other merely dark, Jemima did spare some further thought for the Santo Stefano family. Were these relations? The convent rules were strict enough for it to be unlikely they were mere friends, especially when Mamma Principessa was keeping such a strict eye on access to her daughter. Besides, the woman did bear a certain resemblance to Sybilla, her heavily busted figure suggesting how Sybilla's voluptuous curves might develop in middle age.

Jemima's curiosity was satisfied with unexpected speed: immediately after benediction Sybilla waved in her direction, and with wreathed smiles and much display of dimple, introduced her cousin Tancredi, her Aunt Cristiana and her Uncle Umberto.

"Ah now, Jemima, you come with us, you come with us for dinner? Yes, I insist. You have saved me. *Si, si,* it was her"—to her relations. To Jemima she confided: "I am not expecting them. They come to spy on the naughty Sybilla," dimples again. "But listen, Tancredi, he is very much like my Papa, now you know what Papa looks like, 'andsome, yes? And Papa, he like Tancredi very much, so you come?"

"I don't have a Permission—" began Jemima rather desperately. One look at Tancredi had already told her that he approximated only too wonderfully to her latest ideal of masculine attraction, derived partly from the portrait of Lord Byron at the front of her O-level text, and partly from a character in a Georgette Heyer novel called *Devil's Cub*. (Like many would-be intellectuals, Jemima had a secret passion for Georgette Heyer. Jemima, with Rosabelle, Annie, Pettie and the rest of her coterie, were relieved when from time to time some older indisputably intellectual female would announce publicly in print, tribute perhaps to her own youth, that Georgette Heyer was an important if neglected literary phenomenon.)

Alas, Jemima felt in no way ready to encounter Tancredi, the man of her dreams, at this precise juncture: she was aware that her hair, her best feature, hung lankly, there having been no particular reason in recent days to wash it. Her "home clothes" in which she would be allowed to emerge from the convent, belonged to a much shorter girl (the girl Mrs. Shore had in fact bought the clothes for, twelve months previously), nor could they be passed off as mini-skirted because they were too unfashionable.

One way and another, Jemima was torn between excitement and apprehension when Sybilla, in her most wayward mood, somehow overrode these very real difficulties ("But it's charming, the long English legs; Tancredi has seen you, *ma che bella!* Yes, yes, I am telling you . . .") and also, even more surprisingly, convinced Mother Ancilla to grant permission.

"An unusual friendship, dear Jemima," commented the Reverend Mother drily, before adding: "But perhaps you and Sybilla have both something to learn from each other." Her bright shrewd little eyes beneath the white wimple moved down Jemima's blouse and that short distance covered by her skirt.

"Is that a mini-skirt?" asked Mother Ancilla sharply. "No, no, I see it is not. And your dear mother away . . ." Mother Ancilla's thoughts were clearly clicking rapidly like the beads of her rosary. "What will the Marchesa think? Now, child, go immediately to Sister Baptist in the sewing-room, I have a feeling that Cecilia Clitheroe"—she mentioned the name of a recent postulant, some relation to Annie and Pettie—"is about your size." Marvelling, not for the first time, at the sheer practical worldliness of so-called unworldly nuns, Jemima found herself wearing not so much a drooping blouse and outmoded skirt as a black suit trimmed in beige braid which looked as if it had come from Chanel or thereabouts.

Without the suit, would Jemima really have captured Tancredi in quite the way she did at the dinner which followed? For undoubtedly, as Jemima related it to Rosabelle afterwards, Tancredi *was* captured and Rosabelle, summing up all the evidence, agreed that it must have been so. Otherwise why the slow burning looks from those dark eyes, the wine glass held in her direction, even on one occasion a gentle pressure of a knee elegantly clad in a silk suit of a particular shade of blue just a little too bright to be English? As for Tancredi himself, was he not well worth capturing, the muscular figure beneath the dandyish suit, nothing effeminate about Tancredi, the atmosphere he carried with him of international sophistication—or was it just the delicious smell of *Eau Sauvage?* (Jemima knew it was *Eau Sauvage* because on Rosabelle's recommendation she had given some to her father for Christmas; not that she had smelt it on him subsequently beyond one glorious whiff at Christmas dinner itself.)

As for Sybilla's uncle and aunt, the Marchesa spoke very little but when she did so it was in careful English, delivered, whether intentionally or not, in a reproachful tone as though Jemima's presence at dinner demanded constant explanation if not apology. Jemima's answers to the Marchesa's enquiries about her background and previous education seemed to disgust her particularly; at one point, hearing that Jemima's father was serving in the British army, the Marchesa simply stared at her. Jemima hoped that the stare was due to national prejudice based on wartime memories, but feared it was due to simple snobbery.

Uncle Umberto was even quieter, a short pock-marked Italian who would have been plausible as a waiter, had he not been an Italian nobleman. Both uncle and aunt, after the first unfortunate interrogation, spoke mainly in Italian to their niece: family business, Jemima assumed, leaving Tancredi free for his pursuit of Jemima while their attention was distracted.

The next day: "You 'ave made a conquest, Jemima" related Sybilla proudly. "Tancredi finds you so int-ell-igent"—she drawled out the word—"and he asks if all English girls are so int-ell-igent, but I say that you are famous for being clever, so clever that you must find him so stu-pid!"

"I'm not all *that* clever, Sybilla." Jemima despite herself was nettled; for once she had hoped her attraction lay elsewhere than in her famous intelligence. That might win her the English Prize (she had just defeated Rosabelle) but intelligent was not quite how she wished to be regarded in those sophisticated international circles in which in her secret daydreams she was now dwelling.

Tancredi's letter, when it came, did not however dwell upon Jemima's intelligence but more of her particular brand of English beauty, her strawberries-and-cream complexion (Sybilla's blush-on had been liberally applied), her hair the colour of Italian sunshine and so forth and so on in a way that Jemima had to admit could scarcely be bettered even in daydream. The method by which the letter arrived was less satisfactory: the hand of Sybilla, who said that it had been enclosed in a letter from Tancredi's sister Maria Gloria (letters from accredited female relations were not generally opened). Had Sybilla read the letter which arrived sealed with sellotape? If she had, Jemima was torn between embarrassment and pride at the nature of the contents.

Several more letters followed until one day—"He wants to see you again. Of course he wants to see you again!" exclaimed Sybilla. "He loves you. Doesn't he say so always?" Jemima shot her a look: so Sybilla did know the letters' contents. To her surprise Jemima found that she was not exactly eager to see Tancredi again, despite the fact that his smuggled letters had become the centre of her emotional existence. Tancredi's passion for Jemima had something of the miraculous about it—Jemima smiled to herself wryly, she who did not believe in miracles—and she couldn't help being worried that the miracle might not happen a second time. . . . It was in the end more sheer curiosity than sheer romance which made Jemima continue to discuss Sybilla's daring idea for a rendezvous. This was to be in Jemima's own ground-floor room no less— Tancredi to be admitted through the grille left open for the occasion.

"The key!" cried Jemima "No, it's impossible. How would we ever get the key?"

"Oh Jemima, you who are so clever," purred Sybilla, looking more than ever like a fat black cat denied its bowl of cream. "Lovely Jemima . . . I know you will be thinking of something. Otherwise I am thinking that Tancredi goes to Italy and you are not seeing him. So boring. He has so many girls there."

"Like Papa?" Jemima could not resist asking. But Sybilla merely pouted.

"I could give such a long, long letter to Papa if you say yes," she sighed. "I'm frightened to speak to Gregory now, you know. Papa thinks—" She paused. "He's a bit frightened too. That moving statue." Sybilla shuddered.

"No, Sybilla," said Jemima.

Nevertheless in her languorously persistent way, Sybilla refused to let the subject of Tancredi's projected daring expedition to Blessed Eleanor's drop. Jemima for her part was torn between a conviction that it was quite impossible to secure the key to the grille in front of her ground-floor window and a pride which made her reluctant to admit defeat, defeat at the hands of the nuns. In the end pride won, as perhaps Jemima had known all along that it would. She found by observing Sister Dympna, who swept her room and was responsible for locking the grille at darkness, that the grille was opened by a key, but snapped shut of its own accord. From there it was a small step to trying an experiment: a piece of blackened cardboard between grille and jamb, and the attention of Sister Dympna distracted at the exact moment the busy little nun was slamming the grille shut.

It worked. Jemima herself had to close the grille properly after Sister Dympna left. That night Jemima lay awake, conscious of the outer darkness and the window through which Tancredi would come if she wanted him to come. She began to review the whole thrilling affair, beginning so unpropitiously as it had seemed at the time, with Sybilla's screams in the night. She remembered that night in the chapel with the terrified girl, the smell of incense in her nostrils, and then switched her thoughts to her first and so far her only encounter with Tancredi . . . Her own personal miracle. She heard Sybilla's voice: "*Miraculo.*"

But I don't believe in miracles, said the coldly reasonable voice of Jemima enclosed in the darkness, away from the seductive Mediterranean charm of Sybilla. And there's something else too: my instinct. I thought she was lying that first night, didn't I? Why did the statue move? A further disquieting thought struck Jemima. She got out of bed, switched on the light, and gazed steadily at her reflection in the small mirror over the basin.

"Saturday," said Jemima the next morning; she sounded quite cold. "Maria Gloria had better pass the message." But Sybilla, in her pleasure at having her own way, did not seem to notice the coldness. "And Sybilla—" added Jemima.

"Cara?"

"Give me the letter for your father in good time because I've got permission to go over to my own house to borrow some decent dresses of my mother's, she's coming back, you know. As I may not see you later, give me the letter before I go." Sybilla enfolded Jemima in a soft, warm, highly scented embrace.

By Saturday, Jemima found herself torn between two exactly contradictory feelings. Half of her longed for the night, for the rendezvous—whatever it might bring—and the other half wished that darkness would never come, that she could remain for the rest of her life, suspended, just waiting for Tancredi . . . Was this what being in love meant? For Jemima, apart from one or two holiday passions, for her father's young subalterns, considered that she had never been properly in love; although it was a matter much discussed between herself and Rosabelle (of her other friends the Clitheroe twins, Annie and Pettie being too merrily wanton and Bridget too strictly pious to join in these talks). Then there was another quite different side to her character, the cool and rational side, which simply said: I want to investigate, I want to find out what's going on, however painful the answer.

Jemima made her visit to her parents' home driven by the silent Gregory and chaperoned by Sister Veronica who was cross enough at the waste of time to agree with Jemima that the garden was in an awful state, and rush angrily at the neglected branches—"Come along, Jemima, we'll do it together." Jemima took a fork to the equally neglected beds and dug diligently out of range of Sister Veronica's conversation. (Gregory made no move to help but sat in the car.) Jemima herself was also extremely quiet on the way back, which with Gregory's enigmatic silence, meant that Sister Veronica could chatter on regarding the unkempt state of the Shore home ("Your poor dear mother . . . no gardener") to her heart's content. For the rest of the day and evening, Jemima had to keep the investigative side of her nature firmly to the fore. She found her emotional longings too painful.

Darkness fell on the convent. From the corner of her window— unbarred or rather with a crack left in the grille, so that only someone who knew it would open would be able to detect it—Jemima could watch as the yellow lights in the high dormitories were gradually extinguished. Sybilla was sleeping somewhere up there in the room which she shared with a monkey-like French girl called Elaine, who even in the summer at Blessed Eleanor's was huddled against the cold: "She is too cold to wake up. She is like your little mouse who sleeps," Sybilla had told Jemima. But Sybilla now was certainly watched at night and could not move about freely as she had once done.

On the other side of the building were the nuns, except for those on duty in the dormitories or Sister Veronica in the infirmary. Jemima had no idea where Mother Ancilla slept—alone perhaps in the brief night allowed to nuns before the early morning mass? But Mother Ancilla was another subject about which Jemima preferred not to think; the nun was so famously percipient that it had required some mental daring for Jemima even to say goodnight to her. She feared that the dark shrewd eyes might see right through to her intentions.

In her room, Jemima decided not to change into her convent night gown; she snuggled under the covers in jeans (collected that afternoon from home—strictly not allowed at Blessed Eleanor's)—and a skimpy black polo-necked jersey. In spite of herself, convent habits inspired in her a surprising desire to pray.

Reflecting that to do so even by rationalist standards, could not exactly do any *harm*, Jemima said three Hail Marys.

Oddly enough it was not until Jemima heard the faint—very faint— sound of someone rapping on the window, which was her clue to wind back the grille, that it occurred to Jemima that what she was doing might not only be foolhardy but actively dangerous. By then of course it was too late. She had no course now but to pull back the grille as silently as possible—since Sybilla's escapade the nuns had taken to patrolling the outside corridor from time to time. She raised the window cautiously.

Over the sill, dressed as far as she could make out entirely in black, at any rate in black jersey (remarkably similar to her own) and black trousers, with black rubber-soled shoes, came Tancredi. The smell of *Eau Sauvage* filled the room: for one wild moment the sweetness of it made Jemima regret . . . then she allowed herself to be caught into Tancredi's arms. He kissed her, his rather thin lips forcing apart her own.

Then Tancredi stood back a little and patted her lightly on her denim-clad thigh, "What protection! You are certainly not anxious to seduce me, *cara*," he said softly. Jemima could sense him smiling in the darkness. "This is a little bit like a nun, yes?" He touched her breast in the tight black jersey. "This not so much."

"Tancredi, you mustn't, I mean—" What did she mean? She knew what she meant. She had it all planned, didn't she?

"Tancredi, listen, you've simply got to take Sybilla's packet, her letter that is, it's quite thick, the letter, you must take it and then go. You see, the nuns are very suspicious. I couldn't let you know, but I have a feeling someone suspects . . . Mother Ancilla, she's the headmistress, she's awfully beady." Jemima was conscious she was babbling on. "So you must take the letter and go."

"Yes, I will take the letter. In good time. Or now, *tesoro*, if you like. I don't want to make tr-r-rouble for you." Tancredi sounded puzzled. "But first, oh I'm so tired, all that walking through this park, it's enor-mous, let's sit down a moment on this ridiculous little bed. Now this is really for a nun, this bed."

"I think you should just collect the letter and go," replied Jemima, hoping that her voice did not quaver.

"Collect, you mean you don't have it?" Tancredi was now a little brisker, more formal.

"I—I hid it. By the statue outside. You see we have inspection on Saturdays, drawer inspection, cupboard inspection, everything. I didn't dare keep it. So I used her place, Sybilla's place. Look, I'll explain where you go—"

To Jemima's relief, yes, it really was to her relief, she found Tancredi seemed to accept the necessity for speed, and even for a speedy departure. The embrace he gave her as he vanished into the ill-lit corridor was quite perfunctory, only the lingering smell of *Eau Sauvage* in her room reminded her of what a romantic tryst this might under other circumstances have turned out to be. Jemima sat down on the bed suddenly and waited for Tancredi's return. Then there would be one last embrace, perhaps perfunctory, perhaps a little longer, and he would vanish into the darkness from which he had come, out of her life.

She waited.

But things did not turn out quite as Jemima had planned. One moment Tancredi was standing at the door again, with a clear view of the big statue behind him; he had a pencil torch in his hand and a packet opened at one end. The next moment he had leapt towards her and caught her throat in the fingers of one strongly muscled hand.

"Where is it?" he was saying in a fierce whisper, "Where is it? Have you taken it? Who has taken it?" And then, with more indignation— "What is *this?*" He was looking at some white Kleenex which protruded from the packet, clearly addressed to the Principe Graffo di Santo Stefano in Sybilla's flowing hand. The fingers tightened on Jemima's throat so that she could hardly speak, even if she had some answer to the fierce questioning.

"Tancredi, I don't know what—" she began. Then beyond Tancredi, at the end of the corridor, to Jemima's horror she saw something which looked to her very much like the statue of the Blessed Eleanor moving. Jemima gave a scream, cut off by the pressure of Tancredi's fingers. After that a lot of things happened at once, so that later, sorting them out for Rosabelle (under very strict oath of secrecy—the Clitheroe twins and Bridget definitely not to be informed) Jemima found it difficult to get the exact order straight. At one moment the statue appeared to be moving in their direction, the next moment a big flashlight, of quite a different calibre from Tancredi's pencil torch, was shining directly on both of them. It must have been then that Jemima heard the voice of Gregory, except that Gregory was saying something like: Detective Inspector Michael Vann, Drugs Squad, and Michael Vann of Drugs Squad was, it seemed, in the process of arresting Tancredi.

Or rather he might have intended to be in the process, but an instant after Tancredi heard his voice and was bathed in the flashlight, he abandoned his hold on Jemima, dived in the direction of the window, pulled back the grille and vanished.

Then there were more voices, an extraordinary amount of voices for a tranquil convent at night, and phrases were heard like "Never mind, we'll get him," and words like "Ports, airports," all of which reverberated in the mind of Jemima without making a particularly intelligible pattern. Nothing seemed to be making much sense, not since the statue had begun to move, until she heard someone—Gregory—say:

"And after all that, he's managed to take the stuff with him."

"He hasn't," said Jemima Shore in a small but firm voice. "It's buried in the garden at home."

✝   ✝   ✝

It was so typical of Mother Ancilla, observed Jemima to Rosabelle when the reverberations of that night had at long last begun to die away, so typical of her that the very first thing she should say was: "You're wearing jeans, Jemima."

"I suppose she had to start somewhere," commented Rosabelle. "Personally, I think it's a bit much having the Drugs Squad moseying round the convent even if it is the biggest haul etc. etc. and even if the Principe is a wicked drug pusher etc. etc. Thank goodness it's all over in time for the school play." Rosabelle had recently been cast as Hamlet (Jemima was cast as Laertes—"that dear misguided *reckless* young man," as Sister Elizabeth put it, with a meaning look in Jemima's direction). Rosabelle at least had the school play much on her mind. "Did Mother Ancilla give any proper explanation?" Rosabelle went on.

"You know Mother Ancilla," Jemima said ruefully, "She was really amazingly lofty about the whole thing. That is, until I remarked in a most innocent voice that the nuns obviously agreed with the Jesuits that the ends justify the means."

"Daring! Then what?"

"Then I was told to write an essay on the history of the Society of Jesus by Friday—you can't win with Mother Ancilla."

"Sybilla and Co. certainly didn't. Still, all things considered, you were quite lucky, Jem. You did save the cocaine. You didn't get struck down by Tancredi, and you didn't get ravished by him."

"Yes, I was lucky; wasn't I?" replied Jemima in a tone in which Rosabelle thought she detected just a hint of wistfulness.

The reverberations of that night had by this time included the precipitate departure of Sybilla from the convent, vast amounts of expensive green velvety luggage surrounding her weeping figure in the convent hall the next day. She refused to speak to Jemima beyond spitting at her briefly: "I 'ate you, Jemima, and Tancredi, he 'ates you too, he thinks you are *ugly*." Then Sybilla shook her black head furiously so that the long glittering earrings, which she now openly flaunted, jangled and glinted.

What would happen to Sybilla? The Drugs Squad were inclined to be lenient towards someone who was so evidently under the influence of a father who was both pleasure-loving and poverty-stricken (a bad combination). Besides, thanks to a tip-off, they had had her watched since her arrival in England, and the Prince's foolproof method of bringing drugs into the country via his daughter's school luggage—clearly labelled "Blessed Eleanor's Convent, Churne, Sussex"—had never in fact been as foolproof as he imagined. For that matter, Gregory, the enigmatic gardener, had not been as subornable as Sybilla in her confident way and Jemima in her envious one, had imagined.

Gregory however, as an undercover operative, had not been absolutely perfect; it had been a mistake for example to let Sybilla glimpse him that night by the statue, provoking that fit of hysterics which had the effect of involving Jemima in the whole affair. Although it could be argued—and was by Jemima and Rosabelle—that it was Jemima's involvement which had flushed out Tancredi, the Prince's deputy, after Sybilla had become too frightened to contact Gregory. Then there was Jemima's valiant entrapment of Tancredi and her resourceful preservation of the cocaine.

All the same, Jemima Shore herself had not been absolutely perfect in the handling of the whole matter, as Mother Ancilla pointed out very firmly, once the matter of the jeans had been dealt with. It was only after some very frank things had been said about girls who kept things to themselves, things best confided to authority, girls who contemplated late-night trysts with males (albeit with the highest motives as Mother Ancilla accepted) that Mother Ancilla put her bird's head on one side: "But, Jemima dear child, what made you—how did you guess?"

"I just never believed in the second miracle, Mother," confessed Jemima.

"The second miracle, dear child?"

"I didn't believe in the first miracle either, the miracle of Sybilla's waving statue. The second miracle was Tancredi, the cousin, falling in love with me. I looked in the mirror, and well . . ." Her voice trailed away. Mother Ancilla had the effect of making her confess things she would rather, with hindsight, have kept to herself.

Mother Ancilla regarded Jemima for a moment. Her gaze was quizzical but not unkind.

"Now Jemima, I am sure that when we have finished with you, you will make a wonderful Ca— . . . a wonderful wife and mother"—she had clearly intended to say "Catholic wife and mother" before realizing who sat before her.

Jemima Shore saw her first and doubtless her last chance to score over Mother Ancilla.

"Oh, no, Reverend Mother," she answered boldly, "I'm not going to be a wife and mother. I'm going into television," and having already mentioned one of Mother Ancilla's pet banes, she was inspired to add another: "I'm going to be an investigative reporter."

†

The Witch's Tale

Margaret Frazer

*The gretteste clerkes been noght
wisest men, As whilom to the wolf
thus spak the mare.*
—Geoffrey Chaucer,
The Reeve's Tale

The night's rain had given way to a softened sky streaked with thin clouds. The air was bright with spring, and the wind had a kindness that was not there yesterday. In the fields the early corn was a haze of green across the dark soil, and along the sheltered southward side of a hedgerow Margery found a dandelion's first yellow among the early grass. The young nettles and wild parsley were up, and in a few days would be far enough along to gather for salad, something fresh after the long winter's stint of dried peas and beans and not enough porridge.

Margery paused under a tree to smile over a cuckoo-pint, bold and blithe before the cuckoo itself was heard this spring. Farther along the hedge a chaffinch was challenging the world, sparrows were squabbling with more vigor than they had had for months, and a muted flash of red among the bare branches showed where a robin was about his business. As she should be about hers, she reminded herself.

She had set out early to glean sticks along the hedgerows but there was not much deadwood left so near the village by this end of winter; her sling of sacking was barely a quarter full, and all of it was wet and would need drying before it was any use. But she must go home. Jack would be

coming for his dinner and then Dame Claire at the priory was expecting
her.

Though she and Jack were among the village's several free souls and
not villeins, Margery's one pride was that she worked with Dame Claire,
St. Frideswide's infirmarian. They had met not long after Margery had
married Jack and come to live in Priors Byfield. In the untended garden
behind the cottage she had found a plant she could not identify despite
the herb lore she had had from her mother and grandmother. With her
curiosity stronger than her fear, she had gone hesitantly to ask at the nunnery gates if there were a nun who knew herbs. In a while a small woman
neatly dressed and veiled in Benedictine black and white had come out to
her and kindly looked at the cutting she had brought.

"Why, that's bastard agrimony," she had said. "In your garden? It must
have seeded itself from ours. It's hardly common in this part of England
and I've been nursing ours along. It's excellent for strengthening the lungs
and to ease the spleen and against dropsy, you see."

"Oh, like marjoram. Wild marjoram, not sweet. Only better, I suppose?" Margery had said; and then had added regretfully, "I suppose you
want it back?"

Dame Claire had regarded her with surprise. "I don't think so. We still
have our own." She looked at the cutting more closely. "And yours seems
to be doing very well. Tell me about your garden."

Margery had told her and then, drawn on by Dame Claire's questions,
had told what she knew of herbs and finally, to her astonishment, had
been asked if she would like to see the priory's infirmary garden. One
thing had led on to another, that day and others; and with nothing in
common between them except their love of herbs and using them to help
and heal, she and Dame Claire had come to work together, Margery gathering wild-growing herbs for Dame Claire's use as well as her own and
growing plants in her garden to share with the infirmarian, as Dame
Claire shared her own herbs and the book-knowledge Margery had no
way of having. And for both of them there was the pleasure of talking
about work they both enjoyed, each with someone as knowledgeable as
herself.

Now, this third spring of their friendship, the soil would soon be dry
enough, God willing, for this year's planting. Margery and Dame Claire
had appointed today to plan their gardens together, so that Dame Claire
could ask the priory steward to bring back such cuttings as they needed
when he went to Lady Day fair in Oxford.

But Margery had to hurry. Her husband Jack wanted both her and his dinner waiting for him when he came into the house at the end of the morning's work, and his displeasure was ugly when she failed him. She had left herself time enough this morning, she was sure, even allowing for her dawdling along the hedgerow; but as she let herself into her garden by the back gate from the field path she saw with a familiar sick feeling that Jack was standing in the cottage's back doorway, fists on his hips and a mean grin on his fleshy mouth. He was back early from hedging—Margery would have sworn he was early—and neither she nor his food was waiting and no excuse would make any difference to what he would do now.

Wearily, Margery set down her bundle on the bench beside the door and looked up at him. It was better to see it coming.

"Y'know better than to be late," he accused. "Y'know I've told you that."

"I can have your dinner on in hardly a moment." She said it without hope. Nothing would help now; nothing ever did.

"I don't want to wait!" Jack put his hand flat between her breasts and shoved her backward. He always began with shoving. "I shouldn't *have* to wait!"

Margery stumbled back. Jack came after her and she turned sideways, to make a smaller target, for all the good it would do her. He shoved her again, staggering her along the path, then caught her a heavy slap to the back of her head so that she pitched forward, her knees banging into the wooden edging of a garden bed, her hands sinking into the muddy soil. She scrambled to be clear of him long enough to regain her feet. So long as she was on her feet he only hit. Once she was down, he kicked. His fists left bruises, sometimes cuts. His feet were worse. There were places in her that still hurt from last time, three weeks ago. From experience she knew that if she kept on her feet until he tired, he did not kick her so long.

But her fear made her clumsy. He was yelling at her now, calling her things she had never been, never thought of being. A blow alongside of her head sent her stumbling to one side, into her herb bed among the straw and burlap meant to protect her best plants through the winter. She scrambled to be out of it but Jack came in after her, crushing his feet down on anything in his way.

Margery cried out as she had not for her own pain. "Stop it! Leave my plants be!" Jack laughed and stomped one deliberately.

"Them and you both," he said, enjoying himself "You'll learn to do what you're told."

Margery fumbled in the pouch under her apron and, still scrambling to keep beyond his reach and get out from among her herbs, snatched out a small packet of folded cloth not so big as the palm of her hand. She brandished it at him and screamed, "You stop! You stop or I'll use this!"

For a wonder Jack did stop, staring at her in plain surprise. Then he scoffed, "You've nothing there, y'daft woman!" and grabbed for her.

Margery ducked from his reach, still holding out the packet. "It's bits of you, Jack Wilkins!" she cried. "From when I cut your hair last month and then when you trimmed your nails. Remember that? It's bits of you in here and I've made a spell, Jack Wilkins, and you're going to die for it if you don't leave me alone and get out of my garden!' "

"It's not me that's going to die!" he roared, and lurched for her.

✝ ✝ ✝

After two days of sun the weather had turned back to low-trailing clouds and rain. But it was a gentle, misting rain that promised spring after winter's raw cold, and Dame Frevisse, leaving the guest hall where everything was readied should the day bring guests to St. Frideswide's, paused at the top of the stairs down into the courtyard to look up and let the rain stroke across her face. Very soon the cloister bell would call her into the church with the other nuns for the afternoon's service of Vespers, and she would be able to let go the necessities of her duties as the priory's hosteler to rise into the pleasure of prayer.

But as she crossed the yard toward the cloister door, Master Naylor overtook her. He was the priory's steward, a long-faced man who kept to his duties and did them well but managed to talk with the nuns he served, as little as possible. Bracing herself for something she probably did not want to hear, Frevisse turned to him. "Master Naylor?"

"I thought you'd best know before you went in to Vespers," he said, with a respectful bow of his head. Master Naylor was ever particular in his manners. "There's a man come in to say Master Montfort and six of his men will be here by supper time."

Frevisse felt her mouth open in protest, then snapped it closed. Among her least favorite people in the realm was Master Morys Montfort, crowner for northern Oxfordshire. It was his duty to find out what lay behind unexpected deaths within his jurisdiction, then to bring the malefactor—if any—to the sheriff's attention, and to see to it that whatever fines or confiscations were due King Henry VI were duly collected.

Frevisse had no quarrel with any of that, but Master Montfort had the regrettable tendency to prefer the least complicated solution to any problem and find his facts accordingly. He and Frevisse had long since struck a level of mutual hostility neither was inclined to abate. She was not happy to hear of his coming, and she said, "I trust he's just passing on his way to somewhere else? There's no one dead hereabouts that I've heard of."

Master Naylor shrugged. "It's Jack Wilkins in the village, the day before yesterday. They tolled the village bell for him but you were likely in church for Sext then."

"But why is Montfort coming? Is there doubt about the way this Wilkins died?"

"No doubt. His wife shook a charm at him and cast a spell, and he fell down dead. At least three of their neighbors saw it. I'd not have thought it of Margery," he added. "She's never been known to put her herbs to aught but good, that I've heard."

"*Margery?* Dame *Claire's* Margery?"

"That's her, the herbwife who visits here sometimes."

"Does Dame Claire know?"

"No more than you, I doubt. It was witchcraft and murder certain enough. Montfort will have it done a half hour after he's seen her and talked to her neighbors. He'll probably be on the road to Banbury with her before noon tomorrow and she'll be in the bishop's hands not long after that. I'd have reported it all to Domina Edith come week's end with the other village business." He seemed to think that was all the dealing there needed to be with the matter; Jack and Margery were not among the priory's villeins, and so not his responsibility. The lethal use of witchcraft wasn't usual; on the other hand, all herbwives used spells in their medicines, and it was but a small step to misuse them. He would not have mentioned it except he knew of Margery's link with Dame Claire.

The bell for Vespers began to ring. Frevisse said impatiently, "Where is she being kept?"

Master Naylor pointed through the gateway toward the outer yard. "She's in one of the sheds there. I've two of our men guarding her. She's gagged so it's all right; they're safe. There's nothing to be done."

"Dame Claire will want to see her after Vespers," Frevisse said. "Please you, tell the guesthall servants for me that Montfort is coming. I have to go."

The Vespers she had expected to enjoy was instead a prolonged discomfort of impatience; and afterwards she had to wait until supper was
finished and the nuns went out into the garden for recreation time—the
one hour of the day their Benedictine rule allowed for idle talk—before
she could tell Dame Claire what was to hand.

"*Margery?*" Dame Claire exclaimed in her deep voice. Disbelief arched
her eyebrows high toward her veil. "Killed her husband with witchcraft?
I very much doubt it. In fact I don't believe it at all! I want to see her."

That was easily done. Frevisse waited at the foot of the stairs to the
prioress' parlor while Dame Claire went up to ask permission. Then they
went together, out of the cloister and across the inner yard—Frevisse noting there were lights in the guesthall window so Montfort and his
entourage must have arrived—through the gateway to the outer yard
where a stable hand, surprised to see them outside the cloister, pointed to
the shed at the end of the stables where the prisoner was being kept.

"I should have thought to bring a cloak for her, and something warm
to eat," Dame Claire regretted as they went. "These spring nights are cold,
and she must be desperate, poor thing."

As Master Naylor had said, two stolid stable men were keeping guard
inside the shed door, and Margery was gagged and her hands bound at
her waist. But a clay lamp set in the corner on the bare earth floor gave a
comforting yellow glow to the rough boards of her prison, and by its light
as they stood in the doorway—Dame Claire explaining to the guards that
they were come with permission to talk with Margery—Frevisse saw that
Margery had several blankets, a cloak, and a straw-stuffed pillow to make
her a bed along the farther wall, and that beside it were a pot of ale and
various plates with three different kinds of bread and parts of two
cheeses. Frevisse knew that in such cases as Margery the nunnery provided a blanket and an occasional piece of bread. So who had done this
much for Margery?

Margery herself had risen to her feet as the nuns entered. Despite her
crime, she was much as Frevisse had remembered her, a middling sort of
woman—of middling build, middling young, middling tall, with nothing
particular about her, except—to judge by her eyes above the gag—that
she was frightened. As well she should be.

Dame Claire finished with the men, and crossed the shed to her,
Frevisse following. As Margery curtseyed, Dame Claire said, "Let me loose
your hands so you can take off the gag. I've told them you won't do anything. We want to talk to you."

Dame Claire freed Margery's hands, and gratefully she unknotted the cloth behind her head. "Thank you, my lady," she said hoarsely.

"Have something to drink." Dame Claire indicated the ale kindly. "Have they let you eat?"

Margery nodded over the rim of the clay pot as she drank thirstily. When she had finished, she said, "They've been as kind as might be. And village folk have brought me things." She gestured at her bed and food and lamp. She was clearly tired as well as frightened, worn out by too many strange things happening to her. "But I hoped you'd come, so I could tell you why I didn't come t'other day when I said I would."

"I wondered what happened to you," Dame Claire answered. "But I never thought this."

Margery hung her head. "Nor did I."

"They say you killed your husband."

Margery nodded. "I did that."

"Margery, no!" Dame Claire protested.

"Jack came at me, the way he's done ever since we married whenever I've not done right. But this time we were in my garden and he was trampling my plants." It plainly mattered very much to her that Dame Claire understand. "I told him to stop but he didn't care, and I—lost my temper."

"You truly did kill him?" Dame Claire asked, still disbelieving it.

"Oh, yes. Sure as sure. I didn't know the spell would work that way but it did. Took him off afore he could hit me again, just like that."

"What—exactly—did you do?" Frevisse asked carefully. Murder, serious enough in itself, was worse for the murderer when done by witchcraft. Charms and spells were simply part of healing; every herbwife knew some. But if they were turned to evil, they became part of the Devil's work and a matter for the Church as well as lay law.

Margery looked at Frevisse with mingled shyness and guilt, and did not answer.

"Tell us, please," Dame Claire urged. "Dame Frevisse and I want to help you."

"There's no help for me!" Margery said in surprise. "I killed him."

"How?" Frevisse persisted.

Margery hung her head. She twisted her hands in her apron and, low-voiced with embarrassment, said, "I'd been saving bits of him this while. Hair, you know, and his nail cuttings."

"Margery! That's wicked!" Dame Claire exclaimed.

"I know it!" Margery said piteously. "But I was only going to make a small charm. When I'd money for the wax to make the figure. Not kill him, like, but weaken his arm so he couldn't hit me so hard. That's all I wanted to do. Just weaken him."

"But you hadn't made the figure yet?" Frevisse asked. Margery shook her head dumbly. Frevisse pressed, "What did you do then, that you think you killed him?"

"I had the—things in a little packet. I held it up and told him what it was and that he'd better stop what he was doing. That I'd made a charm and I'd kill him if he didn't stop."

"But you hadn't made a charm yet. You said so," said Dame Claire.

"That I hadn't. But I meant to. I really did." She looked anxiously from one nun to the other. "If I make confession and do penance before they hang me, I won't have to burn in hell, will I? Not if I'm truly penitent?"

"Surely not," Dame Claire reassured her.

"But if you didn't have the charm, what happened?" Frevisse asked.

Margery shuddered. "Jack kept hitting and shoving. I knew he'd near to kill me, once he had his hands on me, and I'd never have another chance to make a charm against him, not now he knew. I was that frighted, I grabbed the first words that came to me, thinking to scare him off with them. I didn't even think what they were. I just said them at him and shook the packet like I was ill-wishing him. I just wanted to keep him back from me, I swear that's all. Just hold him off as long as might be."

She broke off, closing her eyes at the memory.

"And then?" Dame Claire prompted.

Faintly, tears on her cheeks, Margery said, "He stopped. All rigid like I'd hit him with a board. He stared at me with his mouth open and then grabbed his chest, right in the center, and bent over double. He was gasping like he hurt, or couldn't catch his breath. Then he fell over. In the path, away from my herbs. He curled up and went on gasping and then—he stopped. He just stopped and was dead."

A little silence held them all. Frevisse was aware of the two men at her back, and knew that everything they were hearing would be told later all around the nunnery and village.

"Margery," Dame Claire said, "you can't wish a man dead. Or rather, you can wish it, but it won't happen, not that simply."

"But it did," Margery said.

And there would probably be no convincing anyone otherwise. But for Dame Claire's sake, Frevisse asked, "What was it you said to him? A spell?"

Margery nodded. "The one for—"

Master Naylor interrupted her with a firm rap on the door frame. He inclined his head respectfully to Frevisse and Dame Claire, and said, "The crowner wants to see her now."

"So late?" Dame Claire protested.

"He hopes to finish the matter tonight so he can be on his way at earliest tomorrow. He has other matters to see to," Master Naylor explained.

Matters more important than a village woman who was surely guilty, Frevisse thought. A woman who was the more inconvenient because she would have to be sent for examination before a bishop before she could be duly hanged.

"We'll come with her," said Dame Claire.

† † †

Master Montfort had been given the guesthall's best chamber, with its large bed and plain but sufficient furnishings. The shutters had been closed against the rainy dusk, the lamps lighted, and at a table against the farther wall his clerk was hunched over a parchment, quill in hand and inkwell ready.

The crowner himself stood by the brazier in the corner, his hands over its low warmth. He was short in the leg for the length of his body, and had begun to go fat in his middle, but to his own mind any shortcomings he might have—and he was not convinced that he had any— were amply compensated for by the dignity of his office; he no more than glanced over his shoulder as Master Naylor brought Margery in, then sharpened his look on Frevisse and Dame Claire following her. A flush spread up his florid face and over the curve of his balding head.

"You can stay, Naylor," he said. "But the rest of you may go." Belatedly, ungraciously, he added, "My ladies."

With eyes modestly downcast and her hands tucked up either sleeve of her habit, Frevisse said, "Thank you, but we'll stay. It would not be seemly that Margery be here unattended."

She had used that excuse in another matter with Master Montfort. He had lost the argument then, and apparently chose not to renew it now. His flush merely darkened to a deeper red as he said tersely, "Then stand to one side and don't interfere while I question her."

They did so. Master Montfort squared up in front of Margery and announced in his never subtle way, "I've questioned some several of your neighbors already and mean to see more of them before I'm to bed tonight so you may as well tell what you have to tell straight out and no avoiding it. Can you understand that?"

Margery did not lift her humbly bowed head. "Yes, m'lord."

"You killed your husband? Now, mind you, you were heard and seen so there's no avoiding it."

Margery clearly had no thought of avoiding anything. While the clerk's pen scratched busily at his parchment, recording her words, she repeated what she had already told Frevisse and Dame Claire. When she had finished, Master Montfort rocked back on his heels, smiling grimly with great satisfaction. "Very well said, and all agreeing with your neighbors' tales. I think there's no need for more."

"Except," Dame Claire said briskly, knowing Master Montfort would order her to silence if she gave him a chance, "I doubt her husband died of anything more than apoplexy."

The crowner turned on her. In a tone intended to quell, he said, "I beg your pardon, my lady?"

Dame Claire hesitated. Frevisse, more used to the crowner's bullying, said helpfully, "Apoplexy. It's a congestion of the blood—"

Master Montfort's tongue caught up with his indignation. "I know what it is!"

Frevisse turned to Master Naylor. As steward of the priory's properties he had far better knowledge of the villeins than she did. "What sort of humor was this Jack Wilkins? Hot-tempered or not?"

"Hot enough it's a wonder he was in so little trouble as he was," Master Naylor said. "He knocked a tooth out of one of his neighbors last week because he thought the man was laughing at him. The man wasn't, being no fool, but Jack Wilkins in a temper didn't care about particulars. It wasn't the first time he's made trouble with his temper. And he was known to beat his wife."

"Choleric," said Dame Claire. "Easily given to temper. People of that sort are very likely to be struck as Jack Wilkins was, especially in the midst of one of their furies. He was beating his wife—

"As he had every right to do!" Master Montfort declared.

As if musing on his own, Master Naylor said, "There's a feeling in the village that he did it more often and worse than need be."

But Dame Claire, refusing to leave her point, went on over his words,

"—and that's heavy work, no matter how you go about it. Then she defied him, maybe even frightened him when she said her spell—"

"And down he fell dead!" the crowner said, triumphant. "That's what I'm saying. It was her doing and that's the end of it."

"What was the spell she said?" Frevisse interjected. "Has anyone asked her that?"

Master Montfort shot her an angry look; determined to assert himself, he swung back on Margery. "That was my next question, woman. What did you actually say to him? No, don't look at anyone while you say it! And say it slow so my clerk can write it down."

Eyes turned to the floor, voice trembling a little, Margery began to recite, "Come you forth and get you gone . . ."

If Master Montfort was expecting a roaring spell that named devils and summoned demons, he was disappointed. The clerk scratched away busily as Margery went through a short verse that was nevertheless quite apparently meant to call the spirit out of the body and cast it away. Part way through, Dame Claire looked startled.

In the pause after Margery finished speaking, the clerk's pen scritched on. Master Montfort, ever impatient, went to hover at his shoulder and, as soon as he had done, snatched the parchment away. While he read it over, Frevisse leaned toward Dame Claire, who whispered briefly but urgently in her ear. Before Frevisse could respond, Master Montfort demanded at Margery, "That's it? just that?" Margery nodded. Master Montfort glared at his clerk and recited loudly, "Come you forth . . ."

The man's head jerked up to stare with near-sighted alarm at his master. The crowner went on through the spell unheeding either his clerk's dismay or Master Naylor's movement of protest. Margery opened her mouth to say something, but Frevisse silenced her with a shake of her head, while Dame Claire pressed a hand over her own mouth to keep quiet.

When Master Montfort had finished, a tense waiting held them all still, most especially the clerk. When nothing happened after an impatient minute, Master Montfort rounded on Margery. "How long is this supposed to take?"

Margery fumbled under his glare. "My husband—he—almost on the instant, sir. But—"

"Spare me your excuses. If it worked for you, why didn't it work for me? Because I didn't have clippings of his hair or what?"

Keeping her voice very neutral, Frevisse suggested, "According to

Robert Mannying in his *Handling Sin,* a spell has no power if said by someone who doesn't believe in it. Margery uses herbs and spells to help the villagers. She believes in what she does. You don't. Do you believe in your charm, Margery? This one that you said at your husband?"

"Yes, but—"

"She's a witch," Master Montfort interrupted. "And whatever good you claim she's done, she's used a spell to kill a man this time, and her husband at that. Who knows what else she's tried." He rounded on Margery again and said in her face, "There's a question for you, woman. Have you ever used this spell before?"

Margery shrank away from him but answered, "Surely. Often and often. But—"

"God's blood!" Master Montfort exclaimed. "You *admit* you've murdered other men?"

"Margery!" Frevisse interposed, "*What* is the spell *for?*"

Driven by both of them, Margery cried out, "It's for opening the bowels!"

A great quiet deepened in the room. Margery looked anxiously from face to face. Frevisse and Dame Claire looked carefully at the floor. Red darkened and mounted over Master Montfort's countenance again. Master Naylor seemed to struggle against choking. The clerk ducked his head low over his parchment. Nervously Margery tried to explain. "I make a decoction with gill-go-on-the-ground, and say the spell over it while it's brewing, to make it stronger. It provokes urine, too, and ... and . . ." She stopped, not understanding their reactions, then finished apologetically, "They were the first words that came into my head, that's all. I just wanted to fright Jack off me, and those were the first words that came. I didn't mean for them to kill him."

Master Montfort, trying to recover lost ground, strangled out, "But they did kill him, didn't they? That's the long and short of it, isn't it?"

Margery started to nod, but Frevisse put a stilling hand on her arm; and Dame Claire said, "It's a better judgement that her husband died not from her words but from his own choler, like many another man before him. It wasn't Margery but his temper that did for him at the last."

Master Montfort glared at her. "That's women's logic!" he snapped. "His wife warns him she has bits of him to use against him, and cries a spell in his face, and he drops down dead, and it's *his* fault? Where's the sense of that? No! She's admitted her guilt. She was seen doing it. There's no more questioning needed. Naylor, keep her until morning. Then I'll take her in charge."

† † †

The twilight had darkened to deep dusk but the rain had stopped as they came out of the guest hall. Master Naylor steadied Margery by her elbow as they went down the steps to the yard. No matter how much she had expected her fate, she seemed dazed by the crowner's pronouncement, and walked numbly where she was taken. Frevisse and Dame Claire followed with nothing to say, though Frevisse at least seethed with frustration at their helplessness and Montfort's stupidity. Even the acknowledgement of the *possibility* of doubt from him would have been something.

Margery's two guards were waiting at the foot of the steps in the spread of light from the lantern hung by the guest hall door. They stood aside, then followed as the silent group made their way around the rain-puddles among the cobbles to the gateway to the outer yard. Beyond it was the mud and deeper darkness of the outer yard where the lamplight showing around the ill-fitted door of Margery's prison shed was the only brightness. Busy with her feet and anger, Frevisse did not see the knot of people there until one of them swung the shed door open to give them more light, and Master Naylor said in surprise, "Tom, what brings you out? And the rest of you?"

Frevisse could see now that there were seven of them, four women and three men, all from the village. The women curtseyed quickly to her, Dame Claire, and Master Naylor as they came forward to Margery. Crooning to her like mothers over a hurt child, they enveloped her with their kindness; and one of them, with an arm around her waist, soothed, "There now, Margery-girl, we can see it didn't go well. You come in-by. We've something warm for you to eat." Together they drew her into the shed, leaving the men to front the priory-folk.

Tom, the village reeve and apparently their leader in this, ducked his head to her and Dame Claire, and again to Master Naylor before he said, "She's to go then? No help for it?"

"No help for it," Master Naylor agreed. "The crowner means to take her with him when he goes in the morning."

The men nodded as if they had expected no less. But Tom said, "It makes no difference that there's not a body in the village but's glad to have

Jack gone? He was a terror and no mistake and she didn't do more than many of us have wanted to."

"I can't argue that, but it changes nothing," Master Naylor said. "Margery goes with the crowner in the morning, and be taken before the bishop for what she's done."

"She didn't do anything!" Dame Claire said with the impatience she had had to curb in Master Montfort's presence.

Frevisse agreed. "This Jack died from his own temper, not from Margery's silly words!"

"It was apoplexy," said Dame Claire. "People who indulge in ill temper the way Jack Wilkins did are like to die the way Jack Wilkins did."

"If you say so, m'lady," Tom said in a respectful voice. "But Margery cried something out at him, and Jack went down better than a poled ox. God keep his soul," he added as an after-thought, and everyone crossed themselves . Jack Wilkins was unburied yet; best to say the right things for he would make a wicked ghost.

"It wasn't even a spell to kill a man. Margery says so herself."

"Well, that's all right then," Tom said agreeably. "And a comfort to Margery to know it wasn't her doing that killed Jack, no matter what the crowner says. But what we've come for is to ask if some of us can stand Margery's guard tonight, for friendship's sake, like, before she goes."

Dim with distance and the mist-heavy dusk, the bell began to call to Compline, the nuns' last prayers before bed. Frevisse laid a hand on Dame Claire's arm, drawing her away. Master Naylor could handle this matter. There was nothing more for the two of them to do here. Better they go to pray for Margery's soul. And Jack Wilkins', she thought belatedly.

✝   ✝   ✝

Watery sunshine was laying thin shadows across the cloister walk next morning as Frevisse went from chapter meeting toward her duties. She expected Master Montfort and his men and Margery would be gone by now, ridden away at first light; and she regretted there had been nothing that could be done to convince anyone but herself and Dame Claire that Margery had not killed her lout of a husband with her poor little spell and desperation. But even Margery had believed it, and would do penance for it as if her guilt were real, and go to her death for it.

Frevisse was distracted from her anger as she neared the door into the courtyard by the noise of Master Montfort's raised voice, the words unclear but his passion plain. She glanced again at the morning shadows. He was supposed to be miles on his way by this time. She opened the door from the cloister to the courtyard.

Usually empty except for a passing servant and the doves around the well, the yard was half full of villagers crowded to the foot of the guest hall steps. Master Montfort stood above them there, dressed for riding and in a rage.

"You're still saying there's no trace of her?" he ranted. Frevisse stopped where she was with a sudden hopeful lift of her spirits. "You've been searching the wretched place since dawn! My men have scoured the fields for miles! *Someone* has to know where she is! Or if she's truly bolted, we have to set the hounds to her trail!"

Even from where she was, Frevisse could see the sullen set of every villein's shoulders. But it was clear that the main thrust of his words was at Master Naylor, standing straight-backed at the head of the villeins, deliberately between them and the crowner's rage. With a hard-edged patience that told Frevisse he had been over this already more than once, he answered in his strong, carrying voice, "We have no hounds to set to her trail. This is a priory of nuns. They're not monks; they don't ride to hunt here."

Standing close behind the steward, Tom the reeve growled so everyone could hear, "And where she went, you wouldn't care to follow!"

Master Montfort pointed at him, furious. "You! You're one of the fools who slept when you were supposed to be guarding her! Dreaming your way to perdition while she walks off free as you please! What do you mean, 'where she went'? Hai, man, what do you mean?"

"I mean it wasn't a natural sleep we had last night!" Tom answered loudly enough to send his words to the outer yard, to Master Montfort's entourage and a number of priory servants clustered just beyond the gateway. Frevisse saw them stir as he spoke. "Aye, it wasn't a natural sleep and there's not one of us will say it was. We fell to sleep all at once and together, between one word and another. That's not natural! No more than Jack Wilkins falling down dead was natural. We're lucky it was only sleep she did to us! That's what I say! And anybody who tried to follow her is asking for what happens to him!"

Behind and around him the other villeins glanced at each other and nodded. One of the bolder men even spoke up, "Tom has the right of it!"

A woman—Frevisse thought she was one of four who had come to Margery last night—said shrilly, "You can't ask any decent man to follow where she's gone!"

Master Montfort pointed at her. "You know where she's gone? You admit you know?"

"I can make a fair guess!" the woman flung back. "Flown off to her master the devil, very like, and you'll find no hound to go that trail!"

"Flown off?" Master Montfort raged. "*Flown* off? I'm supposed to believe that? Naylor, most of these folk are the priory's villeins! Warn them there's penalties for lying to the king's crowner and hiding murderers. She's around here somewhere!"

"If she is, we haven't found her yet for all our searching," Master Naylor said back. "Twice through the village is enough for one day, and there's no sign where she might have gone across country. As you say, these are our villeins and I can say I've never known them given to such lying as this. Maybe they've the right of it. You said yourself last night she was a witch, and now she seems to have proved it!"

Master Montfort stared at him, speechless with rage.

"What we say," shouted another of the men, "is you're welcome to come search us house to house yourself, you being so much smarter than the rest of us. But if you find her, you'd better hope she doesn't treat you like she did her husband!"

There was general angry laughter among all the villeins at that; and some from beyond the gateway. For just a moment Master Montfort lost the stride of his anger, paused by the man's words. Then he gathered himself together and rounded on Master Naylor. With a scorn that he meant to be withering, he said, "I've greater matters to see to than hunting down some petty village witch. She was in your charge, Naylor, and the loss is to you, not to me. There'll be an amercement to pay for losing the king's prisoner, and be assured I'll see the priory is charged it to the full!"

"I'm assured you will," Master Naylor returned tersely, his scorn stronger than Master Montfort's.

For a balanced moment he and the crowner held each other's eyes. Then Master Naylor gestured sharply for the villeins to move back from the foot of the steps. Crowding among themselves, they gave ground. Master Montfort's mouth opened, then closed, and with great, stiff dignity he descended, passed in front of them to his horse being held for him beyond the gateway, and mounted. He glared around at them one final time and, for good measure, across the courtyard at Frevisse still standing in the doorway, then jerked his horse around and went.

No one moved or spoke until the splash and clatter of his going, and his entourage after him, were well away. And even then the response among them all seemed no more than a long in-drawn breath and a slow release of tension. Heads turned to one another, and Frevisse saw smiles, but no one spoke. There were a few chuckles but no more as they all drifted out of the gateway, some of them nodding to Master Naylor as they passed him. He nodded back, and did not speak either; and when they were gone, he stayed where he was, waiting for Frevisse to come to him.

She did, because there in the open courtyard they could most easily talk without chance of being overheard so long as they kept their voices low. "Master Naylor," she said as she approached him.

He inclined his head to her. "Dame Frevisse."

"I take it from what I heard that Margery Wilkins escaped in the night?"

"It seems her guards and the friends who came to keep her company slept. When they awoke this dawn, she was gone."

"And cannot be found?"

"We've searched the village twice this morning, and Master Montfort's men have hunted the near countryside."

"They think she used her witch-powers to escape?"

"So it would seem. What other explanation is there?"

"I can think of several," Frevisse said dryly.

Master Naylor's expression did not change. "Just as you and Dame Claire could think of some other reason for Jack Wilkins' death besides his wife's words striking him down."

"And the fine to the priory for your carelessness in losing your witch?"

"It was villeins who had the watch of her and lost her. I mean to make an amercement on the village to help meet the fine our crowner will surely bring against the priory."

"Won't there be protest over that?"

"Villeins always protest over paying anything. But in this I think there'll be less arguing than in most. She's their witch. Let them pay for her. Dear-bought is held more dear."

"They still truly believe she killed her husband?" Frevisse asked. "Despite what we told them last night, they still believe she's a witch with that much power?"

"What else can they believe?" the steward asked quietly in return. "They saw her do it."

"What do you believe?" Frevisse asked, unable to tell from his neutral expression and voice.

Instead of an answer to that, Master Naylor said, "I think a straw-filled loft is not an uncomfortable place to be for a week and more this time of year. And that by the time summer comes there'll be a new herb-wife in the village, maybe even with the same first name but someone's widowed sister from somewhere else, freeborn like Margery was and no questions asked."

"And after all, witchcraft in itself is no crime or sin," Frevisse said. "The wrong lies in the use it's put to."

"And all the village knows Margery has ever used her skills for good, except this one time, if you judge what she did was ill. All her neighbors judge it wasn't," Master Naylor said solemnly.

"They mean to keep her even if it costs them?" Frevisse asked.

"They know she's a good woman. And now that they're certain she has power, she's not someone they want to lose."

"Or to cross," Frevisse said.

Master Naylor came as near to a smile as he ever came, but only said, "There'll likely be no trouble with anyone beating her ever again."

✝

Murder Mysteries

Neil Gaiman

The Fourth Angel says:
> *Of this order I am made one,*
> *From Mankind to guard this place*
> *That through their Guilt they have foregone,*
> *For they have forfeited His Grace;*
> *Therefore all this must they shun*
> *Or else my Sword they shall embrace*
> *And myself will be their Foe*
> *To flame them in the Face.*
> —Chester Mystery Cycle:
> *The Creation, and Adam and Eve*, 1461.

T HIS IS TRUE.

Ten years ago, give or take a year, I found myself on an enforced stopover in Los Angeles, a long way from home. It was December, and the California weather was warm and pleasant. England, however, was in the grip of fogs and snowstorms, and no planes were landing there. Each day I'd phone the airport, and each day I'd be told to wait another day.

This had gone on for almost a week.

I was barely out of my teens. Looking around today at the parts of my life left over from those days, I feel uncomfortable, as if I've received a gift, unasked, from another person: a house, a wife, children, a vocation. Nothing to do with me, I could say, innocently. If it's true that every seven years each cell in your body dies and is replaced, then I have truly inherited my life from a dead man; and the misdeeds of those times have been forgiven, and are buried with his bones.

I was in Los Angeles. Yes.

On the sixth day I received a message from an old sort-of-girlfriend from Seattle: she was in LA too, and she had heard I was around on the friends-of-friends network. Would I come over?

I left a message on her machine. Sure.

That evening: a small, blonde woman approached me, as I came out of the place I was staying. It was already dark.

She stared at me, as if she were trying to match me to a description, and then, hesitantly, she said my name.

"That's me. Are you Tink's friend?"

"Yeah. Car's out back. C'mon; she's really looking forward to seeing you."

The woman's car was one of the huge old boat-like jobs you only ever seem to see in California. It smelled of cracked and flaking leather upholstery. We drove out from wherever we were to wherever we were going.

Los Angeles was at that time a complete mystery to me; and I cannot say I understand it much better now. I understand London, and New York, and Paris: you can walk around them, get a sense of what's where in just a morning of wandering. Maybe catch the subway. But Los Angeles is about cars. Back then I didn't drive at all; even today I will not drive in America. Memories of LA for me are linked by rides in other people's cars, with no sense there of the shape of the city, of the relationships between the people and the place. The regularity of the roads, the repetition of structure and form, mean that when I try to remember it as an entity all I have is the boundless profusion of tiny lights I saw one night on my first trip to the city, from the hill of Griffith Park. It was one of the most beautiful things I had ever seen, from that distance.

"See that building?" said my blonde driver, Tink's friend. It was a red-brick art deco house, charming and quite ugly.

"Yes."

"Built in the 1930s," she said, with respect and pride. .

I said something polite, trying to comprehend a city inside which fifty years could be considered a long time.

"Tink's real excited. When she heard you were in town. She was so excited."

"I'm looking forward to seeing her again."

Tink's real name was Tinkerbell Richmond. No lie.

She was staying with friends in small apartment clump, somewhere an hour's drive from downtown LA.

What you need to know about Tink: she was ten years older than me, in her early thirties; she had glossy black hair and red, puzzled lips, and very white skin, like Snow White in the fairy stories; the first time I met her I thought she was the most beautiful woman in the world.

Tink had been married for a while at some point in her life, and had a five-year-old daughter called Susan. I had never met Susan—when Tink had been in England, Susan had been staying on in Seattle, with her father.

People named Tinkerbell name their daughters Susan.

Memory is the great deceiver. Perhaps there are some individuals whose memories act like tape recordings, daily records of their lives complete in every detail, but I am not one of them. My memory is a patchwork of occurrences, of discontinuous events roughly sewn together: the parts I remember, I remember precisely, whilst other sections seem to have vanished completely.

I do not remember arriving at Tink's house, nor where her flatmate went.

What I remember next is sitting in Tink's lounge, with the lights low; the two of us next to each other, on the sofa.

We made small talk. It had been perhaps a year since we had seen one another. But a twenty-one-year-old boy has little to say to a thirty-two-year-old woman, and soon, having nothing in common, I pulled her to me.

She snuggled close with a kind of sigh, and presented her lips to be kissed. In the half-light her lips were black. We kissed for a little, and I stroked her breasts through her blouse, on the couch; and then she said:

"We can't fuck. I'm on my period."

"Fine."

"I can give you a blow job, if you'd like."

I nodded assent, and she unzipped my jeans, and lowered her head to my lap.

After I had come, she got up and ran into the kitchen. I heard her spitting into the sink, and the sound of running water: I remember wondering why she did it, if she hated the taste that much.

Then she returned and we sat next to each other on the couch.

"Susan's upstairs, asleep," said Tink. "She's all I live for. Would you like to see her?"

"I don't mind."

We went upstairs. Tink led me into a darkened bedroom. There were child-scrawl pictures all over the walls—wax-crayoned drawings of winged fairies and little palaces—and a small, fair-haired girl was asleep in the bed.

"She's very beautiful," said Tink, and kissed me. Her lips were still slightly sticky "She takes after her father."

We went downstairs. We had nothing else to say, nothing else to do. Tink turned on the main light. For the first time I noticed tiny crows' feet at the corners of her eyes, incongruous on her perfect, Barbie-doll face.

"I love you," she said.

"Thank you."

"Would you like a ride back?"

"If you don't mind leaving Susan alone . . . ?"

She shrugged, and I pulled her to me for the last time.

At night, Los Angeles is all lights. And shadows.

A blank, here, in my mind. I simply don't remember what happened next. She must have driven me back to the place where I was staying—how else would I have gotten there? I do not even remember kissing her goodbye. Perhaps I simply waited on the sidewalk and watched her drive away.

Perhaps.

I do know, however, that once I reached the place I was staying I just stood there, unable to go inside, to wash and then to sleep, unwilling to do anything else.

I was not hungry. I did not want alcohol. I did not want to read, or talk. I was scared of walking too far, in case I became lost, bedeviled by the repeating motifs of Los Angeles, spun around and sucked in so I could never find my way home again. Central Los Angeles sometimes seems to me to be nothing more than a pattern, like a set of repeating blocks: a gas station, a few homes, a mini-mall (donuts, photo developers, laundro-mats, fast-foods), and repeat until hypnotised; and the tiny changes in the mini-malls and the houses only serve to reinforce the structure.

I thought of Tink's lips. Then I fumbled in a pocket of my jacket, and pulled out a packet of cigarettes.

I lit one, inhaled, blew blue smoke into the warm night air.

There was a stunted palm tree growing outside the place I was stay-ing, and I resolved to walk for a way, keeping the tree in sight, to smoke my cigarette, perhaps even to think; but I felt too drained to think. I felt very sexless, and very alone.

A block or so down the road there was a bench, and when I reached it I sat down. I threw the stub of the cigarette onto the pavement, hard, and watched it shower orange sparks.

Someone said, "I'll buy a cigarette off you, pal. Here."

A hand, in front of my face, holding a quarter. I looked up.

He did not look old, although I would not have been prepared to say how old he was. Late thirties, perhaps. Mid-forties. He wore a long, shabby coat, colorless under the yellow street lamps, and his eyes were dark.

"Here. A quarter. That's a good price."

I shook my head, pulled out the packet of Marlboros, offered him one. "Keep your money. It's free. Have it."

He took the cigarette. I passed him a book of matches (it advertised a telephone sex line; I remember that), and he lit the cigarette. He offered me the matches back, and I shook my head. "Keep them. I always wind up accumulating books of matches in America."

"Uh-huh." He sat next to me, and smoked his cigarette. When he had smoked it halfway down, he tapped the lighted end off on the concrete, stubbed out the glow, and placed the butt of the cigarette behind his ear.

"I don't smoke much," he said. "Seems a pity to waste it, though."

A car careened down the road, veering from one side to the other. There were four young men in the car: the two in the front were both pulling at the wheel, and laughing. The windows were wound down, and I could hear their laughter, and the two in the back seat ("*Gaary, you asshole! What the fuck are you onnn mannnn?*") and the pulsing beat of a rock song. Not a song I recognised. The car looped around a corner, out of sight.

Soon the sounds were gone, too.

"I owe you," said the man on the bench.

"Sorry?"

"I owe you something. For the cigarette. And the matches. You wouldn't take the money. I owe you."

I shrugged, embarrassed. "Really, it's just a cigarette. I figure, if I give people cigarettes, then if ever I'm out, maybe people will give me cigarettes."

I laughed, to show I didn't really mean it, although I did. "Don't worry about it."

"Mm. You want to hear a story? True story? Stories always used to be good payment. These days . . ." He shrugged. ". . . Not so much."

I sat back on the bench, and the night was warm, and I looked at my watch: it was almost one in the morning. In England a freezing new day would already have begun: a workday would be starting for those who could beat the snow and get into work; another handful of old people, and those without homes, would have died, in the night, from the cold.

"Sure," I said to the man. "Sure. Tell me a story."

He coughed, grinned white teeth—a flash in the darkness—and he began.

"First thing I remember was the Word. And the Word was God. Sometimes, when I get *really* down, I remember the sound of the Word in my head, shaping me, forming me, giving me life.

"The Word gave me a body, gave me eyes. And I opened my eyes, and I saw the light of the Silver City.

"I was in a room—a silver room—and there wasn't anything in it except me. In front of me was a window, that went from floor to ceiling, open to the sky, and through the window I could see the spires of the City, and at the edge of the City, the Dark.

"I don't know how long I waited there. I wasn't impatient or anything, though. I remember that. It was like I was waiting until I was called; and I knew that some time I would be called. And if I had to wait until the end of everything, and never be called, why, that was fine too. But I'd be called, I was certain of that. And then I'd know my name, and my function.

"Through the window I could see silver spires, and in many of the other spires were windows; and in the windows I could see others like me. That was how I knew what I looked like.

"You wouldn't think it of me, seeing me now, but I was beautiful. I've come down in the world a way since then.

"I was taller then, and I had wings.

"They were huge and powerful wings, with feathers the colour of mother-of-pearl. They came out from just between my shoulderblades. They were so good. My wings.

"Sometimes I'd see others like me, the ones who'd left their rooms, who were already fulfilling their duties, I'd watch them soar through the sky from spire to spire, performing errands I could barely imagine.

"The sky above the City was a wonderful thing. It was always light, although lit by no sun—lit, perhaps by the City itself: but the quality of light was forever changing. Now pewter-coloured light, then brass, then a gentle gold, or a soft and quiet amethyst..."

The man stopped talking. He looked at me, his head on one side. There was a glitter in his eyes that scared me. "You know what amethyst is? A kind of purple stone?"

I nodded.

My crotch felt uncomfortable.

It occurred to me then that the man might not be mad; I found this far more disquieting than the alternative.

The man began talking once more. "I don't know how long it was that I waited, in my room. But time didn't mean anything. Not back then. We had all the time in the world.

"The next thing that happened to me, was when the Angel Lucifer came to my cell. He was taller than me, and his wings were imposing, his plumage perfect. He had skin the colour of sea-mist, and curly silver hair, and these wonderful grey eyes . . .

"I say *he,* but you should understand that none of us had any sex, to speak of." He gestured towards his lap. "Smooth and empty. Nothing there. You know.

"Lucifer shone. I mean it—he glowed from inside. All angels do. They're lit up from within, and in my cell the angel Lucifer burned like a lightning storm.

"He looked at me. And he named me.

"'You are Raguel,' he said. 'The Vengeance of the Lord.'

"I bowed my head, because I knew it was true. That was my name. That was my function.

"'There has been a . . . a wrong thing,' he said. 'The first of its kind. You are needed.'

"He turned and pushed himself into space, and I followed him, flew behind him across the Silver City, to the outskirts, where the City stops and the Darkness begins; and it was there, under a vast silver spire, that we descended to the street, and I saw the dead angel.

"The body lay, crumpled and broken, on the silver sidewalk. Its wings were crushed underneath it and a few loose feathers had already blown into the silver gutter.

"The body was almost dark. Now and again a light would flash inside it, an occasional flicker of cold fire in the chest, or in the eyes, or in the sexless groin, as the last of the glow of life left it for ever.

"Blood pooled in rubies on its chest and stained its white wing-feathers crimson. It was very beautiful, even in death.

"It would have broken your heart.

"Lucifer spoke to me, then. 'You must find who was responsible for this, and how; and take the Vengeance of the Name on whomever caused this thing to happen.'

"He really didn't have to say anything. I knew that already. The hunt, and the retribution: it was what I was created for, in the Beginning; it was what I *was.*

"'I have work to attend to,' said the angel Lucifer.

"He flapped his wings, once, hard, and rose upwards; the gust of wind sent the dead angel's loose feathers blowing across the street.

"I leaned down to examine the body. All luminescence had by now left it. It was a dark thing; a parody of an angel. It had a perfect, sexless face, framed by silver hair. One of the eyelids was open, revealing a placid grey eye; the other was closed. There were no nipples on the chest and only smoothness between the legs.

"I lifted the body up.

"The back of the angel was a mess. The wings were broken and twisted; the back of the head staved in; there was a floppiness to the corpse that made me think its spine had been broken as well. The back of the angel was all blood.

"The only blood on its front was in the chest area. I probed it with my forefinger, and it entered the body without difficulty.

"*He fell,* I thought. *And he was dead before he fell.*

"And I looked up at the windows that ranked the street. I stared across the Silver City. *You did this,* I thought. *I will find you, whoever you are. And I will take the Lord's vengeance upon you.*"

The man took the cigarette stub from behind his ear, lit it with a match. Briefly I smelled the ashtray smell of a dead cigarette, acrid and harsh; then he pulled down to the unburnt tobacco, exhaled blue smoke into the night air.

"The angel who had first discovered the body was called Phanuel.

"I spoke to him in the Hall of Being. That was the spire beside which the dead angel lay. In the Hall hung the . . . the blueprints, maybe, for what was going to be . . . all this." He gestured with the hand that held the stubby cigarette, pointing to the night sky and the parked cars and the world. "You know. The universe."

"Phanuel was the senior designer; working under him were a multitude of angels labouring on the details of the Creation. I watched him from the floor of the hall. He hung in the air below the Plan, and angels flew down to him, waiting politely in turn as they asked him questions, checked things with him, invited comment on their work. Eventually he left them, and descended to the floor.

"'You are Raguel,' he said. His voice was high, and fussy. 'What need have you of me?'

"'You found the body?'

"'Poor Carasel? Indeed I did. I was leaving the hall—there are a number of concepts we are currently constructing, and I wished to ponder one of them,—*Regret* by name. I was planning to get a little distance from the City—to fly above it, I mean, not to go into the Dark outside, I wouldn't do that, although there has been a some loose talk amongst . . . but, yes. I was going to rise, and contemplate.

"'I left the Hall, and . . . ,' he broke off. He was small, for an angel. His light was muted, but his eyes were vivid and bright. I mean really bright. 'Poor Carasel. How could he do that to himself? How?'

"'You think his destruction was self-inflicted?'

"He seemed puzzled—surprised that there could be any other explanation. 'But of course. Carasel was working under me, developing a number of concepts that shall be intrinsic to the Universe, when its Name shall be spoken. His group did a remarkable job on some of the real basics—*Dimension* was one, and *Sleep* another. There were others.'

"'Wonderful work. Some of his suggestions regarding the use of individual viewpoints to define dimensions were truly ingenious.

"'Anyway He had begun work on a new project. It's one of the really major ones—the ones that I would usually handle, or possibly even Zephkiel' He glanced upward. 'But Carasel had done such sterling work. And his last project was so remarkable. Something apparently quite trivial, that he and Saraquael elevated into . . .' He shrugged. 'But that is unimportant. It was this project that forced him into non-being. But none of us could ever have foreseen . . .'

"'What was his current project?'

"'Phanuel stared at me. 'I'm not sure I ought to tell you. All the new concepts are considered sensitive, until we get them into the final form in which they will be Spoken.'

"I felt myself transforming. I am not sure how I can explain it to you, but suddenly I wasn't me—I was something larger. I was transfigured: I was my function.

"Phanuel was unable to meet my gaze.

"'I am Raguel, who is the Vengeance of the Lord,' I told him. 'I serve the Name directly. It is my mission to discover the nature of this deed, and to take the Name's vengeance on those responsible. My questions are to be answered.'

"The little angel trembled, and he spoke fast.

"'Carasel and his partner were researching *Death*. Cessation of life. An end to physical, animated existence. They were putting it all together. But

Carasel always went too far into his work—we had a terrible time with him when he was designing *Agitation*. That was when he was working on *Emotions* . . .'

"'You think Carasel died to—to research the phenomenon?'

"'Or because it intrigued him. Or because he followed his research just too far. Yes.' Phanuel flexed his fingers, stared at me with those brightly shining eyes. 'I trust that you will repeat none of this to any unauthorised persons, Raguel.'

"'What did you do when you found the body?'

"'I came out of the Hall, as I said, and there was Carasel on the sidewalk, staring up. I asked him what he was doing and he did not reply. Then I noticed the inner fluid, and that Carasel seemed unable, rather than unwilling, to talk to me.

"'I was scared. I did not know what to do.

"The Angel Lucifer came up behind me. He asked me if there was some kind of problem. I told him. I showed him the body And then . . . then his Aspect came upon him, and he communed with the Name. He burned so bright.

"'Then he said he had to fetch the one whose function embraced events like this, and he left—to seek you, I imagine.

"'As Carasel's death was now being dealt with, and his fate was no real concern of mine, I returned to work, having gained a new—and I suspect, quite valuable—perspective on the mechanics of *Regret*.

"'I am considering taking *Death* away from the Carasel and Saraquael partnership. I may reassign it to Zephkiel, my senior partner, if he is willing to take it on. He excels on contemplative projects!

"By now there was a line of angels waiting to talk to Phanuel. I felt I had almost all I was going to get from him.

"'Who did Carasel work with? Who would have been the last to see him alive?'

"'You could talk to Saraquael, I suppose—he was his partner, after all. Now, if you'll excuse me . . .'

"He returned to his swarm of aides: advising, correcting, suggesting, forbidding."

The man paused.

The street was quiet, now; I remember the low whisper of his voice, the buzz of a cricket somewhere. A small animal—a cat perhaps, or something more exotic, a raccoon, or even a jackal—darted from shadow to shadow among the parked cars on the opposite side of the street.

"Saraquael was in the highest of the mezzanine galleries that ringed the Hall of Being. As I said, the Universe was in the middle of the Hall, and it glinted and sparkled and shone. Went up quite a way, too . . ."

"The Universe you mention, it was, what, a diagram?" I asked, interrupting for the first time.

"Not really. Kind of. Sorta. It was a blueprint; but it was full-sized, and it hung in the Hall, and all these angels went around and fiddled with it all the time. Doing stuff with *Gravity,* and *Music* and *Klar* and whatever. It wasn't really the universe, not yet. It would be, when it was finished, and it was time for it to be properly Named."

"But . . ." I grasped for words to express my confusion. The man interrupted me.

"Don't worry about it. Think of it as a model, if that makes it easier for you. Or a map. Or a—what's the word? Prototype. Yeah. A Model-T Ford universe." He grinned. "You got to understand, a lot of the stuff I'm telling you, I'm translating already; putting it in a form you can understand. Otherwise I couldn't tell the story at all. You want to hear it?"

"Yes." I didn't care if it was true or not; it was a story I needed to hear all the way through to the end.

"Good. So shut up and listen.

"So I met Saraquael, in the topmost gallery. There was no one else about—just him, and some papers, and some small, glowing models.

"'I've come about Carasel,' I told him.

"He looked at me. 'Carasel isn't here at this time,' he said. 'I expect him to return shortly.'

"I shook my head.

"'Carasel won't be coming back. He's stopped existing as a spiritual entity,' I said.

"His light paled, and his eyes opened very wide. 'He's dead?'

"'That's what I said. Do you have any ideas about how it happened?'

"'I . . . this is so sudden. I mean, he'd been talking about . . . but I had no idea that he would . . .'

"'Take it slowly.'

"Saraquael nodded.

"He stood up and walked to the window. There was no view of the Silver City from his window—just a reflected glow from the City and the sky behind us, hanging in the air, and beyond that, the Dark. The wind from the Dark gently caressed Saraquael's hair as he spoke. I stared at his back.

"'Carasel is . . . no, was. That's right, isn't it? *Was.* He was always so involved. And so creative. But it was never enough for him. He always wanted to understand everything—to experience what he was working on. He was never content to just create it—to understand it intellectually. He wanted *all* of it.

"'That wasn't a problem before, when we were working on properties of matter. But when we began to design some of the Named emotions . . . he got too involved with his work.

"'And our latest project was *Death.* It's one of the hard ones—one of the big ones, too, I suspect. Possibly it may even become the attribute that's going to define the Creation for the Created: if not for *Death,* they'd be content to simply exist, but with *Death,* well, their lives will have meaning—a boundary beyond which the living cannot cross . . .'

"'So you think he killed himself?'

"'I know he did,' said Saraquael. I walked to the window, and looked out. Far below, a *long* way, I could see a tiny white dot. That was Carasel's body I'd have to arrange for someone to take care of it. I wondered what we would do with it; but there would be someone who would know, whose function was the removal of unwanted things. It was not my function. I knew that.

"'How?'

"He shrugged. 'I know. Recently he'd begun asking questions—questions about *Death.* How we could know whether or not it was right to make this thing, to set the rules, if we were not going to experience it ourselves. He kept talking about it!

"'Didn't you wonder about this?'

"'Saraquael turned, for the first time, to look at me. 'No. That *is* our function—to discuss, to improvise, to aid the Creation and the Created. We sort it out now, so that when it all Begins, it'll run like clockwork. Right now we're working on *Death.* So obviously that's what we look at. The physical aspect; the emotional aspect; the philosophical aspect . . .

"'And the *patterns.* Carasel had the notion that what we do here in the Hall of Being creates patterns. That there are structures and shapes appropriate to beings and events that, once begun, must continue until they reach their end. For us, perhaps, as well as for them. Conceivably he felt this was one of his patterns.'

"'Did you know Carasel well?'

"'As well as any of us know each other. We saw each other here; we worked side by side. At certain times I would retire to my cell, across the city. Sometimes he would do the same.'

"'Tell me about Phanuel.'

"His mouth crooked into a smile. 'He's officious. Doesn't do much—farms everything out, and takes all the credit.' He lowered his voice, although there was no other soul in the gallery. 'To hear him talk, you'd think that *Love* was all his own work. But to his credit, he does make sure the work gets done. Zephkiel's the real thinker of the two senior designers, but he doesn't come here. He stays back in his cell in the City, and contemplates; resolves problems from a distance. If you need to speak to Zephkiel, you go to Phanuel, and Phanuel relays your questions to Zephkiel . . .'

"I cut him short. 'How about Lucifer? Tell me about him.'

"'Lucifer? The Captain of the Host? He doesn't work here . . . He has visited the Hall a couple of times, though—inspecting the Creation. They say he reports directly to the Name. I have never spoken to him.'

"'Did he know Carasel?'

"'I doubt it. As I said, he has only been here twice. I have seen him on other occasions, though. Through here.' He flicked a wingtip, indicating the world outside the window. 'In flight.'

"'Where to?'

"Saraquael seemed to be about to say something; then he changed his mind. 'I don't know.'

"I looked out of the window, at the Darkness outside the Silver City.

"'I may want to talk with you some more, later,' I told Saraquael.

"'Very good.' I turned to go.

"'Sir? Do you know if they will be assigning me another partner? For *Death*?'

"'No,' I told him. 'I'm afraid I don't.'

"In the centre of the Silver City was a park—a place of recreation and rest. I found the Angel Lucifer there, beside a river. He was just standing, watching the water flow.

"'Lucifer?'

"He inclined his head. 'Raguel. Are you making progress?'

"'I don't know. Maybe. I need to ask you a few questions. Do you mind?'

"'Not at all.'

"'How did you come upon the body?'

"'I didn't. Not exactly. I saw Phanuel, standing in the street. He looked distressed. I enquired whether there was something wrong, and he showed me the dead angel. And I fetched you.'

"'I see.'

"He leaned down, let one hand enter the cold water of the river. The water splashed and rilled around it. 'Is that all?'

"'Not quite. What were you doing in that part of the City?'

"'I don't see what business that is of yours.'

"'It is my business, Lucifer. What were you doing there?'

"'I was . . . walking. I do that sometimes. Just walk, and think. And try to understand.' He shrugged.

"'You walk on the edge of the City?'

"A beat, then, 'Yes.'

"'That's all I want to know. For now.'

"'Who else have you talked to?'

"'Carasel's boss, and his partner. They both feel that he killed him-self—ended his own life.'

"'Who else are you going to talk to?'

"'I looked up. The spires of the City of the Angels towered above us. 'Maybe everyone.'

"'All of them?'

"'If I need to. It's my function. I cannot rest until I understand what happened, and until the vengeance of the Name has been taken on whomever was responsible. But I'll tell you something I do know.'

"'What would that be?' Drops of water fell like diamonds from the angel Lucifer's perfect fingers.

"'Carasel did not kill himself!

"'How do you know that?'

"'I am Vengeance. If Carasel had died by his own hand,' I explained to the Captain of the Heavenly Host, 'there would have been no call for me. Would there?'

"He did not reply.

"I flew upwards, into the light of the eternal morning.

"You got another cigarette on you?"

I fumbled out the red and white packet, handed him a cigarette.

"Obliged.

"Zephkiel's cell was larger than mine.

"It wasn't a place for waiting. It was a place to live, and work, and *be*. It was lined with books, and scrolls, and papers, and there were images and representations on the walls: pictures. I'd never seen a picture before.

"In the centre of the room was a large chair, and Zephkiel sat there, his eyes closed, his head back.

"As I approached him he opened his eyes.

"They burned no brighter than the eyes of any of the other angels I had seen, but somehow, they seemed to have seen more. It was something about the way he looked. I'm not sure I can explain it. And he had no wings.

"'Welcome, Raguel,' he said. He sounded tired.

"'You are Zephkiel?' I don't know why I asked him that. I mean, I knew who people were. It's part of my function, I guess. Recognition. I know who *you* are.

"'Indeed. You are staring, Raguel. I have no wings, it is true, but then, my function does not call for me to leave this cell. I remain here, and I ponder. Phanuel reports back to me, brings me the new things, for my opinion. He brings me the problems, and I think about them, and occasionally I make myself useful by making some small suggestions. That is my function. As yours is vengeance.'

"'Yes.'

"'You are here about the death of the angel Carasel?'

"'Yes.'

"'I did not kill him.'

"When he said it, I knew it was true.

"'Do you know who did?'

"'That is *your* function, is it not? To discover who killed the poor thing, and to take the Vengeance of the Name upon him.'

"'Yes.'

"He nodded.

"'What do you want to know?'

"I paused, reflecting on what I had heard that day. 'Do you know what Lucifer was doing in that part of the City, before the body was found?'

"The old angel stared at me. 'I can hazard a guess.'

"'Yes?'

"'He was walking in the Dark.'

"I nodded. I had a shape in my mind, now. Something I could almost grasp. I asked the last question:

"'What can you tell me about *Love*?'

"And he told me. And I thought I had it all.

"I returned to the place where Carasel's body had been. The remains had been removed, the blood had been cleaned away, the stray feathers collected and disposed of. There was nothing on the silver sidewalk to indicate it had ever been there. But I knew where it had been.

"I ascended on my wings, flew upward until I neared the top of the spire of the Hall of Being. There was a window there, and I entered.

"Saraquael was working there, putting a wingless mannikin into a small box. On one side of the box was a representation of a small brown creature, with eight legs. On the other was a representation of a white blossom.

"'Saraquael?'

"'Hm? Oh, it's you. Hello. Look at this: if you were to die, and to be, let us say, put into the earth in a box, which would you want laid on top of you—a spider, here, or a lily, here?'

"'The lily, I suppose.'

"'Yes, that's what I think, too. But why? I wish . . .' He raised a hand to his chin, stared down at the two models, put first one on top of the box then the other, experimentally. 'There's so much to do, Raguel. So much to get right. And we only get one chance at it, you know. There'll just be one universe—we can't keep trying until we get it right. I wish I understood why all this was so important to Him . . .'

"'Do you know where Zephkiel's cell is?' I asked him.

"'Yes. I mean, I've never been there. But I know where it is.'

"'Good. Go there. He'll be expecting you. I will meet you there.'

"He shook his head. 'I have work to do. I can't just . . .'

"I felt my function come upon me. I looked down at him, and I said, 'You will be there. Go now.'

"He said nothing. He backed away from me, toward the window, staring at me; then he turned, and flapped his wings, and I was alone.

"I walked to the central well of the Hall, and let myself fall, tumbling down through the model of the universe: it glittered around me, unfamiliar colours and shapes seething and writhing without meaning.

"As I approached the bottom, I beat my wings, slowing my descent, and stepped lightly onto the silver floor. Phanuel stood between two angels, who were both trying to claim his attention.

"'I don't care how aesthetically pleasing it would be,' he was explaining to one of them. 'We simply cannot put it in the centre. Background radiation would prevent any possible life-forms from even getting a foothold; and anyway, it's too unstable.'

"He turned to the other. 'Okay, let's see it. Hmm. So that's *Green*, is it?

It's not exactly how I'd imagined it, but. Mm. Leave it with me. I'll get back to you.' He took a paper from the angel, folded it over decisively.

"He turned to me. His manner was brusque, and dismissive. 'Yes?'

"'I need to talk to you.'

"'Mm? Well, make it quick. I have much to do. If this is about Carasel's death, I have told you all I know!

"'It is about Carasel's death. But I will not speak to you now. Not here. Go to Zephkiel's cell: he is expecting you. I will meet you there.'

"He seemed about to say something, but he only nodded, walked toward the door.

"I turned to go, when something occurred to me. I stopped the angel who had the *Green*. 'Tell me something.'

"'If I can, sir.'

"'That thing.' I pointed to the Universe. 'What's it going to be *for*?'

"'For? Why, it is the Universe.'

"'I know what it's called. But what purpose will it serve?'

"He frowned. 'It is part of the plan. The Name wishes it; He requires *such and such,* to these dimensions, and having *such and such* properties and ingredients. It is our function to bring it into existence, according to His wishes. I am sure He knows its function, but He has not revealed it to me.' His tone was one of gentle rebuke.

"I nodded, and left that place.

"High above the City a phalanx of angels wheeled and circled and dove. Each held a flaming sword which trailed a streak of burning brightness behind it, dazzling the eye. They moved in unison through the salmon-pink sky. They were very beautiful. It was—you know on summer evenings, when you get whole flocks of birds performing their dances in the sky? Weaving and circling and clustering and breaking apart again, so just as you think you understand the pattern, you realise you don't, and you never will? It was like that, only better.

"Above me was the sky. Below me, the shining City. My home. And outside the City, the Dark.

"Lucifer hovered a little below the Host, watching their maneuvers.

"'Lucifer?'

"'Yes, Raguel? Have you discovered your malefactor?'

"'I think so. Will you accompany me to Zephkiel's cell? There are others waiting for us there, and I will explain everything.'

"He paused. Then, 'Certainly.'

"He raised his perfect face to the angels, now performing a slow revolution in the sky, each moving through the air keeping perfect pace with the next, none of them ever touching. 'Azazel!'

"An angel broke from the circle; the others adjusted almost imperceptibly to his disappearance, filling the space, so you could no longer see where he had been.

"'I have to leave. You are in command, Azazel. Keep them drilling. They still have much to perfect.'

"'Yes, sir.'

"Azazel hovered where Lucifer had been, staring up at the flock of angels, and Lucifer and I descended toward the city.

"'He's my second-in-command,' said Lucifer. 'Bright. Enthusiastic. Azazel would follow you anywhere.'

"'What are you training them for?'

"'War.'

"'With whom?'

"'How do you mean?'

"'Who are they going to fight? Who else is there?'

"He looked at me; his eyes were clear, and honest. 'I do not know. But He has Named us to be His army. So we will be perfect. For Him. The Name is infallible and all-just, and all-wise, Raguel. It cannot be other-wise, no matter what—' He broke off, and looked away.

"'You were going to say?'

"'It is of no importance.'

"'Ah.'

"We did not talk for the rest of the descent to Zephkiel's cell."

I looked at my watch: it was almost three. A chill breeze had begun to blow down the LA street, and I shivered. The man noticed, and he paused in his story. "You okay?" he asked.

"I'm fine. Please carry on. I'm fascinated."

He nodded.

"They were waiting for us in Zephkiel's cell: Phanuel, Saraquael, and Zephkiel. Zephkiel was sitting in his chair. Lucifer took up a position beside the window.

"I walked to centre of the room, and I began.

"'I thank you all for coming here. You know who I am; you know my function. I am the Vengeance of the Name: the arm of the Lord. I am Raguel.

"'The angel Carasel is dead. It was given to me to find out why he died, who killed him. This I have done. Now, the angel Carasel was a designer in the Hall of Being. He was very good, or so I am told . . .

"'Lucifer. Tell me what you were doing, before you came upon Phanuel, and the body.'

"'I have told you already I was walking.'

"'Where were you walking?'

"'I do not see what business that is of yours.'

"'*Tell me.*'

"He paused. He was taller than any of us; tall, and proud. 'Very well. I was walking in the Dark. I have been walking in the Darkness for some time now. It helps me to gain a perspective on the City—being outside it. I see how fair it is, how perfect. There is nothing more enchanting than our home. Nothing more complete. Nowhere else that anyone would want to be.'

"'And what do you do in the Dark, Lucifer?'

"He stared at me. 'I walk. And . . . there are voices, in the Dark. I listen to the voices. They promise me things, ask me questions, whisper and plead. And I ignore them. I steel myself and I gaze at the City. It is the only way I have of testing myself—putting myself to any kind of trial. I am the Captain of the Host; I am the first among the Angels, and I must prove myself.'

"I nodded. 'Why did you not tell me this before?'

"He looked down. 'Because I am the only angel who walks in the Dark. Because I do not want others to walk in the Dark: I am strong enough to challenge the voices, to test myself. Others are not so strong. Others might stumble, or fall.'

"'Thank you, Lucifer. That is all, for now.' I turned to the next angel. 'Phanuel. How long have you been taking credit for Carasel's work?'

"His mouth opened, but no sound came out.

"'*Well?*'

"'I . . . I would not take credit for another's work.'

"'But you did take credit for *Love*?'

"He blinked. 'Yes. I did.'

"'Would you care to explain to us all what *Love* is?' I asked.

"He glanced around uncomfortably. 'It's a feeling of deep affection and attraction for another being, often combined with passion or desire—a need to be with another.' He spoke dryly, didactically, as if he were reciting a mathematical formula. 'The feeling that we have for the Name, for our Creator—that is *Love* . . . amongst other things. *Love* will be an impulse which will inspire and ruin in equal measure. We are . . .' He paused, then began once more. 'We are very proud of it.'

"He was mouthing the words. He no longer seemed to hold any hope that we would believe them.

"'Who did the majority of the work on *Love*? No, don't answer. Let me ask the others first. Zephkiel? When Phanuel passed the details on *Love* to you for approval, who did he tell you was responsible for it?'

"The wingless angel smiled gently. 'He told me it was his project.'

"'Thank you, sir. Now, Saraquael: whose was *Love*?'

"'Mine. Mine and Carasel's. Perhaps more his than mine, but we worked on it together.'

"'You knew that Phanuel was claiming the credit for it?'

"'. . . Yes.'

"'And you permitted this?'

"'He—he promised us that he would give us a good project of our own to follow. He promised that if we said nothing we would be given more big projects—and he was true to his word. He gave us *Death*.'

"I turned back to Phanuel. 'Well?'

"'It is true that I claimed that *Love* was mine.'

"'But it was Carasel's. And Saraquael's.'

"'Yes.'

"'Their last project—before *Death*?'

"'Yes.'

"'That is all.'

"I walked over to the window, looked out at the silver spires, looked at the Dark. And I began to speak.

"'Carasel was a remarkable designer. If he had one failing, it was that he threw himself too deeply into his work.' I turned back to them. The angel Saraquael was shivering, and lights were flickering beneath his skin. 'Saraquael? Who did Carasel love? Who was his lover?'

"He stared at the floor. Then he stared up, proudly, aggressively. And he smiled.

"'I was.'

"'Do you want to tell me about it?'

"'No.' A shrug. 'But I suppose I must. Very well, then.

"'We worked together. And when we began to work on *Love* . . . we became lovers. It was his idea. We would go back to his cell, whenever we could snatch the time. There we touched each other, held each other, whispered endearments and protestations of eternal devotion. His welfare mattered more to me than my own. I existed for him. When I was alone I would repeat his name to myself, and think of nothing but him.

"'When I was with him . . .' He paused. He looked down. '. . . Nothing else mattered.'

"I walked to where Saraquael stood; lifted his chin with my hand, stared into his grey eyes. 'Then why did you kill him?'

"'Because he would no longer love me. When we started to work on *Death* he—he lost interest. He was no longer mine. He belonged to *Death*. And if I could not have him, then his new lover was welcome to him. I could not bear his presence—I could not endure to have him near me and to know that he felt nothing for me. That was what hurt the most. I thought . . . I hoped . . . that if he was gone then I would no longer care for him—that the pain would stop.

"'So I killed him; I stabbed him, and I threw his body from our window in the Hall of Being. But the pain has *not* stopped.' It was almost a wail.

"Saraquael reached up, removed my hand from his chin. 'Now what?'

"I felt my aspect begin to come upon me; felt my function possess me. I was no longer an individual—I was the Vengeance of the Lord.

"I moved close to Saraquael, and embraced him. I pressed my lips to his, forced my tongue into his mouth. We kissed. He closed his eyes.

"I felt it well up within me then: a burning, a brightness. From the corner of my eyes, I could see Lucifer and Phanuel averting their faces from my light; I could feel Zephkiel's stare. And my light became brighter and brighter, until it erupted—from my eyes, from my chest, from my fingers, from my lips: a white, searing fire.

"The white flames consumed Saraquael slowly, and he clung to me as he burned.

"Soon there was nothing left of him. Nothing at all.

"I felt the flame leave me. I returned to myself once more.

"Phanuel was sobbing. Lucifer was pale. Zephkiel sat in his chair, quietly watching me.

"I turned to Phanuel and Lucifer. 'You have seen the Vengeance of the Lord,' I told them. 'Let it act as a warning to you both.'

"Phanuel nodded. 'It has. Oh it has. I, I will be on my way, sir. I will return to my appointed post. If that is all right with you?'

"'Go.'

"He stumbled to the window, and plunged into the light, his wings beating furiously.

"Lucifer walked over to the place on the silver floor where Saraquael had once stood. He knelt, stared desperately at the floor as if he were trying to find some remnant of the angel I had destroyed: a fragment of ash, or bone, or charred feather; but there was nothing to find. Then he looked up at me.

"'That was not right,' he said. 'That was not just.' He was crying; wet tears ran down his face. Perhaps Saraquael was the first to love, but Lucifer was the first to shed tears. I will never forget that.

"I stared at him, impassively. 'It was justice. He killed another. He was killed in his turn. You called me to my function, and I performed it.'

"'But . . . he *loved*. He should have been forgiven. He should have been helped. He should not have been destroyed like that. That was *wrong*.'

"'It was His will.'

"Lucifer stood. 'Then perhaps His will is unjust. Perhaps the voices in the Darkness speak truly after all. How *can* this be right?'

"'It is right. It is His will. I merely performed my function.'

"He wiped away the tears, with the back of his hand. 'No,' he said, flatly. He shook his head, slowly, from side to side. Then he said, 'I must think on this. I will go now.'

"He walked to the window, stepped into the sky, and he was gone.

"Zephkiel and I were alone in his cell. I went over to his chair. He nodded at me. 'You have performed your function well, Raguel. Shouldn't you return to your cell, to wait until you are next needed?'"

The man on the bench turned towards me: his eyes sought mine. Until now it had seemed—for most of his narrative—that he was scarcely aware of me; he had stared ahead of himself, whispered his tale in little better than a monotone. Now it felt as if he had discovered me, and that he spoke to me alone, rather than to the air, or the City of Los Angeles. And he said:

"I knew that he was right. But I *couldn't* have left then—not even if I had wanted to. My aspect had not entirely left me; my function was not completely fulfilled. And then it fell into place; I saw the whole picture. And like Lucifer, I knelt. I touched my forehead to the silver floor. 'No, Lord,' I said. 'Not yet.'

"Zephkiel rose from his chair. 'Get up. It is not fitting for one angel to act in this way to another. It is not right. Get up!'

"I shook my head. 'Father, You are no angel,' I whispered.

"Zephkiel said nothing. For a moment my heart misgave within me.

I was afraid. 'Father, I was charged to discover who was responsible for Carasel's death. And I do know.'

"'You have taken your vengeance, Raguel.'

"'*Your* vengeance, Lord.'

"And then He sighed, and sat down once more. 'Ah, little Raguel. The problem with creating things is that they perform so much better than one had ever planned. Shall I ask how you recognised me?'

"'I . . . I am not certain, Lord. You have no wings. You wait at the centre of the City, supervising the Creation directly. When I destroyed Saraquael, You did not look away. You know too many things. You . . .' I paused, and thought. 'No, I do not know how I know. As You say, You have created me well. But I only understood who You were and the meaning of the drama we had enacted here for You, when I saw Lucifer leave.'

"'What did you understand, child?'

"'Who killed Carasel. Or at least, who was pulling the strings. For example, who arranged for Carasel and Saraquael to work together on *Love,* knowing Carasel's tendency to involve himself too deeply in his work?'

"He was speaking to me gently, almost teasingly, as an adult would pretend to make conversation with a tiny child. 'Why should anyone have "pulled the strings," Raguel?'

"'Because nothing occurs without reason; and all the reasons are Yours. You set Saraquael up: yes, he killed Carasel. But he killed Carasel so that *I* could destroy *him.*'

"'And were you wrong to destroy him?'

"I looked into His old, old eyes. 'It was my function. But I do not think it was just. I think perhaps it was needed that I destroy Saraquael, in order to demonstrate to Lucifer the Injustice of the Lord.'

"He smiled, then. 'And whatever reason would I have for doing that?'

"'I . . . I do not know. I do not understand—no more than I understand why You created the Dark, or the voices in the Darkness. But You did. You caused all this to occur.'

"He nodded. 'Yes. I did. Lucifer must brood on the unfairness of Saraquael's destruction. And that—amongst other things—will precipitate him into certain actions. Poor sweet Lucifer. His way will be the hardest of all my children; for there is a part he must play in the drama that is to come, and it is a grand role.'

"I remained kneeling in front of the Creator of All Things.

"'What will you do now, Raguel?' He asked me.

"'I must return to my cell. My function is now fulfilled. I have taken vengeance, and I have revealed the perpetrator. That is enough. But— Lord?'

"'Yes, child.'

"'I feel dirty. I feel tarnished. I feel befouled. Perhaps it is true that all that happens is in accordance with Your will, and thus it is good. But sometimes You leave blood on Your instruments.'

"He nodded, as if He agreed with me. 'If you wish, Raguel, you may forget all this. All that has happened this day.' And then He said, 'However, you will not be able to speak of this to any other angels, whether you choose to remember it or not.'

"'I will remember it.'

"'It is your choice. But sometimes you will find it is easier by far not to remember. Forgetfulness can sometimes bring freedom, of a sort. Now, if you do not mind,' He reached down, took a file from a stack on the floor, opened it, '— there is work I should be getting on with.'

"I stood up and walked to the window. I hoped He would call me back, explain every detail of His plan to me, somehow make it all better. But He said nothing, and I left His Presence without ever looking back."

The man was silent, then. And he remained silent—I couldn't even hear him breathing—for so long that I began to get nervous, thinking that perhaps he had fallen asleep, or died.

Then he stood up.

"There you go, pal. That's your story. Do you think it was worth a couple of cigarettes and a book of matches?" He asked the question as if it was important to him, without irony.

"Yes," I told him. "Yes. It was. But what happened next? How did you . . . I mean, if . . ." I trailed off.

It was dark on the street, now, at the edge of daybreak. One by one the streetlights had begun to flicker out, and he was silhouetted against the glow of the dawn sky. He thrust his hands into his pockets. "What happened? I left home, and I lost my way, and these days home's a long way back. Sometimes you do things you regret, but there's nothing you can do about them. Times change. Doors close behind you. You move on. You know?

"Eventually I wound up here. They used to say no one's ever originally from LA. True as Hell in my case."

And then, before I could understand what he was doing, he leaned down and kissed me, gently, on the cheek. His stubble was rough and prickly, but his breath was surprisingly sweet. He whispered into my ear: 'I never fell. I don't care what they say. I'm still doing my job, as I see it.'

My cheek burned where his lips had touched it.

He straightened up. "But I still want to go home."

The man walked away down the darkened street, and I sat on the bench and watched him go. I felt like he had taken something from me, although I could no longer remember what. And I felt like something had been left in its place—absolution, perhaps, or innocence, although of what, or from what, I could no longer say.

An image from somewhere: a scribbled drawing, of two angels in flight above a perfect city; and over the image a child's perfect handprint, which stains the white paper blood-red. It came into my head unbidden, and I no longer know what it meant.

I stood up.

It was too dark to see the face of my watch, but I knew I would get no sleep that day I walked back to the place I was staying, to the house by the stunted palm tree, to wash myself, and to wait. I thought about angels, and about Tink; and I wondered whether love and death went hand in hand.

The next day the planes to England were flying again.

I felt strange—lack of sleep had forced me into that miserable state in which everything seems flat and of equal importance; when nothing matters, and in which reality seems scraped thin and threadbare. The taxi journey to the airport was a nightmare. I was hot, and tired, and testy. I wore a T-shirt in the LA heat; my coat was packed at the bottom of my luggage, where it had been for the entire stay.

The airplane was crowded, but I didn't care.

The stewardess walked down the aisle with a rack of newspapers: the *Herald Tribune, USA Today,* and the *LA Times.* I took a copy of the *Times,* but the words left my head as my eyes scanned over them. Nothing that I read remained with me. No, I lie: somewhere in the back of the paper was a report of a triple murder: two women, and a small child. No names were given, and I do not know why the report should have registered as it did.

Soon I fell asleep. I dreamed about fucking Tink, while blood ran sluggishly from her closed eyes and lips. The blood was cold and viscous and clammy, and I awoke chilled by the plane's air-conditioning, with an unpleasant taste in my mouth. My tongue and lips were dry. I looked out of the scratched oval window, stared down at the clouds, and it occurred to me then (not for the first time) that the clouds were in actuality another land, where everyone knew just what they were looking for and how to get back where they started from.

Staring down at the clouds is one of the things I have always liked best about flying. That, and the proximity one feels to one's death.

I wrapped myself in the thin aircraft blanket, and slept some more, but if further dreams came then they made no impression upon me.

A blizzard blew up shortly after the plane landed in England, knocking out the airport's power supply. I was alone in an airport elevator at the time, and it went dark and jammed between floors. A dim emergency light flickered on. I pressed the crimson alarm button until the batteries ran down and it ceased to sound; then I shivered in my LA T-shirt, in the corner of my little silver room. I watched my breath steam in the air, and I hugged myself for warmth.

There wasn't anything in there except me; but even so, I felt safe, and secure. Soon someone would come and force open the doors. Eventually somebody would let me out; and I knew that I would soon be home.

✝

The Bishop and the Hit Man
A Blackie Ryan Story

Andrew Greeley

"I've put down thirty-two men, Father," he told me. "I could give you all their names . . ."

"That won't be necessary," I assured him.

I have often argued that if the rule of celibacy is to be lifted partially for Catholic priests but only for a certain period each week, Sunday night would be the appropriate time. In a dark and lonely rectory, quiet for the only night of the week, the priest who mans the fort feels that he is isolated from the human condition. This is especially true if the rectory is a monumental monstrosity like that of Holy Name Cathedral, a place which at the best of times is filled with silent emanations from the past and an occasional spirit of a departed bishop—or even Cardinal—is said to walk the corridors.

I've never seen one such, however, being the most empirical and pragmatic of men.

It is perhaps an appropriate time and place to open the door at 720 North Wabash in the so-called Windy City (Richard M. Daley, mayor, and Michael Jordan, owner) and encounter a self-professed hit man.

"I don't know," he continued. "Some of them probably deserved it.

But I never asked about that. Like in any line of work, you do what you're told and don't ask questions. It's my line of work, Father."

"Indeed."

He talked like a character in one of the many films about the Outfit (as we call it in Chicago). However he did not look like Robert De Niro or any of the other stars who appear in such films. He was trim, of medium height, and dressed in a conservative three-piece charcoal gray suit (with a faint hint of a line in its weave). His thin brown hair receded only marginally from an utterly unremarkable face, and his skin was pale and bland. Only his hard blue eyes, innocent of emotion or mercy, suggested that he might be a psychopath.

"See this." He opened his expensive attaché case and revealed what looked like a toy weapon. "This is a twenty-five-millimeter automatic. Small, isn't it? Looks like a toy, huh? I don't carve any notches in, but I've put down ten men with it."

"Remarkable."

Who would put out a contract on an inoffensive little priest? I wondered.

"It's not loaded." He fitted an instrument which, from frequent attendance at the cinema, I identified as a silencer. "Some night soon I'm going to walk up behind Mr. Richard Powers as he's taking his walk down East Lake Shore Drive, confident that nothing can happen in that busy and affluent street, yell, 'Hey, Dick,' and put a bullet right between his eyes. No noise, no blood, no mess, and he's facing God."

"Astonishing."

He unfastened the silencer and put the gun away. My guardian angel and I began to breathe again.

"This is all under the seal of confession, isn't it?"

"As you wished."

When I had ushered him into the "counseling room" on the first floor of the Cathedral rectory and hung up his saturated raincoat he told me that he wanted to go to confession, a wish expressed less frequently now than it used to be because Catholics are freer from compulsions about minor matters ("I missed Mass on Sunday, but I was sick") than they used to be.

Multiple homicide was not, however, a minor matter.

"I'm the best there is in the country," my guest insisted. "No one is as neat or as professional as I am. Not a single arrest. The cops don't know who I am. Or where I live. Even my clients don't know who I am.

All the contact is indirect. My family and my neighbors think I have a small business, which I do as a cover. But this is my real line of work."

"Ah."

"I'm known only by my nickname—the Pro. Neat, isn't it?"

"Indeed."

"I don't do too many jobs anymore, Father. One, two a year, and that's all. I get two hundred big ones for each job, half on agreement, half on fulfillment. They don't want to pay that kind of money, they don't ask for the Pro, huh? A man needs that kind of money these days to put his kids through college, know what I mean?"

"A major expense."

"All my kids are in Catholic schools, Father. A boy in college, two high school kids, and one little doll that just made her First Communion. I'm raising them all to be good Catholics, Father."

"Admirable."

"I pray to God every night that they'll never find out what their daddy really does for a living."

Dickie Powers is not one of my favorite people. He is, not to put too fine an edge on things, to the right of Neil of the Nine Hostages, both politically and ecclesiastically. He presumes that because he's a highly successful developer (though he owns a lot of vacant land in our current recessionary times), he would more ably run the Archdiocese of Chicago than Sean Cardinal Cronin, presently, by the Grace of God and the impatient toleration of the Apostolic See, Archbishop of Chicago. Milord Cronin has a long record of more than holding his own against rich and conservative Catholics. However, Dick Powers also thinks that he knows more about how the Cathedral parish ought to be run—down to such tiny details as the Sunday Mass schedule—than the inoffensive and ineffectual little priest who actually does run it. And proposes to continue to run it. Democratically, of course.

His basic strategy for dealing with the problems the Church faces today is to purify it of all who may disagree with certain of its teachings.

"Throw out everyone who won't accept the birth control teaching! Get rid of them all! They're all going to hell anyway! We don't need them and don't want them!"

My problem with such a strategy is not merely that it would empty the Cathedral and that there would be no income to pay the heat and light bills and keep the schools (of which we have two) open. My problem is that even if we tried it, the laity would not leave. Despite Dickie

Powers, we no longer have an Inquisition available to turn the recalcitrant over to the secular arm for suitable disposal.

I would not go so far as one of my young colleagues who, with lamentable lack of charity, remarked at the table the other night, "Dickie Powers is one of the great assholes of the Western world."

I did not dispute the point, however.

"I don't know what this Powers guy did to offend my clients . . . you can guess who they are, Father. Probably welched on a deal. My clients don't like welchers. A deal is a deal, and if they let one guy get away welching, then everyone would, isn't that so?"

"Arguably."

Recently Dickie had done something extraordinary which could have increased the number of people who disliked him. He had taken unto himself a new wife, twenty-five years younger than his fifty-five years, his first wife having finally escaped him to her eternal reward— helped by acute cirrhosis of the liver, in turn the result of, among other things, chronic alcoholism.

"Being married to Dickie," Milord Cronin had remarked, again with scandalous lack of charity, "would drive anyone to drink."

I may have added, "And a new wife would drive to the creature those who have expectations of inheritance at the time of his departure for whatever reward God may be planning for him."

To make matters worse for his allies on the Catholic right, Regina, Dickie's intended young woman (as far as I can see quiet, presentable, and intelligent and perhaps capable of taming Dickie), not only was not of the household of the faith but had been married before—at twenty for a brief period.

"I don't believe in those annulment things," Dickie had bellowed at me. "So don't pull that stuff. Her first husband was a bastard. I want a church wedding just like my first marriage."

Dickie was a big, strong, well-preserved man, handsome in a rugged way with a square blunt face (usually red with anger) and thick iron gray hair. His bride-to-be watched him intently, not with fear but with admiration.

I explained that there would be certain difficulties since both his bride-to-be and her first husband were baptized Christians. There were some steps we might take—

"I don't want to take any steps," he had shouted. "I have been a good

Catholic all my life, and I demand to be married in this Church, by Father Martin, two weeks from today."

I don't make the current marriage rules for the Catholic Church, and I don't necessarily like them. But no way I was going to apply them to everyone else but Dickie Powers, a loudmouth shanty Irishman if I ever met one.

Nor, as far as I could see, would Father Martin, the head of a right-wing "secular institute," dare to violate publicly the Vatican's rules on such matters.

During the shouting match in my office (well, he was shouting anyway), I felt sorry for Regina, who knew nothing of our Church, was not seeing us at our best, and seemed astonished by the anger of her groom. I felt less sympathy with the Powers offspring, who had been brought along to the rectory for reasons that escaped me. Rick and Melissa—the sole issues of the marriage—smirked through the whole session, delighted at the spoke I had thrown into the wheel of their father's marriage bandwagon and triumphant over their prospective stepmother, to whom they blatantly refused to speak.

Both children were economically useless. Rick, an overweight, long-haired snob, who wanted passionately to produce "important" films, ran an "off-Loop" theater group which performed, with notable lack of critical or financial success, obscure modern plays, sometimes made more obscure because they were done in the original language—like Hungarian. Melissa, a brittle blonde, owned a boutique on Oak Street that sold, or rather did not sell, women's apparel that has been described to me by my nieces as "like totally *funky,* you know."

In that context the adjective was not spoken in admiration.

While he disapproved of the occupations of both his children and of their swinging-singles lifestyles, Dickie resolutely funded their efforts and kept them from not only starvation but the necessity of purchasing cheap liquor.

So Dickie and Regina were married in a civil ceremony by an elderly judge who was a friend of his. Most of the invited guests stayed away from the wedding, less for religious reasons than because they didn't like Dickie.

In addition to the union workers, who hated Dickie for hiring scabs, and the other developers, who resented his bidding tactics, and, according to my strange penitent, the Boys Out on the West Side, there were other actors who would benefit from his death before he changed his will to favor the new wife: Rick, Melissa, and Father Martin's happy little band of brothers, who were now, in alleged obedience to St. Paul and in imitation of the Amish, ostentatiously shunning their greatest benefactor.

"I've got cold feet for the first time in my life, Father," the hit man continued, his face narrowing into an anxious frown. "This is a tricky one. He'll probably have his own bodyguards, and there'll be cops, too. I've handled tough ones before, but this will be one of the toughest. What if they get me? What if I don't make it home?"

"Your children will know you are a criminal?"

"Nah. No one will link the hit man with me. I mean, they'll find out my real identity from my prints. But back home I'm someone else and no one has my prints." Tears appeared in his eyes. "As far as the wife and kids are concerned, I'll vanish from the face of the earth."

"Ah."

"No, what I'm scared about is God." He rubbed his hands together nervously. "God is pretty mad at me these days. He's not gonna like to see me when I show up. I don't figure I can cop a plea with him. It'll be curtains for me."

"You fear eternal damnation?"

"What else will I get? And no time off for good behavior either. I mean, I never really thought about dying before. I figured that I'd get a chance on my deathbed, and that way I'd make it. But what if I'm killed while I'm trying to hit someone else? Then it's the pit of hell for me, isn't it?"

I personally hold with the late Cardinal von Baltassar that salvation for everyone is not inconsistent with the Catholic tradition—and himself a favorite of the Pope at that. But I was not about to explain that position just at the moment.

"God's love is without limit," I said, "its fullness beyond our wildest imagination. One always gets second chances, opportunities to turn away from what separates us from God and to begin our life again."

"Yeah, Father"—he shook his head sadly—"but not professional killers."

"Yes, even mass murderers. Compared with some political leaders I might mention, you're small time."

"You mean, I might still make it?"

"Precisely."

"But what if I'm killed during the hit?"

"Cancel the hit, return the down payment, live off the income from your other business."

"My clients wouldn't like it, Father."

"I thought they couldn't find you."

"I'm a pro, Father. I do my work. I keep my promises. Besides, I need the money. I've got family expenses. I can't give it back. It costs a hell of a lot of money to put four kids through college."

"Nonetheless, you know you should get out of your line of work."

"I know that, Father. I know it. This will be the last one, I promise. Can you give me absolution now?"

"How can I invoke God's love to reconcile you with God's people when you tell me that you are going forth to kill someone?"

"Maybe he deserves to die."

"We all do, but in God's time."

"Yeah . . . but a job is a job. I'm a professional, Father. That's why they call me the Pro."

"You believe that God will accept that argument?"

Tears were pouring down his face. "Gee, how could He? I'm caught. Damned no matter what I do . . . You sure you can't give me absolution so I could receive Holy Communion tomorrow?"

I gave up on the new-fashioned theology of reconciliation and stated my position in old-Church terms: "I can't absolve you unless you have a firm purpose of amendment."

"Yeah, I have that, too."

"Not if you intend to kill someone."

"I don't want to kill him. I *have* to kill him. Damn it, Father, don't you understand that?"

"I'm afraid I don't. There is no excuse for murder, and you know that well."

"Yeah, Father, I guess I do."

He continued to weep. "Jeez, what would my ma say if she knew up in heaven?"

"Pretty much what I'm saying. Take this chance to change your life."

"It's too late." He stood up. "I'm damned already. Thanks for listening, Father. I gotta be going. Pray for me."

He extended his hand and shook mine firmly.

"Come back again if you want to," I said lamely.

What the hell do you say in such circumstances?

"You're sure this is under the seal of confession? You can't tell anyone?"

"Not a soul."

"Good-bye, Father," he said to me at the door. "You've been a big help. Remember to pray for me."

"I will certainly do that. Remember, it's never too late to begin again."

"Not for me," he said, and disappeared into the rain and the darkness.

I returned to my room, glanced briefly at the posters of the three Johns of my young adulthood—Pope, President, and quarterback of the Baltimore Colts—poured myself a generous amount of Jameson's twelve-year special reserve to calm my nerves, and sat back on my easy chair to think.

I thought for a long time.

The doorbell rang again. The hit man again.

"Nah, Father." He stood in the rain, water pouring off his anguished face. "Forget about that seal of confession thing. You can tell them that there's a contract out on Richard Powers and there's a professional hit man in town to do the job. Maybe that will help me with God."

Before I bad time to challenge his absurd reasoning, he had faded back into the watery darkness.

Upon return to my study, I found that the poltergeist that shares my quarters, had, as is his custom when I leave for a few minutes, finished my drink. I was constrained to fill my Waterford tumbler again.

Once more I thought for a long time.

Then I dialed Captain John Culhane of the Chicago Police Department, commander of Area Six Detectives, a smart and honest cop, at his private home phone.

"Culhane."

"Father Ryan, John."

"Yeah, what's up, Bishop?"

"Have there been any threats against the life of a certain Richard Patrick Powers lately?"

"How lately?"

"Recent weeks."

"Only four or five, the usual number. Lot of people hate tricky Dickie."

"So I've been led to believe. Any rumors of his being in trouble with the Boys Out on the West Side?"

"He's been in trouble with them for years. They're scared of him."

"Another threat was called to my attention tonight, purporting to be serious."

"Yeah, well, he's got his own bodyguards. Doesn't want us around because he says we're all crooks. I'll tell him about it and offer some police protection. I suspect he'll laugh in my face. Should I say the Outfit is involved?"

"You might mention that."

My obligations fulfilled, I retired for the night and slept peacefully.

After the morning Eucharist (what we now call the mass when we remember to do so) and breakfast, I made a phone call to an acquaintance who is what is known as a "friend of friends." I wanted some information on two questions. He was able to answer them both, as I thought he would, without consulting those friends.

John Culhane called me later in the morning, just as I returned from the grammar school and the eighth graders whom I enjoy greatly. But then I'm not their parent.

"Like I said, Bishop, Dickie Powers laughed in my face. Then, get this, he called back to apologize because his new wife made him. So it ends up with him saying thanks but no, thanks. She may be his salvation."

"Arguably. God usually knows what She is doing."

Two weeks passed, and there was no hit on Dickie Powers.

Then one evening, after I had listened to a husband and wife who once had been deeply in love spew hate at each other, John Culhane was on the phone:

"It went down tonight, Bishop. Dickie Powers. Classic mob hit. Dickie's walking down East Lake Shore Drive with his wife at night, his bodyguards a few yards behind him. A man with a turned-up coat collar comes out from beneath one of those canopies in front of the buildings on the street, calls, 'Dick,' softly, and puts him down with a twenty-two with a silencer. He jumps into a car that pulls up and is gone before the bodyguards see Dickie slump to the ground."

"Dead?"

"No, the hit man blows it. A bullet in the lung, but he's going to make it, I think. He's on his way to Northwestern."

"Lung?"

"Yeah, I know. They usually go for the head. Maybe this guy was going for the heart."

"Or can't shoot straight. I'm on my way to the hospital."

The Hit Man Who Couldn't Shoot Straight, not bad as a title for a film.

In the emergency room Dickie Powers was conscious when I administered the Sacrament of the Sick to him. His wife, her face stained with tears, clung to his hand and answered "amen" with him to the prayers, though there was some confusion with the doxology at the end of the Lord's Prayer.

"Thanks for coming, Father Blackie. I'm through being a bastard. It'll be tough, but I'm going to change my life."

"He means it," Regina said firmly. "He really does."

"I'll try," he whispered, "but you gotta help me."

"Count on that," she said firmly. "And thank you, Bishop. Perhaps I could come over to talk to you in a couple of days."

"Surely." I smiled benignly, figuring that once again Herself had called me in to straighten out the minor messes after She had accomplished Her major goals.

Maybe, just maybe it was not too late for Dickie Powers to undergo a metanoia.

John Culhane, trim and fit, as always, silver blue eyes twinkling behind his glasses, met me in the corridor.

"What do you think, Bishop?"

"If I were in your position, Commander, I would arrest Rick Powers immediately and charge him with the attempted murder of his father. I believe that lacking willpower to match his cleverness, he will breakdown and confess at once."

So it went down.

"You had it right, Bishop," he told me while I demolished my pancakes and bacon at the cathedral breakfast table the next morning. "He broke down immediately. Not much guts there."

"Very little, I fear."

"How did you know?"

"I had a visit a couple of Sunday nights ago from a purported professional hit man, who said he was known as the Pro. He told me under the seal of confession that he had killed thirty-two men and that there was a contract to make Dickie Powers number thirty-three. He went through considerable and, on the whole, credible agonizing about the state of his soul, his relationship with God, and his eternal fate, then departed, having argued that his need for money and his obligation to honor his contract forced him to continue with the hit.

"I was intrigued that he would tell me the name of the intended victim. There seemed to be no need to do that. Then he came back a half hour later and released me from the seal on the grounds that maybe God would be more sympathetic with him if he gave Powers a fighting chance by letting him know there was a mob hit man in town.

"That was clearly nonsense. In his first manifestation the hit man did not want to die because of his wife and family. In the second he was putting his life at enhanced risk for no obvious purpose. The devout Catholic he pretended to be would know that from God's point of view, murder is murder whether you put yourself at risk or not.

"The next morning I called a certain source and asked him two questions. He gave me the answers I expected.

"Patently I had been played for the fool by a very clever actor. I was supposed to put out the word that there was a contract on Dickie. Then, when a few weeks had passed and the hit finally went down in Outfit fashion, we were all supposed to figure the hit was a fulfillment of the contract. Rick hired a good actor—probably from out of town—who carried off the scenario to fit his script.

"The scheme was clearly designed to divert suspicion from him. I doubt that it would have worked in any case. But he failed to carry out his part of the scenario when his hand wavered at the end and he didn't kill his father. Hit men may have occasional guilt feelings, but they shoot straight.

"Which turns out to be fortunate for the hit man who couldn't shoot straight. The charge against him will only be attempted murder. When he comes out of prison, I presume he will continue to aspire to make films. Perhaps he will make one about life in prison. Perhaps then his creativity at plot construction may be of some use to him."

"He wanted the money so he could be a film producer," John told me. "He even had a script for a film. He had almost talked his father into financing it. When the old man met Regina, he changed his mind. With Regina in charge, Rick saw his hopes go up in smoke."

"The actor recited his lines well, but finally the script was inadequate and the direction less than convincing," I said, trying to sound like my good friend Roger Ebert. "One and a half stars."

""What were the two questions you asked your source?" The commander rose to leave.

"The first was whether there was a hit man named the Pro. My source, who would know, said he had never heard of him. The second was whether two hundred big ones were out of line for I hit. He whistled and said he had never heard of anything like that. If Rick Powers's script when he emerges from jail is truly about prison life, presumably he will have, courtesy of the state of Illinois, done better research than he did for this script."

✝

THE SWEATING STATUE

EDWARD D. HOCH

IT WAS THE MIRACLE AT Father David Noone's aging inner-city parish that brought Monsignor Thomas Xavier to the city. He'd been sent by the Cardinal himself to investigate the miraculous event, and that impressed Father Noone, even though he might have wished for more run-of-the-mill parish problems now that he'd reached the age of fifty.

Monsignor Xavier was a white-haired man a few years older than Father Noone, with a jolly, outgoing manner that made him seem more like a fund-raiser than the Cardinal's troubleshooter. He shook hands vigorously and said, "We met once years ago when you were at St. Monica's, Father. I accompanied the Cardinal."

"Of course," David Noone replied, bending the truth a little. The Cardinal's visit had been more than a decade earlier, and if he remembered the monsignor at all it was only vaguely.

"Holy Trinity isn't much like St. Monica's, is it?" Monsignor Xavier remarked as he followed David into the sitting room. "These inner-city parishes have changed a great deal."

"Well, we have to scrape a bit to get by. The Sunday collections don't bring in much money, but of course the diocese helps out." He poked his head into the rectory kitchen, "Mrs. Wilkins, could you bring us in some—what will it be, Monsignor, coffee or tea?"

"Tea is fine."

"Some tea, please."

Mrs. Wilkins, the parish housekeeper, turned from the freezer with a carton of ice cream in her hand. "Be right with you. Good of you to visit us, Monsignor."

When they'd settled down in the parlor, the white-haired monsignor asked, "Are you alone at Holy Trinity, Father?"

"I am at present. When I first took over as pastor five years ago I had an assistant, but there just aren't enough priests to go around. He was shifted to a suburban parish two years ago and I've been alone here with Mrs. Wilkins ever since."

Monsignor Xavier opened a briefcase and took out some papers. "The parish is mainly Hispanic now, I believe."

"Pretty much so, though in the past year we've had several Southeast Asian families settle here, mainly in the Market Street area. We're trying to help them as much as we can."

He nodded as if satisfied. "Now tell me about the statue."

Mrs. Wilkins arrived with tea, setting the cups before them and pouring with a steady hand. "I'll bring in a few little cookies too," she said. "You must be hungry after your journey, Monsignor."

"Oh, they gave us a snack on the plane. Don't worry about me."

"We'll have a nice dinner," she promised. "It's not often we have such a distinguished visitor."

When they were alone, Monsignor Xavier said, "You were going to tell me about the statue."

"Of course. That's what you've come about." David Noone took a sip of tea. "It began two weeks ago today. Our custodian, Marcos, had unlocked the church doors for the seven A.M. Mass. There are always a few early arrivals and one of these, Celia Orlando, came up to light a candle before Mass began. She noticed that the wooden statue of the Virgin on the side altar seemed covered with sweat. When she called Marcos's attention to it, he wiped the statue dry with a cloth. But a few moments later the sweating began again."

He paused for some comment, but the monsignor only said, "Interesting, Please continue."

"Marcos showed it to me when I arrived to say the Mass. I didn't think too much of it at first. Perhaps the wood was exuding some sort of sap.

In fact, I thought no more of the incident until later that day when Mrs. Wilkins reported that people were arriving to view the miracle. I went over to the church and found a half-dozen women, friends and neighbors of Celia Orlando."

"Tell me about the woman."

"Celia? Her parents moved here from Mexico City when she was a teenager. She's twenty-eight now, and deeply religious. Attends Mass every morning on her way to work at an insurance company."

A nod. "Go on with your story."

Father Noone shifted in his chair, feeling as if he was being questioned in a courtroom. "Well, I spoke to the women and tried to convince them there was no miracle. I thought things had settled down, but then the following morning the same thing happened. It kept happening, and each morning there's been a bigger crowd at morning Mass. After television covered it on the six o'clock news the church was jammed."

Monsignor Xavier finished the tea and rose to his feet. "Well, I think it's time I saw this remarkable statue."

Father Noone led the way through the rectory kitchen where Mrs. Wilkins was already at work on dinner. "It smells good," the monsignor commented, giving her a smile. They passed through a fire door into a corridor that connected the rectory with the rear of the church.

"It's handy in the winter," David Noone explained.

"Is the church kept locked at night?"

"Oh, yes, all the doors. It's a shame but we have to do it. And not just in the inner city, either. These days they're locked in the suburbs, too."

The two priests crossed in front of the main altar, genuflecting as they did so. The Blessed Virgin's altar was on the far side, and it was there that the wooden statue stood. "There are no people here now," Xavier commented.

"Since we've had all the publicity I've been forced to close the church in the afternoon too, just to get the people out of here. We open again at five for afternoon services."

Monsignor Xavier leaned over for a closer look at the statue. "There is moisture, certainly, but not as much as I'd expected."

"There's more in the morning."

He glanced curiously at Father Noone. "Is that so?"

The statue itself stood only about eighteen inches high and had been carefully carved by a parish craftsman many years before David Noone's arrival. It was a traditional representation of the Blessed Virgin, with the polished unpainted wood adding a certain warmth to the figure. Monsignor Xavier studied it from all angles, then put out a finger to intercept a drop of liquid which had started running down the side of the statue. He placed it to his tongue and said, "It seems to be water."

"That's what we think."

"No noticeable salty taste."

"Why should it be salty?"

"Like tears," the monsignor said. "I'm surprised no one has dubbed the liquid the Virgin's Tears or some such thing."

"That'll be next, I'm sure."

They were joined by a thin balding man who walked with stooped shoulders and wore a pair of faded overalls. David Noone introduced the monsignor to Marcos, the church's custodian. "That means janitor," the balding man said with a smile. I know my place in the world."

"We'd be lost without you," David assured him, "Whatever you're called."

"You unlock the church doors every morning for the early Mass?" Monsignor Xavier asked.

"Sure."

"Ever find signs of robbery or forced entry?"

"No, not in years."

"When I first came here," David Noone explained, "it was customary to leave the side door facing the rectory unlocked all night. But someone stole one of our big gold candlesticks and that put an end to it. With the covered passageway from the rectory we don't really need any unlocked doors. On the rare occasion when someone needed to get into the church at night, they simply came to the rectory and Mrs. Wilkins or I took them over."

"What about this young woman, Celia Orlando?" the monsignor asked Marcos. "Do you know her?"

"Yes, her family has been in the parish many years. She is a good girl, very religious."

"Tell me, Marcos, what do you think causes the statue to sweat?"

The old man shifted his eyes to the wooden Virgin, then back to the monsignor. He seemed to be weighing his answer carefully. "A miracle, I suppose. Isn't that why you came here from the Cardinal?"

"Have you ever seen wood like that sweat before?"

"No."

"Could it be some sort of sap?"

"It has no taste. Sap would be sweet. And there would be no sap after all these years."

"So you think it is a miracle."

"I think whatever you want me to think. I am a good Catholic."

Monsignor Xavier turned away. "We'd best go see this young woman," he said to David Noone. "Celia Orlando."

† † †

In the car David tried to explain his people to Monsignor Xavier. "They are deeply religious. You are a stranger from another city, someone sent by the Cardinal himself. Naturally they do not want to offend you in any way."

"That old man does not believe in miracles, David. May I call you David? We might as well be informal about this. I'm Tom." He was relaxing a bit, feeling more at home with the situation, David thought. "Tell me a little about Marcos."

"There's not much to tell. His wife is dead and he lives alone. His children grew up and moved away. His son's a computer programmer."

"A story of our times, I suppose."

David Noone parked the car in front of the neat, freshly painted house where Celia Orlando lived with her brother Adolfo and his wife. It was almost dinner time, and Adolfo came to the door. "Hello, Father. Have you come to see my sister?"

"If she's home. Adolfo, this is Monsignor Thomas Xavier. The Cardinal sent him to look into our strange event."

"You mean the miracle." He ushered them into the living room.

Monsignor Xavier smiled. "That's what I'm here to determine. These things often have a natural explanation, you know."

Celia came into the room to greet them. She was still dressed for work, wearing a neat blue skirt and a white blouse. The presence of the monsignor seemed to impress her, and she hastened to explain that she deserved no special attention. "I attend Mass every morning, Monsignor, but I'm no Bernadette. I saw nothing the others did not see. I was merely the first to notice it."

"And you called it a miracle."

She brushed the black hair back from her wide dark eyes, and Father Noone realized that she was a very pretty young woman. He wondered why he'd never noticed it before. "An act of God," she responded. "That's a miracle isn't it?"

"We believe the wood of the statue is merely exuding moisture."

She shook her head in bewilderment. "Why is the church so reluctant to accept a miracle? What the world needs now are more miracles, not less."

"We must be very careful in matters of this sort," Xavier explained. "Have you ever noticed anything strange about the statue before? Anything unusual?"

"No, nothing."

Her brother interrupted then. "What are you after, Monsignor?"

"Only the facts. I must return home tomorrow and report to the Cardinal."

"I have a boyfriend who thinks I'm crazy. He's not Catholic." The admission seemed to embarrass her. "He says the priests are twisting my mind. He should be here now to see me trying to convince you both of the miracle."

Father Noone glanced at his watch. "I have to get back for the afternoon Mass in fifteen minutes. I hadn't realized it was so late."

She saw them to the door. "Pray for me," she said.

"We should say the same to you," Monsignor Xavier told her.

On the drive back to the parish church he talked little. When he saw the crowds at the five-thirty Mass, filling the small church almost to capacity, he said nothing at all.

✝ ✝ ✝

In the evening they sat in David Noone's small study, enjoying a bit of brandy. They were on a first-name basis now, and it was a time for confidences. "How do you do financially here?" Thomas Xavier asked.

"Poorly," David Noone admitted. "I have to go hat in hand to the bishop a couple of times a year. But he realizes the problems. He helps in every way he can."

"What does he think of the statue?"

"Strictly hands off, Tom. That's why he phoned the Cardinal. It's known as passing the buck."

"I know how he feels. If you think the church was crowded this afternoon, just wait till the national news gets hold of this. You'll have people coming here from all over the country."

"There was a call from the *New York Times* yesterday. They said they might send a reporter out this weekend."

"That's what I mean. We have to be very careful, David—"

He was interrupted by Mrs. Wilkins, who announced, "There's a young man to see you, Father Noone. He says it's very important."

David Noone sighed and got to his feet. "Excuse me, Tom. Duty calls."

He walked down the hall to the parlor where a sandy-haired man in his late twenties was waiting. "You're Father Noone?" the man asked, rising to meet him.

"Yes. What can I do for you?"

"My name is Kevin Frisk. Maybe Celia mentioned me."

"Celia Orlando? No, I don't believe so."

"I'm her boyfriend."

"Oh, yes. I think—"

"I want you to stay away from her."

David could see the anger in his eyes now. "I assure you—"

"You came this afternoon with another priest. She told me about it. I want you to leave her alone, stop filling her head with all these crazy notions of a miracle."

"Actually it's just the opposite. No one is more skeptical than a priest when there's talk of miracles."

"I want to marry her. I want to take her away from your influence."

"We have very little influence over Celia or anyone else. We only try to give a bit of comfort, and a few answers to the questions people ask. Do you work with Celia at the insurance office?"

"Yes. And I'm not Catholic." There was a challenge in his words.

"Celia told me that."

"If you think you can hypnotize me with your crazy notions—"

"Believe me, I'm not trying to hypnotize you or persuade you or convert you."

"Then stay away from Celia. Stop filling her head with statues that sweat. If we're ever married it'll be far from here."

"Mr. Frisk—"

"That's all I have to say. Take it as a warning. The next time I might not be quite so civil."

David watched as he left the room and walked out the front door without looking back. He shook his head sadly and returned to the study where the monsignor was waiting.

"No special problem, I hope," Thomas Xavier said, putting down the magazine he'd been glancing through.

"Not really. It was a young man who's been dating Celia Orlando."

"Ah yes—the non-Catholic one. I caught that point when she made it."

"He thinks we're brainwashing her or something. He seemed a bit angry."

"The statue seems to be having a ripple effect on the lives of a great many people."

The meeting with Kevin Frisk had left David dissatisfied. He felt he'd given the wrong answers to questions that hadn't even been asked. "What will you tell the Cardinal when you go back tomorrow?"

"I want to have another look at our statue in the morning. That may help me decide."

It was Father Noone's habit to rise at six-thirty for the seven o'clock Mass, delaying breakfast until after the service. When the alarm woke him he dressed quickly and went downstairs, noting only that the door to the guest room where Monsignor Xavier slept was still closed. Passing through the kitchen he noted that Mrs. Wilkins was not yet up either. The brandy glasses from the previous night sat unwashed on the sideboard, and a carton of ice cream lay melting in the sink. The door to her room, at the rear of the main floor, was also closed.

Through the window he could see a parishioner trying the side door of the church, which was still locked. Had Marcos overslept too? David Noone hurried along the passageway and into the church, switching on lights as he went. It was already ten minutes to seven. He entered the sacristy and was about to open the cabinet where his vestments were hung when something drew him to the stairwell leading to the church basement. There was a light on down there, which seemed odd if Marcos was late arriving.

But Marcus was there, sprawled at the foot of the stairs. David knew before he reached him that the old man was dead.

David knelt by the body for a moment, saying a silent, personal prayer. Then he administered the last rites of the Church. He went back to the rectory and roused Monsignor Xavier, telling him what had happened. "Can you take the Mass for me while I call the police? There are people waiting."

"Certainly, David. Give me five minutes to dress."

He joined David Noone in three minutes and they returned to the

Church together. Staring down at the body, Thomas Xavier said a prayer of his own. "The poor man. It looks as if his neck was broken in the fall."

"He knew these stairs too well to fall on them," David said.

"You think he was pushed? But why, and by whom?"

"I don't know."

"Open the doors of your church. It's after seven and people are waiting. Tell them Mass will begin in a few moments."

"Where are you going now?"

"Just over to see the statue."

David Noone followed him across the sanctuary to the side altar. The Virgin's statue was sweating, perhaps more intensely than before. The monsignor reached out his right hand to touch it, then drew sharply back. "What is it?" David asked.

"The statue is cold, as if it's aware of the presence of death."

† † †

The Mass went on as the police arrived and went through their routine. A detective sergeant named Dominick was in charge. "Anything stolen, Father?" he wanted to know, peering over the rim of his glasses as he took notes.

"Nothing obvious. The chalices are all here. We don't keep any money in the church overnight, except what's in the poor box, and that hasn't been touched."

"Then foul play seems doubtful. He probably just missed his footing in the dark."

"The light was on," David reminded him.

"He was an old man, Father. We got enough crime these days without trying to find it where it doesn't exist."

When they returned to the rectory after Mass, Mrs. Wilkins was busy preparing breakfast. David told her what had happened and she started to cry softly. "He was a good man," she said. "He didn't deserve to die like that."

"The police are convinced it was an accident," David Noone said. "I'm not so sure."

She brought them their breakfast and Monsignor Xavier took a mouthful of scrambled egg. After a moment he said, "This is very good. I wish we had breakfast like this back home."

"What do you think about Marcos?" David Noone asked him.

He considered that for a moment. "I don't know. I did notice that Celia Orlando wasn't at Mass this morning. Didn't you say she comes every day?"

"Yes."

"Perhaps we should see why her routine changed today."

Father Noone had to make some calls at the hospital first, and he was surprised when the monsignor changed his return flight and arranged to stay over an extra day. He wondered what it meant. Then, just before noon, they called on Celia at the insurance office where she was employed.

She was startled to see them enter, and came up to the counter to greet them. "Is something wrong? It's not my brother is it?"

"No, no," Father Noone assured her. "It's just that you weren't at Mass and I wondered if you were ill."

She dropped her eyes. "Kevin—my boyfriend—doesn't want me to go there anymore. He says you're a bad influence on me."

"He certainly can't keep you from practicing your religion."

"He says I should go to another parish. All that business with the statue—"

At that moment one of the office doors opened and Kevin Frisk himself emerged. He hurried over to the counter and confronted the two priests. "Get out of here!" he ordered.

"You can't—"

"I can order you out when you're keeping employees from their jobs, and that's exactly what you're doing. Get out and don't let me see you here again."

David Noone turned to Celia as they departed. "Call me at the rectory. We need to talk."

"Stay away from her!" Frisk warned.

Outside, Monsignor Xavier shook his head. "A hotheaded young man. He could cause trouble."

"If he hasn't already. Maybe he broke into the church and Marcos caught him at it."

"There were no signs of forced entry, David. Perhaps that detective is right about looking for crime where none exists."

"I'm sorry, Tom. I just can't get that old man out of my mind."

As they walked back to the car they saw a headline on the noon edition of the newspaper: MAN FOUND DEAD AT "MIRACLE" CHURCH. Monsignor Xavier said, "I'm afraid this will bring you all the national publicity you've been trying to avoid. It's something more than a miracle now."

"Is that why you're staying over? Did you expect something like this?"

Thomas Xavier hesitated. "Not expect it, exactly. But in a large city we're more in tune with the way the press operates. They couldn't get the right angle on a sweating statue, but now there's a dead old man and they'll have a field day."

"What do you suggest I do?"

"We must have an answer ready when they ask the Church's position on the so-called miracle."

"And what is the Church's position? What will you report to the Cardinal?"

"The answer to that lies back at Holy Trinity."

† † †

There had been no Marcos to lock up the church during the early afternoon, and David Noone realized it had been left open as soon as he drove up to the rectory and saw the streams of people entering and leaving.

"I forgot to lock it," he said sadly.

"I doubt if there's any harm done."

They found Mrs. Wilkins just hanging up the telephone, almost frantic. "It's been like a circus here. Reporters calling from all over the country! The television stations have all been down, filming the statue for the evening news."

"Again? They did that last week."

"There are more people around now. And everyone wants to see where poor Marcos died. I was over there shooing them out of the sacristy myself."

The afternoon Mass was like a bad dream for David. People he'd never seen before filled the church, many with little interest in following the service. Instead they crowded around the side altar where the statue stood. The moisture was not as heavy as it had been that morning, but there was still some to be seen. In his sermon he said a few words about Marcos, then tried to make the point that the phenomenon of the statue was still unexplained. Following the services people lingered around the side altar until finally David had to ask them to leave so he could close the church.

"The only blessing to come out of all this," he told the monsignor over dinner, "is that the crowds, and the collections, have never been better. Still, I'm wondering if I should simply remove the statue temporarily and end all this fuss."

"That would surely bring complaints from some, though it's an option we must consider."

Mrs. Wilkins brought in their coffee. "Sorry there's no dessert tonight. What with all the commotion I didn't get to the store today."

"It'll do us both good," the monsignor assured her.

Later, they walked around the church in the darkness as David Noone checked all the doors to be sure they were locked. "I'll have to find a replacement for Marcos, of course, immediately after the funeral."

Monsignor Xavier stared up at the spire of Holy Trinity Church as it disappeared into the night sky. "I often wish I had a church like this. It would be just the right size for me. In the city, serving the Cardinal, I lose touch with things at times."

"With people?"

"With people, yes, and with their motives."

Later that night, just after eleven, as David was turning out the light and getting into bed, his door opened silently and Thomas Xavier slipped into the room. He held a finger to his lips. "Put on your robe and come with me," he said softly.

"What—"

"Just come, very quietly."

David took his robe and followed Thomas Xavier down the stairs. When they reached the main floor the monsignor headed for the kitchen, then paused as if listening.

"What—"

"Shh!"

He heard a noise from the passageway leading into the church, and then the kitchen door swung open.

It was Mrs. Wilkins, carrying the statue of the Virgin in her arms.

"Let me take that," Monsignor Xavier said with a kindly voice. "We don't want any more accidents, like what happened to poor old Marcos."

✝   ✝   ✝

She gave him the statue, and then the will seemed to go out of her. For a long time she cried, and talked irrationally, and it was only the soft words of the monsignor that calmed her at last.

"We know all about it, Mrs. Wilkins. You carried the statue in here each evening, didn't you, and immersed it in water. Then you left it in the freezer overnight, carrying it back into the church each morning before

Mass. Naturally as it thawed it seemed to sweat. That was why there was
more moisture in the morning than later in the day, and why it was cold
to my touch this morning. I remembered seeing the ice cream melting in
the sink when I passed through the kitchen with Father Noone. You took
it out of the freezer to make room for the statue, and then forgot to put it
back, so there was no dessert for us tonight."

"I only did it so more people would come, so the collections would
be bigger and we could help the poor souls in our parish. I never meant
to do any harm!"

"Marcos caught you this morning, didn't he? If he was already suspicious, my presence might have prompted him to come in earlier than
usual. He hid in the stairwell and turned on the light as you were returning the statue."

"Oh my God, the poor man! He startled me so; he tried to take the
statue away and I pushed him. I didn't realize we were so close to the
stairs. He just went down, and didn't move. I didn't mean to kill him."
Her voice had softened until they could barely hear her.

"Of course you didn't," David Noone said, taking her hand.

"I read about it in a book, about putting the statue in the freezer. I
thought it would help the parish. I never meant to hurt anybody."

Monsignor Xavier nodded. "There was something similar down in
Nicaragua a few years back. I read about it too. When I saw the ice cream
in the sink it reminded me. You see, David, if someone was tampering
with the statue overnight it had to be either Marcos or Mrs. Wilkins. The
church was locked, with the only entrance from the rectory here. It was
locked this morning, when Marcos died. He had a key, and she didn't
need one."

"What are they going to do with me?" she asked sadly.

"I don't know," David replied. "We'll have to phone the police. Then
I'll go down there with you. I'll stay with you as long as I can. Don't
worry."

In the morning Monsignor Xavier departed. He stood for a moment
looking up at the church and then shook hands with David Noone. "You
have a fine church here. Fine people. I'll tell the Cardinal that."

It was after the morning Mass, and as he watched the monsignor get
into his taxi for the airport, Celia Orlando approached him. "The statue
is gone, Father. Where is the statue?"

"I didn't expect to see you at Mass, Celia."

"He can't tell me how to pray. I said that to him. But where is the statue?"

"I'm keeping it in the rectory for a few days. It was all a hoax, I'm afraid. There was no miracle. You'll read about it in the papers."

She nodded, but he wondered if she really understood his words. "That's all right," she said. "I managed to wipe a bit of the sweat off one day with a piece of cotton. I carry it with me all the time. I'll never throw it away."

✝

THE STRIPPER

H. H. HOLMES

HE WAS CALLED JACK THE Stripper because the only witness who had seen him and lived (J. F. Flugelbach, 1463 N. Edgemont) had described the glint of moonlight on bare skin. The nickname was inevitable.

Mr. Flugelbach had stumbled upon the fourth of the murders, the one in the grounds of City College. He had not seen enough to be of any help to the police; but at least he had furnished a name for the killer heretofore known by such routine cognomens as "butcher," "werewolf," and "vampire."

The murders in themselves were enough to make a newspaper's fortune. They were frequent, bloody, and pointless, since neither theft nor rape was attempted. The murderer was no specialist, like the original Jack, but rather an eclectic, like Kürten the Düsseldorf Monster, who struck when the mood was on him and disregarded age and sex. This indiscriminate taste made better copy; the menace threatened not merely a certain class of unfortunates but every reader.

It was the nudity, however, and the nickname evolved from it, that made the cause truly celebrated. Feature writers dug up all the legends of naked murderers—Courvoisier of London, Durrant of San Francisco,

Wallace of Liverpool, Borden of Fall River—and printed them as sober fact, explaining at length the advantages of avoiding the evidence of bloodstains.

When he read this explanation, he always smiled. It was plausible, but irrelevant. The real reason for nakedness was simply that it felt better that way. When the color of things began to change, His first impulse was to get rid of his clothing. He supposed that psychoanalysts could find some atavistic reason for that.

He felt the cold air on his naked body. He had never noticed that before. Noiselessly he pushed the door open and tiptoed into the study. His hand did not waver as he raised the knife.

The Stripper case was Lieutenant Marshall's baby, and he was going nuts. His condition was not helped by the constant allusions of his colleagues to the fact that his wife had once been a stripper of a more pleasurable variety. Six murders in three months, without a single profitable lead, had reduced him to a state where a lesser man might have gibbered, and sometimes he thought it would be simpler to be a lesser man.

He barked into phones nowadays. He hardly apologized when he realized that his caller was Sister Ursula, that surprising nun who had once planned to be a policewoman and who had extricated him from several extraordinary cases. But that was just it; those had been extraordinary, freak locked-room problems, while this was the horrible epitome of ordinary, clueless, plotless murder. There was no room in the Stripper case for the talents of Sister Ursula.

He was in a hurry and her sentences hardly penetrated his mind until he caught the word "Stripper." Then he said sharply, "So? Backtrack please, Sister. I'm afraid I wasn't listening."

"He says," her quiet voice repeated, "that he thinks he knows who the Stripper is, but he hasn't enough proof. He'd like to talk to the police about it; and since he knows I know you, he asked me to arrange it, so that you wouldn't think him just a crank."

"Which," said Marshall, "he probably is. But to please you, Sister . . . What did you say his name is?"

"Flecker. Harvey Flecker. Professor of Latin at the University."

Marshall caught his breath. "Coincidence," he said flatly. "I'm on my way to see him now."

"Oh. Then he did get in touch with you himself?"

"Not with me," said Marshall. "With the Stripper."

"God rest his soul . . ." Sister Ursula murmured.

"So. I'm on my way now. If you could meet me there and bring this letter—"

"Lieutenant, I know our order is a singularly liberal one, but still I doubt if Reverend Mother—"

"You're a material witness," Marshall said authoritatively. "I'll send a car for you. And don't forget the letter."

Sister Ursula hung up and sighed. She had liked Professor Flecker, both for his scholarly wit and for his quiet kindliness. He was the only man who could hold his agnostic own with Father Pearson in disputatious sophistry, and he was also the man who had helped keep the Order's soup-kitchen open at the depth of the depression.

She took up her breviary and began to read the office for the dead while she waited for the car.

† † †

"It is obvious," Professor Lowe enunciated, "that the Stripper is one of the three of us."

Hugo Ellis said, "Speak for yourself." His voice cracked a little, and he seemed even younger than he looked.

Professor de' Cassis said nothing. His huge hunchbacked body crouched in the corner and he mourned his friend.

"So?" said Lieutenant Marshall. "Go on, Professor."

"It was by pure chance," Professor Lowe continued, his lean face alight with logical satisfaction, "that the back door was latched last night. We have been leaving it unfastened for Mrs. Carey since she lost her key; but Flecker must have forgotten that fact and inadvertently reverted to habit. Ingress by the front door was impossible, since it was not only secured by a spring lock but also bolted from within. None of the windows shows any sign of external tampering. The murderer presumably counted upon the back door to make plausible the entrance of an intruder; but Flecker had accidentally secured it, and that accident," he concluded impressively, "will strap the Tripper."

Hugo Ellis laughed, and then looked ashamed of himself.

Marshall laughed too. "Setting aside the Spoonerism, Professor, your statement of the conditions is flawless. This house was locked tight as a drum. Yes, the Stripper is one of the three of you." It wasn't amusing when Marshall said it.

Professor de' Cassis raised his despondent head. "But why?" His voice was guttural. "Why?"

Hugo Ellis said, "Why? With a madman?"

Professor Lowe lifted one finger as though emphasizing a point in a lecture. "Ah, but is this a madman's crime? There is the point. When the Stripper kills a stranger, yes, he is mad. When he kills a man with whom he lives . . . may he not be applying the technique of his madness to the purpose of his sanity?"

"It's an idea," Marshall admitted. "I can see where there's going to be some advantage in having a psychologist among the witnesses. But there's another witness I'm even more anxious to—" His face lit up as Sergeant Raglan came in. "She's here, Rags?"

"Yeah," said Raglan. "It's the sister. Holy smoke, Loot, does this mean this is gonna be another screwy one?"

† † †

Marshall had said *she* and Raglan had said *the sister.* These facts may serve as sufficient characterization of Sister Felicitas, who had accompanied her. They were always a pair, yet always spoken of in the singular. Now Sister Felicitas dozed in the corner where the hunchback had crouched, and Marshall read and reread the letter which seemed like the posthumous utterance of the Stripper's latest victim:

> My dear Sister:
>
> I have reason to fear that someone close to me is Jack the Stripper.
>
> You know me, I trust, too well to think me a sensationalist striving to be a star witness. I have grounds for what I say. This individual, whom I shall for the moment call "Quasimodo" for reasons that might particularly appeal to you, first betrayed himself when I noticed a fleck of blood behind his ear—a trifle, but suggestive. Since then I have religiously observed his comings and goings, and found curious coincidences between the absence of Quasimodo and the presence elsewhere of the Stripper.

I have not a conclusive body of evidence, but I believe that I do have sufficient to bring to the attention of the authorities. I have heard you mention a Lieutenant Marshall who is a close friend of yours. If you will recommend me to him as a man whose word is to be taken seriously, I shall be deeply obliged.

I may, of course, be making a fool of myself with my suspicions of Quasimodo, which is why I refrain from giving you his real name. But every man must do what is possible to rid this city *a negotio perambulante in tenebris.*

Yours respectfully,
Harvey Flecker

† † †

"He didn't have much to go on, did he?" Marshall observed. "But he was right, God help him. And he may have known more than he cared to trust to a letter. He must have slipped somehow and let Quasimodo see his suspicions. . . . What does that last phrase mean?"

"Lieutenant! And you an Oxford man!" exclaimed Sister Ursula.

"I can translate it. But what's its connotation?"

"It's from St. Jerome's Vulgate of the ninetieth psalm. The Douay version translates it literally: *of the business that walketh about in the dark;* but that doesn't convey the full horror of that nameless prowling *negotium.* It's one of the most terrible phrases I know, and perfect for the Stripper."

"Flecker was a Catholic?"

"No, he was a resolute agnostic, though I have always had hopes that Thomist philosophy would lead him into the Church. I almost think he refrained because his conversion would have left nothing to argue with Father Pearson about. But he was an excellent Church Latinist and knew the liturgy better than most Catholics."

"Do you understand what he means by Quasimodo?"

"I don't know. Allusiveness was typical of Professor Flecker; he delighted in British crossword puzzles, if you see what I mean. But I think I could guess more readily if he had not said that it might particularly appeal to me . . ."

"So? I can see at least two possibilities—"

"But before we try to decode the Professor's message, Lieutenant, tell me what you have learned here. All I know is that the poor man is dead, may he rest in peace."

Marshall told her. Four university teachers lived in this ancient (for Southern California) two-story house near the Campus. Mrs. Carey came in every day to clean for them and prepare dinner. When she arrived this morning at nine, Lowe and de' Cassis were eating breakfast and Hugo Ellis, the youngest of the group, was out mowing the lawn. They were not concerned over Flecker's absence. He often worked in the study till all hours and sometimes fell asleep there.

Mrs. Carey went about her work. Today was Tuesday, the day for changing the beds and getting the laundry ready. When she had finished that task, she dusted the living room and went on to the study.

The police did not yet have her story of the discovery. Her scream had summoned the others, who had at once called the police and, sensibly, canceled their classes and waited. When the police arrived, Mrs. Carey was still hysterical. The doctor had quieted her with a hypodermic, from which she had not yet revived.

Professor Flecker had had his throat cut and (Marshall skipped over this hastily) suffered certain other butcheries characteristic of the Stripper. The knife, an ordinary kitchen-knife, had been left by the body as usual. He had died instantly, at approximately one in the morning, when each of the other three men claimed to be asleep.

More evidence than that of the locked doors proved that the Stripper was an inmate of the house. He had kept his feet clear of the blood which bespattered the study, but he had still left a trail of small drops which revealed themselves to the minute police inspection—blood which had bathed his body and dripped off as he left his crime.

This trail led upstairs and into the bathroom, where it stopped. There were traces of watered blood in the bathtub and on one of the towels—Flecker's own.

"Towel?" said Sister Ursula. "But you said Mrs. Carey had made up the laundry bundle."

"She sends out only sheets and such—does the towels herself."

"Oh." The nun sounded disappointed.

"I know how you feel, Sister. You'd welcome a discrepancy anywhere, even in the laundry list. But that's the sum of our evidence. Three suspects, all with opportunity, none with an alibi. Absolutely even distribution of suspicion, and our only guidepost is the word Quasimodo. Do you know any of these three men?"

"I have never met them, Lieutenant, but I feel as though I know them rather well from Professor Flecker's descriptions."

"Good. Let's see what you can reconstruct. First, Ruggiero de' Cassis, professor of mathematics, formerly of the University of Turin, voluntary exile since the early days of Fascism."

Sister Ursula said slowly, "He admired de' Cassis, not only for his first-rate mind, but because he seemed to have adjusted himself so satisfactorily to life despite his deformity. I remember he said once, 'De' Cassis has never known a woman, yet every day he looks on Beauty bare.'"

"On Beauty . . . ? Oh yes. Millay. *Euclid alone* . . . All right. Now Marvin Lowe, professor of psychology, native of Ohio, and from what I've seen of him a prime pedant. According to Flecker . . . ?"

"I think Professor Lowe amused him. He used to tell us the latest Spoonerisms; he swore that flocks of students graduated from the University believing that modern psychology rested on the researches of two men named Frung and Jeud. Once Lowe said that his favorite book was Max Beerbohm's *Happy Hypocrite*; Professor Flecker insisted that was because it was the only one he could be sure of pronouncing correctly."

"But as a man?"

"He never said much about Lowe personally; I don't think they were intimate. But I do recall his saying, 'Lowe, like all psychologists, is the physician of Greek proverb.'"

"Who was told to heal himself? Makes sense. That speech mannerism certainly points to something a psychiatrist could have fun with. All right. How about Hugo Ellis, instructor in mathematics, native of Los Angeles?"

"Mr. Ellis was a child prodigy, you know. Extraordinary mathematical feats. But he outgrew them, I almost think deliberately. He made himself into a normal young man. Now he is, I gather, a reasonably good young instructor—just run of the mill. An adult with the brilliance which he had as a child might be a great man. Professor Flecker turned the French proverb around to fit him: 'If youth could, if age knew . . .'"

"So. There they are. And which," Marshall asked, "is Quasimodo?"

"Quasimodo . . ." Sister Ursula repeated the word, and other words seemed to follow it automatically. "*Quasimodo geniti infantes* . . ." She paused and shuddered.

"What's the matter?"

"I think," she said softly, "I know. But like Professor Flecker, I fear making a fool of myself—and worse, I fear damning an innocent man. . . . Lieutenant, may I look through this house with you?"

He sat there staring at the other two and at the policeman watching them.

The body was no longer in the next room, but the blood was. He had never before revisited the scene of the crime; that notion was the nonsense of legend. For that matter he had never known his victim.

He let his mind go back to last night. Only recently had he been willing to do this. At first it was something that must be kept apart, divided from his normal personality. But he was intelligent enough to realize the danger of that. It could produce a seriously schizoid personality. He might go mad. Better to attain complete integration, and that could be accomplished only by frank self-recognition.

It must be terrible to be mad.

"Well, where to first?" asked Marshall.

"I want to see the bedrooms," said Sister Ursula. "I want to see if Mrs. Carey changed the sheets."

"You doubt her story? But she's completely out of the—all right. Come on."

Lieutenant Marshall identified each room for her as they entered it. Harvey Flecker's bedroom by no means consorted with the neatness of his mind. It was a welter of papers and notes and hefty German works on Latin philology and puzzle books by Torquemada and Caliban and early missals and codices from the University library. The bed had been changed and the clean upper sheet was turned back. Harvey Flecker would never soil it.

Professor de' Cassis's room was in sharp contrast—a chaste monastic cubicle. His books—chiefly professional works, with a sampling of Leopardi and Carducci and other Italian poets and an Italian translation of Thomas à Kempis—were neatly stacked in a case, and his papers were out of sight. The only ornaments in the room were a crucifix and a framed picture of a family group, in clothes of 1920.

Hugo Ellis's room was defiantly, almost parodistically the room of a normal, healthy college man, even to the University banner over the bed. He had carefully avoided both Flecker's chaos and de' Cassis's austerity; there was a precisely calculated normal litter of pipes and letters and pulp magazines. The pin-up girls seemed to be carrying normality too far, and Sister Ursula averted her eyes.

Each room had a clean upper sheet.

Professor Lowe's room would have seemed as normal as Ellis's, if less spectacularly so, if it were not for the inordinate quantity of books. Shelves covered all wall space that was not taken by door, window, or bed. Psychology, psychiatry, and criminology predominated; but there was a selection of poetry, humor, fiction for any mood.

Marshall took down William Roughead's *Twelve Scots Trials* and said, "Lucky devil! I've never so much as seen a copy of this before." He smiled at the argumentative pencilings in the margins. Then as he went to replace it, he saw through the gap that there was a second row of books behind. Paperbacks. He took one out and put it back hastily. "You wouldn't want to see that, Sister. But it might fit into that case we were proposing about repressions and word-distortions."

Sister Ursula seemed not to heed him. She was standing by the bed and said, "Come here."

Marshal came and looked at the freshly made bed.

Sister Ursula passed her hand over the mended but clean lower sheet. "Do you see?"

"See what?"

"The answer," she said.

Marshall frowned. "Look, Sister—"

"Lieutenant, your wife is one of the most efficient housekeepers I've ever known. I thought she had, to some extent, indoctrinated you. Think. Try to think with Leona's mind."

Marshall thought. Then his eyes narrowed and he said, "So . . ."

"It is fortunate," Sister Ursula said, "that the Order of Martha of Bethany specializes in housework."

Marshall went out and called downstairs. "Raglan! See if the laundry's been picked up from the back porch."

The Sergeant's voice came back. "It's gone, Loot. I thought there wasn't no harm—"

"Then get on the phone quick and tell them to hold it."

"But what laundry, Loot?"

Marshall muttered. Then he turned to Sister Ursula. "The men won't know of course, but we'll find a bill somewhere. Anyway, we won't need that till the preliminary hearing. We've got enough now to settle Quasimodo."

He heard the Lieutenant's question and repressed a startled gesture. He had not thought of that. But even if they traced the laundry, it would be valueless as evidence without Mrs. Carey's testimony . . .

He saw at once what had to be done.

They had taken Mrs. Carey to the guest room, that small downstairs bed-

room near the kitchen which must have been a maid's room when this was a large family house. There were still police posted outside the house, but only Raglan and the lieutenant inside.

It was so simple. His mind, he told himself, had never been functioning more clearly. No nonsense about stripping this time; it was not for pleasure. Just be careful to avoid those crimson jets. . . .

The Sergeant wanted to know where he thought he was going. He told him.

Raglan grinned. "You should've raised your hand. A teacher like you ought to know that."

He went to the back porch toilet, opened and closed its door without going in. Then he went to the kitchen and took the second best knife. The best had been used last night.

It would not take a minute Then he would be safe and later when the body was found what could they prove? The others had been out of the room too.

But as he touched the knife it began to happen. Something came from the blade up his arm and into his head. He was in a hurry, there was no time—but holding the knife, the color of things began to change. . . .

He was half naked when Marshall found him.

Sister Ursula leaned against the jamb of the kitchen door. She felt sick. Marshall and Raglan were both strong men, but they needed help to subdue him. His face was contorted into an unrecognizable mask like a demon from a Japanese tragedy. She clutched the crucifix of the rosary that hung at her waist and murmured a prayer to the Archangel Michael. For it was not the physical strength of the man that frightened her, not the glint of his knife, but the pure quality of incarnate evil that radiated from him and made the doctrine of possession a real terror.

As she finished her prayer, Marshall's fist connected with his jaw and he crumpled. So did Sister Ursula.

✝   ✝   ✝

"I don't know what you think of me," Sister Ursula said as Marshall drove her home. (Sister Felicitas was dozing in the back seat.) "I'm afraid I couldn't ever have been a policewoman after all."

"You'll do," Marshall said. "And if you feel better now, I'd like to run over it with you. I've got to get my brilliant deductions straight for the press."

"The fresh air feels good. Go ahead."

"I've got the sheet business down pat, I think. In ordinary middle-class households you don't change both sheets every week; Leona never does, I remembered. You put on a clean upper sheet, and the old upper sheet becomes the lower. The other three bedrooms each had one clean sheet—the upper. His had two—upper and lower; therefore his upper sheet had been stained in some unusual way and had to be changed. The hasty bath, probably in the dark, had been careless, and there was some blood left to stain the sheet. Mrs. Carey wouldn't have thought anything of it at the time because she hadn't found the body yet. Right?"

"Perfect, Lieutenant."

"So. But now about Quasimodo . . . I still don't get it. He's the one it *couldn't* apply to. Either of the others—"

"Yes?"

"Well, who is Quasimodo? He's the Hunchback of Notre Dame. So it could mean the deformed de' Cassis. Who wrote Quasimodo? Victor Hugo. So it could be Hugo Ellis. But it wasn't either; and how in heaven's name could it mean Professor Lowe?"

"Remember, Lieutenant: Professor Flecker said this was an allusion that might particularly appeal to me. Now I am hardly noted for my devotion to the anticlerical prejudices of Hugo's *Notre-Dame de Paris*. What is the common meeting-ground of my interests and Professor Flecker's?"

"Church liturgy?" Marshall ventured.

"And why was your Quasimodo so named? Because he was born—or found or christened, I forget which—on the Sunday after Easter. Many Sundays, as you may know, are often referred to by the first work of their introits, the beginning of the proper of the Mass. As the fourth Sunday in Lent is called *Laetare* Sunday, or the third in Advent *Gaudete* Sunday. So the Sunday after Easter is known as *Quasimodo* Sunday, from its introit *Quasimodo geniti infantes* 'As newborn babes.'"

"But I still don't see . . ."

"The Sunday after Easter," said Sister Ursula, "is more usually referred to as *Low* Sunday."

"Oh," said Marshall. After a moment he added reflectively, "*The Happy Hypocrite* . . ."

"You see that too? Beerbohm's story is about a man who assumes a mask of virtue to conceal his depravity. A schizoid allegory. I wonder if

Professor Lowe dreamed that he might find the same happy ending."

Marshall drove on a bit in silence. Then he said, "He said a strange thing while you were out."

"I feel as though he were already dead," said Sister Ursula. "I want to say, 'God rest his soul.' We should have a special office for the souls of the mad."

"That cues into my story. The boys were taking him away and I said to Rags, 'Well, this is once the insanity plea justifies itself. He'll never see the gas chamber.' And he turned on me—he'd quieted down by then—and said, 'Nonsense, sir! Do you think I would cast doubt on my sanity merely to save my life?'"

"Mercy," said Sister Ursula. At first Marshall thought it was just an exclamation. Then he looked at her face and saw that she was not talking to him.

✝

The Base of the Triangle
A Father Dowling Mystery

Ralph McInerny

I

When Earl Haven showed up at the rectory door, there was fire in his eye and his manner with Mrs. Murkin would normally have drawn a rebuke from the housekeeper but she brought him to the pastor's study without complaint.

"Father, this is Earl Haven."

"I'm not a Catholic."

"I am. As doubtless the collar tells you."

"She's Catholic. Harriet."

"Ah."

"Harriet Dolan," Mrs Murkin said, and her brows lifted in significance.

"The girl that's getting married?"

A groan escaped Earl and he collapsed into a chair. "She can't marry that idiot, she can't."

The reference would be to Leo Mulcahy with whom Harriet had sat in the front parlor not a hour before, making arrangements for their wedding.

"If it's being Catholic she wants, I'll do it."

"Become a Catholic?"

The man's expression suggested inner anguish. "If she'll marry me, yes I will."

Marie stood in the doorway wringing her apron but her expression was not in every way anguished. The housekeeper had a taste for other people's troubles and she found the various permutations of the relations between man and woman irresistible.

"It will never happen," she had said an hour before after Harriet Dolan and Leo Mulcahy had finished discussing with the pastor their impending nuptials and had left the rectory. Ahead of them lay months of preparation before the big day. Father Dowling conducted a weekly class for couples preparing themselves for marriage. Harriet and Leo would have to attend those classes.

"They seem very attached to one another."

"In love with love."

This was not like Marie, who was one of the last romantics, something she concealed beneath a crusty exterior. Father Dowling wondered if she were seeking to deflect trouble from Harriet and Leo by predicting it; there were depths to Marie's Irish superstitiousness that the pastor did not pretend to fathom. But Marie shook away this explanation, like a pitcher not getting the right signal from his catcher.

"She's taking him on the rebound."

"From what?"

"From whom."

But Marie had intuited little more than this fact. She did not then know who the third party might be, it was simply something that Harriet had said. Now, with Earl Haven collapsed in a chair in the rectory study and unable to suppress his groans, Marie had clearly made an identification.

"Have you proposed to Harriet?" Marie asked.

"She knows."

"But have you asked her?"

"I was going to."

"Apparently Leo Mulcahy got there before you," Father Dowling said.

Marie glared at the pastor and Earl doubled over, as if in pain. Suddenly, he looked up and his expression changed. "He can't afford to marry her!"

"Two can live as cheaply as one," Father Dowling said. Although this was an article in Marie's somewhat plagiarized creed, the housekeeper again glared at him. But then she asked Earl in a soothing voice what he meant.

The question restored Earl to the land of the living. Once his attention had been diverted from his broken heart, he spoke with succinct authority of the business in which both he and Leo Mulcahy were engaged.

There are amazingly inventive ways for people to earn their daily bread and one would have had to lack soul not to respond to the entrepreneurial creativity represented by Boxers Inc. The idea had been Earl's and it involved cutting himself in on the thriving business of the package delivery systems that had proved to be such competition for the U.S. Postal Service. Usually these giants had their own depot, at or near the airport, where the client not large enough to be visited by one of the pick-up trucks might go to send off his packages. Earl had opened a storefront in a mall, the first Boxers Inc, and had served as a clearing house for the various national deliverers—UPS, Federal Express, two or three others—making their services convenient for the occasional non-commercial user. A birthday present, something for a son or daughter at school, the odd item that must be elsewhere in a finite period of time. Boxers provided packaging as well as a clearing house for package delivery. At intervals throughout the day, the packages were taken to the depots of the great delivery systems. Earl had declined the offer to have trucks pick up the packages. It was important for the client to see what Earl was doing for them, thus justifying the modest fee he charged which, added to the payments from the deliverers, made Boxers Inc a money making enterprise. With success came the urge to expand. Earl set Leo Mulcahy up in the business.

"He didn't have a nickel," Earl said, almost with contempt. "I didn't either, when I started, but then I started from scratch. Leo's location in the Naperville mall would be the replica of the original Boxers Inc."

"You lent him the money?"

"Twenty-five thousand dollars."

The whistle came from Marie. "How much does he still owe you?"

"With interest, twenty-seven five. Only Leo could take such a simple idea and mess it up."

"He's in debt $27,500?"

"My accountant could kill me." Earl stood, and there was an unattractive expression on his face. "I am going to collect that money now."

Father Dowling, at his desk, listened to Marie as she accompanied Earl down the hall to the front door. The housekeeper cajoled, threatened, pleaded and, in the end, prophesied.

"Harriet will never forgive you!"

"She would never forgive herself if she married that idiot."

2

Life was full of mystery, Marie Murkin felt, and in this she was certainly not alone, but she took the common point to uncommon lengths. To identify the mystery was in some degree to have overcome it. But like everyone before her, she was utterly baffled by the men to whom some women were attracted and of course vice versa. The most improbable combinations formed before one's eyes, defying every law of probability. Father Dowling often cited a seminary definition of man as a rational animal and of course he did not have to explain to her that the phrase was meant to cover women as well as men. But the truth was that it applied to neither men nor women, not when it came to affairs of the heart. Marie was not being cruel when she thought of Harriet Dolan as, well, what she was, and how any man, let alone two of them, could make fools of themselves over the girl, Marie did not understand. Nor did she regard this as merely the limitations of her own abilities. She defied anyone to explain how a girl hardly more than five and a half feet high, with a round plain face, abundant if nondescript hair worn in the current bag lady style, narrow little mouth and the body of a boy could turn the heads of both Earl Haven and Leo Mulcahy. It made no sense, not even when you acknowledged Harriet's smile that transformed her face, crinkled her eyes behind the lenses of her glasses, and was admittedly infectious.

"I hope I'm doing the right thing," the girl had whispered to Marie, when Leo was alone with Father Dowling on the occasion of their first visit.

"How long have you known him?"

"All my life."

"That's good."

"And his whole family," she added significantly.

"Ah. And he is in business for himself?"

"It's his partner who knows things."

Of course a girl was nervous and said odd things when she was on the brink of marriage but Marie found this particularly enigmatic. Until Earl Haven showed up at the rectory door. If Leo was a fine specimen of a man, and he was, Earl Haven was even more so, and his near despair at the thought of Harriet marrying Leo did nothing to detract from his attraction. One of the advantages of age was that Marie could deal with handsome men as she never could have when she was young and they were the same age. All the more did she marvel at the way Harriet had wrapped Leo and Earl around her finger, effortlessly manipulating them. She sent Leo to the rectory as soon as she learned that Earl had been there.

"It's none of his business," Leo almost shouted. His anger added to his imposing presence. He was a larger man than Earl, dark haired, craggy— a term that was much used in the novels Marie read. Earl on the other hand was blonde—golden locked, Marie's author might have said—slim and graceful with the clear blue eyes of a dreamer. Yet he apparently was the business whiz and Leo, in looks the practical man of action, was inept, losing money running a business that, according to Earl, ran itself.

"I understand you and Earl are in business together."

"He leant me some money, Father. Now he wants it back. I don't have it. It's sunk in that lousy business I was talked into starting."

Talked into by whom, Marie wondered. But she did not have to wonder long. Leo's expression had softened.

"I did it for Harriet. I was happy enough working for Midwest Power."

"Why not give up the business and go back to work for Midwest Power?"

Marie could have cheered this suggestion from Father Dowling. She found herself being tugged from side to side in this matter. On the one hand, she did not like to think that a couple would come talk to the priest about getting married, make arrangements for instructions, and then just drop it. On the other hand, if she were Harriet, her choice would certainly have been Earl Haven. But again she was mystified by the fact that little Harriet had her choice of these two paragons.

"I lost my seniority when I quit."

"That could not have been much at your age?" Marie said.

"They gave me a going away party." It seemed clear that Leo had left Midwest Power in such a way that any return would be demeaning. "I can't pay Earl back, not now, I'm losing money."

"He's just bluffing," Marie assured Leo. "Besides, if you don't have it . . ."

"He could take over my business."

Leo's situation was not enviable. He was stuck with a business that was losing money and his partner was demanding repayment of a loan and threatening to take over the business if Leo did not come up with the money. And all this out of spite because Leo had won the hand of the girl Earl loved. Father Dowling would not have thought of Harriet's as a face that would launch a thousand ships. But she was incentive enough for both Leo and Earl.

"I'll talk to Earl," Father Dowling said.

Hope leapt momentarily into Leo's eyes then faded away. "He won't listen to you."

"Let's find out."

3

Peanuts wanted to return some videos he had purchased from a catalog and Tuttle took him to the Boxers Inc store in Naperville to send the merchandise back.

"You know the place?"

"It's just like the ones in Fox River."

Peanuts didn't know them, but how often did he need someone to pack up and return merchandise for him? Tuttle assured him that Boxers Inc was reliable.

"What's wrong with the Post Office?"

"Don't get me started. What's wrong with the videos?"

"I already seen them."

"You're returning them just because you watched them?"

"Not these. I've already seen these. They're not what I ordered."

Peanuts had ordered several dozen old episodes of *The Untouchables*.

"I like Frank Nitty."

"Who doesn't?"

Tuttle meant the actor. He wasn't sure what Peanuts meant. No matter, they were at the mall and Tuttle was searching for a parking spot as close as possible to Boxers Inc.

"There's an ambulance," Peanuts observed.

"I noticed the light." Tuttle was also noticing that it seemed to be stopping traffic right in front of Boxers Inc. This could mean anything, of course. It may or not concern Boxers directly, then again it could be a customer fallen ill. Naperville was beyond the jurisdiction in which Peanuts was an officer of the law and a policeman out of his jurisdiction feels like an imposter. But then Peanuts felt like an imposter in Fox River. His sinecure in the local constabulary was due to the influence of his family. When he was on duty he was given tasks of minimal responsibility. This suited Peanuts fine. He was not an ambitious man and was not personally proud, though fiercely loyal to his dubious family.

"I don't have to send these back right now."

"As long as we're here," Tuttle said. He had maneuvered his car through the lot and now drew up to the curb behind the ambulance. "I wish we had a squad car."

If Peanuts had been driving they could have turned on the warning light and given a little goose to the siren, arriving in style and authority. As it was, an overweight cop signaled imperiously for Tuttle to drive on. Tuttle put the car in neutral and hopped out.

"I got here as quick as I could," he said to the cop, silencing the order he was about to bark.

"Who are you?"

Tuttle took off his tweed hat and extracted a calling card from the crown. While the cop was reading it, Tuttle circled him and saw that the commotion was indeed inside the Boxers.

"That's Officer Pianone in the passenger seat."

Tuttle breezed on past then and swept into the door of Boxers Inc. He did not need any explanation of the scene before him. The store was alive with officers and plainclothesmen and paramedics. A young man in a white coat got up from a crouch and looking at a cop crossed his eyes and drew a finger across his throat. The paramedics were prepared to turn matters over to the medical examiner. Tuttle pressed on through to where the body lay on the floor. A man. Leo Mulcahy! Tuttle had the feeling that he had been brought providentially to this scene.

"His name is Leo Mulcahy," Tuttle said in a raised, authoritative voice.

Heads turned to look at him.

"The deceased is a friend of mine. What happened?"

What happened to Tuttle was that he was collared by two officers and hustled outside and into a patrol car. He tried to wave to Peanuts as he was hustled across the walk to the car but the reflection on the windshield made it impossible to see Peanuts. In the back seat of the Naperville squad car, Tuttle was bracketed by a uniformed officer and a plainclothesman.

"Who are you?"

"You're making a great mistake."

"You want to talk to a lawyer?"

"I am a lawyer."

The plainclothesman, who had a face still bearing the traces of teenage acne, narrowed his eyes. Outside the car, the cop to whom he had given his card tapped on the window. It was rolled down and Tuttle's calling card was passed in.

"This you?" the detective asked.

"Tuttle the lawyer."

"You say you know the dead guy?"

"What happened to him?"

Tuttle posed a problem for his captors. His manner disarmed them and yet they were disinclined to admit to having made a mistake. It was easier to act as if they had pressed Tuttle into service as an informant.

"I was afraid something like this would happen," Tuttle said, letting out a little line, getting in deeper. He hoped Peanuts had enough sense to put his car in a parking space. Peanuts could catch a nap in the back seat then and derive some benefit from this failed effort to return the unwanted videos. As for Tuttle, he was asking himself what kind of bill he could send the Naperville police after they solved the murder of Leo Mulcahy.

4

Cy Horvath drove out to the Fox River mall and parked where he could look at the front entrance of Boxers Inc, what was described in the writeup Cy had downloaded from the Web page of the *Tribune* as the flagship of Earl Haven's little empire. This was the first store Haven had opened and which he had used as a model for the others he had then opened in the area. The store in Naperville where the body of Leo Mulcahy had been found was a spin-off that had been jointly owned by Haven and the deceased.

Cy got out of the car and wound his away among parked vehicles, crossed the access road and pulled open the door of Boxers Inc. There were people waiting at the counter, there were customers availing themselves of the pack-it-yourself facilities, there was soothing music oozing through the place. All in all, a picture of pastel prosperity. Cy looked around and then decided that Haven's office would be down the hall past the computers and faxes and copying facilities. A diminutive woman whose blonde hair seemed shaped like a helmet looked up in surprise. The nameplate on her desk said Rose Hanlon. Cy told her he wanted to see Earl Haven.

"Oh he's over in Naperville."

"At the store there?"

"Can I help you?"

"I'm Lieutenant Horvath."

"Lieutenant?"

"Fox River Police."

"Is anything wrong?"

"Do you know Leo Mulcahy?"

Her expression changed. "Why do you ask?"

"Isn't he Earl Haven's partner in the Naperville store?"

She looked at him with growing disapproval. "If that were so, why would it be of interest to the Fox River police? Or are you asking personally?"

"Leo Mulcahy was found dead in the Naperville store an hour ago." No need to tell her that he had been strangled to death with a scarf.

Her gasping intake of air set her chair in motion and she backed away from him. Her eyes were round as dollars and her lips trembled.

"Dead?"

"Yes."

"That's impossible! He was a young man. His health was good."

"How well did you know him?"

"How well did I know him?" she repeated.

"The Naperville police would like some help in their investigation. This looks like something that spans our jurisdictions. When did Mr. Haven go to Naperville."

"He always went over there on Wednesdays."

"A regular visit."

"Yes."

"He hadn't heard of what happened to Mr. Mulcahy?"

"He must have been there already." After she said it, she seemed to regret having said it.

"I understand that there had been a falling out between the two men."

"I'm not sure I should talk about such things."

"Rose, a man has been murdered."

"Murdered! Oh my God." Tears welled into her eyes and then she was sobbing helplessly. Cy took a chair and waited. He let her cry as long as she wanted to and that turned out to be a long time indeed.

"You did know Leo Mulcahy."

"Of course I knew him. We were engaged to be married. Some years ago"

"You and Leo Mulcahy?"

"Yes." Her chin lifted, as if he had doubted her word.

"You broke off with him?"

She thought for a minute. "It wouldn't have worked out."

Phil Keegan had called the St. Hilary rectory while Cy was checking out the *Tribune* Web page. The call from Naperville reminded the captain of something he had heard from Father Dowling. But it was Marie Murkin he talked with. Leo Mulcahy? He was soon to marry Harriet Dolan. Now, talking with Rose Hanlon, Cy wondered if Leo's one time fiancée knew of his marriage plans.

"Do you know Harriet Dolan?"

An angry expression formed on Rose Hanlon's face. "Whatever happened to Leo Mulcahy is her fault."

5

Phil Keegan was in the study with Father Dowling, telling him what he knew of events in Naperville, and Marie was listening in. The picture seemed clear. Earl Haven had been driven half mad by the thought that the woman he loved intended to marry such an idiot as Leo Mulcahy.

"The Wednesday visit to the Naperville store was apparently a regular event," he said.

"Have you talked with him yet?"

"Earl Haven? He can't be found."

"Who has looked for him?"

"Cy."

Phil as much as said that very little mystery remained as to what had happened to Leo Mulcahy. Not only was Earl Haven the prime suspect, he was the only suspect.

"He left a trail as wide as the Interstate. Half a dozen people noticed him arrive at the Naperville store. Two people who were in the store have told us of a fierce argument between two men. The argument was the kind that would almost inevitably lead to blows."

"Did anyone witness a fight?"

"Haven told Mulcahy he was stupid. He told him he could not run a penny lemonade stand. He just threw insults at Mulcahy."

"What was his reaction?"

"He laughed."

"Laughed."

That was when Haven cleared everyone out of the store. "Being laughed at got to him, that was obvious. Mulcahy was hit on the head, probably with a scotch tape holder made of heavy metal. But it was the scarf that did it."

"Scarf."

"He was strangled with a scarf. It was not a pretty sight."

"Did anyone see Earl leave?"

Phil took the cigar from his mouth, studied it, then returned it to his mouth. clamping it between his teeth.

"Of course we're just assuming the man was Earl Haven."

Whatever the ostensible reason for the quarrel, it seemed obvious that Harriet Dolan was the real explanation. Earl's anger was more easily explained by the fact that he had lost Harriet than that he had lost money.

6

Harriet Dolan was unconvincing in the role of tragic woman. Surrounded by the sisters of Leo Mulcahy, she looked around her as if seeking a cue as to how she should behave. Her fiancé was dead and the man who killed him had professed his love for her and was now the object of a police search. Any of Leo's sisters was more attractive than Harriet but none of them had been the cause of such a romantic tragedy. It seemed assumed that Harriet would be brokenhearted by the events and from time to time she dabbed at her dry eyes with a handkerchief. She might have been concealing the little smile that kept forming on her thin lips. Of course it had not really dawned on her that Leo was dead and that Earl had killed him.

"She is in shock," one of the Mulcahy girls said to Marie Murkin.

"Who could blame her?" the housekeeper replied, but her eye was on Harriet and her tone was not as definite as her words. The chair next to Harriet was offered to Marie and she took it. She patted the girl's arm and sighed.

"You have lost them both."

Harriet looked at her.

"Leo and Earl."

"I didn't encourage him," Harriet protested, and rubbed the forming smile from her lips.

"It's not your fault."

But Harriet was distracted by the arrival of a young woman who turned out to be Rose Hanlon, accompanied by her brother. Their arrival created an awkwardness and when Rose approached her, Harriet grew apprehensive, but Rose just took her hand and shook her head in silent disbelief at what had happened. Steve Hanlon stood unobtrusively against a wall. Everyone seemed to be waiting for Rose to say something, but she held her silence. Finally she drifted off to the side of the room and joined her brother.

"She is affected as much as Harriet," a Mulcahy girl whispered to Marie.

"Why would she be?"

"She and Leo were engaged, you know. Informally."

Marie Murkin looked at Rose with new interest. The young woman had begun to weep and was being comforted. The contrast with Harriet was eloquent.

7

Earl Haven was located in a cabin north of town overlooking the Fox River, a summer place that afforded relief from the Midwestern heat. His car had been parked sideways on the narrow gravel drive and he had appeared in the picture window armed with a shotgun. Phil Keegan had prudently decided to address Earl by bull horn from the road. It added to the drama that Earl replied through a bullhorn of his own, one he had made notorious as a fan of the local high school football team.

"Come on out, Earl. We don't want anyone else getting hurt."

"I haven't hurt anyone."

"No reason not to come out then, is there?" Phil looked around, obviously pretty proud of that retort.

When Father Dowling arrived Phil and Earl were still exchanging one liners. Roger Dowling stood beside Cy Horvath.

"What are they talking about, Cy?"

"Football."

"Football!"

"Earl played for the Fox River Reds. His touchdown pass record to Steve Hanlon, who played wide receiver, will never be broken."

"How long has this been going on?"

Cy thought twenty minutes. Phil and Earl were discussing a game against Naperville played in the misty past when Earl had first become the toast of the town.

"Don't spoil it now, Earl. Face up to this."

"Do you think I killed Leo?"

"It doesn't matter what I think, Earl. We've got to straighten it out. Do you have a lawyer?"

Suddenly, through the no man's land between the police cars and the cabin door a short figure, arms raised, one hand waving a greyish hand-kerchief, waddled toward the door of the cabin.

"It's Tuttle," Father Dowling said.

"Who else?"

A more successful lawyer can wait for clients to come to him. Tuttle was always on the alert for poor devils in need of legal representation and he had been riding in a squad car with Peanuts when he switched the radio dial from Rush Limbaugh and picked up the report of Earl Haven holed up in his riverside summer cottage. Immediately they were on their way to the scene. Tuttle had jumped out of the car, listened for a few minutes and, when his opportunity came, seized it.

His breath came in rapid gasps and he had a stitch in his side before his hand closed over the knob of the front door. He panted for a moment and then lifted his free hand toward the door and knocked. In doing this, his hand turned the knob, the door opened and he tumbled inside, liter-ally sprawling across the uncarpeted floor of the cabin. The windows overlooking the river blinded him with their brightness and he got to his knees and looked blinking about.

"Who are you?"

"Can you pull those blinds?"

"Are you a reporter?"

"No!" Tuttle rose to his feet in indignation. He might be at the bottom rung of his chosen profession but he had not sunk to the level of those purchased pens who hung around the press room of the court house. "I am Tuttle the lawyer." He found his tweed hat and put it on his head. It was like resuming his true persona.

"Oh yeah."

"My advice is that you make no statement whatsoever. We will march out of here, they can book you, but I will do the talking."

"There's nothing to say."

"Exactly."

"I didn't hurt Leo."

Tuttle remembered the scene at the Naperville Boxers Inc. He had not seen Earl there. He could not remember anyone else who had. Rose Hanlon, Earl's secretary, had unwisely told the police that Earl had gone to Naperville.

"That could work."

"What do you mean?"

"Look, I was at the store in Naperville when the cops were investigating. It couldn't have been long after . . ."

Something in Earl's eye caused Tuttle to stop. He did not want to antagonize a potential client.

"What time were you there?"

"I never got there. I got caught in traffic, a jack-knifed semi blocked the road, and finally I just turned around and started back to Fox River. I heard about it on radio, and that I was being sought. I headed here."

"Why?"

"Look out there. I feel like a treed squirrel."

But why would an innocent man run? Tuttle did not ask this question. A lawyer can often represent his client better if he lets innocence remain a presumption. Knowing too much can be a burden.

"Earl, we're going out there. We're going to open that door and march right out to the police, those cameras, everything. You can't stay here forever."

Earl looked as if he wanted to argue about it, but suddenly his shoulders slumped. "You're right. Let's go."

"Let me look at you first."

Tuttle stood in front of Earl and squinted his eyes, imagining what he would look like on television.

"Why don't you take off your cap."

"You going to take off your hat?"

"Okay, leave it on." Tuttle took the door handle, inhaled, and pulled. Silence fell. Tuttle stepped outside first, his eyes shaded by the brim of his hat, and located the television cameras. When Earl came out, Tuttle took his elbow and they walked right at the cameras. Tuttle kept up a non-stop patter as they walked, a lawyer advising his client. Earl looked bewildered but that wasn't bad. It could be mistaken for innocence. All this was being taped. It would be like running a commercial on television. Tuttle moved even closer to his client. He didn't want to be focused out of the picture.

Phil Keegan and Cy Horvath came forward to meet them.

"Remember, Earl," Tuttle said, addressing the media. "You don't have to say a thing."

"I didn't do anything," Earl protested. "I'll say that."

8

There was an unbaptized part of Marie Murkin's soul that took mordant pleasure from the spectacle of Harriet Dolan being deprived of two men, either one of whom had been too good for her. But the fact—or alleged fact, as Tuttle always insisted in speaking to the press—that one of those men had killed the other out of insane desire for Harriet was something it was difficult to accept cheerfully. Harriet rose to her tragic role during the funeral of Leo Mulcahy, sitting in the front pew with the Mulcahy girls, for all the world as if she were a widow. But it soon became clear that Harriet had no intention of going into deep mourning.

"Does she intend to wait for Earl?"

"Ask Phil Keegan about that."

"Does she confide in Phil?"

"She hasn't even been to visit him in jail."

"Well, after all, he is accused of killing her fiancé."

There was no point in trying to explain it to the pastor. One needed a woman's intuition to maneuver through the intricacies of the matter. It was Marie's fear that while she might ignore him while he languished in jail awaiting trial, Harriet would be all too prominent in the court room once proceedings began. What a magnet she would be for the press. The woman whose fiancé the accused had killed because she had spurned him. It was almost too much to bear.

Marie noticed that Harriet came regularly to Mass on Sunday and had to acknowledge that she did nothing to draw attention to herself, not coming late nor leaving early, dressing in a subdued way. Marie was on the verge of thinking that she had misjudged Harriet when she ran into her as she was leaving the mall.

"Hello," Harriet replied warily in response to Marie's greeting.

"I'm Marie Murkin, housekeeper at St. Hilary's."

"Of course I recognize you."

Marie would have liked to chat with the girl but the moment was not propitious. They parted and Marie started for her car. When she got in, she noticed that Harriet was still standing near the door, looking out over the lot. Had she forgotten where she had parked? But then her expression changed as a car drew up to the curb. Harriet, radiant, pulled open the door. Marie had started her engine and managed to drive forward to where she could get a good glimpse of the man behind the wheel of the car that had come for Harriet Dolan. At first she did not recognize him, but then she did.

Steve Hanlon.

9

Earl Haven's trial proceeded with slow inevitability and the apparent fate of the accused could not be ascribed simply to the want of skill on the part of his lawyer. Indeed, when Father Dowling asked Amos Cadbury what he thought of Tuttle's performance, the patrician lawyer, dean of Fox River attorneys, thought for a moment.

"I am only surprised that the prosecution has not called those who said they saw Haven at the Naperville store that morning."

Amos was right. At the time any number of people claimed to have been eye witnesses to a quarrel between Earl and Leo.

"Maybe they don't need that evidence."

"You may be right."

"It looks bad for Earl."

"His chances of acquittal are not good."

"Poor fellow."

"Perhaps he is guilty."

"Perhaps?"

But apparently it was simply the caution of the lawyer. Father Dowling had spoken with Earl Haven and while he was privy to no confidential matters so far as Earl's soul went—as a non-Catholic Earl would not ask to confess his sins—he had the distinct feeling that he was speaking with an innocent man. Or at least with one innocent of the crime of which he was accused. Earl's story about never having gone to the Naperville store on that fateful morning had been difficult to sustain in court. The traffic jam Earl said had decided him to return to Fox River could not be verified. Earl had spoken of a jack-knifed semi, but no police report corroborating the incident had been discovered. Earl said he had never actually seen the semi, but a similar delay three weeks before had been caused by a jack-knifed semi. Tuttle was able to verify that and he produced police reports, subpoenaed half a dozen drivers, proved it beyond the shadow of a doubt. But, as the prosecutor pointed out, that had nothing to do with the traffic on the day Leo was killed. Tuttle then turned to the undisputed negative fact that no one had seen Earl in Naperville that day. The prosecutor did not counter with eyewitnesses. It was soon clear why.

"Ah, but he left proof of his being there," the prosecutor said. A long gray scarf was introduced into evidence. It had been twisted around the neck of the hapless Leo Mulcahy. The scarf was definitely Earl's. It had his name in it.

"I lost that scarf," Earl cried. "I haven't seen it for years."

"Lost it? No, you didn't lose it. But you did leave it behind at the scene where you killed Leo Mulcahy!"

Earl was doomed. The jury withdrew to consider their verdict. Within an hour they were back. They found Earl Haven guilty of causing the death of Leo Mulcahy and with malice aforethought.

"He will be an old man when he gets out," Father Dowling observed to Marie Murkin.

"The poor man."

"There will be no point in the young lady waiting for him."

"There will be no danger of it either."

"Oh?"

Listening to Marie Father Dowling sat very still. It was as if she had suddenly been given the key to recent events. It was unclear that Marie saw the full significance of what she was saying. He said nothing at the time and the housekeeper eventually returned to her kitchen, a little embarrassed at having passed on such gossip. Father Dowling remained at his desk for half an hour, thinking. He got out a piece of paper and prepared to write on it, but did not. He did not need to make a list of what he knew in order to arrive at a conclusion.

He got up and put on a coat and said on his way through the kitchen, "I'm going out, Marie. Would you call Phil Keegan and Cy Horvath to come over tonight?"

"For supper?"

"What a wonderful idea."

✝ ✝ ✝

The one-time wide receiver of the Fox River high school Reds had an office in the same mall in which Earl Haven had opened the original Boxers Inc. Stephen Hanlon was an accountant, a bald man in a blue shirt and striped tie who sat coatless behind his desk, his unblinking eyes concentrating on figures and columns and the quantification of the romance of commerce. He greeted Father Dowling and asked him to be seated. His eyes never left his caller.

"How I marvel at anyone who can do that," Father Dowling exclaimed when Steve Hanlon answered his question as to what he did in this bare and orderly office.

"Who keeps the books at St. Hilary?"

"I keep one set."

The pale brows rose above pale eyes.

"No mortal knows enough to keep a complete account, does he, Steve?"

"There is no mystery about a good set of books."

"Income and outgo, plus and minus, add and subtract?"

Steve Hanlon nodded.

"What sort of balance can there be for taking another life?"

Perhaps if his life had gone differently Steve Hanlon might have become a Trappist. He seemed comfortable with silence. His eyes were all but expressionless as he looked across his neat desk at Father Dowling.

"Was it jealousy, Steve?"

Silence.

"Did it anger you that your old quarterback had teamed up with Leo Mulcahy?"

The fan of Hanlon's computer purred evenly. A digital clock on the wall measured time not quite noiselessly.

"Of course it wasn't that, was it? It was what Leo had done when he jilted Rose."

Steve rose as if he were managed by invisible wires. His hand closed on a large smooth stone that did service as a paperweight.

"You use what's at hand, don't you? How did you happen to be wearing Earl Haven's scarf?"

"You're guessing, I know. But if you can guess, so can others."

"That seems a reason for not compounding your troubles, doesn't it?"

Steve stood there, the rock gripped menacingly in his hand, but he was thinking. What Father Dowling had said was entered into one column, his mind went on to the next. After a moment, he sat down. He put the large stone where it had been and placed his hands on the arms of his chair.

"You're right. It was Rose. She loved him. She still does."

"Does she know?"

"Of course not."

Another item was entered in the ledger in Steve's mind, and Father Dowling feared that he had put himself in danger by the question. But Steve simply looked at him. Finally he said, "What do you want me to do?"

"Come to dinner at the rectory?"

For the first time Steve Hanlon reacted to what Father Dowling had said. His mouth opened in surprise.

1 0

The drive to and from Joliet was not a long one and Father Dowling did not remain long at the prison. Steve Hanlon seemed to appreciate his visits, but he simply did not have the gift of conversation. Besides, his talents had been put to work in the business office and, while he was no longer a free man, he was free to engage in the accounting that had always made up a large part of his life. Only one thing had truly bothered him. He had kept the books for Boxers Inc and picked a quarrel with Leo Mulcahy over his terrible business sense when he heard that his sister's old fiancé was engaged to marry Harriet Dolan, sacking his old quarterback.

"Please explain to Rose, Father," he had asked when, having dined with Phil Keegan and Cy Horvath at the rectory table, he had told the detectives what he had done in Naperville.

"You invited a murderer to dinner?" Phil asked, after Cy had taken Steve downtown.

"Is this a confession?"

"You know what Captain Keegan means," Marie said, coming in from the kitchen. "When I think that I was urging all that food on someone who had taken a human life."

"He did have a good appetite, didn't he?"

"Second helpings of everything."

"Perhaps he figured out how much he was saving."

But the personality of Steve Hanlon was not known to Marie or Phil Keegan. His matter-of-fact admission that he had strangled Leo Mulcahy, dabbing at his mouth with his napkin as he told of it, had not exactly promoted digestion. Nonetheless, Father Dowling was certain he had been right in following his instinct and asking Steve Hanlon back to the rectory for dinner. The police were already scheduled to be there.

"He ate a hearty meal before he was condemned," Phil said. He seemed to have decided to let Marie carry the complaint alone.

"Well, he certainly won't have to worry about where his next meal is coming from," Marie said.

Phil Keegan sighed. "I can still see him gathering in a pass from Earl Haven."

"That will doubtless be Harriet Dolan's game now," Marie said. She widened her eyes and then turned on her heel and went into her kitchen.

Earl Haven had always attracted Harriet. Nor had his attraction suffered from the accusation that he had strangled Leo Mulcahy rather than let him marry Harriet. When it seemed that this act of gallantry would cause Earl to spend most of the rest of his life in prison, it was only human that Harriet should become susceptible to the charms of Steve Hanlon. Of course she misread his interest. He had been motivated by anger that Leo had dropped his sister Rose for Harriet. But Harriet's fickleness had dissolved the charm she had for Earl.

As he drove back to Fox River from Joliet and his visit with Steve Hanlon, Father Dowling checked his watch. Earl Haven would be coming to the rectory for instructions that evening. He professed to be interested in becoming a Catholic.

"Rose has told me to make up my own mind, of course."

"Of course."

"We would like to be married at St. Hilary's."

Whether the ceremony came before or after Earl's entry into the Church was still undecided. He still seemed to think a Hail Mary was a pass rather than a prayer.

✝

Conventual Spirit

Sharan Newman

June 1137, the convent of the Paraclete, France

"Pride, Catherine! Evil, wicked pride! It will be your damnation, girl!"

Sister Bertrada glared at Catherine, their faces an inch apart. "You'll never be allowed to become one of us unless you learn some humility," the old nun continued. "How dare you try to lecture me on the blessed St. Jerome! Do you think you've received a vision of the Truth?"

Catherine bit her tongue.

"No, Sister," she said.

Even those two words sounded impudent to Sister Bertrada, who considered the student novices under her care to be her own private purgatory. And Catherine LeVendeur, with her ready tongue and sharp mind, was her special bane.

"Abbess Heloise has a soft spot for you, though I can't see why," Bertrada went on. "I don't find your glib attempts at rhetoric endearing at all."

"No, Sister." Catherine tried to back up, but Sister Bertrada had her wedged into a corner of the refectory and there was no farther back to go.

"What you need is some serious manual labor."

Catherine stifled a groan. Sister Bertrada did not consider sitting for hours hunched over a table laboriously copying a Psalter to be real work. Never mind that her fingers cramped, her back ached, and her eyes burned at the end of the day. Now she tried to look meek and obliging as she awaited Sister Bertrada's orders.

She succeeded about as well as most sixteen-year-old girls would.

Sister Bertrada had eyes like the Archangel Michael, which glowed with righteousness and ferreted out the most deeply hidden sins. Her cane tapped the wooden floor with ominous thumps as she considered an appropriate penance.

"Go find Sister Felicitia," she told Catherine at last. "Ask her to give you a bucket and a brush. The transept of the oratory has mud all over the floor. You can easily finish scrubbing it before Vespers, if you give the labor the same passion you use to defy me."

Catherine bowed her head, hopefully in outward submission. Sister Bertrada snorted to show that she wasn't fooled in the least, then turned and marched out, leaving Catherine once again defeated by spiritual superiority.

Outside, she was met by her friend and fellow student, Emilie. Emilie took one look at Catherine's face and started laughing.

"Why in the world did you feel you had to tell Sister Bertrada that St. Jerome nagged poor St. Paula to death?"

Catherine shrugged. "I was only quoting from a letter of St. Ambrose. I thought it was interesting that even the saints had their quarrels."

Emilie shook her head in wonder. "You've been here a year and you still have no sense about when to speak and when to keep silent. Sister Melisande would find it amusing, so would Mother Heloise, but Sister Bertrada. . . !"

"I agree," Catherine said sadly. "And now I'm to pay for it on my knees, as usual."

"And proper." Emilie smiled at her fondly. "Oh, Catherine, you do make lessons interesting, if more volatile. I'm so glad you came here."

Catherine sighed. "So am I. Now if only Sister Bertrada could share our happiness."

† † †

If meekness were the only test for judging the worthiness of a soul, then Sister Felicitia should have inherited the earth long ago. She was the only daughter of a noble family, who ought to have had to do nothing more than sing the hours, sew, and copy manuscripts. Her only distinction was that her face was marred by deep scars on both sides, running from temple to jaw. Catherine had never heard how she came by them, but assumed that this disfigurement was the reason she was in the convent instead of married to some lord. Although for the dowry Felicitia commanded, it was surprising that no one was willing to take her, no matter what she looked like.

Felicitia certainly didn't behave like a pampered noblewoman. She always volunteered when the most disagreeable tasks were being assigned. She scrubbed out the reredorter, even leaning into the holes in the seats above the river to scrub the filth from the inside. She hauled wood and dug vegetables. She never lifted her eyes from the job she was doing. She never raised her voice in dispute.

Catherine didn't know what to make of her.

"I'll need the bucket later this evening," Sister Felicitia said when Catherine stated her orders. "I'd help you, of course, but I'm dyeing today."

Catherine had noticed. The woman's hands were stained blue with woad. It would be days before it all washed off. Sister Felicitia didn't appear concerned by this. Nor did she seem aware that the day was soft and bright and that the other women were all sitting in the cloister, sewing and chatting softly while soaking up the June sunshine.

"Sister Bertrada wants me to do this alone, anyway," Catherine said, picking up the bucket and brush. Sister Felicitia nodded without looking up. She did not indulge in unnecessary conversation.

✝ ✝ ✝

Catherine spilled half the water tripping over the doorstop to the oratory. Coming in from the sunlight, it seemed to her that there were bright doves fluttering before her eyes. So she missed her step in the darkness, and then mopped up the puddles before spending the better part of the afternoon scrubbing the stone floor. But, true to Sister Bertrada's prediction, she did indeed have the job finished in time for Vespers, although her robes were still damp and stained at the hem, unsuitable attire for the Divine Office.

And that was how she knew that there had been no muddy footprints on the oratory floor when the nuns retired to the dormitory that evening.

Of course, Sister Bertrada didn't believe her.

"This time, do it properly," she told Catherine as she handed her the bucket the next day.

Catherine fervently wanted to protest. She had scrubbed the floor thoroughly, half of it with her own skirts. It had been clean. Perhaps one of the nuns had forgotten and worn her wooden clogs to prayers instead of her slippers. It wasn't her fault.

But Catherine knew that she would never be allowed to remain here at the Paraclete if she contradicted Sister Bertrada every time she opened her mouth, and she wanted to stay at the convent more than anything else in the world. So she took the proffered bucket and returned to the dark oratory.

She propped the door open to let the light in and knelt to begin the task.

"That's odd," she said as she started on the marks.

"That's *very* odd," she added as she went on to the next ones.

These had to have been made recently, after Compline, when all the women had retired for the night. They were in the shape of footprints, starting at the door and running across the transept to the chapter room, stopping at the bottom of the staircase to the nuns' dormitory. The marks were smudged, perhaps by the slippers of the nuns when they came down just before dawn for Vigils and Lauds. But the muddy prints had certainly been made by bare feet. And they were still damp.

Who could have entered the oratory secretly in the middle of the night?

Catherine wondered about it all the while she was scrubbing. When she had finished, she went to the prioress, Astane, for an explanation.

"These footprints," Astane asked. "You already removed them?"

"Sister Bertrada told me to," Catherine explained.

The prioress nodded. "Very good, child. You are learning."

"But I know they weren't there yesterday evening," Catherine insisted. "I did clean the floor carefully the first time. Someone was in the oratory after we went to bed."

"That seems unlikely." Astane did not appear alarmed by Catherine's statement. "The door is barred on the inside, after all."

"Then how did the footprints get there?" Catherine persisted.

The prioress raised her eyebrows. "That is not your concern, my dear."

"It is if I have to wipe them up," Catherine muttered under her breath.

Not far enough under. Astane's hand gripped her chin tightly and tilted her face upward.

"I presume you were praying just then," the prioress said.

Catherine marveled at the strength in these old women. Sister Bertrada, Prioress Astane; they both must be nearly seventy, but with hands as firm and steady as a blacksmith's. And eyes that saw the smallest lie.

"No, Sister," Catherine said. "But I am now. *Domine, noli me arguere in ira tua* . . ."

The prioress's lip twitched and her sharp glance softened. "'Lord, do not rebuke me in your anger. . .'" she translated. "Catherine, dear, I'm not angry with you and I hope and trust that our Lord isn't, either."

She paused. "Sister Bertrada, on the other hand . . ."

Catherine needed no further warning. She resolved not to mention the footprints in the oratory again.

† † †

But the next morning, everyone saw them.

The light of early dawn slanted through the narrow windows of the chapter, illuminating the clumps of damp earth, a few fresh stalks still clinging to them, forming a clear trail of footprints across the room.

"How did those get there?" Emilie whispered to Catherine, peering down the stairs over the shoulders of the choir nuns.

"They're exactly the same as yesterday," Catherine whispered back. "But I'm sure I cleaned it all. I know I did."

Sister Bertrada and Sister Felicitia walked through the marks, apparently without noticing, but the other women stopped. They looked at each other in confusion, pointing at the footprints, starting at the barred door to the garden, going through the oratory and ending at the steps to their sleeping room.

Sister Ursula shuddered. "Something is coming for us!" she shrieked. "A wild man of the woods has invaded the convent!"

A few of the others gave startled cries, but Emilie giggled, putting a hand over her mouth to stifle the sound. Behind her, Sister Bietriz bent over her shoulder.

"What is it?" she whispered.

Emilie swallowed her laughter. "'Wild man' indeed!" she whispered back. "Maybe Sister Bertrada has a secret lover!"

Bietriz and Catherine exploded in most unseemly mirth.

"*Quiet!*" The object of their speculation raised her cane in warning.

They composed themselves as quickly as possible, knowing that the matter would not be forgotten, but hoping to alleviate the punishment.

"Catherine," Sister Bertrada continued. "Since you and Emilie find this mess so amusing, you may clean it. Bietriz, you will help them."

Catherine opened her mouth to object that she had already removed the marks twice and it had done no good. Just as she inhaled to speak, Emilie stepped on her toe.

"Yie . . . yes, Sister," Catherine said instead.

Privately, she agreed with both Ursula and Emilie. The marks must have been made by a wild man from the forest. For who else could become enamored of Sister Bertrada?

✝   ✝   ✝

"I agree that there is something very strange about this," Emilie told Catherine as they scrubbed. "Who could be getting in here every night? And why doesn't Mother Heloise say something about it? Do you think she knows who it is?"

Catherine wrung out the washrag. Bietriz, whose family was too exalted for floors, leaned against the wall and pointed out spots they had missed.

"Mother Heloise probably doesn't think this worth commenting on," she said. "Perhaps she thinks someone is playing a trick and doesn't want them encouraged. You don't really believe one of us is letting a man in, do you?"

"Who?" Emilie asked. "Sister Bertrada? She and Sister Felicitia would be the most logical suspects. Since they sleep on either side of the door, they have the best chance of leaving at night without being noticed."

Catherine tried to imagine either woman tiptoeing down the steps to let in a secret lover. In Sister Bertrada's case her imagination didn't stretch far enough.

She laughed. "I would find it easier to believe in a monster."

"It's not so preposterous," Emilie continued. "Sister Felicitia is really quite beautiful, even now. I've heard that she had a number of men eager to marry her, but she refused them all. Her father was furious when she announced that she would only wed Christ."

Catherine leaned back on her heels and considered. "I suppose she might have changed her mind," she said. "Perhaps one of them continued to pursue her even here and convinced her that he wanted her despite her looks and had no interest in her property."

Bietriz shook her head. "I don't think so, Catherine. Felicitia made those scars herself, with the knife she used to cut embroidery thread. She sliced right through her cheeks, purposely, so that no one would desire her. That was how her father was finally convinced to let her come here."

Catherine sat back in shock, knocking over the bucket of soapy water.

"How do you know this?" she asked.

"It was common knowledge at the time," Bietriz answered. "I was about twelve then. I remember how upset my mother was about it. Felicitia threatened to cut off her own nose next. It's dreadful, but I benefited from her example. When I said I wanted to come to the Paraclete, no one dared oppose me. Mother even refused to let me have my sewing basket unless she was present, just in case."

"I see." Catherine was once again reminded that she was only a merchant's daughter, at the Paraclete by virtue of her quick mind and her father's money. Bietriz was from one of the best families in Champagne, related in some way even to the count. Bietriz knew all about the life of a noblewoman and all the gossip she herself would not normally be privy to. At the Paraclete they could be sisters in Christ, but not in the world.

"Very well," Catherine said. "I will accept that Sister Felicitia is not likely to be letting a man in. But I don't see how any of the rest of us could do it without waking someone."

"Nor do I," Emilie agreed. "In which case we might have to consider Ursula's theory."

"That some half-human creature came in from the forest?" Catherine snorted.

Emilie stood, shaking out her skirts. Bietriz picked up the bucket, her contribution to the labor.

"Of course not," Emilie said. "Even a half-human creature would have to unbar the door. But Satan can pass through bars and locks, if someone summons him. And it's said that he often appears as a beautiful young man."

Bietriz was skeptical. "So we should demand to know who has been having dreams of seduction lately? Who will admit to that?"

Catherine felt a chill run down her spine. Was it possible that one of them could be inviting Evil into the convent, perhaps unwittingly? It was well known that the devil used dreams to lure and confuse the innocent into sin. She tried to remember her dreams of the past few nights. The memories were dim, so it was likely that she had only had dreams of *ventris inanitate,* those deriving from an empty stomach and of no relevance.

They walked out into the sunlight and Catherine felt the fear diminish. While it was true that Satan used dreams to tempt weak humans, sin could only occur when one was awake. Tertullian said so. We can no more be condemned for dreaming we are sinners than rewarded for dreaming we are saints.

"And why would the devil leave footprints?" she continued the thought aloud. "That doesn't seem very subtle."

Emilie didn't want to give up her demon lover theory.

"There is a rock near my home with a dent in it that everyone says is the devil's toe print," she told Catherine. "So why not the whole foot? Satan is known to be devious. Perhaps he doesn't just want one soul. He may be trying to cause dissension among us so that he may take us all."

Bietriz had moved on to another worry. "Why is it that the feet are only coming in?" she asked them. "How does this intruder get out?"

"Perhaps he turns into something else," Emilie answered. "Satan can do that, too."

She seemed delighted with her conclusions, and her expression dared them to come up with a refutation.

Catherine looked at her. Was she serious? Did she now believe they were being visited by the devil as shapechanger? Emilie was usually scornful of such tales. Why was she so eager to assign a supernatural explanation to this? An answer leaped unbidden to her mind.

Emilie's bed wasn't that far from the door.

Catherine tried to suppress the thought as unworthy, but it wouldn't be put down. Emilie was blond, beautiful, and also from a noble family. Perhaps she wasn't as happy in the convent as she pretended. It entailed a much smaller stretch of the imagination to see Emilie unbarring the door for a lover than Sister Felicitia.

But that explanation didn't satisfy her, either. It wasn't like Emilie. And Catherine was sure Mother Heloise and Prioress Astane didn't believe that one of the nuns had a secret lover, human or demon. If they did, then Brother Baldwin and the other lay brothers who lived nearby would have been set to guard the oratory entrance.

She was missing something. Catherine hated to leave a puzzle unsolved. She had to find out who was doing this. She sighed. It was either that or spend the rest of her life scrubbing the oratory floor.

† † †

It was nearly midsummer. The days were long and busy. Apart from reciting the Divine Office seven times a day, the nuns all performed manual labor. They studied, copied manuscripts for the convent library, sewed both church vestments and their own clothing, as well as doing the daily round of cleaning, cooking, and gardening necessary to keep themselves alive.

Catherine meant to stay awake that night, but after the long day, she fell asleep as soon as she lay down and didn't wake until the bell rang for Vigils.

Even in the dim light of the lamp carried by Sister Felicitia, they could all see the fresh footprints at the bottom of the stairs.

Sister Ursula retreated back up the stairs, whimpering, and had to be ordered to continue to the oratory. The others obeyed as well, but with obvious reluctance.

Mother Heloise and Prioress Astane were already waiting in the chapel. Their presence reassured the women and reminded them of their duty to pray. But Catherine was not the only one who looked to see that the bar was still across the garden door.

"Satan won't distract me," Emilie whispered virtuously as they filed into their places. "He can't get you while you're praying."

Catherine wasn't so confident. Whatever was doing this had thoroughly distracted her. She missed the antiphon more than once and knew that bowing her apology to God would not save her from Sister Bertrada's rebuke.

There was an explanation for this, either natural or supernatural. Catherine didn't care which it was. She only wanted to know the truth.

† † †

The next day was the eve of the feast of the Nativity of St. John the Baptist. There would be a special vigil that night. It was also midsummer's eve, a time of spirits crossing between worlds, a fearsome long twilight. A good Christian could be driven mad or worse by the things that walked this night. These beliefs were officially denied and forbidden, but children learned the folk tales before they were weaned and such stories were hard to uproot. The shimmering sunlight of the morning was not bright enough to dispel fear.

✝   ✝   ✝

Each afternoon while they worked in the cloister, the women were permitted some edifying conversation. Today, the usual gentle murmurs and soft laughter had become a buzzing of wonderment, anger, and fear.

"What if this thing doesn't stop tonight at the bottom of the stairs?" Sister Ursula said, her eyes round with terror and anticipation. "What if it climbs right up and into our beds?"

"All of ours, or just yours?" Bietriz asked.

Ursula reddened with anger. "What are you implying?" she demanded. "I would never bring scandal upon us. How dare you even suggest such a thing!"

Bietriz sighed and put down her sewing. She went over to Ursula and took her gently by the shoulders.

"I apologize," she said. "It was not a kind joke. I make no accusations. I believe you have become overwrought by these happenings. Perhaps you could sleep with Sister Melisande in the infirmary tonight."

"Perhaps I will," Ursula muttered. "Better than being slandered by my sisters or murdered by demons in the dortor."

Sister Felicitia was seated on the grass, her stained hands weaving softened reeds to mend a basket. She looked up.

"There are no demons here," she said firmly.

They all stared at her. It would have been more surprising if a sheep in the meadow had spouted philosophy.

"How do you know?" Ursula asked.

"Mother Heloise promised me," Felicitia answered. "The demons won't come for me here."

She bent again to her work. The others were silent.

"Well," Ursula said finally. "Perhaps I will stay in the dortor. But if anything attacks me, I'll scream so loud you'll think Judgment Day has come."

"If you wake me," Emilie warned, "you'll wish it had."

Before Vespers the Abbess Heloise gathered all the women together in the chapter room. There was a collective sigh of relief as they assembled. Finally, all would be explained.

The abbess smiled at them all fondly. Her large brown eyes studied them, and Catherine felt that Mother Heloise knew just what each of them was thinking and feeling.

"It has been brought to my attention," she began, "that some of you have been concerned about some mud stains in the oratory and chapel. I fear that you have allowed these queries to go beyond normal curiosity to unwholesome speculation. This saddens me greatly. If something so natural and common as wet earth can cause you to imagine demons and suspect each other of scandalous behavior, then I have not done my duty as your mentor or your mother."

There was a rustle of surprise and denial. Heloise held up her hand for silence. There was silence.

"Therefore," she continued, "I apologize to you all for not providing the proper spiritual guidance. I will endeavor to do so in the future and will ask our founder, Master Abelard, for advice on how this may best be done. I hope you will forgive me."

That was all. Heloise signaled the chantress to lead them in for Vespers.

They followed in bewildered obedience. Catherine and Emilie stared at each other, shaking their heads. As far as Catherine could see, they had just been told that the intruder in the convent was none of their business. It made no sense.

Mindful of her earlier mistakes, Catherine tried desperately to keep her mind on the service for St. John's Eve, despite the turmoil in her mind.

"*Ecce, mitto angelum meum . . .*" Behold, I send my angel, who will prepare the way for you before my coming. "*Vox clamitis in deserto . . .*" A voice crying in the wilderness.

She tried to concentrate on St. John. It was hard to imagine him as a baby, leaping for joy in his mother's womb as they visited the Virgin Mary. She always saw him as the gaunt man of the desert, living naked on a diet of locusts and honey. People must have thought him mad, preaching a savior no one had heard of.

"*Ecce, mitto angelum meum . . .*"

All at once Catherine realized what she had been doing. She had looked at the problem from one direction only. Mother Heloise knew the answer. That was why she wasn't worried. When one turned the proposition around, it made perfect sense. Now, if only she could stay awake tonight to prove her theory.

The night, usually too brief, seemed to stretch on forever. Catherine was beginning to believe that she had made an error in her logic.

There was a rustling from the other end of the room. Someone was getting up. Catherine waited. Whoever it was could be coming this way, to use the reredorter. No one passed her bed. She heard a creak from the end of the room, as if someone else were also awake. She peered over the blanket. It was too dark to tell. There were no more sounds. Perhaps it had only been someone tossing about with a nightmare. Perhaps. But she had to know.

Carefully, Catherine eased out of bed. They all slept fully dressed, even to their slippers, so as to be ready for the Night Office. Catherine looked up and down the rows on either side of the room. In the dim light everyone appeared to be accounted for and asleep. Slowly, fearing even to breathe, Catherine moved down the room to the door. It was open.

All the tales of monsters and demons came rushing suddenly into her mind. Anything could be at the foot of those stairs. Who would protect her if she encountered them against orders, because of her arrogant curiosity?

She said a quick prayer to St. Catherine of Alexandria, who had known what it was to wonder about things, and she started down the stairs.

At the bottom she nearly fainted in terror as she stepped onto a pile of something soft that moved under her foot. She bent down and touched it.

It was clothing just like her own. A shift, a long tunic, a belt, and a pair of slippers. The discovery of something so familiar terrified Catherine even more.

What had happened to the woman who had worn these clothes?

Moonlight shone through the open door of the oratory. Catherine looked down at the floor. In her fear, she had almost forgotten to test her conclusion.

She was right. The floor was clean. So far, nothing had entered. Feeling a little more confident, she stepped out into midsummer night.

The herb garden lay tranquil under the moon. Catherine had been out once before at night, helping Sister Melisande pick the plants that were most potent when gathered at the new moon. This time she was here uninvited.

There was a break in the hedge on the other side of the garden. Catherine thought she saw a flicker of something white in the grove just beyond. Before she could consider the stupidity of her actions, she hurried toward it.

Within the grove there was a small hill that was empty of trees or undergrowth. Sheep grazed there by day, but tonight . . . *"Ecce! Mitto angelum!"*

Catherine stopped at the edge of the trees. There was someone on the hill, pale skin glowing silver in the moonlight, golden curls surrounding her face like a halo. It was Sister Felicitia, naked, dancing in the night, her feet covered with mud. Her arms were raised as she spun, her face to the sky, her back arched, moving to some music that Catherine couldn't hear.

A hand touched her shoulder. Catherine gasped and the hand moved to her mouth.

"Make no sound," Abbess Heloise warned. "You'll wake her."

Catherine nodded and Heloise removed her hand.

"How did you find out?" the abbess whispered.

"It was the footprints," Catherine whispered back, not taking her eyes from Felicitia. "We all thought they were from someone being let in. But it made much more sense if they were made by someone coming back. Then only one person was needed to open the door from the inside. What I didn't understand was the prints of bare feet."

"She always leaves her clothes at the bottom of the stairs and puts them on again before returning to bed," Heloise explained.

"But shouldn't we stop her?" Catherine asked. "She must be possessed to behave like this."

"She might be," Heloise said. "I worried about that, too. But Sister Bertrada convinced me that if she is, it's by nothing evil and we have no right to interfere."

"Sister Bertrada?" Catherine's voice rose in astonishment.

"Hush!" Heloise told her. "Yes, she's on the other side of the grove, watching to be sure no one interrupts. Brother Baldwin is farther on, guarding the gate to the road. Not everyone who saw her would understand. Do you?"

Catherine shook her head. She didn't understand, but it didn't matter. She was only grateful she had been allowed to watch. Felicitia, dancing in the moonlight, wasn't licentious, but sublime. She shone like Eve on the first morning, radiant with delight at the wonder of Eden, in blissful ignorance of sin. The joy of it made Catherine weep in her own knowledge that soon the serpent would come, and with it, sorrow.

Heloise guided Catherine gently away.

"She'll finish soon and go back to bed," the abbess explained. "Sister Bertrada will see that she gets there safely. Come with me. Astane has left some warmed cider for me. You have a cup also, before you go back."

When they were settled in Heloise's room, drinking the herbed cider, Catherine finally asked the question.

"I figured out who and how, Mother," she said. "But I don't understand why."

Heloise looked into her cider bowl for several minutes. Catherine thought that she might not answer. Perhaps she didn't know.

At last she seemed to come to a decision.

"Catherine," she asked, "have you ever believed that you were loved by no one? That you were completely alone?"

Catherine thought. "Well," she answered, "there was about a month when I was thirteen, but . . . no, no. Even then I always knew my family loved me. I know you love me. I know God loves me, unworthy though I am of all of you."

Heloise smiled. "That's right, on all points. But until she came here, Felicitia believed that no one loved her, that God had abandoned her, and she had good reason. That is not a story for you to hear. I only want you to understand that I am sure that Felicitia is not possessed by anything evil."

"I believe you," Catherine said. "But I still don't understand."

"I didn't, either," Heloise admitted. "Until Sister Bertrada explained it to me. Don't make such a face, child. Sister Bertrada sees further into your heart than you know."

"That doesn't comfort me, Mother."

Heloise smiled. "It should. Bertrada told me that Felicitia spent all her life being desired for her beauty, for her wealth, her family connections. In all that desire, there was no love. So she felt she wasn't worthy of love and consented to despair. She endured much to find her way to us. The scars on her face are mild compared to the ones on her soul. She struggles every day with worse demons that any Ursula can imagine. And until a week ago, she had nightmares almost every night."

"And then . . ." Catherine said.

"And then," Heloise smiled, "joy came to her one night, and she danced. It has only been in her sleep so far, but if she is left in peace, we are hoping that soon she will also have joy in the morning, all through the day, and at last be healed."

Catherine sat for a long while, until the cider went cold and the chantress rose to ring the bell for Vigils. Heloise waited patiently.

"Are you satisfied, Catherine?" she asked. "You assembled the evidence, arranged it properly, and solved the mystery. There is no need to tell the others."

"Oh, no, I wouldn't do that," Catherine promised. "I only wanted to know the truth."

"Then why do you look so sad?" Heloise prodded.

"It's only—" Catherine stopped, embarrassed. "I'm so clumsy, Mother. If only I could dance like Felicitia, even in my sleep."

Heloise laughed. "And how do you know that you don't?"

For once in her life, Catherine had no reply.

✝

Miss Butterfingers

Monica Quill

I

By the second day, there was no doubt that the man was following her; he showed up in too many places for it to be a coincidence, but Kim let another day go by before she mentioned it to Joyce and Sister Mary Teresa. "Tell him to knock it off," Joyce said, drawing on pre-convent parlance. "Ignore him," Emtee Dempsey said. But Kim found it impossible to follow either bit of advice. Joyce offered to go with her, but then it was hard to say what Joyce would do for several hours in the Northwestern library. And then suddenly one day there was the man, sitting in the reading room, looking about as comfortable as Joyce would have.

To feel compassion for a pest was not the reaction Kim expected from herself. Now, after days of seeing that oval face, expressionless except for the eyes, whenever she turned around, she felt a little surge of pity.

She settled down to work, driving the man from her mind, and was soon immersed in the research that, God and Sister Mary Teresa permitting, would eventually result in her doctoral dissertation. When she went to consult the card catalogue, she had completely forgotten her pursuer, and when she turned to find herself face to face with him, she let out an involuntary cry.

"Don't be frightened." He looked wildly around.

"I am not frightened. Why are you following me?"

He nodded. "I thought you'd noticed."

"What do you want?"

"I know you're a nun."

Well, that was a relief. The only indication in her dress that she was a religious was the veil she wore in the morning when the three of them went to the cathedral for Mass, but of course Kim didn't wear a veil on campus.

"Why not?" Sister Mary Teresa had asked. As far as the old nun was concerned, the decision taken by the order to permit members either to retain the traditional habit, as Emtee Dempsey herself had done, or to wear such suitable dress as they chose was still in force, no matter that the three of them in the house on Walton Street were all that remained of the Order of Martha and Mary. The old nun was the superior of the house, but would never have dreamt of imposing her personal will on the others. She had subtler ways of getting what she wanted. Of course, when it came to the rule, it was not a matter of imposing her will but that of their founder, Blessed Abigail Keineswegs, the authoress of the particular path to heaven they all had chosen when they were professed as nuns in the order.

"I think it has a negative effect on people."

"Perhaps a dissuasive effect is what a young woman your age might want from the veil, Sister."

"Oh, for heaven's sake."

"Indeed."

The day Emtee Dempsey lost an argument would be entered in the *Guinness Book of Records*. What had been particularly annoying about the young man was the possibility that he did not know she was a nun and would ask for a date, and then the explanation would be embarrassing. What a relief, accordingly, to learn that he knew her state in life.

"What is it you want?" She spoke with less aloofness. If he knew she was a nun, perhaps he was in some trouble and thought she might be of help.

"Oh, I don't want anything."

He looked intelligent enough; he was handsome in a way, dark hair, tall, nice smile lines around his eyes. Still, you never know. People with very low IQs don't always look it.

"You can't just follow people around. Would you want me to call a policeman?" The ragtag band of campus guards would not strike fear in many, but they looked like real policemen and as often as not that was enough.

"I am a policeman."

"You are!" Kim stepped back as if to get a better look at him. "Chicago or Evanston?"

"Chicago."

"I can check up on that, you know. What's your name?"

"Your brother doesn't know I've got this assignment. If you tell him, the whole point of it will be lost."

The allusion to Richard dispelled her scepticism. "What are you talking about?"

"There's been a threat against his family. You're part of his family."

"Who threatened him?"

"Does it matter? We're taking it seriously."

"But his wife and kids are the ones you should be looking after."

"We are."

"Nobody is going to harm me."

"I hope you're right. The reason I've been so obvious about following you is to let anyone who might try anything know that I'm around."

It seemed churlish to object to this and silly to ask how long it would continue.

"You didn't tell me your name."

"That's right." His grin was like a schoolboy's. Well, nuns brought out the boy in men, Kim had long been aware of that. Despite her age, she was often addressed as if she were the nun who had once rapped the knuckles of a now middle-aged man. It wasn't necessary that she know her guardian's name, not if she couldn't call Richard and verify that he was a policeman.

After she knew why he was always around, his presence was more distracting rather than less. She felt self-conscious taking notes, every expression was one that might be observed. Within fifteen minutes, she closed her notebook and gathered up her things. All the way out to the Volkswagen bug and on the drive home to Walton Street, she assumed he was just behind her. Now that she knew he was following her, she couldn't find him. But at least she could tell Emtee Dempsey and Joyce what was going on.

"Oh, that's a relief," Joyce said sarcastically. "There's only a threat on your life and all along we thought it was something serious like a persistent Don Juan."

"He said Richard doesn't know?" Emtee Dempsey asked.

"That's right."

"But why wouldn't he be told? Why don't you call him?"

"What if our phone is tapped?"

Emtee Dempsey tried to look outraged but was actually delighted at the thought of such goings-on. "And if we invite Richard to come over, the young man will of course assume you are going to tell him."

✝   ✝   ✝

But Richard stopped by the next day unasked. He was ebullient and cheerful, turned down a beer twice before accepting one, sat in the study and looked around expansively.

"It's nice to stop by here when you're not interfering in my work."

"Richard, I have never interfered in your work," Sister Mary Teresa said primly.

His mouth opened in feigned shock and he looked apprehensively toward the ceiling. "I am waiting for a flash of lightning."

"I do not need dramatic divine confirmations of what I say."

"That isn't what I meant."

"What are you working on now?"

He shook his head. "Nothing important, but I would still rather not let you know."

"Very well. And how is your lovely family?"

"I think Agatha, my oldest, has a vocation."

"Really! What makes you think so?"

"No one can tell her a thing, she already knows it all."

"Richard!" Kim said.

He grinned. "Maybe it's just a stage she's going through."

"It must be very difficult for a child to have a father in the police force," the old nun said.

Richard's smile faded. "Why do you say that?"

"Oh, I don't know. Your work takes you among such unsavory elements. It must sometimes be difficult to protect your family from all that."

Kim gave Sister Mary Teresa a warning glance.

"I never bring my work home."

"Does it ever follow you there?"

"How do you mean?"

"Oh, I think of all the malefactors you have brought to justice. I imagine not all of them are grateful to you."

He laughed. "Sister, there are even some who resent it."

"That's my point."

"What is?"

Sister Mary Teresa hesitated. She had promised Kim she would not tell Richard that he and his family were being provided protection by his colleagues. She had come within an eyelash of saying it already, and she was obviously trying to think what further she could say without breaking her promise.

"Who are some of your victims who might seek revenge?"

"Sister, if I worried about things like that I'd have entered a monastery rather than the department."

"Of course you wouldn't *worry* about it. I don't suggest that for a moment. Certainly not worry about your *own* safety. But just for the sake of conversation, if you had to pick someone who is in jail because of your efforts, blames you, and might want to avenge himself, who would it be?"

Richard adopted the attitude of the man of the world telling a house of recluses what was going on outside their walls. Emtee Dempsey was fully prepared to play the naive innocent in order to keep Richard talking.

"The difficulty would be ruling anyone out," he said. "It's fairly routine for a crook after the verdict is in to turn and threaten any and every cop who was in the investigation. This is especially true if you appear in court during the trial. Some even send letters once they're settled in at Joliet."

"Threats?"

"Kid stuff."

"But that's another crime, isn't it?"

"Sister, if we brought charges for every crime that's committed I wouldn't be able to drop by for a social visit like this."

"You are a very evasive man, Richard."

"Thank you."

"You have managed not to name one single criminal who might actually seek to do you harm because you were instrumental in his arrest."

"I'll give you one.

"Good."

"Regina Fastnekker."

"The terrorist!"

"Miss Butterfingers."

Regina Fastnekker was the youngest daughter of a prominent Winnetka family whose fancy it was to be an anarchist. A modern political theory class at De Paul had convinced her that man and human society are fundamentally corrupt, reform is an illusion, and the only constructive thing is to blow it all up. Something, Regina knew not what, would arise from the ashes, but whatever it was, it could not be worse, than the present situation, and there was at least a chance it might be better. On the basis of a single chemistry class, Regina began to make explosives in the privacy of the apartment she rented in the Loop. Winnetka had become too irredeemable for her to bear to live with her parents anymore. It was when one of her bombs went off, tearing out a wall and catapulting an upstairs neighbor into eternity, that Regina confessed to several bombings, one a public phone booth across the road from the entrance to Great Lakes Naval Base. When she was arrested, Regina's hair was singed nearly completely off and that grim bald likeness of her was something she blamed on Richard. In a corrupt world, Regina nonetheless wanted to look her best.

"You're part of the problem, cop," she shouted at him.

"Sure. That's why you're going to jail and I'm not."

"Someday," she said meaningfully.

"Someday what?"

"POW!"

Emtee Dempsey's eyes rounded, as she listened. "How much longer will she be in jail?"

"How much longer? She was released after two years."

"When was that?"

"I don't know. A couple months ago."

"Richard, won't you have another beer?" Emtee Dempsey asked, pleased as punch. "I myself will have a cup of tea."

"Well, we can't have you drinking alone."

✝ ✝ ✝

Having found out what she wanted, Emtee Dempsey chattered on about other things. It was Richard who returned to the subject of Miss Butterfingers.

"In court she screamed out her rage, threatening the judge, everyone, but when she pointed her finger at me, looking really demented, and vowed she'd get me, I felt a chill. I did. Nonetheless, she was a model prisoner. Got religion. One of the Watergate penitents spoke at Joliet and she was among those who accepted Jesus as their personal savior."

"Then her punishment served her well."

"Yeah."

"Well, that cancels out Regina Fastnekker," Joyce said when Richard had gone.

"We could make a methodical check," Kim said.

"Or you could insist that your guardian angel tell you who has threatened Richard and his family. I should think you have a right to know if you have to put up with him wherever you go."

"I'll do it."

"I'm surprised you didn't insist on it when you talked with him."

Kim accepted the criticism, particularly since she was kicking herself for not finding out more from . . . But she hadn't even found out his name.

2

The next day two things happened that set the house on Walton Street on its ear, in Emtee Dempsey's phrase. At five in the morning, the house reverberated with a tremendous noise and they emerged from their rooms into the hallway, staring astounded at one another.

"What was that?" Joyce asked, her eyes looking like Orphan Annie's.

"An explosion."

As soon as Emtee Dempsey said it, they realized that was indeed what they had heard. The old nun went back into her room and picked up the phone.

"It works," she said, and put it down again. "Sister Kimberly, call the police."

Joyce said, "I'll check to see . . ."

"No." Emtee Dempsey hesitated. Then she went into Kim's room which looked out over Walton Street. They crowded around her. What looked to be pieces of their Volkswagen lay in the street, atop the roof of a red sedan, and shredded upholstery festooned the powerlines just below their eye level.

"Now you know what to report."

Kim picked up her own phone and made the call.

They were up and dressed when there was a ring at the door. Their call had not been necessary to bring the police. Emtee Dempsey was pensive throughout the preliminary inquiry, letting Kim answer most of the questions. At ten minutes to seven she stood.

"We must be off to Mass."

"Maybe you better not, Sister," one of the policemen, Grimaldi, said. He wore his salt-and-pepper hair cut short and his lids lay in diagonals across his eyes, giving him a sleepy, friendly look.

"It is our practice to attend Mass every morning, Sergeant, and I certainly do not intend to alter it for this."

When he realized she was serious, he offered to drive them to the cathedral and Emtee Dempsey was about to refuse when the drama of arriving at St. Matthew's in a squad car struck her.

"Since we might otherwise be late, I agree. But no sirens."

He promised no sirens, thereby, Kim was sure, disappointing Emtee Dempsey.

It was, to put it mildly, a distracting way to begin the day. As it happened, their emerging from a police car at the cathedral door was witnessed by a derelict or two, but otherwise caused no sensation. Once inside, Emtee Dempsey of course put aside such childishness. It was not until Richard joined Grimaldi later that Emtee Dempsey brought up Miss Butterfingers.

Richard squinted at her. "All right, what's going on? How come you ask me about her yesterday and today your car's blown up?"

"Richard, you introduced her into the conversation. I may have asked a thing or two then, but if I ever heard of the young woman before, I had forgotten it. Are you suggesting that she . . ."

"Aw, come on."

"Sergeant Grimaldi, has the lieutenant been told of the concern about him and his family?"

Grimaldi looked uncomprehending.

"Perhaps you weren't aware of it." She turned to Kim. "I think you will agree, Sister, that I am no longer bound by my promise."

"Of course not."

"Richard, your colleagues have been assigned to look after you and your family. Even Sister Kimberly has had an escort these past days."

Richard glared at Grimaldi, who lifted his shoulders. Richard then got on the phone. Emtee Dempsey's initial attitude was a little smug; clearly she enjoyed knowing something about the police that Richard did not know. But her manner changed as the meaning of Richard's end of the conversation became clear.

"There's been no protective detail assigned to my family. Where in hell did you get such a notion?"

Emtee Dempsey nodded to Kim.

"A man has been following me for several days. Two days ago I had enough and asked him what he was doing. He said he was a policeman."

"A Chicago policeman?"

"Yes."

"What's his name?"

"I don't know."

"Didn't you ask? Didn't you ask for his ID?"

"No, Richard. And I didn't call you up and ask what was going on either. At the time, I was relieved to learn why he was following me."

"Relieved that I was supposedly threatened?"

"Well, I was relieved to think that Mary and the kids . . ."

"I don't suppose he'll be following you around today," Richard broke in, "but I guarantee you a cop we know about will be."

"You want Sister to keep to her regular routine?"

"Sister Mary Teresa, I want all of you to follow your regular routines. And if anything relevant to this happens, I want to know about it pronto."

"An interesting use of the word, Richard. In Italian it means ready. It's how they answer the phone. Pronto," she said, trilling the *r.* "You, on the other hand, take it in its Spanish meaning."

There was more, much more, until Richard fled the study. At their much delayed breakfast, the conversation was of the car. Joyce thought their insurance covered bombing. "Unless it's considered an act of God."

"Sister, a bombing is always an act of man. Or woman."

The newspaper lay on the table unattended throughout the meal. After all, the news of the day had happened in their street.

"I'll want to speak to Katherine about this. We don't want her to learn of it from someone at the paper. What is in the paper, by the way?"

Joyce had taken the sports page and Kim, standing, was paging through the front section when she stopped and cried out.

"That's him!"

"He," Emtee Dempsey corrected automatically, coming to stand beside her.

The picture was of a young man, smiling, confident, embarking on life. Perhaps a graduation photograph.

His name was Michael Layton. He had been found dead after an explosion in a southside house. He had been missing for five years. He was the man who identified himself as a policeman in the Northwestern library.

3

Katherine Senski caught a cab from her office at the newspaper and was in the house within half an hour of Emtee Dempsey's call, but of course there was far more to discuss now than the mere blowing up of their automobile. The street had been cordoned off, to the enormous aggravation and rage of who knows how many drivers, while special units collected debris and the all but intact rear end of the car, which seemed to have gone straight into the air, done a flipflop, and landed in their customary parking place.

"Dear God," Katherine said. "They might be out there collecting pieces of you three."

"Nonsense," Emtee Dempsey said.

A first discovery was that the device had not been one that would have been triggered by starting the car. This conclusion was reached by noting the intact condition of the rear of the car.

"But aren't such devices hooked up to starters, to motors?"

"The motor was in the rear end," Joyce explained

"Oh," Katherine said, but the three nuns were suddenly struck by that past tense. Their Volkswagen bug was no more.

They had just settled down at the dining room table with a fresh pot of coffee when Benjamin Rush arrived. The elegant lawyer stood in the doorway, taking in the scene, and then resumed his usual savoir faire.

"It is a relief to see you, as the saying goes, in one piece, Sister. Sisters."

They made room for him, but of course he refused coffee. He had had the single cup that must make do until lunchtime. Joyce brought him a glass of mineral water, which he regarded ruefully, not interrupting Emtee Dempsey's colorful account of Kim's being followed, her confronting the man, their attempt to get information from Richard. And then this morning. By the time she got to the actual explosion, it might have been wondered how she could keep the dramatic line of her narrative rising, so exciting the preliminary events were made to sound. Kim found herself wishing she had actually behaved with the forthrightness Emtee Dempsey attributed to her when she confronted her supposed police escort in the Northwestern library. Emtee Dempsey had the folded morning paper safely under one pudgy hand, clearly her prop for the ultimate revelation. But there was so much to be said before she got to it.

"Regina Fastnekker! Do I remember that one," Katherine said. "My pretrial interviews?" She looked around the table. "I was nominated for a Pulitzer, for heaven's sake."

"Do you still have them?"

Katherine smiled sweetly. "My scrapbooks are up to date, thank you."

Benjamin Rush wanted to know where Regina was now. Katherine, to her shame, had not followed further the Fastnekker saga once the girl had been safely put away. Emtee Dempsey told them of the woman's supposed prison conversion.

"'Supposed' in the sense of 'alleged.' I do not mean to express skepticism. Some of the greatest saints got their start in prison."

"I won't ask you how many lawyers have been canonized," Mr. Rush said and sipped his mineral water.

Katherine said, "Conversion isn't a strong enough word for the turnaround that girl would have needed. I have seldom talked with anyone I considered so, well, diabolic. She seemed to have embraced evil."

"'Evil be thou my good,'" murmured Emtee Dempsey.

"Who said that?"

"Milton's Satan, of course, don't tease. I must read every word you wrote about her, Katherine. I suppose the police will know where she now is."

"I suspect they may be talking with her right now."

"The bombing is in her style," Rush said. "Ominously so. It is why I came directly here. Katherine will know better than I that the Fastnekker crowd had a quite unique modus operandi. There was always a series of bombings, the first a kind of announcement, defiant, and then came the big bang. What I am saying is that, far from being out of danger, you may be in far more danger now than before the unfortunate destruction of your means of transportation. If, that is, we are truly dealing with Regina Fastnekker and company."

"Company? How many were there?"

"It's all in my stories," Katherine said. "I wonder why I didn't read of her big conversion."

"If it is genuine, she might not have wanted it to be a media event."

"Well, you have certainly had some morning. But, as Benjamin says, the excitement may be just beginning. I suggest that you go at once to the lake place in Indiana."

"No, no, no," Rush intervened. He thought that for them to be in such a remote place, where the police were, well, local, far from taking the nuns out of danger, might well expose them fatally.

"We have to assume that you are being watched at this very moment."

"Isn't it far more likely that the next attempt will be on Richard's family?"

Katherine said, "I wonder who that phony policeman was?"

That was Emtee Dempsey's cue. "I was coming to that," she said, unfolding the paper. "This is the man."

"But that's Michael Layton," Mr. Rush said in shocked tones.

"Ah, you know him."

"Sister, that boy, that young man, disappeared several years ago. Vanished into thin air."

"That's in the story, Benjamin."

"But I know the Laytons. I knew Michael. I can't tell you what a traumatic experience it was for them."

Emtee Dempsey turned to Katherine. "Was this young man part of Regina Fastnekker's company?"

"That's not possible," said Mr. Rush.

"Why on earth would he impersonate a policeman?"

"Sister Kimberly, please call your brother and tell him that Michael Layton was the one following you around of late."

It was Katherine who summed it all up, despite the evident pain it caused Benjamin Rush. Alerted by what the young man following Sister Kimberly had said, Emtee Dempsey had coaxed from Richard his belief that Regina Fastnekker was more likely than anyone else to seek to do him harm after she was released from jail. She had masked her intention by undergoing a religious conversion while in prison, and some time had elapsed since she had regained her freedom. Richard himself had been lulled into the belief that Miss Butterfingers had gotten over her desire for revenge. She chose to strike where it would be least expected, at Richard's sister. Accordingly, one of the gang followed Kim around and, when confronted, disarmingly claimed to be part of a police effort to protect Richard's family. This morning, their automobile was blown up, a typical first move in the Fastnekker modus operandi.

By this point in Katherine's explanation, Emtee Dempsey had plunged her face into her hands. But Benjamin Rush took it up.

"Michael was then killed for warning Sister Kimberly that she was in danger." The lawyer's spirit rose at the thought of his friends' son exhibiting his natural goodness at such peril to his life.

"What a tissue of conjecture," Emtee Dempsey observed, looking around at her friends. "In the first place, we have no reason at all to think that Michael Layton was connected with this Fastnekker terrorist gang."

"Of course we don't," Benjamin Rush said, switching field.

"Nor do we have any reason to think this is the work of the Fastnekker gang. The idea that her religious conversion was a ploy must deal with the fact that she tried to keep it quiet."

"The sneakiest publicity of all," Joyce said.

"Salinger," Kim agreed.

"What?" Emtee Dempsey looked at her two young colleagues as if they had lost their minds. But she waved away whatever it was they referred to. "We know only two things. First, that a young man named Michael Layton, who had been missing for years, who was lately following Sister Kimberly and claimed to be a policeman when she spoke to him, is dead. Second, we know that our automobile has been destroyed."

"Our insurance company will probably suspect us of that," Joyce said.

Benjamin Rush rose. "You are absolutely right, Sister. I have entered into this speculative conversation, but I must repeat that I cannot believe Michael Layton could possibly be involved in anything wrong or criminal. Let us hope that the police will be able to cast light on what has happened."

4

It was not only those on Walton Street who were reminded of the Fastnekker gang by the exploding Volkswagen. An editorial in the rival of Katherine's paper expressed the hope that Chicago, and indeed the country, was not on the threshold of a renewal of the terrorism of a decade ago. Readers were reminded of the various groups, including that led by Regina Fastnekker, and the fear was stated that the destruction of the car was only a prelude to something worse. How many like the unfortunate Michael Layton, products of good homes, having all the advantages of American society, suddenly dropped from sight only to turn up, incredibly, as terrorists? The editorial immediately added that there was absolutely no evidence of any connection of Layton with any terrorist efforts, though the explanation he had given of following a member of a Chicago policeman's family and the fact that he had been found in a building that had exploded from unknown causes would doubtless prompt some to make that connection. Lieutenant Richard Moriarity had led the investigation that resulted in the successful prosecution of Regina Fastnekker.

Katherine Senski threw the paper down on Emtee Dempsey's desk and fell into a chair. "That is completely and absolutely irresponsible. It is one thing to sit among friends and try to tie things together, but to publish such random thoughts in a supposedly respectable newspaper, well . . ." She threw up her hands, at a loss for words.

But Katherine's reaction was nothing to that of Benjamin Rush. Under his distinguished snow-white hair, his patrician features were rosy with rage.

"It is an outrageous accusation against a man who cannot defend himself."

"Perhaps the Layton family will sue."

"I am on my way there now. That is precisely what they want to do. Alas, I shall advise them not to. The editorial cunningly fends off the accusation of libel by qualifying or seeming to take back what it had just said. When you add the First Amendment, there simply is no case. Legally. Morally, whoever wrote this is a scoundrel. I now understand the feelings of clients who have urged me to embark on a course I knew could end only in failure. One wants to tilt at windmills!"

"You will be talking to the Laytons today?"

An immaculate cuff appeared from the sleeve of Benjamin Rush's navy blue suit as he lifted his arm, and then a watch whose unostentatiousness was in a way ostentatious came into view. "In half an hour. I have come to ask you a favor. Actually, to ask Sister Kimberly."

"Anything," Kim said. No member of the Order of Martha and Mary could be unaware of their debt to Benjamin Rush. He had saved this house at the time of the great dissolution and had insured that an endowment would enable the order to continue, in however reduced a form.

"It would be particularly consoling for the Laytons if they could speak to someone who saw Michael as recently as you have."

The request made Kim uneasy. What if the Laytons wished to derive consolation from the fact that it was a nun who had spoken to their son? Kim herself had wondered if he had not perhaps thought that she could be of help, directly or indirectly, in some difficulty.

"I should tell you that while Melissa Layton is quite devout, her husband Geoffrey is a member of the Humanist Society and regards all religion as a blight."

"Find out which of them the son favored, Sister."

Having already agreed to help Mr. Rush, there was nothing Kim could do, but she was profoundly unwilling to talk to grieving parents about a son they had not seen in years and to whom she had spoken only once, in somewhat odd circumstances. Mr. Rush's car stood at the curb where the Volkswagen had always been, but the contrast could not have been greater. Long and grey with tinted glass, it seemed to require several spaces. Marvin, Mr. Rush's chunky driver, opened the door and Kim got in, and with Mr. Rush at seemingly the opposite end of the sofa, they drove off in comfort to the Laytons.

On the way, Mr. Rush told her a few more things about the Laytons, but nothing could have prepared her adequately for the next several hours. Kim had somehow gotten the impression that the Laytons would be Mr. Rush's age, which was foolish when she considered that the son had been closer to her age, but Mrs. Layton was a shock. She was beautiful, her auburn hair worn shoulder length, her face as smooth as a girl's, and the black and silver housecoat, floor length, billowed about her, heightening the effect she made as she crossed the room to them. Kim felt dowdy in her sensible suit, white blouse, and veil, and it didn't help to remind herself that her costume befitted her vocation. Melissa Layton tipped her cheek for Mr. Rush's kiss and extended a much braceleted arm to Kim.

"Sister." Both hands enclosed Kim's and her violet eyes scanned Kim's face. "Ben assured us that you would come."

Geoffrey Layton rose from his chair, nodded to Rush, and gave a little bow to Kim, but his eyes were fastened on her veil.

"Come," Mrs. Layton said. She had not released Kim's hand and led her to a settee where they could sit side by side. "Tell me of your meeting with Michael." And suddenly the beauty was wrenched into sorrow and the woman began to sob helplessly. Now Kim held her hand. Mrs. Layton's tears made Kim feel a good deal more comfortable in this vast room with its period furniture, large framed pictures, and magnificent view.

Mrs. Layton emerged from her bout of grief even more beautiful than before, teardrops glistening in her eyes, but composed. Mr. Layton and Mr. Rush stood in front of the seated women while Kim told her story.

"How long had he been following you around?"

"For several days."

"That you know of," Mrs. Layton said.

"Yes. I spoke of it with the other sisters. At first it was just a nuisance, but then it became disturbing. We decided that I should talk to him. On Wednesday morning . . ."

"Wednesday," Mrs. Layton repeated, and her expression suggested she was trying to remember what she had been doing at the time this young woman beside her had actually spoken to her long lost son.

"He said he knew I was a nun."

"Of course," said Mr. Layton.

"I do not wear my veil when I go to Northwestern."

"Why not?"

"I just don't."

"Could he have seen you with it on?"

"I suppose."

"But what did he say?" Mrs. Layton asked. Kim was aware that another woman had come into the room, her hair and coloring the same as Mrs. Layton's, though without the dramatic beauty. Mrs. Layton turned to see what Kim was looking at. "Janet, come here. This is Sister Kimberly who talked with your brother Michael."

The daughter halved the distance between them, but as Kim talked on, answering questions that became more and more impossible, about the Layton son, Janet came closer. The parents wanted to know what he looked like, how he acted, did she think he was suffering from amnesia, on and on, and from time to time when Kim glanced at Janet she got a look of sympathy. Finally the younger woman stepped past Mr. Rush.

"Thank you so much for telling us about your meeting with Michael." Comparing the two women, Kim could now see that, youthful as Mrs. Layton looked, she looked clearly older than her daughter, who made no effort to be attractive.

The Laytons now turned to Mr. Rush to insist that he bring suit against the editorialist who had slandered their son. Janet led Kim away.

"There's coffee in the kitchen."

"Oh good."

"You realize that all this is to put off the evil day. We have not seen Michael's body. It is a question whether we will. As a family. I certainly intend to."

There was both strength and genuineness in Janet Layton, and Kim could see, when they were sitting on stools in the kitchen, sipping coffee, that with the least of efforts Janet could rival her mother in beauty. If she didn't, it was because she felt no desire to conceal her mourning.

"You're a nun?"

"Yes.

"I wanted to be a nun once. I suppose most girls think of it."

"Very briefly."

"What's it like?"

"Come visit us. We have a house on Walton Street."

"Near the Newberry?"

"Just blocks away. Do you go there?"

She nodded. "What is so weird is that I also use the Northwestern library. What if I had gone there Wednesday?"

"I hope I made it clear that your brother seemed perfectly all right to me. But then I thought he was the policeman he said he was and that changed everything. He looked the part."

"It's cruel after years of thinking him dead to find out he was alive on Wednesday, in a place I go to, but now is truly dead." Her lip trembled and she looked away.

"He just disappeared?"

She nodded, not trusting herself to speak for a moment. "One day he left the house for school and never came back. No note, no indication he was going. He took nothing with him. He just ceased to exist, or so it seemed. The police searched, my parents hired private investigators. My father, taking the worst thing he could think of, suspected the Moonies. But not one single trace was found."

"On his way to school?"

"Chicago. He was an economics major."

"How awful."

"I don't know how my parents bore up under this. My mother of course never lets herself go physically, but inside she has been devastated. It is the first time my father confronted something couldn't do anything effective about. That shook him almost as much as the loss of Michael."

"Mr. Rush says your mother is very devout."

"Let me show you something."

They went rapidly through the house, which was far larger than Kim's first impression of it. On an upper floor as they came down a hallway stood a small altar. There was a statue of perhaps three feet in height of Our Blessed Lady and a very large candle in a wrought-iron holder burning before it. Janet turned and widened her eyes significantly as she indicated the shrine.

"Mother's. For the return of her lost son."

There was nothing to say to that. Janet went into a room and waited for Kim to join her.

"This is just the way it was when he disappeared. Michael's room. Maybe now Mother will agree to . . ."

No need to develop the thought. No doubt Mrs. Layton would consider it an irreverence to get rid of her son's clothes and other effects, even though she knew now he was dead. A computer stood on the desk, covered with a clear plastic hood. A bookshelf the top row of which contained works in or related to economics. The other shelves were a hodgepodge, largely paperbacks—mysteries, westerns, science fiction, classics. Michael Layton had either unsettled literary tastes or universal interests.

"The police checked over this room and the private investigators Daddy hired also looked it over. They found no indication Mike intended to leave, and of course that introduced a note of hope. That he'd been kidnapped, for instance. But no demands were made. Every investigation left us where we'd been—with something that made utterly no sense."

"It must have been awful."

"I am glad the waiting is over, after all these years. Does that sound terrible?"

"No."

"I wanted you to see this. I wanted you to know that there are no clues here."

Kim smiled. "You've heard of Sister Mary Teresa?"

Janet nodded.

As they went downstairs, Kim reflected that if Janet was right, and why wouldn't she be, the explanation for Michael Layton's murder would have to be sought in what he had been doing in the years since he left his home for the last time. And no one seemed to know where on earth he had been.

5

"Miss Butterfingers is going to call on us," Joyce whispered when Kim returned to Walton Street.

"Wow."

"Just what I said to Emtee Dempsey."

"Yes," Sister Mary Teresa said, when Kim went into the study and asked about the impending visit. "Miss Fastnekker called half an hour ago and asked if she might come by. I am trying to read these articles of Katherine's before our visitor arrives. Here are the ones I've read."

Kim took the photocopies and began to read them as she crossed to a chair. What a delight they were. This was Katherine at the height of her powers, the woman who had been the queen of Chicago journalism longer than it was polite to mention. Reading those old stories acquainted Kim with the kind of person she preferred not to know. The Regina Fastnekker Katherine had interviewed intensively and written about with rare evocative power was a prophet of doom, an angel of destruction, a righteous scourge of mankind. At twenty-two years old, she had concluded that human beings are hopelessly corrupt, there is nothing to redeem what is laughingly called civilization. Any judgment that what she had done was illegal or immoral proceeded from a system so corrupt as to render the charges comic. Katherine described Regina as a nihilist, one who preferred nothing to everything that was. It was not that the world had this or that flaw, the world was the flaw.

"I am glad you don't have possession of hydrogen weapons," Katherine had observed.

"Atomic destruction is the solution. Inevitably one day it will arrive. I have been anticipating that awful self-judgment of mankind on itself by the actions I have taken."

"Who appointed you to this destructive task?"

"I did."

"Have you ever doubted your judgment?"

"Not on these matters."

"From the point of view of society, it makes sense to lock you up, wouldn't you say?"

"Society will regret what has been done to me."

Katherine had clearly been as awed as Kim was now that a woman who had done such deeds, who had killed by accident rather than design, should continue to speak with such conviction that she was somehow not implicated in the universal guilt of the race to which she belonged.

"You are employing a corrupt logic," Miss Butterfingers had replied.

Katherine had concluded that the only meaning "corrupt" seemed to have was "differing from Regina Fastnekker."

"What a sweetheart," Kim commented when she had finished.

"We must not forget that this was the Regina of some years ago. On the phone she seemed very nice."

"Did you tell her the police would know if she visited us?"

"I saw no reason to say such a thing."

Emtee Dempsey had invited Regina to come to Walton Street on the assumption that she was now a changed woman, radically different from the terrorist so graphically portrayed by Katherine Senski in her newspaper stories. If she was wrong, if Regina had been behind the blowing up of the Volkswagen and if her custom was to announce a serious deed by a lesser one, Emtee Dempsey could be inviting their assassin to visit. She did not have to wonder what Richard would say if asked about the advisability of admitting Regina to their home.

The woman who stood at the door when Kim went to answer the bell wore a denim skirt that reached her ankles and an oversize cableknit sweater; her hair was pulled back severely on her head and held with a rubber band. Pale blue eyes stared unblinkingly at Kim.

"I have come to see Sister Dempsey."

There was no mistaking that this was Regina Fastnekker, despite the changes that had occurred in her since the photos that accompanied Katherine's stories. Kim opened the door and took Regina down the hall to the study. Her back tingled as she walked, as if she awaited some unexpected blow to fall. But she made it to the study door without incident.

"Sister Mary Teresa, this is Regina Fastnekker."

The old nun did not rise but watched closely as her guest came to the desk. Regina put out her hand and the old nun stood as she took it.

"Welcome to our home."

"I must tell you that I consider the Catholic Church to be the corruption of Christianity and that it is only by a return to the gospels that we can be saved. One person at a time."

"*Ecclesia semper reformanda.*"

"I don't understand."

"You express a sentiment as old as Christianity itself. Do you know the story of the order St. Francis founded?"

"St. Francis is someone I admire."

"I was sure you would. Francis preached holy poverty, personifying it, calling it Lady Poverty, his beloved. After his death, his followers disputed what this meant. Could they, for example, own a house and live in it, or did poverty require them to own absolutely nothing and rely each day on the Lord to provide? Did they own the clothes they wore, since of course each one wore his own clothes?"

"Why are you telling me this?"

"It is possible to make Christianity so pure that it ceases to be."

"It is also possible to falsify it so much that it ceases to be."

"Of course."

"You sound as if you had won an argument."

"I wasn't sure we were having one. I am told that you have become a Christian."

"That makes it sound like something I did. It was done to me. It is a grace of which I am entirely unworthy."

"Do you know Michael Layton?"

The sudden switch seemed to surprise Regina. She rearranged her skirt and pushed up the sleeve of her sweater.

"I knew him."

"Before your conversion?"

"Before I went to prison, yes."

"Have you any idea who killed him?"

"I came here to tell you that I have not."

"Have you seen him since you were released?"

"That is the question the police put to me in a dozen different ways."

"And how did you answer?"

"Yes and no."

"How yes?"

"I saw his photograph in the paper."

"Ah."

"It is my intention always to tell the truth, even when it seems trivial."

"An admirable ideal. It is one I share."

There was not a trace of irony in Emtee Dempsey's tone, doubtless because she felt none. Her ability so to speak that she did not technically tell a lie, however much others might mislead themselves when listening to her, was something Kim tried not to be shocked at. Whenever they discussed the matter, the old nun's defense—if it could be called a defense—was unanswerable, but Kim in her heart of hearts felt that Emtee Dempsey should be a good deal more candid than she was.

"The truth, the whole truth, and nothing but the truth," she had reminded the old nun.

"A noble if empty phrase."

"Empty?"

"What is the whole truth about the present moment? Only God knows. I use the phrase literally. Since we cannot know the whole truth we cannot speak it."

"We can speak the whole truth that we know."

"Alas, that too is beyond our powers. Even as we speak, what we know expands and increases and we shall never catch up with it."

"You know what I mean."

"Only by what you say, my dear, and I am afraid that does not make much sense."

"I didn't invent the phrase."

"You have at least that defense."

But now, speaking to Regina Fastnekker, Emtee Dempsey seemed to be suggesting that she herself sought always to tell the whole truth. If they were alone, Kim might have called her on this. But at the moment, she watched with fascination the alertness with which Regina listened to the old nun. In her articles, Katherine had described the ingénue expression Regina wore when she pronounced her nihilistic doctrines. Her beliefs might have changed, but her expression had not. Now she looked out at the world with the innocence of one who had been saved by religious conversion, but nonetheless, however much she had changed, Regina Fastnekker was still on the side of the saved.

"What I have come to tell you is that I did not blow up your car, and I have no intention to harm you."

"I am glad to hear that."

"I tell you because it would be reasonable to think I had, given my sinful past. I am still a sinner, of course, but I have chosen Jesus for my personal savior and have with the help of His grace put behind me such deeds."

"You have been blessed."

"So have you. If I had not been converted I might very well have conceived such a scheme and put it into operation."

"And killed me?"

"The loved ones of those who put me in prison."

"A dreadful thought."

Regina said nothing for a moment, and when she spoke it was with great deliberateness. "I have never killed anyone. I do not say this to make myself seem less terrible than I was. But I never took another's life."

"I had thought someone died when an explosion occurred in your apartment."

"That is true."

"And you were the cause of that explosion."

"No. It was an accident."

"You express yourself with a great deal of precision."

"Praise the Lord."

Seldom had the phrase been spoken with less intonation. Regina put her hands on her knees and then rose in an almost stately manner.

"I challenge you to accept the Lord as your savior."

"My dear young lady, I took the vows of religion nearly fifty years ago. I took Jesus as my spiritual spouse, promising poverty, chastity, and obedience. But I take your suggestion in good grace and shall endeavor to follow your advice."

Regina Fastnekker, apparently having no truth, however trivial, to utter, said nothing. She bowed and Kim took her to the door.

"Thank you for visiting us."

"Did you too take those vows?"

"Yes. But not fifty years ago."

Regina Fastnekker's smile was all the more brilliant for being so rare. Her laughter had a pure soprano quality. Lithe, long-limbed, her full skirt lending a peculiar dignity to her passage, she went across the porch, descended the steps, and disappeared up the walk.

6

Two days later, in the Northwestern University library, Kim looked up from the book she was reading to find Janet Layton smiling down on her.

"Can we talk?" she whispered.

Kim, startled to see the sister where she had had such a dramatic encounter with the brother, got up immediately. Outside, Janet lit up a cigarette.

"There is something I should have told you the other day and didn't. In fact I lied to you. I have known all along that Mike was still alive."

"You did!"

"He telephoned me in my dorm room, within a month of his disappearance. The first thing he said was that he did not want my parents to know of the call."

"And you agreed?"

"I didn't tell them. I don't think I would have in any case. You would have to know how terribly they took Mike's disappearance, particularly at the beginning. If I had told them, they would have wanted proof. There was none I could give. And of course I had no idea then that it would turn into a permanent disappearance. I don't know that he himself thought so at the time."

"What did he want?"

"He wanted some computer disks from his room."

She had complied, putting the disks in a plastic bag and the bag in a trash container on a downtown Chicago corner. She walked away, as she had been instructed, but with the idea of hiding and watching the container. She took up her station inside a bookstore and watched the container. Clerks asked if they could be of help and she shook her head, her eyes never leaving the container. After an hour, the manager came and she moved to a drugstore, certain her eyes had never left the container. After four hours of vigil, she was out of patience. She decided to take the disks from the container and wait for another phone call from her brother. The plastic bag containing the disks was gone.

"I felt like a bag lady, rummaging around in that trash, people turning to look at me. But it was definitely gone. Someone must have taken it within minutes of my putting it there, while I was walking away."

"And your brother called again?"

"Months later. I asked him if he got the disks. He said yes. That was all. His manner made me glad I'd done what I had."

Before leaving the disks in the container, Janet had made copies of them. She opened her purse and took out a package.

"Would you give these to Sister Mary Teresa?"

"You should give them to the police."

"I will leave that up to her. If that's what she thinks should be done with them, all right."

"Did you read the disks?"

"I tried to once. I don't know what program they're written on, but I typed them out at the DOS prompt. They looked like notes on reading to me. The fact that Mike wanted them means only that they were important to him. Frankly, I'd rather not admit that I've heard from Mike over the years. My parents would never understand my silence."

Kim had difficulty understanding it herself, Emtee Dempsey, on the other hand, found it unsurprising.

"But of course it would have been unsurprising if she told them too. Singular choices do not always have moral necessity. There were doubtless good reasons for either course of action and she chose the one she did."

"What will you do with them?"

"What the young lady suggested. Study their contents. Can you print them out for me?"

Before she did anything with the disks, Kim took the same precaution Janet had and made copies of them. There were three disks, of the five-and-a-half-inch size, but only two were full, the third had only twelve thousand bytes saved on it. Running a directory on them, Kim jotted down the file names.

BG&E.one

BG&E.two

TSZ.one

TSZ.two

TSZ.tre

That was the contents of the first disk. The second was similarly uninformative.

PENSEES.UNO

PENSEES.DOS

PENSEES.TRE

The third disk had one file, AAV.

The files had not been written on Notabene, the program Kim preferred, nor on either Word or WordPerfect. Kim printed them from ASCI and began reading eagerly as they emerged from the printer but quickly found, as Janet had, her interest flagging. Michael Layton seemed to have devised a very personal kind of shorthand "Para fn eth no es vrd, Pero an attmpt Para vanqr los grnds."

Let Emtee Dempsey decipher that if she could. The fact that Michael Layton wrote in a way difficult, if not impossible, to follow suggested that the disks contained information of interest. The old nun spread the sheets before her, smoothing them out, a look of anticipation on her pudgy face. Kim left her to her task.

The old nun was preoccupied at table and after night prayers returned to her study. At one in the morning, Kim came downstairs to find Emtee Dempsey brooding over the printout. She looked up at Kim and blinked.

"Any luck?"

"You are right to think that decoding always depends on finding one little key. Whether it is a matter of luck, I do not know."

"Have you found the key?"

"No."

"I couldn't make head nor tails of it."

"Oh, the first two disks present no problem. They are paraphrases of Nietzsche."

"You mean you can understand those pages?"

"Only to the degree that Nietzsche himself is intelligible. The young man paraphrased passages from the mad philosopher and interspersed his own comments, most, of them jejune."

"How did you know it was Nietzsche?"

"*Beyond Good and Evil. Thus Spake Zarathustra.*"

"And the second is Pascal?"

"Unfortunately no. The thoughts are young Layton's, thoughts of unrelieved tedium and banality. Do you know the *Pensieri* of Leopardi? Giacomo Leopardi?"

"I don't even know who he is."

"Was. His work of that name is a collection of pessimistic and misanthropic jottings, puerile, adolescent. If a poet of genius, however troubled, was capable of writing such silliness, we should not perhaps be too harsh with young Layton."

"What is on the third disk?"

She shook her head. "Those few pages are written in a bad imitation of *Finnegan's Wake,* a kind of macaronic relying on a variety of languages imperfectly understood. I had hoped that the first disks would provide me with the clue needed to understand the third, but so far this is . . ."

An explosion shook the house, bringing Emtee Dempsey to her feet. But Kim was down the hall ahead of her and dashed upstairs. As she came into the upstairs hall, she saw that a portion of the left wall as well as her door had been blown away. The startled face of Joyce appeared through plaster cloud.

"Strike two," she said.

7

Sister Mary Teresa wanted to take a good look around Kim's room before calling the police, although why the neighborhood had failed to be shaken awake by the explosion was explained by the incessant street racket that did not really cease until three or sometimes four in the morning. The explosion of Kim's computer would have been only one noise among many to those outside, however it had filled the house. The wall that had been blown into the hall was the one against which Kim's computer had stood.

"Why would it do a thing like that?" the old nun asked.

"I've never heard of it before."

"Was it on?"

"I never turn it off." Kim explained the theory behind this.

They puzzled over the event for perhaps fifteen minutes before Kim called Richard, relying on him to alert the appropriate experts. They came immediately, a tall woman with flying straight hair and her companion whose thick glasses seemed to have become part of his face. They picked around among the debris, eyes bright with interest. This was something new to them as well.

"Computers don't blow up," the girl said.

"There had to be a bomb." Behind the thick lenses her companion's eyes widened.

"When did you last use the machine?"

"I printed out some disks."

"Any sign of them?"

They were in the plastic box that had bounced off the far wall and landed on her bed. She opened it and showed them the five disks it contained.

"Five!" she exclaimed. "There are only five."

"Only?"

She showed them the three copies she had made, and two of the disks she had been given by Janet Layton, And then she remembered.

"I left the third in the drive."

"Can a computer disk be a bomb?" Emtee Dempsey asked.

Her question brought amused smiles to the two experts. The girl said, "Anything can be a bomb."

"Michael Layton delivered his second bomb," Emtee Dempsey said. "Posthumously."

"Janet Layton gave them to me," Kim reminded her.

"Yes. Yes, she did."

Richard came and kept them up until three going over what had happened. Kim let Emtee Dempsey tell the story she herself had heard from Janet Layton. She went over in her mind the conversation she had had with Janet at the Layton home and then what she had said at Northwestern that afternoon. If Janet had told her the truth, the disks she had given Kim were copies of those her brother made, rather than his originals. If one of those disks had been made into a bomb, it had to have been by Janet. But why?

"I'll ask her why. And I don't intend to wait for daylight either."

✝ ✝ ✝

The next time Kim saw Janet Layton was under police auspices. The violet eyes widened when Kim came in.

"Oh."

"I'm alive."

"Thank God."

She, rose and reached a hand across the table. Mastering her aversion, Kim took the hand. Janet turned to Richard.

"Why didn't you tell me she was unharmed?"

"I don't talk to people who don't talk to me."

Janet talked now. What she had told Kim was true as far as it went; well, almost. She had not, years ago, made copies of the disks her brother asked her to bring, but everything else had happened as she had said.

"Regina told me to tell you what I did."

"Regina Fastnekker!"

Janet nodded. "After Michael's death, she called me. She asked me if I remembered delivering some computer disks to Michael long ago. Of course I did. She said she had them and felt they might help solve the mystery of Michael's death. She asked if I would pass them on to you with just the message I gave you. You could decide, or Sister Mary Teresa could decide, what to do with them."

Richard made a face. "She knew she could rely on the nosiness of you know who."

But he was on his feet and heading out of the room. "I'm going to let you go," he said to Janet.

"Come with me," Kim said. There was no substitute for Emtee Dempsey's hearing this story from Janet herself.

† † †

But the old nun merely nodded impatiently as Janet spoke. Her interest was entirely in Regina Fastnekker. Katherine, having heard of the second explosion on Walton Street, hurried over, but Janet stayed on, far from being the center of attention. Katherine was almost triumphant when she heard the news that the supposedly converted Regina Fastnekker had used Janet to deliver a second bomb to Walton Street.

"The brazen thing," she fumed, a grim smile on her face.

"You think she blew up our car?"

"Of course. Your car, Michael Layton, and very nearly Sister Kimberly.

Oh, I never believe these stories of radical conversion. People just don't change character that easily."

"She denied it, Katherine."

"It's part of her new persona. But the gall of the woman, to use the same pattern she always used before."

"As if she were drawing attention to herself."

"More insolence," Katherine said.

✝ ✝ ✝

Regina Fastnekker denied quite calmly through hours of interrogation that she had killed anybody. Richard, when he brought this news to Walton Street, regarded it as just what one would expect.

"But she does talk to you?"

"Talk?" He shook his head. "She goes on and on, like a TV preacher. How she has promised the Lord to tell the truth and that is what she is doing."

"I suppose you have gone over the place where Regina lives?"

Richard nodded. "Nothing."

"And this does not shake your confidence that she is responsible for these bombings?"

"You know what I think? I think she sat in prison all those years and planned this down to the minute. But she wasn't going to risk being sent to prison again. She would do it and do it in a way that I would know she had done it and yet would not be able to prove she had."

"Can you?"

"We will. We will."

Katherine wrote a feature on the Backsliding Miss Butterfingers, in the words of the header. The veteran reporter permitted herself some uncharacteristic forays into what made someone like Regina Fastnekker tick. Prison may not breed criminals, her argument ran, but it receives a criminal and releases him or her worse than he or she was before.

"Wouldn't 'he' be sufficient?"

"I've told you of our manual of style?"

"Style is the man," Emtee Dempsey purred. "Would you be allowed to write that?"

Katherine seemed to be blushing beneath her powdered cheeks. "'Style is the woman' is the way it will appear in my tomorrow's article."

"*Et tu,* Katherine? Didn't Regina take credit for what she had done when she was arrested before?"

"She did."

"And now she continues to deny what she is accused of?"

"'I have not touched a bomb since I left prison.' That's it verbatim."

"Gloves?"

"I thought of that. Something in the careful way she speaks suggested that I do. 'As far as I know I have never been in the vicinity of an explosive device since leaving prison.'"

"What does she say about what Janet Layton told us?"

"She denies it."

"How?"

"She says it is a lie."

"Verbatim?"

"Verbatim."

"Hmmm."

The following morning when they were returning from St. Matthews on foot, creating a sensation, Emtee Dempsey suddenly stopped and clapped her hands.

"Of course!" she cried, and began to laugh. When she set off again, it was almost skippingly, and her great starched headdress waggled and shook. Joyce and Kim exchanged a look. The mind is a delicate thing.

Emtee Dempsey bounded up the porch steps and inside removed the shawl from her shoulders.

"First breakfast, then call Richard."

"Why not ask him for breakfast?" Joyce said facetiously.

"No. Afterward. Let's try for ten o'clock, and we want everyone here. The Laytons, Katherine, Regina Fastnekker, and of course Richard."

"Regina Fastnekker is under arrest."

"That is why we must convey the invitation through Richard."

"He is not going to bring a mad bomber to the scene of the crime."

"Nonsense. I'll talk to him if necessary."

"I'll talk to her," Richard said, "but it's not necessary, it's impossible, as in it necessarily can't happen. I am not going to help her put on one of her amateur theatricals."

"You have every reason to object," Emtee Dempsey said, already on the phone in her study. "But wouldn't you like to clear this matter up?"

"Only what is obscure can be cleared up. This is simple as sin. We have the one responsible for those bombings."

"There's where you're wrong, Richard."

"How in hell can you know that?"

"The provenance of my knowledge is elsewhere. I realized what had happened when we were returning from Mass less than an hour ago."

"Not on your life, Sister Mary Teresa. And I mean it."

With that outburst, Kim was sure the old nun had won. Richard had to bluster and fulminate but it was not in his nature to deny such a request. Too often in the past, as he would never admit, such a gathering at Walton Street had proved a breakthrough. When he did agree, it was on his own terms.

"I will be bringing her by," he said, as if changing the subject. "I want her to see that upstairs bedroom and what's left of the computer."

"That's a splendid idea. Ten o'clock would be best for us."

Mr. Rush agreed to bring the Laytons, and wild horses could not have kept Katherine away.

8

Benjamin Rush introduced the Laytons to Sister Mary Teresa, who squeezed the grieving mother's hand while Geoffrey Layton tried not to stare at the old nun's habit. He looked around the room as if fearful of what signs of superstition he might find, but a man who could get used to the shrine in the hallway of his own house had little to fear on Walton Street. Katherine swept in, a glint in her eye. At the street door she'd whispered that she couldn't wait to see how Emtee Dempsey broke the shell of Miss Butterfingers.

Kim said nothing. It was unnervingly clear that Emtee Dempsey meant to exonerate the convicted terrorist. Katherine might soon be witnessing the first public embarrassment of her old friend, rather than another triumph. Janet was in the kitchen talking with Joyce, so Kim answered the door when Richard arrived. Regina Fastnekker stood beside him, hands joined in front of her, linked with cuffs, but her expression was serene. Behind them were two of Richard's colleagues, Gleason and O'Connell, shifting their weight and looking up and down the street. Kim stepped aside and they trooped in.

"Okay if we just go upstairs?"

"The others are in the living room."

Richard ignored that and proceeded up the stairs with his prisoner. O'Connell leaned close to Kim. "Who's here?"

"I'll introduce you."

Gleason tugged O'Connell's arm and shook his head warningly. They would stay right where they were.

When Richard came into the living room, one hand on Regina's elbow, he feigned surprise at the people gathered there.

"I'm here for an on-site inspection of the bombing," he announced to the far wall.

Mrs. Layton was staring with horror at Regina Fastnekker and her husband looked murderously at the expressionless terrorist. Regina had an announcement of her own.

"Your automobile was blown up by Michael Layton," she said to Sister Mary Teresa.

"Get her out of here!" Geoffrey Layton cried. "Better yet, we'll go."

"Wait," Emtee Dempsey said. "Let us hear what Regina has to say."

She repeated, "Michael Layton blew up your car. I called him as soon as I heard of it on the news." She moved closer to the old nun. "He despised me for being born-again. He meant to force my hand."

Geoffrey Layton sneered. "He blew up their car and then blew up himself and then blew up the sisters' computer? Is that your story?"

"Did you kill Michael Layton?" Sister Mary Teresa asked Regina. "No."

The old nun shifted her hands on the arms of the chair. "Did you do anything that resulted in the death of Michael Layton?"

Regina started. But she did not answer. She looked warily, almost fearfully at the old nun.

"I know you express yourself with great precision," Emtee Dempsey said. "One who has vowed always to tell the truth must be most precise in what he says. I ask you again. Did you do anything that . . ."

"Yes!'

A smile broke out on Richard's face and he looked as if he might actually hug Emtee Dempsey.

"But you didn't murder him?"

"No."

"Richard, let our guest sit down so that she can speak at her leisure."

But Regina shook her head. She preferred to speak standing. "Michael blew up your car, using skills we had learned together. This consisted in planting the device and from a distance activating it. After Michael's phone call, I drove past his house with a transceiver set at the appropriate frequency."

"And there was an explosion."

"Yes."

"So you killed him!" Richard said.

"No. He killed himself. That radio signal could only harm him if he intended to harm someone else. If a man fires at another and his gun backfires and kills him, has his intended victim killed him or has he killed himself?"

It was a discussion that went on for some time. The general consensus in the room was that Regina was lying, blaming a dead man.

"That's how she planned it," Geoffrey Layton said with disgust.

Benjamin Rush sat sunk into himself. Nothing Geoffrey Layton could say would restore his son's honor.

Emtee Dempsey rose and went to Mrs. Layton who was looking around almost wildly, as if she could not at all understand what was going on. Kim felt much the same way. Her eye met Janet's and she went to her. How awful this must be for her. But Janet did not want to be consoled.

"I'm leaving," she said, and started for the kitchen door.

"Wait, my dear." Surprisingly, Emtee Dempsey was at Kim's side. She took Janet's hand authoritatively and led her to Regina.

"Regina Fastnekker," she said, "did you give this girl computer disks to pass on to me?"

Regina looked surprised for the second time.

"No."

"You are not dissembling, are you?"

Regina peered at Janet. "Is that how it was done?"

Janet lunged at Regina, who lifted her manacled hands and staved off the blow. By then Emtee Dempsey had again grasped Janet's wrist and Richard had come to her assistance.

"We're talking about the device that blew up the computer?"

"She's the one," Janet screamed, trying to free herself. "She ruined Michael's life and he waited for her while she was in jail and out she comes a religious freak. No more terrorism for Miss Butterfingers."

Janet threw back her head and began to howl in frustration. Her father seemed to age before their eyes and Mrs. Layton recoiled from the spectacle of her out-of-control daughter. Benjamin Rush tried to calm Janet, but she lowered her shoulder and bumped him away, very nearly sending him to the floor. That's when O'Connell and Gleason came in and subdued her. It seemed a good idea to unshackle Regina and put the cuffs on Janet. Katherine Senski stood, looked around the room, and asked if she could use the study. She had a story to write.

† † †

But her story was incomplete until two days later when a defiant but subdued Janet told of rigging the disks in order to turn suspicion firmly on
Regina. The woman had ruined Michael's life and Janet was sure she had
killed him as well. By continuing with her brother's plan, she hoped to
send Regina Fastnekker back to prison.

That, as it turned out, was her own destination, however postponed
it would be, given the legal counsel her parents hired for her defense. She
released a statement saying that she regretted that anything she might
have done had threatened the nuns on Walton Street. But by then she had
reverted to her story that Regina Fastnekker had persuaded her to deliver
the disks.

Questioned about this at the mall where she was urging shoppers to
repent and be saved, Regina would say only, "When I was a child I spoke
as a child, but now that I have become a man I have put away the things
of a child."

Emtee Dempsey asked Katherine if her paper's policy would necessitate altering the scriptural passage cited by Miss Butterfingers, but her old
friend pretended not to hear.

†

In the Confessional

Alice Scanlan Reach

Blue slipped in through the side door of St. Brigid's and stood motionless in the shadow of the confessional. Opposite him loomed the statue of the Blessed Virgin treading gently on a rising bank of vigil lights. Blue's eyes, darting to the ruby fingers of flame flickering around the marble feet, saw that the metal box nearby with the sign *Candles—10¢* had not yet been replenished. Only a few wax molds remained. Had the box been full, Blue would have known he was too late—that Father Crumlish, on depositing a fresh supply, had opened the drawer attached to the candle container and emptied it of the past week's silver offerings.

So all was well! Once again, all unknowingly, the house of God would furnish Blue with the price of a jug of wine.

Now, from his position in the shadow, Blue's red-rimmed eyes shifted to the altar where Father Crumlish had just turned the lock in the sacristy door, signaling the start of his nightly nine-o'clock lock-up routine.

Blue knew it by heart.

First, the closing and locking of the weather-weary stained-glass windows. Next, the bolting of the heavy oaken doors in the rear of the church. Then came the dreaded moment. Tonight, as every night, listening to Father Crumlish make fast the last window and then approach the confessional, Blue fought the panic pushing against his lungs—the fear that the priest would give the musty interior of the confessional more than a quick, casual glance.

Suppose tonight it occurred to Father Crumlish to peer into the confessional's shadow to see if someone were lurking—

Blue permitted himself a soft sigh of blessed relief. He was safe! The slow footsteps were retreating up the aisle. To be sure, there were torturing hours ahead, but that was the price he had to pay. Already he could almost feel his arms cradling the beloved bottle, his fingers caressing the gracefully curved neck. He could almost taste the soothing, healing sweetness.

It was almost too much to bear.

Now came what Blue, chuckling to himself, called "the floor show."

Extinguishing the lights in the rear of the church and thus leaving it, except for candlelight, in total darkness, Father Crumlish, limping a little from the arthritis buried deep in his ancient roots, climbed the narrow winding stairway to the choir loft.

Blue, hearing the first creaking stair, moved noiselessly and swiftly. In the space of one deep breath he flickered out of the shadow, entered the nearest "sinner's" door of the confessional, and silently closed it behind him. Then he knelt in cramped darkness, seeing nothing before him but the small closed window separating him from the confessor's sanctuary.

By now Father Crumlish had reached the choir loft and the "show" began. Believing himself alone—with his God and Maker, the descendant of a long line of shillelagh wielders ran his arthritic fingers over the organ's keys and poured out his soul in song. Presently the church rafters rang with his versions of "When Irish Eyes Are Smiling," "Come Back to Erin," and "The Rose of Tralee."

It was very pleasant and Blue didn't mind too much that his knee joints ached painfully from their forced kneeling position. As a matter of fact, he rather enjoyed this interlude in the evening's adventure. It gave him time to think, a process which usually eluded him in the shadowy, unreal world where he existed. And what better place to think than this very church where he had served as an altar boy forty—fifty?—how many years ago?

That was another reason he never had the slightest qualm about filching the price of a bottle from the Blessed Virgin's vigil-light offering box. "Borrowing," Blue called it. And who had a better right? Hadn't he dropped his nickels and dimes in the collection basket every Sunday and Holy Day of Obligation from the time he was a tot until—?

The Blessed Virgin and Father Crumlish and the parishioners of St. Brigid's were never going to miss a few measly dimes. Besides, he was only "borrowing" until something turned up. And someday, wait and see, he'd walk down the center aisle of the church, dressed fit to kill, proud as a peacock, and put a $100 bill in the basket for the whole church to see, just as easy as you please!

A small smile brushed against Blue's thin lips, struggled to reach the dull sunken eyes, gave up in despair, and disappeared. Blue dozed a little.

He might more appropriately have been called Gray. For there was a bleak grayness about him that bore the stamp of fog and dust, of the gray pinched mask of death and destruction. His withered bones seemed to be shoved indifferently into threadbare coat and trousers; and from a disjointed blob of cap a few sad straggles of hair hung listlessly about his destroyed face. Time had long ceased to mean anything to Blue—and he to time.

All that mattered now was the warm, lovely, loving liquid and the occasional bite of biscuit to go with it. And thanks to St. Brigid's parishioners, thanks to his knowledge of Father Crumlish's unfailing nightly routine, Blue didn't have to worry about where the next bottle was coming from. The job was easy. And afterward he could doze in peace in the last pew of the church until it came time to mingle with the faithful as they arrived for six o'clock morning Mass, and then slip unnoticed out the door.

Now, kneeling in the confines of the confessional, Blue jerked his head up from his wasted chest and stiffened. Sudden silence roared in his ears. For some unseen reason Father Crumlish had broken off in the middle of the third bar of "Tralee."

Then, in the deathly pale quiet, the priest's voice rang out.

"Who's there?"

Sweet Jesus! thought Blue. Did I snore?

"Answer me!" More insistent now. "Who's there?"

Blue, his hand on the confessional doorknob, had all but risen when the answer came.

"It's me, Father—Johnny Sheehan."

Sinking back to his knees, Blue could hear every word in the choir loft clear as a bell, resounding in the shuttered, hollow church.

"What's on your mind, Johnny?"

Blue caught the small note of irritation in the priest's voice and knew it was because Father Crumlish treasured his few unguarded moments with "The Rose of Tralee."

"I—I want to go to confession, Father."

A long pause and then Blue could almost hear the sigh of resignation to duty and to God's will.

"Then come along, lad."

Now how do you like that for all the lousy luck, Blue thought, exasperated. Some young punk can't sleep in his nice warm beddybye until he confesses.

Confesses!

Blue felt the ice in his veins jam up against his heart. Father Crumlish would most certainly bring the repentant sinner to *this* confessional since it was next to the side-door entrance. Even now Blue could hear the oncoming footsteps. Suppose he opens *my* door instead of the other one? Dear God, please let him open the first door!

Trembling, Blue all but collapsed with relief as he heard the other door open and close, heard the settling of knees on the bench, and lastly, the faint whisper of cloth as Father Crumlish entered the priest's enclosure that separated himself from Blue on one side and from Johnny Sheehan on the other by thin screened windows.

Now Blue heard the far wooden window slide back and knew that Johnny Sheehan was bowing his head to the screen, fixing his eyes on the crucifix clasped in the confessor's hands.

"Bless me, Father, for I have sinned. . ."

The voice pulled taut, strained, and snapped.

"Don't be afraid to tell God, son. You know about the Seal of Confession—anything you tell here you confess to God and it remains sealed with Him forever."

Confess you stole a bunch of sugar beets and get it over with, Blue thought angrily. He was getting terribly tired and the pain in his knees was almost more than he could bear.

"I—she—"

She! Well, what do you know? Blue blinked his watery eyes in a small show of surprise. So the young buck's got a girl in trouble. Serves him right. Stick to the warmer embrace of the bottle, my lad. It'll keep you out of mischief.

"I heard your first confession when you were seven, Johnny. How old are you now? Sixteen?"

"Y—yes, Father."

"This girl. What about her?"

"I—I killed her!"

In the rigid silence Blue heard the boy's body sag against the wooden partition and was conscious of a sharp intake of breath from the priest. Blue was as alert now as he ever was these soft, slow days and nights, but he knew that sometimes he just thought he heard words when actually he'd only dreamed them. Yet—Blue eased one hurting kneecap and leaned closer to the dividing wood.

Father Crumlish shifted his weight in his enclosure.

"Killed?"

Only retching sobs.

"Tell me, Johnny." Father Crumlish's voice was ever so gentle now.

Then the words came in a torrent.

"She laughed at me—said I wasn't a man—and I couldn't stand it, Father. When Vera May laughed—"

"Vera May!" the priest broke in. "Vera May Barton?"

Even in the shifting mists and fog of his tired memory, Blue recognized that name. Who didn't these past few weeks? Who didn't know that every cop in the city was hunting Vera May Barton's murderer? Why, even some of Blue's best pals had been questioned. Al was ready to hang a rap on some poor innocent.

Blue rarely read newspapers, but he listened to lots of talk. And most of the talk in the wine-shrouded gloom of his haunts these past weeks had been about the slaying of sixteen-year-old Vera May Barton, a choir singer at St. Brigid's. Someone had shown Blue her picture on the front page of a newspaper. A beautiful girl, blonde and soft and smiling. But someone—someone with frantic, desperate hands—had strangled the blonde softness and choked off the smile.

Blue was suddenly conscious once more of the jagged voice.

"She wasn't really like they say, Father. Vera May wasn't really good. She just wanted you to think so. But sometimes, when I'd deliver my newspapers in the morning, sometimes she'd come to the door with hardly any clothes. And when I'd ask her to go to a show or something, she'd only laugh and say I wasn't a man."

"Go on," Father Crumlish said softly.

"I—she told me she was staying after choir practice that night to collect the hymnals—"

The priest sighed. "I blame myself for that. For letting her stay in the church alone—even for those few moments—while I went over to the rectory."

"And then—then when she left," the halting words went on, "I followed her out in the alley—"

Blue's pals had told him about that—how one of St. Brigid's early morning Mass parishioners found Vera May lying like a broken figurine in the dim alley leading from the church to the rectory. She wasn't carrying a purse, the newspapers said. And she hadn't been molested. But her strangler, tearing at her throat, had broken the thin chain of the St. Christopher's medal around her neck. It had her initials on the back but the medal had never been found.

"What did you do with the medal, Johnny?" Father Crumlish asked quietly.

"I—I was afraid to keep it, Father." The agonized voice broke again. "The river—"

The weight of the night pressed heavily on Blue and he sighed deeply. But the sigh was lost in the low murmuring of the priest to the boy—too low for Blue to catch the words—and perhaps, against all his instincts, he dozed. Then there was a sudden stirring in the adjoining cubicles.

Blue knelt rigid and breathless while the doors opened, and without turning his head toward the faint candlelight shimmering through the cracks in the door of his enclosure, he knew that Father Crumlish had opened the side entrance and released Johnny Sheehan to the gaunt and starless dark.

Slowly the priest moved toward the first pew before the center altar. And now Blue risked glancing through the sliver of light in his door. Father Crumlish knelt, face buried in his hands.

A wisp of thought drifted into the wine-eroded soil of Blue's mind. Was the priest weeping?

But Blue was too engrossed in his own discomfort, too aware of the aching, ever-increasing, burning dryness of his breath and bones. If only the priest would go and leave Blue to his business and his sleep!

After a long time he heard the footsteps move toward the side door. Now it closed. Now the key turned in the lock.

Now!

Blue stumbled from the confessional and collapsed in the nearest pew. Stretched full length, he let his weary body and mind sag in relief. Perhaps he slept; he only knew that he returned, as if from a long journey.

Sitting upright, he brought out the tools of his trade from somewhere within the tired wrappings that held him together.

First the chewing gum—two sticks, purchased tonight.

Blue munched them slowly, carefully bringing them to the proper consistency. Then, rising, he fingered a small length of wire and, leaving the pew, shuffled toward the offering box beneath the Blessed Virgin's troubled feet.

Taking the moist gum from his mouth, Blue attached it to the wire and inserted it carefully into the slot of the box. A gentle twist and he extracted the wire. Clinging to the gummed end were two coins, a nickel and a dime.

Blue went through this procedure again and again until he had collected the price of a bottle. Then he lowered himself into the nearest pew and rested a bit.

He began to think of what had happened in the confessional. But it had been so long since Blue had made himself concentrate on anything but his constant, thirsting need that it took a while for the rusted wheels to move, for the pretty colored lights to cease their small whirlings and form a single brightness illuminating the makings of his mind.

Finally he gave up. The burning dryness had gripped him again and he began to yearn for the long night to be over so that he could spend, in the best way he knew, the money he held right in his hand this minute.

Two bottles! I should have two bottles for all the trouble I've been through tonight, Blue thought. They owe it to me for making me kneel there so long and robbing me of my sleep. Yes, they owe it to me!

And so thinking, he took out the gum once more and, bringing it to his mouth, chewed it again into pliable moistness.

The first try at the offering box brought him only a dime, but the second try—God was good—another dime, a nickel, and a dollar bill!

Too exhausted to drag himself to his customary last-pew bed, Blue stretched out once more on the nearest wood plank and slept.

✝ ✝ ✝

Some time later, the unrelenting dryness wakened him. This "in between" period was the only time Blue ever approached sobriety. And in the sobering, everything seemed terribly, painfully clear. He began to relive the events of the night, hearing the voices again with frightening clarity. Father Crumlish's and then the kid's—

Blue's own voice screamed in his ears.

"Out! I've got to get out of here! Nobody knows but me—nobody knows about the murder but me. I've got to tell. But first I'll have to have a little sip. I need a little sip. And then I'll tell—"

In a flurry of cloth and dust Blue rushed to the side door. He had never before tried to let himself out this way and had no idea if the door was locked. But the knob gave easily, and in an instant he had closed the door behind him and, leaning heavily against it, was breathing the night's whispering wind.

It had been a long time since Blue had been out alone in the deep dark, and suddenly, with the night's dreadful knowledge inside him, it was overpowering. Shadows rushed at him, clawed at his face and fingers, and crushed him so bindingly that he could scarcely breathe.

In an agony to get away, he plunged into the blackness and began to run.

And in his urgency Blue never heard the shout behind him, the pounding feet on the pavement. He never heard the cry to halt or risk a bullet. He only knew that he was flying, faster and faster, yet not fast enough, soaring higher and higher, until a surprisingly small jagged thrust of sidewalk clawed at him and brought him to his knees.

The bullet from his pursuer, meant to pierce his worn and weary legs, pierced his back.

Suddenly it was calm and quiet and there was no longer any need for speed. He lay on his side, crumpled and useless, like a discarded bundle of rags.

A wave, a wine-red wave, swept over him and Blue let himself rock and toss for a moment in its comforting warmth. Then he opened his eyes and, dimly, in the fast-gathering darkness, recognized Father Crumlish bending over him.

"Poor devil," Blue heard the priest say. "But don't blame yourself, officer. The fellow probably just didn't know you'd be suspicious of his running away like that. Particularly around here, now, after the Barton girl. The poor devil probably just didn't know."

Didn't know? Blue didn't know? He knew, all right! And he had to tell.

"Father!"

Quickly the priest bent his ear to Blue's quivering lips. "I'm listening," he said.

"I—was in the confessional too."

"The confessional?"

The wave rushed to envelop him again. Before he could speak the urgent words, he heard the officer's voice.

"He came out of the church door, Father. I saw him."

"I don't see how that's possible," the priest said bewilderedly.

Blue forced the breath from his aching lungs.

"I heard—the kid confess. I have to tell—"

"Wait!" Father Crumlish said sharply, cutting Blue off. "You have nothing to tell. Maybe you heard. But you don't know about that boy. The poor confused lad's come to me to confess to every robbery and murder in this parish for years. You have nothing to tell, do you hear me?"

"Nothing?"

Blue almost laughed a little. For the pain was gone now and he felt as if—as if he were walking down St. Brigid's center aisle, dressed fit to kill, proud as a peacock, and putting a $100 bill in the collection basket for the whole church to see just as easy as you please.

"There's something—"

His voice was strong and clear as he brought his fumbling fingers from within the moldy rags and stretched out his hand to the priest.

"I was 'borrowing' from the Blessed Virgin, Father. Just enough for a bottle, though. I need it, Father. All the time. Bad! She caught me at it. And she was running to tell you. But if she did, where in the world would I ever get another bottle, Father? Where? So I had to stop her!"

Fighting the final warm, wine-red wave that was washing over him, Blue thrust into Father Crumlish's hand a St. Christopher's medal dangling from a broken chain and initialed V.M.B.

"I've been saving it, Father. In a pinch, I thought it might be worth a bottle."

✝

AUTHOR BIOGRAPHIES

CHARLOTTE ARMSTRONG (1905–1969) was a "modern witch" according to the late and esteemed writer-critic Anthony Boucher. She took common, everyday situations and found the danger and menace in them. Her short novel *Mischief* is a perfect example: Husband and wife going on a business trip to New York hire a babysitter for their young daughter. The trouble is, the sitter is dangerously ill mentally and resents the life the little child leads. Only by the skin of their teeth are they able to rescue their daughter. A truly harrowing novel. Armstrong was one of the leading suspense novelists of her time and died far too young, in her early sixties.

"Among the writers I admire most are Christie, Allingham, Rendell, and Margaret Millar," ROBERT BARNARD once noted. Perhaps this is why his own voice is that of a "pure" detective writer. Whatever else a given Barnard novel may offer (humor, keen social observation, place description that is genuinely poetic) his novels and stories always remain focused on the mystery. While one hates to speculate on which writers of our time will be read by future generations, Barnard, with his grace, his intelligence, and his enormous range of skills, is certainly a likely contender. *Death of an Old Goat* (1977), *Bodies* (1986), and *A City of Strangers* are among his many worthwhile novels, with his latest including *The Lost Boy* and *A Murder in Mayfair*.

Not many writers can sell a manuscript from the slush pile that goes on to be nominated for both the Agatha and Anthony mystery awards. But **JAN BURKE** did just that. And, in a handful of novels about her newspaper protagonist Irene Kelly, Burke has found an ever-expanding audience eager for her next book. She is also a fine short story writer, her story "Unharmed" winning both the Ellery Queen Mystery Readers Award and the Macavity award. Her most recent novels include *Bones* and *Flight*.

G. K. CHESTERTON (1874–1936) was so well known for his Father Brown detective stories that he sometimes grew resentful, feeling that the press tended to overlook his "serious" writings. Good as some of that writing undoubtedly was, it is largely for the Father Brown stories—and one extraordinary novel, *The Man Who Was Thursday*—that we remember him today (Chesterton scholars to the contrary not withstanding). The Browns are some of the best pure detective stories of all times, and deliciously, delightfully British. They influenced, among many others, everybody from Julian Symons to Agatha Christie.

Born in New York, **RICHARD CONNELL** (1893–1949) claimed to be the world's youngest professional author. He covered baseball games at the age of six with his father, who was then editor of the *New York News Press*. He attended Georgetown College for a year, but graduated from Harvard in 1915, after which he served as a reporter for the *New York American*. When World War I broke out, he served with the Twenty-Seventh Division in France. After the war he became a freelance writer, turning out more than three hundred short stories, novels, and scripts. He is best remembered for the classic adventure story "The Most Dangerous Game," which was filmed three times.

P. C. DOHERTY is the prolific author of more than three dozen novels featuring three different characters, all set at different times in the Middle Ages. He has written under several pseudonyms, including Michael Clynes, Ann Dukthas, C. L. Grace, and Paul Harding. His research is always authentic, mostly due to his doctorate in history from Oxford University. His most recent novel is *The Horus Killings*.

KATHLEEN DOUGHERTY's story "When Your Breath Freezes" was one of the seven finalist stories for the Mystery Writers of America's fiftieth anniversary contest. Her novels have been described as "explorations of the dark underbelly of the mind." She has worked as a sales manager for an artificial intelligence company and as a research associate in pharmacology.

Westerns, gangster novels, private eyes, historical novels, Victorian gothics starring Jack the Ripper and assorted other monsters (including the sometimes monstrous Holmes himself), **LOREN D. ESTLEMAN** has had one of those enviable careers filled with kudos and commercial success. His work, mystery and non-mystery alike, constantly appears on annual year's best lists, and his list of admiring critics grows increasingly longer. Here he is working the shadowy streets of crime fiction, where a down-on-his-luck private eye stumbles into a case of a high-ranking member of the Catholic church gone wrong.

LADY ANTONIA FRASER is not only a mystery writer but also a serious student of history, having earned her B.A. and M.A. at Lady Margaret Hall, Oxford. Her father is Lord Langford, a man who writes; and her husband the famous playwright Harold Pinter. She edits *The Kings and Queens of England* books while finding time to write her internationally renowned mystery novels, including the recent *Oxford Blood*. She recently edited the nonfiction book *The Lives of the Kings and Queens of England*.

MARGARET FRAZER is the pseudonym of Gail Frazer, who has been writing mystery novels for years, formerly as the partner of Mary Kuhfield. She has since taken the pseudonym and continued the medieval murder mystery series featuring Sister Frevisse, a great-niece of Geoffrey Chaucer. The series currently spans nine novels, with *The Maiden's Tale* and *The Prioress's Tale* being the most recent. She lives in Minnesota, where she is hard at work on future Sister Frevisse novels.

NEIL GAIMAN is a world-class fantasist. Whether in his graphic novels of *The Sandman* or in his many novels or story collections, Gaiman has elected to show us—and the world around us—in the slightly skewed perspective that writers from Lord Dunsany to Ray Bradbury to Clive Barker to Terry Prachett favor—and, in truth, Gaiman's unique voices manage to incorporate just about every major strain of traditional and modern fantasy—and yet remain just that, unique, and unlike anyone else's. Recent books include *The Day I Swapped my Dad for Two Goldfish,* *Stardust,* and *American Gods.*

Who says a priest can't have a second career as a bestselling author? Father **ANDREW GREELEY** has done just that. In addition to his excellent mainstream novels (*Irish Gold, Irish Lace, Irish Whiskey, Fall from Grace*), he has also graced the mystery field with his Father "Blackie" Ryan series. Greeley is never better than when he gives us a behind-the-scenes look at Church politics and brinksmanship. He couples his priestly devotion with his very real concerns for how the Church conducts itself in this most trying of times. His fiction, in whatever form he chooses to use, is always a pleasure to read.

EDWARD HOCH is probably the only man in the world who supports himself exclusively by writing short stories. He has appeared in every issue of *Ellery Queen Mystery Magazine* since the late 1970s, and manages to write for several other markets as well. He has probably created more short story series characters than anybody who ever worked in the crime fiction field. And what great characters, too—Nichael Vlado, a Gypsy detective; Dr. Sam Hawthorne, a small-town GP of the 1920s who solves impossible crimes while dispensing good health; and, among many others, his outre and bedazzling Simon Ark, who claims, in the proper mood, to be two thousand years old. Locked room, espionage, cozy, hard-boiled, suspense, Ed Hoch has done it all and done it well.

In his all too brief life, Anthony Boucher (1911–1968), who wrote under several pseudonyms, **H. H. HOLMES** being just one of them, managed to be a seminal editor, reviewer, publisher, and writer in not one but two genres: mystery and science fiction. He was the founder and long-time co-editor of *The Magazine of Fantasy & Science Fiction* and the mystery reviewer for the *New York Times* for many years. He was also a writer of great wit, subtlety, and skill—again in both genres—and whether in fantasy or mystery fiction, he showed himself to be a devout and serious Catholic scholar. His short stories of Sister Ursula are especially good. No one has come close to replacing him since his death in 1968. The largest annual mystery convention in the United States—the Bouchercon—is named for him.

RALPH MCINERNY has long been acknowledged as one of the most vital voices in lay Catholic activities in America. He is co-founder and co-publisher of CRISIS, a widely read journal of Catholic opinion, while finding time to teach Medieval Studies at Notre Dame University and write several series of mystery novels, one of which, *The Father Dowling Mysteries,* ran on network television for several seasons, and can now be seen on cable. Scholars are rarely entertainers. Ralph McInerny, both as himself and under his pseudonym Monica Quill, has been both for many, many years.

Just in case you don't think anything exciting happened in twelfth-century France, just consult **SHARAN NEWMAN**'s excellent, lively novels in her Catherine LeVendeur mystery series. A genuine medievalist, Newman won the Macavity with her first novel *Death Comes as Epiphany,* which was also nominated for the Agatha and Anthony awards. The books have continued to grow in popularity and the demands of writing them ever more difficult. But even so, and despite her workload, she is finishing her Ph.D in history at the University of California. Her latest novel is *To Wear the White Cloak.*

ALICE SCANLAN REACH is the creator of Irish priest Father Xavier Crumlish, who made more than a dozen appearances in the pages of *Ellery Queen's Mystery Magazine* and *Alfred Hitchcock's Mystery Magazine* in the 1960s. Her work is characterized by wry insight into the workings—and failings—of the human heart. Unfortunately, the good Father has never appeared in a novel-length work, but there is always hope that that situation might change.

COPYRIGHTS AND PERMISSIONS